D0425971

OLD DOGS AND CHILDREN

Other Books by Robert Inman

A Note in Closing
My Friend Delbert Earl and Other Notes in Closing
Home Fires Burning

ROBERT INMAN

OLD DOGS AND CHILDREN

Little, Brown and Company
Boston   Toronto   London

First Edition

This is a work of fiction. Names, characters, places, and incidents
are either the product of the author's imagination
or, if real, are used fictitiously.

Excerpt from "Old Dogs, Children, and Watermelon Wine," by Tom T. Hall,
© Hallnote Music Co., P.O. Box 40209, Nashville, TN 37204. Used by permission.

Library of Congress Cataloging-in-Publication Data
Inman, Robert, 1943–
    Old dogs and children / by Robert Inman.—1st ed.
        p. cm.
    ISBN 0-316-41897-8
    I. Title.
    PS3559.N449O43   1991
    813'.54—dc20   90-43659

10   9   8   7   6   5   4   3   2   1

MV PA

Published simultaneously in Canada
by Little, Brown & Company (Canada) Limited

Printed in the United States of America

To the women who raised me:
Nell Bancroft Cooper
Emma Margaret Cooper Inman

Ain't but three things in this world
That's worth a solitary dime:
Old dogs and children and watermelon wine.
    —Tom T. Hall

BOOK 1

1

When you top the rise over the River Bridge, the first thing you see is the Birdsong house down at the end of Claxton Avenue, three blocks away, where the street makes a right angle with Birdsong Boulevard. The house is wide and white with a banistered porch running across the front, nestled behind a grove of pecan trees that shades the front lawn. The house sits up rather high off the ground, and it has brickwork all around the bottom with gaps left in the bricks for ventilation, a patchwork skirt. There is a second story, but not much of one—a few dormered windows peeking out from the roofline—as if it had been added as an afterthought. Which is exactly what happened after the Great Flood of 1939.

This early June morning, gray and purple in the half-light just before dawn, Bright Birdsong stands on her front porch looking up Claxton Avenue toward the River Bridge and waiting for the sun. Claxton is quiet and deserted, not a single sign of life in the pools of amber light from the street lamps, not even a dog sniffing about the side loading dock of the Dixie Vittles Supermarket across the street, looking for a stray morsel. There is a car parked in front of the store, but there is no one in it, at least not anyone she can see. Is there someone stretched out in the back seat asleep? Some eager shopper waiting for the store to open to take advantage of the special on ruta-bagas or drumsticks? She considers a number of possibilities, turning them over idly in her mind. As she does, a car approaches from her left on Birdsong Boulevard and turns left on Claxton, moving away from her toward the River Bridge. Its red taillights wink off as the treetops on the low bluff across the river glow orange with the anticipation of the sun.

New sun. The first shards of light splinter the treetops now, and Bright raises her arms slowly, reaching for the new sun. She feels its

< 3 >

warmth flooding her body, stirring something in her that stretches in a single unbroken strand to her childhood some sixty years before, one of the few constants in her life. The new sun blinks at her and then pops, full of itself, into the morning. She embraces it, arms wide, the thin fabric of her flowered print housedress spread like a fan.

The new sun brings memory. Hosanna, the old black woman who helped raise her, has a deep-seated belief in the mysterious, curative effect of new sun. And the small white child knows wisdom when she hears it. So she wakes very early and goes to stand in her long white nightgown on the front porch, watching the sun wink and smile just over the top of the house across the street. She pulls the gown over her head and lets it fall to the floor of the porch, feels the new sun fill her naked body with a strange, light warmth.

The memory of it echoes through the spreading sunlight of this present June morning. *What if I should do that now?* she thinks, and she giggles, pictures the imagined man sleeping in the back seat of the car in front of the Dixie Vittles waking suddenly, peering out the back window and seeing a naked old woman on the banistered front porch of the house across the street. What to do? Wave or ignore him? It is a delicious thought, one that may well entertain her all morning. Until Roseann gets here.

Roseann. The spell is broken. Bright lowers her arms with a sigh and gives herself up to the morning.

Birds chatter in the pecan trees on the lawn, fussing at her because the birdbath in the backyard is nearly empty. It is Monday and the birds are anxious to get about their business. Monday, and that means Roseann will be here within hours—she and her new husband, Rupert, and Bright's grandson, Jimbo, in their Winnebago, stopping by on their way to the beach. Roseann. Perhaps the visit will be quick, like a summer storm.

But that is not all. Monday means it is only three days until Fitz Birdsong Day, in honor of her son the governor, who is running for reelection and wishes to end the campaign triumphantly here among the home folks. A parade, a rousing speech, a barbecue luncheon. Another summer storm, but gentler. Fitz tries to please; Roseann does not. By sundown Thursday it will all be behind her and she can be quiet again, blend in again with the deepening summer.

She stands a moment longer, then gives up the porch reluctantly. She stops briefly in the parlor, surveys the comfortable clutter: a pile of magazines on the table next to the wing-back chair where she likes to read—*Time, Esquire, National Geographic, Southern Lumberman*; a stack of books on the floor next to the chair—an Agatha Christie, a

< 4 >

Louis L'Amour paperback, a new book about the assassination of John F. Kennedy; piles of sheet music on top of the Story and Clark upright piano and more of it spread open above the keyboard—Liszt, Chopin, a Scott Joplin rag. There is no rhyme or reason to the room or its contents, she thinks, taking brief inventory. Her tastes run amok, but she maintains a lively interest in things in general if not things in particular. She will have to tidy things a bit before Roseann gets here. *Mama, don't you ever pick anything up?* Roseann is painfully tidy. Roseann is a pickle.

She pads on, her slippered feet slap-slapping on the hardwood floor of the small breakfast room and the linoleum of the kitchen, stopping to put the coffeepot on to boil and a pan of milk to warm. The kitchen is narrow and cozy. Cabinets, counter, and sink on one side, stove and refrigerator on the other. And comfortably old-fashioned, like the refrigerator that is its centerpiece—an ancient Kelvinator with the motor in a round housing on top. It has been with her since the Great Flood of 1939, when it replaced the icebox that a deliveryman filled once a day with a five-pound block of ice. The refrigerator had looked enormous in 1939, with space enough inside for all manner of foodstuffs on its stainless steel shelves and a small freezer compartment that made its own trays of ice. Bright had felt very elegant, very modern, with her own electric refrigerator. But it is tiny by modern standards. She opened the door to a brand-new refrigerator in Thompson's Furniture last week—gleaming white without even a latch on the front—and it seemed as if she were peering into the entrance to Mammoth Cave.

"About time for a new one, Miz Bright?" Lester Thompson asked. "This model's got a built-in icemaker."

"Why no, I've got a perfectly good Kelvinator at home," she replied, "and it makes perfectly good ice." But there is more to it than that. This refrigerator was the one that Fitzhugh gave her in 1939. Fitzhugh didn't leave very much.

This morning, the Kelvinator is purring at her, the only sound in the kitchen. She opens the door and takes out the sugar bowl, which she keeps in the refrigerator because it attracts ants if left on the counter. Bright has given up trying to rid the world of ants. She simply accommodates, in this as in most things. The last time the Orkin Man came was twenty years ago, in 1959.

Bright steps onto the screened-in back porch and stands there for a moment, waiting for the coffee to boil, listening to the bumping noises that her dog, Gladys, makes under the house. Gladys is an Irish setter, feeble with age, one eye glazed over and sightless from some dog

< 5 >

disease. Gladys has been living under the house since Little Fitz brought her home from school.

It had been about this time, early June, the end of Fitz's second year in law school. Bright had expected Fitz to come home from the University on the bus, so she was surprised to see him climb down from the cab of a truck that pulled up to the curb in front of the house. He went around to the back of the truck, opened the tailgate, lifted out his suitcase and trunk. And then the dog. He picked up the suitcase with one hand and dragged the trunk with the other, across the lawn to where Bright waited on the front porch. The dog just sat by the curb on her haunches and watched him.

"Hi, Mama," he called.

"Hi yourself. Why didn't you come on the bus?"

"They wouldn't let the dog on the bus. So I hitched."

Fitz deposited the suitcase and trunk beside the front steps and went back for the dog. He tried to coax her to follow him, but she simply sat there and stared at him. Then he grabbed her by the scruff of the neck and tried to hoist her to all fours, but she collapsed in a heap by the curb. So Fitz reached down and gathered her up in his arms and marched across the lawn with her. He set the dog down by the steps and she sprawled there on the grass, head resting across her front paws.

"What's wrong with that dog?" Bright asked.

"She has a drinking problem."

"You mean alcohol?"

"Yes'm."

"Where did she acquire a drinking problem, Fitz?"

"In the fraternity house. Her name is Gladys, Mama. She's our mascot. She started out on light bread soaked in beer and then gradually moved on to the hard stuff."

"Who did this?"

"Well, I guess we're all a little responsible."

"You ought to be ashamed," Bright said.

"I am. That's why I brought her home to you."

"Why me?"

"I figured you could rehabilitate her. Get her all fixed up."

"Oh, no," Bright said, crossing her arms across her chest.

"Just for the summer, Mama," he pleaded. "I'll take her back to school with me in the fall."

"And get her drunk again."

"Well . . ."

So Gladys stayed. She never had another drink of liquor, as far as

< 6 >

Bright knew, but her bladder and stomach were already pretty much gone. Long ago, a veterinarian examined her and pronounced her terminal. But she lives on now, defying nature, incontinent and dyspeptic. She pees constantly, in little dribbles. She eats nothing but canned dog food softened with warm milk and spends most of her time in a warm, dry place under the house, just underneath Bright's bedroom. She comes and goes through an open space in the brickwork by the back steps. Lately, she has taken to bumping around in the middle of the night, getting herself tangled in the web of pipes and wires, moaning and clanging until she extricates herself.

Now, in the early morning, she is making her way out . . . *rattle* . . . *clang* . . . *bump* . . . *moan* . . . and Bright follows her halting, half-blind progress. By the time Gladys clears the maze, Bright has fetched and opened the can of food from the kitchen, mixed it with warm milk from the pan on the stove, and placed the bowl by the back steps. She sits on the steps, wrapping her housedress around her knees, and waits for Gladys to poke her head through the opening in the brickwork. The dog pauses, giving the morning a one-eyed once-over, and stares for a moment at Bright, tilting her head this way and that. She gives forth a soft moan. Bright has never heard Gladys bark, not in the many years she has been here. Perhaps her bark fell victim to alcoholism, back there in her profligate days at Little Fitz's fraternity house. Or perhaps she never found anything worth barking at. Gladys steps gingerly into the morning as if expecting to collide with another pipe. She shakes herself, the most vigorous thing she does these days, and dust flies. She looks up at Bright again, expecting a greeting.

The redeeming thing about a dog, Bright thinks, is that it will look you in the eye. A lot of people won't do that. "Good morning," Bright says. "You look in the pink of health this morning. You slept well, I take it?"

Gladys turns to her food dish. Another thing about dogs. They have no truck with nonsense.

Gladys takes her sweet time with breakfast and Bright sits quietly, letting her mind wander, as it does a great deal these days. She drifts, especially here in the warm beginning of summer where thoughts puddle like melting butter in the languid heat. She has often wondered if that is why it is so hard for new ideas to blossom in the South. When it is cold, you have to think fast. But heat is deadening, and you can take refuge in it. You can lose hours, days, even perhaps a lifetime in the heat.

This will be a hot day, the promise of it in the cloudless blue of

< 7 >

the sky, lightening now above her as the day begins to take hold. But it is still very early and the backyard remains cool and soft under the tall oaks and maples, shaded in grays as if ghosts are about.

Ghosts. If there are any here, oozing about on the gray-green carpet of grass this early morning, there are none she knows. Certainly not the ghost of her husband, Congressman Fitzhugh Birdsong. If Fitzhugh's ghost haunts any place, it is the sidewalk in front of the Commercial Bank and Trust where he collapsed on a February morning eight years before. Harley Gibbons, the president of the bank, had taken her hand at the hospital and said, "Bright, he didn't suffer. He was dead before he hit the pavement." Sweet, gentle Fitzhugh. Finally home from Congress after all those years—through Roosevelt and Truman, Eisenhower and Kennedy and Johnson and Nixon. And dead on the sidewalk two weeks later.

There are echoes of Fitzhugh Birdsong, to be sure. The hum of the ancient Kelvinator refrigerator. The stacks of *National Geographics* he loved to read because he was so much a man of the world, chairman of the Foreign Affairs Committee. Papers, books, memorabilia packed away in the attic. And two children, of course. Roseann and Little Fitz, leading their own lives now, no longer Bright's responsibility. But no ghosts. Bright has no time or patience for hauntings.

Gladys lifts her head from her dish, cocks it to one side, stares balefully out of her one good eye. Then she turns toward the opening in the bricks, stops for a moment and sniffs the patch of mint next to the back steps. She looks up at Bright again and Bright gives her a pat on the head, scratching for a while behind her ears. Gladys emits a low, grateful moan and heads back under the house. In a moment, Bright can hear her banging against the pipes, moving in fits and starts toward her cool place under Bright's bedroom. She leaves Bright alone in the soft quiet, thinking that Gladys is just the kind of dog for a woman who has retired from responsibilities and hauntings. They both simply accommodate and have no truck with nonsense.

<   >

Things remain tranquil for only a moment, until Bright hears the whine of machinery from the shed behind Montgomery V. Putnam's house next door. A low, singing whine—some kind of saw, or perhaps his lathe. Buster Putnam (she can't help but think of him as Buster) has been using his lathe a lot lately, turning spindles for a banister. The whole house is falling down around his ears, and Buster is turning spindles.

Buster Putnam is recently retired from the United States Marine Corps, where he was a lieutenant general and very nearly commandant

< 8 >

of the entire business. Except for an incident in Korea, they said, he would have had his fourth star. But he has finished his military career with only three and come home to reclaim a family relic, the house next door to Bright that people have been calling the Putnam mansion since Buster's grandfather, the founder of Putnam's Mercantile, built it in the 1880s, when the town began to prosper. It has never truly been much of a mansion, but for a long time it was the closest thing to the genuine article in town. Now it is just a flaking, fading, two-story white-columned beast of a house. It was cut up into apartments back in the fifties and for the past two years it has stood empty, considered unfit even for apartment dwellers. Buster bought it from a real estate broker for next to nothing, and folks generally said that he got exactly what he paid for.

Decay has descended upon the house like a shroud. The upper story is entirely uninhabitable. Buster lives in two rooms downstairs. A man came to inspect the roof shortly after Buster took up residence, and the minute he stepped off his ladder, he fell through. Bright was standing at the kitchen sink and she heard him bellow as the rotten boards gave way and he crashed into an upstairs bedroom. When she got to her own back steps, drying her hands on a dish towel, she could see the big hole in the roof where he had gone in. The fall did him considerable damage. The Rescue Squad came wailing up in their orange and white truck, and when they carried the roofer down the stairs on a stretcher, they knocked over the banister and sent it crashing into the hallway. Since then, Buster has spent a lot of time in the workshop he has set up in the shed out back, turning new spindles for the banister on his lathe, while the hole in the roof remains covered with a sheet of black plastic, tacked down by boards. No roofer in his right mind will go near it.

Yes, it is the lathe Bright hears now. She has learned its low, singing hum and then the sharper sound as the lathe chisel bites into the wood. In a moment, if he is drunk, Buster will start singing.

"*Down in the valllleeeeyyyyyy . . . ,*" he begins. Then, "Aaarrrgghhh. Aw, SHIT!"

Buster is sitting on the floor of the shed by the time she gets there, clothes and hair speckled with wood shavings, blood dripping from a gash in his left thumb, blood-stained chisel lying on the sawdust-littered floor next to him. The lathe is still humming, the spinning slab of wood a yellow blur. Bright stands in the doorway for a moment, hands on hips, surveying the mess while Buster squints bleary-eyed up at her. Then she finds the switch on the lathe and turns it off. The smell of liquor is powerful.

"Buster, don't you know better than to mess around with machinery

< 9 >

when you've been drinking whiskey?" She laces her voice with disgust, but not too much.

"Gin," he says.

"It's all the same. It's all whiskey. Don't quibble over nomenclature."

Buster holds out his hand. "I'm bleeding to death."

She bends, takes his left hand by the wrist, looks at the gash. "No, you're not bleeding to death, but you're going to need some stitches."

She looks around for something to wrap around the thumb, but there is only a filthy rag on the workbench along one wall of the shed. "Don't you have a first aid kit?"

Buster shakes his head. "Do you think a man who would fool with machinery while he's drunk would have sense enough to keep a first aid kit in his workshop?"

"I suppose not." Bright picks up a knife from the workbench, cuts a slit along the hem of her thin housedress, tears off a strip of the cloth. She wraps it around Buster's thumb several times, then splits one end of the cloth into two strips and ties it off neatly with a little bow.

She works quietly, and as she does she is suddenly aware of the smell of wood, the rich pungent aroma of nature's secret laid open, fresh and raw and sweet. It is powerful, a rush of remembrance. Her father's sawmill, the smell of fresh-cut wood, the whine of machinery, her father towering far above her in his tall leather boots and khaki clothes. She remembers, as if it were yesterday, seeing a man's arm cut off at the elbow by a huge circular saw, the agonized shriek as spinning metal tore flesh and bone, blood everywhere, her father scooping her up in his strong arms and turning her away from the sight. But not before she had seen everything. It is something long buried, along with so much else, but now suddenly sharp and alive, horrible in a strange, delicious way. She draws in a quick breath, drops her hands to her sides, stands there staring at the bandage she has made around Buster Putnam's wound.

Buster looks up at her. "Bright, will you marry me?"

She shakes herself. "Of course not," she says after a moment.

"Why not?"

"You're too young for me. And you're a mess."

Buster nods. "I suppose you're right. I've always felt like a little kid around you."

Buster is only two years younger than Bright, but she remembers him as a little boy in overalls in the long ago when they were growing up in next-door houses on the other side of town, always standing back

< 10 >

at the edge of whatever crowd they were in, too young to be accepted by the older kids but earnestly hoping someone would notice him. Shy, too. Strange, she always thought, that he had become a Marine. And a general at that.

Buster had been quite the celebrity when he came home from his distinguished military career—tall, trim, hair just beginning to fleck gray. He was sought after. He was grand marshal of the Veterans Day parade, became a director of the Commercial Bank and Trust, even addressed a joint session of the legislature at Governor Fitz Birdsong's urging. Widowed ladies and even some with husbands had fawned over him. But then they had seen Buster begin to unravel. The first sign was the day he spoke before the United Methodist Women on World Missions Day. He had shown up smelling strongly of bay rum oil and bourbon and proceeded to say that he had "never seen a foreign country worth pissing on, much less fighting over or saving for Jesus." After that, people began to draw back, and Buster became an object of morbid curiosity.

This morning, he is clad in a faded plaid flannel shirt and an old pair of brown trousers, shiny with wear. He has a stubble of beard on his jowls and his eyes are glazed and bloodshot. Decay has descended on Buster Putnam the way it has descended upon his homestead. Perhaps it is the house, eating at his vitals.

"Have you been up all night?" Bright asks.

"Not only *up* all night, but *out* all night. I have drunk me some terrible gin and paid court to some homely women, and it took all night to do it."

"You ought to be ashamed of yourself," she says.

"Probably." He doesn't seem very ashamed, but he does look perplexed, as if he has lost something.

"What's the matter with you?" she asks.

He holds up his bandaged thumb. "I'm wounded."

"No," she says with a wave of her hand. "I mean in general."

He ponders that for a long moment, and then he says quietly, "I'm not sure who I am anymore. They used to call me General, but I'm not a general anymore. You call me Buster, but I haven't been Buster for years. I got over being Buster, by God. And the boys at the Spot don't know what the hell to call me, so they just call me sir. Except for one asshole who calls me General Patton, even though I keep telling him that Patton was an Army sonofabitch."

"You don't have to curse, Buster," Bright says.

"Sorry. Old habits, you know . . ."

"You don't need anybody to tell you who you are, Buster."

< 11 >

Buster nods. "Maybe you're right. Maybe I need somebody to tell me what to do."

"What you need to do is get hold of yourself."

"Ah, yes. Come to grips. That's the way my father used to say it. *Come to grips with yourself.* I think he always assumed that I had come to grips with myself because I made a career as a military man. And I suppose I thought so too. But now . . ."

"Yes?"

Buster shrugs. "I am as you see me. I don't have anybody to tell me what to do anymore."

"Nobody tells generals what to do. They tell everybody else what to do."

"Oh, no." Buster shakes his head. Flecks of sawdust fall from his hair and cling to the flannel shirt. "Everybody has somebody telling them what to do, all the way up the line. Even the president. He has people telling him what he *ought* to do, which is the same thing, maybe even worse."

Bright looks him over, wondering what his wife was like, if she told him what to do. They divorced several years ago, childless. Buster should be enjoying his retirement now, at ease with a wife in a nice house, perhaps a condominium at Hilton Head within walking distance of a marina or a golf course. Instead. . . . Yes, what he needs to do is get a grip on himself.

"Well, what you need to do now," she says, "is get some stitches in your thumb. Can you drive?" He looks up, gives her a crooked grin. "No, of course you can't drive. You're drunk and wounded."

So Bright quickly changes into a cotton dress, fetches her purse and her old Plymouth, and takes Buster Putnam to the hospital. There is only a nurse on duty in the emergency room, but she finds a doctor making his early morning rounds. Buster is perched on an examining table, holding his injured hand in the other, when the doctor comes in. He is an earnest-looking young man carrying a clipboard and a Styrofoam cup of coffee, wearing a loose white jacket over an open-necked madras shirt, khaki pants, no socks. A stethoscope hangs out of a jacket pocket. He looks vaguely familiar, but Bright can't place him. "Morning," he says. "Got a little problem here?"

"Wounded in action." Buster holds up the bandaged thumb.

The young doctor lays the clipboard and coffee cup aside and pulls up a stool, wrinkling his nose a bit at the gamy smell of dissipation that rises from Buster's body and clothing. He unwraps Bright's homemade bandage from around Buster's thumb and the wound opens and blood flows again, dripping on the green tile floor of the emergency room until the doctor dabs at it with a piece of gauze. Everything is shades of

< 12 >

green and stainless steel here. Things hiss and burble, little green machines on stainless steel tables, everything on rollers. Nothing is permanent in an emergency room. You could clear the place and have a volleyball game in two minutes. Standing here, smelling the antiseptic smell and seeing the impermanence of it, she is glad that Fitzhugh Birdsong died on the sidewalk in front of the Commercial Bank and Trust, not in a hissing green emergency room.

"Well, it's not life-threatening," the doctor says. "A few stitches ought to take care of it. How did you do it?"

"Operating a wood lathe while intoxicated," Buster says matter-of-factly.

"Well, that was pretty dumb," the doctor says mildly.

"Just fix the goddamn thing!" Buster booms, drawing himself up, eyes steely, back and shoulders straight. "Excuse me, Bright."

The doctor gives him a close look. "You're General Putnam, aren't you?"

"Yes. And I don't need any advice, Bubba."

The doctor shrugs. "This is an emergency room, not a counseling center." He peers at the wound for a moment. "I'll put a little shot of novocaine in it, then sew you up."

"Don't bother with the novocaine," Buster orders.

Another shrug. "Suit yourself." He puts a metal tray under Buster's hand and sloshes a good deal of alcohol into the open wound and the blood turns the alcohol pink. Bright starts to turn away, finds that she cannot, that she is gripped by the pinkness, the thin trickle of blood oozing from the wound, and—for the second time in less than an hour—by a powerful remembrance of her father. A look of utter surprise on Dorsey Bascombe's face, a summer morning exploding, blood everywhere, a scream from somewhere so deep inside her it has no sound. She feels a wave of weakness wash over her and she puts her hand quickly to her temple.

The doctor glances up, concerned. "Miz Birdsong, are you all right? Maybe you better go outside and sit down." And that is when she recognizes him or, more accurately, recognizes the family resemblance. He is a Tillman, she thinks, a grandson or perhaps a grandnephew of Finus Tillman, the doctor of her childhood. She feels and smells the house of Dorsey Bascombe's wounded agony as if it were here now, here instead of this green hissing antiseptic room.

She shakes her head, startled and unnerved by the memory. "No!" The doctor starts to rise, but she waves him back, fighting to calm herself. "No. I'll be all right." She looks around, spies another stool. "I'll just sit right over here. I'm fine. Really. You go right ahead."

"Okay. But don't pass out on me, now."

< 13 >

He is a nice young man, she thinks. Tillmans make good doctors. They comfort well. Bright sits on the stool, folds her hands in her lap, gives him a faint smile.

He nods, goes to work silently. He uses a tiny silver needle shaped like a fishhook and very thin black thread, working his way from one end of the gash to the other—a quick stab through the skin on one side of the rupture, then a twist of his fingers to bring the needle up through the other side, tying off each suture with a delicate knot and snipping the thread with a small pair of scissors before starting the next one.

Bright stares, horrified by what she sees, forgetting her own discomfort. Sweat pops out on Buster's upper lip and his jaw muscles twitch. He looks over at her for a quick moment and she sees the pain and panic, raw in his eyes. Clearly, Buster now wishes he had opted for the novocaine. But it is too late. He has committed himself and he is unable to draw back because he is a man and a Marine and a fool, unyielding in his cussedness the way a man will be when trapped between the folly of a bad decision and the rock wall of his own pride. *Stupid! Bullheaded, stupid, self-centered man!* she thinks, the anger rising in her. She wants to scream at him, but she holds it in. *Let him suffer! He asked for it!*

There are eight stitches in all, each one an exquisite violation of flesh. The doctor looks up at Buster once in midoperation, grunts and continues. And finally he is finished, dropping the needle and scissors with a clatter into the metal pan. "Okay?" he asks Buster simply.

Buster nods weakly, relief flooding his face. The stubble of his beard stands out starkly against his pale skin and now there is sweat all along his forehead, a tiny trickle of it just next to his right ear.

The doctor swabs the wound with an orange substance that smells a little like creosote, then wraps it with gauze, around and around the thumb, securing it with strips of adhesive tape until it looks like a small mummy. "It's going to throb for a while, so I'll write you out a prescription for some pain pills." No argument on that from Buster. "You'll need to keep it clean. Change the bandage every day."

"I don't know how," Buster says obstinately.

For the first time, the doctor looks exasperated. "Can you change his bandage, Miz Birdsong?"

She is so mad now, she can hardly speak. "Yes. I'll change his bandage." She gets up from the stool, trembling. "Pay the bill, Buster," she snaps. "I'll be in the car." And she turns on her heel, feeling both their eyes on her as she stalks out.

It takes ten minutes for Buster to reach the car, but she is still

< 14 >

seething, the anger gnawing at her empty stomach like a small razor-toothed animal. He has barely closed the door before she lurches away from the curb in front of the hospital and roars onto Birdsong Boulevard. Buster seems not to notice. He slumps against the door, staring vacantly out the window; he is somewhere far off, perhaps on a landing craft chugging toward some white-hot beach. He was wounded and decorated at Iwo Jima, she knows that. And there had been Korea. Is that what got him in hot water in Korea, his bullheadedness? She doesn't want to know. She has had a bellyful of Buster Putnam this morning.

But they have gone scarcely a block before her anger gets the better of her. She turns suddenly and barks at him, "Why did you do that?"

"Do what?" Buster says absently.

"What are you trying to do to yourself?"

He rouses himself from wherever he has been, turns to her with an odd look, holding his injured hand gingerly, as if it belonged to somebody else. "I don't know what you mean."

"That . . ." Her voice shakes. Her hands grip the steering wheel like a vise. "That *performance* in there."

He turns away again, looks out the window.

"Do you think if you hurt yourself enough you'll find out who you are? Good Lord, Buster. That house, falling down around your ears, the hole in the roof, the way you live"—she is fairly sputtering now, the words pouring out in a torrent—"that . . . that *thumb!*"

He stares at her for a moment, then says mildly, "Don't you think you'd better slow down?"

She realizes suddenly that she is driving much too fast. The old Plymouth is groaning and shaking as it hurtles down the long gentle hill that Birdsong Boulevard takes from the hospital to town, houses on either side whizzing by.

"How I drive is my business!" she bellows, infuriated now.

"And how I act is my business," Buster says. "So if you'll just pull over to the curb here and let me out, I'll walk home and let you proceed on like Fireball Roberts."

She twists the steering wheel and jams on the brake and the car slews to a stop against the curb, the right front tire bumping up on the grass of somebody's lawn, just missing a nandina bush and jostling both of them thoroughly. Buster reaches out with his good hand and braces himself against the dashboard until the car bounces to a stop. But he doesn't say a word until he has opened the door and climbed out, taking his own sweet time about it, then stuck his head back in the open window.

< 15 >

"And what about you, Bright?"

It startles her. "What . . . ?"

"Sitting over there so quiet in that big house of yours. What are you hiding from? Are you trying to figure out who you are too?"

It stuns her. "You go to hell, Buster Putnam!" she cries. And he withdraws his head quickly before she takes it off, stomping the gas again and bumping back onto Birdsong Boulevard with a nasty roar of the Plymouth's engine and a belch of gray smoke from the tail pipe, leaving Buster standing by the nandina bush. She doesn't look back. *Damn him! Who does he think he is!*

A block from home the car begins to sputter, the engine cutting in and out. Bright bangs her hand on the dashboard in anger and, with that, the car quits entirely. She shoves the gearshift into neutral and rolls to a stop against the curb, then sets the hand brake and sits there for a moment, boiling, muttering under her breath at Buster Putnam and the aging Plymouth. Both of them are old and ornery. She doesn't know what is wrong with Buster, but she has no doubt about the Plymouth. Vapor lock. That's what Big Deal O'Neill calls it, vapor lock. When the car gets overheated, the gasoline in the fuel line vaporizes. And the engine quits. Arzell, Big Deal's chief mechanic at the Ford dealership, has clamped wooden clothespins along the length of the fuel line to absorb the heat, and things are fine as long as Bright doesn't drive too far on a hot day or push the car too hard. Which she has just done.

There is no use sitting here. Nothing to do but abandon the car. Later, she will send Big Deal to pick it up and have Arzell tinker with it some more. Big Deal is patient with Bright and her Plymouth, even though he is a Ford man. There is no longer a Plymouth dealer in town, and besides, Big Deal and Little Fitz Birdsong have been lifelong friends.

So Bright gets out of the car, leaves the key in the ignition, walks the rest of the way home, calming herself as she goes. Enough of Buster Putnam, she decides. He can fall through the roof, cut off his head with a table saw for all she cares. She won't be responsible.

As she passes the Methodist parsonage, several doors down from her own, she thinks, *That's what's got your bowels in an uproar, Bright Birdsong. Responsibility.* For a few minutes there, she felt just a tiny bit responsible for Buster Putnam. It is a bad old habit she has meant to be rid of. Responsibility. For most of her life it has been her great burden—the aches, sufferings, worries about the people she has felt responsible for, those who had claim on her life and her heart. She realizes that she has largely defined herself by her responsibilities. She

< 16 >

has a great sense of having poured her own life into the people she felt responsible for, then giving them up—parents, children, husband. Children she has been giving up since the beginning, with the sadness that came from releasing them from the womb. And Fitzhugh, dead on the sidewalk in front of the Commercial Bank before either of them had a chance to set things right.

No, the devil with responsibilities. She wants no burden. No Buster Putnam with his life flaking away like weathered paint, no Roseann, no Little Fitz. They will come and go this week, and she will bear up as gracefully as possible. But she will welcome their leaving. *No, Buster Putnam, I know exactly who I am. A woman who just wants to be quiet. It is precious little to ask after a long life filled with noise. Enough is enough.*

Once home, Bright shakes herself free of it and busies herself with routine. First to the backyard to retrieve Gladys's empty dish, wash it out with the garden hose, and place it on the steps to dry in the morning sun. Then she drags the hose across the yard to splash the birdbath full of water while the birds scold her tardiness from the trees above. She coils the hose neatly beneath the kitchen window and goes back in the house, pours a cup of coffee in the kitchen and takes it to the front porch, sits in a wicker rocking chair, sipping the coffee and watching Claxton Avenue wake to the morning. It is seven-thirty. A refrigerated delivery truck throbs at the front of the Dixie Vittles across the way. The car that had been parked in front is gone, perhaps already home now with a batch of rutabagas. Big Deal O'Neill unlocks the door at his Ford dealership halfway down on Claxton. A steady stream of cars tops the rise on the River Bridge from the new subdivision beyond and traffic has picked up along Birdsong. It is already warm, even out here in the shade of the porch, the new sun climbing white and hot above the trees beyond the river. The quiet, best part of the morning is gone. But Bright means to collect her wits between now and midmorning, when Roseann arrives. She will need her wits for Roseann.

And then, for some reason she can't fathom, she thinks of *Rhapsody in Blue.*

It happens to her often, has, in fact, for all her life. Snatches of music pop into her head and then grow, passages repeating themselves and giving birth to others, sometimes staying with her all day until she drifts into sleep with melodies and words finally fading. It has become something of a game, trying to figure out where they come from and why. Why *Rhapsody in Blue* this particular morning?

< 17 >

Whatever the reason, the music dances in her mind, piano and orchestra, bits and pieces from the score, until finally she gives in to it, sets her coffee cup down on the table beside the wicker chair and goes into the parlor, opens the phonograph cabinet, gets out the album she brought home from Washington in 1942, a gift from Fitzhugh. It is a two-record set of oversized 78's in a cardboard sleeve. There is a picture of a champagne glass on the cover, musical notes rising like bubbles from the glass. It takes one side of each of the thick vinyl discs to get through *Rhapsody in Blue*. On the other record is *An American in Paris*. George Gershwin himself at the piano with Paul Whiteman and his orchestra, the original version from the masters. She has heard the piece played without interruption by Arthur Fiedler and the Boston Pops on television, but it seems strange without the pause for the records to change. She prefers the old 78's, the tiny clicks and scratches like static from an ancient radio, recalling sounds long lost in the ether. Bright stacks the records on the changer, and by the time she gets back to her rocker it has begun—the low trill of the solo clarinet climbing to a siren wail, high and lonesome, beckoning magic.

Sitting now on her front porch with the music drifting through the screen door from the living room, it all rushes back, speaking of time forever lost. It was supposed to be so different. He was supposed to come home from Washington satisfied that he had made an indelible mark on history, satisfied to grow old with Bright in the company of this small Southern town that had revered him and sent him to Congress as many times as he cared to go. And then they would make amends and nobody would have to choose anymore, nobody would have to win or lose. But it took Fitzhugh just two weeks after he'd come home to drop dead of a heart attack, to leave her with the terrible, numbing sense of being abandoned again.

Bright Birdsong does not want to think about all this here on her front porch on this warm June morning. Or does she? Why has she put *Rhapsody in Blue* on the phonograph, if not to stir up old haints and poisons? She just wants to be quiet, to be left alone. Doesn't she? And she wants very much not to be mad as hell at Fitzhugh Birdsong. But she is.

< 18 >

2

Nine o'clock, Bright finally preparing her own breakfast, thick round slices of banana on a bowl of Post Raisin Bran.

She tried to ignore the knocking at the front door, hoping that whoever it was would give up and go away. But it was persistent, and she finally put the knife and the half-peeled banana down on the counter and wiped her hands on a dish towel, then stepped to the breakfast room doorway to see Flavo Richardson standing on the porch. Flavo, unmistakable even in silhouette with the bright morning at his back, short and a bit stooped from age and struggle. Bright smiled. Beginning with the day Flavo Richardson had arrived with his rowboat to rescue Bright and Little Fitz from the Great Flood of 1939, he had always come to the front door. Neither of them would have it any other way.

"Whoever you are," Bright called from the breakfast room doorway, "go away. I don't want to buy any Bibles or detergent."

"You're gonna wish I was selling Bibles or detergent," Flavo said somberly.

Bright walked to the screen door and opened it. Flavo looked decidedly sour this June morning. He was holding a newspaper.

"Why doesn't a smart woman like you take the newspaper, Bright?" he asked.

"Because newspapers are fractious and noisome," she said.

"Humph," he grunted, and handed her the paper, carefully folded to show a picture and article on the front page. The bold black headline said, "FITZ DIDDLES?" Below it, a picture of a man and a woman on the porch of a house, obviously taken at night, with a flashbulb that cast stark shadows on the wall behind them. The man was wearing only boxer shorts and a look of desperate surprise. The woman, clutching a robe tightly about her, didn't look surprised at all. Bright had

< 19 >

never seen the woman, but the man was her son, Governor Fitz Bird-song. And she recognized the porch as that of the old camp house her father, Dorsey Bascombe the lumberman, had built several miles up-river, a very private place deep in a pine forest next to the river. There, on the wall between Fitz and the woman, was the horseshoe Dorsey had nailed up when he finished the camp house in 1919. Dorsey had believed in things like luck and romance. At least, he had in 1919.

Bright looked up from the paper at Flavo. "This morning's paper?"

"Yep."

She read:

> Governor Fitz Birdsong denied vehemently Sunday that any im-propriety was involved in his meeting with a young woman at a rural house in Sumiton County early Sunday morning. An Enquirer-Journal reporter and photographer, acting on an anony-mous telephone tip, surprised the scantily clad couple about 3:00 A.M. Birdsong at first denied he was the governor, then ordered the Enquirer-Journal reporter and photographer from the prop-erty. The woman identified herself as Drucilla Luckworst, 27, a cocktail waitress from Columbus.
>
> Sunday, the Birdsong campaign headquarters issued a statement that read in part: "Governor Fitzhugh Birdsong was resting alone after an arduous day of campaigning at his family's Sumiton County hunting lodge Saturday night when he was roused from sleep by a woman's voice on the front porch of the lodge. When Governor Birdsong stepped onto the porch to inquire about the commotion, a photographer lurking in the yard suddenly snapped a picture of the scene. Governor Birdsong had never seen the woman before, and is convinced that the entire business is a last-minute and desperate attempt to smear his good name by despic-able elements in the camp of his opponent in the governor's race."

"Great God," Bright said with a sharp intake of breath, as if some-one had punched her in the stomach. She looked up at Flavo, back down at the paper. "Hunting lodge," she said after a moment. "It never was a hunting lodge. My father never hunted a day in his life. It was a camp house, not a hunting lodge." She read on:

> Governor Birdsong's wife, Lavonia, reached at the Governor's mansion shortly after the picture-taking incident, said she did not know her husband's whereabouts. "He said he was going to be all weekend at a strategy meeting," Mrs. Birdsong said.
>
> Miss Luckworst, contacted at her Columbus apartment Sunday, refused further comment on the affair, and referred reporters' ques-tions to her attorney.
>
> Lieutenant Governor Maurice Calhoun, Birdsong's opponent in the June 10 Democratic runoff, was unavailable for comment. His press aide did not return the Enquirer-Journal's telephone calls.

< 20 >

There was more. "Please turn to Page 6," it said at the bottom of the article. Instead, she handed the paper back to Flavo, who was standing there with his arms crossed, studying her closely. He tucked the paper under one arm. "Well, are you going to make me stand here on the porch like some common jigaboo, or are you going to invite me in like proper folks?"

She opened the door wider for him, letting more of the morning in. "Excuse me. I forgot my manners. I guess I'm a little . . ."

"Hmmmm. Yes." He stepped past her, stood for a moment in the middle of the cluttered parlor.

"Do you want a cup of coffee?" she asked.

"I don't drink the foul stuff. It rusts your bowels. I'll take a glass of ice water if you have it."

He had seated himself on the sofa when she returned with the glass of water. She handed it to him, sat down heavily in the wing-back chair across from him. The newspaper was open on the coffee table, Little Fitz and Drucilla Luckworst staring up at them in bold black and white. Flavo crossed one thin leg over the other, took a sip of his ice water, uncrossed his legs, drummed his fingers against the glass, crossed his legs the other way.

Bright sat staring at the newspaper for a long time, finally took a deep breath and asked, "What do you think?"

Flavo pursed his lips. "I hope he's been framed."

She shook her head. "I hope so too," she said. "But I tell you this, it's mighty strange that he was at the camp house by himself Saturday night instead of coming on here to stay with me. And another thing is, he hasn't called me yet." She tapped the paper with her finger. "This says it happened Saturday night. Here it is Monday morning and I have to find out in the newspaper."

"Are you going to give him the benefit of the doubt?"

Bright handed the paper back. "I'm just saying what I think."

Flavo looked up at the ceiling. "He had it won," he said. "Fitz had it in the bag. No way Calhoun could have caught him."

"Had?"

"Yes, had. This"—he pointed at the paper—"puts everything somewhat in doubt."

"But what if he was framed," Bright said, realizing as she said it that "what if" was a kind of passing judgment. Was Little Fitz Birdsong capable of a midnight tryst with a cocktail waitress? Was any man?

Flavo snorted. "We vote a week from tomorrow, Bright. You know politics, you of all people . . ."

"Damn politics," she said.

"Damn it all you want. But it's a fact of life. It's the way things get

< 21 >

done. Not just this business"—he waved at the newspaper—"but all the other, too. You've been up to your neck in it all your life."

There was a tinge of disgust in his voice. Flavo Richardson was a little like Gladys, she thought. Neither had any truck with nonsense. "Politics is the art of what's real," he went on, "and what's real is what folks think, not what the truth may be. Damn the truth if you want, but don't damn politics."

Bright thought about that for a moment. "So you think Fitz has lost?"

"I didn't say that. But he's got eight days to convince folks that this"—he indicated the paper again—"ain't real. Especially white folks."

"How about black folks?"

"Black folks ain't as bad hypocrites as white folks. White folks want somebody for governor who pretends he's a little better than they are. Black folks just want somebody that gets the job done, and don't care so much whether he . . ."

". . . keeps his pants zipped up," Bright finished for him.

Flavo nodded, his jaw hard. "Yep." He took another sip of the ice water, then put the glass down on the coffee table next to the newspaper.

They sat there for a while staring at each other, and then Bright said, "Well, what are you going to do about it?"

"Hah! What *can* I do? Stick, that's what. I've got no choice. *We've* got no choice."

"But if you did?"

Flavo hung fire for a moment, and then his face softened. "I'd stick anyhow, I reckon. Little Fitz Birdsong may not be the greatest statesman who ever came down the pike, but his heart is in the right place, far as black folks is concerned. Unlike some I remember."

Bright started to protest that Fitz's father's heart had been in the right place too, he just never did much about it. And of course times were changed. Lots of black folks voted now, and that made white politicians sit up and take notice. But of course Flavo Richardson knew all that.

"God knows, we don't need Maurice Calhoun." The name dripped from Flavo's tongue like bile. "We need to get shet of what Maurice Calhoun stands for. So no, Flavo Richardson ain't going to run out on Little Fitz Birdsong."

He is a calculating man, Bright thought, *keen and cunning.* She remembered him as a very small boy, sitting on the back steps of the Bascombe house across town while his mother, Hosanna, cooked and

< 22 >

cleaned for Dorsey Bascombe and his family inside—quiet, deep inside himself, staring out across the backyard for hours at a time. No bother to anybody, just sitting there thinking, the small dark eyes blinking with some inner rhythm. She never asked him back then what he was thinking. It would never occur to a young white girl that a small black boy had any thoughts worth asking about. And it would never cross the mind of a small black boy to volunteer any. It was not until years later that Bright discovered that Flavo Richardson had not been contemplating june bugs or wild onions there on her back steps. She had never really paid much attention to Flavo until the day he rowed up onto her front porch in 1939.

"You rescued Fitz from the Flood," Bright said now.

A bit of a smile flickered across Flavo's face. "Yes. I did that."

"I don't know what we would have done without you."

"Drowned, prob'ly." Flavo stood stiffly, grimacing. A touch of arthritis in his back added to his stoop and his irritability these days. "Well, I'm gonna do what I can to rescue him again, Bright. That is, if the boat ain't sprung too bad a leak."

She picked up the newspaper from the coffee table, took a last look at it, handed it back to Flavo.

"Keep it if you want," he said.

"No." She shook her head. "I think I've seen quite enough, thank you."

He shrugged, tucked the paper under his arm. She followed him to the door, but before he opened it, he turned to her again. "And you, Bright. What are you going to do about it?"

"Me?"

"He's your boy."

"Well, it's not my fight."

"Hmmmm." He tilted his head up, looked at her down the bridge of his nose. "You done gone to seed, Bright?"

"No," she snapped. "I just mind my own business."

"Times past, you minded lots of folks' business. Made some folks mad, made some folks think you were something special." He opened the screen door, stepped out onto the porch.

"I've done my bit," she said firmly. "As the old song says, I have laid down my burden down by the riverside, and I ain't gonna study war no more."

Flavo frowned, a deep furrow creasing his brow. "War don't never end, Bright. Battles do, but war don't. You can sit here in this old house and ignore it if you want. But don't talk to me about laying down no burden."

< 23 >

Bright opened her mouth to say something mean and spiteful. *Mind your own business! Who do you think you are?* But no. That would not do for a good number of reasons. Chiefly, this stooped old man, still full of combativeness, was part of her history—a strong black link to her childhood. And there was precious little of that left anymore. So instead she said quietly, "Are you going to call him?"

"Of course."

Bright nodded. "When you do, tell him to call his mama."

"Yes. I'll do that." And he closed the screen softly between them and was gone into the morning, leaving her standing there in the quiet of the house, drained and weary.

There was of course nothing she could do. Was there? Hear him out, perhaps, provide a little comfort. Avoid judgment. But Fitz Birdsong was a big boy now, capable of making his own messes and cleaning them up. Like the rest, he was no longer her responsibility. Damn Flavo Richardson for trying to make her think he was.

<   >

No sooner had Flavo gone, taking his newspaper with him, than the phone began to ring. It was as if he had come as the town's emissary, bearing bad tidings, and thus opened the subject for everybody else's two cents' worth.

Bright let the phone ring for a long time before she finally picked up the receiver. "Yes?"

"Shall I come over?" Xuripha Deloach. Plump, powdered Xuripha. Cheerful purveyor of bad news from the sunroom of her white-columned house on the bluff across the river. Newspaper spread across the brass and glass coffee table while she clucked over the hideous picture of Fitz and Drucilla Luckworst.

"Come over?" Bright asked. "For what?"

A huge, bosom-expanding intake of breath on the other end. "Have you seen the paper?"

"Oh, my God," Bright said. "I'll bet the Japanese have bombed Pearl Harbor again. Fitzhugh was always afraid of that."

"No. Little Fitz."

"Little Fitz has bombed Pearl Harbor."

"Worse than that!" Then softly, sadly: "It appears he has stuck his foot in it, Bright."

"Stuck his foot in what?"

"Come to think of it," Xuripha said, "it wasn't his foot at all."

"Let's start over," Bright said. She knew she was being perverse, but there was something about Xuripha that could summon perversity.

< 24 >

They had been friends since childhood in the way two women who live together in the same small town all their lives will of necessity carry on a friendship of one sort or another. But it was a friendship edged by rivalry, and Xuripha had always felt the rivalry much more keenly than Bright. Bright realized that Xuripha had simply never gotten over the fact that Bright had won, at least in those things which truly mattered to Xuripha. Bright had married the handsome and successful Fitzhugh Birdsong. And Xuripha had settled for Hubert Deloach, a young man so homely that people called him Monkey. To his face. Only in recent years had Xuripha begun to gain what she perceived to be the upper hand as Bright was widowed and, in effect, retired. Monkey Deloach had proven to be an exceptionally astute businessman. He had made a good deal of money from what had once been Bright's father's lumber business. And Xuripha had become the town's reigning matron—social arbiter, giver to worthy causes, theological conscience of the Baptist Church, five-time president of the Study Club. She worked tirelessly at it, exerting an iron-willed influence and fending off the younger women who nipped at her heels. But despite all that, the past rankled. Even now, Bright imagined, Xuripha took some exquisite satisfaction in a bit of scandal involving a Birdsong. Perversity on both their parts.

"Let's start over," Bright said now. "There's something in the paper about Fitz?"

"Lord God Almighty!" Xuripha exploded.

"Read it to me," Bright said. "I don't take the paper."

"Well, there's an enormous photograph . . . ," she began. Bright put the telephone receiver down softly on the table and went to the kitchen to retrieve her breakfast. By now, the raisin bran was soggy and the milk lukewarm, but the banana slices were still firm. Bright could not abide soft, overripe bananas. She liked to buy them fresh, even a tad green, two or three at a time. This was the last one in the house. She took the cereal back to the telephone table and took her time eating it, listening abstractedly to the unintelligible buzz of Xuripha's voice. When she had finished, she took a pad and pencil from the drawer underneath the phone and wrote down "bananas." Then she took the empty cereal bowl back to the kitchen. As she finally picked up the telephone receiver again, Xuripha was reading, " ' . . . reported huddling behind closed doors with his political advisers through the day Sunday . . .' "

"Merciful heavens!" Bright cried. "No more! I feel faint!"

"I'll be right there . . ."

"No! It's a private agony!"

< 25 >

There was a long moment of silence. Then Xuripha said firmly, "He's been framed, of course."

"Of course."

"A hussy and a couple of newspapermen," she snorted. "Birds of a feather. And Maurice Calhoun. He'd drive over a carload of nuns to get elected."

Bright smiled. That was the thing about Xuripha Deloach. There was, at the bottom of the rivalry, the friendship—strange, perhaps, but long-suffering. Only over a long time spent in one place could such an accommodation come about. As Dorsey Bascombe had liked to say, it is pretty hard to stay mad at a man when you have to look him in the eye day after day. You make do with each other, warts and foibles and all. So for Bright Birdsong and Xuripha Deloach, the friendship transcended the other, at least at the moments when it counted. And at this particular moment, there was Little Fitz Birdsong, a local boy and Bright Birdsong's son. And damn the man or woman who attempted to blacken his name, rightly or wrongly. So there.

"Has he called?" Xuripha asked now.

"No," Bright confessed. "He may be trying just this minute."

"Are you sure I shouldn't come over?"

"No. Truly."

"Take two aspirin. I'll call back."

"Yes. 'Bye now." Bright hung up and sat there for a moment. Then the telephone rang again.

"Bright?" Henry Wimsley, the Methodist minister.

"Yes, Henry."

"The paper . . ."

"I know."

"Is there anything I can do?"

"I can't think of a thing, Henry."

"Has Fitz called yet?"

"Not a word."

"I guess he's busy." Henry was trying to sound hopeful, she knew, but it came out wrong. Busy. Yes, he must be up to his keister in alligators about now.

"Um-hum, I imagine he is."

"Well, should I lead us in prayer?"

"It's sweet of you to offer, Henry, but somehow I have a hard time with the notion of praying on the telephone, like we were asking God to eavesdrop."

"Yes, I suppose so. Well, I'll just say a prayer here in my study."

"Thank you, Henry."

The telephone rang again almost the instant she put the receiver

< 26 >

back in the cradle. She jerked her hand away, startled, sat staring at it for a good long moment. It rang and rang. She thought not to answer. *Go away and let me be quiet and think about this thing!* Then she snatched it up.

A thick, harsh voice on the other end. "You tell that boy of yores to stop dippin' his wick—"

Bright slammed the receiver down, waited an instant, picked it up again, heard a dial tone, dropped the receiver with a clatter on the table. That would be quite enough of that business.

Bright sat there, stunned and confused. Then she got up quickly, went to the door and stood looking out at the porch, half expecting Little Fitz Birdsong's big black limousine to wheel into the driveway and Fitz to jump out with his big warm smile enveloping her like new sun. "It's all right, Mama! All a mistake! No sweat!" But no, the driveway was empty and the morning clanked and clamored at her, all raucousness and discord now—the traffic rumbling by on Birdsong, a stock boy banging about at the Dixie Vittles loading dock, the whine of machinery down the block at the rear of Big Deal O'Neill's Ford dealership, a man standing in the doorway of the Western Auto on the other side of the street, hollering something unintelligible to someone unseen in a pickup truck parked at the curb.

The morning assaulted her ears and her sensibilities. Bright stood there a moment longer and then retreated in confusion to the piano, an old refuge. She began to play mindlessly, hands wandering about the keyboard with a life of their own, unheard. After a while, she began to hear what they played, the old familiar melody at last beginning to break through the babble. Schumann's *Träumerei.* It was the most beautiful piece of music she knew, and she could still play it with a lovely grace, the way she had done fifty years before at the Atlanta Conservatory of Music competition, the day she had met Fitzhugh Birdsong. Afterward, the slim young man had introduced himself and said, "Miss Bascombe, you made me cry." And she had believed him.

Bright had always insisted that her own piano students, at a certain stage in their development, learn the *Träumerei.* She stuck to it over the years as her classes dwindled until there were just a handful now, mostly children of former students who remembered fondly the soft afternoons in Bright Birdsong's parlor with the metronome clicking its discipline and small fingers coaxing notes from the upright console Story and Clark piano; who remembered the day when Bright turned off the metronome and opened the piano bench and spread the pages of Schumann's *Träumerei* across the stand and said, "I believe you're ready for this." For those few, it would be a magic moment.

She played it now, hearing—as she always did—the mellow ghost

< 27 >

of Dorsey Bascombe's trombone floating above the piano, matching note for note. "A trombone," Dorsey Bascombe had said, "is the sound of God's breathing." A lost duet, so unspeakably beautiful and sad it made Bright Birdsong's heart ache. She played on, seeing Dorsey standing beside her piano in the choir loft in the Methodist Church on a warm summer's Sunday night, eyes closed and fingers poised lightly on the gliding slide of the trombone. They played, now as then, in perfect unison. And when the last note had taken wing through the window into the June morning, she lifted her hands from the keyboard and placed them gently in her lap and sat there quietly.

She waited for the return of tranquillity. But instead, she heard a small voice inside her brain asking, "What on earth now?"

< 28 >

3

The bleating of the Winnebago's horn startled her, and she rose from the piano bench and went to the front door in time to see the van turn the corner onto Birdsong Boulevard and then lumber into her driveway like a huge amiable beast, the spreading branches of the pecan trees scraping along its top with a screech. She could see Roseann in the passenger seat, her son-in-law, Rupert, behind the wheel, pipe clamped in his teeth, Jimbo's small head peering between them. Bright stepped onto the porch as the Winnebago wheezed to a halt and Roseann jerked the window open.

She was holding a newspaper in her right hand, waving it. "Did you see it? Did you see what he did?"

Bright could feel her stomach knotting, the old dread taking hold. Roseann had always been a tattletale, never happier than when she was delivering some piece of bad news about her brother, the worse the better. She thrived on crisis, and if she didn't have one ready-made, she would resort to invention. Who else but a woman looking for trouble would marry a professional golfer whose eye wandered farther than his tee shots? Not Rupert; Rupert was the second—a solid, plodding man, totally unlike the golfer, whose name Bright was already having trouble remembering.

Roseann flung open the door of the Winnebago and leapt out, her shoes making tiny explosions in the sand of the driveway as she marched toward the steps, still waving the paper. "All over the front page!" she cried. Roseann's hair, already streaked with gray at thirty-six, was disheveled, galloping off in all directions. She still plucked at her hair. She had done it as a child, pulling and tugging at the fine brown strands until Bright finally cut it in exasperation to a short bob. It had been a mistake. Roseann fretted and fumed until there was a wildness in her eyes and her asthma flared up, racking her frail body

< 29 >

with fierce coughing fits. Her fingers danced about her head, even in sleep. Bright let the hair grow back, but it scarcely made Roseann less difficult, then or now.

Bright met her at the bottom of the steps. "Roseann, it's good to see you," she said. She reached out, brushing past the newspaper, and hugged her daughter. She could see Rupert still in the front seat of the Winnebago, tidying up. Rupert was a tidy man. She wondered for a brief moment if he was miserable yet, if Roseann had driven him to distraction. Roseann was obsessively neat, but not tidy in the comfortable way Rupert was.

Roseann gave her a quick squeeze, then stepped back and thrust the newspaper out again. "Have you seen it?"

"Yes, I've seen it."

"Well?" Roseann demanded.

Bright glanced down at the photograph, the startled man in boxer shorts and the bored woman in the robe, frozen in black and white. "Fitz is getting a little paunch, don't you think? All that rich food at these political do's. Your father never had to worry about that. The Birdsongs could always eat until their eyes bulged out and never gain an ounce. Fitz takes after the Bascombes in that regard, I'm afraid. I had an uncle . . ."

"Mother!"

"What do you want me to say?"

"Well, it's wretched." She waved the paper again. "How could he *do* it?"

"How do you know he did it?"

"It's right there"—Roseann poked the photograph with her finger—"in black and white."

"Don't be too quick to judge, Roseann. You know politics."

"No." She shook her head angrily. "I don't know politics. I never did know politics. I *hate* politics."

And that was the truth, Bright thought. Fitzhugh Birdsong had always been the one who could manage Roseann. She would sit calmly in his lap for hours while he read or talked to her. Nights when he was home from Washington they would sit together in a wicker rocking chair on the front porch while the evening grew soft and velvet around them, while the town grew still, and Bright could hear the faint rise and fall of their voices until finally Roseann would drift off to sleep in Fitzhugh's arms. He might sit there for another hour, rocking her, until he finally rose and took her gently to bed. But those nights were so few, so preciously few. Yes, Roseann must truly hate politics.

"Has Fitz called you?"

"No," Bright admitted.

< 30 >

"Well . . ."

"He may have tried, but the phone has rung all morning. I've got it off the hook now."

"And yesterday. Was it off the hook yesterday? All this happened Saturday night. Fitz had all day yesterday to call."

"Don't grill me, Roseann," Bright flashed.

Roseann shrugged, unchastened.

"Hello, Rupert," Bright called to her son-in-law as he stepped out of the door of the Winnebago and started across the bare patch of yard toward the steps. He was wearing seersucker Bermuda shorts and an argyle knit shirt, black socks and bright blue running shoes with big red stars on the sides. Rupert had a wide, open face and thinning black hair that he parted just above his right ear and swept across the top. He took the pipe out of his mouth and gave her a hug. The golfer she never hugged. With Rupert, it seemed the thing to do. "My father," she told him, "always said he'd never hire a man who smoked a pipe because he didn't believe a fellow could hold down two jobs at once."

Rupert laughed. "How are you, Bright?" He had called her Bright from the day more than a year before when Roseann had brought him home and introduced him as her new husband. That too seemed the thing to do. Rupert was in his midforties, several years older than Roseann and light-years ahead of her in stability. Bright had heard Roseann refer to Rupert as a professor at the University, but in fact he was not. He was a technician, a man who worked in the Engineering School, designing and building instruments and machines for faculty members' experiments.

"I'm fine, Rupert. And you? Are you bearing up?"

Rupert laughed again. "Yes, that's a good way to put it. Bearing up. Definitely bearing up. Ready for a vacation."

"I thought you'd be here earlier," Bright said.

Rupert stuck his pipe back in his mouth and Roseann gave Bright a pained look. "Well, I had a little, ah . . ."

Rupert pulled the pipe out and held it, stem poised next to his lips. "Asthma attack," he said. "She got a little excited with all the packing and loading and then this"—he nodded toward the newspaper. "She couldn't catch her breath. We had to take her to the hospital."

"Good Lord," Bright said softly. "Are you all right?"

"Of course," she snapped.

"I'm afraid it gave Jimbo a bit of a scare," Rupert said.

"What's he doing in there?" Bright looked toward the open door of the Winnebago.

"Jimbo," Roseann called.

< 31 >

"He reads a lot," Rupert said. "And he has an alligator . . ."

"A what?"

"Well, it's an imaginary alligator. Named Josephus. When I was a kid, my dad was in the Army, and we traveled all over the country towing a house trailer. We had this imaginary alligator named Josephus who lived under the trailer. Whenever we got ready to move, we'd hitch up the trailer and Dad would put us all in the car, and then he would go back and get Josephus out and put him in the trailer. And whenever we stopped, Dad would make us stay in the car while he let Josephus out."

Bright studied him as he talked, smiling, waving the pipe, the strands of his thinning hair snaking down across his forehead. A good man for a small boy, she thought, a man who grew up with an alligator under the house. She couldn't imagine the golfer with an alligator, except on his shirt.

"Anyway," Rupert said, "I was the oldest, so I inherited Josephus. And I gave him to Jimbo."

"And he lives under the house," Bright said.

"Yes, but he goes on trips."

"He'll grow out of it," Roseann said. She seemed impatient with the alligator business.

"I hope not." Rupert shook his head. "I didn't."

"Jimbo," Roseann called again. And finally he poked his head through the open doorway of the Winnebago and Bright saw with a pang how small and frail he seemed, how pinched the features of his thin face. She saw Jimbo perhaps once a year, on Roseann's infrequent visits. How old was he now? Nine? Ten?

Bright stepped around them and walked over to the Winnebago. "I hear you've got an alligator in there."

Jimbo gave her a thin smile, but he didn't say anything.

"Rupert says it used to be his alligator."

"Uh-huh."

"But he gave it to you."

"Uh-huh."

"Well, are you so busy with your alligator you can't give your grandmother a hug?"

He stepped out then and put his arms around her neck as she bent to him, clasping his small body, smelling his fresh-scrubbed smell, thinking that it was unnatural for a boy to smell this clean this late on a summer morning.

"Will you come in and sit a spell?" she asked, straightening.

Jimbo looked back at the Winnebago. "I suppose so."

"Do you want to put your alligator under the house?"

< 32 >

"We're not gonna be here that long. I'll just let him rest inside."

"Well, come on and let's talk about what we're going to have for lunch." Jimbo closed the door of the Winnebago and she took his hand and led him to the steps, where Rupert and Roseann waited.

"We can't stay—," Roseann started to say.

"Of course you'll stay for lunch," Bright said firmly. "You've got to eat lunch somewhere. I've got ham and potato salad in the refrigerator. And iced tea. That's better than somebody's greasy hamburger with who knows what kind of germs and hair in it."

She herded them into the parlor and got them seated, Rupert and Roseann on the sofa, Jimbo on the piano stool. He eyed the keyboard of the piano, but he didn't touch it, just sat there watching his mother. Roseann perched rather than sat on the edge of the sofa, running her hands over the worn edge of the fabric and looking about the room, taking in the clutter of magazines and books that Bright had not had time to straighten up, the long thin cracks in the ceiling plaster and the faded wallpaper coming loose in places and the threadbare Oriental rug on the hardwood floor. *All right*, Bright thought, settling herself into the wing-back chair next to the window, *say something*.

"Your phone's off the hook," Roseann said. She still had the newspaper in her hand, and she waved it in the direction of the telephone table next to the front door.

"Yes, it is," Bright said evenly. "I just told you, I took it off the hook. That's why I don't know whether Fitz has called or not."

"I suppose everybody in town has been calling."

"Not anymore."

Roseann flounced a bit on the sofa, straightening her skirt beneath her. "I'm just glad we'll be at the beach all week so we won't have to answer people's snotty questions and hear their snide remarks."

Bright glanced over at Rupert. He was working hard on his pipe, looking out the window across the front yard, a thin wreath of smoke encircling his head. She turned back to Roseann. "You're not coming back Thursday?"

"What's Thursday?"

"Governor Fitz Birdsong Day."

"You mean they're actually going ahead with it? After *this*?" She thumped the paper again.

"I imagine they are. They've got the parade all arranged, and they sold so many tickets for the luncheon, they had to move it to the gymnasium at the high school."

"Who's *they*?"

"Francis O'Neill is the chairman."

"Francis? You mean Big Deal?"

< 33 >

"I've always thought of him as Francis," Bright said. Francis and Fitz had been the best of boyhood friends. She remembered them sitting for hours in the wicker chairs on the front porch on long summer afternoons, reading the Tom Swift and Hardy Boys books that were stored away now by the shelfful in the attic. Bright had always called him Francis O'Neill.

Roseann looked out the window up Claxton Avenue at the Ford dealership with the big sign on the front that said BIG DEAL O'NEILL NEW AND USED CARS. "Everybody calls him Big Deal, Mama."

"I don't," Bright said simply.

Roseann laughed. "I'll bet you even call him Francis when you go in there to get your car worked on. And I'll bet he just wants to go back in the men's room and hide."

Bright could hear the faintly mocking tone in Roseann's voice. She really wanted to say, *You're so old-fashioned, Mama.* But she wouldn't say that, not out loud anyway. It would just be there, an undercurrent.

"No," Bright said, "as a matter of fact I don't call him Francis when there are other men around. But I don't call him Big Deal, either. I just don't call him anything. When it's just the two of us, I call him Francis."

"So Big Deal O'Neill is the Grand Lama for Governor Fitz Birdsong Day."

"That's right."

"Well, we'll be at the beach all week."

"Fine," Bright said. "We'll make out."

Roseann spread the newspaper out on the coffee table, just in the spot where Flavo Richardson had left his copy open an hour or so before, out where they could all keep Little Fitz Birdsong and Drucilla Luckworst in full black-and-white view. Then she picked up a magazine from the table next to the sofa, an ancient edition of *National Geographic* with a picture of some round-bellied African children on the front, and started flipping through the pages absently, seeing nothing. Rupert took his pipe out of his mouth and stared at it for a moment, then fished in the pocket of his Bermuda shorts for his pipe tool and started poking about in the bowl. Jimbo just sat, his head cocked a bit to one side, watching everybody. And the silence grew like a toadstool, filling up the room.

Finally, Bright said, "Would anybody like some iced tea?"

"Coke," Jimbo said, brightening.

"You know better than that," Roseann said, still flipping pages. "Coke at this time of the day?"

< 34 >

"Well, I don't have any Coke," Bright said, "so that settles that. But the iced tea is excellent."

So she got up and went to the kitchen, leaving them to the strained silence of the living room. She poured three glasses of iced tea, then surveyed the contents of her refrigerator and cupboard. She had plenty of sliced ham and a bowl of potato salad, but there were only two slices of bread left in the wrapper. So she took the iced tea glasses to the living room, wrote down "bread" just below "bananas" on the telephone table pad, and went to fetch her purse.

"I'm out of bread," she said, returning with it from the bedroom.

Rupert heaved himself off the sofa. "I'll go."

"Nonsense," Bright said, waving him back to his seat. "It's just across the street. Won't take but a minute. You rest yourself." She looked at Jimbo, who sat on the piano bench with one finger poked into his iced tea glass, swirling the ice cubes around and around, making small motions with his mouth. "Come help a little old lady across the street," she said. Jimbo looked up at her, then over at Roseann, who seemed at the moment to be powerfully absorbed in the *National Geographic*. Then to Rupert, who winked at Jimbo and nodded. Jimbo got up, put his iced tea glass on the coffee table, and followed Bright out the door.

They stood for a moment on the sidewalk, waiting to cross Birdsong Boulevard to the Dixie Vittles Supermarket, feeling the heat of late morning radiating from the concrete. The leaves of the pecan trees in her front yard drooped in the hot, still air. Only June, and already summer clutched the town in its first fevered heat wave.

"Is this street named for you?" Jimbo asked, pointing to the BIRD-SONG BOULEVARD sign across the way, where Claxton intersected.

"Your grandfather," Bright said.

"Why did they name a street for him?"

Bright looked down at him in surprise. "Why, he was a congressman. He was very distinguished."

"Was he on TV?"

"Well, yes he was. A number of times, in fact. He was a rather well-spoken man. And handsome, too. He came across very well on TV."

Indeed he had. There had been a story on Huntley-Brinkley when Fitzhugh Birdsong retired from Congress. "A master of compromise, an architect of American foreign policy under six presidents," David Brinkley had called him. Brinkley and the others had been surprised when he retired and went home to the small town where they named a street for him. Birdsong Boulevard. Bright had never considered it

< 35 >

very boulevardish. It looked pretty much like any other street in town, not like you would imagine a boulevard, with two broad lanes on either side of a landscaped and tree-lined median. But it had been the town's way of honoring Fitzhugh, who had brought them a measure of fame. They had the ceremony the day after he arrived home from Washington, and there was nothing particularly grand about it—no parade, no pomp and circumstance, nothing like they would have this Thursday on Governor Fitz Birdsong Day.

"Were you on TV?" Jimbo asked.

"No," Bright said. "I was not on TV. I left all that business to your grandfather."

Which was not precisely true, she thought. A fellow with a TV camera had been there at Fitzhugh's reception. Bright and Fitzhugh had walked downtown at midmorning to City Hall, where there was a nice gathering of local folks, and Mayor Harley Gibbons had said a few words and read a proclamation renaming Hill Street (so named because it climbed a hill as it wandered out of town) as Birdsong Boulevard. The town council had gone to some lengths to find a street that wasn't already named for someone else, to avoid ruffling any feathers, but no one seemed too proprietary about Hill Street. There were no Hills in town. Fitzhugh had made a short speech about how he was glad to be back home among the people who had sent him to Congress for so many years, how much he looked forward to being just plain folks for a change, away from the weighty issues of Washington. When he was finished, they had punch and cookies inside City Hall and everybody went home in time for dinner. That night, they sat down and watched the six o'clock news, and there was a nice story about Fitzhugh's retirement party, a good shot of him shaking hands and making his speech, with Bright standing off a bit to the side, next to Xuripha Deloach. Bright had on a nice pink dress that day, but you couldn't tell it on the evening news because their set was a black-and-white. Fitzhugh remarked that they would have to get a color set, now that he was home to watch it. But two weeks later, Fitzhugh was dead. Now, eight years later, Bright still had the black-and-white set.

"The cars sure do go slow," Jimbo said.

Yes, she thought, things move so slowly for so long, and then change comes suddenly, without warning. You can have a heartache for a long, long time—and then have your heart completely broken in an instant.

"That's so little boys and little old ladies won't get run over," Bright told him.

Conversation froze when Bright and Jimbo pushed through the

< 36 >

big glass door into the fluorescent cool of the Dixie Vittles. Doris Hawkins, at the cash register, swept up the newspaper that was spread out on her counter with a noisy rattle and stuffed it underneath, but not before Bright got a glimpse of the photograph of Fitz and the woman on the front porch of the camp house. "Lord, howdy, MIZ BRIGHT!" Doris tossed the name back over her shoulder loudly enough to alert the rest of the store. "Ain't it a scorcher already!" Bright could see another woman, a shopper, peering around the corner of the canned goods section and Fonzel Baker, the butcher, craning his neck from behind the meat counter in the back.

"Good morning, Doris."

"Who's that handsome young man you got with you, Miz Bright?"

"This is James Randolph Blasious," Bright said, putting her hand on Jimbo's shoulder. "Better known as Jimbo. Passing through on his way to the beach."

"Yeah, I saw the mobile home pull in over yonder."

"It's a Winnebago," Jimbo said.

"This Roseann's boy?" Doris asked.

"That's right." Bright picked up a small shopping basket from the stack next to the door, just big enough to hold a loaf of bread and a few bananas.

"Blasious," Doris mused. "I thought she was a Poteet or something like that."

"Poquette," Bright said, remembering the golfer's last name for the first time that morning. Kip Poquette. Tall, slightly slump-shouldered from bending over golf clubs for so many years. He had started playing when he was five years old, that's what he had told Bright one time. She thought it odd. Five-year-old boys were supposed to play with frogs, not golf clubs. Kip Poquette had unruly blond hair and a big toothy smile and, to hear Roseann tell it, an absolute lack of a sense of responsibility about anything but golf. Roseann, of course, was as mean as a snake, and it had been a disastrous marriage, which ended amiably on Kip's part when, five years earlier, he simply declined to come home after the golf season was over. Kip might have been amiable about it, but Roseann was not. The next year, Kip had almost won some enormously big golf tournament. Bright remembered that he was leading by five strokes after the third round, but Roseann had called him on the telephone in Georgia or wherever it was and told him she was putting a curse on him. Kip went out the next day and sprayed golf balls all over the course and missed a three-foot putt on the last hole to lose the tournament by a stroke. He had never been the same. Roseann had said the newspapers started calling him "Yip"

< 37 >

Poquette. The last time Bright had heard anything about him, he was an obscure club pro somewhere in South Carolina.

"Kip Poquette," Bright said again, looking down at Jimbo. "But Roseann is remarried." She started to say that Rupert had adopted Jimbo, but then she thought that it was really none of Doris Hawkins's business, no matter how harmlessly she intended her busybodyness. Doris was the one who always called the radio station whenever she saw Little Fitz's big black limousine pull into Bright's driveway. Just to let everybody know the governor was visiting his mama.

"Well, let's see—," Doris started.

"Is the bread fresh?" Bright interrupted.

"Oh, yes. The Golden Hearth man was just by here an hour ago. Fresh week, fresh bread. You know the old saying." Doris laughed. Doris was just a little too loud this morning, a little nervous, trying hard to say too much of just the right thing to keep from saying the wrong thing. She wrinkled up her nose as if the newspaper she had stuffed under the counter had begun to smolder.

"Where's your car this morning?" Doris asked, looking out the big plate glass window that gave her a cinemascope view of Birdsong Boulevard and Bright's house across the street with the Winnebago hulking under the pecan trees in the driveway.

"It's up the street," Bright said. "It expired this morning."

"Oh?" Doris paused for a moment, waiting. Then, "I reckon you'll have to get Big Deal on the case."

"I reckon," Bright said, and left Doris standing there while she and Jimbo fetched a loaf of bread from the shelf at the side of the store and a clump of three good, firm bananas from the produce section. They brought their items back to the counter, where Bright paid Doris with a wrinkled dollar bill from her purse.

Doris rang up their purchase on the cash register, a new device that whirred and hummed and slowly ejected a piece of paper out of the top, as if it were sticking out its tongue. Doris bagged the bread and the bananas, ripped off the receipt and dropped it into the bag. "Here," Doris said, as she handed Bright the bag and a few coins in change. "Don't forget your Casino Caper card."

"My what?"

"Ain't you heard about the new contest?" Doris asked, reaching under the counter and handing her a card. It said DIXIE VITTLES CASINO CAPER at the top and SCRATCH AND WIN at the bottom, and there were three large black rectangles in between.

"It starts today. It's like playing the slot machines in Las Vegas," Doris said. "You scratch off that black stuff on them rectangles there,

< 38 >

and underneath is fruits and so forth. Then next time, you get another card and scratch off the black and if the fruits match up, you win a prize. They got a Cadillac automobile and a trip to Las Vegas and even cash money."

"Why?" Bright asked.

Doris stared at her, puzzled. "What do you mean, why?"

"What has Las Vegas got to do with a grocery store? Goodness, grocery stores don't even smell like grocery stores anymore. You used to be able to walk into a grocery store and smell food. Fresh bread and vegetables and meat and soap powder. Now, they've got it all in cans and plastic. Grocery stores smell like linoleum." She looked at the DIXIE VITTLES CASINO CAPER card. "And now the fruits are on cardboard."

Doris laughed. "Folks just want to have a little fun, I reckon. Think they're getting something for nothing, you know."

"I suppose." Bright handed the card to Jimbo. "Here, you hold on to this. And if you get rich, let me know."

"If you win a trip to Las Vegas, you can take your grandmama in your Cadillac," Doris said. Jimbo just stared at her.

They went out again into the bright hot sunshine and Jimbo held her hand as they waited at the corner for a tractor-trailer to rumble down Claxton, squeal to a halt with a wheezing of air brakes, and make a wide turn onto Birdsong Boulevard.

"Are you excited about going to the beach?" she asked as they crossed the street.

"I suppose so."

"You don't sound much like it."

"Mama gets upset when I get in the water," Jimbo said. "Rupert puts on lots of sunburn stuff and wears a big floppy hat and sits under the umbrella. And every time I get in the water, Mama starts yelling for me to be careful and watch for sharks and don't go out too far and finally Rupert has to get up and take off his hat and get in the water with me. At least, that's what happened last summer when we went to the beach, right after Mama and Rupert got married."

"Is Rupert much fun in the water?" Bright asked as they stepped up on the curb. She wondered if he wore his black socks on the beach.

"He's okay. He can't swim."

"Good Lord," Bright said softly.

Bright looked over at Buster Putnam's house next door. The front door was standing wide open, but that was nothing particularly new. Buster didn't seem to care much about whether the front door was open or closed, whether flies or even large animals wandered in and out at

< 39 >

their pleasure. His pickup truck was parked in the driveway, an old green GMC with fading paint and a battered tailgate. But there was no sign of Buster.

"Whose house is that?" Jimbo asked as they crossed the lawn.

"General Montgomery V. Putnam," Bright said, "who was almost the commandant of the entire United States Marine Corps."

"Does he live there?" Jimbo said, taking in the sagging shutters and peeling paint.

"After a fashion." Probably inside sleeping it off, Bright thought, oblivious to chaos. Of course, Buster Putnam was a warrior, no stranger to death and madness. Perhaps it was peace and tranquillity, after a life in bedlam, that had him buffaloed. She supposed that it depended on your perspective and what you considered normal.

As for herself, Bright discovered as they climbed the steps, she was strangely at ease for the first time since early morning, and she wondered why. Perhaps, she thought, it was the presence of this strange, silent child holding her hand. He had taken her mind off all the rest—Buster, Flavo, Little Fitz, even Roseann. She looked down at him curiously, wondered for an instant what he was like under all the silence. She realized that she would probably never know. Roseann wouldn't let her.

The refrigerator went *clunk* as Bright was fixing the sandwiches. She stopped, knife poised over the mayonnaise jar, and stared at the Kelvinator, realizing that the faint, almost inaudible hum of the refrigerator had been an undercurrent in her kitchen since 1939, as much a part of it as the air she breathed. Now it was so awesomely quiet that the knife made a jarring rattle when she set it down on the counter. She opened the door of the Kelvinator and felt the cool air on her face as she bent to stare into its innards, looking for some clue among the small Glad Wrap–covered bowls of leftovers, dibs and dabs of mashed potatoes, veal patties, broccoli, and carrots. She closed the door and looked up to see Rupert standing in the doorway.

"The refrigerator went *clunk*," she said. "I've had it since 1939, and it never went *clunk* before."

"It's a museum piece," Rupert said.

"I beg your pardon."

"No offense. They don't build 'em like this anymore." He rapped the top of the Kelvinator with his knuckles. "They don't build anything like this anymore. It's all plastic and cheap sheet metal now. Lots of plastic. Nothing wrong with plastic, mind you, but it doesn't make for very sturdy appliances." Rupert got up on his tiptoes and peered down into the round motor housing on the top of the refrigerator, then

< 40 >

sniffed. "Motor's gone." Bright could smell it now, the faint acrid aroma. "How long have you had this motor?" he asked.

"Since I've had the refrigerator."

Rupert shook his head, marveling. "Can you imagine that? An electric motor that's been running for forty years."

Bright's heart sank. She didn't want a new refrigerator. Giving up the old Kelvinator would be giving up another small piece of Fitzhugh Birdsong. She could remember, as clearly as if it had been yesterday, Fitzhugh standing there next to it, smiling broadly. Fitzhugh had rescued the house from the ravages of the Flood and built on the second story, but it was the refrigerator he was proudest of. It made her heart ache to think of it. And suddenly, standing there in her tiny kitchen with Rupert Blasious staring at her, she discovered that she was crying.

"Oh, my goodness," she said, the words barely a whisper.

He stepped quickly, instinctively to her and put his arms around her and she leaned against him, hiding for a moment in the warm space of his comfort. He was very gentle, very solid, and she let him enfold her, snuffling softly against his knit shirt.

"There now," Rupert said, patting her on the back. "Don't worry, I can fix it."

She took a deep breath, trying to compose herself. "You can?"

"Of course. It's just a motor."

She drew back and he released her, looking down into her eyes. "All right now?"

She nodded, blushing with embarrassment. "I don't know what got into me." Bright felt stupid and foolish. She hadn't done that for a long time, not even at Fitzhugh's death. But now she was crying over him here in the kitchen on a warm June morning, eight years after he was gone, after she thought she had put it all behind her.

Rupert smiled. "Maybe you've just had a hard morning."

"Yes. I suppose that's it." She plucked a paper towel from the roll by the sink, wiped her eyes and blew her nose softly. "Thank you."

"Now," Rupert said, clearing his throat, turning away to give her a bit of space to collect herself. "Let's see what we can do about this antique here." He bustled about, pulling in a chair from the breakfast room and standing up on it in his sock feet, peering down into the motor housing. "It's a standard-sized motor. Might have to monkey around with the fittings a bit, but I can probably salvage enough off the old one to make do." He looked down at Bright. "Mind you, they don't make motors like they used to, either. A new one won't last forty years."

"Well, when the new one goes *clunk*, I'll call you back," she said. She felt much better now. The sight of Rupert up on the chair in his

< 41 >

seersucker Bermuda shorts and black socks was somehow very comforting.

He smiled. "Fair enough."

Roseann poked her head through the doorway, frowning. "What's the matter? What are you doing up on that chair?"

"The refrigerator went *clunk*," Rupert said. "I'm gonna fix it."

"*Fix* it? What do you mean?"

"It needs a new motor."

"Good grief! We'll never get to the beach!" Roseann's hand went to her hair.

"Of course we will." Rupert climbed down off the chair and headed past her into the parlor with his jogging shoes in his hand. "I'll just get my tools out of the camper . . ."

"Rupert!" she called after him, but he was gone, letting the screen door bang behind him. Roseann turned to Bright. "He just can't stand it!" she cried. "He's always got a project going!" The color was high in her face. "You should see the house. He's been adding a room for nine months now. Nine months! Wires hanging out of the walls, dust everywhere. And pieces of fiberglass insulation. Do you realize that if you breathe fiberglass insulation it will give you lung cancer?"

Bright stared at her. "Roseann, you're going to have another asthma attack if you don't watch it . . ."

Jimbo appeared at Roseann's side. "What's the matter?"

"Rupert has gone into the refrigerator repair business," she said with a disgusted toss of her head.

"Oh," Jimbo said, and went back to the parlor.

"Roseann," Bright said, "go sit down at the breakfast room table. I'll bring you a sandwich. Do you want potato salad?"

"No, Mama. I don't want potato salad. I want to go to the beach."

Bright ignored that. She turned back to the counter and picked up the knife, stuck it in the mayonnaise jar, and spread a thick coating of mayonnaise on a slice of bread.

Roseann stood there in the doorway, fidgeting, one hand plucking at her hair. The silence hung heavy between them, punctured only by the sound of Bright's knife against the jar. Finally, Roseann took a deep, noisy breath that seemed to suck all the air out of the kitchen. She took a step into the room. "Mama, can I ask you something?" Her voice was low, conspiratorial.

"Of course." Bright kept working, spreading mayonnaise on another slice of bread, placing a piece of ham and some crisp lettuce between the slices.

"Can Jimbo stay here with you this week?"

Bright stopped, set the sandwich down on a plate, and wiped her

< 42 >

hands on her apron. She waited a moment, then turned to Roseann. "Here? Why?"

"Rupert and I need some time."

"For what, Roseann?" She could hear the accusing tone in her voice. *Have you messed up something else?*

"Oh," she said quickly, "nothing's wrong. We're doing just fine. We just need some time off by ourselves, you know, where we can talk . . ."

"About?"

"Things."

"Such as?" It was an old, familiar, wearying pattern that went back to Roseann's childhood—the two of them faced off, firing words at each other, Bright trying to hit the moving target, Roseann bobbing and weaving, hand tugging at her hair the way she was doing now.

"Well . . ."

"Roseann!" Bright said sharply. "Stop!" Roseann froze. "Now explain to me what's going on."

Roseann took another deep breath. "I want Rupert to go into business for himself." She paused, waiting for Bright to ask why. Bright crossed her arms over her chest. "He's wonderful with his hands," Roseann went on after a moment. "I complain about the mess, but he can fix anything or make anything. He builds these marvelous machines for the faculty members. Lots of wires and computer chips and little bitty machine parts. But he's just on the payroll, and everything he does belongs to the University. He could do it under contract, have his own shop, and everything would be *his*. If he invented something, it would be his—the patents, the royalties, all that. He's got this idea . . . well, it could be worth a lot."

"And what does the University think about it?"

"Oh, it's fine with them. They've talked about it. He's been thinking about it for years, in fact. But he just won't *do* anything."

"He's a deliberate man," Bright said.

"Oh"—Roseann gave a short laugh—"*is* he. When I try to talk to him about it, he just sits there and puffs on that pipe and stares off into space and smiles and says, 'Maybe someday.'"

"So you want to force the issue," Bright said.

Roseann shook her head. "We just need to talk about it."

Bright could imagine it, a week on the beach with Rupert huddled under the umbrella, wearing his floppy hat, slathered with sunblock lotion, Roseann's voice beating down on him like the fierce noonday sun. If Rupert Blasious were not miserable by now, he would be by week's end. And she imagined Jimbo, small and quiet, just sitting and watching and listening. She turned back to the counter, feeling the

< 43 >

hopeless anger rising in her, Roseann trying to hem her in, dumping a ten-year-old boy in her lap when what she really needed was some peace and quiet, some time to put things back in order. Jimbo was not Bright's responsibility. Jimbo . . . *Oh, drat!*

She picked up the plate with the sandwich on it. "Your sandwich is ready. Go get your glass and I'll pour you some more iced tea."

"Mama . . ."

"Not now!"

Roseann stood staring for a moment, then gave a final tug on her hair and turned away with a jerk.

Rupert came, lugging a large gray metal toolbox, and set it down on the floor next to the Kelvinator. "You want to finish fixing the lunch before I start making a mess?"

"That's fine," Bright said. "You come and sit down and eat and then you can get to work in here. Are you sure you want to fool with this old thing?"

Rupert waved his hand. "A fellow doesn't get a chance to work on a fine piece of machinery every day. It won't take long, really."

They ate at the breakfast room table, Roseann wrapped in a sullen silence, Bright and Rupert making desultory talk. Bright watched in fascination as Jimbo picked at his food, carefully plucking out all the bits of pickle from the potato salad and making a neat pile of them at the edge of the plate, then opening up the sandwich, tearing the sliced ham into small pieces and eating them one by one, leaving the bread and lettuce. He worked at it arduously, and when he had finished, the plate was a round white disaster area, littered with the shucked-off remains of the lunch. He had eaten only the ham and a few pieces of potato. Roseann seemed to pay him no attention until he finished, and then she told him to go brush his teeth. They had a long discussion about the difficulty of retrieving his toothbrush from his suitcase in the Winnebago, and finally she snapped at him and he shrugged and got up from the table and left.

Roseann wiped her mouth primly with her paper napkin, folded it in half and tucked it under the edge of her plate, then placed her fork squarely in the middle and polished off the last swallow of iced tea. She looked over at Rupert. "How long is this . . ."—she waved her hand in the direction of the kitchen—". . . thing going to take?"

Rupert crumpled his napkin, dropped it onto the plate, sat back and rubbed his stomach. "Half hour, maybe. Why don't you go lie down for a while. Bright, can Roseann lie down for a while?"

He is an incredibly patient man, Bright realized, *probably almost impossible to anger.*

"Of course," Bright said. "Go stretch out on my bed."

< 44 >

"All right," she said with a resigned sigh, and left them. Bright gathered the dishes and took them to the sink while Rupert started to work on the refrigerator, removing the round white housing on top and exposing the motor and compressor, pointing out the parts to her as she washed up the dishes.

"Should I take the food out while you work on it?" Bright asked. "I could take it over to the Dixie Vittles and put it in the freezer."

"Oh, I don't think that's necessary. It should be all right." He ran his finger around the edge of the door. "Nice tight seal, even after all these years."

"Well, there's potato salad in there. Potato salad spoils easily. You shouldn't ever take potato salad to a picnic because it spoils easily."

Rupert nodded. "I've heard that. In fact, I don't think I've ever seen potato salad at a picnic. But I think the inside will stay cool for a while longer. It shouldn't take long."

He pulled the refrigerator away from the wall a bit, reached behind and unplugged it, then climbed back up on the chair and unhooked several wires and started to work on the bolts holding down the motor, giving a sharp tug with his wrench to loosen them. By the time he finished, his hands were grimy with accumulated dust and beads of sweat stood out on his high forehead. He lifted the motor and stepped off the chair, holding it with both hands, a fat gray cylinder with wires dangling from both ends. He looked around the kitchen. "Where can I put this for a moment? Don't want to get grease and dirt all over your counter."

She remembered the newspaper, fetched it from the coffee table in the parlor, brought it back to the kitchen and spread it out on the counter next to the sink. Little Fitz and Drucilla Luckworst stared up at them from the front porch of the camp house. Rupert started to put the motor down on it, paused. "Do you . . . ah . . . mind messing up the paper? This thing's dirty." He blushed with embarrassment. "I meant the motor."

Bright stared at the picture, wrinkled her nose. "Yes, it is," she said. "Go right ahead."

He set the motor down, stared at his hands, cleared his throat. "I . . . ah . . . don't know anything about politics."

"Good for you," she said, putting him at ease, remembering at the same time that the telephone in the parlor was still off the hook, had been since midmorning. Fitz would have tried to call by now. Surely. "If I were you, I'd stick to motors."

"Yes," he smiled. "Speaking of which, where's the best place in town to buy an electric motor?"

She went to the parlor for the telephone directory, and thought

< 45 >

for a moment of placing the receiver back in its cradle so Fitz could call. But no, she decided that she didn't want the phone ringing and waking Roseann from her nap. Fitz would keep trying until he got her. She took the directory back to the kitchen and flipped to the yellow pages while Rupert looked over her shoulder, holding his grimy hands away from them. MOTORS, ELECTRIC—REPAIR. THOMPSON'S FURNITURE. Rupert washed up at the sink with a bar of Lava soap while Bright gave him directions and told him to charge the motor to her account. Then he left with the old motor, wrapping the newspaper around it to keep from getting his hands and the Winnebago dirty.

Bright stood for a while in the kitchen, looking at the old refrigerator, remembering Roseann and Fitz as children, making Kool-Aid Popsicles on a rainy summer afternoon. Roseann would have been about four, and that would have made Fitz eleven, already sprouting out of his jeans and shirts, giving evidence of the tall man he would become. Bright had bought plastic Popsicle makers at a Tupperware party at Xuripha Deloach's house and stashed them away in the cupboard for just such a day. The children made grape Kool-Aid, measuring out the sugar, mixing everything in a pitcher. They stood together at the sink, Fitz pouring while Roseann held the plastic devices, both of them engrossed in the work and Roseann, for once, keeping her tart tongue civil. Then Bright helped them store the six Popsicle holders in their plastic tray in the tiny freezer compartment of the Kelvinator. They spent the next hour sneaking peeks, waiting for the Kool-Aid to freeze, and then suddenly the rain stopped and the sun reappeared and Fitz dashed out to find Francis O'Neill. It was not until after supper that he remembered the Popsicles. Bright heard his enraged bellow from the kitchen. He flew into the dining room as Roseann clambered down from her chair and darted out the back door. "She ate every one!" he screamed, his eyes popping with indignation. "Every goddamn one!" Bright banished him to his room for two days for cursing and spanked Roseann and sent her howling to bed. Roseann, she thought, never seemed to get over being two years old.

Bright went now to the bedroom, stood just inside the door, watching Roseann. She was stretched out on Bright's bed, arms stiff at her side, brow furrowed even in slumber, as if sleep were an act of contrition. As always, Bright felt at a loss, as incapable of reaching the grown woman as she had been the small girl who fretted and tugged at her hair, troubled by some nameless, restless animal that nibbled at her insides, opening raw wounds deep down where no one could truly soothe and heal. Only Fitzhugh Birdsong could keep it at bay.

< 46 >

She took a step toward the bed, drawn by the immutable sadness of her sleeping daughter's taut body. She wanted to cover Roseann with a light spread, to touch the deep lines of her brow, to comfort. To make the smallest of amends. But she froze with her hand outstretched, afraid of waking her. It would not do. Awake, there was only the dark undercurrent of rancor, of their inability to simply get along. They should be long past the necessary disagreements of mother and child to a time of easy friendship, shared wisdoms. That was the way it was supposed to work. Instead, there was only a profound separateness made of equal parts of Roseann's long-simmering anger and Bright's . . . What?

Bright lowered her hand slowly to her side. *No, not now. But there is this one small thing I could do, and that might be an opening . . .*

She turned away from the bedroom, leaving Roseann in troubled sleep, and went to the porch. Jimbo sat reading in one of the wicker chairs, perfectly still except for his right hand idly playing with the short strands of his brown hair, reaching every so often to turn a page of the book.

Bright sat next to him, but he didn't look up. "What are you reading?" she asked after a moment.

He put his right index finger on the place where he had been reading, turned and looked up at her. "*Encyclopedia Brown*," he said.

"What's it about?"

"A smart kid who solves stuff."

"Would he know how to stop a runaway truck?"

"Well, he's not one of these action guys like G. I. Joe or anything. But yeah, I suppose he would."

"Would you?"

Jimbo shrugged.

"Well, it could happen at any moment," Bright said. Jimbo cocked his head, gave her a curious look. "In fact," she went on, "it almost happened last month."

He waited. *All right, what kind of old-lady foolishness is this?*

"Right up there is the River Bridge," she pointed, and he followed her aim down Claxton where the street rose to cross the river. "And there at the bottom of the bridge, you see, is a stoplight." Jimbo nodded. "Last month, a truckload of logs crossed the bridge and it didn't even slow down. It ran right through the red light and kept coming."

"Did you see it?" Jimbo asked.

"From this very chair."

Jimbo was wide-eyed now. He put *Encyclopedia Brown* on the chair seat beside him. "What did you do?"

< 47 >

"Not a thing," she said. "About midway the block, the truck swerved to the right and snapped off a telephone pole clean down to the ground. And stopped. As it turned out, the driver had had a heart attack."

"Was he dead?"

"As a doornail."

"What would you have done if he hadn't hit the telephone pole?"

"Gone upstairs," she said. "That's what the upstairs is for. Emergencies. Floods and runaway trucks and such."

They both sat quietly for a moment, watching the early afternoon traffic along Birdsong Boulevard and Claxton, contemplating disaster and its consequences. Henry Wimsley passed on his motorcycle, going back to the Methodist Church after dinner at the parsonage. And then Harley Gibbons drove by in his dark gray Oldsmobile, heading back to the bank with his tinted windows rolled up to keep the air-conditioning inside. It was a tradition that died slowly in a small Southern town, she thought—the notion of people going home for dinner in the middle of the day, sitting at their own tables, eating a good meal with two meats and four or five vegetables, the way her father had always done, the way Henry Wimsley's and Harley Gibbons's fathers had done. It was a way of measuring the day, dividing it properly into its halves, putting commerce in its proper place. One should not conduct commerce over dinner, like they did nowadays at the Three Square Café downtown. Taking one's dinner at home helped preserve the particular rhythm of life that made a small town worth living in, no matter its other warts and foibles. Young Jimbo Blasious, sitting next to her now in his wicker chair, might come to understand that if she showed him, if she had time enough . . .

"I've never been upstairs," Jimbo said, breaking into her thoughts.

"Really? Well, it's nothing much but junk anyway."

"Can I take a look?"

"Gracious, it's too hot right now. You'd faint dead away up there. Maybe tomorrow. We'll go up early in the morning and you can see what it looks like."

He stared at her. "I'll be at the beach tomorrow."

"Yes," she said quickly, realizing that she had decided. "Of course." She tried to keep her voice light. "Unless you wanted to stay here with me this week and let your mama and Rupert go on to the beach."

There was something a little like panic in his eyes. At the very least, uncertainty. She realized that he didn't know her, not really, not the way a grandson might know his grandmother. A funny old woman, living alone, babbling about runaway trucks.

"I'd like it very much if you would," she said softly. "In fact, you

< 48 >

would be doing your grandmother a very great honor if you would stay here with me. I've got an attic full of books, and we've got a nice swimming pool on the other side of town, and there are some things I could show you about being a small-town boy."

"I don't know," he said. He looked very small and frail, hunkered down in the chair. Too quiet, too compliant, she thought. He should be rowdy and rumpled. He picked up his book again, finding the page he had marked.

"Well, you think about it," she said, and then she heard the screech of pecan limbs on metal and looked up to see the Winnebago pulling into the driveway. Rupert gave them a wave and blew a little puff of smoke out of one side of his mouth, around the stem of his pipe. The Winnebago eased to a halt and he got out after a moment, carrying a large box under one arm.

"We'll have you perking in a moment," he said as he climbed the steps. "Good as new. Well, almost. This one"—he patted the box— "only has a one-year warranty. They don't make anything these days with a warranty more than one year."

"Roseann's still asleep," Bright said, opening the screen door for him, looking back to see Jimbo engrossed in *Encyclopedia Brown* again. She followed Rupert to the kitchen, where he set the box on the counter, took the motor out, pulled up the chair, and started to work.

"Had to get some of the holes in the mounting brackets rebored to fit," he said. "No charge for that."

Bright left him to his work and fussed around on the back porch for a few minutes, then stood just inside the kitchen door, watching him.

"This shouldn't take long," he said, wiping a forearm across his brow. His thinning hair was dark and plastered with sweat.

"I hope not," she said. "I'm ready for you to clean up your mess and go on to the beach."

Rupert gave her a strange look. "Well . . ."

"That didn't sound right," Bright said hastily. "I'm obliged, really." She shook her head. "I'm a little sharp-tongued sometimes, I suppose. It's what happens when you get old and live by yourself."

Rupert put down his wrench and looked down at her with a smile. "No offense. I like for people to say what they mean. That's the worst thing about working with college professors. They hem and haw a lot. You don't hear a lot of plain speaking around college professors."

"Or politicians," Bright said. "Except for Fitzhugh. He was a plainspoken man. Not sharp-tongued, mind you, just plainspoken. Fitzhugh once had a man from the State Department before his

< 49 >

committee, testifying about some blunder or another, and when the man got through with his long-winded explanation, Fitzhugh looked him square in the eye and said, 'I don't believe you.' And the man broke down and cried, right there in front of the committee, right on national TV. Fitzhugh was a kind and gentle man, but plainspoken."

Bright wondered why she was telling all this to Rupert Blasious. She hardly knew the man. But then, there was something in his face akin to that in Dorsey Bascombe's, something that invited you to tell him what you knew. Dorsey had been the kind of man who dealt with you straight on, at least until the end, when he had retreated deep down inside himself where nobody else could go.

Rupert paused now to take his pipe out of its little leather holster on his belt, pack it with tobacco from the pouch in his rear pocket, and light up. An aromatic cloud filled the kitchen, swirling about his head and drifting toward the open doorway to the porch where Bright stood.

"You know that Roseann wants to leave Jimbo here with me," she said.

"Yes," he said around the stem of the pipe. He didn't look down.

"You know why."

He nodded.

"Well, what do you think?"

Rupert stopped, took the pipe out of his mouth, laid it on the top of the refrigerator. "To tell you the truth, he might have a better time here. Not that I don't want him at the beach. I do. But Roseann wants to work on me a little, and when she's got something on her mind, everything else is a little extraneous. Roseann wants me to go into business for myself, and I've given it a lot of serious thought. There's pros and cons."

Bright crossed her arms. "Let me ask you this, Rupert. Has she made you miserable yet?"

Rupert stared at her, but there was no rancor in it. "You really are plainspoken, aren't you. No, she hasn't made me miserable. Roseann has a lot of . . . ahhh . . . energy. She's spunky. I tend to cogitate too much, and I'm as dull as dishwater. So we sort of complement each other, I suppose. We accommodate."

"What was your first wife like?" Bright asked.

"Too much like me. We bored each other to death. It was like sleepwalking." He picked up his wrench again, inserted a bolt through the bottom of the motor mount and began tightening it.

"So now you've got a wife with a lot of, as you put it, energy. And a ten-year-old boy."

< 50 >

"Yes," he grinned. "And maybe that's the biggest change. My first wife and I didn't have any children. Thank goodness. They would probably have been as boring as we were, and the world doesn't need any more boring people. Jimbo's anything but. The kid's got quite an imagination. He just needs a little space to let it work."

"Roseann, you mean."

"She mothers a lot," he said reluctantly. "But that's natural, I guess. She's had him all to herself most of this time. She doesn't want to make any mistakes with him, doesn't want *him* to make any mistakes. So she . . ."

"Smothers him."

Rupert shrugged. "Hmmmmm. I suppose. A little."

"A lot."

"Yes. A lot."

Rupert appeared almost finished now, the new motor bolted into place and connected by a belt to what he had told her was the compressor. "I don't know how long the motor will hold out," he said, "but the rest of this old gadget ought to last for at least forty more years."

Forty years? She imagined herself long dead, dust to dust, while the Kelvinator hummed on in this kitchen, keeping potato salad safe from bacteria. Surely, though, they would tear the house down and replace it with a washateria. She would be glad not to be here.

"All right, then," she said.

"All right what?" Rupert asked. His pipe was back in its holster, waiting to be drawn again when he needed to wrestle with his thoughts or keep the rest of the world at bay.

"He can stay. I'll be glad to have him."

"Jimbo."

"Yes." She nodded. "While you go to the beach and work out whatever it is you need to work out."

Rupert stepped down from the chair, then reached around behind the Kelvinator and plugged it into the wall socket. The refrigerator gave a tiny shudder and hummed to life again, a slightly different sound now with the new motor powering its innards. It would take a while before she would stop hearing it, before it became part of the great silence of this house. Rupert stepped back up on the chair and gave the works on top a good look, craning his neck to see the motor and compressor from several directions. Finally he grunted, satisfied. "I hope it's not an imposition," he said. "Jimbo, I mean."

"No, not an imposition. A little strange, I reckon, having a boy around the house. But no imposition."

Rupert replaced the round white metal housing on the top of the

< 51 >

refrigerator and tightened it into place with four screws, working me-thodically, taking his time. There was a smudge across the bridge of his nose. A dark stain spread down the back of his shirt.

"I suppose I ought to think about air-conditioning someday," Bright said.

Rupert waved his hand. "Oh, I wouldn't bother. A house like this, it would be a waste of time and money. They built 'em like fortresses back then, but they didn't build 'em for air-conditioning. It would be like trying to cool the whole town. A window fan is about all the good you'll do. Just keep the air stirred up, take advantage of the natural drafts. Do you have a window fan?"

"Up in the attic. The motor . . ." Rupert's eyes brightened. "Oh, no," she said firmly, raising her hands. "You've done enough. Quite enough for one day. Wash your hands and face and go to the beach."

"All right," Rupert said, "I'll take a look at it on our way back through the end of the week. You could put it right in there"—he pointed at the breakfast room window—"and pull a lot of air through the front door and the back and even the window of your bedroom. Surprising what a window fan . . ."

"Stop!" she commanded, reaching for the bar of Lava soap by the sink and pressing it into his hand. "Wash." He was probably a little maddening at times, she thought. It probably made Roseann a bit frantic.

"Well, are you finished?" Roseann at the breakfast room door, hands on hips. Sleep had not smoothed the deep furrows of her brow. *Does she truly rest? Ever?*

"All done," Rupert said cheerily. He turned on the cold faucet at the sink and water came out with a splat.

"Jimbo can stay," Bright said.

From Roseann, "All right." That was all.

"Have you talked with him about it?"

"No."

"Let me talk to him," Rupert said. He didn't look up from the sink.

"Fine." Roseann turned away, left them there in the kitchen. Ru-pert finished washing up, dried his hands on a towel Bright fetched from the back porch. Then he put his wrenches and pliers and screw-drivers neatly away in the gray toolbox and closed the top with a snap. "I guess that does it."

"I'm obliged," Bright said.

"Think nothing of it. I'll let you fix something for me someday." He cocked his head to one side and Bright could see a little twinkle in his eye.

< 52 >

"I think you might do to hunt with, Rupert," Bright said.

"Do what?"

"Do to hunt with. An expression I heard from my father. He said you wouldn't go hunting with a man unless you trusted him, because you might get your head blown off. My father never hunted in his life, but he knew who he could trust and who he couldn't. It was the best thing my father could say about another man. 'He'll do to hunt with.' I never heard him say it about a woman."

Rupert bowed slightly. "I accept the compliment in the spirit it's offered. I wish I'd known your father. Would he do to hunt with?"

"Oh, yes," she smiled. "Yes indeed."

"Well, I'll go have a talk with Jimbo."

"Yes. You do that."

Bright worked in the kitchen, straightening up, wiping the counter and the refrigerator. She gave Rupert a good ten minutes and then she dried her hands and took off her apron and went to the front porch. Rupert was at the Winnebago, Jimbo still in the wicker chair. He looked up at her as she came through the screen door, then ducked his head back into his book. Rupert came up the steps with Jimbo's small brown suitcase. "In here," Bright said, and showed him the small spare bedroom at the back of the house. Rupert set the suitcase on the bed.

"Is he all right about this?" Bright asked.

"Oh, I think so. It's hard to tell with Jimbo sometimes. He won't be any trouble. Just feed him and give him a book, and he's all right."

"Surely there's more to him than that."

"Yes," Rupert smiled. "No telling what you'll find."

Roseann was standing in the driveway now, arms crossed, giving the house a good looking over. "The house needs painting," she said.

Bright looked at the house. It was a bit weathered in places, but it was certainly nothing like Buster Putnam's monstrosity next door. "Perhaps you're right," Bright said. *Just let her go on to the beach now.*

"And where's your car?" Roseann asked.

"Up the street."

"Where?"

"Down by the Methodist parsonage."

"What's it doing there?"

"Vapor lock."

Roseann shook her head. "You ought to get rid of that old piece of junk."

Bright could feel the anger rising like prickly heat up the back of her neck. But she kept her mouth shut, and after a moment Roseann

< 53 >

gave a shrug and looked past her at Jimbo, sitting quietly on the porch, glancing at them now and then over the top of his book. "Well, aren't you going to come down here and tell us good-bye?" Jimbo placed his book carefully on the chair, facedown, and walked down the steps to them. Roseann bent and gave him a hug. "Mind your grandmother. Remember to take your pills. Don't get too hot. And brush your teeth three times a day." Jimbo nodded.

"And have a good time," Rupert said, pulling his pipe from his mouth. He stuck out his hand and Jimbo shook it solemnly. Then he fished in the back pocket of his Bermuda shorts for his billfold, pulled out a twenty-dollar bill. "Here's a little mad money in case you decide to run away."

"Rupert, don't give the boy ideas," Roseann said.

"If you're still here when we get back, you can keep it," Rupert said. Then he turned to Roseann. "Ready?"

"I was ready three hours ago," Roseann said.

"Well, let's go, then." And he held the door open while she clambered in and settled into the passenger seat up front. Rupert climbed in beside her and they looked like two very casual astronauts there in the high-back bucket seats of the big Winnebago. Rupert started the motor and waved to them. But as he started to put the Winnebago into gear, Bright signaled to him to hold up and she stepped quickly to the open passenger-side window. Roseann stared at her curiously. "Roseann," Bright said, "when you come back later this week, I want us to have a talk."

"About what?"

"About us."

There was a quick, unguarded look of surprise there, and something else, which Bright could not fathom. Roseann's mouth opened, and then she gave a little jerk of her head. But she didn't say anything, and Bright stepped back away from the Winnebago and gave Rupert a wave. Roseann stared at her as Rupert backed out of the driveway. Then as the Winnebago pulled away, she closed the window and picked up a map and spread it out before her. Bright and Jimbo stood, a bit apart there in the sandy driveway, as the Winnebago made the turn onto Claxton and lumbered away, a great tan beast moving slowly in the afternoon heat, and finally topped the bridge and disappeared around the curve at the other end.

Roseann, Bright thought to herself, *you are a pickle, but I have got your curiosity up.*

Suddenly she remembered another time long ago, the only time she ever knew of Roseann being openly angry with Fitzhugh. It had

< 54 >

been a lovely fall evening with the leaves on the pecan trees turning yellow and orange out on the lawn and the first bare hint of coolness in the air. It was Bright's favorite time of year. They had sat on the front porch, Bright and Fitzhugh and Roseann, while Little Fitz ran about under the trees, playing tag with himself, his laughter mocking the night sounds. Roseann nestled in Fitzhugh's arms in the wicker chair while he read to her from a huge beautifully illustrated storybook he had brought home with him from Washington the day before. He had selected the tale of Hansel and Gretel, and as he read the story of the two children wandering lost in the woods, Roseann began to squirm in his arms and pluck at her hair, making small whimpering noises. Fitzhugh patted her head and read on. Then suddenly she tore the book from his hands. "No! No! They weren't lost!" she cried. She flung the book to the floor of the porch, ripping pages from its spine, and burst into anguished sobs, thrashing about in Fitzhugh's grasp.

Bright jumped up from her chair and reached for Roseann. "Let me . . ."

"No!" He looked up at her, badly frightened.

Little Fitz came rushing up from the yard, pounding up the steps. "What's wrong?" he asked.

Fitz and Bright stared at each other, the sobbing child a wall between them. "I don't know," Fitzhugh said hoarsely. "I don't know." Then Roseann suddenly started to wheeze and cough, her eyes bulging with the tortured effort to breathe. An asthma attack. Fitz snatched her up quickly and ran for the car. "I'm going to Finus Tillman's!" he tossed back over his shoulder. Bright put Little Fitz to bed and then sat on the porch waiting for them to return. Fitzhugh was still shaken. He looked at Bright as he climbed the steps with the now-sleeping child, but he didn't stop or say a word, went straight on to Roseann's room and put her to bed. They never spoke of it again. But it never quite went away.

Fitzhugh, she thought now, should be here to help them make peace. But he wasn't.

Bright looked down at Jimbo. He was standing there with his hands jammed in his pockets, wrinkling his nose, staring at the empty spot at the top of the bridge where the Winnebago had disappeared.

"I'm sorry," she said. Jimbo looked up sharply at her. "I don't reckon you're too happy about staying here while they go off to the beach."

Jimbo thought about it for a moment. "It's okay." And then, almost to himself, "I bet he'll have his schlong out five miles down the road."

< 55 >

"Who? *What?*"

"Schlong. You know, what you make babies with. The mama lays an egg and the daddy takes out his schlong and pees on it."

Holy Sweet Jesus. "Who told you that?"

"Alvie Bernelli. He's from New Jersey."

Bright's mouth dropped open, but nothing came out.

"Mama wants a baby," Jimbo said. "I heard 'em talking about it."

Why, Bright wondered, would a woman who hovered on the edge of crisis look for ways to create chaos? A baby. At thirty-six. "Does your mama always get what she wants?"

"No. Sometimes Rupert just puffs on his pipe and looks like he's thinking hard about whatever it is she's talking about, and then goes on about his business. But this time I think she'll win." Jimbo nodded. "Rupert'll have his schlong out five miles down the road." Then he left her there in the yard, speechless, walked back up the steps, picked up his book from the seat of the chair, sat down, and started reading.

< 56 >

4

At midafternoon, Bright decided three things. First, she decided to put the telephone receiver back on the hook so Little Fitz could call. But for an hour, nothing. Not only did Fitz not call, neither did anybody else.

So then Bright decided to call Flavo. When he answered, she could hear a radio playing gospel music in the background, a spatter of voices—the early afternoon crowd lounging about Flavo's small grocery store, wandering in and out and buying nothing more serious than soda pop and pork skins.

"No," said Flavo, "the governor has not favored me with a call as of yet. But I have spoken with Doyle Butterworth."

"Doyle Butterworth." She snorted. "Hah!" He was a weasel-faced little man who was Fitz's campaign manager, about as colorless as a used tea bag. Bright had met him only once, at Fitz's inauguration. *This is a man who would cheat at cards,* she had thought to herself.

"And what did you tell Doyle Butterworth?"

"I told him that number one, Fitz Birdsong was in a peck of trouble, and number two, if he didn't call his mama, he'd be in a peck more."

"And what did Doyle Butterworth say?"

"He said a great deal, and I can't remember that a single word of it made much sense," Flavo said dryly. Then, "Just a moment." He put the telephone down with a clunk on the counter. She could hear him ringing up a sale on the cash register, passing the time of day with a customer, and then he picked up the phone again. "You sound a trifle addled, Bright," he said.

"I've got Jimbo here."

"Who?"

"Roseann's boy. She left him with me while she and Rupert—that's her new husband—go to the beach."

< 57 >

Flavo gave a snort. "My goodness, Bright. All these men in your life all of a sudden."

"What do you mean?"

"Wellll," he drawled, "you and Buster Putnam riding up and down the street early this morning . . ."

"Good Lord!" she exploded. "Can't you do a simple favor for somebody without it becoming public business? Where did you hear that?"

"Round and about," he said. "One thing about this new age of integration, Bright, black folks and white folks hear the same gossip nowadays. Hell, I got white customers now, and they all gossip. A whole truckload of pulpwood workers stopped in here this morning. Some of Monkey Deloach's boys, headed to the woods. Some black, some white. All of 'em smelled like pulpwood workers. They all sweat just the same. And all gossipin'."

"Good-bye, Flavo," she said.

"Top of the afternoon to you, Bright."

He hung up and she sat for a moment with the receiver in her hand, then let it fall with a clatter into the cradle. And then she made her third decision. That was to get her automobile fixed and see what was up with Francis O'Neill. He was Fitz's county campaign chairman. If Fitz was going to call anybody at all, it might be Francis. She could have called Francis and had him send someone to fetch the car, but she decided to go and look him in the eye.

She got her purse and hat from the bedroom. Jimbo was still in the chair on the porch, deep in another book. "Do you want to walk down to the Ford dealership with me?" she asked.

"It's too hot," he said, glancing up. "Mama said for me not to get too hot."

"Yes, in fact, she did. Well, I'll be back in a while."

It was indeed hot. Heat phantoms radiated from the street and the sidewalk and Bright could feel an occasional gust of hot wind on her face underneath the wide-brimmed hat. She was not accustomed to being out in the midafternoon sun. By the time she reached Francis O'Neill's, halfway down Claxton, a little trickle of perspiration was coursing down her spine.

Bright could hear some kind of machine whining fitfully back in the big open-bayed garage area of the auto dealership, and the banging of metal against metal. But it was cool and quiet in the air-conditioned showroom, the afternoon tempered by the big, lightly tinted plate glass windows. A sporty new red two-door Ford convertible sat gleaming on one side of the showroom floor, top down to show the white vinyl interior. Verlon Hawkins, Doris's brother and Big Deal's only salesman, was slumped in a chair by the back wall of the showroom, mesmerized

< 58 >

by the newspaper he was holding, the one with the photograph of Fitz and the waitress splashed across the front. Verlon had it opened to the midsection. *Please turn to page 6.* Verlon's head nodded slowly, his mouth forming the words as he read. Then he looked up, stared at her, folded the newspaper slowly into his lap. "Lord," he croaked. "Miz Bright. Just reading the comics." Then he blushed deeply, realizing what he had said. "I mean . . ." Verlon looked stricken.

"The thirst for knowledge is a noble thing, Verlon," she said. "Where's Mr. O'Neill?"

"Back yonder in the office." He pointed down a hallway toward the back of the building.

Bright could hear Big Deal talking on the telephone in his office, the words amplified by the tacky imitation-pine-paneled walls, the linoleum floor, the metal and vinyl furniture. She didn't want to interrupt, so she took a seat in a chair outside the door and waited.

"Godawmighty, Doyle," Big Deal said, and Bright realized he was talking with Doyle Butterworth at the Reelect Fitz Birdsong headquarters. "I feel like a one-legged man at an ass-kicking contest. I got folks calling me from all over the county wanting to know what the hell's going on, and I don't know what to tell 'em." He paused for a moment, listening. "Well, that's easy for you to say. Look, I ain't asking you to tell me if he did or he didn't. That's between you and Fitz and the Lord. But I know this, Doyle, sooner or later Fitz has got to say something to the *folks.* And it better be sooner, because it's later than you think. We gonna vote a week from tomorrow, and I'm telling you, Doyle, it's squirrelly as hell around here, and this is *home.* What?" He listened again, and Bright could hear the faint buzz of the voice on the other end of the phone, talking fast and loud. "Sure, we're gonna go ahead with Fitz Birdsong Day. But you-all better have this thing straightened out by Thursday, or we gonna have a mess on our hands. And you can bet every damn reporter in the state is gonna be here." Doyle Butterworth buzzed again. "Yeah, you gotta get him on TV. Lots. Every time folks turn on the TV, you gotta have Fitz there telling 'em he's Clean Gene." *Buzz-buzz.* "We done raised a lot of money down here, Doyle, and you folks done spent it all. Y'all worse than my wife at spending other folks' money. But I'll do what I can." There was a long pause and Bright could hear Big Deal O'Neill scratching himself. Then he laughed. "Yeah, she's got big tits, all right. Fitz always did appreciate a good set of knockers on a woman."

Bright stood up then, moved into the open doorway of Big Deal's office. He was reared back in his swivel chair, legs splayed across the cluttered top of the desk, staring at the ceiling. He looked at her and the color drained from his face. "Oh, SHIT!" he muttered softly, and

< 59 >

went over backward in the chair with a crash, arms and legs waving, pulling the telephone with him. Bright stood there, clutching her purse in front of her. The telephone buzzed angrily. After a moment, she heard him say, "I'll call you back, Doyle." He hung up the receiver, then reached up and placed the telephone back on the desk. He climbed slowly to his feet, rubbing the back of his head where it had banged the floor, straightening his clothes. Big Deal was a tall, balding man going to pot, belly lapping over his belt, two buttons unbuttoned on his shirt to reveal a vee of hairless skin and a ribbon of thin gold chain around his neck. She remembered him as a gangly boy. "Miz Bright, I ah . . ." He gestured vaguely at the telephone.

"Doyle Butterworth," she said.

He nodded, then swallowed hard and ran his hand over the slick top of his head. It seemed to give him some comfort. "I'll tell you this, Miz Bright, we ain't gonna run under a log. We gonna stick by Fitz on this."

"That's what Flavo Richardson told me," she said.

"Yes'm. I talked with Flavo this morning. Flavo's folks'll stick. Me and Flavo will stick." He shook his head. "But Lord, Fitz has got to *say* something. If he'd just . . ." He gestured at the phone again.

"Has Fitz called you?" she asked.

"No ma'am. Just Doyle."

"He hasn't called me, either," Bright said.

Big Deal's face fell. "Well, gee, he oughta . . ."

"But I didn't come to talk politics. I've got a sick car down by the Methodist parsonage."

His voice lifted, glad to be done with Little Fitz. "What's wrong with your car, Miz Bright?"

"I suppose it's the same old thing, Francis. Vapor lock, I think you called it."

Big Deal rubbed his head again. "Lord, Miz Bright, we 'bout done all we can do to that car of yours. What you need is a new car."

"Francis," she said, eyeing him evenly, "I don't want a new car. I like my old car. I like things the way they are. Or were. Quiet. And fixed."

"Yes'm." Resigned. A Ford man dealing with a balky Plymouth. Friendship transcending franchise.

"Roseann has left her boy Jimbo with me this week, and I need transportation. Can I depend on you?"

Francis nodded. "Sure. I'll get it taken care of. I'll send Arzell up yonder to get the car and look it over. Just leave it to me. Consider it done."

< 60 >

Bright smiled. "After all, they don't call you Big Deal for nothing. And one other thing, Francis . . ."

"Yes'm."

"When you talk to Mr. Doyle Butterworth again, you tell him to tell Fitz Birdsong to call his mama."

"Yes'm."

By the time she got back to the house, walking slowly in the heat, a pickup truck with BIG DEAL O'NEILL NEW AND USED CARS on the side was turning the corner in front of the Dixie Vittles, creeping up Birdsong Boulevard toward the parsonage. Arzell, the mechanic, waved to her. She wondered if he had a bag of wooden clothespins with him.

Bright went straight to the kitchen and fixed two glasses of lemonade and two oatmeal cookies on a plate and took them to the porch, set them on the table at Jimbo's elbow while he watched her, then sat down in the other chair with the table between them.

"Drink up," she said. He closed his book and took a glass of lemonade and a cookie.

Out beyond the porch, the afternoon baked—bright spikes of sunlight riddling the pecan trees and dappling the lawn, Claxton Avenue and the River Bridge floating above themselves on a shimmer of heat. Bright got up and pulled the long cord on the paddle porch fan. It turned slowly, barely whispering, sending small warm ripples of air down toward them. Bright sat, listening, then wondering what she was listening for, then realizing it was the telephone. The house was quiet. Just the sound of the afternoon outside and the whoosh of the ceiling fan.

"Are you enjoying your book?" she asked.

Jimbo shrugged his small shoulders. "I suppose."

"You what?"

"I suppose."

"What kind of language is that for a ten-year-old boy? Repeat after me: 'I reckon.'"

He stared at her. "I reckon," he said finally.

"Do you ever use the word *ain't?*"

"Mama won't let me."

"It's a perfectly good word for people your age. Adult people should not say *ain't.* But young folks, especially boys, should flavor their speech with an occasional *ain't!*"

"Why?"

"Because it shows you don't go around with starch in your

< 61 >

britches. And because it's emphatic. When you say 'I'm not going to,' that's one thing. But when you say 'I ain't,' that's emphatic. Final. Kaput." She snapped her fingers.

"But Mama . . ."

"Your mama is a fine and upstanding woman and a good mother. She is also a bit of a stiff-neck at times."

"I suppose she is." Jimbo nodded. He took a sip from his glass of lemonade and bit off a piece of one of the oatmeal cookies, chewing slowly. Bright wondered how many times Roseann had told him to chew his food.

"Reckon," Bright corrected.

He put the cookie back on the plate and gazed up into her face for a moment. Then he blurted, "You know what Rupert told me before they left?"

"What's that?"

"He said I ought to keep my eyes and ears open because you're a savvy old gal and I might learn something."

"Hah! Rupert said that?"

"Yeah."

"He said it exactly that way? 'A savvy old gal'?"

"Just like that."

"Well, we'll see." Bright picked up her own glass of lemonade. "I haven't had a boy around the place for a long time, so I'm not sure what I'm up to here. You'll just have to bear with me. I have three rules: don't mess with Gladys, don't let the faucet drip in the kitchen, and flush the commode when you get through going to the bathroom. The rest of it is up to you."

"Who's Gladys?"

"The dog."

"You've got a dog?"

"An ancient, decrepit dog. She lives under the house. If you sit here long enough and listen carefully enough, you will hear her banging around amongst the pipes. Her favorite place is just below my bedroom."

Jimbo's eyes widened. "Josephus is under the house."

"Who?"

"The alligator. I put him under the house before they left. He's under there right now. Taking a nap."

"Ahhhh. Yes. Well, Gladys doesn't eat alligators. She eats canned dog food soaked in warm milk. Does your alligator eat dogs?"

"Of course not. But he's not used to anybody else sleeping under the house with him."

< 62 >

Bright stifled a smile. He looked so terribly earnest, so somber about it.

"Well," she said after a moment, "let's give 'em a chance."

Jimbo made a small frown. "I suppose so."

"I reckon."

He cocked his head to one side. "All right. I reckon. But Josephus won't like it."

They sat drinking their lemonade and finishing their cookies, pondering the thought of an old dog and an alligator coexisting underneath the house.

"Where did Gladys come from?" Jimbo asked after a while.

"Your uncle Fitz brought her home from law school. Lord, that was twenty years ago. Maybe a tad longer."

"Dogs don't live that long," Jimbo said.

"This one does. She's pickled. A recovering alcoholic."

Jimbo gave her a long, curious look.

"You think I'm a bit daft, don't you," she said. He shrugged. "Well, I suppose I am. You get that way when you live by yourself for a long time. You get set in your ways and you do odd things without thinking they're odd. For me, it's odd having someone else around. Nice, but odd." And it was, she thought. Odd to have someone to talk to in this house where there was so much silence, where the faint humming of the old Kelvinator and the whoosh of the ceiling fan on the porch became imbedded in the silence that wrapped you like a cocoon, like the heat on a June afternoon. Time ticked away and you didn't even hear it, only felt it sometimes in your bones. Not time itself, but the soft underbelly of time, the almost imperceptible eddies it left in its wake.

She heard the banging at the back door then. Buster Putnam, standing on the steps, peering through the screen. "May I use your bathroom?" he asked.

"What's wrong with your bathroom?" She put a little starch in her voice, letting him know she hadn't forgotten the morning.

"It's out of commission," he said. "The plumber's over there now."

So she let him in, showed him the tiny bathroom off her bedroom, went back to the front porch.

"Who was that?" Jimbo asked.

"General Putnam."

"Is he a real general?"

"He used to be," Bright said, "but I don't think he's quite sure anymore."

They sat and finished their lemonade and cookies, watching the

< 63 >

traffic on Birdsong Boulevard glide by in the heat, a few cars with their windows rolled up and a shirtless teenage boy on a bicycle with a white towel draped around his neck, heading home from the city swimming pool, pedaling slowly. "Do you want to go swimming?" she asked.

Jimbo looked over at her. "Now?"

"Tomorrow. There's a public pool." Then she thought of something else. "Or, there's the river. We could go out to the camp house."

"You have a camp house?"

"Oh, yes. In fact, it's rather famous right now. Did you see the newspaper your mother had this morning?"

"The one with the picture of Uncle Fitz and the floozy?"

"The, ah . . . yes. Well, that was the camp house."

Jimbo thought about it for a moment. "Mama says Uncle Fitz is too big for his britches. Is that why he took 'em off?"

She tried to think of an answer for that, but Buster Putnam rescued her, banging loudly on the bathroom door. "Bright! Dammit, Bright!"

She went to the door. He was shaking it violently from the inside, rattling the doorknob and growling. "What's the matter?" she shouted above the din.

"The damned door won't open," he said, exasperated. "I can't turn the knob. It's broken."

"Are you decent?" she asked.

"Of course."

She opened the door. He stood there, red-faced, sweating. She glowered at him, then turned the inside knob lightly with her fingers, like a thief delicately opening a safe.

"It's broken," he repeated.

"No, it's not broken, but it would have been in a few seconds the way you were beating on it. You just have to know how to work it."

He thrust his jaw out. He was freshly shaven, but it was a bad job. There were flecks of blood on his chin and upper lip, patches of stubble he had missed. The bandage on his thumb was soiled. "It's broken," Buster said stubbornly. "It doesn't work so that ordinary people can use it. Something inside the mechanism isn't right. You ought to get it fixed."

"It works better than your commode," Bright said evenly.

"I'll fix my commode if you'll fix the doorknob on your bathroom."

"If you'll fix your commode, you won't have to worry about the doorknob on my bathroom," she shot back. "And besides, you have a foul mouth, Buster. I've got a small boy out on my front porch, and you sound like you're in a barracks or something."

< 64 >

"What small boy?"

"Jimbo. Roseann's son. He's staying with me while Roseann and Rupert go to the beach. Come on and I'll introduce you. If you'll keep a civil tongue."

He followed her to the door, but the front porch was empty. They found him in the backyard, down on all fours, peering through the hole in the brickwork by the steps into the dark underneath of the house, being careful not to let the knees of his pants touch the bare ground. They both stopped and looked at him, and Jimbo rose to his feet.

"This is Jimbo," Bright said. "Jimbo, this is General Putnam."

"Don't you like the beach?" Buster demanded.

Jimbo looked him up and down for a moment. "I suppose not."

"I'm trying to get him to say *reckon*," Bright said.

Buster pointed to the hole in the brickwork. "What are you doing down there?"

Bright could see a little flash of something across Jimbo's face, almost a smile, and then he said, "I was looking to see if my alligator has eaten Gladys."

Jimbo and Buster studied each other for a moment, Buster working his jaw and Jimbo standing there with his hands at his sides, everything neat and tucked and clean. Finally, Jimbo said, "You don't look like a general."

Buster glowered at Jimbo. "And you don't look much like a boy," he pronounced. "What you need is some overalls." Then he turned to Bright. "Listen, about this morning . . ."

"What about it?"

"I didn't mean to meddle."

"I hope not," she said. "Neither did I."

Buster rubbed his face, his hand making the patches of stubble sound like sandpaper. "I saw the newspaper just now. About Fitz."

"Yes."

"Well," he said with a twitch of his nose, "things aren't so quiet over here after all, are they."

She fixed him with an icy stare. "We've all got plenty to keep us busy."

Buster Putnam gave her a little wink and then turned without another word and disappeared through a gap in the hedge. Bright stood staring at the hedge, Jimbo looking up at her curiously. In a moment, she heard the whine of the band saw from his toolshed.

"What is he doing?" Jimbo asked.

"Renovating," Bright said. "And you stay away from over there.

< 65 >

He's either going to disappear through the floor or get eaten by one of those machines."

Jimbo looked down at himself then, at his neat khaki pants and madras shirt and nearly white tennis shoes. "Do I need overalls?"

"About that one thing," Bright said, "he may be right."

In the late afternoon, with the heat still clinging to the pavement on Birdsong Boulevard, they crossed the street again to the Dixie Vittles. They had had a long discussion about supper and settled on a peanut butter and banana sandwich, and then Bright remembered she was out of peanut butter. So they headed for the supermarket, and Bright found herself feeling strangely light and alert here in the shank of the day, when she normally would be sitting quietly on the porch with the light going soft and pale out under the pecan trees and fireflies beginning to wink above the grass and insects making night music. She should be exhausted, with all that had happened. Perhaps it was Jimbo. Or maybe waiting for Fitz, who still had not called. Or maybe it was something else altogether. But what more could there be in a day such as this?

Jimbo held the door for her and they stepped into the noisy clatter of the Dixie Vittles, busy with the last-minute rush before closing time. Doris Hawkins looked up from her cash register, brushed back a strand of hair that flopped across her forehead, gave them a tired wave.

Monkey Deloach was standing just inside the door, hands clasped behind him, bending slightly forward as if ready to set sail but not quite sure of the heading.

Bright and Monkey and Xuripha had been children together years ago—Monkey wretchedly homely, with ears so big they seemed like wings. The others, Bright included, called him Monkey. And over the years he came to accept it with quiet resignation. The thing that saved Monkey was that he was also as smart as a whip, and Xuripha Hardwicke had seen it and allowed Monkey to pursue and finally marry her. Monkey had worked for Bright's father, Dorsey Bascombe, and finally bought the lumber business himself and made a fortune with it. But the year before, he had turned it over to his son Donald. Without the business, with only Xuripha to deal with, he seemed to lose track of himself. He spent a good bit of the day downtown, making the rounds of the business district, stopping people to talk until they could edge away and escape. Monkey had developed a strange pattern of speech, like a car left parked at the curb with its motor running.

Just now, Monkey turned and saw Bright and Jimbo as they entered the Dixie Vittles. His face brightened. "Ah, uh,

< 66 >

hummmmmmm . . . top of the . . . hmmmmmmm . . . ," he started.

She clasped his arm. "Monkey, I want you to meet my grandson. Jimbo, this is Mr. Deloach."

Jimbo looked up at him. "Why do they call you Monkey?" he asked.

Monkey's small bright eyes twinkled. "Because I have big ears," he said without a stammer. He stuck out his hand and Jimbo shook it.

"Well, we came to get peanut butter," Jimbo said.

Monkey laughed, then looked perplexed. "I, ah, hummmmm . . . "

"Monkey, may I help you?" Bright interrupted.

He nodded. "Xuripha needs . . . ah . . . hummmmm . . . "

"Do you have a list?"

"Yep. Right here . . . hummmmm . . . " He fished in the pocket of his shirt and pulled out a neatly folded piece of paper that he handed to Bright.

She unfolded it, looked at both sides. "No, this is from the state, telling you it's time to renew your driver's license."

"Well, that's all . . . hummmmm . . . I've got," he said, taking the paper and putting it back in his shirt pocket. "And Xuripha . . . hummmmmm . . . won't let me get my license renewed. She . . . hummmmm . . . says I'll leave for the store and end up in . . . hummmmm . . . Bangkok."

Poor Monkey, she thought with a pang, growing old and wizened and confused. She owed him a debt. He had rescued her father's business from ruin, had insisted all these years in keeping the original name. Bascombe Lumber Company. There was a loyalty there that went beyond names. And now, this. Xuripha spoke of the early stages of Alzheimer's. Bright thought it might be more like aimlessness. Monkey Deloach should have stayed at the lumberyard. Or, he should find something else. You couldn't just muddle along.

"Should I call Xuripha for you?" Bright asked.

"Nope."

"Well," Bright said, "let me suggest this. Why don't you stand here and watch the checkout line. Somebody may come through with something that triggers your memory. If not, I imagine Xuripha will be along presently."

Monkey smiled. "That's a . . . hummmmm . . . good idea."

They left him there, leaning slightly forward, watching the conveyor belt at Doris Hawkins's checkout counter, shaking his head slightly as food items slid by. Bright and Jimbo selected a medium-sized

< 67 >

jar of peanut butter—smooth, because Jimbo did not like crunchy food—and stood in line at the counter. Bright could feel the stares of the dozen or so other customers. *They have all read the paper and they all know that Little Fitz Birdsong has made a damfool of himself. But they are too polite, or too embarrassed, to say anything about it. Thank God. If they were to ask, what could I say? "Sorry, I don't know a thing about it. The governor hasn't called his mama."* Then a black man at the front of the line called out, "Miz Bright, you come on up here and get checked out. No sense you waiting with that one jar back yonder."

The other customers gave them a little chorus of agreement. "Thank you, I'm much obliged," she said, and she and Jimbo slipped past them to the front of the line, in front of the man who had called out to her and behind a woman whose large order Doris was checking through. The man looked vaguely familiar. "My daddy worked for your daddy," he said. "I'm Luther Fox."

"Babe Fox's boy," she smiled.

"Yes'm."

She remembered his father, a squat, barrel-chested man who drove one of Dorsey Bascombe's logging trucks.

"Your father . . ."

"Dead thirteen years," Luther Fox said.

"I'm sorry. I'm afraid I've lost track."

"Yes'm."

She looked down the line of people. There was nobody else here she knew. It was a small town, and she should know at least some of them. But they were all strangers. And it struck her then that she was the stranger here. She had hidden away in the house across the street, and in the past, and this town had left her to her privacy. Mostly, that was her doing. But theirs too, perhaps, because she was the congressman's widow and a bit beyond their everydayness, the only thing they had that resembled a celebrity. And she had drifted away from them in the quiet stillness of her life, dwelling as she did upon memory. She walked the streets of this town and did business with its people without taking notice of them, and they had let her do that, as they would leave her to deal privately with the present business of her son the governor.

Standing here among these people now, she felt an instant of shock, of awakening. She blinked in the bright fluorescent light of the Dixie Vittles, a bit bewildered and disoriented.

"Miz Bright, are you all right?" Luther Fox asked. His brow wrinkled with concern.

She took a deep breath, saw the rest of them staring at her. "Fine,"

< 68 >

she said a bit too loudly. "I'm just fine, Luther. Thank you." She turned and saw Doris grinning at her, the counter empty. She put down the jar of peanut butter.

"Hi-dee, Jimbo," Doris said. "Let me guess. Y'all gonna have peanut butter and jelly sandwiches for supper." She turned the jar, searching for the price, then entered it on the cash register and added tax.

"Peanut butter and banana," Jimbo said.

Doris arched her eyebrows. "Goin' gourmet tonight, eh?" She giggled. "Seventy-nine cents, Miz Bright."

Bright took the money from her coin purse, the exact change, and Doris rang it up. "Want it in a bag?" Doris asked.

"Please," Bright said.

Doris slipped a small bag from underneath the counter, flipped it open with a snap of her hand, and dropped the peanut butter jar inside along with the cash register receipt. She handed the bag to Bright. "And here's your Casino Caper card."

"You mean you give away those things for peanut butter?"

"One to a customer, every purchase, no matter how large or small. That's the rule."

Bright took the small white card and handed it to Jimbo.

"Roseann still over yonder?" Doris indicated Bright's house with a shake of her head.

Bright stepped out of the way to let Luther Fox up to the checkout counter. "No, she and Rupert have gone on to the beach." Of course, Doris would have seen the Winnebago pulling out of the driveway at midafternoon, at a time when she had little to do but slouch against the cash register and watch the world ooze by in the heat. "Jimbo is staying with me this week."

"That's real nice," Doris said. "I remember I used to go to my grandmama's house out in the country every summer and stay for a week or so. We'd pick lots of blackberries and make blackberry nectar and preserves. My grandmama had a big old crock jar she used to put the blackberries in, and let 'em sit for a day or so, then she'd cook 'em on the stove in a big iron boiler and squeeze everything through a piece of muslin to get the seeds and stuff out . . ."

Luther Fox was beginning to twitch a bit. He set down his gallon of milk and a box of Aunt Jemima Instant Grits. He cleared his throat politely, but Doris went on. "Grandmama would take some of the juice and put some Sure-Jell in it and make preserves, and then she would bottle some up as nectar, and a little bit of it, she'd put some yeast in it and let it work and make blackberry wine." Doris threw her head back, laughing. "I remember I come in one afternoon and Grandmama

< 69 >

was drunk as a lord. She'd got into the blackberry wine and thought it was nectar."

"'Scuse me," Luther Fox said, impatient. Bright backed away, looked over her shoulder and saw Jimbo and Monkey Deloach standing by the door, examining something.

"Well," Doris said, reaching for Luther's items, "I just wouldn't take nothing for spending them weeks in the summer out in the country with my grandmama. A young'un needs to get away from his parents and learn something from the older generation, doncha think?"

"Yes," Bright said. "Well, I suppose we best be—"

Monkey Deloach tapped her on the shoulder. "I . . . hummmmm . . . I, ah, hummmmm . . ."

Doris stared at him. "Spit it out, Mr. Deloach, spit it out."

"He's got two cherries," Monkey said.

"I beg your pardon?"

"Actually," Monkey said, "he's got . . . hmmmmmmm . . . four cherries. Two on each card."

Jimbo held up the two cards, the ones that said DIXIE VITTLES CASINO CAPER at the top and SCRATCH AND WIN at the bottom, the one Bright had gotten just now and the one from the morning. Jimbo had scratched off the black rectangles to reveal two sets of bright red cherries on stems.

"Cherries?" Doris's eyes bulged. "Gawdamighty," she bellowed. "He's got FOUR CHERRIES!"

"What, what?" Bright could hear a ripple of noise go down the checkout line.

"Holy guacamole!" Doris shouted. "Miz Bright, you done won FIFTY THOUSAND DOLLARS!"

Bright stood there with her mouth open, feeling a bit faint, the noise exploding around her, people yelling, running from all over the store, Jimbo tugging on her dress, Monkey Deloach at her elbow weaving back and forth and humming like a high-voltage wire, Doris leaping up and down and screaming, "FOUR CHERRIES! FIFTY THOUSAND DOLLARS!"

All Bright Birdsong could think was *I hope I don't make a fool of myself.*

< 70 >

BOOK 2

5

First memory of her father, Dorsey Bas-
combe: knee-high leather boots, scuffed and wrinkled from long wear
in the woods, rich with the smell of neat's-foot oil.

Bright hunkers deep in the kneehole beneath Dorsey's big wooden
desk, safe in the dark cool cavity, listening to the sounds of the lumberyard outside— the rattle of chain and singsong calls of the black
men hoisting logs from the flatbed wagons, the chug and whistle of the
big steam engine that powers the mill, the slap-slap of the long conveyor belts, the bite and whine of the huge saws. She smells the good,
clean smell of freshly cut wood, secret growth opened and pungent.
The spring morning splashes across the smooth wood floor of the one-
room lumberyard office and across Dorsey's swivel chair with its tattered cushion. She hears her father's voice outside, clear and strong
and sure of itself, the words indistinguishable, and then the creak and
slam of the screen door. He stops for a long moment and she can sense
his eyes sweeping the room. She is very still and quiet, a mushroom
growing in a cave. After a moment, Dorsey strides across to the desk,
sits down in the swivel chair. She can see the rising tan sweep of his
boots and the khaki twill pants above, rough and faded at the knee.
The boots are enormous, taller than her head, and they fill the opening
of her cave as Dorsey eases the chair up to the desk. She wants to reach
out and fling her arms around the boots, bury her nose in the cleft
between them, smell their oil and sweat, feel the wrinkled leather
against her cheek. But she remains quiet, deep in the kneehole. She
hears the scratching of Dorsey's pen overhead, imagines the strange
black scribbles he makes in neat rows on paper. He stops, leans back in
the chair, pondering, then hunches forward again. *Scratch-scratch.*

Another pause, longer this time. "Ahem." He clears his throat. "I
wonder if the termites are under my desk again."

< 73 >

Bright reaches up and taps lightly on the bottom of the long middle drawer with her knuckles.

"Yes, by goshen, I believe they are. Termites in a lumberyard. Verrrrry dangerous. Why, they could eat through the floor and we would fall, desk and all, clear to China."

Bright stifles a giggle, thinking of them tumbling softly together down a dark, magic hole, her cheeks pressed against the leather of her father's big boots. She taps again on the underside of the drawer.

"Best keep 'em distracted," Dorsey says with a sigh. She hears the clink of heavy glass and then Dorsey eases the chair back a bit and stretches his long khaki arm under the desk with a piece of rock candy in his palm. Bright plucks it from his hand and stuffs it in her mouth, savoring the warm sweetness. Then she reaches out and pats his hand and his huge hand closes about her tiny one and gives her a soft squeeze.

"Ahem," he says again, his voice wrinkled with gentleness like the leather of his boots, "soft-shell termites. Baby soft-shell termites. The most dangerous kind. Well, maybe that'll hold 'em for a while."

He releases her hand and she sits back in the corner of the knee-hole as he returns to his work. *Scratch-scratch.* Buzz and whine. Pen on paper, lumberyard droning outside, the air sweet and warm with wood smells, the candy flooding her insides with its own sweet warmth, the spring morning a cocoon about her. She sleeps.

<   >

"A lumberyard is no place for a small child, especially a girl," Elise Bascombe fretted. "She could . . ." She trailed off with a shudder, imagining the worst.

"Nonsense," said her husband, Dorsey. "It's perfectly safe as long as she does what I tell her." And he said it with a finality that brooked no argument. Dorsey Bascombe would take care of things.

So Dorsey took his small daughter frequently to the lumberyard in the warm months, waking her gently in the early morning with the sky just beginning to pale outside, helping her dress while the smell of Hosanna's biscuits and ham and grits drifted up the stairs and filled the house. They ate quietly in the kitchen while Bright's mother slept in the big front bedroom with the flowered wallpaper and chintz curtains. After breakfast, Dorsey would go to the stable in back of the house and saddle his horse and bring it around to the front steps, looping the reins around a nandina bush, and go back inside and sweep Bright up in his arms and climb into the saddle with her in front. And then they would ride across town to the lumberyard by the river as the morning

< 74 >

blossomed, Bright high and safe in Dorsey's arms, senses brimming with the smell of leather and horse and Dorsey's after-shave and the clip-clop sound of hooves on bare earth.

Dorsey Bascombe was a progressive man. He would eventually be the first citizen of the county to have a motorcar, and he would be one of the first lumbermen in the entire South to use portable sawmills and logging trucks.

The portable sawmill came first, and it marked him as an imaginative entrepreneur, a man worth watching. Before his time, sawmills were cumbersome, fixed operations, and the woods came to them. Logging crews went deep into the forest and cut the trees, sawed off the branches, and hauled the whole logs to the mill on mule-drawn wagons. It was slow and inefficient, and the output of the sawmill was governed by the backbreaking process of getting the logs to the mill, often over miles of bad road from remote locations. But Dorsey Bascombe invented a portable sawmill and changed the lumber business. It was a simple thing, no more than a big circular saw driven by a steam engine, all of it compact enough to be loaded onto wagons and taken directly to the woods where the trees were being felled. Slabs of bark and waste wood were used to fire the steam boiler, and the mule-drawn wagons came from the woods loaded with rough-sawn lumber, ready to be stacked in the lumberyard to air-dry in neat crisscross piles that looked like rows of new houses on the sprawling lot; and later, to be sized and smoothed at Dorsey's big planer mill. When one tract of timber had been cut, the mill could be taken apart and moved to another location, set up and operating in a day's time. Other lumbermen laughed at first at the notion of taking a piece of machinery into the deep woods. But when Dorsey's operation doubled and tripled its output, they came hat-in-hand to study what he had done and marvel at the simple common sense of it. Weekly, railroad cars loaded with Dorsey Bascombe's fragrant pine went lurching off toward Atlanta and New Orleans and Memphis from the rail spur that ran alongside the lumberyard, the one the railroad men had built when they saw what Dorsey was doing to the lumber business. Railroad men, Dorsey said, could smell money a mile away.

Over the years, Dorsey would stay a step ahead of the competition. At the end of the Great War, he would purchase his first logging truck, as powerful engines were developed to heave the mechanized equipment of war through the muck and mire of Europe. Not long after, he would strike upon the idea of using the big steam boiler that powered the planer mill to provide heat for a kiln, a large tin shed

< 75 >

where the rough-cut lumber could be dried in a fraction of the time. Even later, he would initiate the practice of replanting what he had just cut, scoffing at the notion that the South had so much virgin timber at its disposal that you would always be able to just walk away from a denuded tract of land and give it fifty years or so to regenerate. "Timber's a cash crop," he would tell anyone who would listen, "or should be. Just like corn and cotton. Yes, we've got lots of wood in the South. We've also got lots of blockheads trying to cut it down. The South doesn't have anything to waste."

But in the beginning, Dorsey had only the small lumberyard, a crew of no more than ten or twelve black men, his wits, and a sixth sense about cruising timber—the process of determining the number of board feet of finished lumber in a stand of trees. Dorsey could stride into the woods in his big leather boots, look the trees up and down for a few minutes, do a few quick calculations on the back of an envelope, and give you the best fair price you were likely to get for your timber rights. People said that Dorsey was a shrewd man and he had an odd gleam in his eye, but he would deal with you fair and square. That was the Dorsey Bascombe of Bright's early childhood.

Before Bright, there was Elise. It was the one time, Dorsey liked to say, when he had gladly made a fool of himself.

She was slim and delicate with porcelain skin and strawberry hair and long tapering hands that held a cup and saucer as if she cradled baby birds, a New Orleans girl whom Dorsey met on a business trip in 1909. Dorsey was thirty-five years old. Elise was nineteen. He loved her instantly and incurably. He postponed his return from New Orleans a week, then two, while he paid ardent court, calling on her daily at the wide-verandaed two-story white house just off St. Charles Street. Her mother watched the proceedings with growing alarm. It was not unusual for an older man to court a younger woman. But my goodness, she fretted, this man was practically middle-aged. Elise's father, a cotton trader, was less distressed. He made inquiries about Dorsey Bascombe and found that while he had an unorthodox approach to the timber business, he had interesting prospects. He treated Dorsey civilly but didn't interfere, neither encouraged nor discouraged, leaving the matter to the women of the house. Dorsey kept at it doggedly, making little headway with any of them until finally, with an urgent wire in hand from his banker back home, he appeared on the doorstep one oppressive summer afternoon.

The black maid met his knock, a gnarled old prune of a woman. "You again," she said through the screen door.

< 76 >

Dorsey stared at her for a moment. "Miss Elise," he said. "May I . . ."

"She's napping. Young ladies nap this time of day. Least, *proper* young ladies." By the way she said it, he could tell that no proper young New Orleans gentleman would call on a proper young lady at such an hour. Dorsey felt like an idiot, a backwoods bumpkin smelling faintly of pine tar and decaying undergrowth. He decided to throw himself upon the mercy of the court.

"I'm desperate," he croaked, cringing as he said it.

The old woman's eyes widened. "You some sort of preacher?"

"No. Why?"

"Preachers act crazy sometimes."

Indeed they do, Dorsey thought, indeed they do. So it is with fools in love, who are somewhat like preachers in that love becomes a religion. Fools are born to worship women, even unto madness.

"Well, I'm not a preacher, but I've got to see Miss Elise."

Something in the ancient woman's eyes softened then, and she said, "Well, I say you can't bother Miss Elise while she's taking her nap back yonder on the sleeping porch round *this* side of the house." She pointed a long bony finger. "Now go!" And she motioned him with an impatient wave of her hand in the general direction of Galveston, Texas, and disappeared back into the dark bowels of the house.

Dorsey stepped off the porch and peered around the side of the house and saw the thick high hedge blocking access to the rear of the premises. To hell with it, he thought, and waded in, thrashing about in the lush, tangled growth, the foliage tearing at his coat and skin, trying to keep quiet but growing increasingly desperate and enraged until he bellowed an oath and flailed mightily with his arms and sprawled through the far side onto an open space of Bermuda grass, carrying a large dense patch of the hedge with him. "Gawd Awmighty," he heard softly from an open window to his left and looked up to see the old black maid duck back from view. He stood, brushing himself off, trying to regain his dignity. The left sleeve of his coat was ripped nearly away from the rest of the garment and he could feel the sting of a raw scrape along his left cheek. His chest heaved with exertion. He bent over and put his hands on his knees, catching his breath, then looked up and saw the wide screened window of the second-floor sleeping porch.

"Miss Elise," he called softly, cupping his hands around his mouth. He called again, then looked around in the grass for something to toss against the screen, saw nothing. So he shucked off his tattered coat and balled it up tightly and flung it toward the screen. It hit with a

< 77 >

thud and he heard a tiny cry inside. After a moment she appeared at the screen, hair tousled from sleep, rubbing her eyes. His heart stopped for an instant and he felt faint. She was a child, really, soft and vulnerable.

"Miss Elise," he said, "I'll come right to the point. You must marry me or I'll lose my business. Not to speak of my mind."

She brushed the hair from her face. "What do you mean, lose your business?"

Dorsey fished the telegram from his shirt pocket, held it toward her. "My sawmill is stuck in the mud halfway between town and my logging site, things are at a standstill, the note is overdue, and the bank is threatening to foreclose."

"Then you best go home and take care of your sawmill and your bank," she said, starting to turn away.

"Given the choice," he called, "I would choose you."

She stared at him, a tall man with a sun-browned face, hair already beginning to gray slightly at the temples, slightly bowlegged. But handsome in a sort of rough-hewn way. Yes, definitely handsome, even though he looked quite ridiculous just now with a snippet of hedge embedded in his hair and blood oozing down his cheek and a wild look in his eye.

"Go home," she said. His face fell and his shoulders slumped. "But come back when you've taken care of the sawmill and the bank."

His jaw dropped open, then he straightened, ran his hand through his hair, combing out the bit of hedge. "I'll always take care of you, I promise that," he said. He had a strong vibrant voice, the kind that bade men do what he said. The kind of voice you could put stock in.

"I believe you will," she said. Then she turned from the window and climbed back into bed. She lay there for a long moment, listening to the pounding of her heart, wondering what strange thing she had set in motion, then smiling as she heard Dorsey thrashing about again in the high hedge.

"Tell me about the hedge," Bright would cry as a small child, and they would tell her the story over and over, Dorsey's eyes bright with the memory of it, adding details, embellishing the tale, Elise crossing her hands primly in her lap, her face scrunched with earnestness, taking a deep breath, "Now let me see . . . ," until Bright knew by heart how each of them had looked and exactly what they had said and thought there in the sweltering New Orleans afternoon, how Dorsey had gone home and straightened out his business and then returned to pay pa-

< 78 >

tient court to daughter and mother. All through the summer and fall, Dorsey journeyed back and forth until finally, by year's end, he had worn them down. They married in the spring, and by summer, Elise was pregnant.

"Bright," Dorsey said the first time he laid eyes on the baby, when Dr. Finus Tillman brought the child from the upstairs bedroom where Elise had given birth. The doctor gave him a grunt and a curious look. When he filled out the birth certificate before he left the house, he entered the name Bright Bascombe in his neat hand, and Dorsey laughed when he saw it. "Yes," he said. "I hadn't meant it as a name, but it fits."

"Bright," he repeated to Elise, who was groggy from childbirth, propped on a mound of pillows in the bed with the baby cradled in the crook of her arm. "That's her name. She has your eyes and my optimism." He sat gently on the bed and touched the baby's smooth pink cheek with the tip of a finger. "You don't mind, do you?"

"What?" She closed her eyes, drifting away from him.

"The baby's name. Bright."

"Ummmm."

Hosanna was hovering nearby, and as she reached to take the baby she said, "You give a young'un an uncommon name, you better make shore it's an uncommon young'un."

"Yes," Dorsey said. "I'll make sure of that."

Hosanna gave him an arch look. "I 'speck you will."

By the time Elise awoke several hours later it was done, the certificate recorded at the courthouse. Elise protested: there were several perfectly good female names on both sides; the relatives would be put off by their having given an offspring a strange and undignified name such as Bright. But the protest was mild. In this as in most matters, Elise Bascombe allowed her husband to take care of things, as he had promised he would do.

So, too, with the visits to the lumberyard that began when Bright was barely out of diapers. Dorsey brushed aside Elise's concern and took Bright with him, and she grew up with the noise and smell and feel of the yard. Dorsey had only one rule: *Don't go outside without me.* Bright never broke it. She sensed the gravity of it. She would stand for hours at the open window of the small lumberyard office, watching the teeming life outside, or play with a doll in the dark kneehole of the big desk, while her father came and went, bringing the smell of sawdust and resin through the door when he entered, leaving a powerful resonance behind when he departed.

She went in the early morning and stayed until lunchtime. Just

< 79 >

before the noon hour, Dorsey would bustle in and hoist her on his shoulders and they would tour the yard, checking every facet of the operation as Dorsey's long strides took them from one end to the other, his boots crunching softly in the thick matting of sawdust that covered everything. From the giddy height she could watch the sweating mill hands wrestling with the lumber-laden wagons, checking them as they came through the gate and noting the size of the load in rude cross-hatch arithmetic on a pad, unloading the rough boards and stacking them to dry. Then to the shed, where the giant saws of the planer mill shrieked and whined, first crosscutting the dried boards into eight- and ten-foot lengths, ripping them lengthwise into their proper dimensions. On by conveyor to the planer itself, where the boards disappeared into the whirling blades and emerged naked and white, smooth-cut on two sides, carried directly to a growing stack inside a gaping boxcar on the spur next to the mill. Bright Birdsong could see all of the world that was worth seeing from Dorsey's shoulders, arms wrapped tightly around his head while he held his battered felt hat in one hand and pointed out things with the other.

In the years of her early childhood, they were the only white people on the entire lot. It was backbreaking, dangerous work that only blacks would do. You could lose an arm or your life in the blink of an eye. But there was something primitively beautiful about the work and an intensely physical dignity about the way they did it, a powerful rhythm that seemed to flow from inside the wood into the heaving muscles of the mill hands. The black men shouted to Dorsey over the din, waved to Bright on her lofty perch, their own musty smell mingling with the rich aroma of the wood. They would end the tour at the big steam engine that powered the mill and Dorsey would pull his gold watch out of his pocket, flip open the cover, and, precisely at noon, he would nod to the man operating the steam engine, who would give a tug on the lanyard and let loose a blast from the steam whistle—*whooooooo-whoot-whoooooooooo.* The air sang with its clear call and the lumberyard pulsated with vibrant life and Bright grew with it humming inside her like music.

<   >

Music . . . the first vivid memory of her mother. Notes, like fireflies, floating in the air above her bed, so close you could reach up and touch them, but so clean and sweet you only watched and listened for fear of damaging their tiny, delicate bodies.

Dorsey had brought his bride home to a new two-story frame house on a quiet street two blocks from the business district, built with

< 80 >

lumber from his mill. He had started construction immediately after returning from New Orleans the first time he had met Elise, smiling at friends' suggestions that it was much too big for a bachelor. It was finished and furnished by the time he had won her hand, complete with a small music room on the side of the house next to the living room—a bright, airy place with large windows on three sides, kept open in the warm months to let the music drift outside. "My studio," Elise called it. Dorsey had a Story and Clark upright piano shipped by train from Atlanta in a big wooden crate. It was just right for the narrow rectangular room, a tall, stately piano, dark mahogany, with a hinged lid over the keyboard and a bench to match with its own hinged seat that opened to reveal neat stacks of Elise's sheet music.

As a very small child, Bright would sit quietly in the big green overstuffed chair in the corner of the room, watching her mother play, fascinated by the way her long slim fingers made the fireflies dance at the right end of the keyboard, then coaxed the deep, somber bass notes from the other. The music vibrated deep inside her, the way the new sun filled her with warmth when she stood on the front porch on a clear early morning. Bright would watch for a long time, aching to be close to the music, and then Elise would turn and beckon with a smile and Bright would climb into her lap and sit, very still and quiet, while her mother played for a few moments more. And finally, Elise would give a nod and Bright would reach and put her small hands on the black and white keys and press them gently. Then, with Elise's index finger guiding her own, she would tap out a simple melody, marveling at the sounds beneath the smooth ivory that floated out at her bidding. A magical thing it was, to make music one note at a time. *Three blind mice . . . See how they run. . . .*

It was not until much later, when she had become an accomplished pianist, that Bright realized that her mother's playing was pleasant but quite ordinary. As a young girl, Elise had memorized Debussy's *Clair de Lune* for a recital before an audience of New Orleans grandees, who gave her a lovely ovation, and it remained her favorite and best piece, a bit of artistic refinement in what was otherwise a repertoire of popular songs of middling difficulty. But to Bright the child it was a wondrous gift to be able to summon such sounds from a piece of furniture; and to Dorsey Bascombe it was the essence of romance.

"The first time I saw your mother, she was at the piano," he told Bright, recounting how he had met Elise's father, the cotton trader, at a New Orleans men's club and had been invited home for dinner, how he stepped through the front door to the sight and sound of her, a wisp

< 81 >

of a girl in a chiffon dress, seated at the Steinway grand in the living room, her long slender hands curved gracefully over the keyboard as she played "I Dream of Jeanie with the Light Brown Hair." Elise was partial to Stephen Foster. Dorsey Bascombe was smitten. "It was a delicious moment," he said. "I knew at that instant what angels do in heaven. They play the piano."

The evenings of Bright's childhood were filled with music. Dorsey would arrive late in the afternoon from the lumberyard, smelling of pine tar and wood shavings, give Elise and Bright a quick peck on the cheek, and retire to the upstairs bathroom to soak in the big white claw-footed tub (another evidence of Dorsey Bascombe's progressiveness, indoor plumbing) while Bright hunkered in the hallway outside, listening to the splash of water and his slightly off-key baritone: *"I'se coming, I'se coming, for my head is bending loooooooow. I hear de gentle voices calling, Old Black Joooooooooe."* Dorsey too was partial to Stephen Foster. Then after supper (they called it *dinner* in New Orleans, Elise said, but Dorsey insisted upon *supper*), with Bright bathed and nightgowned, they would gather in the music room off the parlor, where Dorsey would sit in the big green overstuffed chair with Bright nestled in his lap and Elise would play.

In the warm months, with the windows open on three sides of the room, the notes from Elise Bascombe's piano would mix and mingle with the music from the gathering night outside, the cricket symphonies and bird études, soft and delicate things. On the evenings when the windows had to be shut against cold or rain, her repertoire tended toward minor keys and plaintive popular melodies. But all of it she played with a light and pleasant touch, the notes floating above the piano like dandelion seeds, so that the chill or storm outside seemed unthreatening, only a bit sad and self-absorbed. Her only piece of any real spirit was "Yankee Doodle," which she said was considered a bit unpatriotic back home in New Orleans. Whenever she launched into it, Dorsey would clasp Bright's small hands in his and they would clap in time to the music while Bright cackled with laughter.

No matter what the weather, at the end of a half-hour or so concert by Elise, Dorsey would rise from the chair, seat Bright deep in its cushions, kneel and open the long black leather case that always lay next to the chair, and remove his trombone from its velvet resting place. "The coffin," he called it, even though it made Elise shudder. He would attach the slide to the body of the trombone, place a few drops of oil on the slide, working it up and down with a long flowing motion of his arm, then tune it while Elise tapped out an E-flat on the piano. "What shall it be tonight, my dear?" he would ask. It was always

< 82 >

her choice, usually something with a nice, simple melody, and always a piece written in a key with flats so that it would be easy for Dorsey to transpose on his trombone. There were no duets for trombone and piano in the stacks of music beneath the hinged lid of the bench; he simply picked out the melody and played by ear. He had been introduced to the trombone by a local bandmaster when he was a boy and had fallen in love with it. "The trombone," he said, "is the sound of God's breathing." He had a nice firm lip and good lungs and he could entice smooth, rounded tones from the instrument. The golden trombone seemed an extension of him as he stood by the piano, eyes closed, the slide gliding back and forth as they played. His favorite piece was Beethoven's *Klavierstück*, written for Beethoven's own Elise, his mystery woman. At the end of whatever they played, he would bend down and kiss Elise on the forehead and say, "Ah, lovely, my dear." That was Bright's signal to cry "Play it again." And they would repeat their selection for the evening while Bright fell asleep deep in the pillows of the chair with the music falling about her like a shroud, tiny crystal notes from the piano and big round golden ones from the trombone. Sometimes she would wake in her bed far into the night, hearing the music swirling about in her head. Or perhaps, she thought, it was the sound of God breathing outside her window.

⟨   ⟩

There was music, and then there was wisdom. Hosanna. The rise of the strong black voice over the kitchen stove as she prepares breakfast, indoctrinating the white child with her black notions, the tantalizing smell of them mingling with the aroma of grits and ham and perking coffee: "White girls ain't s'pozed to be out in the broad-day sun. It sprockles the skin and makes 'em look trashy."

"What does *sprockled* mean, Hosanna?"

"Hush, child, and listen to what I'm tellin' you. Broad-day sun ain't nothing but hot and wore out with hisself. Ain't nothing but leftovers. Black folks ain't got no choice but to be out in the broad-day sun 'cause black folks don't get nothing but leftovers nohow." *Hiss . . . sizzle . . . a dollop of butter goes skittering across the smoking surface of the frying pan . . .* "But what folks s'pozed to have is the new sun. He been down there hiding all night, storing up power, and then he peeks up and winks at you and then gives a big smile." *Gurgle . . . plop . . . tiny pockets of air rise from the depths of the grits boiler, bulging the surface and then erupting with puffs of steam . . .* "New sun got power to heal and clean. That's what yo' mama needs, some new sun. That's why she act strange sometimes.

⟨ 83 ⟩

She needs to get up and get some new sun 'stead of stayin' in bed 'til midday." *Smack! . . . a plump brown hand wallops a yellow wad of biscuit dough against the floured kneading board. . . .* "And that's the truth, young'un." It is more than truth. It is wisdom. She suspects that in some things, Hosanna Richardson is wiser than Dorsey Bascombe. He knows all there is to know about horses and trees. But if you asked him about the power of new sun, he would likely give you a strange look. Some things are best left to Hosanna.

<   >

Music and wisdom formed the strong, sure bedrock of Bright's early childhood. It was mostly warmth and light, an airy goodness like fresh-risen biscuits.

But there was also what Hosanna referred to darkly as "the baby bidness." Bright understood little of it, only that it took her mother away from her for long periods of time when there was no music from the piano and a pall of nervous anticipation settled over the house. It was a cycle, like the seasons: Elise weak and nauseous, taking to her bed, Dr. Finus Tillman bustling in and out periodically, Dorsey pinch-faced and hopeful. Elise made infrequent trips downstairs, slow migrations with Dorsey's strong arm around her; and Bright was allowed a daily visit to Elise's room, where she propped herself beside her mother on two pillows while Elise read to her. But there was mostly quiet, heavy with the mystery of what was going on in the bedroom upstairs and by Bright's notion, communicated unwittingly by the adults in the house, that if she asked too many questions, it would somehow disrupt the process. Inevitably, something did. There was a crisis—like a cold blast of winter—and everything was over: Dorsey stonily silent and sad, Elise pale and wasted against her pillows, barely able to raise her hand to Bright's cheek, Hosanna wrapped in a deep funk of disapproval over the entire business. Bright took frightened refuge in the kitchen, where Hosanna explained just enough of it to keep her questions at bay, but not enough to satisfy her about the dark and mysterious details. The only thing she knew for sure was that, at some point, "the baby bidness" was over. There had been angry men's voices in the hall-way upstairs on a cold February evening and Bright had heard the un-mistakable words from Dr. Tillman: "No more, Dorsey. Give it up, or you'll kill her." Then, the slamming of a door and Dr. Tillman, grim and smelling of camphor, had left the house carrying something in a white porcelain pan covered with a piece of cloth. Hosanna stood at the bottom of the stairs, wiping her eyes with her apron. Bright lurked in the kitchen doorway nearby, trying to see and hear without being obtrusive. "Well, that's the end of the baby bidness," Hosanna said.

< 84 >

"What did the doctor do to Mama?" Bright asked in a very small voice.

Hosanna whirled on her, eyes flashing. "Curiosity killed the cat!" she barked, and stormed past Bright into the kitchen, leaving her alone and confused. She crept upstairs after a while to her own room and put herself to bed, drifting off to troubled sleep in a muddle of dreams about dead cats and too many questions. The next morning, Dorsey descended the stairs for breakfast cloaked in gloom and disappointment. There was something very close to anger naked on his face. Bright decided to keep her mouth shut and risk no more disaster.

< >

It was five months after the end of "the baby bidness" when the woman appeared at the front door. She had a big brown mole protruding from her chin with two black hairs growing from it. Bright stared, fascinated, through the screen as the woman bent, peering into the gloom of the hallway at her. "I've come to see your mother," she said.

"Yes'm, Miz Elise'll be right down," Hosanna said, looming behind Bright. She reached around Bright to open the screen. "You just come on in, Miz Hardwicke. Just have a seat in here in the parlor and I'll tell Miz Elise you're here."

"I hope I'm not calling too early," the woman said, arching her eyebrows in a way that seemed to invite confession.

"Oh, no ma'am," Hosanna said resolutely. "Miz Elise been up for hours."

Bright knew that wasn't so. It was very late in the morning, the sun high and hot outside, and she had only heard her mother moving around upstairs in the past few minutes. Hosanna gave her a good, sharp look as Bright followed them into the parlor, where the woman spread herself on the sofa. Hosanna didn't say anything, but Bright knew what she was thinking. *You don't tell nobody else yore bidness.* Hosanna could tell you a lot without ever opening her mouth. She clomped off up the stairs and Bright stood in the middle of the room, with the coffee table between her and Mrs. Hardwicke, and stared some more. The mole seemed to grow bigger as you looked at it, the black hairs longer. The woman squirmed a bit. She had an ample behind, and even the tiniest squirm moved a lot of area. "How old are you?" she asked Bright.

"Five."

"My little girl Xuripha is five. You'll meet her in school next year. You would have met her already, but y'all go to the Methodist Church, and we go to the Baptist." The way she said *Baptist*, it sounded like something pretty special. Bright had an ear for the way people said

< 85 >

things, the way you could play a note on the piano several different ways. Hearing Mrs. Hardwicke say *Baptist* just now reminded Bright somehow of the way Hosanna said *Big-Ikey.* Bright didn't know who Big Ike was, but when Hosanna said somebody was acting Big-Ikey, you knew she was talking about being *too big for your britches.* Hosanna, like the Bascombes, was a Methodist and given to suspicion about anyone who wasn't.

"Yes ma'am," Bright said, and kept staring. It was hard to take your eyes off a mole that big, especially one with two long black hairs growing out of it.

Mrs. Hardwicke gave another squirm. "Are you excited about going to school?" she tried again.

"No ma'am." In fact, she wasn't. She couldn't imagine anything more interesting than going to the lumberyard with her father, or out into the deep pine woods, or playing hide-and-seek with her dolls in the backyard, or listening to an evening piano and trombone concert. And she couldn't imagine anybody smarter than Dorsey Bascombe or wiser than Hosanna. No, school didn't seem like much of a bargain. She thought she might just stay home next year and ask questions. She had a lot of questions, and so far, Dorsey Bascombe and Hosanna had been able to answer everything to her satisfaction except for "the baby bidness." Right now, Bright had quite a few questions about Mrs. Hardwicke's mole. Her eyes bored in on it. It wasn't particularly menacing. In fact, it reminded her a great deal of a toadstool, the kind you would find out in the broad green backyard after a good rain, poking its head up between the thin blades of the Saint Augustine grass in a shady spot next to the stable or under one of the pecan trees. You wouldn't dare put a toadstool in your mouth, especially after Hosanna told you about the man who ate one and went crazy and ran all the way to Columbus foaming at the mouth until he dropped plumb dead. But the fascinating thing about a toadstool was, you could study it for a long time and then reach down and snap it off right at the . . .

"Bright!" her mother cried. Bright's hand froze in midair.

Mrs. Hardwicke recoiled, horrified, on the sofa. "You little snip!"

"Bright, go to your room!" Elise commanded. "No, first you apologize to Mrs. Hardwicke for your behavior!"

"Yes ma'am. I'm sorry for my behavior." She did a little curtsy and backed out of the room, making a good deal of noise as she climbed the stairs, and then sneaking back down on tiptoe a few minutes later to crouch in the back hallway so she could hear the conversation in the parlor. By this time, Hosanna had brought iced tea and it seemed to have cooled Mrs. Hardwicke down a bit. Bright could hear the tin-

< 86 >

kle of ice in the heavy crystal glasses, the rustle of a paper fan. Mrs. Hardwicke, no doubt. Elise Bascombe never fanned herself. She never seemed to get hot.

"Well," Mrs. Hardwicke was saying, "enough about children. I've come to invite you to the Study Club." She said *Study Club* about the way she did *Baptist*. "In fact, we'd like for you to come and give the program. It's something we ask our, ah, prospective members to do."

"Oh, my," Elise said. "What's the Study Club?"

"It's . . . well, we study things. Topics of general interest. World affairs and the like."

"Oh." A long pause. Then, "Why?"

Bright could imagine her mother sitting there primly on the edge of her chair, birdlike, ready to take flight, face very earnest, a bit bewildered. Elise looked like that a great deal of the time. Bright understood in a basic way that she and her mother were children together. Her mother could play dolls in the most earnest way. *And will you take cream with your tea, my dear?* And she could imagine Mrs. Hardwicke leaning forward on the sofa, pressing her point, the long black hairs from the big mole dancing a bit in the air.

"Why, to inform. To illuminate. To *edify,*" Mrs. Hardwicke said. It sounded a bit stuffy to Bright. "To bring a little culture to our community. We can't all live in *New Orleans,* you know." The way she said *New Orleans* made it sound like *Big-Ikey.*

"I see," Elise said, her voice sounding smaller with every word.

There was the clink of ice and glass again as both women sipped their tea and let the Study Club marinate there in the warm air of the parlor for a moment. Bright could hear the whoosh-whoosh of Mrs. Hardwicke's fan, stirring things about. She considered the idea of Hosanna putting in an appearance at the Study Club, standing up before a group of plump, powdered Mrs. Hardwickes and telling them about the man running all the way to Columbus, foaming at the mouth after he ate a toadstool. She stifled a giggle.

"For instance," Mrs. Hardwicke said after a moment, gathering herself, "we're studying the Orient now. Don't you find the Orient terribly mysterious, with all those dark people and strange customs?"

"I suppose," Elise said. "Yes, I suppose it is terribly mysterious." Bright could tell that her mother was trying very hard, and that she was not enjoying herself particularly.

"Well," Mrs. Hardwicke said with a little clap of her hands, "we'd like for you to give a program on Borneo."

"Borneo?"

"Yes."

< 87 >

Elise took a deep breath. "But I don't know anything about Borneo."

"Oh, that's no problem. I have a book. I'll send it around by my girl." Bright understood by the way she said *girl* that Mrs. Hardwicke wasn't speaking of her daughter, Xuripha, but of her version of Hosanna. There were girls, and there were *girls*. "Just read the book and give us a presentation. The highlights, you know. Some interesting facts. So that we'll get the flavor, the mystery of the place."

There was a long, deep silence and then Elise said softly, "No thank you."

"I beg your pardon?"

"I can't."

"What do you mean?"

"I just can't. I'm no good at all in front of a group of people. Except playing the piano. Perhaps I could play some music from Borneo. But I couldn't talk. No, I just couldn't." Elise sounded frightened, like a small animal caught in a corner by a bright light.

Then there was a rustle of fabric and Bright knew that Mrs. Hardwicke was shifting her bulk forward on the sofa, leaning across the coffee table. "Well, we're not a music club. But my dear, you'll find us very easy to know if you'll give us a chance."

"I'm sure, but . . ."

And then a hard edge in Mrs. Hardwicke's voice. "You must. Really, you must. You have obligations, Mrs. Bascombe. You can't sit here in this house forever. People will think you . . ."—a deep breath, a long pause—". . . odd."

"Oh." A tiny, hollow word, almost a whisper.

Then Mrs. Hardwicke rose from the sofa. "I'll send the book around this afternoon. We'll expect you next Wednesday." Her voice brightened. "I'm sure you'll be charmed by the mystery of Borneo. We'll all be charmed."

She chattered her way to the door, and then Bright heard the screen close behind her. Bright peeked from her hiding place in the back hallway and saw her mother standing there in the doorway, dark outline against the noon brightness, hand raised tentatively in goodbye as Mrs. Hardwicke faded into the midday, leaving the parlor heavy with the scent of lilac water. Elise lowered her hand and stood for a long time, very still, arms clutched about her as if warding off a chill. Bright watched and then tiptoed up the back stairs to her room, wondering what it was about the mysteries of Borneo that could make her mother so frightened, so sad. Surely there was nothing about Borneo half so mysterious and frightening as "the baby bidness." After a while she heard the long high wail of the steam whistle from Dorsey Bas-

< 88 >

combe's lumberyard across town, signaling noontime. Her father would be home in five minutes, bustling in the door, smelling of the woods on a summer morning. And he would take care of everything.

Huge, steaming bowls of field peas, fried okra, squash, butter beans; a platter of pork chops smothered in rich brown gravy, another of roast beef carved in thick slices, well-done on the outside, slightly pink at the center; a cut-glass platter of sliced tomatoes and cucumbers and rings of fresh onion; a wicker basket of hot buttered rolls, covered with an embroidered cloth; boats of food floating on the white sea of the damask tablecloth. Hosanna hovering in the background, her presence mingling with the rich smells drifting up from the table.

"What's *noliminny?*" Bright asked as they lifted their heads from the blessing.

Dorsey Bascombe reached for the platter of pork chops and helped himself to two large ones. "What's who?"

"*Noliminny.* When you say the blessing, you say, 'Thank you, Lord, for these and *noliminny* blessings.'"

Dorsey threw his head back and laughed. "*Noliminny.* That's rich. I'm saying *all-our-many.* 'Thank you, Lord, for these and *all-our-many* blessings.'"

Bright nodded. "Are you thankful for toadstools?"

"Toadstools. Yes," he nodded, "I suppose so."

"Did you ever eat a toadstool?"

"No, and don't you. Goodness, all these questions." He passed the platter of pork chops to Elise, at his left. She sat there, staring at the platter, her face ashen. Dorsey held the platter for a long moment, then said softly, "Elise? Hon!" She shook her head finally. Dorsey passed the platter over to Bright and held it while she speared a pork chop with her fork, sliding it onto her plate and being careful not to drip any gravy onto the tablecloth, the way Elise had showed her. Elise's mother had brought the damask tablecloth all the way from New Orleans on her last visit. It was a very fine tablecloth, Grandma Poncie said. She looked a little unhappy when Dorsey Bascombe bustled in from the lumberyard in his sweat-stained khakis and knee-high leather boots and sat down to eat dinner off such a fine New Orleans tablecloth. Dorsey commented on what a privilege it was to dine at such an elegant table, and went on about his business. Bright thought Grandma Poncie was a bit stiff. Grandma Poncie would probably enjoy the Study Club.

They helped their plates in silence, *clink-tinkle*, Dorsey casting glances at Elise, who took little dibs and dabs of food, a small mound of butter beans, a bit of okra, a slice of tomato. They looked lost and

< 89 >

forlorn on her plate. She poked about with her fork, moving the food this way and that, eventually taking a small bite of okra. She chewed with tiny movements.

"Well," Dorsey said after a moment. "I understand you had a visitor this morning."

Elise looked up, stricken. Hosanna retreated to the kitchen, leaving the door swinging in her wake, squeaking softly on its spring hinges.

"Fincher Hardwicke dropped by the lumberyard this morning," Dorsey went on. "He said Fostoria was going to come by for a visit." He picked up his knife and fork, cut off a piece of pork chop, chewed thoughtfully. Bright sat small and quiet, watching, listening. "Did you have a nice visit?"

Elise nodded.

"Well. Well, that's nice." Dorsey worked at his food for a while, concentrating on it, finding the butter beans and tomato slices particularly interesting. A wagon creaked by on the hard-packed clay street in front of the house. In the warm stillness of the dining room you could hear every small noise it made. It sounded so close Bright thought it might just come on inside, up the front steps and through the screen door and into the dining room, where it would stop while the mule ate some butter beans from the bowl on the table. Bright thought about that very hard, imagining the mule peering at her while he chewed, his bottom jaw moving in a circular motion, the way mules' jaws did when they were eating. She liked to imagine things the way they *might* be. It seemed more interesting that way. She put a hand over her mouth. Now didn't seem to be a very good time to giggle.

"And, ah, what did you talk about?" Dorsey asked.

Elise sat holding her fork in her right hand, staring at Dorsey. She put the fork down next to the plate. "Borneo," she said.

"Ah, yes, of course. Borneo. And how are things in Borneo this morning?" He was trying to keep his voice light.

"Fostoria Hardwicke wants me to come speak to the Study Club about Borneo. Next Wednesday."

"And what did you say?"

"I said 'No thank you.'"

Dorsey nodded, thought about that for a while, and then said, "I see. And why not?"

Elise took a deep breath and said, "Dorsey, I can't. I just can't."

"Why not, dear?"

"I just . . . a group . . ." She shook her head firmly. "I've never done anything like that before. I just can't."

Then Bright piped up and said, "Miz Hardwicke is sending a

< 90 >

book. By her girl." And the moment it came out, she wished she had kept her mouth shut. Elise stared at her and Bright felt like a traitor.

Dorsey took a deep breath and gave Elise a big, winning smile. "Well, there, now. Fostoria is trying to be helpful. You'll do just fine, dear. I daresay you'll know more about Borneo than anybody in the room when you get through with the book. You could probably tell them that Borneo is made of green cheese, and they'd believe it. And, too, I'm sure the Study Club is perfectly harmless. A little stuffy, maybe, but essentially harmless. It's a nice gesture. They want to include you. Now that . . ."

It hung in the air, unspoken. *Now that . . .* And Bright thought, *Now that the baby business is over with.*

"Ahem." Dorsey cleared his throat, leaned forward, looked over the cut-glass platter in front of him carefully. "I, ah, think I'll have a piece of onion. I'll pay for it later, but there's nothing quite like a bit of onion to spice up your meal." He lifted a ring of onion off the platter with his fork, dropped it on his plate, cut off a piece, chewed. Finally he smiled into the silence. Dorsey didn't smile a great deal, but when he did it was big and warm and wrapped itself around everything and everybody within reach. And you just knew when he turned that smile on you that everything would be all right. He put his fork down then, clasped his hands in front of him, resting his elbows on the arms of his chair, cleared his throat again. "I want you to try," he said. "It will go just fine, I'm sure." Elise stared at him, eyes large, the color drained from her face. He paused a moment, then went on. "You've got to *live* here, Elise, here in this town."

Elise dropped her head, stared at her plate, and Bright thought how small and lost she looked, like a child who had wandered away and didn't know how to get back home. "Fostoria Hardwicke said people will think I'm odd," she said quietly.

"Yes," Dorsey said. "They will. She's right about that."

Elise raised her head, looked him straight in the eye for the very first time since dinner had begun. "So? What if they do? Don't I have the right to be odd if I want to? After all, I'm from *New Orleans.*" There was something very sad and self-mocking in her voice.

Bright sat very still, not really wanting to be there but caught in the web of whatever was going on between her mother and father, knowing that it was very important, something awfully big and grown-up scary. Her parents seemed to have forgotten that she was there.

Dorsey stared at her for a long moment and then his eyes broke away and he looked down at his clasped hands, and Bright could see how white his knuckles were. Finally he looked up at her and said, "No, you don't have the right. If not for your sake, then for mine." He

< 91 >

paused, searching. "Fincher Hardwicke told me something this morning. He told me some of the men want me to run for mayor. I don't really want to. I've got a full plate right now." Bright glanced at his plate, thought that he had made a pretty good dent in his food already, but decided not to say anything. "But when you choose a place, choose to live in it, you take from it and then you give part of yourself back. This happens to be a good place, but it can be better. And I aim to do what I can. But I need you . . ." His words trailed off into the stillness of the room, and he lifted his hands in a gesture of supplication. Then he reached out a hand to her, palm open, across the table. She looked up at him and after a moment she put her small, slender hand in his big one and he closed it about hers; Bright could see the tiny movement of muscles in his powerful hand as he squeezed ever so slightly.

"For me?" he said softly.

Bright held her breath, frozen by the moment, by the anguished fright in her mother's eyes and by the enormous presence of her father, the powerful aura about him that seemed to bend things ever so gently but inexorably into the shape in which he willed them. He seemed to tower above them, even sitting as he was now. Bright thought, *I would never want to disappoint him.*

And finally Elise let go of Dorsey's hand and put her own hand in her lap and said, in a voice so tiny it could have been a mouse's, "All right. I'll try."

< >

Suds flew. Bright sat on a stool next to the counter by the sink while Hosanna washed the dinner dishes. It was her second-favorite place in the house, next to the big green overstuffed chair in the music room where she snuggled with her father. That was like being deep down in a warm, safe cave. This was like sitting on the edge of a cliff, watching a drama unfold below. Hosanna attacked the dishes, scrubbing them so hard it seemed she would rub the shininess clean off, flinging suds in all directions, carrying on a running commentary as she worked.

"They ought to leave that young'un alone," she muttered now, brow creased in dark wrath. "Ought to let that young'un get her rest, get over this *bidness*." Hosanna referred to Elise as "that young'un," and said it in a way that let you know she felt like a mother hen. "Some folks *do* and some folks *don't* and some folks do *sometimes* and some don't *never*."

Bright wondered what it was that some folks *do*. Hosanna talked in disconnected bursts of sound, like beginning a piece of music in the middle of the one just before. Slosh-scrub-splash. She dunked each

< 92 >

dirty dish in the pan of suds, scrubbed fiercely, held it up for inspection, then doused it in another pan of rinse water, stacked it with a clatter on the drainboard next to the sink. Bright had never seen her break a dish. Hosanna seemed to know exactly how much each of them could take.

"Can God eat toadstools?" Bright asked.

Hosanna never missed a beat. Slosh-scrub-splash. "Course He could if He wanted to, but He don't want to. He don't *have* to. God don't have to eat nothin'." She snorted. "Folks think God gets up every mornin' and puts on His hat and shoes and goes to work, just like everybody else. Folks want God to be just like them, only cuter. Folks get down on they knees and pray, 'Oh, God, send me a mess of turnip greens!'" She made a wail out of it, and Bright giggled. Hosanna was getting good and warmed up now. Bright thought Hosanna could have been a great actress. "God don't *send* turnip greens, he lets turnip greens *grow*. And before they *grow*, you got to *hoe*. God do the growin', but you does the hoein'."

"You don't have to hoe toadstools," Bright said, clasping her arms around her knees. She knew a thing or two about toadstools. She had studied toadstools pretty closely, out in the backyard under the shade of the pecan tree. She figured she already knew about as much about toadstools as anybody could teach her in school, just from direct observation.

"No, but you don't eat toadstools, neither," Hosanna said. She gave the gravy boat a vigorous scrub, dishcloth sloshing about in the water. "Ain't no reason for toadstools except God wants 'em there. You go out yonder under the pecan tree and look down and say, 'Hey, Mr. Toadstool, what you be about?' And there ain't no answer. God just took a notion once upon a time to make toadstools and let 'em grow. And that's the be-all and end-all of toadstools. It's just a mystery. Life's a mystery. God's a mystery. He's powerful mysterious. That's why you don't never know how things are gonna turn out. Except"—she flung her head in the direction of the dining room, empty now—"sometimes you can see 'em comin'. God don't keep folks from making *fools* of theyselves. Even smart folks. Even folks way up on the peckin' order."

"What's a peckin' order?"

Hosanna gave the gravy boat a dip in the rinse water and set it carefully on the drainboard with the growing pile of dishes. Then she dried her hands on her apron before she picked up another plate. "Peckin' order is the way folks is arranged," she said. "God's at the top, then the President. After that is a bunch of folks that's got good sense,

< 93 >

including yore daddy most of the time. I say, *most* of the time." She rolled her eyes back in her head, as if the rest of the peckin' order were printed somewhere above her eyebrows on the inside. "Then there's ordinary folks. And slap-dab at the bottom is Big-Ikeys."

"Does God make Big-Ikeys?"

"Course He does. He makes everything. Most Big-Ikeys He makes is white folks, 'cause white folks likes to *pose* a lot, like they having they picture took all the time, 'fraid somebody's gone see 'em without they hair just right and they airs in place. White folks can't jest *be*, they got to *pose*."

"Why does God make Big-Ikeys?" Bright asked, making a mental note to see if Fostoria Hardwicke was posing the next time she laid eyes on her.

Hosanna gave a great sigh. "That's a mystery. Big-Ikeys is just like toadstools. God just lets 'em grow." She looked over at Bright, perched on the stool. "You a figurin' young'un," she said. "But don't you go around tryin' to figure out God. He just *be*."

Bright understood a little of that. The Sunday school version was a little confusing. They told you that God was in heaven, and then they told you He was everywhere, watching everything you did. And then they told you that God was in the First Methodist Church, which was God's house. But Bright also knew from personal experience that He was in the African Methodist Church, because she had been there and felt Him. On a Wednesday evening a month before, with Dorsey gone on a business trip and Elise abed upstairs with what Hosanna vaguely referred to as "vapors," Hosanna had taken Bright to what she called "singing" at the small, neat frame church on the edge of the Negro section.

"Yore daddy built this church," she told Bright as they walked down the rutted clay street to where a crowd was gathering at the door. "He said to me ten years ago, 'Hosanna, I'm going to build two churches in this town. And they're both going to be Methodist churches.' So yore daddy gave the lumber, and the men that worked in his lumberyard put up this church, and yore daddy came to the first service and when we sang the first hymn, Dorsey Bascombe stood up at the front of the church smiling the biggest smile God ever put on a man, and tears rollin' down his cheeks like cat's-eye marbles, they was so big. Pride tears. Mr. Dorsey was *proud* that day."

Inside the church, surrounded by the broad smiles of the congregation, Dorsey Bascombe's little girl, she stood on the pew beside Hosanna as the singing began, and she felt it grow and grow, the powerful ring of their magnificent voices all joined together as if they were holding hands without touching, and it warmed her like the warmth of the

< 94 >

new sun. Midway through the first long resounding hymn, the beautiful golden voice of a young woman broke through the rest and soared up in the rafters of the church while the congregation swayed below. Bright reached over and tugged on Hosanna's sleeve and whispered loudly in her ear, "Is that God?" And Hosanna gave her a long, penetrating look, her face all soft in a way that Bright had never seen it. "Yes, honey," she said, "that's God."

She pondered God for a moment now in the kitchen, perched on the stool, while Hosanna splashed noisily in the sink beside her. She pondered God and toadstools and music and the baby business and her mother upstairs and the Study Club and Big-Ikeys and the posing of white folks and the mysterious wisdom of colored folks. And she decided after a while that God had an awful lot of things He could be bothered with if He allowed himself to, and that was probably why He just let lots of things be.

Then she looked up and saw the black girl at the back door, her face pressed hard against the screen. "Hosanna?" the girl said.

Hosanna turned, glowering, flinging soapsuds across the floor. "MIZ HOSANNA TO YOU," she thundered. She gave the girl a good once-over. She was holding a book, a slim volume with a brown binding. "You come from Borneo?"

The girl gave a flounce of her head. "Naw. I come from Miz Fostoria Hardwicke's," she said.

"Same thing." Hosanna walked over to the door, drying her hands on her apron. The girl stepped back and Hosanna opened the door and took the book, then closed the door again, leaving the girl on the steps, looking at them through the screen. She opened the book and thumbed through several pages. "My, my," she said, "they shore is some right interesting things goin' on in Borneo these days. They is *powerful* stuff goin' on in Borneo. Have to be, or high-fashion ladies wouldn't be messin' with Borneo, I tell you that. It says right here that folks in Borneo grows precious jewels in they gardens, right alongside the turnip greens and rutabagas." She looked up at the girl, then flipped a few more pages. "And it says here"— she tapped the page with a finger— "that they sacrifices virgins in a pot of boiling blood." The girl's mouth dropped open, and so did Bright's. Hosanna closed the book with a smack. "You tell Miz Fostoria Hardwicke we is *mortified* to get all this stuff on Borneo."

The girl backed down the steps into the yard, wide-eyed. "Yes'm, I'll tell her. Miz Hardwicke be glad to hear that. Mighty glad." And she disappeared.

Hosanna held the book up in the light from the open door. "Borneo," she muttered softly. "My ass."

< 95 >

6

Wednesday morning was gray outside, the tree just beyond the open kitchen window rustling with the first stirrings of birds anticipating daybreak. Bright sat, fully dressed, a huge glass of milk untouched on the table before her. The kitchen seemed an alien place now, cold and harsh in the bright light from the overhead bulb, not the warm sanctuary to which she was accustomed. She was still fuzzy from sleep and she held her head very still to keep the starch in the lace collar of her Sunday dress from scratching her neck. Her mother stood at the sink, fumbling noisily with the coffeepot. There was a trail of brown coffee beans across the counter to the sink. Bright watched, fascinated, wondering what would happen when and if Elise finally got the coffeepot organized, then discovered that you had to start a fire in the stove to get anything hot. She could not *ever* remember her mother being in the kitchen before.

The door from the dining room swung open, creaking on its springed hinges, and Dorsey stood there, wearing khaki pants and an undershirt and bedroom slippers, eyes bleary. His gaze swept the kitchen and he ran his fingers through his thick gray-speckled hair. Elise turned and looked at him, then went back to her work, trying to fit parts of the coffeepot together.

"Well, ahem," Dorsey began, then he reached into the watch pocket of his khaki pants and drew out his watch, snapped open the cover, squinted at it. "It's not quite five o'clock," he said, a bit of wonder in his voice.

Elise dropped part of the metal coffeepot into the sink with a clatter. Her hand went to her mouth. "Damn," she said. Then she set the rest of the pot on the counter and turned again to Dorsey, the color high in her cheekbones. She wore a loose-fitting beige lace dress with a low waist and long narrow skirt, and she looked, Bright thought, as

< 96 >

if she could step away from the sink and out the front door at any moment, gathering her hat and gloves from the table in the front hall as she went. "Where the devil is Hosanna?" Her voice was high and tight, stretched like a piano string.

Dorsey glanced at his watch again. "Isn't it a bit early, hon?"

"Early? What's early when you haven't slept a wink all night?"

Dorsey closed the watch gently and slipped it back into his pocket, then gave Bright a long look. "And what in heaven's name are you doing up at this hour, young lady?"

"She's going with me," Elise answered for her.

"I really don't think—"

"She'll be *fine!* Just *fine!*" Bright thought her mother looked like a piece of china, that kind of statue you would find on a parlor whatnot shelf, very fragile. She had been pacing the upstairs bedroom for two days now, Bright hunkered outside the closed door listening as Elise recited fact and figure about Borneo, her voice rising and falling in a singsong cadence, the words coming faster and faster until finally she would collapse into a chair and there would be a long exhausted silence. Then the rustling of papers, and the pacing and reciting would begin again. Bright could feel panic oozing out from under the door and it terrified her. She wanted to fling open the door and rush in and wrap her arms around her mother. But she sat quietly, trembling, afraid that Elise might shatter if touched.

Dorsey crossed the kitchen to the sink now and stood before Elise, placed his hands on her shoulders. She stood rigid for a moment, but she yielded, let him guide her gently to a chair at the table. Then he bent to her, looked straight into her eyes. "Elise, hon, don't get all wrought up about this. Look, let's just tell them you're not feeling well, that you'll do it another time."

"No!" she flashed. "I've got to do it TODAY! I can't wait. I said I'd do it, and I will." Her hands fluttered to her face, but then she caught herself, lowered her hands to her lap, stared at them until they finally became still. Bright could see the very great effort it took, the force of will. *Mama is stronger than I thought. Maybe stronger than Hosanna thinks she is.*

Elise finally looked up again at Dorsey. "I'm fine," she whispered, "just fine."

He searched her face for a moment longer. "All right," he said, then stood. "Well, let's have some breakfast, what do you say. How about some scrambled eggs and fried ham with redeye gravy and some grits. I'll get things started, and then Hosanna will be here in a bit and she can do the biscuits. I'll catch the devil for being in her kitchen,

< 97 >

but I won't go so far as to try to make biscuits. She'd stuff me in the oven for that." His voice bounced hollowly off the walls of the kitchen and out through the window by the sink, where the birds were beginning to chatter in earnest now. Bright looked at the window and she could see a hint of gray-blue peeking through the branches of the pecan tree.

"I think," she said solemnly, then paused for a long moment. Her parents looked at her curiously. "I think," she said again, "that I don't much like milk this early in the morning." Then she laid her head down on the kitchen table and went back to sleep.

Shortly before ten, they walked the few blocks to Fostoria Hardwicke's house. Bright barely remembered being carried up to bed in her father's strong arms, and being reawakened an hour ago by her mother, redressed, led downstairs, where Hosanna was bustling about in a dark funk, muttering about menfolks dirtying up her kitchen. "Looks like a lumberyard in here," she said, holding up a black cast-iron skillet that had the yellowed remains of scrambled egg in the bottom, dousing it with a splash into a sinkful of dishwater. Elise left Bright to be fed, but she picked idly at her food, her mind swirling with the anticipation of the Study Club. Finally, they set off in the warming day while Elise chattered in a determined singsong. "*Borneo is the third-largest island in the world. Borneo was settled by European explorers in the 1500s. Borneo has about a million people, called Dyaks, who follow a heathen tribal religion. Borneo makes teakwood and diamonds.*" She walked fast, the heels of her shoes clicking along the sidewalk, the ostrich plume on her wide-brimmed hat bouncing like a horse's tail. She gripped Bright with a gloved hand, a little too tightly, and Bright's feet fairly flew over the pavement as she tried to keep up. "*Borneo has four territories, ruled by Great Britain and Holland. The equator runs through Borneo . . .*" Bright wondered when she would get to the part about precious gems growing alongside the turnips and virgins being boiled in blood.

Fostoria Hardwicke's house was big and green, trimmed in white, with a wide, banistered porch across the low sweep of its front and lush, bright green ferns drooping like eyelids from baskets that hung above the banisters. As they climbed the steps, Bright could hear the faint mutter of voices through the screen door, deep inside the green cave of the house. "*Borneo's coastline is mostly swampland . . .*"

Bright was quite out of breath. Elise paused for a moment at the door, dropping Bright's hand to give a tug on her gloves and smooth the front of her dress. Then she knocked, and Fostoria Hardwicke ap-

< 98 >

peared in the doorway. "Oh, good morning!" she chimed, "so glad to see . . ." Then she looked down and saw Bright. "Oh," she said. Then, after a moment, "Well, Xuripha is in her room. I suppose you . . ."

Bright sensed that she was her mother's ally here. She reached up and took Elise's hand. "I came to hear about Borneo," she said firmly, giving the large mole on Fostoria Hardwicke's chin a good, hard look. Did it have two black hairs, or three? Could it have grown another in the space of a week?

"Well, we don't—"

"She'll be *just fine*," Elise said. Bright looked up at her mother, saw the wide-eyed look of desperation.

Fostoria Hardwicke must have seen it too. She opened the door. "Of course," she said gently, taking Elise's arm, guiding her into the dim interior of the house. "We're just so glad you came, dear. Really, we are. I hope we haven't asked too much." Elise stared at her dumbly.

There was a great deal of furniture in the parlor and all of it was filled with ladies, a dozen or so, a garden of crinoline and lace, chiffon and brocade, stirred by the soft whoosh of the ceiling fan. Conversation ceased as they appeared in the doorway and Bright felt her mother's hand tremble. Fostoria Hardwicke led them around the room through a puddle of pleasantries. *You remember . . . of course, my dear . . . how very nice . . .* All of the women were older than Elise, a couple of them fairly ancient. They were soft ladies, pastel and flower-scented. Mrs. Artesia Gibbons had a little silk handkerchief stuffed into her glove, just the corner peeking out, and after Elise pressed her hand lightly, Mrs. Gibbons withdrew the handkerchief and dabbed at the corner of her mouth. Mrs. June Deloach (how nice, Bright thought, to be named for a lovely month, or perhaps for a june bug) had a trace of dark hair above her upper lip, so small and delicate you would not think to call it a moustache. When she spoke, she sounded wispy and out of breath, as if she had teeny-tiny lungs. In fact, Bright observed, she didn't have much of a bosom. On the other hand, Miss Eugenia Putnam (Bright noticed how Fostoria Hardwicke put the emphasis on the *Miss*) had an ample bosom and a big strong voice, even though she was frightfully old and had dark liver spots on her arms. She was slightly hard of hearing. She bent forward in her chair with her left hand cupped behind her ear, and spoke rather loudly. "Eh? Dorsey Bascombe's wife? Didn't know Dorsey Bascombe had a wife. Is she from around here?" as if Elise were not even there. Bright took it that Miss Eugenia Putnam was given to saying whatever came to mind, which Bright thought was rather fun.

The ladies of the Study Club eyed Bright curiously and Bright

< 99 >

gave each of them a little smile and curtsy, as Elise had drilled her to do, and then they sat down, Elise in a huge flowered-print chair next to the arched entrance to the room, Bright on an ottoman beside her. Elise looked small and lost in the great expanse of the chair, as if she had fallen backward into a pansy patch and couldn't get out. Conversation bubbled up around them and Bright watched as her mother sat primly, gloved hands in her lap, feet barely touching the floor, a stricken smile on her face. *She's afraid,* Bright thought. Bright could never remember being afraid of anything herself. With Dorsey Bascombe towering above her in his rich brown leather boots and Hosanna filling the kitchen with dead-certain wisdom and God whispering outside her window at night, what was there to be afraid of? Whatever happened, Dorsey would come home and take care of everything. She could almost feel him here now, watching, nodding. The ladies of the Study Club seemed perfectly harmless, as he had said. But there her mother sat, lost and afraid and fragile, nodding mindlessly as Fostoria Hardwicke at her left chattered and the conversation bubbled up around them like a lilac-scented fountain . . . *the most delicious chicken . . . looked so natural lying there in the coffin, like she might reach up . . . Nigra asked for a book at the library, can you believe . . . his sermon, you know . . . all the way to Philadelphia to buy a motorcar . . . allow dogs in the house . . .*

Mrs. June Deloach, seated on the other side of the doorway, leaned toward her. "We're not accustomed to having young ladies at our gatherings," she said breathlessly.

Bright placed her hands together in her lap and tucked her feet up under the ottoman. She pretended for a moment that she was Miss Eugenia Putnam, ancient and plainspoken and a bit hard of hearing. "I might not come again," she said loudly. "I wanted to hear Mama talk about how they boil virgins in blood."

Conversation positively stopped. Mrs. June Deloach drew in a sharp breath, Mrs. Artesia Gibbons whipped out her silk handkerchief, and Miss Eugenia Putnam cupped her hand behind her ear. "Eh? What? Virgins?"

Fostoria Hardwicke leapt to her feet. "Well," she exploded into the silence, "it's time for a little refreshment before we have our program." They all started talking at once and Fostoria bustled out of the room, clattering down the hallway toward the back of the house. Bright looked up at her mother. Elise's eyes seemed glazed, uncomprehending. Her mouth moved silently, reciting Borneo. Bright hoped she wouldn't forget the part about the virgins.

Mrs. Hardwicke came back in a moment, carrying a large silver tray piled high with tiny sandwiches. Behind her was the black girl

< 100 >

who had delivered the book on Borneo to the Bascombes' back door, gingerly balancing another tray, laden with small plates, cups and saucers, and a stack of cloth napkins, folded neatly in triangles. They made the rounds of the room, each lady taking a plate, cup and saucer, napkin, and two of the little sandwiches. Bright felt her empty stomach grumble and she took three, arranging them tidily on the plate in her lap. Instead of a cup and saucer, Mrs. Hardwicke had a small glass of milk for her. Bright held the glass of milk in her left hand and took a nibble of a sandwich with the other, and then she discovered a very unfortunate thing. Pimento cheese. She didn't like pimento cheese. In fact, she positively *dis*liked pimento cheese. The thought of those little red bits of pimento lurking down there inside the yellow cheese made her feel queer. She wished she had taken only two of the sandwiches, or perhaps none at all. She sat staring at the small white rectangles on her plate while Mrs. Hardwicke and the black girl made the rounds of the room again, Mrs. Hardwicke pouring coffee from a silver pot while the black girl held a tray of sugar and cream. The ladies of the Study Club nibbled and sipped daintily, chattering around their morsels, utterly unaware of her dilemma. Bright stared at the sandwich for a moment. *I just won't think about it. I'll just think about delicious candied yams. I'll take a big bite and a big swallow of milk and . . .*

PIMENTO CHEESE, her stomach said.

She looked around the room. The ladies were all eating their pimento cheese sandwiches and drinking their coffee, even her mother, who also detested pimento cheese. Elise was eating the pimento cheese sandwiches as if there were nothing wrong, as if she couldn't even taste them. All of these soft, elegant ladies, eating pimento cheese. Every crumb of it. Not a single one of them leaving a trace of sandwich on her plate. Bright wanted desperately not to embarrass her mother, who was sitting there numb and afraid, a small fragile petunia amid all the lush foliage of the Study Club. She took a deep breath and told herself *I cannot taste anything!* and began stuffing the pimento cheese sandwiches into her mouth very quickly, taking big gulps of milk, washing everything down, every last bite and drop until it was all gone. She sat there for a moment, not breathing, and then she thought, *It's down there!* She looked up and saw Fostoria Hardwicke staring at her, wide-eyed, mouth formed in a shocked O. Then Mrs. Hardwicke snapped her mouth shut and gave a tiny, disgusted shake of her head. *Oh dear,* Bright thought, and her stomach gave a lurch of protest.

In a moment, Mrs. Hardwicke got up with a rush of crinoline and she and the black girl collected the empty dishes while Bright sat miserably on the ottoman, feet tucked underneath. The room felt hot and close now, the air so sickly sweet with the mingling of perfumes that

< 101 >

she could hardly breathe. Overhead, the fan went around and around and around. Bright forced herself to look at a spot on the Oriental rug where a yellow deer pranced on a red background, and desperately wished herself out somewhere in the woods or at the lumberyard with her father or back home safe in the kitchen with Hosanna.

Fostoria stood in the arched doorway, hands clasped in front of her. "Now, ladies," she said, and the murmur of conversation trailed off. "Ladies, it's so good of you to come today. I believe we have every single one of our members here today, and one"—she nodded toward Elise—"prospective member. Shall we call now for the reading of the minutes of the last meeting?" Mrs. June Deloach got up then and opened a small notebook and read about the meeting the month before at Mrs. Artesia Gibbons's house, where they had had cucumber and cream cheese sandwiches and iced tea and Fostoria Hardwicke herself had presented a study of Australia. Bright wished she had been at that meeting, because she liked cucumber and cream cheese sandwiches, and Australia sounded like it might be interesting. She wondered if they had virgins in Australia—whatever virgins were. Mrs. June Deloach sat down and Fostoria said, "Any corrections to the minutes?" Silence. "Then the minutes stand as read. Now"—she gave a small clap of her hands—"we have a special treat in store today as we continue our study of the far-flung"—she flung her arm—"nations of the world. Elise Bascombe has consented to give us a view of the island nation of Borneo. Let's welcome Elise."

There was a little round of gloved applause as Fostoria sat down and Elise got unsteadily to her feet. She stood next to the chair, one hand gripping the back of it tightly, towering over Bright's ottoman. Bright thought she looked very tired and pale—and doomed, like a chicken about to have its neck wrung. She had a sudden urge to stand up next to her mother and hold her hand, but she thought that would not do at all, and besides, any movement might bring the precarious pimento cheese into action. There was a long silence and the ladies of the Study Club sat expectantly, faces upturned. Bright thought they looked kindly, helpful. But she could feel the fear, thick and poisonous, radiating from her mother.

Elise stood there for a very long time, staring at a spot where the ceiling and wall came together at the far end of the room, and then she took a deep breath. "Bah . . . ," she said, and the sound choked in her throat and died. She swallowed hard. "Bah . . ."

Miss Eugenia Putnam leaned forward in her chair and cupped her hand behind her ear. "Eh? What she say?"

Elise opened her mouth again and Bright saw the horror twist her mother's face. One hand went to her cheek and the other clutched the

< 102 >

back of the chair so fiercely that her knuckles turned white. She croaked again, "Bah . . . bah . . ."

Down at the other end of the room, Mrs. Artesia Gibbons pulled her silk handkerchief out of her glove, dabbed at the corners of her mouth, and said softly, "Poor dear."

Elise stared at her, and then suddenly the fear left her and her face went slack and she got a dreamy look in her eyes. "To hell with it," she said softly, and there was a stunned silence and then a whoosh of air being sucked into scented bosoms. *She's going away from us now,* Bright thought. It took a moment longer. Elise swayed a bit and then she looked slowly around the room, searching each face, and gave them a tiny soft smile. And finally she took a little breath and her eyes rolled back in her head and she fluttered like a leaf to the floor at Bright's feet. She lay there, small and crumpled in the lace dress, her face ghostly white, while everyone else in the room sat frozen, staring at her. Bright looked at her mother for a moment and felt immensely relieved. Then she thought, *I'd best do something.* So she screamed as loud as she could and all the ladies of the Study Club jumped up at once and rushed to where Elise lay, crowding in around her, all talking excitedly at the same time, their words a tittering babble in Bright's ears. Bright was caught in the middle, hemmed in by a rustling, chattering nightmare of cloth and perfume and clutching hands. *Get away!* she tried to cry out, but her own voice froze. She felt a hand on her arm, pulling her roughly away from her mother. Her head swam dizzily. And then the pimento cheese in her stomach said, *I'm coming up.* And it did.

< >

She was sitting on the front steps of the Hardwicke house, wearing one of Xuripha's dresses, when Dorsey Bascombe steered the buggy to the curb, leapt out, and hurried up the front walk, taking long strides in his tall leather boots. There was a dark sweat stain on the front of his khaki shirt. He had been out in the woods when they called for him an hour ago. It was almost noontime now. The whistle at the lumberyard would blow any minute, Bright expected, and then they could go home.

He stopped, bent over Bright, put his hand gently on her head. "Honey, are you all right?"

"Yes, Papa. And Mama's all right too. She's lying down. All the ladies have left. Except Miz Hardwicke. I threw up."

"That's all right." He stood again. "I'll go get Mama, all right? You just wait here. I won't be a minute. Then we'll go home."

"All right, Papa."

< 103 >

Dorsey went inside and Bright sat quietly, waiting for them, feeling empty and drained. She was thirsty and hungry and her eyes felt scratchy out here in the bright sunshine, but she hadn't wanted to complain. Mrs. Hardwicke had been a little hysterical for a while, and she had just now calmed down. Bright wanted to go home and have something small and light for dinner and perhaps take a little nap and then sit quietly in Hosanna's kitchen while things got sorted out. Hosanna could help sort things out, she was sure of that. Bright could see her now, splashing at the sink, muttering "That young'un . . ."

Bright heard the screen door open behind her and she stood, smoothing the front of Xuripha's dress, as they emerged from the house, Dorsey's arm firmly around Elise's waist, followed by Fostoria. Elise looked pale and she wobbled a bit, but she didn't have the wild, frightened look in her eyes anymore. Dorsey was tall and broad-shouldered beside her, and she looked tiny in the protective crook of his arm.

"I'm so sorry," Fostoria was saying. "We're all so sorry. Perhaps after Elise has had a little more time . . ."

"No," Dorsey said firmly. Bright could see how the muscles along his jaw bulged under the skin, how the tiny crow's-feet around his eyes seemed deeper.

"Oh, I'm sure . . . ," Fostoria started to say.

He stopped, turned a little toward her. "Fostoria, I appreciate everything. You've been more than kind. But no more."

"Well," she said, giving a little shrug. "Well, then . . ."

"I'll get the dress back to you this afternoon."

"Yes. Well, there's no hurry."

They left Fostoria standing on the porch and Bright followed her parents to the buggy. Dorsey helped Elise up, then took Bright around to the other side and lifted her to the seat and climbed in himself.

As they pulled away, Bright leaned out and gave Fostoria a little wave. Fostoria must not have seen it, she thought. She stood there at the edge of the porch with her arms crossed, staring at them, and then she turned and disappeared inside the house.

Bright sat back in the seat between her parents and looked up at them, first one and then the other, their heads framed by the bright noonday outside the canopied shade of the buggy. And it was then that she realized how angry her father was—angry and disappointed. It was as clear on his face as if it had been painted there in big black words. And just as quickly, she realized why he was angry and disappointed, because that was etched just as clearly in the look of resigned failure on her mother's face. She sensed the very great gulf between the two

< 104 >

of them, here where Bright sat on the buggy seat, a big and lonely space that smelled of leather and her father's sweat and her mother's perfume.

Bright sat there, feeling wretched and frightened, as the horse clip-clopped along the clay of the street toward their house and the noon whistle from the lumberyard screeched high above the town, splitting the day into halves and calling a brief respite from labor. Finally, she could stand it no more. She reached over and touched her father's hand, the one that held the reins. "Can I sit in your lap, Papa?" she asked.

He looked down at her and she thought for an instant that she saw something very close to tears in his eyes. "Yes," he said softly, then put his arm around her and helped her into his lap. She put her hands on the reins and he put his big hands around hers and the horse took them home. Bright did not look over at her mother again. She was afraid of what she might see.

< 105 >

7

The spring of 1919 came with a rush that left her a bit breathless. It had been a hard, bone-aching winter with ice rimming the puddles on the sidewalks and the stark limbs of trees seeming almost to cry out with loneliness against bare gray sky. Then suddenly Bright stepped into a warm morning's sunshine, stretching and blinking in the brightness, seeing that the world outside had changed in small ways that had escaped her notice—a bush beside the front steps grown slightly taller, a corner of the stable roof in the backyard sagging a bit from decay because Dorsey now had a motorcar and no use for a horse at home, a new nest of pigeons in a high eave on the side of the house next to the chimney. It made Bright wonder if more than a single winter had come and gone, and if so, where she had been. And, she wondered if the changes had been more within herself than in the world outside her door that seemed to blossom so forcefully to life.

But if Bright Bascombe took notice of spring, it seemed that her parents did not. They were still in the thrall of winter—a lingering sense of things dormant, of expectations unfulfilled, of marking time and waiting for something to reveal itself. She had begun to take note of them, as children of eight will do, as people unto themselves, not just as parents whose sphere was circumscribed by their relationship to her own small world. As her vision expanded, people and things shifted and took on broader meaning. As for Dorsey and Elise, they became husband and wife in Bright's mind, not just mother and father. And as her sense of their otherness grew, she realized the distance between them and their ineffectual attempts to reach across it and the pervading sense of disappointment on both their parts for having failed. They were good parents. They loved her, took care of her, lavished her with attention—especially Dorsey. But she was struck by the

< 106 >

strange notion that their very acts of parenting were somehow an attempt to reconcile what they were not able to touch in each other, that she was in some ways a conduit through which they tried to connect.

The household had been busier than ever. Dorsey's business grew and prospered in the years of the Great War. He was away from the house for days at a time to places like Memphis and New Orleans, Atlanta and Louisville, where there was a great appetite for the pine and hardwood timbers that his crews harvested from the woods and shipped by the boxcarload from the lumberyard beside the river.

And Elise Bascombe had quite surprised everyone. Far from letting the disaster of the Study Club three years before make her a recluse, she had sallied forth with a fairly determined set to her jaw. She was a regular attendee at Methodist services, shopped frequently in the small business district, and even took in a few piano students in the room off the parlor. She traveled several times to visit her parents in New Orleans and once accompanied Mayor Dorsey Bascombe on an overnight journey to the state capital, where they attended a meeting of the League of Municipalities.

But Bright sensed that all of their activity masked the deeper thing that was amiss. She suspected that whatever grew from her parents' joint cultivation was shallow-rooted, like a mushroom, easily plucked from the earth and a bit withered in appearance. It was not something she could ask Hosanna about, because it was not something she could put into words.

There was, however, plenty she *could* ask about, a great deal to think about. And at least in some respects, as children of eight will do, she began to leave her parents and the mystery of their lives behind and embark upon her own.

Bright started to school and found to her surprise that there was, indeed, a great deal to learn about things, each new bit of information spawning its own questions. She brought them to Elise, to Dorsey, to Hosanna, who answered them as best they could with a combination of fact, supposition, and folk wisdom.

Frequently, Hosanna was the first convenient object of Bright's curiosity as she dashed in breathless and ravenous from school for a midafternoon snack in the warm, rich-smelling kitchen. "Lord, young'un, yo' brain like bread risin'," Hosanna would say. "What they feed you down yonder at the schoolhouse? Yeast?" If pressed beyond the limits of her knowledge and common sense, she would simply roll her eyes and retreat to her favorite nostrum: "Life's a mystery." A bit earlier, it might have been enough. Now it was not. There was

< 107 >

nothing, Bright decided, so mysterious that it was unfathomable if you asked enough questions and thought long and hard enough about it.

And then there was music. There were echoes of it everywhere in the house. There were still occasional evening concerts in the music room with Bright, no longer small enough to sit on her father's lap, squeezing into the big chair beside him while Elise played, always from her familiar repertoire. She seemed uninterested in learning anything new. At the end, she would invite Dorsey to play with her and he would take the golden trombone from its case and tune it and stand beside her, making a mellow counterpoint to her piano. But their playing, like everything they did together, was tentative. *They are too gentle*, Bright thought. *They tiptoe.* Still, the music lingered long after the trombone was put away and the cover closed over the piano keyboard. She heard it in the deep recesses of her mind—the familiar songs her parents played and things new and unknown. Sometimes the music awakened her at night, so real and immediate she would think that Dorsey and Elise were playing, and she would slip quietly downstairs to find the music room dark and quiet. It made her a bit uneasy at first, all this music announcing itself suddenly inside her brain, full-blown melodies that might begin with a phrase from one of her mother's pieces and then take strange and unexpected turns. The music drifted through her mind like smoke, curling and twisting as the currents caught it. She learned to be still and listen, fascinated with its possibilities.

It sometimes got her in trouble. At school, she would occasionally find her teacher standing over her, glowering. "Bright Bascombe! What's wrong with you? Don't you hear me speaking to you?"

She would blush, with the titter of the other children's laughter bubbling up around her. "No ma'am."

"Where on earth do you go when you drift off like that?"

"Nowhere," she would answer. That was not true; it was simply not worth explaining. She suspected that other people did not hear music in their minds quite the way she did, and that they probably would think her daft if she told them what went on in her own. She also realized that other people thought her a somewhat odd child, a trifle distracted and distant, and that it would be useless to try to make them understand that the music she heard was ever so much more interesting than almost anything they had to say, certainly more interesting than her friend Xuripha Hardwicke's ceaseless babble.

Finally, she presented herself beside the piano one afternoon as her mother was playing, waited until the piece was finished, and then said, "I want to learn."

< 108 >

Her mother put her hands in her lap and turned to look at Bright. "You do?"

"Yes," Bright said. "I hear music up here all the time." She tapped her head. "It needs to get out."

"Well," said Elise, "I'll call Mrs. Bobbitt." Mrs. Bobbitt also taught piano students in her home a block away and had a small recital each spring in the basement of the Baptist Church. It was said that Mrs. Bobbitt did not take kindly to Elise Bascombe, who after all did not need the income, dipping into the limited local supply of young piano students. Perhaps Elise wanted to placate Mrs. Bobbitt by sending Bright to her for instruction. But Bright knew from Xuripha, who took lessons from Mrs. Bobbitt, that she had a habit of rapping her students on the head with her knuckles when they made a mistake. And that did not sound much like a pleasant way to learn piano. She probably did not like children who asked a lot of questions, either.

Bright shook her head. "No, I want you to teach me."

Elise pursed her lips, considering it. "You might find you positively don't like it, having your piano teacher in the house all the time, reminding you to practice. Goodness knows, I wouldn't have liked it when I was learning. Grandma Poncie plays, but she always sent me to someone else for lessons."

"But you're not Grandma Poncie," Bright said stubbornly, "and I'm not you. Besides, I wouldn't want to take piano lessons from Grandma Poncie, even if I *were* you."

"Why not?"

"Because Grandma Poncie doesn't have much patience."

Elise allowed herself a tiny smile, just a tug at the corners of her mouth. "Well, Grandma Poncie is very sweet."

"Yes ma'am. Will you teach me to play?"

Elise scrunched her face up earnestly. "My goodness. Well . . ."

Bright didn't give her mother another moment to think about it. She climbed up on the piano bench next to Elise, who slid to the right to give her room at the middle.

"You must promise me this," Elise said. "You'll tell me if you get tired of it, or tired of having me for a teacher. We shouldn't have any, ah, conflict over the piano."

Bright couldn't imagine having much of a conflict with her mother over the piano or anything else. Elise avoided conflict of any kind, and Hosanna, as much as anyone in the house, took on much of the burden of keeping Bright reined in. "Yes ma'am. I promise."

"All right, then." Elise took a deep breath. "Let's see. All good students of the piano start at the beginning, and that's middle C."

< 109 >

Bright didn't think that made a good deal of sense, beginning in the middle. But for once, she didn't ask any questions. She placed her right thumb where her mother showed her and gave middle C a good, strong strike. And she could feel it vibrate as if the string were somewhere deep inside her own body instead of in the piano. It was certainly not the first time her fingers had touched the piano keys. But it was the first time when there was purpose and direction to it, when it meant something more than just random sound. If you could play middle C, and *know* you were playing middle C, then that must inevitably lead to all the other, to that vast swirl of music loose inside her head. *Yes. This is it.*

That evening, as they sat at the supper table, Bright announced to Dorsey, "Mama's teaching me to play the piano."

"Oh?" he said, raising his eyebrows and glancing over at Elise, who was still finishing her meal, taking dainty bites of fresh sliced tomato. "When did this start?"

"Today," Bright said. "We started today with middle C."

Dorsey wiped his mouth, folded his napkin and tucked it under the edge of his plate. He stared at the plate for a moment, considering something, then cleared his throat and folded his hands in front of him. "Well. I think that's just fine." He paused, then looked at Elise. "In fact, I think you ought to just concentrate on Bright."

She jerked her head up quickly, stared at him. "You mean . . ."

"These other children"—he waved his hand in the general direction of the parlor. "I can't imagine why you bother, Elise. Send them to Mrs. Bobbitt. Lord knows, you don't need the money. I'm sure she does."

"It's not that," she said in a small but even voice. "I enjoy it. It gives me something to do."

"To do? Goodness, you've got a house to manage, a child to raise, a husband to put up with. And I would think there are a thousand other things you could do to occupy your time. It's not New Orleans, but there *are* things going on here." Bright could tell he was trying to keep his voice light, but she could hear the edge in it, something that no doubt echoed from other times and places and encounters, from the mysterious and secret part of her parents' relationship.

Elise put her fork down on the plate and placed her hands in her lap and then Bright saw something wholly unexpected—an almost imperceptible tightening of her mother's mouth. She stared, amazed, and then she thought, *She is going to say no.* Silence covered the table like the still, glassy surface of a pond and Bright held her breath, waiting to see what curious thing would shatter the calm. *She is going to defy him.*

< 110 >

But then Dorsey reached across the expanse of New Orleans linen, reached into Elise's lap, took her right hand in his left and lifted it to the table. Their two hands rested there, his big and sun-reddened with the hairs along the back of it a forest of gold strands in the light from the chandelier, hers very small and smooth and pale, the two hands in strange union against the white of the tablecloth.

"Didn't I promise I would always take care of you?" he said quietly. "And haven't I always?"

Elise closed her eyes very slowly and her jaw went slack and she nodded. "Yes."

Bright sat frozen in her chair, transfixed by the sheer, raw, quiet exercise of power, of maleness. And she felt something twist inside her, something at once fascinating and frightful. Suddenly she felt, as she had felt on Fostoria Hardwicke's doorstep three years before, her mother's ally.

"I'll go to Mrs. Bobbitt," she said, almost feeling the painful rap of knuckles against her skull.

Dorsey looked at her, blinked, as if he had forgotten that she sat there, seeing everything, listening to everything, feeling everything. He studied her for a moment, then released Elise's hand, which slid back into her lap, defeated. Dorsey sat back in his chair. "No," he said. "I won't have it."

And Bright, like her mother, did not argue.

<   >

By the early spring of 1919, the boys were coming back from the Great War in Europe, and some of them were bringing their flying machines. Suddenly, the air above America was full of them, bi-winged one- and two-seaters with fabric stretched over their fragile wooden frames and the whole business held together precariously with wires. Sometimes, the pilots flew while other foolish young men walked on the wings of their planes, and others dipsied and doodled acrobatically above gawking crowds at county fairs. Quite often they crashed, and there was an element of morbid curiosity about the whole affair.

The Air Age came to Bright Birdsong on a brisk, dappled day in late March as she stood in the backyard, handing wet items of clothing to Hosanna, who draped them over the clothesline and fastened them down with wooden clothespins she took from a pocket of her white apron. Camisoles and undershirts flapped wetly in the chill wind and Bright stuffed her raw hands into the pockets of her coat until Hosanna was ready for the next garment. Hosanna seemed not to mind the cold. She was clad only in a light cotton dress that moved easily around her lumps and bulges. She had a bright green scarf tied about her head,

< 111 >

knotted at the back. Hosanna's boy Flavo stood solemnly at his mother's elbow, watching them. His great round eyes followed their movements, a small black Buddha swallowed by a tattered jacket several sizes too large for him. Flavo was a quiet presence in the kitchen these days, a small dark ghost who communicated largely by nods and shakes of his head and seemed to be pretty much at peace with things. He was four. Bright took scant notice of him most of the time. He didn't interfere with her running discourse with Hosanna, didn't intrude on the life of the house. He was simply there.

They heard the buzzing sound overhead and they all looked up at once, Hosanna's hands poised over the thin wire of the clothesline. Bright saw it then, a tiny moth among the scudding white puffs of cloud, spiraling down toward them in big, lazy circles. They stood mesmerized as the plane seemed to stop in midair, then tumble sideways in a wingover with a sparkle of sunlight dancing off the spinning propeller at its nose. "Lord A'mighty," Hosanna said softly. "God done give the bullfrog wings."

"It's an aeroplane!" Bright cried.

Hosanna snapped a clothespin over the top of a sock and put her hands on her hips. "Course it's an aeroplane. You think I don't know an aeroplane when I see one?"

The plane righted itself now, and it was low enough that Bright could see it clearly—gaily painted with a stubby red and blue fuselage and white wings, a man sitting inside. The wings waggled from side to side as the plane made a wide circle of the town, disappearing momentarily behind a tree and then reappearing, held aloft by magic. Then it turned and headed straight for them, veering off just as it passed with a roar, and the pilot turned the plane a bit and leaned over the side and waved to them. "G'wan! Git outta here!" Hosanna shook her fist and bellowed, her voice lost in the noise. Bright stood frozen, mouth open. And then as the plane disappeared over the trees, just about the place where Abner Carlisle's pasture began a half mile or so away, Bright took off running, leaving Hosanna and Flavo at the clothesline. She could hear Hosanna's voice at her heels, but she never even looked back.

Bright was the first one there, except for the small herd of Abner Carlisle's frightened milk cows that lumbered toward the near end of the pasture, bumping into each other and mooing loudly, teats swinging, like a committee of old women rousted from a Women's Missionary Union meeting. Bright paid them no mind. Her eyes were on the aeroplane down at the far end, bumping slowly along the ground, turning now in her direction, the backwash from its propeller churning up a

< 112 >

whirlwind of dead grass. As she got closer, the engine died and the propeller gave a few more turns and then stopped with a shudder. She could see some writing on the side, and as she reached the plane she read RIDES $2.

She stopped just beyond the edge of the wingtip, unsure of how close she should go, and stared at the pilot, who sat up in the front seat, fiddling with something in front of him. When he pulled off his leather helmet and goggles and grinned at her, she could see that he was not much more than a boy, with a thick mat of tousled brown hair and big white rings around his eyes where the goggles had been.

"Hi," he called down from the cockpit.

"Hi yourself," Bright called back.

"Wanna go for a ride?"

She looked the plane over carefully, front to rear and back again. It looked pretty sturdy, sitting here on the ground, not the fragile swooping bird she had seen up there among the clouds a few minutes before. "Yes sir," she answered.

"Got two bucks?"

"No sir. But my papa does."

"Where's your papa?"

"I imagine he'll be here pretty soon. He's the mayor."

The pilot stood up and eased one leg over the side of the plane, then the other. He dropped to the ground, bouncing easily on the balls of his feet. He had on a leather jacket and khaki puttees and tall brown boots, much like Dorsey Bascombe wore. "Well, the mayor gets a free ride. For you, it's two bucks."

"Mr. Abner Carlisle is going to be mad as a wet hen at you for scarin' his cows. He won't let any young'uns close to this place. He must not be at home, or he'd be out here with his shotgun."

The pilot grinned and ran his hand through his mop of hair. "I been shot at by the Huns. Ain't no cow farmer gonna scare me. Anyhow, I had to set 'er down someplace. What you folks need is an aerodrome."

"A what?"

"Place to land aeroplanes. And fix 'em."

"We don't have any aeroplanes around here. This is the first aeroplane I've ever seen outside of a picture in the newspaper."

"Oh," he said, "you'll see lots more before long. We'll have aerodromes all over the country. Even in little piddly towns."

Bright put her hands on her hips. "This isn't a little piddly town."

The pilot laughed. "You wait 'til you see 'er from the air. I've flown over New York City and Chicago, Illinois, little lady, and I'm telling

< 113 >

you, alongside the great metropolitan areas of the country, this is a piddly town."

Bright heard a noise behind her and she turned to see a crowd of people climbing the fence, heading across the pasture toward them, dodging the cow pies, pointing and chattering as they ran. Hosanna's white apron and bright green scarf were a splash of color in the crowd and she was pulling little Flavo along with her, his feet barely skimming the ground.

"Looks like a welcoming committee," the pilot said. "And there ain't a shotgun in the crowd."

Hosanna grabbed Bright by the arm as the crowd boiled up around the plane. "What you mean, runnin' off from me, child? You come on away from here."

"I'm going for a ride," Bright said, digging in her heels. "As soon as Papa gets here with two bucks."

"In *that?*" Hosanna pointed at the aeroplane.

"Of course."

"Well, I'll tell you what, when Mr. Dorsey Bascombe gets here, there ain't gonna be no riding in *that* thing. He's gonna shoo it off from here."

But he didn't, as Bright thought he probably wouldn't. Dorsey Bascombe was a farsighted man, and when he strode up a few minutes later, she could see the twinkle in his eye. He had come home from a business trip to Nashville a few years before talking about the aeroplane he had seen at an exposition, and he had read to her from the paper one evening a year ago about how aeroplanes had started carrying the mail from Washington, D.C., to New York. Dorsey thought aeroplanes were here to stay, he said then, the way trucks were here to stay in the logging business. He said that people might one day as easily go places on aeroplanes as they did on trains.

Bright squirmed out of Hosanna's grasp and ran to meet her father. He was wearing a black band around the sleeve of his coat, still mourning the death of Theodore Roosevelt two months before. Dorsey Bascombe considered Theodore Roosevelt a consummate American— the kind of man, Bright thought, who would jump at the chance to take a ride in an aeroplane. "You get to ride free," she called. "It's two bucks for me."

He laughed as he took her small hand in his big one. "Whoa, wait a minute, sugar. Let's see what this is all about." Bright thought she probably wouldn't say anything about the pilot calling their town piddly.

"Here comes the mayor," somebody called, and the crowd parted

< 114 >

to let them through, Dorsey and Bright with Hosanna and Flavo right behind them.

"Dorsey Bascombe," he said, shaking hands with the pilot.

"Ollie Doubleday," the young man said. "From Oklahoma."

"Long way from home, aren't you, son?"

"This here is home," Ollie Doubleday said, patting the side of the plane. "She's a Curtiss Jenny and she'll fly a hundred and fifty miles an hour, and I can be anywhere I want to go in a heartbeat. That's the marvel of flying, sir. A guy from Oklahoma can go anywhere he takes a notion. I been to France, I been to New York City. Not a lot of folks from Oklahoma been either place. You're the mayor?"

"Some of the time," Dorsey said.

Ollie Doubleday indicated his plane with a twist of his head. "You ever been up?"

"No, I can't say as I have."

"You goin' up in that thing, Dorsey?" a man called from back in the crowd.

Dorsey turned to the man. "Think I ought to?"

"You prob'ly got too much sense to go up in an aeroplane," the man said, "but you also prob'ly the only man here with two bucks in his pocket." The crowd laughed at that.

"Hmmmph," Hosanna grumbled at Dorsey's elbow. "Ain't every man that's got two dollars also got a lick of sense." And that got another laugh.

"Well," Ollie Doubleday said, "it ain't even going to cost you that, Mayor Bascombe. Every place I land, the mayor gets a free ride. I figure if I can get the mayor up, it's good for business."

Bright studied Ollie's face. He had a big wide breezy smile, and though he was young, he had a lot of tiny wrinkles around his eyes, probably from being up there in the air so much, so close to the sun. She wondered what he saw up there. She had to see for herself. She tugged on her father's hand. "How about me?"

Dorsey gave her a long look. "You wouldn't be afraid?"

"Of course not."

"Shoot," Ollie said, "I've had lots of kids up in my plane. Long as they sit still and don't try to climb over the side while we're in the air, they're okay. You ain't predisposed to lose your cookies, are you, young lady?"

"Do what?"

"Throw up."

"No," Bright said, "as long as I don't eat pimento cheese."

"Can she sit in my lap?" Dorsey asked.

< 115 >

Ollie looked her up and down. "How much you weigh?"

"Twenty pounds," Bright said quickly, trying to make herself look small.

"Oh, I imagine you're a tad more than that," Ollie laughed, "but I reckon the two of you together won't be too much."

"Great God, Mr. Dorsey!" Hosanna exploded. "For sure, you and that child ain't gonna go tootin' off in THAT!" She flung a hand in the direction of the plane. "Y'all gone fall out the sky and then they gone have to bury me and Miz Elise from grief."

Bright could see the genuine fear in Hosanna's eyes. She really, truly did care about them. Bright threw her arms around Hosanna's neck and hugged her tightly. "We'll be all right," she said fiercely. "Don't you worry. My papa will take care of me."

"Hosanna, why don't you go on back to the house," Dorsey said. "You'll catch your death of cold out here. But let's don't say anything to Miz Elise just yet. Let me tell her about it when we get back."

Hosanna thrust her chin out. "I'm stayin' right HERE," she said, planting herself defiantly. "You and that child fall outta that thing, I'm gonna be here to catch you."

Dorsey smiled and patted her on the shoulder. "All right. That's fine." And then Ollie helped them climb up the side of the plane into the rear seat, first Dorsey and then Bright. He strapped them in, adjusting the harness to go around both their bodies. He moved the crowd back a good distance and then went around to the front of the plane and hauled down hard on the propeller several times and jumped back as the engine finally caught and roared to life and the propeller spun in a silvery circle, like one of the big saws at Dorsey's sawmill. Ollie climbed into the front seat, fastened his harness, and pulled on the leather helmet and goggles. Then he turned around to Dorsey and Bright and gave them a thumbs-up and a big Oklahoma grin. They gave him a thumbs-up back and he gave the plane some gas and it eased forward. They all waved briefly to the crowd and everybody waved back except Hosanna, who stood with her arms crossed over her bosom, hugging herself, glaring at them. *Foolishness and nonsense. A bullfrog with wings.* Dorsey held tightly to Bright as the plane headed down the length of the pasture, bouncing roughly at first and then smoothing out as it picked up speed, easing gingerly off the ground and then lifting with a breathtaking swoop into the air as it roared over the scattering knot of cows down at the other end. There would be sour milk in Abner Carlisle's pail tonight, Bright thought.

The flight must have lasted no more than fifteen minutes, but it seemed like hours up there circling the town, time suspended. It was

< 116 >

terribly cold and the wind stung her face and sent shivers down inside her coat, but Dorsey's strong arms around her made Bright feel safe and secure. The awesome roar of the engine made conversation impossible, so they flew in silence, leaning first over one side and then the other as the plane banked and dipped, Dorsey pointing out one landmark after another.

For the first time, she got a sense of the town as a whole, the way it fit together down below them, everything in plain view with tree limbs still bare from winter—the broad main street that ran for several blocks through the heart of the town, opening up onto the courthouse square, with tiny people on the sidewalks gawking up at them and waving; the squat red brick schoolhouse where she would be an object of powerful curiosity and envy on Monday; their house nestled on its patch of brown grass like a white laying hen, the pecan trees out back under which toadstools would soon be growing as the ground warmed and gave birth. And at the edge of the town, next to the river, the sprawling expanse of Dorsey Bascombe's lumberyard with its toothpick stacks of drying boards making neat rows next to the railhead, the scattering of tin-roofed sheds that covered the big saws, the growing mound of sawdust a tan tepee at the end of the long chute that carried the sawdust from the mill, and a truck creeping onto the grounds with a load of lumber like an insect dragging a captured foe. The river ran brown and smooth in a great bend at the perimeter of the town, intersected by the single bridge at the end of Claxton Street and the railroad trestle near the lumberyard. From up here she could see how the low hills beyond the town on either side formed the valley through which the river flowed. And on every side, as far as you could see, the green-gray of the forest, pine and hardwood, encircling it all, nestling the town in its bosom. *So that's what it is,* she thought. *My town.* She thought then that Ollie Doubleday, up there in the front seat, was surely wrong. This was no piddly place, her town. It grew up out of the land like a garden, neatly tended rows of living things nourished by the rich brown soil and the river. You could see it all from up here, every street and building and tree, all of a piece. It was small enough to make sense, with a beginning and an end and the rest of the world out there beyond if you cared to venture into it. But she could not imagine that would ever be necessary. This down below her seemed quite enough for anybody to ever want. It fit, like a good, well-worn shoe, and it was anything but piddly.

And then she heard the music—the wind playing harplike through the thin wires that held the two wings of the plane together, the deep steady bass of the engine, the air rushing past her ears like a

< 117 >

thousand woodwinds in unison. She hummed down deep inside herself, becoming part of the lovely, perfect symphony. Her mind stretched out beyond the fragile singing aeroplane into the thin air, up and up past the scudding clouds, and she heard then the tiny crystal notes of her mother's piano and the soft mellow tones of her father's trombone. *This is where it all comes from*, she thought, *up here where God lives*. She twisted in her father's lap and looked up into his face. He looked enraptured, mesmerized by the spectacle that sprawled below them, the lines of his face deeper but softer. He smiled and nodded. *He feels it too*, she thought—the sense of the place, the powerful allure of the land and all that springs from it, the thing that takes him to the woods each morning in his tall leather boots. They were cut from the same bolt of cloth, Dorsey Bascombe and his eight-year-old daughter, up here in this frail craft held aloft by faith. She leaned back against him and he gave her a squeeze and she closed her eyes, feeling her face go numb from the cold, smelling the rich smell of canvas and wood and engine exhaust, listening to the music, hearing after a moment the slight change in pitch in the plane's engine as Ollie began to bring it gently down to earth again.

They bumped down softly onto the pasture and rolled to a stop near the crowd, which had grown much larger now. Bright spotted friends—Xuripha Hardwicke for one, Harley Gibbons for another, and just in front of Harley, little Buster Putnam with one overall strap undone and hanging down about his waist. She waved to them and they gawked back at her, stunned by her incredible great fortune. Ollie left the engine running and stood up in his seat, reaching back to undo the harness, lifting Bright out of the rear seat and handing her to a man waiting below on the ground.

Then a strange thing happened. Flavo Richardson—small, silent Flavo—slipped free from Hosanna's grip and dashed up to the plane. "How 'bout me?" he yelled up at them. "How 'bout me?"

They all stared at Flavo, and a gale of laughter swept through the crowd. Dorsey looked down at Flavo, and he laughed too, a great booming laugh. Flavo did not. He stood planted there beside the plane as if he had sprung up through the sod, a solemn black sprout announcing spring. And it was then that Bright truly took notice of Flavo for the first time, saw how resolutely he occupied his own small piece of earth with a miniature dignity. Flavo looked at Bright Bascombe and their eyes met and he saw that she did not laugh, either. There was a brief exchange of some kind—she could not have said what it meant or even in which language it was transmitted. And then Hosanna was there, grabbing Flavo by the arm, pulling him back. "Law, child, you

< 118 >

come away from here. Stay outen the white folks' bidness!" And Bright watched their backs as Hosanna led Flavo away, through the parting crowd, through their laughter. Flavo did not look back.

For them all, the day became something of a benchmark, the day when the future arrived in their small town. For Bright, there was something quite beyond the day and the event, something she realized as she sat in the parlor late in the afternoon, describing the adventure in breathless tones to her astonished mother. Elise listened earnestly, hands in lap and brow furrowed in concentration. But Bright realized that she could not understand, not really, what it was like to break free, to soar in a tiny fragile craft just below the place where God lived, to hear music such as Bright had heard. Bright had gone where her mother would never think of going, held in her father's strong arms. In a way she only vaguely understood, she sensed that she was beginning the long journey out of childhood and leaving her mother behind.

< >

The road from town followed the river for several miles after it crossed the bridge at the foot of Claxton Street, and then curved away to the northeast. Her father told her that if you stayed on the road long enough, it would take you to Columbus, thirty-five miles away, a town so big that it had a full-time policeman instead of a constable, and a drugstore with a soda fountain where you could sit at a small round table under a paddle fan in the summer months and eat real ice cream in a crystal dish, served up by a young man in a white apron. Dorsey said that someday, their own town would have a policeman and a soda fountain. Dorsey would see to that, as he saw to a great deal. When Dorsey Bascombe spoke of things like policemen and soda fountains, paved streets and manufacturing plants, you believed him, because Dorsey was a man who, by the force of his character, made things happen. That was the main reason people had been glad to see him elected mayor.

For now, though, there was Columbus—something to aspire to. It was the county seat of the next county, and thus had a courthouse like their own where Dorsey went periodically to record transactions as he bought land and timber rights for his expanding business. It took all day to get to Columbus and back, and if you wanted to go on beyond Columbus to the state capital, it meant an overnight journey. That was beyond comprehension, Bright thought, sleeping in someone else's bed. Dorsey had promised to take Bright to Columbus on her thirteenth birthday, because she would be a grown-up young lady then.

Now, on the last Saturday in March, Bright had no idea where

< 119 >

they were going as they headed across the bridge in the early morning in Dorsey's automobile, chugging along the hard-packed clay road toward what Dorsey had told her was a surprise. For now, she thought, a surprise was better than a trip to Columbus, which would be no surprise at all because she already knew all about Columbus.

The early morning air was chill and damp and Bright was bundled in a blanket in the seat next to her father, her teeth chattering from the cold and from the bouncing of the car as it jarred along the ruts and potholes, made worse by the winter just past. She could see the occasional glint of early sun off the river through the bare trees to their left. The trees were beginning to show the faintest hint of green, and if you looked closely, you could see the buds beginning to break through. In another week or so, they would blush with growth as April yawned and waked itself in the glow of new warmth.

They had left the isinglass side curtains of the motorcar rolled up on their metal rods. They were practically useless. They did little to keep out the drafts and only served to trap the noxious smell of engine fumes in the passenger compartment. Besides, this way they could see the world better. This way, Bright thought, perhaps she could spot the surprise before they were upon it.

A mile or so out of town, the radiator boiled over and steam spurted from under the hood with a hiss. Dorsey brought the car to a bouncing stop at the edge of the road.

"Old horse is lame again!" Bright cried.

"Reckon we ought to shoot him?" Dorsey pulled an imaginary pistol from the broad belt of his coat.

"No, let's fix him up and see if he'll get us on down the road."

They climbed out of the car and Dorsey raised the hood and they surveyed the smoking radiator. "The fellow that laid out this road alongside the river must have had a vision about radiators," Dorsey said. He got a bucket out of the compartment in the back of the car and while Bright waited, he struggled through the underbrush to the river and got a bucketful of water.

"Don't you want to stay in the car?" he asked as he climbed back up the bank.

"It's warmer out here," Bright said. She looked up at the clear sky, the early sun climbing above the trees to their right.

They sat on the running board, waiting for the radiator to cool down before they poured the water in, and Dorsey put his arm around Bright and drew her close to keep her warm. She nestled in the crook of his arm, cheek against the rough fabric of his coat, feeling like a small animal burrowing into warm earth.

< 120 >

"One of these days, somebody will invent a radiator that doesn't boil over," Dorsey said.

"Maybe somebody will invent a road with no ruts," Bright said, massaging her jaw.

"Oh, they've got those already. It's called macadam. Black stuff. Hard as a rock. It makes a nice, smooth surface and no ruts."

"Do they have macadam in Columbus?" Bright asked.

"No, not yet, but they will have before long. Lots of streets in places like Nashville and Atlanta and New Orleans have macadam already. One of these days, you'll see macadam everywhere. And then folks will get soft and lazy because they won't get any exercise fixing cars that fall apart from bouncing over ruts and potholes."

"Will this road have macadam on it?" She tried to imagine a ribbon of black stuff all the way to Columbus.

"Of course."

"How do you know?"

"Because I can see the future," Dorsey said simply.

She looked up at him curiously. "How do you do that?"

"Nothing hard about it. You just think about the way you'd like things to be, and then you start working to make them that way, and that's the future. One day, every street in this town"—he waved in the general direction of town—"will be paved with macadam. I'll see to that."

"Because you're the mayor," she said.

"Not just because I'm the mayor. Because I can see the future. What I have to do as mayor is help other people see the future, so they'll help me work toward it. That's what progress is all about. Getting other folks to see the future the way you do." He leaned back against the side of the car, ruminating. "Back some time ago, I went to the bank and told Pegram Gibbons I wanted to borrow some money to buy a truck. Pegram said, 'What for?' And I said, 'To haul lumber out of the woods.' And Pegram said, 'What's wrong with mules?' I could see I wasn't making much progress with Pegram, so I painted him a word picture of what it would be like using trucks instead of mules to haul logs, how much faster and more efficient it would be and how much more money I could make. I kept talking until I got Pegram to see the future with me, and then he lent me the money. That's what you have to do."

Dorsey released her from the curve of his arm, got up and walked around to the front of the car and studied the radiator for a moment.

"Are you the only one who sees the future?" Bright asked.

He looked around the edge of the car and smiled at her. "Lord,

< 121 >

no. Anybody can see the future if they learn how to look for it. It's just a way of thinking about things." He glanced over toward the river. "Take the fellow who thought about damming up the river downstream a few years ago so we could have electricity. There wasn't a soul in these parts with an electric light bulb. Lots of 'em were probably like Pegram Gibbons. Probably said, 'What's wrong with oil lamps?' But this fellow could see the day when lots of people would have electricity. So he convinced other folks to build the dam."

Bright got up and walked around to the front of the car and stood next to him. "You see the future like I hear music," she said.

"Do what?"

She tapped her head. "Up here. I hear music all the time. Some of it is Mama's music, and yours. But some of it I never heard before."

Dorsey nodded. "It's the same thing. Music that nobody has written down yet. That's the future. Once you write it down, that's history."

"I heard music up there in the aeroplane last Saturday," she said.

"And I saw the future." Dorsey swept his arm in a big circle. "All this land around here, I saw it the way it will be, with houses and stores and schools and churches on it, and all the streets paved with macadam, and boats on the river taking lumber downstream all the way to the Gulf. A big, wide river with dams all along it making electricity and locks to let the boats through. That's what I see up here." Dorsey tapped his own head. "In my mind's eye."

"You have a mind's eye, and I have a mind's ear," Bright said.

Dorsey laughed. "I suppose that's so. What you want to do is to make the best of the place you are and work with what you've got." Bright thought instantly of her mother, still asleep now in the upstairs bedroom, oblivious to the green, sparkling morning. Elise, who seemed unable to make a place for herself in the here and now. Elise never seemed livelier than when she had just returned from a visit with her parents in New Orleans, talking animatedly about the social affairs she had attended, especially during the Mardi Gras season—the glittering balls with ladies in sequined gowns, men dressed as buccaneers, everyone masked in mystery, everything very gay. Bright could not go along, of course, because she was in school. But Elise would return with a box full of trinkets and favors, remembrances of all she had seen and done. And she would regale Bright with details of it for days, spinning it out, making it last as long as possible. Then slowly, the magic would fade and the dancing light would go out of her eyes to be replaced by a sort of opaqueness that separated her from this place, this time. *She doesn't belong here,* Bright thought to herself now.

< 122 >

Dorsey touched the lip of the radiator gingerly, loosened the cap and let the last pent-up steam whoosh out with a sigh, then picked up the bucket and poured the water in. The radiator filled and the water sloshed over the top and Dorsey waited for a moment before he put the cap back on. Then he took the bucket around to the rear of the motor-car and put it away, wiping his hands on an old diaper he kept in the rear compartment.

Bright followed him, stood watching as he stowed everything neatly. Then she asked her father, "Are you sorry Mama didn't have any more babies?"

He didn't look at her at first, and she wondered for a moment if he had heard her. Then he closed the lid of the rear compartment, snapped the latch, turned to her. She could see a flicker of something across his face, something a bit wistful. "Some things . . . ," he said after a moment, then paused again, searching for words. He shook his head, tossing away whatever he had been about to say, then smiled. "You're all the baby girl I ever wanted. A baby girl who hears music inside her head, for goodness' sake."

They laughed and climbed back into the car and headed on down the Columbus Road with the morning brightening, the sun chasing the shadows away from the roadway and warming the inside of the car. As they drove, Bright forgot about her mother and began to anticipate the surprise ahead. They were well into the country now. A rabbit darted across the road in front of them and skittered into the woods on the other side. A mile or so beyond, they clattered across a wooden bridge and scared up a covey of doves feeding in the grass next to the creek bed. Farther on, they passed a wide field dotted with the yellow stubble of last year's corn, and on the back side of the field, a black man following a mule-drawn plow, the harrow biting into the gray surface of the field and exposing rich brown earth ready for seed. They waved as they passed, and then just beyond the field, they turned off the main road and plunged into the woods along a narrow double-rutted trail with tall pine trees close on either side making a cave. Bright could hear the sound of the engine bouncing off the trees that grew shoulder to shoulder, their branches spreading over the roadway so that you saw only flecks of sunlight overhead. It was dark and cool underneath the canopy and Bright pulled the blanket around her again. Dorsey drove slowly and carefully, peering out through the windshield as he eased the automobile along. They were headed in the direction of the river now. Every so often, the cave would open into a small clearing, then narrow again. The trail got rougher as they went and the car bounced from side to side, tilting close to the trees as it

< 123 >

lurched along. "Old logging trail," Dorsey said over the noise of the bouncing car. "I logged this area fifteen or so years ago, before you were born, back when I was just starting out. We used mules and horses." A road like this might do for mules and horses, Bright thought, but it was not much for a motorcar. She held on to her seat with both hands and clamped her jaw tightly to keep her teeth from banging against each other.

Then suddenly they broke free of the woods into a wide sandy clearing with a huge, gnarled live oak tree off to one side and low scrub brush at the perimeter. Under the oak tree was a neat stack of lumber, higher than Bright's head, fresh-sawn and yellow. She eyed it curiously, but she didn't say anything. Dorsey stopped the car at the near end of the clearing and turned off the engine and they sat there for a long moment, neither of them speaking, letting the quiet take over. Then underneath the quiet she heard the faint gurgle of the river. She followed the sound, saw the gap in the trees, how the land dropped off just beyond the clearing.

She climbed out of the car and ran to the edge of the clearing and stood, looking down the sloping embankment, seeing the glint of the river through the brush, flowing swiftly, gorged by the winter rains. Down the bank she could see bits of litter, brush and twigs, caught in the branches of the bushes.

The water had risen here, as it had all along the river, a month before. She had stood then on the bank of the river next to her father's lumberyard and watched the angry red water as it tumbled over itself, swirling past the town. It had only flooded a few low-lying fields and pastures along the river bottom, painting the land with a thin coat of mud that would be plowed under as soon as the land dried out. But another ten feet, and it would have gotten out of its banks. It worried Bright, imagining the river sweeping through her town. She wondered why people would build a town here at all, daring nature. But Dorsey said you couldn't sit around waiting to see when a river would flood. It was rich land, eager to be plowed and built upon, and you had to get on with your life.

Dorsey stood next to her now at the edge of the clearing. "Is this the surprise?" she asked.

"Part of it," he said. He took in the clearing with a sweep of his arm. "The best part is that lovely little camp house there."

"Where?"

"Come back over here by the car and you can get a better view," he said, and she followed him. The clearing lay open before them, bare except for the stack of lumber. She stared at it for a moment, and then she understood.

< 124 >

"I think I like the porch the best," Bright said.

"Hmmmm. The porch. Yes, I think that's a nice touch. I'm glad we decided to add the porch, aren't you?"

She nodded and crossed her arms. "I think you should have a place to play when it's raining that's not inside and it's not outside."

"You have just described a porch, I think. And what about the door?" He cocked his head to the side a bit. "I think it looks nice right there in the middle. We could have put the door off to one side, but I think a door should go in the middle of a house, with windows on either side. At least, a front door should."

"It looks more symmetrical that way," Bright said.

"My, what a big word!"

"I learned it in school. When you fold a piece of paper in half and cut out something, like a doll or a Christmas tree or a tepee, then unfold it, you have a symmetrical."

Dorsey studied the clearing for a moment. "What do you think about having the chimney on the right side?"

Bright thought about it. "That's all right, because the big tree is on the left. And that makes it symmetrical. Sort of."

"Yes," Dorsey said, "I can see that."

They stood together a while longer, looking at the place where the camp house would be, Bright imagining what it would be like to spend the night there and wake up early in the morning and stand on the front porch facing the new sun, then go inside, where her father would be frying ham, the lovely aroma of it filling the house and drifting out the windows.

"I haven't been inside yet," Bright said. "Does it have beds?"

Dorsey considered the matter. "Yes, as a matter of fact, it does have beds. There are two big rooms on the inside, one for sleeping and the other for living. The one for living has a cookstove in it and a table and some chairs, and the one for sleeping has two beds."

"One for you and one for me," she said quickly.

"Well," he said, "for whoever comes to visit."

Bright looked around the clearing, at the big oak tree, at the woods close on both sides. It was quiet here except for the occasional call of a bird in the woods, the shrill sing of a cricket in the tall grass at the edge of the clearing, the murmur of the river beyond. You could hear all sorts of music in a place like this, she thought. It would make its own music, but you would have to be very still and quiet to hear all of it. It was a good place, and she already felt at home here, as if the camp house stood in reality just to the right of the big oak tree and smoke curled from the chimney, from her father's breakfast fire. A place you could belong to.

< 125 >

Bright reached and took her father's hand. "Will Mama come to the camp house?" she asked.

He thought about that for a moment, his face pensive. Then he said carefully, "I don't think we'll tell her about it just yet. We'll build it just like we see it, and it will be a pretty little camp house. Then we'll just put Mama in the car and bring her out here and surprise her." He paused, then nodded. "She'll like it. She likes pretty things."

< 126 >

8

As spring blossomed, they began to build the camp house. They worked at first only on Saturdays while school was still in session. Dorsey would get her up early and they would be away from the house by seven, carrying the lunch Hosanna had fixed the night before and left in a paper sack on the kitchen table—biscuits with thick slabs of ham, hard-boiled eggs wrapped in a piece of muslin, slices of pound cake, apples. By eight, they would be at work.

The second weekend they went to the clearing, there were more supplies next to the pile of lumber: a neat stack of bricks, several bags of cement covered by a canvas tarpaulin, a pile of yellow sand, a metal bucket, a long-handled shovel, and a shallow wooden box. Dorsey handed Bright the bucket. "You get the water," he said.

"Where from?"

"There's a whole river full of it down there," he said, pointing.

"Aren't you afraid I'll fall in?"

Dorsey gave her a long look. "Yes," he said, "I'm afraid you'll fall in."

"Then why are you letting me go to the river by myself?"

"Because I think you can do it," he said simply. "And it's more important for you to do it than it is for me to be afraid. If you get in trouble, holler." Then he turned and walked toward the car to get his tools, leaving her there with the bucket in her hands.

Bright carried the bucket down the sandy embankment to where a small shelf jutted out into the river. The brush was thick on either side but she could see that the river made a big sweeping curve here, nestling the clearing in the crook of its arm like a mother would a baby. It was shallow on this side, just a foot or so deep, but several feet out into the river she could see where it dropped off into greenish-brown and then the bottom disappeared. On the far side, the current had undercut the high bank and exposed tree roots that dipped down into

< 127 >

the water like the arms of an ancient, gnarled octopus. The water swirled under the roots, digging out a small dark cave, and she stared at it for a moment, wondering what river creatures lived there.

She stooped and held the bucket out into the water, letting the current fill it, then tried to stand and found that it was much too heavy to carry. So she poured the water out and tried again, letting it fill only partway before she lifted it from the river. It was still heavy, but she could carry it now. She struggled up the embankment with the bucket, feet digging deep into the sand and getting it down in her shoes. Almost to the top, she slipped and went down in the sand, and the bucket spilled, splashing her dress and leaving a dark wet spot on the sand. "Damnation," she said, using one of Hosanna's favorite words but saying it under her breath so that Dorsey would not hear. She sat there for a while, wondering if she really wanted to help build a camp house, then got up and brushed herself off and went back to the river. This time, she only got a little bit of water in the bottom and she toted it up the sandy bank without mishap. Dorsey was sitting on the stack of lumber, legs crossed, waiting for her. He had opened a bag of cement and had poured some of it, dry gray powder, into the shallow wooden box along with several shovelfuls of sand. "In there," he said. The inch or so of water in the bottom of the bucket scarcely wet the top of the mound of cement.

"Is that enough?" she asked.

"No." Dorsey shook his head. "I'd say another dozen trips or so should do it."

Bright set the bucket down beside the cement trough and put her hands on her hips. "Why do I have to do the hard part?"

Dorsey laughed, rubbing his nose. "Oh, there'll be plenty of hard parts for both of us. If you do all the easy parts and I do all the hard parts, then when the camp house is finished, you won't have any sweat in it."

"Little girls aren't supposed to sweat," Bright said. "Mama told me that."

"Hmmmm. Yes, I imagine she did. And that may be true. But people who build camp houses sweat, especially when the weather gets hot, as it's about to do. So you'll have to make up your mind whether you want to be a little girl who doesn't sweat or somebody who builds a camp house."

"I'm not sure," she said.

He gave her a hard look. "Well, make up your mind right now, because if you're not interested in building the house, I'll take you back to town and get on with the business."

< 128 >

She could tell he meant it. He had that same look in his eyes that he did when he was running the lumberyard, issuing orders in his strong clear voice. Nobody at the lumberyard asked questions. They just did what Dorsey Bascombe said. Just about everybody did pretty much what Dorsey Bascombe said.

"Well," Bright said, "I'm not going to be one of your niggers."

She knew instantly that she had done something terribly wrong. She saw the hot flash of anger cross his face and he opened his mouth to speak, but stopped. He looked away from her then, staring at something in the trees over her head, and he sat there for a long time, nothing moving but a faint ripple of muscles in his lean jaw. Finally, he said, "Where did you hear that word?"

"What?"

"I'm going to say it just once so you'll understand, and then I'm not ever going to say it again. *Nigger.* Where did you hear it?"

"Xuripha Hardwicke," Bright said.

"Xuripha Hardwicke, excuse my French, is a damned fool. And if you use that word, you're a damned fool, too."

It stung her. She felt tears well up suddenly and fought them back. "I'm sorry," she whispered.

"It's not enough to be sorry," he said. "Would you call Hosanna that?"

"No," she said.

"Why not?"

"Because . . ." She stopped, confused, thinking about Hosanna, who was not black or white, just Hosanna. "I don't know," she said.

"Because you love her. Right?"

Bright nodded.

"And you wouldn't do anything in the world to hurt her or make her feel bad. Right?"

"Yes, Papa."

"Hosanna's skin is the same color as the men who work in my lumberyard. The good men I work with. And they are *not*"—his hard voice lashed out at her and she took a half step back—"what you called them. Do you understand me?"

Bright gulped and nodded.

Dorsey sat there for a long time, jaw still working. Bright stood frozen before him, stomach churning with the dread bile of his displeasure, wishing the ground would open and swallow her and she would tumble all the way to Heathen China. It was the most terrible feeling she could remember.

"I'm sorry, Papa," she said after a while, her voice very tiny.

< 129 >

He softened then, the hard lines easing from his face. "Then come here."

He folded his arms around her and pressed her to him, and she melted against him, feeling the great strength in his body, the love pouring out, and she began to cry then. He let her go on for a moment and then he pulled a handkerchief out of his back pocket and wiped her face. "Now," he said. "That's done. Done and over." She calmed herself and sat on his knee, catching her breath. Then he set her down on the ground in front of him and held her by her arms. "Now, do you want to build a camp house with me, or do you want to go back to town?"

Ah, she thought, *I do love him truly and dearly.* But there was the other. She remembered her mother at the dinner table, melting in the hot glare of his disapproval, the helpless and desperate look on her face. It was a terrible thing, the moment itself and all that followed, the way her mother had seemed to shrink, to become separate and alone. Bright would do most anything to escape that. Even the thought of it filled her with a cold dread beyond bearing.

"I reckon I'll stay," she said finally.

He dropped his hands and gave her a big smile that warmed her to her toes. Then she picked up the bucket and went back to the river.

< >

They would build the house well up off the ground, Dorsey said, in case the river ever got this far out of its banks. You could never tell about a river, he said. They have a mind of their own, and sooner or later they will do what rivers naturally do. So they started with brick piers, three feet high and eighteen inches square, nine of them evenly spaced like the outline of a tic-tac-toe game. Bright carried the bricks one at a time from the pile while Dorsey laid them. He was a meticulous worker. A trowelful of mortar was spread across the surface of the pre-viously laid brick like gray cake icing, a new one placed carefully on top, tapped this way and that with the butt of the trowel while Dorsey squinted along the edges to line it up with the string that stretched along a wooden frame next to the pier, then scraped the excess mortar from the edges where it had squeezed out. And finally a spirit level laid on top of the brick to make sure everything was true and square.

"Why are you so picky?" Bright asked, impatient to get on with it. He reminded her of an old woman, fussing over her needlepoint.

Dorsey, kneeling next to the pier, straightened from his work, massaging his lower back. "If the foundation's not right, the whole business is wrong. If I'm off an eighth of an inch down here, it gets

< 130 >

worse as we go up. Then first thing you know, the whole house is catty-whompus."

Catty-whompus she knew. It was one of Hosanna's favorite words, alongside *damnation*—*catty-whompus* generally standing for anything that was physically out of kilter. Bright supposed that when the house was finished, they would bring Hosanna out here to see it, and if Hosanna stood in the yard with her fists on her hips and looked at it and said it was catty-whompus, that was the worst condemnation she could give it. Except, perhaps, for Big-Ikey, and this camp house would definitely not be Big-Ikey. It already felt cozy and comfortable, like a favorite corner of your own room or the space below her father's desk at the lumberyard or the burrow you made down under the covers of your bed when it was cold.

It took them a month of Saturdays to finish the brickwork, and by then spring was in full explosion, the woods around the clearing green and alive, insects busily at work in the grass, new growth poking up through the sandy soil, the river singing just beyond where they worked. They arrived one Saturday in April to find a heron standing in the middle of the clearing, as if waiting for them with a message. Dorsey stopped the car at the edge of the clearing and they all watched each other for a moment, the heron tall and gangly on his stilt legs, head turned in profile, his large round unblinking eye fixed on the automobile. Then he took two lurching steps and was airborne in a magnificent slow-motion swoop of his blue-tinged wings, flying directly over them as he gained altitude, the ungainly body now a graceful curve of white. Dorsey and Bright sat for a moment longer, spellbound, then looked at each other and smiled and climbed out of the car without speaking.

There were three huge timbers now laid across the sets of brick piers, added during the past week. Bright was disappointed. "You've been out here working without me," she said accusingly.

Dorsey nodded. "It takes four grown men to lift one of those timbers," he said. "They're eight by eight, solid heart pine. They'll be there long after you and I are gone."

She tried to imagine that, being gone. She thought about it all day, as they began to lay the floor joists for the house, big two-by-eights that Dorsey notched with a handsaw and hoisted crossways onto the timbers, fastening them with long silver twenty-penny nails that he drove through the joists and into the timbers with sure, powerful blows of his hammer. She watched the way he moved, the grace of his body, the smooth ripple of muscles in his arms after he had taken off his shirt and hung it on a tree branch, working in his ribbed cotton undershirt. He

< 131 >

seemed very permanent, she thought. She could imagine her mother being gone, because her mother seemed wispy and impermanent, with a tenuous hold on life. She could even imagine herself aged and shriveled like Miss Eugenia Putnam at the Study Club, passing slowly out of this life like a yellowing flower after first frost. But she was quite sure that Dorsey Bascombe was here to stay. He was so very sure of himself.

As summer began, the work went quickly. They went to the clearing by the river every Saturday and usually an afternoon or two during the week, leaving the lumberyard after Dorsey had checked things over following the noon break to make sure everything was running smoothly. They would stay through the long afternoon, losing themselves in the work, arriving back home in the warm twilight just before supper. Bright drifted off to sleep at night with the house taking shape in her mind, a fascinating puzzle you put together with every piece going just so. It was only a matter of time until she spilled the beans.

It happened as she sat at the piano with Elise on a late June morning for her weekly piano lesson. Her mind was not on the business at hand. She played poorly, her fingers fumbling absently with the keys, Elise patiently correcting her errors until finally she asked, "Where on earth *are* you this morning?"

And before Bright could catch herself, she said, "At the camp house."

"The what?"

Bright froze, appalled. It was their secret—hers and her father's—and she had spoiled it. Her heart sank.

"What did you say?" Elise asked again, and there was a bit of an edge in her voice, and something else—perhaps a tinge of satisfaction, as if she had stumbled upon something she had been searching for.

Bright took a deep breath. *All right, get it over with. Face the music.* "Papa and I are building a camp house. On the river."

"What kind of a camp house?"

"Just a little house with a porch."

"For what?"

For what? Because . . . well, because it's ours. Mine and Papa's. But I can't tell you that. Instead she said, "To go camping." She squirmed with discomfort under her mother's cold stare. She had never seen Elise quite this way.

"And how long has this little project been going on?"

"Just a little while."

"I see." She reached up, closed the music book they had been working from. "A secret."

"We wanted to surprise you," Bright said quietly.

< 132 >

Elise took one of Bright's hands in her own, turned it over, looked closely at the rough skin, released it. "You and Papa. Building a camp house. My, what ladylike work." There was ice in her voice.

Bright felt small and grubby, and at once ashamed of feeling that way, and in turn resentful. But she said nothing.

Elise got up from the piano bench. "Well," she said, "if you're that busy with Papa, I don't suppose you'll have time for the piano." And she walked out, leaving Bright speechless.

Bright sat through supper that evening in a dread gloom, wondering when her mother would reveal that she had spoiled the secret. She tried to eat, but her food lay in a dead lump in her stomach. At the end of the table, Dorsey had a second helping of everything. He talked idly about the affairs of his day—a tract of timberland he had bought in the next county, the town council's plan for a street lamp outside City Hall—oblivious to Bright's discomfort. Elise did not look at her, not even a glance, until the meal was over. And then she wiped her mouth daintily, put her napkin aside, and looked straight across the table at Bright. "Bright tells me you two have quite a project going," Elise said.

Dorsey looked up, his gaze sweeping from one to the other, and then he put his fork down on the edge of the plate. He sat quietly, considering the matter. He nodded and looked at Bright and said, "It's well nigh impossible for an eight-year-old to keep a secret." Bright wished he would smile, just a little, but he didn't. He didn't look angry, but he didn't smile, either. And she could hear the faint echo of disappointment in his voice.

"A camp house," Elise said.

"That's right. We were going to surprise you when it was all finished. But now that the cat is out of the bag, you can come out and see it any time you like. And when it's finished, we'll take you camping."

"I've never been camping in my life."

Dorsey gave her a long look. "No," he said, "I suppose you haven't."

Elise sat there for a moment with her hands in her lap and then she said, "Building a camp house is not an appropriate activity for a child, especially a young lady."

"Oh? And what is?"

Elise looked him in the eye, unflinching. "Music. Playing with children her age. The things little girls do." Her voice began to rise. "Not spending all day at a dirty, dangerous lumberyard with all those Nigras and all that machinery. And not a construction project, for goodness' sake."

< 133 >

Dorsey's jaw tightened and Bright could see the color rising in his neck. He struggled to keep his voice under control. "Bright can be anything she wants to be, Elise. I see nothing wrong with exposing her to the real world."

He said it with finality, the way he ended discussions. But Bright stared at her mother and saw that Elise was not wilting now, not this time. There was a glint in her eyes, something hard there, something almost desperately angry. "Your idea of the real world and mine are quite different." She bit off the words.

Dorsey's face went pale and he sat for a moment, very still except for the tiny ripples along his jaw. Finally he nodded. "They are that. Quite different."

Bright huddled in her chair, caught between them now, afraid that everything would be spoiled on both sides—the music, the camp house project, everything else. The air in the room was electric and frightening. She wanted to leave them, but she was frozen in place and she dared not speak, for fear it would be a spark that caused something even worse. She had done quite enough damage for one day, she thought. Just now, she must be very quiet and still.

Blessedly, Hosanna intervened. The doorway from the kitchen opened with a creak of its hinges and Hosanna stuck her head through the opening. She looked at each of them in turn, black and impassive, and then she asked, "Y'all want some apple pie for dessert?"

"No," Elise said. "I think we're quite finished here."

Hosanna surveyed the table. "Miss Big Britches here don't look like she ate enough to keep a bird in the air. You sick, young'un."

"No," Bright said. "Yes. I don't feel so well, I guess."

"Then you may go to your room and lie down," Elise said.

Hosanna withdrew, easing the kitchen door slowly shut behind her, and Bright got up and left her parents at the table, staring at their plates in stony silence.

She slept wretchedly, waking once in the night to hear voices down the hall. She couldn't make out the words, but she could feel the anger, the frustration, the sounds beating against her door like waves lapping at the riverbank. Finally they fell silent, leaving a chill emptiness.

She woke with the touch of her father's big, gentle hand on her forehead and she looked up at him, sitting there on the side of her bed, a dim figure in the early light peeking around the edges of her window shade. He looked very tired and drawn, the lines and shadows deep in his face. But he smiled down at her. "Early bird gets the worm," he said, and she could hear the great sadness in his voice that belied his smile. "Let's go build us a camp house."

< 134 >

Bright's eyes felt scratchy and she blinked, struggling awake. "I'm sorry I spilled the beans," she said, and felt tears spring to her eyes.

He lifted her up, cradled her in his arms, and stroked her hair for a long time. She nestled against him, letting his strength envelop her like a warm cloud. Finally he said, "Don't worry, sugar. I'll make it all right."

But for the first time in her life, she heard doubt in his voice.

It was not all right. There was a pall over the house, the air sucked dry by the oppressive heat of summer and her parents' silent conflict. There were no more late-night voices. Through the rest of June and into July, they spoke little to each other at all. Elise spent a good deal of the day in her room. She said nothing about music lessons, leaving Bright to muddle idly at the keyboard with the rudimentary material she had already learned. There didn't seem to be much point in it, and she left it off altogether after a week or so. Dorsey arrived home late in the evenings, drained and weary, barely capable of conversation. He made no further mention of the camp house to Elise. They all went to bed early and Bright slept fitfully in the heat that clung to the upstairs bedrooms, purpling her dreams. She waited, holding her breath, hunkered in her own silence, caught between these two people in their profound unhappiness with each other, fearful of making things worse. Hosanna's kitchen provided her only safe haven, the one place in the house where no one passed judgment. But there was not much Hosanna could do.

Finally, in early July, Elise went to New Orleans. It was a regular thing with her each summer, and she usually took Bright with her. But this time she mentioned nothing about the trip to Bright. Dorsey took her to the train in Columbus and she spent three weeks with her parents—a week longer than usual—leaving behind a household limp with relief at the respite from trouble.

While she was gone, Dorsey and Bright threw themselves anew into the building project, and Dorsey said nothing about Elise's opposition. Bright felt the tiniest bit guilty about it at first, but then she decided that she would not let the lurking sense of her mother's disapproval spoil things.

First the floor—tongue-and-groove pine planking laid across the joists, so that when it was finished, they could stand on it and say, *This is a house, and the rooms go just thus and so.* Next, they began to frame the walls, leaving spaces for the doors and windows, Bright measuring and marking, Dorsey cutting the two-by-fours with his handsaw, Bright passing the boards up to him as he nailed them into place, forming the exterior skeleton of the house. Then the hardest part, with Dorsey

< 135 >

balancing on the top of the skeletal walls while he labored over the roof joists. It would have been easier with two men, she knew. But it was their house.

It was exhausting work, especially in the fierce heat, and Dorsey was careful to take frequent breaks for rest and water. But he expected her to shoulder her share of the load, and she did, fetching and lifting until the muscles in her legs and arms and shoulders cried out. She felt herself, as the days passed, growing stronger. She learned to use the saw and hammer herself, to drive a nail straight and true, to follow a carefully measured pencil line as she cut a board, standing on a little platform next to two sawhorses to give her a good cutting angle. "Measure twice, cut once," Dorsey said. Her hands became roughened and calloused, and when she looked at them in her bath at night, she thought to herself, *No, these are not a lady's hands. And that's just fine, because I don't want to be a lady. I'd rather sweat and build a camp house, no matter what Mama says.*

She began to feel too Dorsey Bascombe's sense of creation—the goodness of building something, of doing it with your own hands and bathing it in your own sweat, of watching something take shape because you made it. The boards with which they built the house were rough and they would send wicked splinters deep into your flesh, but she began to feel the strength in the wood, flowing out into her own body as she handled it, like the warmth of the new sun. There were secrets locked inside the wood, ready to be revealed if you knew just where to put your hands. The big secret was that a house, a grand little house, could rise up out of the wood at their bidding and stand tall and sturdy and proud at the edge of their clearing with its own special kind of music making—the rhythm of hammer and saw, the gurgle of the river nearby. Everything fit. It belonged there because they had picked the right spot and built carefully and well and put the best of themselves into it. You couldn't ask for much more.

On a late afternoon toward the end of July, they stood back from the house and looked at it, the framing finished so that it was beginning, finally, to look like a real house, even if you could see clear through to the other side. And they had a little toast, apple juice in tin cups that they clinked together before drinking.

"It's rather nice, don't you think," Bright said.

"Rather nice?" Dorsey cried. "I should say it's a bit more than that. I'd call it downright magnificent! Fit for a king and his princess."

"When can we stay in it?" she asked.

"Oh," he laughed, "we've got a lot to do yet. Sides, roof, interior walls, all that. One thing about a house, it's not finished until it's finished."

< 136 >

"Is it going to have a bathroom?"

"Of course. In a little house behind the house." Bright gave him an arch look. "Goodness knows," he said, "you don't have indoor plumbing in a camp house. We'll get a well drilled here in the side yard with a hand pump for water, and we'll build a privy right over there." He pointed to a spot near the woods, a few paces from the house. "You'll smell the honeysuckle as you take care of your business."

Bright turned up her nose. "Mama won't like going to the privy."

She wished instantly she had not said it. Dorsey's face clouded.

"Or," Bright said hastily, "maybe she'll think it's quaint." It was a word Elise used frequently to describe something she found a trifle odd and unfamiliar. Much about their town she found quaint. It was such a far cry from New Orleans with its trolley cars running down tree-shaded St. Charles Street and gay laughter from the parlors of the great old houses. "How quaint," she would say, speaking of something like the way Pegram Gibbons, the banker, kept a cow in his backyard. This—this two-room cabin with no indoor plumbing—well, she could imagine Elise standing at the edge of the clearing, giving it a long, slow look, and saying, "How quaint." But that wouldn't mean she didn't like it. Just that she didn't know quite what to do with it.

Standing here now, studying her father's troubled face, she was torn between hoping Elise would come to like the house and hoping that she would not like it at all. It was their house—hers and her father's. But perhaps it would be worth giving up some of that to make peace.

"Mama will come here," Dorsey said, as if reading her mind. "It'll be all right. You'll see. I'll make it all right." He said it resolutely, and then he gave her a big smile. He sounded more hopeful than positive.

Elise returned a few days later, and Bright could instantly see the change that New Orleans had wrought. Her eyes sparkled, her face was alive and clear, and she seemed to move with a light grace. There was still a reserve, a coolness there. But she did not mention the camp house and there was none of the cold anger of before. Bright understood that she didn't want to spoil the magic of her visit. There was a tacit truce, and for Bright, that was quite enough.

Dorsey remarked at dinner her first night back, "The trip seems to have done you a world of good."

She looked at him for a moment before she said, "New Orleans will always be my home."

"Yes," he said, nodding. "I understand that."

As the summer waned, they began to finish the house, and though Bright longed to stretch the days out and make them last, they sped by.

< 137 >

The boards seemed to leap from their hands onto the walls, entire sections going up in a day. Some of the work was too much for the two of them, and they reluctantly brought in help—two men from the sawmill to help put on the tin roof, and a brickmason who came during a week in August to build the fireplace and chimney with old bricks, their edges rounded with age. Dorsey and Bright finished up the walls inside and out—pine boards that would be left to weather naturally—and finally the windows and doors.

On a Saturday in September, after school had resumed, they finished. Bright hammered a nail into the front doorsill, and suddenly there was nothing left to do. She looked around, blinked, took a deep breath of the aroma of fresh-cut pine.

"It's done," she said.

Dorsey was in the yard, gathering up scraps of lumber, stacking them under the front porch of the house to be split for kindling. He looked up at her, a bit wistful. "Yes," he said, "I believe it is."

Bright stood, smoothing her plain brown dress, worn at two spots on the front from where she had knelt at her work. She had worn the same dress every day since they had started building the camp house and it was faded and thin from Hosanna's frequent washings. She felt the smooth length of the hammer in her hands, so awkward and ungainly when she had first lifted it to strike a nail, so familiar to her now. It seemed years ago that they had started.

Her father looked her up and down appraisingly. "You've grown," he said. "You've become a young lady."

Bright looked down at her hands. She didn't tell him, but Xuripha Hardwicke had made fun of her hands at school. "Gracious, you've got hands like a field young'un," Xuripha had said. "Have you been chopping cotton all summer?" Bright kept her own counsel. She had grown strong and wiry from her summer's labor and she could outrun any boy in the class. She didn't think Xuripha would understand at all about building a camp house. And the thought of Fostoria Hardwicke doing her business in a privy, even one fragrant with the smell of honeysuckle, made her giggle.

She sat down on the edge of the porch, feet resting on the steps, and pulled the dress tight around her legs. It was still warm, but there was already a hint of autumn—squirrels busy in the trees, the foliage dry and wilted by the hot blast of summer. Before long, the leaves would begin to turn and then the brisk October wind would send them skittering across the clearing, a red and brown snowfall. It would be very pleasant to sit here on the porch of the camp house and watch autumn take hold.

< 138 >

"Did you want a boy?" she asked.

Dorsey kept working, loading his arms with wood, then depositing the armload under the house atop a growing pile. Finally he straightened and ran his hand through his hair, gray at the temples. "Yes," he said. "At one time I did want a boy. But I wanted a boy *too*, not a boy *instead*."

"Did Mama want to have a boy?"

"Yes. She tried awfully hard, but it just didn't work out."

It was the first time they had talked about it, but somehow it seemed the thing to do just now. It was a warm, fine day full of the satisfaction of work done, things put right.

"If I hadn't wanted to help build the camp house, would you have been disappointed?"

"Yes," he said simply.

"But I did," she said. "Even though sometimes I got pretty tired."

He nodded. "Bright, don't ever let anybody tell you what you've got to do or got to be. People have set ideas, but things change. And they change because a few people kick over the traces and do things they weren't supposed to do, or supposed to be able to do."

"Did you always do just what you wanted to do?" she asked.

"Well, pretty much, I suppose. I was the youngest child in my family, and until I was in high school I was a scrawny runt of a boy." Bright couldn't imagine him being a scrawny runt. He was the tallest man she knew, towering above the world in his leather boots and khakis. "Nobody expected much of me," he went on, "so I could be what I wanted to be. I could surprise folks. It's better to surprise folks than disappoint them."

She got up from the steps and helped him finish the work, gathering up the last scraps of wood and stacking them away. Then he got their lunch from the car and they sat on the steps eating sandwiches made of Hosanna's homemade bread with big slabs of ham and cheese and slices of sweet pickle, washing them down with iced tea from a mason jar they passed back and forth, finishing with bittersweet yellow apples picked from the tree in their backyard. They spent the afternoon clearing brush from the edge of the building site, Dorsey whacking away at the low-growing scrub plants with a small ax and Bright helping him drag it all to the middle of the clearing, where they made a tall pile. Then Dorsey used the paper sack from their lunch to start a fire at the bottom of the brush pile. It had rained little in the past few weeks and the dry brush caught with a quick crackle, the flames leaping up through the branches until the entire pile was ablaze, sending up a thick bluish column of smoke that a light breeze caught at treetop

< 139 >

level and whisked away. They circled the fire, stamping out sparks that fell in the dry grass nearby, watching to see that nothing spread, coughing and laughing in the sweet acrid smoke that seemed to follow them.

When the fire had died down, they sat on the steps together in the fading afternoon, Bright wishing the day could go on and on and the sun would hang suspended, low in the sky just above the trees. Dorsey put his arm around her and she leaned against him.

"We've done good work," he said softly. "And we've done it together. You and me. It's something to be proud of." He leaned down, kissed her forehead. "You're my very special girl and I love you very much."

"I love you too, Papa."

They sat that way for a long time, and then Dorsey took a deep breath and released her, clasped his hands in front of him. "Bright, Mama and I are going to take a trip."

She didn't say anything for a moment. "Where?" she asked finally, her voice small.

"To San Francisco. All the way across the country on the train, and then up the coast to Vancouver. And then back again."

"Oh."

"We'll be gone for most of a month. Hosanna will stay with you, and you'll be just fine."

She looked up sharply at him. "But what about the camp house?"

"It'll be here when we get back."

She started to cry out in protest. But then she saw the raw, naked look of desperation in his face and it stopped her cold. *Something is still terribly wrong. It seems better, but it's really not. He's trying to make it right. And he's afraid he'll fail!* It stunned her, seeing him thus. Dorsey Bascombe was not afraid of anything. But this . . .

She turned her head, trying to hide her disappointment.

"It's very important for Mama and me to do this," he said. "It's important for you too. We both love you, and we love each other . . ." His voice faded away for an instant and then caught up again. "We've had some differences. You know that. You're a smart and sensitive girl and you know things haven't been exactly right. And we haven't been as good parents as we should."

"Oh, no," she protested with a cry. "You've been just fine!"

"Well"—he took a breath—"we want to be better. We need some time together, just the two of us. I've got my business taken care of for a few weeks, and Hosanna will be right there every minute. When Mama and I get back from our trip, we'll have everything all worked

< 140 >

out. And we'll come to the camp house for a long weekend. Just the three of us."

There didn't really seem much to say. She thought about them being gone, about the emptiness they would leave—both of them. But she wanted things to be good and whole again. If this was what it took . . .

Dusk and silence stole across the clearing and they sat for a while longer, then Dorsey got up and went to the car, opened the rear compartment and took out the long black leather case that she recognized as his trombone. He sat beside her on the steps and began to play, the notes drifting out across the clearing and mingling with the last wisps of smoke from the brush pile—"Old Black Joe" and "Deep River," "Juanita" and "In the Sweet Bye and Bye"—the notes round and golden and mellow and sad like the setting sun. Bright sat very still and quiet, letting the music fill and soothe her. When he had finished with a number she looked up at him. Dorsey's eyes were closed and she could see the tiny glint of a tear at the corner of his eye. She put her hand on his knee and they sat there for a moment longer, lingering in the twilight, before he took her hand gently and they rose and went home.

< >

Bright awoke deep in the night, hearing the wind making grace notes as it plucked at the edges of the camp house window and blew a deep baritone across the top of the chimney.

November, almost Thanksgiving, the kitchen at home these days awash in the aromas of Hosanna's magic, the trees outside bare-limbed, gaunt with the anticipation of bitter cold, morning skies broken by thick scudding clouds that made you hope deliciously for the snow that would not come until January at the earliest. A quickening of the blood that made you ache to be away from the cramped desk in the schoolroom, cringing at the screech of chalk across the black-board—consonants and long division; made you long for the stark beauty of the clearing in the woods, the clean smell of new pine in the camp house, the rattle of branches as squirrels dashed about in the tops of the trees, the swift gurgle of the river hurrying toward winter.

November: perhaps a strange time to think of rebirth. But it was a hopeful time, fragrant with the rich incense of promise, dressed in the warm reds and browns of autumn.

Dorsey and Elise had arrived home from their long journey flush with renewal, Elise wearing an enormous diamond and sapphire pendant and Dorsey's face wreathed in a great, warm smile, obviously quite

< 141 >

pleased with themselves. They swept through the door and enveloped Bright with a rush that quite took her breath. And in the ensuing days they filled the house with the undercurrent of their murmurings and touchings. Bright was astonished at the change. It was almost as if a new set of parents had arrived on her doorstep, laden with baggage and presents, transformed by something they had found along the way. Whatever it was, it enlivened everything, charged the air in the house with a hopefulness that made Bright feel almost giddy.

Hosanna, bustling about in the kitchen, rolled her eyes and spoke of them as "the lovebirds." "The lovebirds gone come down to supper, or they gone stay up yonder all evening?" The way she said it made Bright tingle with curiosity. There was something secret and delicious going on here, some intimate transaction of the mysterious world of adults that she could not be privy to, that she didn't know enough about to even begin framing questions. But better not to ask, not now. Better not to risk killing this cat with curiosity.

At length, they would come down the stairs to supper, their arms linked, and Dorsey would lean over and kiss Elise lightly on the cheek after he had held her chair at the table. He always made a point of giving Bright a kiss too, but she felt a pang of jealousy, seeing him so in thrall. She told herself not to be a ninny, not to mind too terribly much being left just outside the boundary of whatever strange and special territory they occupied now—not a participant, but certainly a beneficiary. It was no longer a fragile house, tiptoeing about, afraid of itself. There was no struggle and she was not caught in the middle. That should be quite enough, she told herself. Quite enough.

On this chill November night, Bright lay now in the dark in the single bed, nose and eyebrows cold, the rest of her warm beneath the mound of quilts, listening to the wind-music, hearing God breathing trombone breaths just outside the camp house, knowing she would drift off into sleep again in a few moments. But not just yet.

It was their first trip to the camp house, the three of them together. They had left home at midafternoon with the rear seat of the car piled high with blankets and hampers, enough provisions to last for days. Dorsey had supervised the packing, badgering Hosanna with endless details.

"Y'all gone stay in the woods the rest of the year?" she grumbled.

"No," Dorsey said. "Just 'til tomorrow. But I want to have everything we'll need." He looked a bit nervous, Bright thought. And hopeful. They had not spoken of the camp house since Dorsey and Elise had returned, at least not in Bright's presence.

"I 'speck you got everything the U.S. Army need," Hosanna shot

< 142 >

back. "If Gen'ral Pershing come through with the troops, you can invite 'em in." General Pershing had become Hosanna's hero. He had whipped the Huns, who had been acting Big-Ikey. Anybody who whipped Big-Ikeys was a hero in Hosanna's book.

She stood on the porch waving them off as they pulled away from the house, Bright in the middle of the front seat between her parents, she and her mother bundled in a lap robe, Bright wearing a toboggan cap to keep her head warm and Elise a wide-brimmed hat that tied under her chin with large ribbons. It was a sparkling afternoon with the last lingering embers of autumn mingled with the brisk promise of colder weather moving in. They drove across the bridge and out the Columbus Road, the motorcar puttering noisily and Dorsey dodging ruts and potholes.

"I hope the old horse doesn't go lame!" Bright cried.

"He wouldn't dare. Not with such lovely cargo." Then Dorsey broke into song, his slightly off-key voice mingling with the rattle of the engine. "*The old gray mare, she ain't what she used to be.*" Bright joined in, and then Elise with her thin, bright soprano. They sang on through the afternoon—"The Blue Tail Fly" and "Over the River and Through the Woods," even though it wasn't quite yet Thanksgiving, and "Comin' Through the Rye." And soon they were turning off the Columbus Road and bouncing down the rutted trail toward the river underneath the canopy of tall pines and hardwoods, Elise bracing herself with one hand against the dashboard, holding on to her hat with the other, glancing wide-eyed now and again at Dorsey. Then they broke free into the clearing and Dorsey eased the car to a stop and they sat there for a while, all looking at the little camp house sitting neat and squat at the other end, beckoning them with its wide porch and window-eyes. Elise composed herself and then opened the door and stepped out, and Dorsey and Bright followed her, looking at each other as Elise studied the house for a long moment. Then she said, "How quaint." And they both roared with laughter.

"My goodness," Elise said. "Did you . . ." Her hand swept the air in the direction of the house.

Dorsey took a deep bow, then put his big hand on the top of Bright's head. "Bascombe and Bascombe, Builders of Quality Camp Houses, at your service."

"Do you like it, Mama?" Bright asked. "We did it all ourselves. All but the timbers and the chimbley."

"Well!" She turned again, looked at the house, her eyes sweeping across the porch. "I'm overwhelmed, I suppose."

Bright took her by the hand and led her around the house, show-

< 143 >

ing Elise how they had built it, chattering about joists and studs and rafters, with Dorsey following along behind, letting Bright be the tour guide. "My goodness. Yes, my goodness," Elise kept saying over and over. Then they went inside and showed her the two rooms, the bedroom with a double bed and a single; the living room simply furnished with a wood-burning cookstove in one corner, a table and four chairs next to the fireplace, and a long bench under the window next to the front door.

Out on the porch again, Dorsey pointed to the small privy house a short way from the main building, at the edge of the woods. He had had it moved in on the back of one of his logging trucks, after two men from the sawmill had dug the pit beneath and lined it with boards. "The facility," he volunteered.

Elise looked a little unsure about that.

"Simple but functional," Dorsey said.

"Yes, of course. I suppose that's exactly right. Simple but functional. Do you, ah . . ."

"It has seating arrangements," he said, smiling. "Just like at home. Almost."

Dorsey unloaded the car, piling boxes and hampers in the main room for the time being, and then he fetched an old blanket and they went down the path through the underbrush to the river. He spread the blanket and they sat together on the small sandy shelf that jutted out into the water. They had been there only a few minutes when, as if waiting for a stage cue, the heron swooped down with a wide flap of his wings and settled on his stilt legs in the shallows perhaps thirty yards downriver from where they sat. He surveyed them for a moment and then walked about, taking slow gangly steps, raising his feet high up out of the water, looking for dinner. Then there was a flash of his head, a quick dipping movement into the water, and he came up with a silvery splinter of fish that disappeared quickly down his throat. He cast about for another minute or two while they sat spellbound on the blanket, then was airborne with a shudder of his angular body, trailing droplets of water that sparkled in the late sun. No one spoke for a long time, and then Elise said, "That's one of the most beautiful things I've ever seen."

"He's a local fellow," Dorsey smiled. "Here a long time before we were, I imagine. I wonder what he thinks about us roosting in his territory."

"Is this the same river that flows through town?" Elise asked.

"One and the same. It goes all the way to the sea if you stay on it long enough."

< 144 >

She shook her head. "Strange, I never thought about it going much of anywhere. It's such a little river."

"Nothing like the Mississippi," he said, "but it goes somewhere, just the same. One of these days, it will be a thoroughfare." His arm swept the length of river they could see. "Boats will ply up and down carrying people and things, and this whole area will boom because of it."

"Papa can see the future," Bright said.

"Oh?" Elise looked up at him.

"Well," he said, taking her hand. "Some of it, perhaps. Enough to make me an optimist."

Dorsey sat between them, and he put his arms around them and they stayed a while longer by the riverside, letting the quiet speak for itself as the day waned, casting long cool shadows over the river. Bright felt utterly at peace, here in the place she had come to love over the space of the past few months, with things set straight and right now. She would preserve this if she could, at least in some lockbox in her mind where it would wait for another time when she might need the memory of it. She leaned against her father, barely breathing, hoping that she might make time stand still, and all that went with it. But Dorsey rose finally and said, "It's getting late. I don't want you ladies getting cold."

Back in the camp house, he built a roaring fire in the fireplace and another in the firebox of the iron cookstove.

"Is Mama going to cook?" Bright asked, realizing that they had left behind the most essential ingredient for a meal—Hosanna.

Elise looked a bit alarmed. "Goodness, I hope not. We'll either starve or come down with some unspeakable ailment."

"Mama and I are going to cook," Dorsey laughed. "It may not be a gourmet dinner, but it will stick to our ribs."

While the camp house warmed, he organized dinner, unpacking a food hamper and laying out the ingredients on the table. When the cookstove had heated, he plopped pork chops into an iron skillet crackling with grease and then set Elise to work kneading dough for biscuits, showing her how to work the dough with her fingers and then pull off small, pale chunks and pat them into thick rounds, placing them on a greased baking pan. He showed Bright how to shuck and skewer corn on the cob, which would roast in the oven alongside Elise's biscuits. The camp house filled with warm rich smells and they chattered, marveling at the heron they had seen, laughing at a smudge of flour on Elise's cheek. Dorsey drew a bottle of wine and three glasses from a hamper, uncorked the bottle, and poured—even a bit for Bright.

< 145 >

"A Beaujolais," Dorsey said, "in honor of the fair ladies of the great state of Louisiana." He and Elise held their glasses up, clinked them lightly together, looked for a long slow moment into each other's eyes, then sipped.

"*Tu es très galant, monsieur.*"

Bright looked up at Elise. "What did you say, Mama?"

"It's French," she smiled. "I said, 'You are very gallant, sir.'"

"And you, my dear," Dorsey said softly, still gazing at Elise, "are very beautiful." And he turned quickly to Bright, as if remembering that she was there with them, and gave her a huge smile. "And you, little sugar, are also beautiful and not only that, but a bonny good camp house builder." Then they all three clinked their glasses together and Bright took a sip from her own, tasted its strange tartness. She wrinkled her nose. "It's very delicious, sir," she said bravely. And they all laughed at that.

Dorsey went back to his pork chops. Elise and Bright to their work. Bright stole glances, studying her mother's face, earnest and absorbed with the bread dough. She was still a girl, Bright thought, so much younger than the mothers of most of her friends—a graceful and beautiful girl, her eyes dancing now in the light from the fireplace and the oil lamps Dorsey had lit. There was a reserve there, a distance you might never completely broach, fashioned partly of the very fact of her grace and beauty, partly of some innate reticence of spirit. But Bright began to think that Elise might, in the flush of whatever she and Dorsey had found in San Francisco, begin to open herself to the small neat world Bright had seen from the aeroplane. *Make a place for yourself where you are.* A great deal seemed possible now, and she told herself again that she must not be jealous, that having things right and good and whole was the most important thing of all.

After dinner, Dorsey refilled Elise's wineglass and they began to talk about their courtship, telling Bright again the story of how they met. Elise's voice tinkled with laughter and her slim, graceful pianist's hands caressed the air as she spoke of the "tall, handsome gentleman presenting himself beneath my window with bits of hedge in his hair." The warmth of the room and their laughter filled Bright like new sun and her eyelids grew heavy. She barely remembered being undressed and tucked into bed, surrendering to sleep with a last image of Dorsey and Elise standing, framed in the doorway of the bedroom with the firelight dancing behind them, holding hands.

Bright lay now deep in the night, reconsidering it all, warm and fuzzy with half sleep, beginning to drift back into the soft darkness. But before she did, she turned under her covers to face the double bed next

< 146 >

to her single one, expecting to hear the sound of her parents' breathing. But there was only silence, and as she stared into the dark, she realized the bed was empty. She sat up, looking about the room, and then she heard a flutter of sound from the next room and saw through the doorway the flicker of light from the fireplace. She climbed out of bed, feeling the boards of the floor icy against her feet. She padded quietly to the doorway and stood there, blinking, her eyes adjusting to the dim light. And then she saw them on the floor in front of the fireplace, their bodies pure and golden in the light, moving against each other. Elise's hair spread like a fan across the blanket beneath her, and her arms encircled Dorsey's broad back, her long delicate fingers dancing along his skin. He hovered above her, lighter than air, their bodies joining and then parting, keeping time with some unheard music, making small involuntary sounds. Bright stood for a long time, unseen, both puzzled and entranced by what she saw, unable to turn away, though she sensed that it was the most private of things, something forbidden to her, something at once beautiful and fearful. Then their bodies began to quicken and they strained against each other, calling softly like swans, and she felt a sudden rush of something strange and frightening well up inside her—a nameless jumble that spun inside her head and made her feel angry and weak and terribly alone. She wanted to turn and flee to the warm safety of the bed, but she could not move. The two golden bodies held her spellbound, powerless. The muscles along Dorsey's spine and buttocks rippled in the light now, hills and valleys undulating as Elise raised her long, slim legs, bent at the knee, and stroked them against his sides. Then Elise began to cry out softly and her body began to jerk rhythmically and Dorsey rose up, bending at the waist, towering above her, and Bright stared at the glistening thing he shared with her, giving and then taking back.

Something must have caught his eye. His head turned and he stared toward the open doorway of the bedroom and he froze, suspended there above Elise. "Oh, my God," he cried softly. "Oh, no." Elise opened her eyes and looked up at him and then her head snapped around and she saw what he saw and she screamed. The sound ripped from her throat, an explosion that shattered the brittle air of the room.

Bright took a halting step into the room, held her arms out toward them. "Papa, Mama . . ."

"Get out! Get out!" Elise screamed, flailing at Dorsey, slashing at his face, driving him off her and back onto his haunches with the long thing between his legs dancing in the firelight, a thing suddenly wicked and alive. His hands went down instinctively, trying to hide him-

< 147 >

self, then one hand went out, beseechingly, to Bright. "Sugar. Go back . . ."

She turned then in the doorway, thoroughly frightened now. *I have ruined everything. I don't know what I've done, but I've ruined it all.* And then she heard the rush of feet behind her. Elise seized her by the arm, spun her around. Bright looked up, saw the wild, terrible thing that her mother's face had become, the naked hatred and shame. She cringed from it, but she could not escape the hand that flashed toward her like a striking snake. "You little bitch!" The blow flayed her face, snapped her head back. The sound of it was more terrible than the pain, exploding inside her head, drowning out everything else except her mother's piercing scream. "Bitch! Bitch! Bitch!" And then Dorsey, back beyond them, crying out in anguish, "Elise! No!" Her mother's body jerked back as Dorsey pulled her roughly away, making no attempt now to hide himself, his own face contorted with rage. Terror seized Bright's body and flung her away from them, away from the two naked furies looming above her like beasts, tearing at each other. She staggered toward the front door and jerked it open and fled across the porch and down the steps into the night, holding her hands over her ears. Elise's screams and Dorsey's bellowing cry seared her brain, obliterating everything, beating at her back as she stumbled around the edge of the house and blindly into the protection of the underbrush, branches tearing wickedly at her flesh and nightgown.

It was a good while before Dorsey found her huddled in the sand by the riverbank, sobbing and shivering with fright, the awful sounds still reverberating in her head, crashing against each other until she tore at her hair, trying to make them go away. She saw the light dancing toward her and then Dorsey's face in the glow of the lantern as he knelt. He looked horrible, old and gaunt, near death. Blood oozed from the three parallel slashes across one cheek, mingling with the tears that streamed from his fevered, bloodshot eyes. He set the lantern down on the sand and reached for her, but she recoiled from him and he had to grab her and press her roughly against the flannel shirt he wore now. She fought him, and then his viselike strength suddenly overcame her and she collapsed in his arms and everything went black.

< 148 >

9

*F*or a long time, she did not speak. She woke from a long, fevered sleep several days after the terror at the camp house and found that her voice had shattered into small silver shards and fallen into a dark well in the pit of her stomach. She opened her mouth, but nothing came out, not even the tiniest sound. And then she found there was a refuge in her own quiet, a cave she created deep inside herself. So she didn't try to speak anymore. The voices of others rang hollowly in her ears. And the music stopped entirely.

Dorsey was grief-stricken, caught between Elise, who cowered in shame in her room, and Bright, whose silence followed him everywhere. Bright sensed that Dorsey felt accused by them both, but she was powerless to tell him that he was not to blame, that no one was to blame, really. An agonized pall hung over the house and the air inside seemed dead, like the rot of old leaves. They moved, they breathed, they ate and slept, but there was no life to it. And they avoided each other's eyes. There seemed to be nothing to say, and even if there were, no way of saying it. Even Hosanna was struck dumb, aware that something unspeakable had happened, that something had been destroyed, and that for once she was utterly powerless to do or say anything.

When it became apparent that Bright would not talk, Dorsey took her in desperation to Dr. Finus Tillman. She sat alone in his examining room for a long time, hearing the faint mutter of voices from the doctor and her father in the adjacent office, looking at the framed certificates and diagrams of the human body on the walls, the rows of bottles inside glass-fronted cases, the skeleton dangling from a wooden frame in the corner with a bolt in the top of its head. Finally Dr. Tillman came in alone and gave her a thorough examination, holding down her tongue with a small wooden paddle while he peered down her throat, probing with his hands around the outside of her neck,

< 149 >

listening to her insides with his stethoscope. Then he pulled up a chair and sat in front of the examining table, facing her.

"You're a fine, healthy girl, Bright," he said. He waited, looking up into her face. She stared back at him, first at his eyes and then at the bald spot on the top of his head. She sat very still, hardly breathing. She had learned that when you were very quiet, you could take very tiny breaths because you needed so little air.

"You could talk if you wanted to," Dr. Tillman said. "You have good, strong vocal cords. There's no sign of trouble in there, not even so much as a hint of redness." He arched his eyebrows, making question marks. His eyes broke away and he looked down at his hands, then back up at her, fixing her with his gaze. Bright wanted to help him. But she couldn't.

He sighed. "But it's obvious you don't want to, or can't for some reason that is not physical." He fell silent for a moment. "Bright, I want you to know that there was nothing wrong with what you saw." He paused, searching for words, and she looked away at the window, at the dust motes dancing in the pale winter sunlight. "When two people are married, they make love. A man and a woman lie down together, and they touch and express their love for each other, and sometimes their touching starts a baby growing in the woman. But starting a baby is not the only reason. It's simply the most wonderful way they can say to each other, 'I love you.' There's nothing shameful about it, and I don't want you to think of it that way. It's just that it's a private and secret thing between a man and woman. I'm sure it must have been a very great shock . . ."

You were not there! She wanted to cry out, to tell him of how the strange and beautiful thing she had witnessed had turned into an unspeakable terror, a dark wickedness—not the thing itself, but what it had done to all of them. She wanted to tell him how lost and alone she felt, separated from those she loved, isolated by the silence. Obviously, Dorsey had not told him all of it. Bright might have told him, but her voice was deep down there in the well and wouldn't come out. Even if it could, she was not so sure that she wanted it to. She just wanted to be quiet in a way that went far beyond words.

"Is there anything you want to ask me? Anything I can tell you? You can write it down if you want."

He started to reach for a pad and pencil on his desk, but she shook her head.

"Well, then," Dr. Tillman said, "I think we'll just let things take their course, Bright. I could recommend that your father take you to a specialist in Atlanta, but I don't think that's necessary just yet. We'll

< 150 >

wait it out and let time heal things, as I'm sure it will." Dr. Tillman reached out and took her hand in his. "I want you to know this, that your mother and father love you very much. I'm sure of that. And I'm always here to help. If you need anything, you just come here. You can tell me whatever you want, and I'll keep it perfectly to myself. You can count on that. Do you understand?"

She nodded. She thought that he was a kind and good man and probably a very good doctor. But he couldn't see where her voice had gone. Nobody could see down that far.

Dorsey waited until January to take her back to school. Mrs. Arbuckle met them at the classroom door and took Bright's hand and led her to the empty desk in the front row. She had sat midway the room before, but they had moved all her things to the new desk in front, just in front of where Mrs. Arbuckle herself presided. The room buzzed with noise, and the rest of the children stared as Bright sat down and lifted the lid of the desk and saw that all her things were there—books, ruler, pencils. She closed the lid and looked to see her father still standing at the door, watching her. Then he closed the door and went away.

She was a curiosity at first, but after a few days they grew used to her silence. She did her work, filling pages of paper with words and numbers, catching up on adverbs and long division. And on the playground she found that she could send a kickball spinning just as fiercely as ever. She was simply mute and everything sounded far away, as if the world went on next door and she viewed it through a window.

Even in school, surrounded by the bustle of activity and learning, she found there was really not much worth saying, after all. Only once was she tempted to try. Xuripha Hardwicke had decided to take Bright's silence personally. She jostled Bright roughly as they stood in a milling crowd of children on the playground one morning and hissed, "Dummy!" Bright stared at her for a moment and then kicked her in the shin. Xuripha's howl of pain brought Mrs. Arbuckle running from her accustomed place under an oak tree as the rest of the children backed away and formed a small tight circle.

"She kicked me!" Xuripha bawled, writhing on the ground and holding her shin with both hands.

Mrs. Arbuckle grabbed Bright roughly by the arm. But then Hubert Deloach, who stood at the edge of the chattering crowd, stepped forward and tugged on Mrs. Arbuckle's sleeve and said quietly, "Xuripha called Bright a dummy."

"Is that true?" Mrs. Arbuckle demanded. Xuripha just howled louder. Mrs. Arbuckle still held Bright in her grip. "Is that true?" she

< 151 >

repeated. Bright hesitated and then nodded. Mrs. Arbuckle released her arm. "I don't condone violent behavior," she said, then looked down at Xuripha and added, "usually. Xuripha, get off the ground and go clean yourself up. And Bright, don't you ever let that happen again."

Xuripha wiped her nose on the sleeve of her coat and went snuffling off to the bathroom, and the rest of the children drifted back to their games and Mrs. Arbuckle to her place under the oak tree, leaving Bright and Hubert Deloach standing alone, huddling inside their coats in the January wind that plucked at their hair and sent tiny swirls of red dust spinning on the bare clay of the playground. Hubert looked down at his feet and scuffled the dirt with the toe of one shoe. He was small and shriveled and painfully homely, and they called him Monkey to his face with the special mocking cruelty of children. The only thing about him that seemed to be growing was his ears. For the first time in a good while, Bright had something she wanted to say. But when she opened her mouth, nothing came out. Not a peep, not the tiniest fragment of sound. She shook her head vigorously in frustration, and then Hubert said, "It don't make no mind. It's all right." She reached out and hugged him then very quickly, pressing her face against his, and stepped back to look at his astonishment. And she vowed that someday, when Hubert Deloach least expected it, she would repay.

Dorsey Bascombe, for his part, threw himself into his work. It seemed that everybody in the South wanted to build something in this spring of 1920, and that a good percentage of them insisted on having fine pine lumber from Bascombe Lumber Company to do it. Dorsey put on extra crews to work in the woods, where the sawmill whined from first light until it was too dark to see, slicing freshly cut logs into raw lumber. Mule-drawn wagons and his new trucks shuttled constantly back and forth to the lumberyard next to the river, where the planer mill worked feverishly to keep up with the demand. The railroad put extra cars on its daily freight run and as it crawled east across the trestle every afternoon, laden with its bounty, the flatcars stacked high with pine boards looked like a trail of yellow insects.

Dorsey left the house before dawn and returned well after dark, letting the lumberyard consume him. He grew thin and gaunt, and Hosanna fussed. "Mr. Dorsey, you wastin' away. You gone make folks think I unlearnt how to cook. You gone have Dr. Finus shipping you off to Philadelphia to see what's eatin' you up."

"I'm just working hard, that's all," Dorsey said. "Lots of folks need lumber. Got to get it while the gettin's good."

< 152 >

"Humph," she snorted. "Jes' make sure you save some for the casket."

Bright went with her father on Saturdays, sitting mutely beside him in the car while they bounced along rutted dirt roads into the deep woods to wherever the sawmill was set up, watching through the windshield as Dorsey's leather-booted strides took him across the work site, issuing orders, checking the operation, pausing to encourage the black men who strained and sweated in the growing warmth of April. Then back to town, where Bright spent long quiet hours in the tiny office at the core of the lumberyard or climbed into the spreading branches of the elm tree outside to watch the frantic beehive of activity around her. Dorsey would check on her periodically, but he was absorbed in the work. Bright was content just to be there, away from the strange silent house where Elise still cowered in the upstairs bedroom, sleeping away the mornings and sitting idly by the window through the lengthening afternoons with a book, her silence mocking Bright's muteness.

Here, in the lumberyard, there was life. It reeked with the sweet pungent odor of pine and resin, it rattled and clanked and whined and shouted, and if you were not very careful, it would run over you in a heartbeat. But she sat high and safe in the tree and the black men who passed smiled and waved to her, not caring whether she could speak or not. She let the teeming life of the lumberyard bubble up around her and fill her own silence. She still had no power of speech, but she began, ever so slowly, to feel her senses reawaken.

<   >

In the spring, Dorsey hired a foreman. His name was O'Marron and he was a short, elfish man with yellowed teeth and red hair. He came from North Carolina, where he had straw-bossed a lumber operation in the forests near Asheville before the war. Dorsey had put out the word among Southern lumbermen that he needed an experienced foreman, and O'Marron had written a brief, polite letter setting out his credentials and references. Dorsey checked them out, found them excellent, and hired him by mail. O'Marron climbed off the train on a Saturday afternoon in mid-April, carrying his belongings in a cloth satchel, and presented himself at the door of the lumberyard office. Bright was inside, watching as he crossed the yard, stepping around the puddles from a downpour the night before, dressed in canvas britches tucked into puttees and an olive drab Army-issue jacket with a wide-brimmed hat pulled low over his brow. He had a pronounced limp, and his upper body lurched as he walked. Bright opened the screen door as he stepped onto the small stoop. He stared down at her, then peered

< 153 >

inside the office. "I'm lookin' for Bascombe," he said. He had small steel-gray eyes, set deep in his face. He stood there for a moment, waiting for an answer. "Did you hear me?" She nodded. They looked at each other a while longer. "Well?" Bright could see that he was an impatient man. "Who are you?" he demanded finally.

"My daughter," Dorsey said as he rounded the corner of the office building.

The man looked him up and down. "O'Marron," he said simply, then with a jerk of his head toward Bright, "She dumb?"

"She doesn't speak," Dorsey said evenly. He offered his hand and they shook. "Wipe your feet and come in." Dorsey held the door for him. O'Marron looked around, then scraped the bottoms of his shoes on the edge of the stoop, leaving a crust of mud. Inside, he set his valise down on the floor, but he left his hat on his head. Dorsey showed him to a chair and then sat down behind the battered desk while Bright returned to her perch in the rear window, watching the men in the long shed at the planer mill carrying two-by-fours to a growing stack on a flatcar at the edge of the high platform.

"You had a good trip?" Dorsey asked.

O'Marron grunted. "Tol'able." He had a flat, hard voice and his words sounded like pebbles dropping out of his mouth.

Bright heard the rattle of paper behind her. "Your letter says you're just back from the war," Dorsey said.

"That's right."

"Did you see action?"

"Marines. Belleau Wood. Until I caught a bullet in the leg. It don't give me any trouble, if that's what you're getting at. I can get around."

"I'm not getting at anything," Dorsey said. His chair creaked as he leaned back. "You have family?"

"Not no more." That was all. Just a dead silence now, leaving Bright to wonder about Mr. O'Marron's family—how many there had been, what had happened to them. She imagined a huge tree falling, a train plummeting off a mountainside, fire racing through a frame house in the dead of night. Or perhaps Mr. O'Marron arriving home one evening to find wife and children simply gone. She shuddered.

"Well," Dorsey said after a moment, "I suppose it's easier to move about if you don't have a family to worry with."

"They never did worry me noways," O'Marron said. "Makes no difference. Man offers you a good job, you go."

"Yes," Dorsey said, "it is a good job. Good wages and an opportunity. My business is busting loose at the seams. And it's going to get a lot bigger. The South's the place to be. It's ripe for boom times. Peace

< 154 >

and prosperity. I think you boys who went over have pretty much guaranteed us that. I'm a patriotic man, Mr. O'Marron, and I'm pleased to have a veteran working for me."

"Well, I don't know about that," O'Marron said. "I just know timber."

"What kind of logging were you doing around Asheville before the war?"

"Hardwood, mostly. Good deal of oak. Walnut and maple. Some spruce and pine."

"We cut mostly pine around here. Construction lumber."

"Trees is trees," O'Marron said. "Cut 'em down and haul 'em off."

Dorsey shifted in his chair. "I've got one rule about my operation, O'Marron. We don't clear-cut."

O'Marron gave a little snort. "You waste a lot of time, then. But if that's the way you want it done, so be it."

Dorsey waited for a moment before he spoke, and Bright could tell that he was trying to keep his voice light. "You'll find that the crews know how to get what we need. It's been a while since you've worked crews, I take it."

"Coupla years," O'Marron said. "But it ain't something you ferget how to do. I've worked all kinds." He paused and then added, "Except niggers. There ain't no niggers to speak of in the mountains."

There was a long silence and Bright waited, holding her breath. Dorsey said quietly, "We don't use that word around here."

Curiosity got the best of her then, and Bright turned from the window to see O'Marron shrug. He didn't take his eyes off Dorsey's face. "You're the boss, I reckon."

"That's right." Dorsey's voice was firm now. There was no banter in it at all. "You come highly recommended, Mr. O'Marron. I've got more here than I can say grace over. I need someone who can take on a good deal of the work in the woods, get the most out of the crews. I'm prepared to pay top dollar for it."

"Then let's get on about it." O'Marron stood up and looked over at Bright, gave her a hard stare. She thought that she would not like to work in the woods with Mr. O'Marron.

She stood at the window watching as Dorsey gave him a tour of the lumberyard. O'Marron hobbled along gimp-legged, fists stuffed into the pockets of his jacket. It was warm enough that a man ought not to have to wear a jacket, but he clutched it about him as if he were cold. And then she thought, *No, Mr. O'Marron is not cold, he's angry.* She wondered if the Great War had made him angry, or if he had been angry before he left, or if his anger had something to do with whatever had happened to his family. And then she wondered how much of Mr.

< 155 >

O'Marron's anger Dorsey could sense. Bright could tell it right away from his movements, the way he sat impatiently on the edge of his chair, the gray glint of his eyes, the flat unmusical quality of his voice. She had come to notice over the past few months of her own silence how much you could tell about people if you just listened, if you weren't so busy getting ready to talk that you missed the tiny signs that told who they really were and what they were about. But Dorsey didn't seem to pay much attention to it. Out there in the lumberyard now, he was talking a lot, gesturing, in high spirits, like a man who had been rescued. Mr. O'Marron wasn't saying a word.

Bright wondered too, over the next few weeks, if Dorsey could sense the subtle change in the lumberyard. It was a matter of rhythm, of tone and vibration. The pace quickened perceptibly under O'Marron's hand, took on an impatience that Bright could feel as soon as she entered the yard. Her visits with Dorsey became less frequent because he was away much of the time, making deals for land and timber rights, expanding his operations across several counties in the area; taking long trips to places like Memphis and Atlanta, Birmingham and Jackson, to sell the lumber his crews hauled from the woods from dawn to dark. The groaning trucks and wagons deep-rutted the road into the yard; the stacks of drying lumber grew, spilling across the boundaries of the woodlot onto adjacent land Dorsey bought and cleared. And it seemed the planer mill ran at a higher, more urgent pitch, the black workers tending it like bees around a queen who devoured the fruit of their labor, spitting it out onto the flatcars lined up along the rail spur.

O'Marron seemed to be everywhere. Dorsey bought another automobile, a Model T, and O'Marron shuttled back and forth between the logging and sawmill operations in the woods and the lumberyard in town, driving the operation like a sergeant. He was a nimble man despite what the war had done to his leg. He was born to the woods, and he scrambled about the logging sites like a rooster, hopping over the felled trees, barking orders, paying little attention to anything but the work, not even to Dorsey when he drove out to inspect. Dorsey all but stopped going to the woods. O'Marron had things in hand, and there was better use for his time.

It was Hosanna who first gave voice. She stood in the doorway between the kitchen and dining room early on a Thursday morning in mid-June, watching Bright and Dorsey hover over their breakfast of sliced pork and eggs. Bright looked up at her and Hosanna gave a little flick of her hand. *Eat, eat.* Hosanna wasn't satisfied unless you were eating. If you couldn't talk, you could at least eat. If Hosanna ever died, which was unlikely, she would go to a heaven of nothing but fat people

< 156 >

who begged her all day to cook for them. God would come to Hosanna for wisdom and a plate of pork chops and scrambled eggs.

Bright took another bite of scrambled egg and chewed slowly and watched her father. He looked tired this morning, even after a night's sleep. He had arrived late, long after Bright had gone to bed, after a two-day trip to Nashville. But he had waked her early. They would spend the day at the lumberyard.

It had been two weeks since she had been with him, and summer vacation was already dragging wearily through the first hot days of June. She was bored and fidgety, frequently alone despite Hosanna's attempts to keep her occupied. Her silence put people off, kept them at arm's length. Other children found her difficult to play with and quickly abandoned the effort. And her mother was virtually a ghost in her own home, keeping to her room, her own silence mocking Bright as Bright's mocked her father. Bright felt increasingly isolated, trapped inside the dread silence. She had come to hate it now, hate what it did, hate that she was powerless to end the silence and her pervading sense of loss. If she could have spoken, she would have asked them each in turn, *Do you love me anymore?* But then, she was afraid of what they might say if they spoke honestly.

Now, at the table, Dorsey ate and talked, trying to fill the silence. ". . . take along a book," he was saying. "I'll have to spend most of the day at my desk, I'm afraid. It just piles up. I don't know where it all comes from. Thank God for O'Marron. The man's a wonder."

Then Hosanna took a deep breath and said, "The devil take him."

They both stopped in midbite and stared at her. Dorsey put his fork down on his plate, then wiped his mouth with his napkin and held it wadded in his hand. "I beg your pardon."

Hosanna crossed her arms. "They all afraid of that man."

"O'Marron?"

"Mose say they call him Crawdad."

Dorsey arched his eyebrows. "Crawdad?"

"Yeah. He skitter around sort of sideways and ever' so often he reach out and bite. Crawdads got a mean temper."

Dorsey shook his head. "Well, O'Marron's a no-nonsense fellow, I'll give you that. But still . . ."

"Mose say he talk nasty. Mose say his cousin Blue was sittin' on a stump late afternoon the other day, all tuckered out from being worked so hard, and that man come over and jerk him up and say, 'Git yo' black ass back to work.'"

Dorsey cut his eyes over at Bright. "Hosanna, that'll do," he said sharply.

"Well, that's what he say, Mr. Dorsey. I'm just tellin' it like it is."

< 157 >

His nostrils flared. "Well, *don't* tell it *exactly* like it is!"

Hosanna hung fire for a moment and then she tilted her head back a bit and looked down her nose at Dorsey. "Plain truth ain't got no honey on it," she said. "And truth is, Mr. Dorsey, you done turnt yore bidness over to the devil's disciple hisself."

"Hosanna—," he started, warning her.

But she bulled ahead, gathering her courage about her, speaking fast so he couldn't interrupt, her voice urgent. "He mean as a snake and he takin' it out on mens that give you the honest sweat of they brow. They gettin' the trees out of the woods, jes' like you want. But that man gone kill somebody 'fore long. You ax 'em. They tell you what he does, how he talk. You ax 'em Mr. Dorsey. 'Bout time you was axin' 'stead of tellin'."

"By God, that's enough!" Dorsey roared, and his fist came crashing down on the table, rattling the dishes. Bright cowered in her chair, stunned. Mostly by Hosanna. No one, *no one* had ever talked to Dorsey Bascombe like that, at least not in her hearing.

Hosanna stood there for a moment and her eyes never left his face, and Bright understood suddenly what an incredible thing it was that Hosanna had done. And then Hosanna said quietly, "You keep on, folks gone think you Big-Ikey." And she turned then and disappeared into the kitchen, leaving the door swinging softly behind her, leaving Dorsey openmouthed, staring at the space she had left.

It hung over them like a cloud all day, unspoken. Bright took refuge from Dorsey's smoldering silence in the spreading branches of the elm tree just outside the office, shaded from the sun, watching the lumberyard boil with activity—the relentless stream of wagons and trucks from the woods, crews of men scrambling to unload and stack the pine boards, the unending screech of the planer mill. It was feverish, kicking up a haze of dust in the hot June day. The dust drifted up to where she sat, coating her skin with a fine powder, making her eyes dry and scratchy—a nettlesome emanation from the lumberyard, troubled, unsettled, unhappy with itself. And through the open window of the office, she could see her father hunched over the desk, his pen darting across the papers and ledger books in front of him.

Just before the noon hour, he rose suddenly from his work and strode out the door, headed across the lumberyard. Bright scrambled down and followed, keeping a safe distance. Dorsey seemed to pay her no attention. He went straight to the planer mill, where Mose Richardson's brother, Jester, was feeding two-by-fours into the whirling jaws of the planer. He signaled to Jester to stop the machine, and he heaved

< 158 >

on a big metal handle and disengaged the long flapping belt that transferred the power from the steam engine to the planer. The machine ground to a halt and Jester stepped away from it, waiting, cautious.

"Jester," Dorsey said.

"Yes sir, Mr. Dorsey."

"Everything going all right here?"

Jester fetched a bandanna out of his pocket and mopped at his sweat-slick brow. The muscles on his arm bulged, like small animals burrowing under the coal-black skin. It was backbreaking work, feeding the planer. Bright had seen men topple from exhaustion in the heat. But Jester Richardson could keep at it hour after hour, an extension of the machine. Dorsey Bascombe's workers were all strong men, and they wore their great strength like a cloak that fit easily on their shoulders. Any one of them could pick up the foreman O'Marron and break him like a matchstick. Bright understood perfectly that they wouldn't. "Yes sir," Jester said, "it's running jest fine."

"No, I don't mean the machinery."

His face was impassive. "Don't rightly know about nothing else."

"But you hear talk," Dorsey said. "From the crews in the woods."

Jester's eyes never left Dorsey's and they never revealed a thing. "I jest take care my bidness," he said. "I let other folks take care they bidness."

"You'd tell me if anything were wrong," Dorsey said. It was a statement, not a question. "You'd tell me right away."

Jester looked away. "I reckon."

They drove home and ate in silence, Dorsey's face gray and troubled. Hosanna served them without a word and left them alone in the dining room to eat. Bright watched him, knowing as surely as if she could look inside his head what was going through his mind. *He has made a mistake, a very grave one. He misjudged. And because he is a proud man, he doesn't know what to do about it.* And then it struck her—terrible, blinding in its clarity. *It is not the first time.*

<   >

"You'll stay home this afternoon," he said, and there was something in his voice that warned her not to plead with her eyes or pluck at his sleeve. She nodded. He left shortly, banging the screen door behind him, leaving silence and dread.

After he was gone, Bright went to the front porch and sat on the top step for a long time, thinking about Mr. O'Marron. There was a kind of craziness in him. You could almost smell it, an odor of bile and malice that seeped around his small, closely guarded eyes, the smoke

< 159 >

of some terrible poisonous fire that ate at his insides. She feared for the men who were in the woods with him this afternoon.

Hosanna too felt the dread. Trouble settled about her shoulders like a shawl and furrowed her brow. In the kitchen, as Bright watched her sloshing dishes in the sink, she talked in fits and starts, little snippets of conversation that rattled about and then trailed off into silence. Bright could fill in all the blank spaces, the unsaid, from years of listening to Hosanna. White folks' trouble. The worst kind. Colored folks had their own troubles, but they kept it to themselves and dealt with it in the confines of their secretive world. White folks' troubles had a way of washing over everyone, like the river when it jumped out of its banks, angry and red, sweeping things helplessly along whether they wanted to go or not. When white folks' trouble came, no matter who won, colored folks lost.

As dusk came, Bright could stand it no longer. She slipped out the back door and started walking toward the lumberyard across town. She sneaked in by the back way, darting behind the stacks of drying wood, unseen, until she reached the office. Dorsey wasn't there. The door was open, the swivel chair pushed back from the littered desk, a solitary irritated fly beating against the screen of the window. Out in the lumberyard, the planer was running, but there was something else here, an ominous rumble, a smell of something brewing. She walked out onto the stoop and stood there listening to it for a moment, then climbed into the elm tree, secreting herself high in the spreading green foliage, and settled in to wait.

It was after dark before the crews returned, and by then Dorsey was back, working at his desk, shoulders hunched. She heard them way off down the road that led from the River Bridge—two trucks, one of them running badly, its motor limping. It took them a long time to make the entrance to the lumberyard and they rumbled slowly through the gate and into the weak pool of light from the electric bulb on the front porch of the office, opposite the elm tree. She climbed down to a lower branch and she could see the trucks over the top of the small building and Dorsey getting up from the desk. She heard the screen door bang behind him as he stepped onto the porch. The drivers of the two trucks killed the engines—O'Marron in the lead truck, the one with the wounded engine, Mose Richardson in the second.

No one said a word. O'Marron climbed down from the cab and went around to the front of the truck and stood there, hands on hips, glaring at the men crowding the stacks of lumber on the backs of both vehicles. There was the strong, palpable smell of raw fear and anger

< 160 >

here. You could touch it. Then O'Marron turned with a jerk and opened the hood of the lead truck and peered into its darkened innards. Mose sat in his own cab for a moment before he got out and closed the door behind him. None of the men on the trucks moved an inch until Mose did, and then they eased themselves down and stood back a bit in a group, waiting. Mose stood for a while next to his truck and then something powerful rippled through him. He took one slow step and then another, like a heron gathering wing for flight, and they all waited, holding their breath as he passed O'Marron's truck and moved on toward the office building where Dorsey stood. That's when Bright climbed down from her perch in the tree and stood next to the back window, just out of the light.

Dorsey closed the wooden door behind them and the two men stood facing each other in front of the desk, a bit apart, just looking at each other. It was then that Bright noticed the angry welt on Mose's face, just under his right eye. After a moment, Mose said, "He struck me, Mr. Dorsey."

A look of exquisite pain wrenched Dorsey's face and he drew in his breath. "Why?"

"He wanted me to clear-cut. I tole him Mr. Dorsey don't allow no clear-cutting. But he say we ain't got time to study what Mr. Dorsey say, we got to get the logs out the woods. So I say, 'Beggin' yo' pardon, we got to do it like Mr. Dorsey say do, or else he get somebody else.'" He paused, and then he looked away from Dorsey for the first time and his voice broke a little. "That's when he struck me. Knock me down, call me a dumb nigger."

"And what did you do?" Dorsey asked, his voice leaden.

"I cut down lots of trees, me and the boys. And then I fix the truck, the one Mr. O'Marron drivin', so it take us a long time to git back to town and I have time to get my head clear 'fore we get here. Right now, I'm 'bout as clear as can be."

Dorsey stood frozen for a moment and Bright could almost feel the heat of his gathering fury. Then he said softly, "Goddamn him."

When Dorsey reached for the door, Bright eased around the side of the building, keeping to the shadows, and watched as her father crossed the narrow space between the stoop and the truck, the tall leather boots making enormous strides until he reached O'Marron. The man looked up, his small eyes fierce even in the dim light, and he stepped back from the truck, but not far enough. Dorsey's long arm lashed out and his fist caught O'Marron dead on the mouth and there was a loud sickening crack, and then a ripple of sound from the crowd of men, a rumbling affirmation. O'Marron's head snapped back and

< 161 >

small white things sprayed from his mouth and he dropped like a shot and lay motionless on the ground, arms and legs splayed. *He has killed him,* Bright thought. But no, after a moment O'Marron raised up a bit, shaking his head and spitting a wad of blood and teeth; then he crawled to his knees. Dorsey reached down and grabbed him by the front of his shirt and jerked him to his feet and hit him again, this time in the stomach. O'Marron flew backward and crashed into the door of the truck and then stood there, reeling. Still he hadn't uttered a sound and Bright marveled at the raw angry stubbornness that kept him on his feet. He peered at Dorsey, his eyes narrow hate-slits, and then he staggered forward, raising his fists. Dorsey let him get within a couple of feet and lashed out, striking him this time on the side of the head, wincing with the force of his own blow. O'Marron went to his knees and Dorsey reached for him again and that was when Mose Richardson cried, "No, Mr. Dorsey!" He grabbed Dorsey quickly by the arm and Dorsey turned with a jerk and stared at him and Bright could see the crazed look in her father's eyes. "You gone kill him, Mr. Dorsey!" O'Marron looked up at them, his face blasted and bloody, and he toppled onto the ground, out cold. Mose held Dorsey's arm for a little longer and then let it go gently and stepped back. Dorsey stood over O'Marron like a beast over conquered prey, his body bent slightly at the waist, shaking visibly. And then he looked over at the knot of men standing back by the other truck. Shadowy figures appeared at the edge of the group—the crew from the planer mill. Here, well after dark, they had not left yet. They had been waiting.

Dorsey stared at them and his voice lashed out at them like a fist. "What the hell are you looking at? You satisfied? I've whipped a white sonofabitch in front of you. Is that enough?"

No one spoke or moved for a long time. Finally, Dorsey straightened, and from the shadows, Bright could see the great effort it took to get control of himself, calm the rage. When he finally spoke, his voice was low and strangled and his words hung like acrid smoke in the still, soft night air. "From now on, Mose Richardson is the foreman in the woods. You do what Mose tells you. And Jester is the foreman here at the yard." Dorsey looked beyond them, at the sprawling lumberyard out there in the blackness. "We don't need any help."

He looked down at O'Marron again, then at Mose. "Get him out of here," he ordered, his voice flat and hard.

Mose hesitated, afraid to touch the crumpled white heap at his feet.

"Pick him up," Dorsey said harshly. "Tote him over there by the gate and dump him. Outside the property. By God, do it!"

< 162 >

Mose bent and hauled O'Marron up from the ground like a rag doll and slung him over his broad shoulders. O'Marron's head lolled loosely, blood and spittle from his ruined mouth drooling down the back of Mose's shirt, mingling with the dark blotch of sweat stain that ran from his collar to his pants. The knot of men standing by the truck made a wide path for him as he moved through them and disappeared into the dark, toward the lumberyard gate. After a moment, they heard the thump of O'Marron's body up by the road, then the soft crunch of Mose's boots as he returned. Then the men closed in around Mose protectively and they stood a way back from Dorsey, and Bright could see how the distance separated them, the lone white man and the crowd of blacks.

Bright wished deeply to step from the shadows of the building, to go to her father and take him by the hand, have him lift her up and hold her tightly while she rubbed the deep lines from his face. But she knew it would not do. She understood again his grievous error, his great private shame, and that the brutal thing she had just witnessed was both admission of guilt and administration of grisly justice. It was no place for her to be, no thing for her to have seen, and she must never tell him that she had been there. So she turned and stole away in the fevered dark toward home.

<   >

A great storm boiled up from the south during the night, a fury of wind and lightning and driving rain. Bright woke, frightened and disoriented, at its height. She lay there and listened to it and tried to calm herself and after a while she began to think, for the first time in a very long time, about music. There was a terrible dissonant beauty to this. It came all at once, the smashing peals of thunder chasing each other, a tortured howling of wind, a ceaseless drumroll of rain against the window and the side of the house. She imagined God the conductor clutching the podium with rain streaming down His face and wind lashing His long hair and flowing beard, the orchestra of archangels gone mad at His feet. *It's Mr. O'Marron,* she thought suddenly. She thought about the crumpled body, lying beside the gate to the lumberyard, with God and His insane orchestra pealing out judgment from a sky rent by chaos. If O'Marron were not already dead, he would surely not survive the storm. And then she thought about the river nearby, how it could rise so quickly and angrily from its banks and send its red rushing octopus arms out in all directions, gathering the land and all that was on it to its raging belly. The house shook with the great explosions of thunder and lashing of the wind and she imagined it breaking

< 163 >

loose from its foundation, being swept along downstream, passing the lumberyard and heading toward New Orleans. *The house and Mr. O'Marron's body swept along together, the lifeless eyes at her window, clutching hands rising from the blood-red water.* Something broke deep down inside Bright and the tiniest sound flew small and frightened toward her throat, a dread sound. She sat up in bed and her arms flew out involuntarily. She heard footsteps in the hall, her father coming to save her. And then she heard her mother cry out, a high, pitiful wail. Storms always frightened her terribly. The footsteps stopped and Bright could imagine him there in the dark hallway, tall and stooped from the weight of it all, torn between silent child and beseeching wife. Then he took two more steps and before he could open the door, she dived beneath the covers and huddled there, trembling with fear, wretched in her aloneness. *Go on! Go to her!* She did not know whether Dorsey opened her door or not. The house shuddered beneath her and then a bolt of lightning struck very close by, so close she could feel the tingle through her body and smell the bitter copper-stench of blasted air. Elise screamed like a banshee down the hall and Bright heard a muffled crashing of limbs outside in the yard. Then suddenly, it was over—nothing left but the distant rumbling of aftershock and the smell of spent air, all the life washed out of it. When she finally peeked out from under the covers, the room was still, the door closed—the only sound in the house her mother's soft whimpering down the hall. Bright listened to it for a long time before she finally slept.

Dorsey was out at daybreak, and by seven o'clock he had rounded up crews from the lumberyard and started the cleanup, clearing a tangle of fallen limbs from streets and yards.

The biggest mess was right next door, where the lightning bolt had splintered a maple and toppled a huge limb onto O. P. Putnam's house, smashing through the roof into Buster's bedroom. A big crowd gathered in the puddled yard as Mose Richardson and three of his men shinnied up the trunk and began cutting away the limb with their long saws and double-bitted axes and pulling it back through the gaping hole in the roof. Buster stood in the middle of the crowd and everybody kept looking at him as if he had been raised from the dead, especially the kids—all the big kids who generally ignored Buster because he was the youngest in the neighborhood except for the Gibbonses' baby. As Bright squeezed through the crowd, Buster was telling again how he had escaped certain death. "I got up to go to the bafroom," he said, "and when I came back, I couldn't get in the bed because there was a tree in it. It'da kilt me, shore as shootin'."

< 164 >

"Was you scared?" one of the big kids asked.

"Naw, but Mama came runnin' in and started screamin' and she didn't quit 'til Dr. Finus come and knocked her out. She's in yonder sleeping now."

Elsewhere, the town was littered with debris from the storm, two of the streets blocked by fallen trees, every yard filled with branches and leaves. Bright rode with Dorsey as he hurried from place to place, supervising the work. When he was finally satisfied that things were in hand, they drove out of town along the river road, and Bright realized after a moment that they were headed toward the camp house.

It was the first time Bright had been there since the past November. Her father kept glancing over at her as he drove, but she sat quietly, wondering as they bounced through the deep puddles under the canopy of still-dripping trees if the house were still there, if perhaps the river had carried it away in the night, and if it had, whether it carried with it the ghosts of the frigid, terror-stricken night that took her voice. But there it was, sitting squat and eyeless with its windows boarded up, unscathed.

It had been a close thing. The river was swift and red behind the cabin and they could see where it had gotten up during the night, almost to the top of the embankment. Debris clung to the underbrush and the lower branches of the trees, and the sandy ground underneath was scoured by the rushing water. They stood at the top of the embankment and looked at it for a while, and then they went back to the house and sat on the porch steps. The sky overhead was breaking now, the remaining clouds from the storm front scattering before a freshening breeze until there was mostly blue and the sun began to warm and dry the ground.

"It's not a very good place for a camp house," Dorsey said after a while. "One of these days, the river's going to get it. Maybe we should think about moving it. Or just starting over someplace else."

Bright looked up at him, studying his face. He looked bone-tired, the lines around his eyes etched deeply, as if someone had taken a sharp knife and scraped them out. Some of it, she thought, was disappointment. And she felt powerless to do anything about any of it.

They heard the truck then, turning off the main road and heading toward them down the rutted trail, whining in low gear, the engine growling as it bounced through the mud puddles. She recognized it immediately, the peculiar sound of one of Dorsey's logging trucks. His head jerked up and he listened for a minute, and then he rose quickly, took two steps into the yard and stood listening, his body tense and alert. The truck rounded the last curve in the trail and roared into the

< 165 >

clearing toward them. Sun glinted from the windshield and they couldn't see who was inside. Not until the truck stopped with a lurch, the motor still running, and the door flew open. O'Marron had a shotgun.

Dorsey whirled to her. "BRIGHT, RUN!"

But she was frozen there on the steps where she sat—frozen by the wild, bloodshot craziness in O'Marron's eyes, the raw stench of whiskey she could smell even from here, and most of all by the huge twin black holes in the end of the shotgun.

O'Marron lurched around the front of the truck, raising the gun as he came. "Bascombe, you sonofabitch!" he cried, the words strangled in the bloody pulp of his ruined mouth.

"O'Marron, put the gun away!" Bright leapt to her feet on the steps, driven finally by terror boiling up in her throat.

"I'm going to blow your ass to kingdom come!" O'Marron screamed. Then he looked up at Bright and she could see the raw hate in his eyes, the great craving madness.

The muzzle of the gun swung upward and she could see the sinew in his finger move, pulling the trigger. Then Dorsey took one long, swift step toward O'Marron just before the yard exploded, the sound louder than creation. The roar of the shotgun, screams—O'Marron's, Dorsey's, and somewhere deep in her own belly, a sound louder than any other, wrenched from the dark pit where her voice had been hiding.

The blast caught Dorsey in his left shoulder and spun him around, arms flailing the air, and smashed him against the steps next to her in an eruption of blood and flesh, everything suddenly covered in red. She sat there, dumb with horror, and then she saw O'Marron sitting on the ground in front of the truck, the shotgun next to him in the grass. He stared at her, eyes hollow, and as he reached for the gun she flung herself across Dorsey's body and clutched him tightly, waiting. But then she heard the truck's door slam, the clash and whine of gears as the truck backed and turned, roaring away from them, going very fast along the trail, faster and faster. And then a terrible crash, the splintering of metal and glass and a sharp crack of wood.

She forced herself, after a moment, to release her grip on Dorsey and she sat up slowly, seeing the terrible wound, the shirt and the flesh underneath shredded, the arm nearly torn away at the shoulder, a white sliver of bone glinting through the red. Blood spurted from the wound and ran in rivulets down the steps, dripping from one to another. So much blood. It covered the front of her dress, smeared her bare arms and hands. Bright opened her mouth, tried desperately to speak, couldn't, even now. Dorsey's face was ghastly white beneath the

< 166 >

flecks of blood that spattered his face. *He's dead!* And then one eyelid fluttered, just the tiniest movement. Bright began to tremble and then to shake violently, spasms racking her body. She stood, backing away from him, and then her legs collapsed under her and she stumbled and fell. *Papa! Papa!* she cried wordlessly, stretching out her arms. But he sprawled across the steps, and the blood dripped and dripped, reaching the ground now and soaking into the sand.

Bright lurched to her feet and stood there wobbling like a calf for a moment, and then she turned and started running, across the clearing and down the trail toward the main road, weaving crazily, splashing through the deep puddles, losing a shoe in one of them and ignoring the rocks and fallen branches that lashed at her bare foot. She reached the first clearing and saw the truck. It had smashed head-on into a tree, had struck it with such force that it splintered the tree several feet from the ground and toppled it onto the cab of the truck. She stopped, looked at it for a moment, then walked closer, stopped again. There was no sound but the hiss of steam from the radiator. She stepped up on the running board and parted a branch and saw O'Marron there, slumped over the twisted steering wheel. There was a long deep dent in his forehead, already turning purple. His eyes were open. Bright reached in, poked him in one eye with her finger. Nothing. *Bastard!* she screamed silently. It was the worst word she knew.

She stepped backward to the ground and started running again. There was the main road ahead, a splash of red clay beyond the opening in the trees. As she reached it, she looked across the road at the plowed field on the other side, saw the colored man standing in the middle, hands on hips, looking toward her. The storm had turned the field to muck and it pulled at her feet as she struggled toward him. She sprawled headfirst, fought her way up, fell again.

"Hey, yonder! You gone trample all the plants!" the colored man yelled at her. "Hey!" He headed toward her, stepping across the rows of tiny cotton plants. He reached her, saw the blood and gore, stopped with his eyes wide. "Lord, sweet Jesus," he breathed.

She looked up at him, beseeching him with her eyes, but he stared dumbly at her. *Help.* But there was no sound to it. She opened her mouth again and felt the grief rent her gut and then the dam broke and the words spewed out, an eruption of sound—screams, howling wind and thunder, a primitive and vicious storm of words, all the sounds that had been locked away for so very long. "My papa's dead!" she cried over and over. "My papa's dead!" And then the sound rushed in on her and carried her back into the black hole deep inside, obscuring everything.

< 167 >

BOOK 3

10

*T*here is someone in the house.

She woke in the deep quiet of midnight, suddenly alert and wary, tingling with the sense of something alive, something disturbing the rhythms of the old house.

She and the house had been together longer than any other thing in her life. She knew without looking when something was out of place, when there was the slightest alteration in sound or feel, as she had felt instantly this morning the change in the house's tone when the refrigerator went *clunk*. Now, there was something else. Something she could sense.

She thought first of Fitz, perhaps driving down from the capital in the middle of the night to see her, slipping quietly into the spare bedroom to surprise her in the morning. But no, it was unlike Fitz to do anything quietly. He attracted attention the way a dog attracted fleas—a man frozen in black and white on the front page of the newspaper in his boxer shorts. No, it was not Fitz in the house this night. Fitz had not come home. Fitz had not called. Fitz was in hot water with his mama.

Then she remembered Jimbo. How could she have forgotten, with all that had transpired since the Winnebago lumbered into the yard this morning with Roseann yelling out the window?

And there was something else. What was it? Ah, yes. Fifty thousand dollars, locked away in somebody's safe with her name on it. Now she was wide awake.

She lay there for a while, thinking she might drift back into sleep, realizing after several minutes that she would not. Now what? She was never up in the middle of the night. Never. By timeworn habit, she and the house and Gladys settled into sleep together—Bright ticking off the events of the day until they began to jumble together with old

< 171 >

memories, the house creaking and sighing, shifting about the ancient dust in its cracks and crannies, Gladys bumping against the pipes as she came in from her nightly ablutions and flopped into her favorite hole just below Bright's bedroom. Finally, all three gave up the day, weary with time, and slipped into the long night. Bright dreamed of things real and imagined, the accumulation of sixty-eight years, and it suited her fancy to think the house and Gladys did too. At their age, it seemed apt. But now, here she was wide awake with a boy in the spare bedroom and fifty thousand dollars in the bank and all the rest— Fitzhugh and Roseann and Flavo and Buster—dancing like dervishes in her brain. *What the devil is going on here?*

She threw back the sheet and got out of bed, slipping on her robe and house shoes, and went to the spare bedroom. She stood for a long time in the doorway, watching Jimbo sleep in the soft gray light from the street lamp out on Birdsong Boulevard—mouth open in an oval, hair tousled, arms and legs splayed across the bed. There was nothing very neat and buttoned-down about a sleeping boy, she thought, even one who was so carefully scrubbed and pressed when he was awake.

A boy in the house. Lord, it had been a long time since there was a boy in the house. What did you do with a boy? Buy him some overalls, Buster Putnam had said. Yes, perhaps that was it. A boy in overalls.

She was heading back toward her bedroom when she glanced out the front window and saw all the lights at the end of Claxton, up near the bridge. She thought for an instant that it must be some sort of a chase, something like *Dragnet*. But no, there was nothing that seemed in any particular hurry up there—the lights of automobiles moving slowly back and forth across the bridge, the flashing blue light of a police car, another one that flashed red, and a very bright glow that seemed to come from a spotlight of some kind. It was too far away to tell exactly what was going on. She stepped out onto the front porch and watched for a moment, then went to the telephone and dialed the police station.

"PO-leese," a young man answered.

"Who is this?" she asked.

"Butch Holley," he said. She could hear a radio playing in the background. Some kind of boogie music.

"Are you a police officer?"

"Shore am. What can I do for you?"

"What's all the commotion up by the bridge?"

"Aw," he said with a bored drawl, "just a little nigger kid drowned."

Bright caught herself, then said quietly, "Don't use that word, young man. It makes you sound like a redneck."

< 172 >

There was a long pause and then he asked, "Who is this?"

"Mrs. Fitzhugh Birdsong."

"Oh." She heard the spring in his chair squeak.

"Is Chief Sipsey there?"

"No ma'am. He's up at the bridge. They're dragging the river for the . . . ah . . . the little boy."

"Do you know who he is?"

Another pause, and then the policeman said reluctantly, "Yes'm."

"Well, who?"

She heard the shuffling of some papers. "Well, I reckon I can release the name since the next of kin's been notified. His name is Lester Flavo French."

"Flavo?" Her heart caught in her throat. "That's Flavo Richardson's grandson."

"Yes'm. I think it is."

She was halfway to the bridge before she gave Jimbo a thought, and she was torn for an instant between concern for him alone there in the house and the thought of the child drowned underneath the bridge. She stopped, turned back and looked at the house sleeping under the protective awning of the pecan trees. Jimbo would be safe for a while, if indeed there were any place that was truly safe. She would not be long. But she must go to Flavo. She turned again and kept walking toward the lights, pressing uphill against the cold dread of what she would find when she got there, thinking about the small boy in the black water.

Drownings happened with some regularity, this being a town bounded by a river. There would be an occasional article in Ortho Noblett's weekly newspaper, often about a fisherman whose boat had capsized, perhaps a picture of the Rescue Squad boat out on the river filled with men holding long poles, or of men carrying a sheet-covered body on a stretcher. But this was infinitely more personal, a friend's tragedy, and somehow even more grim and ghastly because it was happening in the middle of the night right here at the end of Bright's street.

As she approached the bridge, she could see that it was not such a terribly big commotion. The lights, blinking and revolving, made it seem more than it was. A single police cruiser and a Rescue Squad ambulance and several cars were parked along the approach to the bridge. Another emergency vehicle out on the span itself had a large spotlight on top that was trained over the side of the bridge, down toward the water. Just past it, at the crest of the span, a policeman stood in the middle of the bridge, waving a flashlight, directing an

< 173 >

occasional passing car around the emergency truck. There was a small crowd of onlookers standing at the near edge of the bridge, flashing red and blue in the revolving lights of the police car and the Rescue Squad ambulance. The only one of the crowd she knew was Homer Sipsey, the police chief, who turned and saw her as she puffed up the incline.

Homer took a step in her direction. "Miz Bright, that you?" He gave her a curious look.

"Yes, Homer. I saw the lights and called the police station. The young man said Flavo's grandson has drowned."

Homer hitched up his britches, shifting the weight of the big revolver slung on his hip. "Yes'm. I'm afraid so. He and some of his friends were swimming underneath the bridge late this afternoon, and he just went under. Got the cramps, I reckon."

She looked down the incline where the riverbank sloped from the levee to the edge of the water. The spotlight danced on the river, and out in the middle she could see in its reflected light the Rescue Squad boat with four men in it. There was a man at either end, tossing grappling hooks out into the water, pulling them slowly back with the ropes. A third was sitting midway, manning the oars, keeping the boat turned into the current. The fourth was hunkered just behind him, wearing a rubber suit that made him look like a seal, slick and shiny. He had a diving mask perched on the top of his head and an oxygen tank on his back. The river was black and sluggish, eddying around the edges of the boat and the ropes that stretched out into the water. The boat was working its way slowly downstream toward the bridge. It seemed a pitifully small effort, sad and defeated here in the soft dark of early morning.

"Is Flavo here?"

Homer pointed down toward the darkened edge of the riverbank below the bridge. "Down yonder, Miz Bright. Flavo and the boy's mama and daddy."

"Take me," she said.

"Miz Bright," he protested, "it's a right steep path down there. I'd hate for you to twist an ankle or something. How 'bout I just go get Flavo."

"No," she insisted. "I'll go to him."

She held out her hand to Homer and he shrugged and took it, pulling a huge flashlight from its holster in his belt and training the beam on the edge of the sidewalk where the dirt path dropped off toward the riverbank. "Let's just take it real slow and easy now," he said, and they headed down, Homer keeping a good grip on her arm as she picked her way, stepping carefully along the rutted path.

"You've been here all night?" she asked as they went.

< 174 >

"Yes'm. Since about eight o'clock, when we got the first report. I think it happened about six or so. The rest of the young'uns run home after it happened, scared to death, I reckon. One of 'em finally told his mama and she called us. We'd have waited until morning to start dragging, except it's Flavo's grandson."

"It's a bad place for boys to be swimming," she said.

"Yes'm." Homer nodded. "We chase 'em off when we catch 'em down there, but it's hard to keep a lookout all the time."

She could see now, as her eyes began to adjust to the darkness, a small knot of people huddled on the bank near the water's edge, faintly visible from the reflected light off the water. Dear Flavo, she thought. Flavo, the silent, invisible child who had suddenly presented himself in her consciousness on a brisk March day when he had stood beside Ollie Doubleday's aeroplane and said, "How 'bout me?" Flavo, the young man who had come in a rowboat to rescue Bright and Little Fitz from this very river, from the Great Flood. Flavo, the ally of her adulthood. He was, she thought, the one constant of her life, the one person who spanned its entire course. All the others had come late or left early.

He heard their footsteps in the trampled weeds and turned to peer at them in the dim light. "Flavo," she called out to him softly as they drew near. Homer released her arm and stood back, letting her go on alone.

"Bright?"

"Yes, it's me." She went to him and put her arms around him, feeling the stares of the others, black and white. He was strangely unyielding and she wondered for a brief instant if she had offended him in some way. She drew back, still clutching his arms, and even in the near-darkness she could see the dull yellow pain in his eyes, and something else, something smoldering. Rage. It startled her. Grief, dignity in the face of grief—all that she could understand. "I'm sorry," she said. "I'd give anything in the world if I could undo it."

He seemed to rise up, the smoldering thing flaring in him. "What are you doing here?" he asked. His voice was cold and hard and she flushed, embarrassed.

"I came because it was the right thing to do," she said simply.

He stared at her for a moment and then turned his head away and looked out over the river. "He was just a little boy."

"Yes. I know."

She wanted to reach out again, touch his arm, but his anger was an unyielding thing between them. *There is something else here. Something besides the mere fact of death.*

She held back, baffled and a bit hurt, unsure of what to say or do.

< 175 >

They stood apart there on the riverbank, watching the small boat work its way methodically downstream toward the bridge, the men at bow and stern tossing out the grappling hooks with a muffled splash, hauling in the ropes hand over hand, pulling them free from the dark water, repeating the process. Once, the man in the stern rose up, tugged hard on the line. "Here!" he called, and one of the other men helped him pull while the spotlight from up on the bridge trained its round white beam on the water. But it was only a snag, a rotting piece of limb.

Flavo seemed to pay no attention to her, made no move to introduce her to the others nearby, a man and several young women. Relatives or friends, no doubt, possibly the boy's parents. Bright thought for a moment to go over to them, but there was something in the way they formed a tight knot that seemed to exclude everyone else, even Flavo. Bright realized that she didn't know a great deal about Flavo's family. There were children; his wife had died a few years ago. Beyond that, nothing. Strange to have known this man for more than sixty years and know that little about the essentials of his life. Had it been a friendship? Or transactions?

After a moment, Homer Sipsey stepped up to her. "Miz Bright, you want to go up now?" He could sense the awkwardness.

"No," she said, patting his hand. "But you go on back up to the bridge if you need to. I'll be fine down here."

Homer shrugged. "Nothing to do up there, I reckon. I'll just wait until you're ready."

She waited awhile longer, and then she stepped across the breach to Flavo Richardson and took him by the upper arm. "Flavo, what is it?"

He turned to her then, stung her again with the raw hostility that flashed in his eyes. She flinched.

"Ask me"—he bit off the words—"ask me why those boys were swimming here in the river underneath the bridge when we've got a perfectly good swimming pool across town."

"All right. Why?"

"Because they can't get in."

"What do you mean, Flavo? The swimming pool is integrated. I read about it in the paper."

"Hah! Some judge said five years ago they couldn't keep black young'uns out of the swimming pool. So do you know what the town council did, Bright? They made a rule that young'uns can't go to the pool unless they have a season ticket. You know what a season ticket costs? Fifty dollars." His voice was rising now, full of fury. "How many black young'uns got fifty dollars unless they steal it? So they come

< 176 >

down here and swim. And you see," he cried out, his arm sweeping the river, "what that gets 'em."

"But you . . ."

"Yes. I'm on the council," he said bitterly.

He blames himself! That's it! He blames the rest of us, but he also blames himself!

Bright could see the terrible pain in his face, the weight of damning accusation. And then he turned away from her again with a jerk, leaving her alone and wretched on the riverbank. Bright felt the crushing, desperate weight of the old despair, the old misery. All those years of looking into people's eyes—black and white—and seeing the hard cussedness there, the back-bowed stubbornness, and then trying to prod them gently past it. All that and still, obviously, so much undone. She wanted to take Flavo Richardson by the shoulders, shake him hard, tell him she understood. But this was not the time or place. She could not reach him. Perhaps she should just go home, try again when the hot flames of his grief and fury had eased a bit.

Just then she heard a muffled shout from the river and the banging of the oars against the wooden sides of the boat. "I got something," a voice called. "Over here." The boat was nearly to the bridge now and the narrow round beam of the spotlight shone almost straight down. It flashed across the water to where the rope from one of the grappling hooks disappeared, straining tautly against the surface of the river. The man on the other end tugged on it. "Feels like this might be it." And then the man wearing the rubber suit rose up a bit, pulled the mask down over his eyes and stuck the mouthpiece from the oxygen tank in his mouth, slipped over the side with a quiet splash. He bobbed in the water for a moment, only his head showing on the other side of the boat. Then he began to ease himself across the river, holding on to the rope, a stark figure bathed in the white beam of the light. Flavo and Bright and Homer Sipsey and the others moved a few steps closer to the bank, peering out across the river, watching silently. The diver reached the point where the rope disappeared under the water, and then he gave a flip of his body and went under, roiling the surface. He stayed down for a long time, and all they could see in the beam of light was an occasional rush of bubbles from his air tank. Then something broke the water and they stared at it and saw that it was a hand, a small brown hand, and Bright's heart leapt into her throat. "Oh, God!" one of the young women screamed. And then the diver came up with a rush, clutching the limp body around the waist, straining to stay above water as the men in the boat rowed quickly to him, reached out and pulled the dead boy over the side. They handled him gently, sadly, in

< 177 >

the stark light, and Bright thought to herself, *These are not mean people here. They do not hate, especially now at a moment like this. Surely that terrible part of it has passed. But maybe when the memory of grief has passed, they don't love quite enough. Or understand.*

The men in the rowboat and the others up on the bridge called back and forth to each other now, their voices bouncing hollowly off the water and the underside of the bridge.

". . . come on with the stretcher . . ."

". . . body bag?"

"Naw, we'll just cover him with a sheet."

"Be right down."

". . . some coffee for Hobart. Water's still a little cold this time a' year."

"I'll bring the thermos."

Then the voices stopped and the night was still and quiet now except for the muffled bumping about in the rowboat out in the river as they headed for the bank with the dead boy, and the soft moans of the women in the group onshore. The air felt chill now, and Bright shivered, holding her arms close. And then she thought suddenly of Jimbo, sprawled in sleep in the spare bedroom, vulnerable in the way a little black boy was vulnerable in the dark waters of a river. What if fire broke out, or an intruder. . . . She felt panic rise in her, an old beast with hot yellow eyes that danced with the reflection of the still and bleeding form of Dorsey Bascombe, sprawled across the steps of the camp house, a beast that snarled, *Something will be taken from you . . .*

She turned to Homer Sipsey, who had moved now to the edge of the riverbank, watching as the rowboat neared. "Homer?"

He turned to her. "Yes'm."

"Help me back up now."

"Just be a minute, Miz Bright. Let me give the boys a hand here . . ."

"No," she said, her voice rising. "I need to go *now.*" She did not want to be there when the boat reached the shore, when they lifted him out and covered him with the sheet. She wanted to flee back to the comfort of her home and bed. It was too sad here, too confusing. She was not ready for any of this, especially the pain of Flavo's harsh anger.

Homer heard the panic in her voice, and he turned abruptly and peered at her in the dim light, then shrugged and started toward her. "Sure, Miz Bright. The boys can handle things, I reckon." He took her arm gently and they started up the narrow path, the beam of his flashlight darting in front of them.

< 178 >

"Roseann's boy Jimbo is staying with me this week," she explained. "He's there in the house by himself. I shouldn't have left him."

"No problem, Miz Bright. I'll drive you home myself." He took his time, steadying her with a firm hand as they climbed. She was quite winded when they reached the bridge and they stopped for a moment while she caught her breath. Then Homer helped her into the squad car, turned off the flashing blue light on top, and then eased off down Claxton, away from the bridge. She peered ahead, past the soft amber glow of the streetlights along Claxton, but she could barely see her house under the shadows of the pecan trees in the front yard. At least she could see no angry flash of flame.

She looked over at Homer, saw in the dim light from the dashboard how very tired he looked, the lines in his face deepened by fatigue. He was no longer young, probably in his late forties, unlikely to ever become the police chief of a larger town, certainly too old to be running up and down the road in a highway patrol car. Homer, she thought, was a man at people's beck and call, at least those upon whose goodwill his job depended, those above him in the pecking order. She wondered where in the pecking order of things Homer Sipsey put her.

"I'm sorry to put you to this trouble," she said after a moment.

"No trouble, Miz Bright. No sense you having to walk home alone this time of night. Things ain't as safe as they used to be." He fished a cigarette out of the pack in his shirt pocket, stuck it in his mouth, then punched in the cigarette lighter on the dashboard. "Two nights ago, somebody broke in Folmar's Drug Store. They cut a hole in the roof, of all things. Lowered themselves down by a rope and got in the pharmacy. They took a bunch of drugs, stuff like Demerol and Valium and so forth. I said to myself, 'Homer, things has changed around here. When you got hopheads breaking in Folmar's Drug Store, things has changed.'" The lighter popped out and Homer lit his cigarette, inhaling noisily and then blowing a stream of smoke out his window, away from her. "Then too, Miz Bright," he went on, "you got all that money now. You got to be more careful."

"All that what?"

He glanced over at her. "All that money you won at the Dixie Vittles last evening. Fifty thousand, I hear it was."

"Good Lord," she said softly. "I had forgotten."

Homer laughed. "I don't see how anybody could forget fifty thousand dollars. That's more money than anybody around here will ever see at one time. I want to be there to see a check with 'fifty thousand dollars' printed on it."

"Well, I suppose I do too."

< 179 >

"You want to be careful, now."

"About what?"

"Flimflams. All sorts of folks out there with schemes to take folks' money. Especially old folks."

She started to say that she wasn't old, but she stopped herself. That wasn't true. Not anymore. Bright clutched her purse, thinking about the fifty thousand dollars lying in somebody's bank with her name already on it. As they turned into her driveway, she said absently, "I hope I'd know a scheme when I saw it."

"Well, Miz Bright," Homer said, easing the car to a stop in front of the steps, "folks sometimes don't think straight when they get to thinking about money."

"They make fools of themselves," Bright said.

"Yes'm. I reckon that's the whole of it."

He got out of the car and came around to the passenger side and opened the door for her and put his arm under her elbow to help her out.

"Thank you, Homer," she said, giving him her hand. "I'm really very grateful. I shouldn't have left Jimbo alone here in the middle of the night. But I'm glad I went."

"Yes'm."

"Flavo Richardson is as good a man as there is in this town," she said.

"He's a fine man, yes ma'am. Good councilman."

"It's still a good town, Homer. Despite folks breaking in Folmar's Drug Store."

"I wouldn't want to be anywhere else," he said. She could tell he wanted to go now. He still had business at the bridge, things to be done before he could go home and get some sleep.

"We need to find a way to keep little black children from swimming in the river," she said.

"Well, I've tried everything I know." There was a little edge in his voice. "I guess me and the boys have run 'em off a dozen times since the weather got warm."

She touched his arm. "I'm sure you're doing all you can," she said. "We'll think of something. We've always worked things out here, one way or the other."

"Can I help you up the steps?"

"No. I can manage fine. You go on back now. Thank you again."

He touched the edge of his cap. "Glad to help, Miz Bright. You take care of yourself, now. Be careful about that money. You ever got a question about anybody, you just call me. I'll be right over."

< 180 >

He waited by the car until she got up the steps and in the door, and then she gave him a little wave to let him know she was all right. He got in the car and backed out of the driveway, then turned the corner onto Claxton and headed back toward the bridge. She watched him for a moment, then went to the spare bedroom and looked in on Jimbo. He seemed not to have moved an inch—arm thrown over the side of the bed, mouth slightly open, deep in the cave of sleep that only a small child could inhabit.

Bright got undressed and lay in bed for a while, thinking back over the night, and when she got to the part where she was talking with Homer Sipsey in the patrol car in her driveway, she remembered saying "we." "*We'll* think of something," she had said. How strange, she thought, perhaps her strangest utterance on a strange night. It was something Dorsey Bascombe might have said. But not Bright Birdsong, who had not thought of this town in terms of "we" for a very long time. What was she getting at? And what would Dorsey do if he were here? What would he have said to grieving, angry Flavo Richardson on the riverbank in the dead of night? He knew a lot about loss, but he hadn't been so successful at getting beyond loss. Perhaps Dorsey would not have had any answers at all. Maybe just now, if he saw and heard from wherever he was, he would say, *Work it out for yourselves. I'm not interested anymore.*

She was thinking about Dorsey, remembering the tall leather boots that filled the opening of the cave underneath his desk at the lumberyard as she hunkered, waiting for a piece of candy, when she finally drifted off to sleep again.

< 181 >

11

She dreamed that Little Fitz was calling, but she could not get to the telephone. She knew it was Fitz, knew somehow by the way the telephone rang. But she was immobilized by something — dread? laziness? Whatever it was, she gave in to it finally and drifted away and then the ringing stopped.

But a moment later: "Mama Bright . . ."

She opened one eye, saw Jimbo standing over the bed. He had a book in one hand, held open with his thumb. It was late, she could tell that by the light in the room. Much later than she ever slept. She had missed the early sun. She felt rotten.

"Uncle Fitz is on the phone," Jimbo said.

"What?"

"Uncle Fitz. He says he's talking on the telephone from his limousine. That's neat, huh?"

"Neat," Bright said groggily. "Good Lord."

"He says he wants to talk to Old Lazybones. I told him you were still in bed."

Bright threw back the sheet and eased her legs over the side of the bed, tucking her nightgown around her, then searched with her feet on the rug until she found her house shoes. Jimbo turned and left and she heard the screen door to the front porch slam behind him. She stood, wobbling a moment, holding on to the bedpost until she gained her balance. Her head hurt and she struggled against a shroud of sleep that clung to her like cobwebs. She shuffled to the parlor, sat down in the chair by the telephone table, picked up the receiver.

"Hello, Fitz."

"You been out cattin' again, Mama?" Fitz laughed, his lovely honey laugh. Fitz enveloped you with his laugh, made your toes tingle, made you feel that you were standing with him in the middle of a wide green field with the sun warm on your face, just the two of you sharing

< 182 >

a deliciously special moment. He was a tall man, like his grandfather Dorsey Bascombe, and gentle like his father. When Little Fitz Birdsong laughed, people wanted to give him their firstborn.

She could hear music in the background. Country music, some guitars and a whiny-voiced woman. She had raised Fitz Birdsong on Chopin and Schumann (not that he had any musical talent himself) and now he listened to country music while he tooled around in his limousine. "Where are you?" she asked.

"In my limousine," he said.

"Jimbo told me that. But where?"

"We're just riding around, looking at the morning. Me and Corporal Dodson. Soon to be Sergeant Dodson. He's gettin' a promotion next week. It don't look good for the governor to be driven around by a corporal. Oughta be at least a sergeant, don't you think, Dodson? Here, Dodson, say hello to my mama."

The telephone rustled as it was passed from hand to hand, and then a young voice said, "Morning, Miz Birdsong."

"That's Dodson," Fitz said, taking the receiver back. "He's been learning to drive stately. Dodson used to race cars on the dirt tracks, and he likes to scratch off at the traffic lights. But you do that in a brand-new Lincoln Continental limousine, and you'll tear the transmission right out of the sucker." He laughed again, filling the car with it, making the telephone line hum.

"Is your limousine the only place you've got a telephone?" Bright asked.

That sobered him. She could picture him in the broad rear seat of the limousine, his face suddenly somber. He had always been eager to please, quick to accommodate. He floated like a winged seed on a spring breeze, looking for just the right place to light.

"I tried once and the line was busy," he said.

"Once," she said. "Do you realize it's Tuesday morning?"

"I been up to my ying-yang in alligators up here," he said quietly.

Bright shifted in her chair, put the telephone receiver in her left hand, kneaded her temple with the right. "So I've heard. And read."

"Actually," he went on, "I've sort of been out of pocket."

"What do you mean?"

"Well, I've been staying up at our place on the lake. Lavonia ain't very happy with me right now, and I'm just trying to stay clear until things die down a little."

"Hmmmmm."

"But I got up this morning and told Dodson, 'Dodson,' I said, 'it's time to hitch up our britches and get this thing took care of.'"

< 183 >

Took care of. Fitz Birdsong was a college graduate, more than that a middling lawyer and somewhat literate man. But he had worked so long and hard at being one of the boys that *took care of* came naturally to him.

"So," he went on, "I put on my best blue pinstripe suit and a baby blue oxford cloth button-down shirt and a nice red tie and me and Dodson got in the limo and headed for town. When I get to the Capitol, I'm gonna call me a press conference and tell 'em Fitz Birdsong is back. And then I'm gonna go over to the mansion and tell Lavonia to get her fanny off her shoulder and let's get on with things. Ain't that right, Dodson?"

She heard a muffled reply from the front seat of the car, then a brief silence. "Well," he said after a moment. "Enough about me. I hear you've been right busy yourself."

"What do you mean?"

"Big Deal O'Neill called this morning and said you won fifteen thousand dollars at the Dixie Vittles."

"No, as a matter of fact it was fifty thousand." She felt a throbbing at her temples. She didn't want to think about the money, didn't want to talk about it.

"Whewwwww." Fitz gave a long whistle. "I thought Big Deal said *fifteen.* I'm surprised you aren't off to Acapulco with all that money."

"Why would I want to go to Acapulco?"

"Well," Fitz said, "with that kind of money, I reckon you could go just about anyplace you wanted."

"I'm not going anywhere. I've got Jimbo here with me."

"Yeah. He told me that Roseann and what's his name have gone to the beach."

"Rupert. His name is Rupert."

"I've only met him once," Fitz said. "At the wedding. I invited 'em to a big do at the mansion a few months ago, but I never heard from 'em. Jimbo told me Rupert can't swim."

Bright pictured Roseann and Rupert on the beach this morning, Rupert's pale knees showing between the bottom of his Bermuda shorts and the top of his long black socks, Roseann huddled under a striped umbrella with a can of diet soda pop and a romance novel, glowering behind her sunglasses. *She has a lot of energy,* Rupert had said.

"You should get to know Rupert," Bright said. "I think you'd like him. He's very good with refrigerators."

"What?"

"My refrigerator broke yesterday while they were here. Rupert put a new motor on it."

< 184 >

"Next time the refrigerator at the mansion breaks, I'll tell Lavonia to call Rupert."

"Don't be sarcastic, Fitz."

"You're right," he said. "I need to get to know the man. I can't imagine anybody who'd put up with Roseann. Does he get combat pay?"

"Fitz, that'll do," she snapped.

"Sorry, Mama."

"We're talking in circles here," she said, exasperated. It was like him, talking all around the edges of something. She supposed it was part of what made him a good politician. His father had had the same talent. What you had to do with a politician was tie him down and make him get to the point. "Get to the point, Fitz," she said now.

"Ah, yes," he sighed. "The point. Well, I'm in a peck of trouble, Mama. That's the point."

"I guessed as much," she said.

Fitz took a deep breath. She could hear it through the phone, a great whoosh of air passing over the mouthpiece. "I need the money," he said.

"What money?"

"That fifty thousand dollars you won at the Dixie Vittles. Just a loan. I'll pay you back as soon as the campaign's over. I'm having a little cash flow problem right now, and I need to buy some TV time right away. It's the only way I can lick this thing, Mama." He was talking rapidly now, his voice urgent and insistent. "We're gonna vote a week from today and I've got to get on TV and talk to the folks."

"What are you going to say?" she asked.

"I'll think of something," he said.

"You and Doyle Butterworth will think of something," she said.

"Yes. That's right. We'll try to save Little Fitz Birdsong's political hide," he said.

"Well, I don't have the money."

"What do you mean, you don't have it?"

"It just happened last night, Fitz. They haven't given me the money yet."

"When are they going to give you the money?"

"I don't know. Look, we'll talk about this when you get here Thursday."

"Thursday."

"Are you still going through with it?"

"Oh. You mean Fitz Birdsong Day. Yeah, I guess we are. Big Deal says it's all set up. The parade and a luncheon at the high school. I

< 185 >

want you to ride in the parade with me. We'll get Dodson to drive. How 'bout that, Dodson?" Another muffled reply from up front. "Hold up here, Dodson. Mama, we're turning in the driveway at the Capitol now, and there's a whole gaggle of press folks up there by the steps waiting for me. Somebody musta told 'em I was coming. Damn, you can't keep nothing to yourself these days."

"Well, you go take care of your business," Bright said. "There's just this one thing —"

"Mama," he interrupted her, "will you help me?"

"Fitz, I just can't think about it right now. I can't think about anything right now." She stopped, remembering the riverbank in the dead of night, the small brown hand breaking free of the dark water . . .

"Flavo Richardson's grandson drowned last night," she said.

There was a long silence on the other end. "My God," Fitz said softly. "I'm sorry. I didn't know. How did it happen?"

"Swimming in the river. Underneath the bridge."

"I'll call him as soon as I get rid of these press hyenas." Bright could hear shouts now, and she imagined the pack of reporters surrounding Fitz's limousine, cameras and microphones bearing down on him.

"Yes," she said. "You call him. Don't wait as long to call Flavo Richardson as you did to call me."

"I won't, Mama. I promise." He would call, she was sure of that. Little Fitz Birdsong, whatever his shortcomings, was a man who was loyal to a fault. He had gotten that from his father. "Mama . . ." The shouts were getting louder now. She could hear a banging noise. Somebody beating on the top of the car?

"Yes."

"Don't judge me," he said.

"It's not my place," she said gently. "I'm your mama."

"Will you still vote for me?" he asked, and she could hear the lift in his voice — girding himself, getting ready to step out of the limousine with that big warm grin on his face.

"Of course I'll vote for you," she said.

"I love you, Mama."

"I love you too, Fitz." She hung fire for a moment. "Fitz . . ."

"Yes, Mama."

"Think about what your father would do at a time like this."

She thought for a moment that she had lost the connection. There was nothing but silence on the other end. Then she heard the shouts of the reporters again. And finally he said, "Mama, for one thing, Papa never would have gotten himself in this kind of fix. And

< 186 >

for another . . ." He paused again and then his voice went hard and flat. "Papa never took the time to teach me a damn thing." And he hung up.

She sat staring at the telephone, hearing the bitter echo of his voice, then placed the receiver gently into its cradle and gave a great sigh. *Ah, the old poison, the old hurt and disappointment. He never truly got over it, did he. And now, in a moment when his guard is down, when he is painfully vulnerable and probably a bit sick of himself, it all bubbles to the surface again like foul-smelling gas from the bottom of a pond.*

A sudden flash of memory now — a photograph from a newspaper. The early fifties: Little Fitz, a sophomore in college, eating a goldfish. He was standing on the sidewalk in front of his fraternity house, head thrown back, holding the small fish over his open mouth. There was a big crowd in the background, boys and girls, most of them holding paper cups. The caption under the picture said the fraternity boys were reviving some of the college high jinks of the Roaring Twenties. Fitz looked very pleased with himself.

Bright remembered it now with a flash of anger, the photograph and what she had done. She got in the car and drove straight to the University. Then she marched in the door of the fraternity house with the newspaper in her hand, past a gawking rabble of young louts sprawled about the living room, and up the stairs before they could utter a protest. She searched the second floor, sending half-dressed boys scurrying, until she found his room. Fitz was asleep, his face against the wall. It was midafternoon. The window was open, and outside on the lawn of the fraternity house she could hear the shouts of a football game in progress.

"High jinks from the Roaring Twenties," she said. "Tommyrot!"

He woke with a jerk at the sound of her voice, but he didn't turn over. She heard a muffled "Oh damn."

"Look at me," she commanded.

"I'd rather not," he said.

"Turn over, or I'll pick you up and throw you out the window."

He turned toward her then and stared with sleep-bleared eyes. She unfolded the newspaper and tapped the picture with her finger. "I didn't send you here to make a spectacle of yourself," she said. "If you're so fond of fish, I'll sign you up for the Navy."

He sat up in the bed and rubbed his hand across his puffy face. "I love you, Mama, you know that."

"I love you too, Fitz. I wish that were enough to keep you from acting the fool."

"I won't let it happen again," he said.

< 187 >

"That's right, you won't. Pack up, buster, we're going home."

Actually, she had saved him from academic ruin. At midsemester, his grades were teetering on the precipice of abject failure. Bright withdrew him from school and handed him over to Monkey Deloach, who now owned Dorsey Bascombe's sawmill and timber business. Monkey, in turn, put Fitz to work in the woods.

In the meantime, Bright wrote straightaway to Fitzhugh, telling him what she had done. He called immediately. Yes, that was exactly the right thing. Get the boy straightened out before he ruined himself. She had handled things, just like she always did.

But she sensed, even as she handled things, that she was dealing with something much deeper than goldfish eating. Little Fitz Birdsong didn't want to be Little Fitz at all. He was trying in perhaps the only way he knew to distance himself from his father the now-famous congressman. Some of that was the independence of youth. Some of it was deep resentment over the long absences, the moments missed, the experiences unshared. But what was done was done and probably irreparable. So the only way she knew to deal with it was to have Monkey put him in the woods and let him take out his anger on trees, test himself, do battle with the beast that ate at his gut until he either won or fell exhausted from the combat. Her instinct proved correct, at least in the short run. After five months of the hardest labor Fitz had ever known, he left the woods lean and fit and more sure of himself, the beast held at bay. He returned to the University in the fall, moved out of the fraternity house, eventually graduated with respectable grades, good enough to get into law school. She and Little Fitz had never really talked about it in so many words. He had emerged from the experience no longer a boy, but a young man who kept his own counsel. And as for discussing it with Fitzhugh, the whole business of who was responsible in the larger sense had by that time left them long ago defeated and exhausted.

Now, sitting here beside the telephone with Fitz's sudden, bitter words echoing about in her mind, the question of responsibility came back like an old ghost. Unfinished business. Who had been responsible then, and who now?

When you married and had children, you assumed a responsibility to put them above all else, care for them, pick up after them, guide them as best you could. Bright Birdsong had done that with a firm hand, and she suspected that she had often erred on the side of firmness. With Fitzhugh simply not there much of the time, it had been the only thing to do. But then part of responsibility is knowing when to let go and let people become responsible for themselves. She had done that too as best she knew how. So now, in the quiet of her late

< 188 >

life, she said to herself over and over, *I did what I had to do. I did the best I could.*

But now, in the space of twenty-four hours, all that had been thrown out of kilter and she was forced to confront the possibility that what she had done for Fitzhugh and Roseann had not been enough, or not right. If there was any blame, she was willing to share it. But if there was any present responsibility, it was hers alone. *Fitzhugh, damn your hide, you have left me here again to face the music. And this time I don't even know the name of the tune.*

She sat for a moment, trying to gather her wits and calm herself, rubbing her temples with her fingers and staring blankly out the front window at the bright green of the pecan trees and Claxton Avenue beyond, not really seeing any of it. *All right,* she said to herself finally, *there is not much you can do about Roseann or Fitz right this minute. But there is something else you can do. You can go to Flavo Richardson. It may be a faint attempt at sanity.* She took a deep breath. *So hitch up your britches and get on with it.*

She stood resolutely, glancing at the clock on the mantel. Nine o'clock, the morning half gone. Then she heard voices on the front porch and stepped to the door to see Jimbo and Buster Putnam sitting in the two wicker chairs. Jimbo had put his book down on the table between them and was giving Buster all his attention. Buster was talking animatedly, gesturing with his hands, and she heard the word "Inchon." That had been in Korea, hadn't it? She remembered reading about it, a great victory for the Americans, an amphibious landing behind the enemy lines. General Douglas MacArthur had been the brilliant strategist behind Inchon. And Buster Putnam's Marines had done the work. Little Buster Putnam, who had escaped death from a falling tree because he got up in the middle of the night to go pee.

Buster looked up now, saw her at the door, stopped in midsentence. "Good morning," he said. "Aren't we the late riser today."

"Humph," she said, opening the screen door and stepping onto the porch. The sun was full-bore on the morning and it was already getting hot. A big white truck was parked across the street in front of the Dixie Vittles with its air-conditioning unit throbbing, keeping meat and vegetables cool in the rear. Through the big plate glass window of the store, Bright could see what appeared to be the driver leaning against the counter, talking with Doris Hawkins. She wondered if they were talking about the fifty thousand dollars. Probably.

"And what are you doing out of bed before noon?" she asked Buster.

< 189 >

He raised his hands in surrender. "Hey, I came to make peace, lady. Since you got rich, I figured I'd better get on your good side."

"Hah! Rich! Fifty thousand dollars doesn't make anybody rich. If I gave it to you, would you fix up your house?"

Buster shook his head. "Nope. I'd buy new pickup trucks for all the boys out at the Spot. Even the sonofabitch that calls me General Patton."

"Buster!" she warned him.

"Excuse me. Old Marine Corps habit." He glanced over at Jimbo, who was staring raptly up at him. "Here," Buster said to Jimbo. "Get up and offer the lady a chair."

Jimbo got up, taking his book with him, and perched on the porch banister. Bright sat, gathering her robe around her, and gave Buster a close inspection. He looked as if he had been out most of the night. He had a rough stubble of beard on his face and a faintly rank smell about him. He was clad in the same pair of faded brown pants and plaid shirt he had been wearing yesterday when she had taken him to the hospital.

Buster let her appraise him for a moment and then he asked Jimbo, "What are you reading there?"

He looked down at the book, then held it up for them to see. On the cover was a picture of a large green thing with flaming red eyes reared up on its hind feet, a rocket blasting off in the background. "*The Gargoyle of the Asteroids*," Jimbo said.

"What on earth is a gargoyle of the asteroids?"

"It's not anything on earth. It's a space monster."

"Oh," Buster said. "Of course. Any Marines in there?"

"No sir. But there's Captain Zartor. He tricked the Gargoyle."

"And how did he do that?"

Jimbo scrunched up his face earnestly. "Well, the Gargoyle is real smart. He can tap into giant computers and absorb all of the information in them. But that's how Captain Zartor defeated him. He tricked the Gargoyle into absorbing some phony information, and he programmed himself to blast off into hyperspace."

"If Captain Zartor is that canny, he must be a Marine," Buster said.

"I don't think so. But he's the leader of the Intergalactic Space Patrol."

"Sort of like Buck Rogers," Buster said.

"Who's Buck Rogers?" Jimbo asked.

"Good Lord." Buster snorted. "And I'll bet you've never heard of Tom Swift, either."

< 190 >

"No sir."

Buster turned to Bright. "See, I told you. The boy needs overalls."

"What do overalls have to do with Buck Rogers and Tom Swift?" she asked.

"It's all a matter of cultural development. A boy without overalls runs the risk of missing the best part of being a boy," Buster said. "There are lots of places you'd go wearing overalls that you wouldn't go dressed in" — he gave a wave at Jimbo's khaki pants and knit shirt— "fancy duds."

Jimbo looked down at himself. "These aren't fancy."

"Compared to overalls they are."

"Well, then," Bright said, exasperated, "for goodness' sake go buy the boy some overalls."

"Me?"

"Yes, you. It's your idea."

Buster thought about it for a moment, then slapped his knee and stood up. "Fine. Right now. Let's go do it."

"After Jimbo's had breakfast," Bright said.

"I've already had breakfast."

"Oh? What?"

"Cereal. I found some in the cabinet. Grape-Nuts Flakes. And milk in the refrigerator."

"Good Lord," she said. "That's no breakfast for a growing boy. Milk and cereal is what old ladies eat."

"It's what I have all the time. Mama lets me get up and fix breakfast before I go to school."

"Well, I'm not your mama and you're not in school. But I suppose Grape-Nuts Flakes will do just this once. Tomorrow, you get grits and eggs."

"I don't like grits and eggs," he said.

"You're a finicky child," she said bluntly. "A few mornings of grits and eggs will improve your disposition."

"And some overalls," Buster said. "You ready, Jimbo?"

"I suppose so."

"I *reckon,*" Bright corrected. "If you're going to wear overalls, say 'reckon.' Now go to the bathroom and brush your teeth and don't keep General Putnam waiting."

He scrambled down from the banister and disappeared inside.

When he had gone, Buster edged over toward the steps, leaned against the porch post for a moment. "Well, are you enjoying the limelight, Bright?"

"What do you mean?"

< 191 >

"You're quite the local celebrity this morning. All that money. It's all anybody's talking about. I was in the café for coffee and the place was buzzing. Everybody's speculating about what you'll do with it."

"Humph. What I'm going to do with it is get rid of it as fast as I can. I'm entertaining requests. I've already had one this morning."

"Siding salesman?"

"No, my son the governor."

"Ah, yes." Buster nodded. "That's the other thing they were talking about at the café. The other celebrity Birdsong. That, and the drowning. Flavo Richardson's grandson, I heard."

"Yes," she said quietly. "I was down there on the riverbank when they found him early this morning." The picture flared up in her mind again, the spotlight white-hot on the river, the small brown hand breaking the surface, dripping gems of water. And Flavo's anguished rage. "I've got to go see Flavo," she said. "He thinks it's my fault."

Buster's eyes widened. "Yours? Why the hell does he think it's your fault?"

"Mine, yours, everybody else's. He says the reason they were swimming in the river was because they couldn't get in the city pool. Everybody has to have a season ticket." It sounded so mundane, so trivial in the face of a death. People didn't die because of season tickets. That would be too stupid.

Buster crossed his arms over his chest and looked down at his feet for a moment. "So, what are you going to do about it?"

"I'm going to go talk to Flavo. Beyond that, I can't imagine what I *could* do."

"Hmmmmm," Buster said, twisting his mouth to the side.

"What does that mean? Hmmmmm."

"Oh, nothing. Just thinking that things have gotten awfully unquiet over here all of a sudden. Sort of hard to vegetate with all that going on, isn't it."

"Vegetate?" she said hotly, irritation dancing up the back of her neck like prickly heat. "Look, Buster, you just mind your own business."

"Well," he said mildly, "you're pretty quick to talk about me going to seed next door, Bright."

"Just look at yourself," she shot back.

Buster looked down at himself, gave her a crooked grin. "Dressed for combat, Bright. Doing battle with my devils. Just like you."

"I don't have any devils," she said. She glared up at him, getting ready to spear him with another retort, when Jimbo came through the screen door. His hair was neatly combed, his knit shirt tucked into his

< 192 >

pants, the laces on his shoes tied with an equal length of bow on either side. He still had his book in his hand. Bright felt a pang. There was something almost sad about him, so scrubbed and buttoned-down, even with his mother not there to tuck and fix and fuss. So quiet and cautious and unboy. What had Roseann done to him? *And what did I do to Roseann?*

"I think you can leave that here," Bright said gently, reaching for the book. "You can't read and try on overalls at the same time." Jimbo reluctantly handed her the book and she put it down on the table next to her. He seemed almost naked without it, unsure of what to do with his hands. He jammed them finally into his pockets.

"We'll probably stop somewhere and get a hamburger when we're finished," Buster said, putting his hand on Jimbo's shoulder. "Take your time at Flavo's."

Bright stared at him, felt herself soften. "Thank you, Buster."

He gave her a little salute, a flip of the hand at his forehead, and then he and Jimbo walked down the steps together and across the yard to the old green pickup truck parked in his driveway. Bright sat for a moment longer and watched them back out of the driveway into Claxton and ease off toward the downtown business district with a clashing of gears and a growl of ancient engine. And she thought, as she watched them go, *Yes, he's right. It has become decidedly unquiet over here.* And then she wondered to herself, *Will it become quiet again? And how will I act if it doesn't?*

< 193 >

12

They had gone together to Harley Gibbons thirteen years before, she and Flavo, to integrate the high school. It was near the end of the school year in 1966, and the newspapers were full of the fire and blood of the civil rights movement all across the South, the aftermath of Selma and the beginning of Black Power. Their small town had been a quiet backwater, virtually untouched except for a small group of blacks, led by Flavo Richardson, who had marched one hot morning to the county courthouse to drink from the WHITE ONLY water fountain. They had done it in a dignified, peaceful fashion and the county commissioners, in a rare fit of good judgment, had decided to pretty much ignore the gesture. Flavo and his band drank, milled about the first-floor hallway for a moment, and then left. Several days later, the WHITE ONLY sign disappeared. And that was that. White folks didn't talk much about it, hoping it would go away and leave them alone. What they didn't want was the kind of thing you saw nightly on television — chanting, surging mobs of Nigras led by white-collared preachers, bearing down on stolid-faced rows of truncheon-carrying state troopers and deputies. No, if it meant giving up the WHITE ONLY sign on the courthouse water fountain, so be it. White folks could get a drink of water at home before they went to transact their business.

The schools were a different matter. Bright's fellow members on the school board dug in their heels stubbornly.

"Sooner or later, we've got to face it," Bright said. "It's the law."

"Later," the others said. "Wait for a court order. That's what the community expects us to do."

And Bright figured for a while that that was what everybody — black and white — was waiting for.

Then Flavo Richardson came alone to her door one evening about nine o'clock.

< 194 >

They sat in the wicker chairs on the front porch in the soft, fragrant late-spring dark, watching an occasional automobile pass on what would later be named Birdsong Boulevard. Nine o'clock, and already the town was at rest. Downtown, along Bascombe Street, only the pool hall and a single service station would be open. In another hour, the service station would close. A quiet, peaceful town.

"It's time, Bright," Flavo said.

Bright sighed, wishing for a moment that they could just sit here and pass the evening, two old friends who transcended time and space. Finally she said, "You know that, and I know that, but getting the people who run this town to realize it is a different matter."

"You're one of the people who run this town," Flavo said, and there was a little bit of accusation in his voice.

Bright bristled. "Don't you pull that on me, Flavo Richardson," she said. "I've done what I could."

And she had. For thirty years, she had quietly and insistently pleaded the case of the black schools before the school board — indoor plumbing, playground equipment, better books, a blackboard for each room, lunchrooms with hot meals, the list went on and on. She had stepped on toes and raised ires and pricked consciences. And the community had borne her as graciously as it could, reminding itself that her father, Dorsey Bascombe, had worked only Negroes in his lumber operation years before and that the Bascombes had deep ties to the Negro community. On top of that, Bright was a single-minded woman, in the mold of her father. So over time, the school board reluctantly did most of what she asked. And Flavo Richardson, she decided now, need not try to burden her with guilt.

"I don't mean I'm ungrateful," Flavo said. "But I'm not here with my hat in my hand, shuffling my feet and saying 'Yazzum,' neither."

"What *are* you doing, Flavo?"

"I'm here to close a school."

She turned to him in the dark. "What?"

"I want to close Booker T. Washington."

It took a moment to sink in. She sat there, wondering how many Booker T. Washington high schools there were across the South, how many white school boards had named their local Negro high school for that one man. Booker T. Washington was fairly safe. He had educated black youngsters with their own kind and he hadn't been uppity about it. To speak of closing a Booker T. Washington said everything about a black world turning its back on its own past, throwing a deep, inbred caution to the winds, and all the upheaval that went along with that.

"They'll never do it," Bright said after a moment. "It's too much, too quick."

< 195 >

"They will if you tell them to."

"Me?"

"Yes, you. You're Dorsey Bascombe's daughter."

"No." She shook her head. "That's not enough, Flavo. Not anymore. There have been a few things I could do because of that, but not this. They've got to have a better reason."

"How about because it's right."

"It's been right for a hundred years, but that hasn't made a hill of beans."

Flavo stood up suddenly, the force of it setting the chair to rocking violently. "Then how about fear?" he snapped. "Black folks understand it. I wonder if white folks do?" He strode to the edge of the porch, bent forward with his hands on the banister, looking out across the lawn. She could see, even here in the dim light of the porch, how agitated he was. His shoulders shook.

Bright sat quietly for a moment. Then she said, "It's come to that?"

"Yes."

"I don't want to see this town torn up, Flavo."

"I know you don't. Like I said, you're Dorsey Bascombe's daughter." He fell silent and the night sounds took over — the rustling of a bird in a pecan tree on the front lawn, the singing of crickets in the grass, the rumble of a tractor-trailer up at the end of Claxton, making the turn at the stoplight and groaning up over the bridge on its way to Columbus. "Bright, there are people on both sides who have more to gain out of this by an uproar. The question is, Are we gonna let 'em? One way or the other, it's gonna get done. It's right. And it's time."

"The school board will never make a move on its own," she said.

He turned with a jerk, his eyes flashing now. "They'll move, by God, or we'll move 'em."

She considered all that it would mean — to the town, to Bright herself as keeper of a kind of legacy her father had left, to Congressman Fitzhugh Birdsong, nervous about an election year when the mere mention of civil rights set people to howling. And she decided, very quickly, before she could talk herself out of it. "No," she said, "they'll move if Harley Gibbons tells them to."

They met two days later in Bright's parlor — Harley stiff and nervous, Flavo cloaked in a kind of calm stubbornness. Bright served them iced tea and they sat for a moment staring into their glasses before Bright finally said, "Harley, I think we ought to close Booker T. Washington High School."

The color drained from Harley's angular face. He had been reluc-

< 196 >

tant to come. Now he plainly wished he had refused, as difficult as it was to say no to Bright Birdsong. Harley Gibbons was a good banker, like his father before him, a man of probity and discretion, and a middling good mayor. Not progressive in the way Dorsey Bascombe had been, but a servant who took the public trust seriously. Harley and Bright had grown up together, and long ago in high school he had been a beau of sorts. But he had never known quite what to do with her, even back then.

"You know what that means," he said quietly now.

"Yes."

"Everybody in one place." She could see his banker's mind ticking off the numbers. More than two hundred black students, all at once, plopped down in the middle of what had been for its entire history a lily-white high school. Almost half the student body in grades nine through twelve. A sea of black faces in the Wednesday assembly program, in the stands at the Friday night football games, marching in the band, using the bathrooms, eating in the lunchroom. No Little Rocks or Tuscaloosas here, one or two black students making the first bold token step. Everybody in one place. All at once. A tremor shuddered through Harley Gibbons's broad shoulders.

"Yes," Bright said. "All at once. Over and done with, at least at the high school."

"And the rest?" Harley asked, his voice faint.

"Later," Flavo said. "But not too much later."

Harley set his jaw. "The school board won't do it. They want a court order."

Bright could see the anger rising in Flavo. "No," she said quickly, shaking her head. "They aren't waiting for a court order, Harley, they're waiting for some leadership. I think you call it biting the bullet."

"It's not my place," Harley protested.

"Yes," she said firmly. "It's your place. And mine. And Flavo's. This — this town — is our place. We can make of it what we will, Harley."

Harley looked from one to the other. Flavo had himself under control now, and he said quietly, "Mayor, I want to make this as easy on everybody as possible. I'm determined to make it work from my side. It won't be easy for those little black young'uns to leave what they know. And they'll have to be on their *p*'s and *q*'s. Every time one of 'em slips up, folks will say, 'See, it didn't work.' I'm going to do everything in my power to see that they mind their business and their manners."

Harley tightened, fixed Flavo with a steely stare. "You? What makes you think I'm going to deal with you, Flavo?"

< 197 >

"Because," Flavo said gently, "you can either deal with me or you can deal with folks like Stokely Carmichael and Rap Brown." Harley blanched and Flavo leaned forward, boring in on him. "We got a young firebrand minister up there in the Quarter, name of Whitelaw Pinckney. Came last month. You ain't heard much about him, I imagine, because he's gathering hisself. 'Scuse the expression, Bright, but the young man is full of piss and vinegar and he'd like nothing better than to make a name for hisself right here. He's got *friends*" — he drew out the word—"who'd like nothing better than to come here and help him do it."

Bright could see the pictures parading across Harley's mind, the black and white of the six o'clock news. The nice little towns of the South with their quiet tree-lined streets and gracious courthouse squares never looked as attractive in the black and white of television.

"Now," Flavo continued, "if we was to do something like Bright here just suggested, don't you reckon it would pull the rug out from under the Reverend Whitelaw Pinckney? And don't you imagine he and his friends would look for greener pastures?"

Still, Harley toughed it out. "Or," he said, "we could insist that everybody in this community abide by the law, as soon as we find out what the law is in this case."

"Who you want running this town," Flavo flashed, "Whitelaw Pinckney and the highway patrol?"

"Look here, dammit . . . ," Harley sputtered.

"Would you gentlemen like some more iced tea?" Bright asked calmly. They both stared at her as if she had suddenly grown tusks. She was buying time, searching desperately in her mind for just the right thing to say before this all fell apart right there in front of her. Then she thought of something her father had said a long time ago, something about Harley's father, Pegram Gibbons. Get a man to see the future as you see it, Dorsey Bascombe had said, and he will help you get there.

"This is a good town, Harley," she said, choosing her words carefully. "It has had the good sense to elect you mayor for a long time now because this town believes deep down in what is decent." Harley grunted. He was having nothing of flattery and smooth talk. *Make him see.* "I can see two towns from here on out, and one of them I don't even want to think about. The other is a town that other folks look at and say, 'They took care of their own business. They didn't need the governor or some judge or the National Guard or any outside agitators of one stripe or another to tell them what to do. A town with good people, a good mayor. A good town to do business in.'"

< 198 >

Bright drew out her words, let them hang there in the air, and then sat back in her chair and let everything marinate for a moment. She thought, *If we could all just go home right now and sleep on it and let good sense take its course. But we don't have time for that. We need a little luck.* She offered up a silent prayer for good sense and luck and then sat and listened to the quiet of the house, the clock on the mantel and the gentle hum of the Kelvinator back in the kitchen and Gladys bumping and banging under the house. *O Lord, just a little luck.*

It took a long time, a long spinning out of the afternoon in the quiet. But finally, Harley Gibbons breathed a great sigh and said, "I can't do it by myself."

And Bright Birdsong knew then that the Lord, once in a very great while, when things were at their trickiest, did meddle in the squalid and pitiful affairs of mankind. He must take a certain perverse pleasure in deciding just when and where. This time, he had.

"No, Harley," she said, committing herself in a way that she realized full well was fraught with danger of a very personal kind. "You won't have to."

Bright and Harley started quietly making the rounds of the people who molded opinion in the community — town council and school board members, ministers, teachers, businessmen, club women. With some, they used logic; with others, religion. With a few, they invoked the names of the Reverend Whitelaw Pinckney's friends who were itching to get their hands on a virgin town, unscathed by the civil rights uproar. Bright and Harley worked hard and fast, sunup to midnight for five days, wheedling and cajoling and pushing and shoving the white community while Flavo carried the message to his own people: make this work, or risk chaos. Several times during the enterprise, faced with stubborn resistance from a handful, Harley grew fainthearted. He was a cautious man at heart, a conservative banker, a path-of-least-resistance politician.

At one point, when O. P. Putnam smacked his hand on the counter at Putnam's Mercantile and declared his undying and violent enmity of anything resembling race mixing, Bright thought she had lost Harley. He began backing toward the door, and Bright grabbed him by the arm and held him fast while she just kept talking, scarcely knowing what she said, wearing O. P. down and finally conjuring up the image of a good number of steady black customers taking their business elsewhere. They finally extracted from O. P. a promise to leave his gun at home and stay off the school grounds. That was all.

But for every O. P. Putnam, there were a surprising number who

< 199 >

grudgingly accepted the idea, and a handful who actually welcomed it. Yes, they said. Get it over with. It's not what we agree with, but it's immutable, like crabgrass. We want no tackiness, no unseemly and unsightly milling about in the streets.

It was, Bright reminded herself, a moderate community — nothing like the fevered towns of the Southern Black Belt where white minorities hunkered behind barricades of what they perceived to be self-preservation, where Kluxers and White Citizens Council firebrands with their shotguns and torches and Rebel flags made it virtually impossible to speak with any sense of sanity. This, Bright's town, had little of that. And perhaps that was one of Dorsey Bascombe's abiding legacies. Some had called Dorsey in his prime a civic dictator, a man who ran pell-mell over dissent. And they said in their darkest mutterings that he had left it a dull town, without much character to it. But better dull than bloody. And now, faced with this business of the schools, most people seemed to come to a consensus: this is nobody's business but ours.

Bright and Harley worked all week, and then on Friday night the school board met in special session. Acting on Bright's motion, they threw everybody out except the school superintendent, closed the door, and went at it tooth and tong. Ortho Noblett, the editor of the newspaper, stood pounding on the door and yelling threats for fifteen minutes until Police Chief Homer Sipsey escorted him bodily from City Hall and locked the front door behind him.

It started mildly enough, the five members of the school board stepping softly and couching their debate in careful terms while Harley sat at the end of the table, legs crossed and one fist propped pensively under his chin, watching and keeping his own counsel. That lasted for an hour, and then the air conditioner broke and they got down to business. Going in, Bright knew she could count on two votes — hers and Harley's. As mayor, he was also the chairman of the school board, a quirk in local law that dated from Dorsey Bascombe's day. But then there were two other men and Xuripha Deloach. Xuripha, Bright thought, might well be the most difficult. Simply because she was Xuripha.

After two hours of pitched battle, one of the men, a Church of God preacher, reluctantly agreed to the idea. That was when Xuripha stood up abruptly and turned her chair over with a clatter and said, "Well, the hell with you all. You've got the votes to do it now. I'm going home."

"Sit down, Xuripha," Bright said. "Nobody's leaving until we get a unanimous vote. We've got to go out of here of a single mind, or else it won't work."

Harley Gibbons gave her a grateful look.

< 200 >

Xuripha drew herself up, nostrils flaring. "I can leave when I damn well please, Bright Birdsong. You're not the chairman of the school board."

And that was when Harley, God bless his heart, took charge. "No, you can't, Xuripha," Harley said. "The doors are locked and Homer Sipsey's got the key and he's not going to open up until I tell him to."

Xuripha glowered at him for a moment and Harley sat there unmoved, blinking back at her. And then Xuripha sat back down and they went at it for another hour, working on Xuripha and the fifth member, an insurance salesman who was O. P. Putnam's second cousin. They brought the school superintendent into it and began to talk about how it would work — squeezing all the students into the aging school buildings, organizing teachers to patrol the halls and bathrooms and keep order. Xuripha held out stubbornly, and the insurance salesman kept nodding every time she raised an objection.

Finally, near midnight, Xuripha began to wear down. They were all limp and exhausted in the heat, but they didn't dare raise a window and let the rest of the community hear the ruckus. Xuripha got up out of her chair again and began to pace back and forth at one end of the room, sweat trickling in rivulets down the side of her face, hair matted. "It's not right," she said. "And I'll tell you one thing for sure." She stopped, faced them. "Hubert and I are not going to sit in the stands at the football games and let folks from these other towns yell about us being Jigaboo High."

"Is that it?" Bright said quietly. "The football team?"

Monkey Deloach was the head of the Football Boosters' Club, and he and Xuripha were a Friday night fixture in the bleachers, twelfth row, fifty-yard line. Xuripha might not have known a tackle from a water bucket, but she took high school football, or at least the social occasion, very seriously. She had a grandson who played snare drum in the band. "Yes," she said. "That's some of it. And the band and the glee club. And clubs and such. Social activities."

"For God's sake, Xuripha," Harley started, "the glee club —"

Bright interrupted. "If we didn't integrate the football team and the band and the glee club, would that make you happy, Xuripha?"

"None of it's going to make me happy."

"But would you be less *unhappy*?"

Xuripha looked down her nose at Bright for a long moment. Finally she said, "Perhaps."

Bright looked over at Harley Gibbons. "Harley, may I use your telephone?"

His eyebrows went up. "Of course, Bright."

< 201 >

She stepped into his office next to the council room and called Flavo Richardson.

"Did I wake you?"

"I've been waiting for you to call."

"Flavo, I need a favor."

She could hear the suspicion in his voice. "What?"

"I want you to get the Booker T. Washington students to agree not to go out for the football team or the band or the glee club. Just go to school. That's all. No extracurricular activities."

"What the hell kind of high school is that?" he exploded.

"Wait a minute, before you get your bowels in an uproar. Just for the first year."

"Why?"

"Because we need a unanimous vote from the school board, and we won't get it unless we can satisfy Xuripha Deloach. And she has the football team and the band and such stuck in her craw. Sideways."

There was a long pause on the other end and she could hear a radio playing softly in the background, some late-night boogie music. "I'll have to think about it," he said finally.

"No. I need a commitment right now."

"Hah! You think I can just hand you two hundred young'uns on a platter, Bright?"

"Yes, I do." She let that sink in for a moment, and then she said, "We've been cooped up in a sweaty, smelly room for five hours, saying nasty things to each other, for exactly that reason. Because of you. It's your idea, but we're doing the dirty work. Now you can either help us make this work, or we can turn out the lights and go home and you can deal with the Reverend Whitelaw Pinckney."

It stung him, as she meant it to. Flavo had pretty much had things his way for a long time in the black community, dispensing wisdom and direction from behind the counter at his small grocery store and from his deacon's pew in the A.M.E. Zion Church. It was a matter of power, and beyond that, a man's vanity. So she waited now while Flavo wrestled with his archangel and finally said, "All right."

"Thank you," she said and hung up.

And just after one o'clock in the morning, the school board took a unanimous vote to close Booker T. Washington High School.

What she wasn't prepared for was Fitzhugh's reaction. An aide was waiting to give him the news, passed on from a political crony back home in the district, when he stepped off a plane at Andrews Air Force Base from a trip to inspect U.S. military installations in the Mediter-

< 202 >

ranean. He came straight home, and when he walked in the house, his jaw was tight with barely controlled anger.

"Three weeks before the primary!" he cried, dropping his suitcase with a clatter just inside the door.

Bright was sitting in her wing-back chair, reading Ortho Noblett's account of the school board decision in the paper. She folded it carefully and laid it on the ottoman at her feet.

"Why *now*, for God's sake? Couldn't you have waited at least three weeks before you got the entire congressional district in an uproar over this cockeyed . . ." He lost the word and waved the air with his arms, indicating the general political mess he had arrived home to.

In truth, she thought, she had scarcely given Fitzhugh a thought once the idea of closing Booker T. Washington had taken hold in her mind. She had just done it because it seemed the thing to do, and once you decided a thing needed doing, it did little good to cogitate over it. You could think yourself right out of doing it. But she could not admit that now because it would be acknowledgment of the dimensions of the rift between them.

Instead, she said, "We had to do it before school's out, to give everybody the summer to get used to the idea and give the school people time to get ready."

"We."

"Harley, the school board . . ."

"Flavo Richardson."

"Yes. And Flavo."

"It was his idea, wasn't it."

"Yes. It was his idea, at the beginning. But it was my doing, at least a good deal of it."

"Well," he said bitterly, "I'm glad you took care of Flavo Richardson's agenda." He towered above her, fairly trembling with anger. She had never seen him quite so upset. It would do no good to argue with him. So she stood, reached for his hand. He drew back, sat heavily on the sofa across from her.

"I'm sorry," she said after a moment. "If I had thought it would have any effect . . ."

He sat very straight, very rigid, looking away from her out the window. He was wearing a three-piece pin-striped suit, a nice dark gray, and he looked very distinguished, very statesmanlike, very Washington. Except for his agitation. Fitzhugh rarely looked agitated.

Bright sat down beside him, determined to take the edge off his anger if she possibly could. "It will be all right," she said firmly. "You'd be surprised how people have accepted the idea."

< 203 >

"One town! Bright, I've got a nine-county district to worry about, and parts of it are as hard-nosed as anyplace in the South."

"But you have practically no opposition," she protested. "A . . . what is he . . . storekeeper?"

"A rival! Somebody people can vote for. An alternative. And even if I get past him, there's the general election."

"A Republican? For goodness' sake, Fitzhugh. This district hasn't elected a Republican dogcatcher since Reconstruction."

He stared at her. "Maybe not here, Bright. But do you realize how many Republicans got elected across the South two years ago on Goldwater's coattails? Nobodies, most of them. All because of Goldwater, because Southern whites thought for some reason that he could keep the place in the Dark Ages. Great God!" His eyes flashed and he chopped the air angrily with his hands. "They turned out county commissioners, sheriffs, legislators — all by marking the Republican slate so they could make sure they voted for Goldwater. Then they woke up the next morning and realized how stupid they had been. But they're perfectly capable of doing it again, because stupidity lasts a lifetime." His shoulders slumped then, the fire gone out of him, and he sat kneading his hands while she watched and waited. "Bright," he said finally, "you don't understand what it's like."

"Civil rights."

"Yes. There's no way to win. If you win, you lose."

There was a touch of naked desperation in his voice, and she did understand a bit how it must be for him, always having to be so careful, using the right code words, dodging the messier aspects. Especially Fitzhugh, who was a decent and honorable man and who did take what he did in Washington so earnestly to heart. She understood a bit how much it had taken out of him to vote against the Civil Rights Bill and the Voting Rights Bill — legislation he considered both common decency and political suicide. Civil rights was not something he ever talked about unless pressed, and then only to recite by rote, unenthusiastically, the worn phrases about states' rights and self-determination. The politics of avoidance, practiced by Fitzhugh and dozens of otherwise forthright Southerners for whom it was inevitably a private shame. He and they paid a price for being Southern.

Bright thought about all that as they sat there for a long time with the house sad and exhausted around them and finally she said, "Come home, Fitzhugh."

"Don't start on me again," he snapped. "Not now, for God's sake. Come home! When we're up to our eyeballs in Vietnam and Johnson's acting like it's a damned range war or something! Come home! No, by God, I'm going to stay as long as I have to. Unless" — he stood now

< 204 >

and turned on his bitterness full-bore — "you and Flavo Richardson have pulled the rug out from under me."

He was spooked. She could see it in his eyes, hear it in his voice. Desperately afraid of losing his seat, and more than that, a way of life, something that was as natural to him as breathing. He walked out, letting the screen door bang shut behind him. She watched out the front window as he crossed the lawn in long strides, heading toward downtown, toward the small storefront headquarters his campaign was operating on Bascombe Street near City Hall. He didn't come home until late in the night, after she had already gone to bed. She heard him at the door, then watched his slim, shadowy form as he undressed in the near-dark and slipped into bed beside her.

She waited. "I'm sorry," she said quietly. "Have I ruined it for you?"

He sighed. "I don't know. I've been on the phone. It may hold together."

That was all he said. And he made no move toward her. It was a long time before she slept.

Fitzhugh Birdsong survived the election. His opponent, the store-keeper, kicked up a minor fuss about the school business, but he had neither the time nor the political organization to orchestrate the kind of smear and innuendo campaign that could have toppled Fitzhugh. In September, the white high school absorbed its new black population with a minimum of trouble and the 1966 general election turned out to be a disappointment for Republicans all over the South. The dentist from Columbus who ran against Fitzhugh got barely forty percent of the vote, though it was the best anyone had done against him — primary or general election — in years.

They rarely spoke of it. But the wound was there, scabbed over and visible if you knew where to look for it. And the business seemed to weary him like a slow-acting poison, leaving the smell and taste of bile.

On election night in 1968, as they sat watching the national returns on television — the sore, angry nation giving the presidency reluctantly to Richard Nixon — Fitzhugh took her hand quietly and said, "That's it. I've run the course." And when he went back to Washington, he announced on the floor of the House that it would be his last term. There was no victory in it for Bright, only a pale sense of relief that it would finally be over, that he would come home and they would see what could be made of their lives.

< >

< 205 >

She thought about Booker T. Washington as she drove the Plymouth, running smoothly now, through the late June morning toward Flavo's house. It seemed like a very long time ago — ancient battles, inscribed on parchment. And after all that, still unfinished business.

It was like going back in time, entering the black section of town. Physically, there were still a good number of landmarks from her childhood: clapboard houses, the white frame A.M.E. Zion Church her father had built at the same time he had erected the new Methodist Church for the white folks. But beyond the physicality was the feel of the place, a mysterious and fascinating world to which she had always had entrée because she was Dorsey Bascombe's daughter. Sitting beside him in the front seat of their motorcar years ago as they took Hosanna home after supper, she could sense the crossing-over, almost a change of seasons — the smell of fatback and greens cooking, the fine powder boiling up from the dirt road behind their car, the impassive faces of the children watching from the bare yards and sagging porches of the houses as they passed, dusk settling over everything and softening edges like a watercolor.

She knew from the beginning that there was much more here than met the eye. It was like watching a pond, sensing a vibrancy below the placid surface, lives intermingled in a teeming stew. On Wednesday nights when Hosanna would take her to prayer meeting at the church, she sat deep in the pew surrounded by the close, powerful presence of the people and the great harmonious blend of their voices and felt things stir inside her — the essence of all things musical, the roots of life itself.

She sensed instinctively that she could never truly know this place, only its surfaces and perhaps a bit more. But still she felt, in the crossing-over, that in some strange way a part of her belonged here, even if she was only allowed because she was Dorsey Bascombe's daughter. More than any other man in town, white or black, Dorsey Bascombe had been the economic lifeblood of this black enclave. She came to understand over the years that life was hard here, close to the bone. But it would have been a good deal harder and closer had it not been for Dorsey's lumber company. Dorsey paid regularly and in cash. More than that, he took care of his people and their kin.

Things had changed over the years, most of them long after Dorsey was gone. Most of the streets were paved now and the main thoroughfare had street lamps. There were a number of fairly new houses — brick and mason-board siding with neatly kept yards. But there was the same feel about the place — much of it the mystery of the unknowable.

< 206 >

Flavo Richardson's small grocery store and attached house were in the center of the Quarter, both literally and figuratively. In the years before Dorsey had built the A.M.E. Zion Church, the community gathering place had been a huge oak tree in a clearing beside a small creek. Flavo had built his store in the clearing with the creek at its back side and the oak tree at its front. And this, as much as anything else, marked him as an essential man in the community. Directly across the street was Booker T. Washington High School — now just a boarded-up hulk.

The small parking area around the oak tree in front of Flavo's store was crowded with cars this morning, so she eased her Plymouth onto the shaded grass in front of the school building. She turned the engine off and sat there for a moment, looking at the school and thinking of Dorsey Bascombe. Dorsey would not have approved of the closing of Booker T., because he was of a different era and his vision did not stretch that far. But she thought Dorsey would have understood Bright's seeing a need for change in a changed time and acting upon it. When you lived in a place, you made an investment in it. He had truly believed that. And he most certainly would have approved of her being here this morning, of doing a difficult thing because it was the right and decent thing to do. What Dorsey Bascombe had taught her was right and decent had guided virtually everything she did for an entire lifetime. It had never occurred to her to be guided any differently.

She stepped out of the car now and crossed the street and threaded her way through the tangle of cars, past the oak tree, to the front of Flavo's store. It had a low porch with a smooth-worn floor, benches on either side of the wide front door, and there was a small crowd of people this morning, mostly men and a couple of women, lounging about the benches and leaning against the porch posts. Beyond them she could see that the door to the store was closed and a black wreath hung upon it, next to the Nehi Grape thermometer.

Conversation froze when they spotted her, and Bright, about to speak, stopped in her tracks. There was a shifting about on the porch, an uneasy silence, a looking away. And then she sensed the hostility, like a low growl from an animal. *They don't want me here. I don't belong.* It stung her. She had never, in all the years she had come here, felt shut out. Something had changed. Something ominous was happening. And she could only link it to the small brown body being lifted from the river last night. *But why? Do they blame me? Flavo, what have you done here?*

"Where is Mr. Richardson?" she asked finally.

< 207 >

Nobody said anything for a moment, and then one of the women turned her head aside and said, just loud enough so that Bright could hear her, "Shit." It dropped into the silence like a rock into water and rippled out into the morning, and Bright felt her cheeks flush. She clutched her purse tightly and almost turned to go, retreat to her car and drive away. Then suddenly one of the men pushed his way through the crowd and stepped off the porch. She recognized Luther Fox, the man she had seen in the checkout line at the Dixie Vittles the evening before. Babe Fox's boy, probably the only man in this crowd who had ever heard of Dorsey Bascombe.

"Flavo's in the house, Miz Birdsong," Luther Fox said.

"I'd like to see him if I could," Bright said.

"He's wore out this morning. We trying to let him get a little rest."

"Is he asleep?"

"No'm, I don't think he's able to sleep."

"Well, I won't be long," she insisted. She felt like a supplicant.

Luther looked down at his feet and she could see a blood vessel rippling at his temple. Finally he shrugged. "All right, then. I'll take you to him."

She could feel the cold stares of the rest of them on her back as he led her around the side of the store to the house. They climbed the steps to the wide front porch and Luther knocked lightly on the door. After a moment Flavo appeared, blinking out into the sunlight. "Miz Bright Birdsong come to see you, Flavo," Luther said.

There was a long pause and Bright was afraid for a moment that he might turn her away. Then he finally said, "Ahhhh, yes," and pushed open the screen door. "Come in the house, Bright."

"Thank you," she said to Luther, then left him on the porch and stepped into the dim hallway and Flavo closed the screen behind her. She reached and took his hand and gripped it tightly. "Flavo, I don't have the faintest idea what to say. There's no right thing. So I just came."

"That's the truth, Bright. There's no right thing to say." There was an ancient weariness in his eyes and his voice and he stooped more than usual. They stood for a long moment in the hallway with the silence heavy between them. Then he shook himself and she released his hand. "But you were right to come," he said. "Come on into the parlor and sit for a minute."

"Is your daughter . . ."

"Sleeping," he said. "We finally had to take her to the hospital early this morning. They gave her a shot to knock her out. She's about half-crazy with it."

< 208 >

He led the way into the parlor, showed her to a seat on the sofa. It was a neat room with lace curtains at the open windows, stirring faintly in the cat's breath of breeze outside, solid old furniture, a large kerosene stove in one corner with a black flue that rose up and elbowed into the wall. A massive radio cabinet against one wall, no television set. She remembered Flavo saying one time that he disdained television because it gave people unreasonable expectations like Cadillacs and free sex. She sat now, composing herself on the sofa with her purse in her lap, and Flavo eased himself into a large chair across from her. There was an ashtray on the table next to the chair with a chewed stump of a cigar resting against its edge, and a photograph album, open to reveal pages of old yellowing pictures. Flavo crossed one bony leg painfully over the other. He looked near collapse. She wouldn't stay long. "You ought to be sleeping yourself," Bright said.

Flavo squeezed his eyes shut and pinched the bridge of his nose for a moment, then looked at her. "No, I don't imagine I'll sleep for a while yet."

"Flavo, I'd go get him back if it were in my human power."

"Well," he said flatly, "you can't do that."

"No."

He closed his eyes again and spoke into the darkness. "No way I could tell you what that boy meant to me, Bright. He was my second chance."

"What do you mean?"

He opened his eyes, looked away from her at the open window. "I was hard on my own children. Prob'ly too hard."

"They turned out fine," Bright said. "They've all done well. Your mother would have been proud of them."

"Yes," he sighed. "But they don't come back home much now, and when they do it don't seem we've got much to say to each other."

She thought of Little Fitz and Roseann. Especially Roseann. *Is there a right way? Is it the lot of a parent to always be haunted? When you say to yourself, "I did the best I could," and it turns out not to be enough, then what?* And then she thought of Jimbo. Yes, a second chance there if she were wise enough, wiser than before. "I think," she said, "I know a little of what you're talking about."

He gave her a curious look. "Yes, maybe you do. Anyhow, when Ancie and her husband split up and she and the boy moved back here with me it was like getting a fresh start. I told her right off I didn't want to be that boy's daddy. I wanted to be his granddaddy. And . . ." His voice trailed off and Bright looked down at her purse, giving him a little privacy.

< 209 >

They sat in silence for a while and then he took hold of himself and when he spoke again there was the cold, hard thing in his voice, the same thing she had heard on the riverbank early that morning. "We let you off too easy, Bright."

She looked up at him, confused. "What are you talking about, Flavo?"

His eyes were bloodshot and angry and the white stubble of his whiskers stood out against the black of his sunken cheeks. She thought of the people out on the front porch of his store, the smoldering resentment she had felt radiating from them. *Flavo has started something here, something that may be dangerous. Tread softly.* "We should have caused some uproar, some pain," he said. "Maybe even shed a little blood."

And then she looked out the window and saw the white fading hulk of the old high school across the street, the one they had closed thirteen years before. "You mean the school business?"

"I mean the *whole* business. Booker T. and all the rest. But especially Booker T."

"You think that was easy?" she said, her voice rising. "People sweated blood over that, Flavo."

He ignored her. "You all thought that was all there was to it. Close down the nigger school and maybe they will shut up and leave us alone. And that" — he nodded slowly — "was exactly what we did."

"Flavo, I think you're dead wrong about that. I think you're overwrought."

"Damn right I am, Bright," he said, his voice low. "I'm mad as hell. We didn't change a thing."

"You're talking about the swimming pool?"

"The way people think."

"But things *have* changed, Flavo," she protested. Surely he had to concede that things weren't the way they used to be, when the atmosphere of fear and hatred and suspicion was so thick you could cut it with a knife, when whites had hunkered down behind the barricades and blindly lobbed their defiance over the top. People had come a long way in a short time. She truly believed that. Not all the way, but a long way.

"What about yourself, Flavo? You're on the town council. You're living proof that things have changed. And look at this place." She waved her hand in the direction of the window. "*It* has changed. And you're the biggest reason."

"Ahhhh," he said, "but I'm part of the problem, Bright. I accuse myself. I've sat there for four years on the council voting on resolutions

< 210 >

commending the high school band, purchase orders for new dump trucks. Back in the back room, a little compromise here and a little deal there to get something done. Get along by going along. No, I'm as guilty as anybody."

"Nobody's guilty, Flavo."

"Yes!" He brought his fist down on the arm of the chair with a thump, startling her with his vehemence. She gave a little jump and she realized how on edge she was, sitting here in Flavo's parlor with all that hostility out there on the front porch of his store and her visit of comfort and condolence gone all wrong.

She tried to keep her voice even. "Flavo, we did what you wanted thirteen years ago. You came to my house and sat in my parlor and said, 'Let's close Booker T. Washington.' And I stuck my neck out. I stuck my husband's neck out."

"Yes." He gave a short, mirthless laugh. "The only time Fitzhugh Birdsong's neck was ever stuck out was when somebody did it for him. All he did was hunker down. Hell, Fitzhugh Birdsong didn't retire from Congress, he cut and ran. But . . ." — he held his hands up, stopping her — "we all went along with going halfway. And now the young'uns, the black young'uns, don't even know what it's all about anymore. They go to the big high school, play in the band, join the Beta Club, eat in the same cafeteria as everybody else. On Friday nights they run up and down the football field while the white folks cheer. One of 'em even went off and played football for Bear Bryant and scored a touchdown on national television. So" — he shrugged — "you say the word *struggle* and they look at you like you're crazy. What's to struggle for?"

"All right," she said quietly, "so it's not over. But it's not all still to do, either."

"Maybe the hardest part is."

"I don't believe that."

"Then you're fooling yourself, Bright Birdsong. It's all papered over with laws and court orders. But they don't mean a damn thing if a little black boy has to go swimming in the river because the white folks don't want him in their pool. I stood on that riverbank early this morning and I said to myself, 'Flavo Richardson, you are the worst kind of fool because you have fooled yourself.'"

"And you think some pain and some blood would undo it?"

"No, it won't undo it, Bright," he snapped. "But it might wake everybody up."

"You're wrong," she said stubbornly, her own anger growing. "There are good people in this town and they've done the right thing, by and large. And for you to sit there and say . . ." She threw up her

< 211 >

hands. Then she took a good grip on her purse and stood up. "I came here to say I'm sorry, Flavo."

Flavo watched her for a moment and then he folded his hands in his lap. "If you're sorry, then do something," he said.

"What?"

"Integrate the swimming pool."

"The swimming pool is already integrated," she said.

"No, it's not. White chillun and black chillun don't swim in it together."

"They could . . . ," she started, and then she hung fire. "All right. The season ticket business. But you could have bought that boy a season ticket. You could have bought him a hundred season tickets. You've probably got more money than most white people in this town."

"Yes, I could, Bright. But what's the use buying a boy a season ticket when his friends can't have one?"

"Then you could have bought them all season tickets."

"You miss the point," he shot back. "It's not season tickets. It's not even the swimming pool, Bright. It's what it all stands for. It's hate."

"People here don't hate, Flavo. Not anymore. There's still some ignorance and a little fear, I imagine. But not hate."

Flavo shook his head. "How would you know, Bright? You've been hidden away in that house of yours for eight years."

"Well, you haven't been," she said hotly. "You're on the council. Do something!"

"No, like I said, I've failed. Now it's your turn. I want you to do it."

"Me? Why?"

"Because you're Dorsey Bascombe's daughter."

"This has nothing to do with my father!"

"This has everything to do with your father. He started it."

"What do you mean?"

"Dorsey Bascombe kept us, Bright. Long years ago, he was the *man*. Need a job? Go see Mr. Dorsey. Young'un sick? Mr. Dorsey fetch the doctor. Need the creek unstopped so the raw sewage'll float on down to the river instead of stinking up the Quarter? Shuffle over to Mr. Dorsey with yo' hat in yo' hand and see what he can do. 'Cause he the *man*.' And you" — he stabbed the air with his finger — "you made this town a shrine to him."

"I did not!"

Flavo's eyes flashed. "Then why did you stay, Bright? Why didn't you go to Washington with Fitzhugh? He begged you, Bright! I know

< 212 >

that. But no, you stayed here and kept your fingers in everything. Good deeds, good intentions. Just like Dorsey Bascombe would have done if he hadn't —"

"Stop!" she shouted, close to tears now. "Don't you dare!"

She hovered over him, rage gripping her, and for the first time he softened, and his face went slack and he slumped back in the chair.

"I went too far," he said softly. "I'm sorry I did that."

She sat down heavily on the sofa and tried to catch her breath, fearful of the pounding of her heart, a tired old heart in a tired old body, inflamed now by this maddening man.

It took a while, but she finally calmed herself, and then she opened her purse and pulled out a handkerchief and dabbed at her eyes with it.

"Friends don't do things like that," she said.

"I know," Flavo said quietly. "But I speak the truth, and you know it."

Bright stuffed the handkerchief back in her purse and closed it with a snap. "So. What do you want?"

"Just what I said. I want that swimming pool integrated."

"All right," she said. "I suppose you've heard by now about my great good fortune at the Dixie Vittles last night."

"Yes, the word's gotten around."

"Fifty thousand dollars. When I get the money, I'll go to the swimming pool and buy a season ticket for every black child in this town. And then I'll put the rest in the bank and we'll keep doing it every year until it runs out."

Flavo shook his head. "That's no answer, Bright. That's just papering over again. I want change, not paper."

"And how do you think I'm going to do that?"

"You'll think of something. You're a smart woman."

She stood again, determined to go now. "And what will you do if something doesn't come along?"

"I will cause this town some pain," Flavo Richardson said without blinking an eye.

"Why do you always come to me to do your dirty work?"

"Like I said. You're Dorsey Bascombe's daughter. You chose. You have to live with the choice. The man casts a long shadow, don't he."

She stood for a long moment looking down at him, resenting him, letting her anger feed on itself, thinking back to the battle over the school thirteen years before. Finally, she became aware again of the morning outside, the coming and going of traffic in front of Flavo's store, cars in the yard, voices. She thought about the crowd of people

< 213 >

out in front of the store, the hostility. You could make a mob out of them if you said just the right things. Or just the wrong things. She felt very tired now and she wanted to go home. She had intended to come here and console an old friend. She hadn't wanted this.

"Flavo, go to bed. Get some rest."

He nodded.

"When is the funeral?"

"Thursday," he said. "Thursday morning."

"I'll be there. I'll see that Fitz is there."

"I don't want him to come if it's politics," Flavo said bluntly.

"He'll be there because it's the right thing to do," Bright said.

"If the swimming pool business isn't resolved by then," he said, "don't either of you bother."

And with that, she turned and left, stunned and hurt and angry, blinded by it, so that she was halfway home in her old Plymouth before she came to herself. "Damn you!" she cried out, thumping her hand against the steering wheel. "Damn, damn!" And then she wondered whom she was damning. And beyond that, what in the name of God she was going to do.

< 214 >

13

*H*arley Gibbons was sitting on Bright's front porch when she got home, his automobile parked at the curb in front. He stood as she climbed the steps. "Morning," he called out.

Harley was tall and spare, the kind of man you wanted for a banker. Bright would have been suspicious of a fat banker. But Harley had the look of a man who took home only what he needed from the bank, even a family-owned bank. People trusted Harley with their money and their private affairs. He would not take advantage of you or gossip about you. And they trusted him enough to keep electing him mayor. A fat banker couldn't have been elected mayor, she thought.

"Morning yourself," she answered. "What brings you out of the air-conditioned comfort of the Commercial Bank on a warm June day?"

Harley gave her a big banker's smile as he extended his hand. "Just passing by, and thought I'd drop by and see how you were doing," he said.

"Just passing by," she repeated. "Well, sit down for a spell before you pass on someplace else, Harley. Can I get you a glass of iced tea?"

"Hmmm. Yes, Bright. That sounds good. Some iced tea would be right nice."

She left him sitting in one of the wicker chairs and returned in a moment with two glasses of tea, a sprig of mint peeking from the top of each, picked from the small patch by the back steps. She handed him a glass and sat down in the other chair and they sipped their tea for a moment and studied the morning, the occasional cars passing on Birdsong Boulevard, a woman with a double armload of groceries struggling through the door of the Dixie Vittles across the street while a young child hauled hard on her dress. Bright thought about Flavo Richardson and the swimming pool, started to say something, thought better of it. Not just yet.

< 215 >

"Hmmm," Harley said after a moment, taking a sip and pursing his lips, "the tea has an unusual bite to it. I never tasted any iced tea exactly like this before."

Yes, Bright thought, come to think of it, the tea was just a trifle different. "It must be the mint," she said. "New growth. It may be a little stronger this time of the year. I can get you another glass if you like. Without the mint."

"Oh, no," he hastened. "It's *real good,* mind you. Just a bit unusual." He took a big gulp, held it in his mouth for an instant, swallowed. They sat a moment longer, and Harley crossed and uncrossed his long legs and then said, "Well, we sure could use some rain."

"Yes." Bright nodded. "I suppose so, Harley."

"It's been a couple of weeks, I think."

"At least that."

"It's just too early in the summer to be having a dry spell." Harley nodded emphatically. "It makes folks a little skittish. Reminds folks of the drought two years ago. Lots of farmers went out of business then. Tough on farmers, tough on bankers."

"Well," Bright said, "it seemed like an awfully wet spring to me. Surely a couple of dry weeks won't drive us to ruin."

"No," he said, "I suppose not. But the way folks *feel* is about as important as the way things *are.* Psychology, you know. Psychology has a lot to do with things."

"Yes," she said, "folks put a lot of store by psychology."

Bright felt suddenly at ease for the first time all morning, felt the tension in the back of her neck beginning to slip away. It felt good to sit here watching the day marinate with Harley Gibbons on the front porch, feeling the easy rhythm of speech keeping time with the morning. Harley had something on his mind, but he would arrive at it eventually by circumlocutions, the way a hawk would make lazy circles before swooping down on prey. There was something good and reassuring about conversation that took its time getting to its destination. She had learned the rhythms at her father's side, the way he and another man would lean against the hood of a car with their talk mingling like soft, slow music in the morning air, until finally they parted with a handshake and you realized, on reflection, that a piece of business had been transacted, an understanding reached, perhaps even a disagreement resolved. You had to be very quick, very finely tuned to the nuances of the conversation, to know it had transpired. Bright herself had always been quick of tongue, prone to go directly to the heart of things. But as a child she had been able to hear and understand the measured cadence of good, slow talk just as she heard music in her

< 216 >

head. It was the sound of patience, of tolerance, of compromise and getting along. Now, on this June morning, it returned as a welcome and soothing echo from the past. And she thought, *This is the way we do things here, not by causing pain. And perhaps we can work this new thing out if we give it a little time and don't try to butt heads.* Then she thought, *There I go again.* "We."

"Fitzhugh put a lot of stock in psychology," Harley said now. "Fitzhugh would study a thing, and then he might say, 'The time's not quite right, Harley. No matter what the fact of a thing is, it's what people perceive it is. Politics is timing.' But when he sensed that the time was right, he'd go right ahead and do a thing, and ninety-nine percent of the time it would work out right."

All right. A perfect opening. I will tell Harley about the swimming pool now, and we will start . . . But just as she was about to speak, Harley said, "Actually . . . ," and she stopped, because he said it rather forcefully and she could tell he had arrived at what he had come for. It must be important, because his circumlocution had been fairly brief.

"Actually, what I came by to say has something to do with timing," he said, crossing and uncrossing his legs again.

"Hmmmm," Bright said. "I thought you were just passing."

"Well, I was. But I thought it might be a good time to stop and chat for a moment." He paused, looking into his tea glass. "I've sold the bank," he said.

Bright set her glass down on the table. "What on earth for?"

"Because some people offered me a lot of money for it."

"What people?"

"Some of the big boys. You're one of the few folks who know about it outside of me and their top people. They're buying up small banks all over the state now."

"But your family has had that bank for a hundred years, Harley," she said.

"Not anymore," he laughed, shaking his head. She could hear a little undercurrent there. Bitterness? "Just not any room for a small-town banker anymore. If I didn't sell, they'd come in here anyway, put up one of their branches, and cut the rug out from under me. No way a little guy can compete with them. They've got too much money, too many people, too many computers. They lend money cheaper than I can borrow it."

"That's a shame," she said.

"Well," he said dryly, "I have your son to thank, in a way."

"What do you mean?"

< 217 >

"Little Fitz got the legislature to pass a statewide branch banking bill. It was one of the first things he did when he got into office. The big banks put a lot of money in his campaign, and they called in the IOUs. So now you've got a few big banks gobbling up all the little banks."

"Well, I'm sorry he did that," Bright said, genuinely distressed. She couldn't imagine Harley Gibbons not owning the bank, standing near the front door to greet customers as they came in. "What are you going to do?"

"Oh, they'll keep me on for a while," he said with a shrug. "That's good business. Keeps folks from getting upset, you know. But they'll ease their own people in. First thing I'll get is some bright-eyed, bushy-tailed young fellow not long out of college with a lot of flashy ideas about how to run a bank. And then one day one of the big vice presidents will walk in from state headquarters and tell me it's time to retire. Thing is, he'll be right. I'm getting old, Bright."

"You're not seventy yet," she protested.

"No, but I'm gaining on it."

"Well," she said, "I don't know what to say, Harley."

He laughed, but there was no mirth in it. "No need to feel sorry for me. I'm making a pile of money off the deal. It's cheaper for them to buy me out than compete with me, so they've been downright lavish with their money. I'll never have to worry about a thing. Evelyn and I could get on a plane tomorrow and start flying around the world and never come back."

"But you won't," she said.

"No, I won't. I don't like to fly. I like to bank."

"That's what you're supposed to do. You were cut out for it, just like your father was cut out for it."

Harley reflected on that a moment, took off his glasses, stared at them, put them back on, and looked out down Claxton Avenue as if searching for something.

"Bright," he said, "banking's not going to be the same in this town anymore. These new folks, they'll run it by the book. There won't be any more of this business of looking a fellow in the eye, hearing him out, and then deciding by the seat of your pants if he's worth a loan. We've managed to do business that way since the bank was founded. But these new folks will put your life history down on paper and crank it into a computer and then say yea or nay based on a cold, hard formula. They'll come in here and go through my books with a fine-tooth comb, and they'll be hard-nosed about folks who owe us money."

She stared at him a moment, and then it dawned on her. "Like me," she said.

< 218 >

She and Fitzhugh had put a small mortgage on the house nine years before when he had made the decision to come home. They had spruced up the house and bought the Plymouth. And she had added small amounts to it over the years for one project or another. Harley sent her a bill for the interest each year and kept rolling over the principal. She had paid little attention to it. But now . . .

Harley nodded, still looking off down the street. "I looked at your file this morning, Bright. Your mortgage is just over thirty-eight thousand dollars. Interest rate is still five and a quarter. Unheard of." He turned to her now, and fell silent.

"It's not a good loan," she said, helping him.

"No, it's not a good loan. This house" — he indicated it with a wave of his hand — "probably wouldn't appraise for thirty-eight thousand."

"It's a good house," she said.

"It's not in the best of shape," he countered. "But the loan is in worse shape than the house."

"Why haven't we had this conversation before, Harley? Business is business."

He shook his head. "Not entirely, Bright. Business is people, or at least that's the way I've run my business. And it *is* my business, or has been until now. As long as I don't break the law, I can do what I want. If a bank examiner comes in here and arches his eyebrows over a loan, I can look him in the eye and say, 'That's none of your business.' And the directors who sit on my board don't own enough stock to amount to a hill of beans." He sighed, raised his hands in resignation. "But that's about to change."

She felt genuinely sad for Harley Gibbons then, for what he was giving up. She could hear the echoes of his words, going way back in time. The earnest sound of the child Harley's voice in a classroom on a spring morning, gravely reciting, " 'The boy stood on the burning deck,' " the measured cadence of his words telling you, if you listened carefully enough, that he would be his father's son, a man you could depend upon when he grew to manhood, that he would be serious about his life but not too serious. And now, all he had invested in his life, irrevocably altered. You didn't call that change. You called it disruption.

But now Harley Gibbons smiled at her, a nice warm smile, the kind with which he had been greeting his customers all these years. "But Providence has blessed you, Bright. Honestly, I'd call it a miracle."

"What do you mean?" she asked.

"The money."

< 219 >

"What money?"

"Why," he said, raising his eyebrows, "the fifty thousand dollars. You can pay off your loan. I imagine you'll have just enough, when you get through paying taxes on the money. It should come out just about right."

"Taxes?"

"Well, of course Uncle Sam's going to want his share. A prize like that is treated as income."

"Income?" *What is going on here? You walk in off the street, minding your own business, and suddenly somebody thrusts fifty thousand dollars on you. And then people immediately start asking for it, all these folks who say you've got a responsibility to them — son, banker, tax man.*

"Are you all right, Bright?" Harley asked, wrinkling his brow, bending toward her a bit, putting his hand on her arm.

"A bit overwhelmed, Harley."

"Can I get you something? Some more iced tea? Just tell me where it is."

"Oh, no," she said quickly. "I'm fine. Really. I've just had a lot happen the last couple of days."

"Fitz . . ."

"That, yes."

"Well, don't you worry about Little Fitz. He's a heckuva politician. He'll get through this. We're all pulling for him."

"Even after what's happened to your bank?"

Harley shook his head adamantly. "That's business, Bright. This is home folks. Little Fitz is our boy."

And he meant it. She could tell that. Good, solid, dependable Harley Gibbons. He would stick. And this other thing . . . they would work it out. Somehow.

"Harley," she said, "I've been thinking back about the school business. Closing Booker T. Washington back yonder."

He looked at her curiously. "What about it, Bright?"

"We did the right thing back then, Harley. Especially you. We never could have pulled it off without you."

"Ah," he sighed. "It wasn't easy."

"But it worked out. Things have changed a lot since then, and that's what started it. We've done the things that needed to be done."

"Yes," Harley said. "One thing led to another, I suppose." Harley took off his glasses again and rubbed the bridge of his nose where they made deep indentions in the skin. His eyes were pale and watery. He looked much older without his glasses, Bright thought, older and tired. "Other than that demonstration over the water fountains at the court-

< 220 >

house, we've never had an organized protest by the coloreds in this town. We never had anybody sit down on the sidewalk, or stop traffic, or parade around with signs."

All right. It's time. "You've heard about Flavo's grandson, I suppose," she said gently.

"Yes," he nodded. "Terrible thing. We thought about canceling the council meeting tonight, out of respect, but we've got some business that just can't be put off."

"The council meets tonight?"

"Yes. Tuesday night, seven o'clock. Same as always."

"Well. Yes. I suppose I forgot. It's been a long time since I've been to a council meeting."

Harley gave a wry, soft laugh. "Well, I remember *some* you came to."

She smiled. "We've had some moments over the years on one thing or another."

"But always remained friends," Harley said.

"Yes. I'm grateful for that. I was thinking about old friends when I drove up just now. Old friends who know each other's history." She paused. "I'm sorry about the bank, Harley."

He ducked his head, just a tiny motion. "As I say, time moves on," he said. "Time gets away before you know it."

"About the loan. I'll do the right thing, Harley. You can count on that."

"I knew you would, Bright. Better to take care of things before they become a problem, you know. Always try to anticipate. Avoid surprises. Fitzhugh was that way, I remember. Never saw him do a thing he didn't think out ahead of time."

"Except the last thing he did," she said.

"Yes, I suppose that's right. I'm afraid he didn't plan that very well." Harley looked around at the house, sagging and graying with age. "Fitzhugh intended to come home and take care of you," he said.

"We both had intentions," Bright said.

Harley rose. "Well, I'd better be getting on. Almost dinnertime. Evelyn will be looking for me."

"You still go home for dinner?"

"Of course."

"My father always did that."

"So did mine."

He shook her hand and then walked down the steps to his car. She sat watching as he pulled away from the curb, waved as he headed off up Birdsong Boulevard toward home. Bright picked up her iced tea

< 221 >

glass from the table beside her, took a sip, tasted again the unusual tartness. She held the glass in her hand for a moment, staring at the dark tea inside and the green sprig of mint peeking out of the top of the glass. It looked all right. Then suddenly it hit her. *Gladys has been peeing on the mint! Good grief, what rancid poisons there must be in that ancient bladder!* And then she thought, *My God! Gladys!* She jumped up and headed for the back porch and out the door. Gladys was sitting there on her haunches next to the opening in the bricks, looking mournfully up at her with her one good eye.

Bright threw up her hands in surrender. "I'm sorry," she said. "So much has happened . . ." She trailed off lamely, thinking how silly she was to be standing here in her backyard making excuses to an unfed dog, especially one that peed on the mint. She went quickly to the kitchen and heated up a pan of milk, then took it back to the steps and poured it over some dog food in Gladys's bowl and sat down on the steps, watching her eat.

Harley Gibbons lingered in her thoughts. He had been her high school beau, tall and earnest and a little out of breath with pursuing her. Would she have been better off with Harley? They were both of this place and bound by it through ties that ran deep. There would have been no conflict between them, at least not over that. The problem was, she didn't love Harley Gibbons. She did love Fitzhugh Birdsong, then and now, despite all the disappointments and missed connections. And because she loved him, she was willing to take equal blame for the failures. If Harley had disappointed her, she would have been tempted to blame him completely, not loving him enough to share. No, she thought now, he was better off with Evelyn and his bank and his mayor's job. And she was better off with the friendship that spanned their lifetimes, especially right now, when she might have to ask Harley to stick his neck out for her one last time.

She looked up at Gladys, who was licking the last morsels of food from the bottom of her bowl. "And," she said to Gladys, "Harley Gibbons might not have allowed a decrepit old dog under his house. What would you have done then?" Gladys cocked her head to one side, gave her a curious look, then disappeared under the house.

"Hah!" Bright called after her. "I wish I could get under there with you!" But she knew that it would be a good long while before her head hit the pillow in repose.

She should be exhausted after her chaotic night and morning, on top of everything else that had happened since she had welcomed yesterday's early sun. But for some reason she felt strangely refreshed, even exhilarated. Things were possible here. Something, as Dorsey Bas-

< 222 >

combe was wont to say, might just come along. And after it did, after she was done with this, then she could forsake the field of battle for good. She would be quiet again. You could count on that.

The telephone was ringing when she got back in the house, and she let it jangle for a moment while she filled Gladys's bowl with water and left it to soak in the sink.

"Miz Bright?" Doris Hawkins said from the other end when she finally picked it up. "I figured you'd fell in."

"Fell in where?"

"The commode. I saw you was home, but the phone rang so long I figured you'd got stuck or something."

"No, Doris, I'm fine." She looked out the front window and she could see Doris behind the checkout counter at the Dixie Vittles, the phone cradled between her head and shoulder while she rang up an order on the cash register. Bright could hear the rattle and jingle of the register in the background.

"Well," Doris said, "you're about to be a lot finer. They want to give you your money tomorrow."

"Tomorrow?"

"Yes'm. Fellow just called from the big office over at Columbus, said they'll be here in the morning for the ceremony. They want to do it tomorrow so Ortho can get it in this week's paper. Is ten o'clock all right?"

"Yes," Bright said, "I suppose that will be fine. But do they have to put it in the paper?"

Doris cackled. "Lord, yes, Miz Bright. It ain't every day the Dixie Vittles gives away fifty thousand dollars, and they want to get all the goody out of it. I'm surprised they ain't sending a limousine to pick you up. Thirty-nine forty-five."

"What?"

"'Scuse me, Miz Bright. That was Miz Poteet's order here. Thirty-nine forty-five."

"Well, I don't think we'll need a limousine to get across the street, Doris."

Doris bellowed another laugh. "I reckon not. Well, we'll see y'all in the morning. Bring your wheelbarrow."

< >

She heard the alligator under the house. Jimbo's alligator. Josephus, he called him. She wondered at the implausibility of such a strange creature coming to visit, taking up residence for a while, disturbing dust

< 223 >

and ghosts and the old dog who had been the sole resident for so long. A child's alligator, grown to life in the dark underbelly of the house in the heat and ferment of imagination. They face each other warily, squatter and intruder. The dog — ancient breath, stale eyes, coat armored with the dust of centuries, grumpy from sleep. *Go away. You're a passing fancy, and not much to look at, at that. The stuff of turgid dreams. I've been here much too long to give you the time of day.* The alligator — snout probing the close air, powerful tail sweeping to and fro, eyes blinking slowly, patiently. *I can wait, old dog. I am a child-beast, and I have time on my side. And because I am a child-beast, I can be tiny and quiet or I can be large and noisy. And if I become big enough, I can drive you out of here, old dog, out into the light.* Old dogs and child-beasts, creatures of past and future. And what about the here and now?

She woke, blinking, sleep-logged and headachy. She lay there for a long moment, climbing into consciousness, and realized that it was midafternoon. She had lain down after a light lunch, intending to rest her eyes for just a few minutes. That had been two hours ago.

She heard voices outside now, children's voices, along the sidewalk in front of the house. Tatters of careless sound echoing across the surface of the afternoon. It reminded her of another afternoon so very long ago, an autumn afternoon but one very much like this one, when she had waked from a nap to hear the voices of children at play in the street in front of her house, soft music in the shades of orange and gold that colored the tree outside her bedroom window. The house was very still and quiet and she nestled like a small animal under the light blanket that covered her, feeling safe and warm. Then something tugged at her mind, something dark and frightening. And she suddenly saw the still form of her father sprawled across the steps of the camp house, the blood everywhere. "No," she cried softly into the silence of her pillow. And the voices of the children outside mocked her, calling back, "Yes. Yes."

She shook it away, rose now, rumpled from sleep, steadied herself with a firm hand on the bedpost, went to the kitchen and took two aspirin, washing them down with tap water. Then she walked to the living room and looked out the window. The children were playing in her front yard in the shade of the pecan trees. It had been a very long time since children had played in her yard. There were a half dozen of them now, darting about in the warm speckled afternoon, touching the trees and shouting to each other in some sort of game. She watched them for a minute or so before she realized that one of them was Jimbo, and he was wearing overalls. Blue denim bib overalls with straps over

< 224 >

his shoulders and big loose legs that flapped around his ankles. A red T-shirt under the overalls, sneakers on his feet, white with newness. It was an ungainly costume, something resurrected from Buster Putnam's memory of his long-ago childhood, but it didn't seem to bother Jimbo, who moved with a sort of awkward grace, like a heron lifting into flight. Bright stepped to the front door, looked through the screen, saw a book open on the seat of one of the wicker chairs. She wondered how long he had been back, where he and Buster had been and what they had done. She pictured them in a roadhouse with the jukebox playing hillbilly music and Buster guzzling beer while Jimbo sat gawking on the stool next to him, awed by riotous living.

"Jimbo," she called, and he stopped in his tracks and whirled to look up at her in the doorway.

"Hi, Mama Bright. We're playing."

"Yes. I can see that. Hello there," she called to the others. She didn't recognize any of them. She hadn't paid much attention to children for a long time.

"What have you been up to?" she asked.

"Just messing around," Jimbo said, impatient to get back to the game.

"Doing what?"

"Uncle Buster took me to Columbus."

"*Uncle* Buster?"

"He said y'all might be getting married, so he'd be my uncle."

"Good grief!"

He stood there, waiting for her to be finished with him, and she said finally, "I like your overalls."

He looked down at himself, shrugged.

"Well, be careful," she said.

He gave her an odd look and went back to his play, and she turned from the door and glanced at the clock on the mantel. Three-thirty.

She sat down for a moment on the sofa, reconnoitering, her mind revolving slowly like the ceiling fan overhead, trying to sort everything out. She was still a little groggy from sleep and there was quite a jumble of things. First order of business, Harley and the town council. She thought for a while about what she might do about that. She went to the telephone table, took the receiver out from under the pillow where she had stuffed it when she went to lie down, placed it back in the cradle. Then she picked it up and dialed Flavo Richardson.

< 225 >

14

*F*itz called around four o'clock and she started to tell him about what she had decided to do, but then thought better of it. For one thing, she wasn't exactly sure what she *had* decided. For another, she didn't want him trying to talk her out of it, whatever it was. And for still another, there was no need to worry him with anything, as much as he had on his plate right now. By the time he got here Thursday, things would be taken care of. It was a small thing, really, a local matter, not something that would affect the governor's race. The thing about politicians was, they worried about everything they remotely suspected had "vote" written on it.

Fitz sounded frazzled and out of sorts. "It's been a helluva day, Mama. I won't burden you with details." She heard someone speaking in the background and then Fitz, angry, his voice muffled but still discernible as he put his hand over the mouthpiece. "Tell the asshole to get lost. No, don't tell him that. I'll be with him in a minute." He spoke again into the receiver. "Sorry. Hyenas."

"I just talked to Flavo. He said you called." That was the most important thing, she thought.

"Yes'm. That's why I called you. He sounded kinda strange, Mama."

"Well," Bright said, "he's been through a lot."

"No, I don't mean just losing the boy. He sounded angry. There's nothing wrong down there, is there?"

She started to tell him about the swimming pool, thought better of it. Instead she said, "Are you coming to the funeral?"

"I'm supposed to be clear at the other end of the state Thursday morning," he said. "I was going to fly in just in time for the parade."

"I think you should be here," she insisted.

"Yes," he said. "I should be there. All right. I'll just shuffle things around. Hell, there may not be anything to shuffle by Thursday."

< 226 >

Bright heard the great weariness there, almost despair. He paused for a moment and then he said, "Are you all right, Mama?"

"Of course I'm all right, Fitz. Why do you ask?"

"Oh, I don't know. Just checking."

"Well, that's nice."

"You know what I'd like to do, Mama?"

"What's that, son?"

"I'd like to get in the car right now and come down there and sit on the porch with you and drink a glass of iced tea." There was something wistful in his voice, something she hadn't heard in a long time.

"You'd draw a crowd," she said, "you always do. But why don't you anyway."

"Ahhh," he sighed. "Too many hyenas to keep at bay. I'm up to my keister in hyenas."

"Maybe I should be asking you if *you're* all right," Bright said. "Are you?"

"Lavonia took the kids and went to the beach," he said by way of answering. "I'm staying up at the lake house at night. Me and Sergeant Dodson."

"Well, if you came down here you could have the camp house." And she was instantly sorry she had said that. "I didn't mean . . ."

"I know."

"The camp house is a good place to get away," she hurried on, trying to explain.

"Mama," Fitz said, "I could never in a million years tell you how sorry I am about the camp house. I'm sorry about the embarrassment. About everything —"

"Stop, Fitz," she interrupted him. "Now go take care of the hyenas. And when you're finished, come down here and sit on the front porch and have some iced tea. Whenever that is."

"Yes," he said. "Thursday. We'll have some iced tea after all the folderol is over. Just a quiet glass of iced tea."

When he had hung up, Bright thought for a fleeting moment about getting in the car and going up there to the Capitol and sitting down next to his desk and telling all the hyenas to go away and leave him alone. But no, that would not do. He was a big boy and this was his fight.

She wondered if she had prepared him for it. He had been full of mischief as a child, but she had always been able to get his attention with just a snap of her voice. And then he would look up at her with a sorrowful eagerness, pleading with his eyes to be forgiven. He wasn't the kind of child who talked back. It was entirely possible that she had done too much, given him too much direction, made him too

< 227 >

quick to please. Looking back, she thought she might have done things a little differently, been a little less quick of tongue. But that was hindsight.

She sat pondering all that, and then she realized after a moment that he had not said a single solitary word about the money.

< >

Bright heard the roar of Buster Putnam's riding lawn mower around four-thirty and she walked to her front door and looked out as he made a wide curving slash through his overgrown front yard, aiming the mower in no particular direction. He had a Budweiser can in his hand and he polished off the last of its contents and gave the empty can a fling toward his front porch, where it landed with a rattle. He reached into the cooler between his legs, pulled out another beer, and popped the top one-handed with an expert flick of his wrist. He saw her then and waved grandly and she walked across the porch and down the steps toward him. He cut the engine back to a throaty idle and coasted to a stop, waiting for her. The grass was above her ankles and she stepped carefully, wondering if there were snakes and small animals about.

"Beer?" he said as she reached him, drawing another can, dripping with water, from the cooler. Buster was wearing a shapeless green jumpsuit with a large grease stain on one leg. His face was flushed with the beer and heat and the white stubble of his whiskers stood out against the skin.

"You're going to fall off that thing dead drunk and run over yourself," she said, waving the can away. "No, I don't want a beer."

"Loosen up, Bright," he said as he dropped the can back into the cooler, then indicated his yard with a wave of his arm. "I have carefully calculated the size of my property here. It is a six-beer lawn. Six Budweisers will not make me dead drunk. Drunk, but not dead drunk."

"Well, if you don't fall off the thing, you'll keel over from heatstroke."

"Another good reason to drink beer," he said.

"I hope you weren't imbibing while you had Jimbo with you."

"Imbibing." He grinned. "How quaint. Matter of fact, we did duck into the Spot and take the chill off the morning." Then he held his hand up. "Just kidding. I was as sober as a judge. So was he. Gad, the kid is sober. He, too, needs to loosen up."

"I have some business to transact with you," Bright said.

He gave a little bow from the waist, sloshing a bit of the beer out of his can. "At your service, madam."

"If you tell another soul in this town you're going to marry me, I'll shoot you dead," she said, trying to put some starch in her voice.

< 228 >

"That's what the Chinese Communist Army said," Buster deadpanned.

"You weren't trying to marry the Chinese Communist Army," she shot back.

Buster put his hand over his heart. "If I have offended you, I am grievously sorry."

She gave a disgusted shake of her head. "Put your beer down and come have some iced tea."

"Delighted," he said, and cut off the lawn mower engine and followed her back to the house. She got two glasses of tea from the kitchen and they sat on the front porch, watching the children playing out in the shade under the pecan trees. They had a ball now and they had divided themselves into two teams of three, using the trees for bases and sending the ball spinning through the hot afternoon while they ran, shouting, to touch the trees. One strap of Jimbo's overalls had come undone and it flapped loosely, but he didn't seem to notice.

"Jimbo says you took him to Columbus," Bright said.

"Yeah, we got the overalls and stuff at Putnam's and then we rode over to Columbus for a hamburger and a milk shake. You were asleep when we got back, so I went down to the preacher's house and rounded up some kids for him to play with." He nodded toward the group in the front yard. "He seems to be doing all right. At least he doesn't have his nose stuck in a book."

"Roseann overprotects him," she said. "What the boy needs is some space."

"What the boy needs is to do something outrageous," Buster said. "Something unscheduled and totally outrageous. You know what he told me? He told me that when he comes home after school he has to stay in the house and call his mama at work every thirty minutes."

They sipped their iced tea for a few minutes and then Bright told Buster about Gladys's peeing on the mint and Harley Gibbons's reaction and Buster got a good laugh out of that. Then they watched the kickball game under the trees, Jimbo and the others shouting to each other, arguing over the score, cheering a good kick.

After a while, Bright said, "Flavo Richardson's grandson drowned because he didn't have a season ticket."

Buster turned and looked at her. "A what?"

"To the swimming pool. You can't swim in the city pool unless you have a season ticket. They cost fifty dollars. Black children can't afford that. So they swim in the river."

He studied her for a moment the way she thought he might have studied a white stretch of Pacific beach from the bow of a landing craft. "Bright," he said, "what are you up to?"

< 229 >

"I'm not exactly sure. A little voice in the back of my head keeps telling me it's not my fight."

"Is it?"

"Ten years ago I would have said yes. Twenty-four hours ago I would have said no."

"What happened?"

"Flavo."

"Hmmmm." He fell silent for a moment, sipping his tea, and then he said, "What is Flavo going to do?"

"Right now, nothing. He wants me to do it for him."

"Why?"

"He says, because I'm Dorsey Bascombe's daughter."

"Hmmmm. And if you don't?"

Bright shook her head. "I think there might be trouble, Buster. I could feel it when I was over there this morning. Real trouble."

"Over season tickets?"

"Over an injustice. Flavo's distraught, he's grieving, and he blames the white folks. There's a death involved, and I think he looks at it as a kind of lynching."

Buster gave her a long, careful look. "I hear you used to cut a wide swath, Bright."

"Not anymore. I retired. Or at least I thought I did."

"Just like me," Buster said. "I've been shot at all I want." And that was probably true, Bright thought. Buster had gone into the Marine Corps in 1942 and over the years he had seen a good deal of combat. World War II, Korea, Vietnam. He had come home with a chest full of ribbons.

"You've earned the right to drink beer and go to seed," Bright said.

"Yes ma'am," he said flatly. "Damn straight." Then he put his iced tea glass down on the table and stood up. "Speaking of which, I have miles to cut and beers to drink before I sleep. I smell a fight over here, and I think I'll just get back to my dissipation."

"A fight," she said. "Well, I don't think it will come to that." Then she thought for a moment and added, "But it might, I suppose."

Buster looked down at her, a bemused expression on his face. "Just make sure your sword ain't all rusted up when you ride into battle, m'lady."

<   >

The city swimming pool was on a wide flat shelf of the riverbank, nestled among a grove of huge oak trees dripping with Spanish moss. There were rough-hewn picnic tables scattered underneath the trees

< 230 >

and a small parking area next to the high chain-link fence that surrounded the pool itself.

"Why can't I swim?" Jimbo asked as they bounded down the gravel driveway from the street in Bright's Plymouth. The color was high in his cheekbones, sweat beads stood out on his forehead, and he gave off a powerful aroma of boy-at-play smell. Not at all unpleasant, she thought. It brought back memories. She thought again of Fitz at his desk at the Capitol, keeping the hyenas at bay.

"Maybe tomorrow," she said. "Maybe you can swim tomorrow when there's more time. I just want to see about something." She parked next to the fence and they both got out and looked it over. There wasn't much of a crowd here in the late afternoon — a few young mothers watching small children splash about in the wading pool, a handful of children about Jimbo's age leaping off the diving board to retrieve pennies from the pool bottom, a gaggle of teenagers lounging about on a patch of grass. All of them white. There were several round umbrella-covered tables on the concrete apron that surrounded the pool and a row of lounge chairs, but they were mostly empty. There was plenty of room here for everybody, she thought.

The pool manager looked vaguely familiar — middle thirties perhaps, with a broad forehead and thinning hair that he parted just above one ear and flipped over the top. He sat on a stool inside a small shelter at the pool gate. There was a big soft drink cooler behind him and a counter with boxes of candy bars and crackers.

"I'm Mrs. Bright Birdsong," Bright said, stepping up to the counter.

"Oh, yes ma'am," the manager said, smiling. "Haven't seen you in a while, Miz Bright. Don't think I've ever seen you over here at the pool."

"It's my first visit in a good long while," she said. "This is my grandson, Jimbo Blasious. He's visiting me for a few days."

The manager looked over the counter at Jimbo. "Your mama and I graduated from high school together. She doing all right?"

"She's at the beach. She and Rupert."

"Rupert, huh? Well, when she comes back to pick you up, tell her to come over and see Roger at the swimming pool."

"Yes sir."

"Roger Sipsey," Bright said.

"Yes ma'am."

Bright recognized him now. The thinning hair had once been a jet-black, slicked-down ducktail. Roger and Roseann had dated off and on in high school. Everyone Roseann dated, she dated off and on.

< 231 >

Roger Sipsey had been more patient than most, but he eventually gave up like the rest.

"Well, it's nice to see you after all this time." Bright placed her purse on the counter between them. "I'd like to bring Jimbo over to swim while he's here this week, but he doesn't have a season ticket. Could you explain that business to me?"

"Well, it's all right here," Roger said, indicating a sign tacked to the wall next to him. It read:

SEASON TICKETS ONLY

INDIVIDUAL $50

FAMILY $100

"But I suppose we can make an exception for Jimbo."

"An exception?" Bright felt her eyebrows shoot up.

"Sure. We'll just charge him fifty cents. Since he's from out of town and only gonna be here a few days, it'll be all right."

"Hmmmm. Do you make many exceptions?"

He gave her an odd look and then he said, "No ma'am. Not hardly any at all."

"How long have you had this policy?"

"Oh, a good while, I reckon. I've been pool manager now for five years. It goes back before that."

"Do you know why, Roger?"

"No ma'am," he said. "I just run the pool. In the summers, that is. Rest of the year, I teach vocational education at the high school."

"I see."

"Y'all gonna swim today?"

"No," Bright said, "but we'll be back."

She turned to go and then Roger Sipsey said, "Anytime. And by the way, Miz Bright, when you talk to Little Fitz, you tell him folks down here are behind him. One hundred percent."

"He'll be here Thursday," Bright said. "You can tell him yourself."

"Yes ma'am. I'll do that."

<   >

Heads turned when she and Jimbo walked into the town council meeting room a few minutes after seven o'clock. The meeting had already started. Harley Gibbons, seated at one end of the long rectangular council table in the middle of the room, gave her a curious look and a little wave. The others looked up, but didn't pay her much attention. A window air conditioner throbbed fitfully at one side of the room and droplets of condensation fell *ploink-ploink* into a metal bucket underneath the unit. The room looked a little down at the heels, she thought, with dingy beige walls and a crack that ran the length of the ceiling. She hadn't been here in a long time. She didn't remember it looking this way.

There wasn't much of a crowd tonight, just the council members seated around the table and Ortho Noblett alone in the row of chairs next to the wall with his pad and pencil, scribbling notes for the newspaper. Bright remembered council meetings of the past when the room had been packed and the crowd overflowed into the hallway outside and down the stairs. Bright and Jimbo took seats next to Ortho and he leaned over and whispered, "Understand we got big doings tomorrow."

"What?" she whispered back.

"At the Dixie Vittles."

"Oh, that."

"Who's your young friend here?" Ortho asked.

"My grandson. Jimbo."

"Well, bring him along. We'll get his picture in the paper."

Ortho went back to his writing while the council meeting droned on and Bright took stock of the men sitting around the table, the three members of the council who were there. One seat was empty tonight. Flavo's. Bright knew these men as passing acquaintances, saw their photographs frequently in Ortho Noblett's paper. But she didn't *know* them in the way she had known councilmen in the past when she had been a regular here, when she had come and spoken her mind on one thing or another — the library, the hospital, the schools, recreation, street maintenance. She had known those men as the town's leading citizens, and she had known what they were apt to do in a given situation. She could call them on the telephone or go by their place of business and reason things out in advance, so that when she got to a council meeting and had her say, she knew with some certainty how the vote would come out. But these men. All but strangers. Buck Stewart ran a barbershop and kept a penny-a-point pinochle game going in the back room. Cicero Parsons called himself a contractor, but what he did was little more than carpentry — additions and renovations. Clyde Lee Lovett was the only one who was under fifty and the only one here besides Harley who was wearing a tie tonight. He had on a short-sleeved white shirt and a blue-and-white-striped tie and a plastic holder in his shirt pocket full of ballpoint pens. And gold-rimmed glasses. Clyde Lee didn't even work here, for goodness' sake. He drove every day to Columbus, where he was personnel manager for some sort of factory. And there was Harley, of course. Harley looked out of place, she thought, among these people.

< 233 >

They were talking about building a concession stand for the high school football stadium.

Jimbo tugged on her sleeve. "What are they doing, Mama Bright?"

"Spending money," she whispered in his ear.

"Whose money?"

"Ours."

The discussion around the council table was desultory, mired in detail. Cicero Parsons seemed to have appointed himself resident expert on construction, and a great deal of the talk dealt with joists and studs. Then they moved on to wider issues. How big would the concession stand be? No, that was too small. You needed to get five members of the Band Boosters Club behind the counter at a time to serve hot dogs and Cokes, take money and make change. Five? No, that was too big. You'd end up with a concession stand that was bigger than the press box, and that wouldn't look right. So what? There wasn't anybody in the press box except a fellow from the radio station and the PA announcer. Ortho Noblett spoke up and said he didn't need room in the press box because he stayed down on the sidelines, where he could take better pictures. But he sure did hope they'd build a good-sized concession stand so you didn't have to wait so long in line for a hot dog and a soft drink at halftime, because he had to be back on the sidelines when the second half started. Then, somebody suggested, why didn't they paint the concession stand a different color from the press box so that you weren't so prone to make comparisons? What color? Well, how about green. Like the grass. A big green concession stand wouldn't be all that conspicuous. Harley Gibbons doodled on the back of a manila folder with a pencil. Once, he looked over at Bright and rolled his eyes a bit.

Jimbo tugged on her sleeve and she leaned down so he could whisper in her ear. "Can we go now?"

"No, not yet," she whispered back.

"When?"

"In just a little while."

"How long?"

Clyde Lee Lovett turned around in his seat and looked at them. He didn't say anything, just looked. Clyde Lee looked like he didn't take to people whispering behind his back at council meetings. Bright looked straight back at him and he turned around again to the table. "Not long," she whispered to Jimbo. "Why didn't you bring a book?"

"I didn't think it would take this long."

"Neither did I."

< 234 >

"I'm bored."

"I'm bored too," she said, just loud enough for Clyde Lee Lovett to hear. But this time he didn't turn around.

On and on it went and Bright, who had entered the room full of purpose, felt the vitality drain from her and puddle on the floor. It was like wading through molasses, listening to these men. Bright looked over at Jimbo. He was slumped in his chair now, eyes glazed and heavy. She thought she probably should get up and take him home and then come back. But by then the council might have concluded its business and closed shop for the night, and they wouldn't meet again for another week. She couldn't wait that long.

The concession stand business finally concluded with a motion to appoint a committee to study the matter and report back within a month. And it was ten o'clock before the council stumbled to the end of its agenda by fits and starts. Ortho was nodding off in the chair next to Bright, his thick-leaded pencil making a scraggly slash down the page of his pad from the last word he had written.

Harley Gibbons closed the manila folder in front of him and looked over at Bright. "Before we adjourn," Harley said, "I think we should acknowledge the presence of Mrs. Bright Birdsong, the daughter of a former and very distinguished mayor of our community. And the young man, I believe, is Bright's grandson." The council members all turned and looked at her and nodded.

"Good to see you, Bright," Buck Stewart said.

Bright stood up. "I'd like to say a word to the council," she said.

Harley's eyebrows shot up. "Oh?"

"You used to have an item on the agenda called Comments from Citizens. The last item, I believe."

"We ain't had a citizen want to speak in a good while," Cicero Parsons said. "We figured everybody thought everything was fine." That brought a little round of polite laughter.

Clyde Lee Lovett said, trying to be very pleasant about it, "We do accept comments in writing. A week in advance."

"No, I'd like to speak out loud right here and now," Bright said firmly.

"It's getting pretty late . . . ," Buck Stewart whined.

But then Harley leaned across the table and spoke up, his voice good and strong. "Gentlemen, I move we suspend the rules of the council and let Mrs. Birdsong speak." His gaze swept the table and then he quickly said, "Without objection it is so ordered. Bright, the floor is yours." He sat back in his chair and the rest of them shifted around in their seats while Bright moved around to the other end of the table

< 235 >

so they all could see her without craning their necks. Ortho was wide awake now, pencil poised above pad, and Jimbo was sitting up straight in his chair, watching her.

"It's about the swimming pool," she said. "We have a public swimming pool in this community but the public can't use it. Not all of the public."

"Of course they can," Buck Stewart piped up, but then Harley cut him off. "Buck, let's hear Bright out." Harley was looking straight at her now. He had figured out what was up and she could tell he didn't like it. Some old mischief here.

Bright plowed on. "The rule says you have to have a season ticket. Fifty dollars for an individual, a hundred for a family. That alone is ludicrous. And I happen to know that exceptions are made to the rule." She took a deep breath. "The bottom line is, black children can't swim in the public pool."

"Of course they can," Buck Stewart chimed in again. "All they have to do is buy a season ticket."

Bright stared at him. "How many black children do you know who can afford a fifty-dollar swimming pool ticket?"

An awkward silence settled over the room, except for the *ploink-ploink* of the air conditioner and the faint scratching of Ortho's pencil. She wondered if Ortho would put this in the paper in his account of the council meeting. Ortho didn't always put everything he saw or heard in the paper.

"Bright," Harley said gently, sitting up straight now with his elbows on the table, "the policy isn't meant to exclude anybody. It's designed to give us an idea of how much money we'll have to operate on at the start of each summer so we can budget properly."

"Of course," Clyde Lee Lovett said. "You can't just run a swimming pool willy-nilly. You've got to pay Roger Sipsey's salary and hire lifeguards and buy chlorine and so forth."

"And lounge chairs," Cicero Parsons said. "We had to replace every one of them lounge chairs this year. Do you know how much lounge chairs cost? Good ones?"

"No," Bright said, "and I don't want to know. I don't give two hoots about lounge chairs, Cicero. I know this" — she pointed at the empty chair — "the grandson of one of your fellow council members drowned in the river last night because he and his friends don't have season passes to the swimming pool. And they don't have lounge chairs and lifeguards at the river." She tried to keep her voice steady but it was rising now, like the hairs on the back of her neck. "Now what you good gentlemen need to do, before Flavo Richardson comes back here, is do away with that silly rule. It's unfair and it's unconscionable."

< 236 >

They all just sat there and stared at her. Then Clyde Lee Lovett took one of the ballpoint pens out of his pocket and looked at it, clicked it a couple of times, stuck it back in the holder. Cicero Parsons looked down at his lap, coughed, ran his hand through his thinning hair. And finally Buck Stewart said, "Well, we ain't gonna do that."

And they wouldn't, she could see that plainly. They were pig-headed men. And she had to assume that at some point in the past they had reasoned themselves into a corner where prejudice masquer-aded as logic. They were a motley collection of nobodies and upstarts. All except Harley Gibbons. "Harley . . ."

Harley ducked his head, opened the manila folder in front of him, closed it again. And then she saw very clearly how it was with Harley, with this council, indeed with this town.

"Dolts," she said, and then she reached for Jimbo's hand and he scrambled out of his chair and took her hand and she fairly pulled him out the door, leaving the council members slack-jawed behind them.

Harley Gibbons caught up with them before they had turned the corner at Putnam's Mercantile. "Bright!" he called, and she stopped and looked back and saw him walking fast, the street lamps casting long shadows, black on amber, as he strode toward them, his manila folder under his arm. "Bright, wait!" He was a little winded by the time he reached them and he stopped and stood there for a moment on the corner, catching his breath. "Why did you do that?" he asked finally.

She looked past him at City Hall halfway down the block, saw the light go off in the council chamber upstairs. "Harley," she said, "there's going to be trouble."

Jimbo stood next to her, looking first at one and then the other, mouth slightly ajar, taking it all in. She hadn't told him anything about this business, just that they were going to the council meeting. She hadn't told anybody, in fact, except Flavo.

"What kind of trouble?" Harley asked.

"Flavo. And his people. The Quarter's in a stew, Harley."

"He sent you? Why didn't he come himself?"

"Because he's in mourning. Grieving for a little brown boy they pulled out of the river early this morning."

Harley's voice was accusing. "Why didn't you come see me first? Why didn't you tell me this morning? Did you think you could just walk into the council meeting and turn things upside down?"

"I suppose I thought people would listen to reason."

"Reason?" he exploded. "That wasn't reason. That was beat-ing folks over the head. You of all people should know you don't do it that way."

"Why didn't you do something?" she shot back.

< 237 >

"Do something? You backed us all in a corner, demanding we change the rules right on the spot and then calling us dolts when we didn't."

"If the shoe fits . . ."

"Like it or not, Bright," he said angrily, "we are the elected representatives of the community."

She opened her mouth to speak again, but then it struck her suddenly that she might indeed have blundered. One time, after all these years, she had stuck her neck out. And failed. Had failed to get them to see the future. But then, she thought, you could look at that bunch around the council table and tell that they couldn't see any farther than their own noses.

It seemed that Harley read her thoughts. "It's not like it used to be, Bright." He thumbed back over his shoulder in the direction of City Hall, where the rest of the council members were leaving now, calling to each other as they climbed into their cars at the curb.

"No, it's not, Harley," she said. "I've been away too long. I suppose it's not much fun for you anymore."

"No. That's why this is my last time around."

"Well, I'm sorry," she said. "There used to be men of stature on the town council."

Harley looked at her long and hard. "You still want it to be Dorsey Bascombe's town, don't you."

She didn't answer him. Instead, she took Jimbo's hand and they turned and walked away, leaving Harley on the corner under the street lamp. She didn't look back. It was his problem now.

"What happened, Mama Bright?" Jimbo asked at her side.

"Nothing happened."

"Well, what was all the fuss about?"

"About nothing happening," she said.

"Are the little black kids still gonna swim in the river?"

"I don't know," she snapped.

He fell silent then and she could feel him drawing away from her in the dim light, even though she held fast to his hand as they walked.

"I didn't mean to snap," she said after a moment, but he didn't answer.

They crossed Birdsong Boulevard in front of the Dixie Vittles now, then walked up the driveway toward the front steps.

"How'd it go?" Buster Putnam's voice came from the dark of his front porch. She couldn't see him, just the glowing end of his cigar.

"Go on in and get ready for bed," Bright told Jimbo. "I'll be in in a minute and tuck you in."

< 238 >

"I don't need tucking in," he said and there was something stubborn there, an echo of the child his mother had been years before.

"All right." He climbed the steps without her and as he went through the screen door she called out, "Don't forget to brush your teeth." The door slammed behind him.

Buster was sitting in a rocking chair on his porch, legs stretched out, and she could see a tall glass of something on the floor next to the chair. The smell of whiskey and cigars clung to the warm night air. She stopped at the bottom of the steps. "Can I get you a chair?" he asked.

"No," she said. "It's late."

"Long meeting?"

"Crashing boredom," she answered. "Terminal lethargy and rampant ignorance."

"I take it," he said dryly, "that things didn't go well."

"No, they didn't go well at all."

Buster picked up his glass and she heard the tinkle of ice as he took a swallow, set it back down again. "So, what now?"

"Now? Nothing, as far as I'm concerned. I'm going to go call Flavo and tell him what happened. And I'm going to tell him that I wash my hands of the whole business. I can't for the life of me understand why I tried in the first place."

"Not much fun getting shot at, is it?"

"No," she said. And it wasn't. She was feeling more than a little humiliated just now, stung not only by their rebuff but by having gone about it so clumsily. She hadn't even escaped with her pride.

"Well, if you're going to sit over there and go to seed, marry me and we'll do it together." There was something strong and compelling in Buster Putnam's voice, something she remembered from her father and her husband, who bade people do what they wished. But no, she had had quite enough of that for one woman's lifetime, she thought. So she didn't answer him. She turned and left him there on the porch and went home to call Flavo.

< 239 >

15

Bright slept soundly and rose early and clearheaded when she heard Gladys banging about under the house and the birds fussing about in the trees in the front yard. She put on her housedress and stood for a few minutes on the front porch, taking the new sun and gathering the day about her, letting it open itself to her on its own terms. The front lawn, under the pecan trees, was soft green and gray in the beginning light and Claxton Avenue stretched out emptily beyond it to the River Bridge. You could make sense of things, she thought, if you were willing to get up early enough and be quiet enough. So she stood on her porch with the first rays of sun on her face and made sense.

She was still a little puzzled by Flavo Richardson, who had been curiously composed, almost amused, when she had called him last night to tell him about the council meeting. It occurred to her this morning that he had expected exactly what he heard. Flavo knew the council better than she. He was part and parcel of it. He compromised, got along. So why had he sent her there? And then she thought, *Actually, he didn't. He never said anything about going to the council meeting. He said, "Integrate the swimming pool." He didn't say how. He left me to blunder about in the dark, tripping over my own feet and getting my feelings hurt. But the devil with all that. I tried in the only way it occurred to me to try. Now it's their affair, his and the council's. It's their town now.*

So that was over and done. No sense puzzling anymore. Let things take their course and Bright Birdsong would mind her own business, which this particular morning centered on matters a great deal more personal. To wit, fifty thousand dollars, waiting for her across the way at the Dixie Vittles Supermarket. If anything, last night's experience with the council had reminded her of an old lesson. Don't rush too

< 240 >

much. The fifty thousand dollars would take care of itself if she let it. The thing to do was be quiet, be watchful. Take the money and keep her own counsel. If she did, she was bound to do the right thing about it. Whatever that was.

So Bright Birdsong faced the new morning with a sense of calm. Corners turned, things put behind, possibilities faced tranquilly. She turned from the porch now and looked in on Jimbo, sprawled in profound sleep across the bed in the spare bedroom. Something outrageous, Buster had said. Well, what could be more outrageous than fifty thousand dollars? The new pair of overalls hung carefully across a chair. She picked them up and took them with her to the back porch and put them in the washing machine. They would be drying on the line by the time he woke, and ready to wear by ten o'clock. He would look like a country boy in his overalls when Ortho Noblett took their photograph at the Dixie Vittles ceremony. That would be at least a little outrageous.

After she had started the washer, she went to the kitchen and heated up Gladys's breakfast. Gladys was waiting for it next to the back steps, mournful-eyed. As Bright set the bowl down, she said, "A bath today, old girl. Like it or not. No alligator in his right mind would mess with a clean dog." Gladys ignored her and buried her nose in the bowl, snuffling at the food as she ate. Birds chattered at them from the trees overhead, and Bright pulled the garden hose across the backyard and filled up the birdbath. Then she coiled up the hose next to the house and sat down on the back steps, gathering her housedress about her knees, watching the wrens and towhees and jays splash about in the water, while Gladys finished. She felt soothed by familiar habit, time-worn routine. It was good to be as near back to normal as she could hope until week's end, when they all went away and left her alone.

Gladys finished her breakfast now, gave the bowl a last lick, and looked up at Bright. "Gladys," she said, "you've been peeing on the mint." The old dog snorted and struggled painfully through the opening of the bricks and banged her way back to her place in the cool dirt under Bright's bedroom. Back with the alligator Josephus.

She woke Jimbo with a glass of orange juice and he sat up in the bed, groggy with sleep, took a sip, and put the glass on the night table next to the bed.

"Are you grumpy in the mornings?" she asked.

He nodded, looking up as she stood beside the bed. She raised the shades at the windows, letting the morning fill the room, then sat down on the side of the bed while he drained the glass of orange juice. "Well, I'm not. I sleep like a log and wake with a clear conscience.

< 241 >

Always have. Gladys, now, she's a different story. She's a little grumpy in the mornings. She's very old and not in the best of health. And you know what else?"

"What?"

"She's been peeing on the mint. By the back door." He looked up at her curiously, perhaps not quite sure of what to think. "I discovered it yesterday when Mr. Gibbons came by for a glass of iced tea and he remarked about the odd taste. And then I realized what Gladys had been doing."

"Did Mr. Gibbons *know?*" he asked, wide-eyed.

"No, and we'll let that be our secret."

"Well," Jimbo said, "that's what he gets for not letting the little black kids swim in the swimming pool." He was very earnest about it. She wondered how much of the doings last night at the council meeting he had truly taken in. Perhaps more than she had given him credit for. What did ten-year-old boys perceive, anyway? It had been a very long time since she had truly encountered one.

"Yes," she said. "Well, howsomever."

"What?"

"Howsomever. Haven't you ever heard that word?"

"No ma'am."

"It's a perfectly wonderful word. In the same category as *reckon* and *ain't* for richness of expression. If you can't think of anything else to say, just say *howsomever.*"

He thought about that for a moment. "Is it like *thingamajig?*"

"In what way?"

"Well, when Rupert can't think of what you call something, he calls it a *thingamajig.*"

"Same premise," she said, standing now and picking up his empty orange juice glass. "Howsomever, time's wasting. We've got business to transact this morning."

"The fifty thousand dollars?"

"Exactly. So let's get cracking." She pulled back his covers. "I'm washing your overalls as we speak and I'll have your breakfast ready when you get through taking your bath."

While he showered, she fixed poached eggs on whole wheat toast, Cream of Wheat with a pat of butter melting in the middle, a tall glass of milk for Jimbo and a cup of black coffee for her. She was putting it on the table in the breakfast room when he came in, hair still damp. She sat down at the table and Jimbo slid into his chair across from her and gave his plate a sour look. "I usually have cereal."

Bright picked up her spoon and wiggled it at his bowl. "Cream of Wheat is cereal."

< 242 >

"I mean like Froot Loops."

"What?"

"Froot Loops. Little round things. They float in the milk."

"And I imagine they float in your stomach," she said. "Cream of Wheat sticks to your ribs. What do your mama and Rupert eat for breakfast?"

"They eat Froot Loops too."

"Well, this week, until they get back from the beach, you eat a decent breakfast. Dig in."

Jimbo picked at his breakfast for a while, taking small tentative spoonfuls of the Cream of Wheat and then poking the poached egg with his fork until he broke the soft yolk and the yellow ran out on his plate. Bright didn't say anything. After a few minutes, his hunger began to get the best of him and he ate with relish, down to the last bite of whole wheat toast.

Bright went to the kitchen and refilled her coffee cup, and when she sat down again she asked, "How do you feel about people speaking their minds?"

"What?" He looked up at her curiously.

"Do you think people ought to say what they're thinking, no matter what?"

"Well," he hesitated, "Mama says if you can't say something nice, don't say anything at all."

"Hmmmm," Bright said. "Interesting idea, coming from your mama. Despite that good advice, have you ever had something stuck in your craw that you just wanted to blurt out?"

"Sure. Lots of times."

"Well, for the remainder of this week, I want to encourage you to speak your mind, at least between the two of us. No matter how outrageous a thing is, if you're thinking it, you can tell me."

"You mean *everything*?"

"Well, almost. Be a gentleman about it."

"Gee."

"Want to try it?"

"I suppose."

"I reckon," she corrected. "Now try something. Something you've been thinking but hesitated to say."

Jimbo thought for a moment, staring at his empty plate, then raised his head. "Are you a rich old lady?"

"Who said that?"

"Bonnie Wimsley, one of the kids I was playing with yesterday. She said you're a rich old lady."

Bright plucked her napkin from her lap, wiped her lips carefully,

< 243 >

and tucked it under the edge of her plate. Ask for a thing, she thought, and you might get it. "No," she said, "I'm not a rich old lady."

"But you're gonna get fifty thousand dollars," Jimbo said, eyes wide with the contemplation of it. "Doesn't that make you rich?"

"If you had fifty thousand dollars, would that make you rich?"

"You betcha," Jimbo said.

"Well, I don't consider fifty thousand dollars any great deal of wealth. Your grandfather Congressman Birdsong used to deal in billions. He gave it away to places like Borneo."

"Didn't he bring any of it home?" Jimbo asked.

She stood and picked up their plates and moved toward the kitchen with them. Then she stopped in the doorway and turned back to him. "No," she said, "as a matter of fact he didn't."

Jimbo looked up at her. "Can I say anything I want?"

"That's the rule."

"Grandfather should have kept a little for himself."

<   >

Bright and Jimbo were about to walk out the door just before ten when Xuripha Deloach called.

"Well, you've made a fine stew, Bright Birdsong," she said.

"Beg pardon?"

"It's all over town."

"What's all over town?"

"The council meeting."

There was a long silence while Bright waited for Xuripha to come to whatever point she was working toward. Finally she said, "I would think you'd leave well enough alone."

"The swimming pool."

"Yes. Of course the swimming pool."

"I didn't know you were a frequenter of the swimming pool, Xuripha. Do you wear a one-piece or a bikini?"

There was a little exasperated intake of breath on the other end. "Bright, you're deliberately trying to stir up trouble."

"No, I'm deliberately not," Bright said firmly. "I went to the council meeting and spoke my mind, and that's the end of it."

"Well, I hope so." Xuripha sniffed. "I just hope you haven't got Flavo Richardson and his crowd riled up now. If there's a ruckus —"

"Tell me," Bright interrupted. "What is it you object to, Xuripha? About the swimming pool. Please be frank. You're among friends here."

"Think of . . ." — she hung fire for a moment — ". . . sanitation."

< 244 >

"Sanitation?"

"Yes. All those little unwashed . . ." She trailed off.

"Ah yes," Bright said. "I hadn't thought about that. Sanitation."

"Hadn't thought," Xuripha said. "Yes, I don't suppose you did."

"I always was a bit impetuous," Bright smiled. "You'd think at my age I would have grown out of it."

"Yes, you would," Xuripha said emphatically. "I would think at your age you'd be content to be quiet for a change. Let somebody else besides the Bascombes run things."

"Well, that's why I've got friends like you," Bright said. "To set me straight when I wander from the path. We are still friends, aren't we?"

"Of course. I'm just finding it a little hard to defend you this morning."

"Well, I appreciate your trying." She looked through the screen door at the Dixie Vittles. The parking lot was crowded with cars. "And now I've got to go pick up my winnings," she said. "When the shooting starts, I plan to be in Acapulco."

Harley Gibbons was standing in front of the Dixie Vittles when Bright and Jimbo arrived. He had a funny look on his face, as if he were not at all sure he should have come.

"Good morning, Harley," she called from the street, and she held her hand out as she reached him. "I'm glad to see you."

"About last night . . . ," he started.

"Never mind about last night," she said. "I'm sorry I got involved, and I'm doubly sorry we got crossed up. I hope you'll accept my apology."

"No apology needed, Bright. Not between old friends." Harley looked down at Jimbo and patted him on the head. "Good morning, Jimbo. Come to help your rich grandma tote home her winnings?"

Bright thought suddenly what she had said about Jimbo speaking his mind and felt a little rush of panic. But Jimbo didn't say a word about Gladys and the mint. Instead, he looked up at Harley with a big smile and said, "Yes sir. Howsomever." Bright squeezed his shoulder.

A fair-sized crowd was milling about inside. The store was noisy with shoppers clattering about with their buggies, more than Bright had ever seen in the Dixie Vittles on a Wednesday morning. Ortho Noblett was there from the newspaper with his big Speed Graphic camera.

"Well, here comes the big winner! And hizzoner the mayor!" Doris cried as Harley opened the door and the three of them stepped into the damp coolness. The buzz and hum of voices went up a notch, as if somebody had turned on a big machine. *Dear me, I've become a*

< 245 >

little infamous. Doubly infamous. Fifty thousand dollars AND a public commotion.

Monkey Deloach was standing just inside the door, looking rather festive this morning with a dandelion stuck in the top buttonhole of his open-necked shirt. "Ah, uh, hmmmmm . . . ," he began. "Top of the . . . hmmmmmm . . ."

"Day," Bright finished for him.

"Right . . . hmmmmmm. . . ."

"You look downright festive this morning, Monkey," she said, nodding toward the dandelion in his lapel. "Did Xuripha fix you up with a flower?"

"Nope," Monkey said. "That was my . . . hmmmmmmm. . . ."

"Idea."

"Right . . . hmmmmmm . . ."

"Well, this must be a special occasion."

"Of course it is," Monkey said without a hitch. "And bully for you, calling the town council a bunch of pissants."

"Dolts," she corrected.

"What . . . hmmmmmm . . . ever."

Bright touched his arm. "Well, I'm glad you came. I need a little support. This is all a bit overwhelming."

Doris Hawkins was standing just beyond Monkey, hopping from foot to foot, trying to maneuver around him. Finally she reached over and took Bright protectively by the arm and guided her toward the counter. "Mrs. Fitzhugh Birdsong," Doris announced, "and her grand-son, Jabbo. And Mayor Harley Gibbons."

"Jimbo," Jimbo corrected.

Hank Foscoe, the manager of the store, was there, along with a fellow named Bert Bottoms from the regional office of the Dixie Vittles chain in Columbus. They were wearing little round white hats and red jackets with Dixie Vittles labels on them and they looked as if they had just stepped out from behind the meat counter.

"What a pleasure," Bert Bottoms warbled as Doris introduced everybody. He took Bright's hand and bent toward her, giving her a strong whiff of an after-shave that made her think of cowboys. "Having such a distinguished citizen as our grand-prize winner. And so *early* in our contest, too!" Bright thought from the way he said it that Bert Bottoms probably wished she had waited a couple of months to win the grand prize.

"Pleased to meet you," Bright said, and he leaned down to shake Jimbo's hand too.

"I met your son last year when we had the grand opening of our new distribution center in Columbus," Bottoms went on, straighten-

< 246 >

ing. "He came down and made a speech for us. Guess he's pretty busy these days with the campaign and all . . ." His voice trailed off and there was a bit of an awkward silence while they all contemplated Fitz and his predicament.

Bright rescued them. "You'll have to come back tomorrow, Mr. Bottoms. We're having Fitz Birdsong Day. I'm sure he'd be glad to see you again."

"Well, I'll just have to see if I can't do that." He smiled broadly. "Now, we've got some important business to transact here this morning. Hank, have you got the grand prize?"

"Right here," Hank said, and he reached behind the counter and pulled out a huge cardboard replica of a bank check, perhaps three feet by six, with Bright's name on the "Pay to the order of" line and FIFTY THOUSAND DOLLARS in big bold black letters just below it. Bright stared at it for a moment. *So that's what fifty thousand dollars looks like.*

As he held it up, Bright saw a white van pull up in front of the Dixie Vittles with big red letters on the side that said LIVE EYE 5. The television station from the state capital. *Good Lord.*

"Good Lord," Doris cried. "Look a'yonder. The TV folks. Hank, did you call the TV folks?"

"Not me," Hank said. "Mr. Bottoms, do you reckon the regional office called the TV folks?"

"Not that I know of," Bert Bottoms said. "They don't ever cover things like this, so we gave up trying a long time ago. If it ain't a wreck or a fire, they don't bother. They wouldn't come to the groundbreaking for the distribution center last year, even with the governor there."

There was an excited buzz inside the Dixie Vittles and Bright could hear the clatter of grocery buggies back in the store as the shoppers crowded up toward the front. They watched as a young man got out of the van on the driver's side and a young woman from the passenger side. She waited by the van, digging in her purse for a pad and pencil, while the young man went around to the back and opened the door and pulled out a big gray camera and hoisted it onto one shoulder, then connected some wires to a box he slung over the other shoulder. Then she held the door while he maneuvered through. Inside, everybody stood watching, fascinated. It was the first time Live Eye 5 had been to town since Fitzhugh Birdsong had retired from Congress eight years before. And then it hadn't actually been Live Eye 5, but a fellow from the same station with a little dinky camera that he wound up with a crank, and a tape recorder.

Monkey Deloach was waiting just inside the door for them. "Hmmmmmmm . . . Holly, ah . . . hmmmmm . . . Hardee."

< 247 >

He stuck out his hand and the young woman gave him a curious look and a quick shake. Then she looked at the rest of them, crowded about the counter, gawking at her.

"I'm Holly Hardee from Live Eye Five," she said.

Bert Bottoms broke from the pack and rushed over to her. "I'm Bert Bottoms from the Dixie Vittles regional office," he said. "What a nice surprise."

"The governor's office called this morning," she said with a shake of her blond hair. "They said Birdsong's mother had won a bunch of money. We drove like a bat out of hell to get here."

"Well, you're just in time," Bottoms said. "We're about to present the grand prize to our lucky winner." He brought Holly Hardee over to them. "This is Mrs. Birdsong," he said, "and her grandson Jabbo."

"Jimbo," he said, raising his voice just a bit.

"Pleased ta meetcha," Holly Hardee said, shaking hands all around. She seemed impatient to get on with things. Bright imagined that Holly Hardee thought of this as a dinky story. She would probably rather be somewhere covering a disaster. They should have sent the man with the dinky camera and the tape recorder. He hadn't been in a hurry at all. In fact, he had stood around eating cookies and drinking punch for a good long while after the ceremony was over. Holly Hardee didn't look much like a cookies-and-punch person. "Well, what's the drill here?" she asked.

"Beg pardon?" Bert Bottoms said.

"How are you gonna do this?"

"Well," he said a little uncertainly, "I guess we're just going to give Mrs. Birdsong the check here." He indicated the big cardboard check that Doris and Hank were holding.

"Is that it?"

"That's it."

"Okay," she said, tossing her head again. "Let's get the show on the road."

They all lined up in front of the counter, Doris and Hank on either end holding the big check, Bright and Bert and Jimbo in the middle. "Wait a minute," Bright said. "We need to get the mayor in the shot. Harley, come stand with us. And we've got to get Jimbo out where they can see him." So Harley edged in on the right side of the group and they put Jimbo out in front of the check, down at the left end in front of Doris, so he wouldn't cover up Bright's name or the FIFTY THOUSAND DOLLARS.

The cameraman turned on a light on the top of the camera and it flooded the front of the store and made them blink in the glare.

< 248 >

"Ortho, do you want to get your picture now?" Doris asked Ortho Noblett.

"Naw, no hurry," he said. Ortho was lounging against a display of soft drinks, his Speed Graphic resting on top. "I got all day. Paper don't come out 'til tomorrow. Y'all get through with the TV stuff and I'll get my picture."

"Roll it, Charlie," Holly Hardee said, and the cameraman turned on his camera. It whirred and hummed. "Shake hands," she commanded, and Bert Bottoms reached over and took Bright's hand and gave it a vigorous pump. "Get a close-up of the handshake, Charlie." Bert kept pumping while the cameraman zoomed in on their hands. "And some tight shots," she said. He moved around the group, getting shots of their faces from different angles, while Bert kept shaking Bright's hand and grinning. Bright felt exceedingly silly, but then she remembered feeling silly eight years before when the man with the crank camera took her picture at Fitzhugh's party.

"Awright, let's get an interview." Bert dropped her hand and Holly Hardee stepped in front of the camera, holding a microphone now, thrusting it in Bright's face. "What's your reaction to the mess your son's gotten himself into?" she asked.

There was a stunned silence in the store. Bright looked Holly Hardee straight in the eye. "That's an impertinent question, young lady."

"Do you think he's guilty?"

"Of course not," Bright said without hesitation. "My son is an upstanding man and a credit to his family. He has made a fine governor and the people of this state would be foolish not to reelect him."

"I'll tell you what," Doris chimed in, "you won't find a solitary soul in his hometown got a word bad to say about Little Fitz Birdsong."

"Damn straight," Monkey Deloach piped up from over near the door, and there was a titter of laughter.

Holly Hardee shrugged. "Do you plan to contribute your prize money to the governor's campaign, Mrs. Birdsong?"

Bright smiled sweetly. "That's none of your business."

Holly Hardee lowered the microphone and turned to the cameraman. "Okay, cut it, Charlie." Then to Bright she said, "I wasn't trying to be rude, Mrs. Birdsong. Just doing my job."

"Of course," Bright said and then there was a long silence while everybody in the store stared at Holly Hardee.

"Well, that's it, I guess," she said to the crowd, flashing them a big smile. "Got to run now."

"So glad you came," Bert burbled.

< 249 >

"Sure," she breezed, and they bolted out the door, leaving the place a little breathless in their wake.

"Gosh," Doris said as they watched Holly Hardee and the cameraman loading their gear into the van. "She's a cheeky little thing, ain't she. At least she didn't ask you about the town council meeting."

"Guess I can get my picture now," Ortho said, hoisting his big Speed Graphic. "Just hold what you got, folks."

"Do you want us to shake hands?" Bert asked.

"Naw, this ain't TV," Ortho said. "Just look this way and smile so I can get all your faces real good." Ortho took a flashbulb out of his shirt pocket, wet the end of it with his mouth, and stuck it in the flashgun, then peered through the viewfinder, focusing. "Ritz crackers," he called out.

"Ritz crackers," they all said together, and the flashbulb popped, leaving a big black speck in Bright's vision. Then Ortho put his camera down and took a scrap of paper and pencil out of his shirt pocket and wrote down all their names, left to right.

"Do you want an interview, Ortho?" Bright asked.

He grinned. "Naw, I reckon I got all I need."

"I guess that just about does it," Bert said, and Hank Foscoe took the big cardboard check and laid it over on the counter behind them.

Bright turned to Harley Gibbons. "Harley, we'll just go on around to the bank with you, and you can cash my check."

They all laughed at that. "We'll have the real thing in the mail to you in a couple of days," Bert said.

"You mean that's not the real thing?" Bright pointed at the big piece of cardboard.

Harley looked the check over, one end to the other. "Well, legally I guess you could say that it qualifies as a check. It's got everything that's required — date, payee, amount. Is that an authentic signature, Mr. Bottoms?"

"Oh, yes," Bert said. "Our treasurer signed it himself this morning, so it would look just right."

"But no bank would ever cash something like that," Harley went on. "But when you get the check, Bright, you bring it right on and make a deposit. You don't want to leave something like that lying around." Harley smiled and she could almost hear the adding machine clacking away in the back of his head, toting up the mortgage on her house.

"Good advice, Harley," she said. "Never can tell what I might want to do with the money, but the first thing I'll do is put it in a safe place."

< 250 >

"Can we have this one?" Jimbo chimed in, holding up the big cardboard check.

"Well, sure," Bert said. "It's just a prop. No good to any of us. Keep it as a souvenir."

"Want me to carry it home for you?" Harley asked.

"No, I think we can get it," Bright said. "Here, Jimbo. You grab hold of the back and I'll get the front."

They said their good-byes then and Monkey Deloach held the door for them and Bright and Jimbo went out into the morning, holding the big piece of cardboard between them. They were standing at the curb, waiting to cross Birdsong Boulevard, when Bright heard a loud honk behind her, a vehicle approaching along Claxton. She turned to see the Winnebago bearing down on them. Roseann was leaning out of the passenger-side window, waving and yelling.

"Oh, damn," she said softly under her breath.

<   >

Roseann was climbing out of the Winnebago as Bright and Jimbo stepped up on the curb and started across the lawn with the big piece of cardboard between them. She stood in the driveway, arms crossed, waiting for them.

"Hi, Mama," Jimbo called out to her.

Roseann called back, "What the dickens have you got there?"

"Fifty thousand dollars!" Jimbo said.

"Good morning, Roseann," Bright said pleasantly as they reached her. "We didn't expect you so soon. Did you decide to come back early for your brother's big day?"

"What?"

"Fitz Birdsong Day. Tomorrow."

Roseann gave her a strange look. "Well . . ." She shrugged.

"How was the beach?"

"Just fine," Roseann said. "It was fine."

Bright thought there was something odd, something amiss here. It took her a moment to put her finger on it. Then it struck her. *Roseann is remarkably composed this morning.* Her hair was neat, unplucked. She was calm, under control. *The beach appears to have done her a world of good.*

Rupert appeared in the open doorway of the Winnebago. He was wearing the same knit shirt, seersucker Bermuda shorts, black socks, and jogging shoes he had had on two days earlier. The only difference was that his knees were sunburned.

"Hello, Rupert," Bright said. "I see you didn't drown."

< 251 >

"Morning, Bright." Rupert, she thought, looked a little peaked this morning. Indigestion perhaps. "No" — he gave them a weak smile — "I didn't drown. I hardly got in the water, in fact. How's it going, Jimbo?"

"I got overalls," he said.

"I see you did. Are you becoming a country boy?"

Jimbo tapped on the big cardboard check. "Mama Bright's rich! She won fifty thousand dollars!"

"Is that it?" Roseann stared at the check.

"No, that's just what they took the picture with. For the newspaper. They said the real one's coming in the mail."

They all stood there looking at each other and the check for a moment and then Roseann said, "I read about it in the paper."

"At the beach?" Bright said.

"Rupert went out to get a paper this morning and I was propped up in the bed reading it and there on the back page was this story about Governor Fitz Birdsong's mother winning fifty thousand dollars! I near about fell out of the bed!" Roseann pointed at the cardboard check. "What are you going to do with that thing?"

"Mama Bright said I could have it," Jimbo said.

"Nonsense," Roseann said.

"Well, I'm gonna," Jimbo said stubbornly.

"No, you're not."

"Yes, I am."

"Whoa," Bright interrupted. "Time out. Let's just lay it down here by the steps and we can decide what to do with it later. Now let's go in and get out of the heat. Rupert, you look a little ill this morning. Something in the water at the beach?"

"No," he said, "I'm just fine. Really."

Bright gave him a careful once-over. *What is going on here?*

"Look," he said, brightening, "I think I'll go get us some fried chicken for lunch. Save you having to fix anything. We passed a chicken place coming in."

"Yes," Roseann said. "That's a good idea, Rupert. Why don't you go get some chicken."

"Fine," Bright said. "When you get back, you can unload your things, since you're staying for the big doings tomorrow. Fitz will be delighted."

Roseann started to say something, stopped herself. She turned and headed up the steps, leaving them there in the yard. Rupert watched her go, disappearing into the house; then he looked down at Bright. Then it dawned on her. *The man is embarrassed about something.* "Go get the chicken," Bright said gently. "And then maybe I can

< 252 >

find something for you to fix. Maybe the washing machine will go *clunk* while you're gone."

"Ahhh," he said with a grateful smile. "Yes."

"Take your time. It won't be lunchtime for another hour yet."

He nodded. "I'll do that." He closed the door to the Winnebago and climbed into the driver's seat and started the engine, and Bright and Jimbo stepped back to the edge of the driveway and watched him back out into Birdsong Boulevard. Across the street at the Dixie Vittles, Bert Bottoms was getting into his car, heading back to Columbus. Hank Foscoe and Doris Hawkins stood in the parking lot, seeing him off, and they all gave Bright a little wave.

Bright looked down at Jimbo. His forehead was scrunched in a frown. "I wish they'd stayed at the beach," he said.

So do I, she thought, but she didn't say it.

"They musta made the baby already," Jimbo said. "Or maybe Rupert wore his schlong out."

Bright cleared her throat noisily. "Well, howsomever."

Jimbo looked up. "Yeah. Howsomever."

Bright stood in the driveway for a moment, ruminating, wondering what on earth was going on here. Nothing to do, she thought, but go in the house and deal with Roseann. Then she heard Buster Putnam's saw going in the workshop behind his house. The band saw, it sounded like. "Jimbo," she said, "why don't you go over to Buster's house and see what he's doing. I'll come get you when it's lunchtime."

Jimbo brightened. "Okay." He started toward Buster's backyard. "And stay back from that machinery," she called. He waved and disappeared around the corner of the house.

Now. Bright took a deep breath and climbed the steps.

So it was just the two of them there in the parlor, Roseann in the big wing-back chair by the secretary and Bright on the sofa. *Now,* she thought, *let's get to the bottom of things.*

But instead of getting to the bottom of things, Roseann prattled, and that too was puzzling. Roseann was not one who ever talked in circles, especially when that was the very thing she should do. Usually she went directly, nakedly to the point, bowling over everything in her path. *Like me,* Bright thought with a flash of insight. *Like me at the council meeting last night, beating those old dolts over the head like I did.* Roseann sat there now and talked on about the beach, and as she did, the mental image bubbled in Bright's imagination: Roseann under the umbrella in a low chair with her diet Coke in one hand and romance novel in the other, clad in a one-piece bathing suit with a little pleated

< 253 >

skirt affair about the hipline, a rubber thong sandal dangling from the end of one foot as her leg bobbed nervously, smelling of sunscreen and perfume, face scrunched, hand tugging idly at her hair. Bright cringed at the thought. And then on its heels, a pang of old remorse, old guilt. Roseann could do that to you, always could — make you want to take her by the shoulders and shake her, and then fold your arms around her, ashamed that she could make you so intensely dislike her. A mother could be allowed anger, but not dislike.

She resolved now to be gentle with Roseann. Whatever had brought her racing back from the beach, whatever held her now in the wing-back chair, so fiercely in check — Bright would deal with it gently.

She waited, and finally Roseann's voice trailed off in the middle of a sentence and she looked away, out the window, as if she had exhausted herself with chatter. She studied the morning for a moment and then she looked down at her hands. Bright saw how tightly they gripped each other in her lap, a telltale. Finally Roseann said, "Mama, Rupert needs that money."

Ah, so. How obtuse of me. "Rupert?"

"To start his business. I told you about it. He wants to quit the University and go out on his own. We've talked about it a lot while we've been at the beach."

"*He* wants?"

"Yes."

"And he wants the money."

"Well, he didn't want me to ask you." She hesitated for a moment, and her hands rose of their own power, beginning to pull at her hair. Bright winced. She wanted to grab Roseann's hands, still their plucking and tugging, wrap her arms around her daughter and restore the fragile calm she had brought with her from the beach. But she sat frozen, staring. Roseann rushed on, talking very fast now. "Fifty thousand dollars would get him started, Mama. He could borrow the rest and buy some tools and be all set up. It would be a loan, Mama. I don't want . . . *we* don't want you to *give* us the money. We'll pay it back. With interest. What's interest these days? Ten percent? We'll pay it back at eleven percent. We'll put it in writing."

She finished, breathless. Then she seemed to come to herself. She stared at her hands as if they belonged to someone else, then pressed them quickly together in her lap, capturing them. It was a painful thing to see and Bright felt something very close to tears. But what to do? How to answer? Bright prayed for wisdom, found none. So she tried to buy time. She said, "Fitz asked me to lend it to him."

< 254 >

"Fitz!" An angry explosion of sound. "His mess is all over the papers and the television news at the beach. You can't get away from it."

"No, I suppose not. He needs help, Roseann."

"What he needs," she snapped, "is to keep his pants zipped up."

"Roseann!"

"It's always Fitz, Mama. Why?"

And Bright thought suddenly again of their childhood: Roseann's small hand reaching across the table to her brother's plate, snatching a piece of bread, a drumstick. Nothing she truly wanted, just something to make him bellow with the indignity of invasion. And Bright, striking out with a stinging pop to her hand. *Don't grab!*

"Honey, it's not . . ."

"Yes, Mama. With you, it's always been Fitz."

Bright held her tongue, waited. She didn't want to fight. "He's in a fix right now."

Roseann shook her head violently. "Politics!"

"Yes." Bright nodded sadly. "Politics."

Roseann didn't say anything for a moment. She looked away and Bright could see her lips moving ever so slightly. Words unformed, things unsaid. A wrestling there. Then she seemed to make up her mind, taking a long breath, reaching down deep. She turned back to Bright. "You should know."

This time, she could not turn away. "What do you mean?"

"You were always up to your neck in it. The school board, all that mess. Always going to council meeting. This issue and that." She was trying very hard to keep her voice low and calm, but there was something hard and insistent there. Now they were on the old, familiar, poisoned ground. And despite herself, Bright could feel her hackles rising.

"I'm out of politics now," Bright said firmly. She started to tell Roseann about the town council meeting, then thought better of it. No need to go into that.

"It's a little late," Roseann said tightly. There was a long silence, and then Roseann seemed to gather herself, to make a last stab at conciliation. "If you give the money to Fitz, you will never see it again. It will be throwing good money after bad."

"That may be," Bright said.

"But you're going to do it anyway."

Bright threw up her hands. "I don't know what I'm going to do with the money, Roseann!" She stood suddenly, riven with frustration. "Damn the money! It's nothing but trouble. People pulling and tugging

< 255 >

on me! Fitz and Harley Gibbons. And now you! I don't even have time to think! So you'll all just have to be patient!"

Then Roseann was on her feet too. "Patient? PATIENT? I've been patient all my life!"

The air in the room was electric now, popping and crackling between them.

"What do you mean? You've never been patient about a thing!" Bright's hands slashed the air. She felt a great fury taking hold of her, was powerless to stop it. All the old poisons, loose in the air, acrid and choking.

Roseann took a step toward Bright, eyes flashing, color high in her cheeks. "I waited all my life for things to be *normal*, Mama! But they never were! I wanted to be like everybody else! But I never could!"

"No, you couldn't. You were always busy being impatient and angry and hard to manage! No matter what I tried, it wasn't enough, Roseann!"

They glared at each other across the great gulf of their separateness. Finally Roseann's eyes broke away. "You kept me from Papa."

Yes. That's it, of course. That's been it from the beginning. "I did the best I could! We both had to choose, and I chose what I thought was best for you and Fitz. Growing up here, where people cared about you! But now," she spat bitterly, "I'm the only one left to blame. Well, I won't have it!"

"Oh, yes, you will. You've always had it. Always had it your way."

"Your father —"

"Begged you!" Roseann cried, her voice breaking now, the glint of tears in her eyes. "He begged you!"

Enough! "Stop it, Roseann!"

Roseann thrust her face forward, very close to Bright, menacing, her voice a growl. "Well, to hell with all that, Mama. One thing about you, you were never sorry for a damn thing you said or did. So I shouldn't expect it now. All I want is the money."

"Well, you can't have it!" Bright flashed. "I won't buy your approval, Roseann!"

"Damn you!" Roseann cried out. "You owe it to me!"

Bright clamped her hands over her ears, and her voice was hollow and far away as she shouted, "Don't you damn me! I owe you nothing!"

Roseann grabbed Bright's hands then, her face full of fury, and pulled them roughly away from Bright's head. "You killed him!"

Bright lashed out before she could stop herself, her hand a swift weapon. The force of the blow snapped Roseann's head back and left the flaming imprint of Bright's hand across her cheek. Roseann rocked

< 256 >

back on her heels and stood there, frozen, eyes wide with shock and hurt. Then her hand went to her face and she gave a short, vicious cry and rushed past Bright, into the bedroom. Bright heard the bathroom door slam with bone-rattling force.

Bright stood, hardly breathing, horrified. *All this time, all that rancor and conflict, and it never quite came to this.* Then she thought, *It's the money! It's like a beast, gnawing at me! It will consume me if I don't do something! Now!* Bright stood there for a moment, trying to gather her wits. Then she went quickly to the bathroom door, listened to the anguished sobs, tapped lightly. "Roseann, honey, I'm sorry. Come on out now. We've got to talk about this."

"Go away!" Roseann screamed. "Just leave me alone! Don't ever speak to me again! I'll take Jimbo away from here and we'll never come back!"

Bright blanched, the anger suddenly alive in her again. "The hell you will!"

Roseann screamed and the door handle rattled violently. Bright stepped back, suddenly afraid. Such raw, hateful fury! The door rattled again and then shook as Roseann tried harder to open it. "Let me out, damn you!" She raged at it with her fist and her cries were incoherent now, the awful noise pounding at Bright, driving her away. Then the breaking of glass, jars and bottles swept from the vanity top and sent crashing to the tile floor.

"No!" Bright cried. She imagined blood, suddenly saw her father splayed across the front steps of the camp house, blood everywhere, flowing bright red and dripping off the wooden steps onto the hot sandy ground. She backed away from the bathroom door with terror stalking her, stumbling, reaching to steady herself on the bedpost, the door-frame, until she was into the living room with the awful noise following her, beating at her ears. And then suddenly it ceased and Bright stopped, stunned now by dread silence. She took a step toward the bathroom, then she heard Roseann again, quietly sobbing. She turned away and opened the screen door and stepped out onto the porch, staggered over to one of the wicker chairs. She collapsed into it, shaking uncontrollably, her heart beating wildly. *My God, I'm going to have a heart attack!* Then the pounding from the bathroom started again, measured and powerful now, like a battering ram. Then silence again. *I can't face this! I can't face her if she gets loose!* And she fled, down the steps into the yard, just as Jimbo rounded the corner of the house. He stopped, stared at her.

"Mama Bright! What's wrong?"

"Nothing," she choked out. Then she looked down, saw the big

< 257 >

cardboard check propped against the steps. *The money. The damned money!* And the idea struck her, powerful and consuming. She knew what she had to do, and do right now.

"Get in the car," she said.

"Where are we going?"

"To the bank. With this." She picked up the check and stuck it through the open back window of the Plymouth. It protruded a foot or so, but it would have to do. She opened the door. Jimbo stood staring at her. "Get in!" she commanded, and there was something in her voice that propelled him. He blinked once at her, then climbed in on the passenger side and closed the door, sat watching her curiously. Then she remembered her purse. It had her driver's license in it. "Don't move," she ordered, and she went back in the house and got her purse from the table by the sofa. It was quiet now, but as she turned to go, the bathroom door rattled again. "Mama!" Roseann yelled. "You let me out of here!" She pounded on the door, making it dance with the force of her blows. *She might hurt herself. I don't want that.* Bright picked up the telephone, dialed the police station.

"PO-leese," said the young voice on the other end.

"Tell Homer Sipsey to send the Rescue Squad quick," Bright said. "There's somebody trapped in Bright Birdsong's house."

Then she closed the screen door softly behind her and went to the car, where Jimbo was waiting, looking hard at her, his face a mask of suspicion.

"What's that noise in the house?" Jimbo asked.

"Not a thing." Bright started the car, put it into reverse, backed out of the driveway into Birdsong Boulevard. Then she turned onto Claxton, headed toward the River Bridge. As the Plymouth topped the rise over the bridge, she could hear the siren on top of the fire station downtown, summoning the Rescue Squad. And she could hear too Roseann's anguished voice flailing away at her. "You killed him!" Bright stomped hard on the accelerator and bluish-gray smoke belched in a great cloud from the rear of the old car as it struggled away from the pursuing furies.

< 258 >

16

She had not been to the state capital in more than three years, not since Little Fitz's inauguration. That had been a blustery January day with the wind whipping the state flag atop the Capitol and chilling the crowd gathered in front of the big platform built over the wide Capitol steps. The cold and wind had reddened their faces, and so, a bit, had Bright Birdsong.

She had created quite a stir when she stepped out of the car with Flavo Richardson at her side. Fitzhugh had sent a nice young highway patrolman to fetch her early in the morning, and she had directed him first to Flavo's house, where she badgered Flavo until he finally put on a suit and went with her, grumbling about uppity white folks. The highway patrolman pulled up to the edge of the platform a few minutes before the inaugural parade began, and when she and Flavo alighted from the car, she could hear the astonished buzz from the crowd, could feel their gape-jawed stares. Then Fitz was there, eyebrows at full mast. *What will you do next, old girl?* He handled the surprise nicely, enveloped her in a big hug and his huge warm smile and gave Flavo a hearty handshake. Then he escorted them up to the platform, where they made a place beside her in the front row for Flavo. The next day, the newspapers wrote about how he was the first black man to sit on an inaugural reviewing stand since Reconstruction. "It broke the ice," Fitz said later. He liked to put the best face on things. He was at heart an optimist, as she had intended he be. She had also raised him a progressive, as her father had been. Like most politicians, she thought, he just needed an occasional nudge in the right direction.

Bright thought about all that as she and Jimbo approached the capital in the fierce humid heat of the June midafternoon, coming up from the south across the broad flat plain of the river.

She was calm now, in control of herself and very sure of what she

< 259 >

wanted to do, at least in the short run. Beyond that, she couldn't think just yet. She would get her money and give Roseann time to calm down and then she would deal with the rest of it. It would be easier with cash. She could give it away, throw it in the river, bury it. Whatever. But she would deal with it. She and Jimbo. She felt fiercely protective of him now. They had stopped in Columbus for hamburgers and chocolate malts. Then they had had a rambling conversation as she drove on, not about anything in particular, and he had loosened up a good bit. He sat up straight in the front seat now, right elbow propped on the open window, overall-clad, hair a bit tousled by the wind.

"Is that the capital up there?" he asked as they crept along the four-lane, traffic swooshing by on their left. She had been driving slowly and carefully, trying to avoid vapor lock, and it had taken them most of the afternoon to make the trip.

"The seat of power," she said. "Big government and big banks."

He turned, looked back at the big cardboard check sticking out the rear window. "Nobody's gonna cash that thing," he said.

"Why not?"

"It's too big."

"It's a perfectly good check," she said. "Harley Gibbons said so."

"Then why didn't he cash it? He has a bank."

Questions. He has that much of his mother in him. "A little bitty bank. We're going to a big bank."

"Are you sure it's all right with Mama?"

"I'm in perfect control of the situation," she answered.

He fell silent as the city grew larger in the windshield, watching the road and the river that ran alongside, dark green and sluggish. Ahead, the capital shimmered in the heat like a desert outpost.

It was a middling city, nothing like Atlanta or Nashville, where government coexisted with bustling commerce. The downtown was a low cluster of buildings, dominated by the white-domed Capitol set on a slight rise in the middle with the chunky buildings of the various state agencies splayed around the base like matrons-in-waiting. Where Bright came from, folks had always considered the capital a bit pretentious, full of its own social self-importance, when in fact without the presence of state officialdom it would have barely existed. As it was, the capital had sort of created itself with wide tree-lined boulevards and a good number of presentable homes and, in later years, ribbons of concrete expressway to whisk you from the countryside.

The expressway widened to six lanes as it eased toward the city and soared up and across the river on a towering bridge. There had been some sort of scandal about the construction of it in the administration before Fitz took office. There was always some sort of scandal or

< 260 >

another. Contractors rigging bids, lobbyists delivering caseloads of whiskey, men making fools of themselves over women half their age. Politics, Dorsey Bascombe had once said to her, was a genteel front for the violation of the Commandments. All of them. Of course he considered local politics quite apart, more a matter of stewardship. A mayor wasn't really a politician. And Fitzhugh Birdsong had looked at it from a quite different perspective too. He disdained what he considered the mean and grubby business that went on in the state capital and practiced a far different art and craft at the congressional level. Bright, for her part, didn't make much distinction. Politicians, she thought, didn't so much fool other folks as they fooled themselves.

The first thing she did was to find a policeman. And that happened just after she exited the interstate onto the broad, tree-lined avenue that led uphill to the Capitol, all white-columned and majestic with the late-afternoon sun full on its face and dome. She saw a police car in front of her and she pulled right up behind it and mashed down on the horn.

"Jeezus!" Jimbo yelped, startled. "You're gonna get us arrested!"

The policeman behind the wheel jerked with surprise and snapped his head around to look in his rearview mirror. Then he turned on his blue light, slowed, and eased against the curb with Bright at his bumper. They both stopped and Bright put the Plymouth in park and turned off the ignition. They all sat there for a moment, marinating, and then the police officer opened his door and climbed out, putting on his blue cap and hitching up his britches. He walked back to Bright's car, the heel of one hand resting lightly against the butt of his big pistol, leaned over and peered inside at her. Then he straightened and looked at the big cardboard check sticking out the rear window, a bit wind-tattered at the edges from the trip.

"Ma'am?" he said finally.

"I'm looking for a bank."

"Any particular bank, ma'am?" the officer asked. He pushed his cap to the back of his head and squinted at her.

"A big bank," she said, "to cash a big check."

The policeman looked again at the check, examined it closely, tilting his head to read it. She could see him mouthing the words: FIFTY THOUSAND DOLLARS. "Is that a real check?" he asked.

"Perfectly legal," she said. "Signed personally by the treasurer of the Dixie Vittles Supermarket chain."

He nodded. "For fifty thousand dollars."

"That's right."

He looked again, read silently: MRS. BRIGHT BIRDSONG.

< 261 >

"My son is the governor," she said, helping him.

"Little Fitz?"

"Yes."

He lifted his cap all the way off his head now, scratched at his hair for a moment, plopped it back on.

"Just any old big bank?"

"Right again," she said pleasantly.

"Uh-huh." He blinked, looked the check over for a final time. Then he wiggled his finger at her. "Follow me." And he walked back to his car and climbed in and pulled away from the curb. As he did, he turned on his siren.

"Hey!" Jimbo cried. "That's neat, Mama Bright!"

Bright flushed with embarrassment, but she followed him as they moved slowly up the boulevard toward the Capitol past gawking knots of people on the sidewalks. *My Lord, I hope he's not taking me to Fitz's office. I don't want to see Fitz.* But a couple of blocks short of the Capitol he pulled over again and stopped in front of a big office building, and the siren whined to a halt. Bright eased her own car over behind him at the curb. He got out and came back to them. "Well" — he pointed to the building — "there's your big old bank." The big brass letters on the granite face of the building read OLDSOUTH TRUST.

"I'm much obliged," she said, reaching for her pocketbook. "What do I owe you?"

"Not a thing, ma'am. I wouldn't take a million dollars for the experience." He tipped his cap. "Y'all be careful now, y'hear. And tell Little Fitz I said hello. I met him one time. He's a right nice fellow. Tell him I said to give 'em hell, y'hear."

"We'll do that."

He left them, glancing back again through the mirror as he drove away. Bright turned off the ignition, let the engine die, and then turned to Jimbo. "Buster Putnam said you needed to do something outrageous," she said.

He eyed her warily. "Huh!" he grunted.

"Do you want to go home," she asked him, "or do you want to stick around and see what kind of nutty maneuver I'm going to pull next?"

He considered it for a moment; then he said, "I reckon I'll stay."

"You reckon you will. Well, good. Let's transact our business and get on with things."

They got out of the car and hoisted the check out the rear window, one holding each end, and headed across the sidewalk toward the entrance of the bank. A young man with a briefcase held the big glass door while they went through into the lobby. It was a big, high-

< 262 >

ceilinged, open room with a lot of marble and brass and potted plants, several desks off to one side, nestled on thick carpet, the people behind them busily putting things away, tidying to go home. Straight ahead was a row of elevators with gleaming doors that opened with a whoosh, disgorging little packs of scurrying people who boiled through the lobby, men in suits and women in snappy dresses, brushing by them with curious looks.

"We better get out of the way, or we're gonna get run over," Jimbo said, tugging on his end of the check.

Bright stood her ground, surveying the confusion. "It doesn't look much like a bank," she said. And then, off to one side, she spotted the only thing that really looked like a bank, a long high counter. There weren't any customers there, just a couple of women busily working at calculators.

"Over there," Bright said, and they edged through the rush of people to the counter and stopped in front of one of the women. She looked very prim, very efficient, punching away at her calculator with one hand while she riffled through a stack of papers with the other. She was absorbed in the work. Bright cleared her throat. "Is this a bank or not?"

She punched a few more times at the calculator and then stopped, gave them a thin smile. "Yes," she said, "this is a bank."

"Do you have fifty thousand dollars?"

The woman looked a trifle alarmed.

"It's not a holdup," Bright hastened. "We just want to cash our check. Jimbo, turn around this way so the lady can see the check."

She stared at it for a long moment, opened her mouth, closed it again, then tried another tight smile. Finally she said, "You've got to be kidding."

"Young lady," Bright said, "I didn't drive all the way up here to kid around. It's a perfectly good check, and it's worth fifty thousand dollars." She tried to look pleasant but firm.

The young woman stared at them for a moment longer, then picked up a telephone, punched a number, and turned her back to them while she mumbled into it. No sooner had she put it down than a man appeared magically at their side, a balding middle-aged man, one of those Bright had seen at a desk on the other side of the room.

"Lou Purcell," he said. "The branch manager." He seemed nice enough and he looked her straight in the eye, avoiding the check. "May I be of assistance?"

"Yes, indeed, you may be of assistance," she said. "You may cash our check."

He looked at it then, gave it a careful going-over. He rocked back

< 263 >

and forth from his heels to the balls of his feet a couple of times, like a pendulum on a clock, as if to remind her that it was late in the workday and everybody here wanted to end it neatly and quietly, without any fuss. Then he looked at the check again, and his eyes stopped on the "Pay to the order of" line and his eyes narrowed and his nose twitched like a rabbit smelling greens. "Mrs., ah, Birdsong . . ."

"Mrs. Fitzhugh Birdsong," she said.

"The ah . . ."

"Widow of the congressman, mother of the governor."

Within minutes they were in one of the gleaming elevators, floating toward the upper floors of the building, shepherded by the branch manager, the check now in the custody of the young woman behind the counter, with the manager's assurance that it would be quite safe in her custody. When they stepped off the elevator, a tall, distinguished-looking man was standing in the big open double doors of a spacious office, smiling broadly, offering his hand.

"Mrs. Birdsong. What a lovely surprise. And honor. I'm Foxhall Beaulieu, the president of the bank. I was just talking with Fitz about you this morning, after we read about your good fortune in the newspaper. Quite an exciting time for you, I imagine."

Bright shook his hand. "You know my son."

"Ah, of course," he said with a wiggle of his eyebrows. "Fitz and I go way back." She thought about what Harley Gibbons had told her. Fitz and the big banks.

"This is my grandson, Jimbo," she said, "my daughter's boy." They shook hands and Foxhall Beaulieu ushered them into his inner sanctum on a cloud of pleasantries, to big leather armchairs in front of a huge polished table, with ornate, curving cabriole legs, that served as a desk. It was empty except for a telephone console, a blank notepad, and a pen-and-pencil set with a marble base. There was a lot of brass and marble and potted greenery here too, but also a good deal of mahogany, grass-cloth wallpaper, gilt-framed artwork. Two of the walls were entirely glass, covered by sheer, gauzy curtains, one of them strategically parted to reveal a splendid view of the Capitol nestled on its hill a couple of blocks away, the state flag drifting lazily above the dome in a late-afternoon breeze off the river. Purcell, the branch manager, appeared in a moment with a tray of crystal glasses filled with ice and a clear, bubbly liquid. They each took one while Foxhall Beaulieu babbled on about the weather, the traffic, the sterling attributes of the downstate where Bright lived. Everything but the check.

"Something's wrong with the water," Jimbo said, taking a sip and wrinkling his nose.

< 264 >

"Perrier," said Foxhall Beaulieu. "May I get you something else?"

Jimbo looked over at Bright.

"Would you like a Coca-Cola?" she asked. "I'll bet a big fancy bank like this has a Coca-Cola somewhere on the premises. Even Harley Gibbons's bank has Coca-Colas, and it's a little bitty old bank." She glanced over at Foxhall Beaulieu. "Or, at least it used to be."

"A Coke?" Beaulieu asked.

"Yes sir," Jimbo asked. He looked lost in the expanse of the green leather of the armchair and his feet dangled six inches from the thick carpet.

"Of course. And you, Mrs. Birdsong?"

"No," she said. "Soda water is just fine."

Beaulieu nodded to the branch manager, who took Jimbo's glass and disappeared again. "Gosh, I haven't seen Harley Gibbons in a couple of years," he said to Bright. "I don't think he came to the last Bankers Association meeting. How's he doing?"

Bright took a sip from her glass and thought of Harley, drinking tea on her front porch, the sprig of mint peeking over the top of the glass.

"Just fine for a man who's lost his business," she said.

Foxhall Beaulieu's eyebrows went up. "Lost? Oh yes," he said, smiling. "He's merging with First Commercial, I think."

"Merging," Bright said. That was an interesting way to put it.

"Well, I'm sure he'll do well with First Commercial. They're competitors, of course, but good folks."

"It won't be Harley Gibbons's bank anymore," Bright insisted. "Things won't be the same. Harley likes to stand right at the front door and shake hands with all the customers when they come in. I didn't see anybody standing by your front door."

Foxhall Beaulieu laughed, but she thought it was a trifle forced. "Maybe you've got a point there. We'll have to look into that. Might be a good public relations gimmick. Have somebody stand at the door of every branch and shake hands." Beaulieu swiveled back in his chair and clasped his hands under his chin. "Might even make a good advertising campaign: 'The Bank That Wants to Shake Your Hand.'" He waved a hand, showing a flash of gold cuff link, as if the slogan might magically appear in the air above them. The branch manager was back now, handing Jimbo a glass of Coca-Cola. "Purcell," Beaulieu said, "I think Mrs. Birdsong has just given us an idea. What do you think of 'The Bank That Wants to Shake Your Hand'?" He made another wave. "Put somebody at the door of every branch to greet customers when they come in."

"Sounds good to me," the branch manager said agreeably.

< 265 >

"Well, we'll look into it," Beaulieu said.

"That's fine," Bright said. "Now can you cash my check?"

Foxhall Beaulieu leaned forward slowly in his chair, propped his elbows on the desk. "Gosh, that's a mighty big check, Mrs. Birdsong. In more ways than one." He gave them a nice laugh.

"It is to me," she said. "And it might be to Harley Gibbons. But I'll bet a big bank like this has got millions stashed away in a vault somewhere."

"Well," he said, dismissing the notion of millions with a flick of his wrist.

"It's a perfectly good check," she said. "Harley told me that."

"Then why didn't he cash it?"

She hung fire for a second. She didn't want to tell this pleasant man, this friend of Fitz's, a bald-faced lie. "Because I didn't ask him to," she said.

"Oh."

The telephone on Beaulieu's desk beeped softly then, and he picked up the receiver, leaned back in the chair again. "Fitz!" he said. "I was hoping they could track you down, old buddy. Guess who's sitting right here in the office with me. Your mom. And your nephew. Yes, that's right. Well, she wants to transact some business with us." He listened for a moment, then nodded. "Sure. I'll put her on." He put his hand over the mouthpiece, looked across at Bright. "Would you like to take this somewhere, ah, more private?"

She hesitated. She didn't really want to talk to Fitz right now. But there didn't seem to be much way around it, with Foxhall Beaulieu sitting there, expectantly holding the receiver. So she said, "Yes, I suppose I'd better." He put the call on hold and ushered her into a small room next to his office with just a desk, chair, and telephone. He closed the door behind him and she sat down, picked up the receiver, punched the blinking light. "Fitz?"

"Mama, what the hell's going on?"

"What do you mean, son?" she asked innocently.

"I just called your house and talked to what's his name . . ."

"Rupert."

"Yeah, Rupert. He said you locked Roseann in the bathroom and ran off with Jimbo."

Bright blanched. "Well, that's not the way it happened at all. Roseann locked herself in the bathroom and Jimbo left with me quite voluntarily."

"Rupert says Roseann is under sedation."

"Good Lord."

< 266 >

"Did you have a fight, Mama?"

"Yes, as a matter of fact we did. We had a right serious fight."

"Over the money?"

"That's none of your business, Fitz. That's between Roseann and me."

"Okay. Okay." She could tell that Fitz was trying to be calm and patient, and having a very hard time of it. "Do you know why I called your house, Mama?"

"No, why?"

"Because I had just gotten off the phone with Harley Gibbons. And do you know why I called Harley Gibbons?"

I don't want to hear this. "Why, son?"

Fitz measured out the words, his voice tight and controlled. "Because a newspaper reporter called me to ask what I thought about your uproar with the town council last night. That was the word he used. *Uproar.*"

"No," Bright said firmly, "there definitely wasn't an uproar. I spoke my piece and walked out and then they all went home. I wouldn't call that an uproar. Nothing was thrown or burned."

"Did you call them dolts, Mama?"

"Yes, I did."

"Well," he said, "I think you'll find all those words in the paper tomorrow morning in the story about how the governor's mother is battling the town council over integrating the swimming pool."

"Why on earth would the paper up here be interested in our little old controversy way down there?" she asked.

"Because, Mama, there's a governor's race going on and this particular paper has taken particular interest in me lately. I've been the source of an exceptional amount of news."

The photograph flashed before her, Fitz in his boxer shorts and the woman in her bathrobe on the front porch of the camp house. "Oh," she said. "That paper."

"Yes, that paper."

There was a long silence while the phone line hissed and sizzled across the distance between them. Then she heard noise in the background, the rumble of engines, somebody shouting. "Where are you, Fitz?" she asked.

"I'm at a phone booth outside a truck stop upstate. On my way to a campaign rally."

"Why on earth are you calling from a truck stop?"

"The highway patrol got us on the radio. They said it was an emergency."

< 267 >

"Well, it's not an emergency, and I can't imagine why they bothered you. I'm just trying to cash my check."

There was another long pause and she could hear the blast of a truck's air horn, some whiny music from a radio. Finally Fitz said, "Why do you want to cash your check, Mama?" His voice was low and strained now, as if he were chugging uphill in low gear.

"To get the money," she said.

He sighed. She could hear it clearly, a long sad sigh that went way beyond desperation. "I'm not even going to ask you any more questions about that. But I'll tell you what, Mama. I just don't need any more problems right now. Why the devil did you think you had to take on the town council *now?*"

"Because it needed doing. And because Flavo . . ." She stopped.

"Flavo Richardson?"

"His grandson drowned because they make children buy a season ticket to get in the swimming pool." It sounded confused and stupid. If he were here right now, she could explain it all, explain it so that he would understand how urgent it had seemed. And she could tell him how she had blundered, gone about it all wrong, stuck her neck out, had it chopped off, and left a mess on the floor. But he wasn't here. He was at some fool truck stop.

"Mama, your timing was exquisite," he said.

"You're angry," she said matter-of-factly.

"I'm wore out," he answered.

"Fitz, I'm sorry. I didn't think . . ."

He didn't say anything for a good while. There was a long, thick silence and something changed in his voice. When he finally spoke he said quietly, "No, you're not."

"Not what?"

"Sorry. You did this to Papa once. You and Flavo. The high school. You just went ahead and did it. You didn't ask him what he thought. You didn't think about whether it affected him. You just did it."

"Fitz . . ."

"You've always done pretty much what you wanted, Mama." His voice was tight and bitter now.

"Listen . . . ," she started. And then she heard the echo of Roseann's voice: *You were never sorry . . .* It might be the only thing Little Fitz and Roseann had ever agreed on. This one thing.

"No, Mama," Fitz broke in. "I've got to go now. Put Foxy on the line and I'll tell him to cash your check."

"Fitz . . ."

< 268 >

"I'm about at the end of my rope, Mama. I'll see you tomorrow."

She held the receiver for a moment and then she punched the button that said hold and placed the receiver back in its cradle. Her hands were trembling. She put them in her lap and sat, trying to collect herself. Finally she got up and opened the door. Foxhall Beaulieu was standing at the big plate glass window with Jimbo, pointing out the Capitol and its outbuildings. "Mr. Beaulieu," she said, and he turned to her. "My son wants to talk to you again."

He gave her an odd look; then he left Jimbo at the window and went back to his desk, picked up the telephone, listened for a moment before he said, "Whatever you say, good buddy. We'll work something out. Look, I'll talk to you later. Give me a call at home when you get back in."

He hung up, then rose from his chair. "Purcell," he said to the branch manager, "cash Mrs. Birdsong's check."

"Yes sir," Purcell said. "What are we going to do with that big cardboard check, Mr. Beaulieu? The Federal Reserve will never accept it."

Beaulieu thought for a moment, pressing his fingertips together. "When the supermarket people send you the check, Mrs. Birdsong, get it in the mail promptly to us if you would. Special delivery would be nice, addressed to me personally. We'll consider this transaction today a loan. Until the other check clears."

"No interest," Bright said.

"Of course. Purcell, take care of it."

Purcell looked doubtful. "This is pretty irregular, Mr. Beaulieu."

Beaulieu fixed him with a stare. "Just do it, Purcell. On my authority. Bring me all the papers."

"Yes sir," Purcell said, backing toward the door.

"How do you want the money?" he asked Bright.

"Fifties will be fine."

"I'm a little concerned about you having all that cash on you," Beaulieu said. "Are you staying overnight?"

"No," Bright said, "we're going to get a bit of supper and go straight home. The straighter the better."

Foxhall Beaulieu got up from behind the desk, came around to where she and Jimbo stood now in the middle of the room. "Mrs. Birdsong, I think the world of your son," he said.

"I'm glad to hear that. So do I."

"I realize . . ." He stopped, cleared his throat. "I want him to win this race if it's humanly possible."

Bright thought of Harley Gibbons. "Because you run a big bank?"

< 269 >

Then she thought, *I shouldn't have said that. I've caused enough trouble. I need to curb my tongue and get my money and get out of here.*

"No," Beaulieu said. "Well, that has something to do with it. But Fitz is a friend and he's a man who'll look you in the eye and do what he says. You and the congressman raised him right."

Bright thought for just an instant that she was going to cry then, but she took hold of herself quickly. "That's very kind of you," she said softly.

The branch manager and a security guard walked out with them to their car, the guard holding the manager's nice leather briefcase filled with the money. A thousand fifty-dollar bills, she calculated.

"I'll get your briefcase back to you as soon as we get home," she promised. "I'll put it on the bus."

"No hurry," Purcell said. He still looked a little stunned by the whole business.

There was a parking ticket on the windshield of the Plymouth and the security guard plucked it off, stuck it in his pocket, handed Bright the briefcase through the open window. She passed it to Jimbo, who held it in his lap as they drove away, waving back to the two men from the bank standing on the sidewalk, watching them.

"What am I gonna do with this?" Jimbo asked. "I can't ride all the way home with it in my lap."

"You're my bodyguard," she said. "Both the money and I are your responsibility."

He thought about it for a moment and his shoulders straightened. "I'll sit on it." He rose up from the seat, tucked the briefcase under him, sat down again. "There," he said, giving her a firm look. "I won't let anything happen to you."

They stopped at a nice little café in a town just outside the capital and had a good meal while Jimbo sat protectively on the briefcase. And then they headed south toward home as the night closed in, turning things purply soft. Jimbo fiddled with the radio for a while, listening to snatches of music and talk from St. Louis, New Orleans, Nashville. But the tired old tubes wouldn't hold a station for long, and he gave up eventually and turned it off with a click, then leaned his head back against the seat.

"Tired?" she asked.

"Ummm-hmmm."

"You can crawl in the back seat and go to sleep if you want."

"No." He shook his head. "I'll stay up here with the briefcase." He sat up high in the seat with the leather case underneath him.

< 270 >

"Isn't that uncomfortable?"

He shrugged. "Not much."

"Well, I think you could slide it down under the seat and it would be just as safe. Then you'll know it's right under you in case you have to grab it and run."

"Why would I do that?"

"Oh, in case terrorists attack the car."

He laughed at that, the thought of the car under attack. Then he stowed the briefcase away under the seat and sat for a long time looking out the window at the gathering night, trees and fields, houses and crossroads stores fading into darkness, replaced with warm squares of lights in windows and stark blue-white security lamps in the farmhouse yards. "You better turn on your lights," he reminded her, and she switched them on and they splayed weakly across the road ahead.

She slowed to forty and crept on into the night while the wind at the open windows sang in baritone, a low, fitful song. Traffic was light, on occasional car or truck that appeared suddenly behind her and then whisked past. She had not driven at night for a very long time, but there was something comforting about it, like pulling a thick winter quilt about you, feeling the nubby texture of stitches made by deft hands — in and out, in and out, weaving time itself into the fabric. She felt the same kind of familiarity now — the wind at the window, the swish of the tires, the low throb of the motor, all of it swaddled by the night. You didn't need to see the landmarks when the road led so surely home, long stretches of warm, velvet blackness speckled by lights that kept the night at bay.

"I used to go to the capital with my father when I was a little girl," she said, speaking as much to the night as to Jimbo.

"Was he the guy in Congress?"

"No, that was my husband. Your grandfather."

"Who was your father?" He turned to her, his face pale and fragile in the dim light from the dashboard.

Ah, where to begin? "He was a lumberman," she said.

"What's a lumberman?"

"Well, he owned a sawmill by the river in town, and he had a lot of men who worked for him. They cut timber all through the forests, even up in this part of the state sometimes."

"Like Paul Bunyan," he said.

Bright smiled. "He didn't have an ox, but he had teams of horses at first and then he had big trucks. He was a very progressive man, my father. He was the first timberman in this part of the country to use trucks. His crews would go to the woods and cut the trees—huge trees, so tall you couldn't see the tops of them from the ground. And

< 271 >

then he figured out how to take his sawmill to the woods, and they would cut up the trees right there on the spot and haul the lumber to town. Daybreak to dawn." She talked on, telling him about the lumberyard, the big whining planer mill under the long tin-roofed shed, the sawdust matted underfoot, the smell of fresh-cut wood and resin thick in the air, her favorite spot in the elm tree just outside the window of the small office building. She lost herself in the story, deep in the cocoon of the rushing night and the humming wheels of the car. *She felt Dorsey Bascombe's strong arms lifting her out of the tree onto his shoulders. When she looked down, his tall leather boots seemed to be a mile below. They strode the grounds like a two-headed giant, calling out to the sweating black men who tended the great throbbing mill, waiting for the noon whistle. It was noontime only when Dorsey Bascombe said it was. He was the most powerful man in the world, a man who held sway over time itself. They stopped and Dorsey pulled his watch from his pocket, snapped open the cover, gave a nod. And the whistle sang out across the yard, across the shimmering river nearby, across Dorsey Bascombe's town . . .*

She stopped abruptly, blinking herself back to the present, and looked over at Jimbo. He had fallen asleep, his head lolling against the seat back, mouth open. She reached for him, pulled his head down into her lap. He nestled there, cuddling against her like a small, tired animal.

He had withdrawn into his own world of dreams, but he had left her with her own — the man in the tall leather boots and the other one who strode the landscape in a much different but still powerful way. One man whose world had consumed her, the other whose world she had never truly known. She faced them both now, memories she had had tucked away for so long, like musty remnants of childhood dresses in a cedar chest, hidden in a corner of the attic. One got on with things and got along, because the alternative was abiding despair. And Bright Birdsong had never been a despairing woman. She coped, she took responsibility for herself, she did what needed to be done. When you didn't have time or inclination to bother with ghosts, they kept to themselves. They were shy creatures.

But as she rolled on through the night, she felt the palpable presence of her ghosts, and for the first time in a long time, the old sense of loss and abandonment. Things lost, things missed, things left unfinished.

Her children. She thought of Roseann and Fitz, both of them angry with her now, one violently so. Their bitterness, she realized, had little to do with the money or with the business of the town coun-

< 272 >

cil. It was the old thing, the thing given voice by both of them in the space of five hours today. *You were never sorry.* An ancient grievance, a ghost of another sort, this one a beast that had ripped open old wounds and exposed them to the fetid air. This ghost, joining company with the others, filling the car now with their presence, no longer the shy and unthreatening creatures she had imagined them to be. She felt a growing panic, her old heart racing with apprehension. She wanted to shake Jimbo awake and cry, "What must I do?" But he wouldn't know. He stirred in sleep, made a soft snuffling sound and edged closer to her.

So she rolled on through the night, haunted by ancient spirits. Her brain swirled and eddied like a storm-choked river, and from the dark water, hands reached up to her. And then voices, emboldened by her sudden vulnerability. Fitzhugh, pleading: "Come away with me and be mine and only mine!" Roseann, accusing: "You killed him!" And Fitz, scolding: "You've always done pretty much what you wanted."

She gasped, her eyes wide with fright. And then she began to cry, the tears coming despite all she could do to hold them back, coursing down her cheeks and blurring the night through the windshield. The car lurched and she gripped the steering wheel in terror, realized that a wheel had slipped off the shoulder of the road. She jerked it back and then she mashed on the brake and stopped the car dead in the road and sat there, her heart in her throat and her breath coming in labored wheezes. The voices all cried out at once now. "Why? Why?"

And then it came to her, an illumination, an answer wrenched from the depths of her soul. *Because I never came down from Dorsey Bascombe's shoulders.*

< >

They came at long last to the outskirts of town, the old woman and the young boy in the old rumbling car, refugees from the night.

As they topped the rise on the River Bridge, Bright saw the glow on the horizon, well beyond the dark place at the end of the street where her own house would be. She thought first of the football stadium. She could sit on her own porch on cool fall evenings and see its lights like something atomic over the treetops, hear snatches of cheering and the thump of a bass drum. But no, the football stadium was well off to her right now, not far from the riverbank. This was something different. Then she saw the lick of flame against the sky and she realized with a flash of horror what it was. *Booker T. Washington is burning!*

She fled from it. At the bottom of the bridge she turned into a

< 273 >

driveway, backed into the street and retreated over the bridge. She drove fast out the road along the river, the car devouring the highway as if it might outrun the pale glare of its old headlamps. Eventually, she reached the place she was looking for and turned off the pavement down the dirt road. The car bumped and heaved along the ruts with the trees close on either side.

Jimbo awoke with a start. "What's that?" He rose up in the seat, rubbing his eyes.

"Nothing," she said, trying to keep her voice calm. "Go back to sleep."

He looked at her for a moment, then put his head back down in her lap. She slowed, picking her way along the rutted path, tall weeds scraping the underside of the car. Finally they broke from the woods into the clearing and the lights of the car bathed the front porch of the camp house and she saw it as she had seen it in her imagination that very first day when she and Dorsey had come here together. She stopped the car in front of the house and turned off the engine, sat listening for a moment.

He was still here, she thought, the tall man in the brown leather boots who passed pieces of unbearably sweet candy under his desk to the tiny creature who burrowed there in the safe darkness. His very blood was deep in this ground. The river ran through his veins, and his voice was carried on the wind that rustled the trees with a faint breeze. She was afraid, terribly afraid. But she took a deep breath and calmed herself. Dorsey was here. And now, he was the only refuge she knew.

Dorsey Bascombe would talk to her, and she would listen. And then she would know what to do.

< 274 >

BOOK 4

17

The house of death. It had been lifeless for so long, and now it teemed with people, a constant stream of them, ebbing and flowing across the yard, through the front hallway and into the parlor, like a river out of its banks. They came because Dorsey Bascombe was the one man their town could not afford to lose, and yet he lay upstairs with a great, gaping hole in his shoulder, his heartbeat a mere flutter, his life slowly draining into the blood-soaked mattress.

The men who went rushing to fetch Dorsey back to town from the camp house had gone back later, had handled the body of the dead foreman O'Marron roughly, had tossed it into a hastily dug shallow grave without benefit of coffin or clergy. It was whispered in the house of death that one of the men had urinated on the corpse before they covered it with earth. But they didn't dwell on O'Marron. He was better forgotten.

They came to tend the living and the dying and they brought food, great heaping bowls and platters and hampers full of it, as if they could by the sheer weight of okra and fried chicken and fruit salad stop the hand of death, or at least delay it for a while until they had had proper time to intercede for Dorsey Bascombe's soul. Hosanna took it all to the kitchen, muttering darkly, "Folks don't think I can cook?" Much of it went fairly quickly out the back door to her part of town. "Nigras ain't never eat so good," she said. "Mr. Dorsey would like that."

They came to console, to pray (the town's ministers took turns leading an around-the-clock prayer vigil in a corner of the parlor), and to see how the young widow to be was holding up.

They found Elise Bascombe remarkably composed, tragically pretty, seemingly in complete control of both herself and the situation. She greeted the guests solemnly at the front door, made them feel at ease, accepted their offerings, guided them to the parlor, and then withdrew discreetly at regular intervals to go upstairs to her husband's

< 277 >

side. They marveled. Was this the same Elise Bascombe who had collapsed from sheer fright at the Study Club meeting? This young woman had poise, backbone, breeding. She seemed to draw on some secret reservoir of strength and grace in her husband's darkest hour. She was much admired, much complimented. Only a few wagging tongues wondered why it had taken the approach of death to bring her out of her shell.

The one constant in the house was the doctor, Finus Tillman, perhaps Dorsey's best friend in this town. It would not do, he said, to try to move Dorsey to the hospital in Columbus. It was too risky. So Finus Tillman moved in, black satchel and suitcase, and they set up a cot for him in Dorsey's bedroom. For two days he hovered over the blasted near-corpse on the bed, doing what he could to stanch the steady drip of blood from the horrible wound, grinding his teeth in frustration as the pulse became weaker and the patient slipped farther into darkness. So very much damage had been done. The left side of Dorsey's chest was torn away. Several pieces of buckshot were lodged perilously close to the heart. The doctor did not dare touch them. The left arm was riddled and withered—bone shattered, flesh shredded, blood vessels severed. On the morning of the second day, Finus told Elise that Dorsey could not live. She must prepare herself. Elise nodded, pulled a chair next to her husband's bed, took his limp hand into her own, and waited for the end.

Bright knew little of this until later, because they had sent her straightaway to the Hardwicke home. A house of death, Elise said, was no place for a child. Bright never forgave her for that.

Fincher and Fostoria didn't seem to know what to do with Bright, and so they did too much. They hovered about her like dark angels, clucking and cloying, until she thought she must scream from suffocation. Bright could tell that the whole business was a great strain on them, trying to fill the silence, hoping to God it would soon be over and they could be relieved of this awkwardness. She wanted them to go away and leave her alone, or better still to take her to her father. But she didn't say any of that because it would be mean and tacky and she didn't want to do anything to make anyone mad with her. If she was bad, her father would die Godless. She was petrified with fear of that.

So she said not a single word to the adult Hardwickes. As far as they knew, she was still mute. In truth, the horrible blast of O'Marron's shotgun had loosened the grip of whatever beast had gripped her tongue in its hoary fist these past months. Words had come spilling from her mouth in a torrent there in the field when she had run for help. She had spoken because she simply had to. But when the first

< 278 >

feverish babble had died in her throat, she closed her mouth again and retreated into the silence of her own counsel.

She revealed herself only to Xuripha, and then only in the deep silence of night. The Hardwickes established Bright in Xuripha's room, where there were twin beds, and Xuripha's disapproving silence let her know that she was an interloper and, more than that, a freakish curiosity.

On the evening of the first night, Fostoria tucked them both into bed and turned off the light, and Xuripha waited until the door closed and Fostoria's footsteps faded down the hall. And then she said, quite loudly, "Your father's almost dead. I heard 'em talking. He won't last 'til daybreak."

Something snapped in Bright. She threw back the covers and leapt from the bed and stood trembling with rage over Xuripha's prone form. She hissed. Like a snake. She felt the venom surging through her veins, the furious sound seething through her clenched teeth, and she raised both her hands, curled into wicked claws, preparing to strike. "If you say another word to me, I will bite you on the neck and you will die a horrible death!"

Xuripha cried out in terror, clutching the sheet up around her neck.

"Shut up!" Bright hissed. "Just shut your stupid mouth!" She stood frozen with rage for a moment longer, making sure that Xuripha was thoroughly terrified, and then she got back into her own bed and lay there listening to the wretched whimpering.

It stopped after a while and Xuripha said in a tiny voice, "I didn't know you could speak."

"Yes, I can speak."

"When did it happen?"

"When the man shot my daddy."

Xuripha sat up in the bed. "Why didn't you speak all that time?"

"None of your business," Bright said shortly.

Xuripha didn't say anything for a long while and Bright huddled under the sheet, listening to the crickets in the grass outside the window, hoping Xuripha would leave her alone with her misery. Finally, Xuripha said, "I'm sorry. Truly I am." And then after another moment she got out of her bed and came to Bright's and climbed in with her and put her arms around Bright and hugged her very tightly. Bright stiffened, wanting her to just go away, feeling the ache and grief hard like a rock inside her. But they lay there together for a long time and Bright began to let go a little and then the tears came and it was better.

Xuripha, ever the tattletale, managed somehow to keep Bright's secret. She tried, as best she knew how, to comfort. But Bright was still

< 279 >

much alone with her own dark terrors. She wished fervently to die, to escape at the same moment that life fled her father's wasted body. He would die, she knew that. In truth, he had gone from her in that one horrible instant in which he had stepped toward the gaping black twin holes of the shotgun barrel. She would have stopped him if she could. She would have reached out and plucked at his sleeve and turned him gently away, out of danger, and then turned to stare calmly at the death-flame herself. But it had happened too quickly, even though the moment seemed frozen, all except for Dorsey's brief step and the tiny movement of the finger on the trigger. Dorsey Bascombe had died in that instant, and Bright had lived.

On the second night, she lay awake for a long time after Xuripha had gone to sleep, hearing the strange house creaking and settling about her in the empty hours toward midnight. Then there was a tap on the window screen. She paid no attention at first, thinking it a moth or a night bug. But then there was another tap, and a whisper. "Child," it said, and she stifled a cry of sheer joy. Hosanna!

She rose softly from the bed, found the latch at the bottom of the screen, loosened it and pushed the screen away from the window frame. There wasn't much of a moon, and Hosanna's blackness was a shadow in shadows beneath the window.

"Come with me, child. We gone see your sweet daddy."

She was out the window in an instant and into Hosanna's arms, hugging her tightly, losing herself in the softness of her arms, barely feeling the chill dew on her bare feet. "Oh, you *knew!*" she cried softly.

"Course I knew, child. Come on, let's get away from here before we wake the house."

Her bare feet flew above the pavement of the sidewalks and her nightgown billowed about her as they walked swiftly the few blocks to the Bascombe house, Bright clutching Hosanna's hand. They entered through the dark kitchen and crept up the back stairs, cringing at each creak the boards made under their careful feet. And then at the top of the stairs, Hosanna released her hand. "He's in yonder," she whispered, pointing at the closed door of the death room. "Doctor's in there too, but he's near dead hisself. You be quiet, you won't wake him."

Suddenly, she could smell death here. Not just the strong odor of camphor and medicines that hovered in the close air of the narrow hallway, but death itself. She turned to Hosanna, afraid. Hosanna folded Bright in her arms again, then took her gently by the shoulders. "I know, I know. It'll be all right, child. That's your daddy in there. Can't nothin' change that. You don't have to say nothin' if you don't want to. Just be with him a minute. He's mighty sick, but you'll do him a world of good."

< 280 >

Bright eased open the door and stuck her head in. There was a soft light on a table near the open window, a single oil lamp turned low. She saw the cot, the sleeping form of the doctor sprawled across it, fully clothed. And then the big high four-poster bed. And her father. Her fear fled right out the window, into the deep black midnight, and she felt a great loving joy squeezing her heart. And the music came back, just a few faint chords now, but music just the same. For the first time in a very long time. She crossed to the bed and stood looking down at him. The sheet was pulled up to his chin, and his face seemed to hover above the pillow in the golden light from the lamp, very peaceful, very still. The only physical evidence of near-death was the dark stain where the sheet covered the wound. She leaned over and kissed his cheek. The stubble of his whiskers was rough against her lips and they lingered there. She felt a faint breath from his nostrils, the merest hint of air. She drew back slowly, then looked around and saw a chair not far away. She drew it quietly to the bed, then reached under the sheet and felt for his hand and pulled it to her.

She sat for a long time, holding his hand, watching the soft lines of his face in the lamplight. She had missed him so terribly much, had imagined him in pain, racked by fever, crying for death to bring him mercy. It had broken her heart. It was hideous what her mother had done. But no more. After a while, she leaned over very close to her father's ear and whispered, "Papa, I'm going to stay with you now. I'll be here until you're ready to go, and then I'll hold on to your hand and we'll go together. I'm not going to leave you anymore."

He didn't answer, of course, because he was grievously ill and might not even be able to hear what she said. But then again he might. Perhaps some music would help. She began to hum softly, making up a tune as it came into her head, imagining Dorsey's golden trombone anchoring the melody with its smooth round tones, the sound of God's breathing, and the light graceful notes of her piano dancing above like angels on the head of a pin. She hummed for a long time, pouring her soul softly into the music, until finally she felt at peace and the silence of the room enveloped the last sweet notes of the song. She wanted for just a brief moment to cry, but then she thought there was nothing to cry about, not now. So she rested her cheek against her father's hand, feeling the rough lumberman's skin, so strong and reassuring. And for a time, as dawn approached, she slept safe in the warmth of his touch, waiting.

She woke with a start, hearing a footstep outside the room. Then the doorknob clicked and turned and her mother stood there, staring at her.

"Get out of here," Elise said simply.

< 281 >

Fear leapt into Bright's throat—fear of being separated again from her father. She fought the panic, gained control of it, turned it slowly into a cold anger. "I'm not leaving, Mama," she said. "If you try to make me leave, I will kick and scream and wake up the whole house and tell them all that you beat me."

Then Hosanna appeared in the doorway behind Elise and even from where she sat by the bed, Bright could see her eyes flashing, full of fury. "Come away from there, Miss Elise," she hissed.

Elise whirled on her. "Don't you tell me what to do!" she cried.

Hosanna didn't flinch. She reached around Elise, grabbed the door handle and pulled it closed. But Bright could hear their voices plainly in the hall. "You leave that child alone with her daddy!" Hosanna said. "You done broke her heart, sending her off like that."

"What is she doing here?" Elise demanded, her voice rising.

"I went and fetched her, that's what!"

"How dare you!"

There was a small terrible silence and then Hosanna's voice again, quiet and measured now. "What you afraid of with that young'un, Miss Elise?"

"Damn you!" Elise cried. "Damn you all! When this is over I'll take that child back to New Orleans and raise her among proper people where she can learn some manners!"

Bright's entire body convulsed with terror. No! She couldn't! She leapt to her feet, still holding on to her father's hand, looking wildly about the room while the shouting of the women in the hallway beat against her ears. She would escape, take her father with her!

But just then, Dorsey squeezed her hand and his eyes popped open. And he said in a voice so faint you could hardly hear it, "No, she won't."

Bright froze, stared down at him. Dr. Tillman woke with a start and sat bolt upright on the cot. "What? What's that?" he called out. His voice was thick, his hair tousled, his eyes sunken and haggard. Then he saw Bright. "What are you doing here?"

Her eyes never left Dorsey's. "I'm tending to my father," she said. "He's going to be all right now."

Dorsey Bascombe was not all right, but for the moment he was at least alive and showing some signs of rallying. Finus Tillman said it was medically impossible. He had lost an incredible amount of blood, his body temperature had dropped precipitously, his pulse was so weak it hardly registered. He had for all intents and purposes been a dead man from the moment the shotgun blast hit him. Yet he lived. The parlor

< 282 >

prayer group took much of the credit and gave some to God. Dr. Tillman, to his credit, claimed no credit at all.

But even then, it was a tenuous thing. The doctor warned them that chances for Dorsey's survival were slim, even now. And two days later, what he dreaded most happened: infection. The wound began to fester and Dorsey was racked by delirious fever. He moaned and babbled, drifting in and out of consciousness, finally lapsing into a coma. Finus Tillman stayed on. He did what he could, changing the bandages often, trying to keep the wound as clean as possible. The prayer group took up their vigil again in the parlor. Elise put on another air of stoic composure. But this time, Bright stayed put. She had nothing to say to her mother. She simply went to her father's room when she wanted, sat by the bed, held his hand, patted his flushed skin with cool washcloths. She hummed and sang. And when she was there, Elise stayed away.

Bright could tell the doctor was uncomfortable with her being there, a child in a room where death hovered. "Step outside now, while I change the bandage," he said to her at first.

"No," she said, "I don't mind."

He gave her a curious look, shrugged, and went about his work. It was a hideous sight, raw flesh oozing with yellow poisons, but she swallowed hard and forced herself to look as he peeled the clotted bandage away, dabbed at the wound with a clean white cloth, then swabbed on an antiseptic that smelled like creosote.

"Is that yellow business the germs?" she asked.

"That's what the germs cause. They're in the flesh."

"Can you get rid of them?"

"No," he said, shaking his head as he covered the wound with a fresh bandage. "Only your father's body can do that. It has to fight back. I can help, but not much."

"Is he fighting very hard?"

Dr. Tillman straightened, wiping his hands on the cloth he had used to clean the wound. "Yes. But he doesn't have very much left to fight with." He hesitated a moment, then said, "Bright, don't get your hopes up."

"You think he's going to die, don't you."

He nodded. "Yes. But then, I thought he was going to die two days ago. It's what the praying bunch downstairs might call a miracle that he's still here. But there's only so much . . ."

She looked at him a moment. He was painfully weary, the lines of fatigue etched deeply in his face, his eyes bloodshot.

"Is it very hard being a doctor?" she asked gently.

< 283 >

He thought about that a moment. Then he said, "No, not if you just do your job and leave the rest to nature. But it's hard being a doctor to a friend." His voice sagged with weariness and she reached over and patted him on the hand and gave him a nice smile.

"You keep doctoring, and I'll keep singing," she said, "and we'll let Papa do the rest."

But nothing either of them did seemed to help, and Dorsey seemed to slip away from them into the deep reaches of his fever. Bright could feel Dr. Tillman's resignation and she began to despair.

The morning of the third day, she woke very early, dressed, and started for her father's room down the hall. But she stopped outside the door and her hand froze on the doorknob. Dread welled up in her, and she turned, ashamed of her cowardice, and crept downstairs to the kitchen, seeking solace. It was empty, hollow and dim in the pale light from the windows above the sink. The faucet dripped methodically, big round droplets that went *ploik-ploik* as they landed in the dishpan below. She felt wretched, afraid and alone. *He will leave me,* she thought. *He will leave and he won't take me with him. I really can't go, even if I want to so desperately.* She thought fleetingly of running to the river and throwing herself in, sinking silently beneath the eddying green water. But no, that would be a very great sin and she would rot in hell and never see Dorsey again, and that would be the worst possible thing.

Right now, this instant, she must get out of the house. The thought of it without her father seemed to close in, smothering. She crossed to the back door and opened it, and then she looked down and saw Buster Putnam sitting on the bottom step, sitting very still and quiet with his arms locked around his drawn-up knees. He heard the rattle of the doorknob and turned and looked up at her.

"What are you doing here?" she asked.

"I come to see the angel," he answered.

She closed the door behind her and walked down the steps and sat beside him. The backyard was cool and plushly green in the half-light under the trees, holding its breath in the expectant moments between dark and dawn.

"What angel?" she said, tucking her dress around her knees.

"The angel of death," Buster said. "I heard Mama and Daddy talking about it last night. They said the angel of death was nearby. I always thought that death was a big old black boogeyman."

Bright stared at him for an instant, and then she felt her face collapsing and she started to cry. She put her face down in the folds of her dress and sobbed quietly, letting the ache wash over her. Then she felt Buster's arm around her shoulder, comforting.

< 284 >

"I'm sorry, Bright," he said. "I didn't mean to make you cry."

She looked up at him, her tears blurring the lines of his face. "I'm tired of being brave, Buster," she said. "And I'm scared."

"Course you are. Just like I was the other day when the big tree fell down on my bedroom. If I'da been in there, it woulda squooshed me like an old june bug. I reckon the angel of death just flew in the window and right back out again, but I just missed him. Or at least, he just missed me. It's a good thing I had to pee." Buster fished in his back pocket and pulled out a grimy handkerchief and handed it to her. She dabbed at her eyes and tried to get control.

"Well, at least you won't be an orphan," Buster said.

She stared at him. "What do you mean?"

"You'll still have a mama. Even when your daddy dies. An orphan ain't got either one and he has to go live at the poorhouse and eat soup with cabbage floating in it. I read about it in a book."

Bright thought about Elise then, and she felt a flash of anger. Her mother, growing strong as Dorsey lay near death, seeming to take strength from his weakness. She had been a lost soul until now, cowering in her room, drawing a veil of silence over the house that sucked the very life from the air. Why, she was no mother at all, Bright thought with a sudden burst of revelation. She didn't do the things mothers do. A cold rage gripped her. "I'd rather be an orphan," she said bitterly.

"Bright!" Buster looked quickly at the back door, as if expecting to see Elise standing there, hands on hips, listening to them.

"I'd rather . . ." She almost said "Live with the Hardwickes," but then she thought about that for a moment and instead she said, ". . . live at the mule barn."

"Jesus is listening to you," Buster said, edging away an inch or two on the step.

Bright looked up slowly, past the spreading limbs of the trees at the brightening sky beyond. "Jesus," she said, "my mama is a damn fool!" And at that, Buster Putnam leapt up as if he had been shot and took off running across the backyard, disappearing with a crash through the hedge without a backward glance. Bright sat for a moment longer, then stood, shaking out her dress, waiting to see if lightning would strike her. After a moment she thought, *See, Jesus thinks Mama is a damn fool, too.* Then she thought how wicked she was, how un-Christian and perverse, and panic rose in her throat. Her father, hovering at death's door while his daughter blasphemed on the back steps! *Jesus, I'm sorry.*

Upstairs, she opened the door of the sickroom and saw Finus sitting in the chair by the bed, his head in his hands. Her heart nearly

< 285 >

stopped and a great terror seized her. *I can't go in there!* But she took a deep breath and closed the door behind her and crossed to the bed and bent over her father's still form. Dorsey was breathing easily, the flesh of his face cool to the touch. Bright felt giddy with relief and joy.

"He did it," the doctor said quietly, looking up at her. He was near collapse. "The fever's broken. God only knows how. Dorsey Bascombe will live. He'll live to be an old man, I think."

<   >

It was a long, slow recovery. Dorsey was so weak at first that he couldn't hold his head up. He drifted in and out of sleep, his face slack and sallow, the stubble of his beard stark against his pale skin on the days between the barber's visits. He had never been a heavy man, but the wound withered him until the bones of his face and hands strained against the thin, wasted flesh.

"Food," Dr. Tillman said. "Food is the best medicine. The more the better." So they took turns feeding him—Elise and Bright and Hosanna—thin gruel at first and then a thicker soup with bits of finely chopped meat and vegetables in it. Hosanna kept a kettle of it simmering on the stove, adding to it bit by bit, filling the house with the rich, reassuring smell. They spooned it through Dorsey's dry, cracked lips until he groaned in protest, and he began slowly to gather strength. The first hints of color returned, the bones receded ever so slightly from his gaunt face.

Then there was the pain—at times, only twinges; at others, great waves of it that washed over him, made the sweat spring from his pores and mingle with silent tears and trickle in rivulets down the sides of his face, and then subsided with a shudder. "It's a good sign," the doctor said. "His body has been in shock. It's been protecting itself. But now it's beginning to heal and it's letting down some of its defenses and it hurts. I can ease it some, but not much."

Dorsey bore it mostly in silence. An occasional groan would escape his lips, and when he opened his eyes Bright could see the pain deep down in there, great molten pools of it. She wished desperately to take it from him, but she realized that it was a personal agony that only he could bear. He did, and after a few days he seemed to gain some control over it. In a strange way, the battle appeared to make him stronger. *He is very, very brave,* Bright thought, awed by it. Then the worst of it went away, and Dorsey emerged from the pit with a flush in his cheeks.

It was an afternoon more than a month after the shooting. Dorsey was propped on a mound of pillows, eyes closed, as Bright sat next to the bed feeding him from a soup bowl, his mouth opening automatically as the spoon touched his lips. Outside in the Putnams' yard, she could hear the shouts of a gang of boys playing tree tag, their voices mocking each other. Summer would soon end and school would start and she would have to leave him for most of the day. She felt a pang of grief. Then Dorsey's eyes suddenly snapped open and he said in a hoarse whisper, "Where's my lumberyard?"

Bright stared at him. She said, "Why, it's down by the river. Right where you left it. Did you think it was going to float off downstream?"

"Get Hosanna," he said, and she sat the bowl on the bedside table and flew down the stairs.

"What's going on at the lumberyard?" he asked when the two of them had returned.

Hosanna gave him a long appraising look. "They makin' lumber," she said. "Same as always."

"They're working?"

"Course they workin'." She crossed her arms over her bosom. "Humph. You ain't the only man in the world knows how to cut down trees. Only difference is, they ain't selling nothing. You the one does that. You better get yo'self up off that sickbed, Mr. Dorsey, or else they ain't gonna be no place to stack all that stuff they haulin' in."

"God bless 'em," he said weakly.

"God'll bless 'em just fine. But God ain't paid 'em."

He closed his eyes for a moment. Then he said, "Get Elise."

When she had been summoned and stood at the foot of the bed, he asked, "Do you know how to write a check?"

"No." She shook her head.

"Go to Pegram Gibbons. He'll help you pay the men."

"How much?" she asked, bewildered.

"They'll tell you how many days they've worked."

Elise glanced over at Hosanna. "How do you know—"

"Because they're my men," he said, cutting her off, and Bright could hear just the tiniest little bit of steel in his voice. She wanted to hug his neck, but she stood there silently, watching them. Dorsey gave a tiny wave of his hand. "Now go away." He closed his eyes, exhausted. "Tell 'em I'll be there tomorrow."

Of course, that was foolishness. It was another two weeks before he could even sit up on the side of the bed. But Elise went straightaway to Pegram Gibbons at the bank and then to the lumberyard, and to everyone's astonishment she began to take over.

First she paid the men and gave each of them a five-dollar bonus and told them to keep doing whatever it was they did. If they had a question they were to bring it to her, and she would get an answer from

< 287 >

Mr. Dorsey. Then she opened all the mail that had been accumulating on Dorsey's desk and separated it into neat piles: bills, orders, correspondence regarding land transactions, miscellaneous matter. She handwrote a letter to each of Dorsey's customers, advising them that the business was very much in operation despite his misfortune, and inviting their continued patronage. Return mail brought a flood of orders.

Elise rose early each morning, ate a hearty breakfast, and was driven to the lumberyard by Hosanna's husband, Mose. She returned at midafternoon with a stack of notes and mail and took it straight to Dorsey's room, where she sat at his bedside and went through each item. School began, and Bright would rush home to find them there together, Elise prim and straight-backed in the chair, brow furrowed in concentration, her voice lively and precise as she talked of board feet and skidders, Dorsey sitting up with a mound of pillows at his back, eyes twinkling, watching her with an air of slightly amused fascination. Bright was riven with pangs of jealousy at first, but Dorsey invited her to stay, tried to involve her in the conversation. So she pulled up another chair at the foot of the bed and sat listening, making an occasional comment. She knew the lumberyard almost as well as her father, at least the rhythm and feel of the place. "My lumberwomen," Dorsey began to call them. "By God, Elise," he groused, "they won't want me back. Enough of this bonus business. The men will rise up and elect you president of the place and then I'll have to spend the rest of my days rocking on the front porch."

Bright felt her heart softening. Her mother blossomed, and as she did she seemed to reach out for Bright. The piano lessons resumed in the music room at night, and even when the evenings began to turn cool, they left the windows open so Dorsey, in his bed just above them, could hear. The house quickened with their music and as fall deepened it seemed to Bright that they were all surrounded with rich, vibrant color that glowed most brightly in Dorsey's cheeks. He mended swiftly now, sitting first on the side of the bed, then in a comfortable chair next to the window where he could look out and see the occasional traffic on the street in front of the house and the play of the children in the Putnams' big side yard next door.

The twinges of pain came less frequently now in his left shoulder. The wound itself was healing, the blasted flesh scabbing over and then giving way to bright pink scar tissue, thin and wrinkled like a newborn infant's skin. The arm was saved, but it was wasted and withered and Dr. Tillman told Dorsey he would never have use of it again. Too much of the flesh and sinew were simply ripped away. As the healing pro-

< 288 >

gressed, they fitted him with a leather contraption that buckled about his torso like a corset and held the arm securely at an angle against his side. The first time they strapped it on him, he winced with pain and sweat beaded his brow and upper lip. He gave it a long look and said, "I am half man and half satchel." There was no mirth in it. And Bright thought to herself, *This may be the hardest part of all because it will never go away.*

When October came, he began to walk. There was nothing wrong with his legs but atrophy, and as soon as he got his balance and began to work the muscles, he gained strength and confidence quickly. At first he took a few slow, shuffling steps from the bed to the doorway and back, always with someone at his elbow. Then he ventured down the hallway alone, leaning for support on a cane. And finally he negotiated the stairs and went outside to the front porch, where he sat in a wicker chair in his bathrobe and slippers and waved to passersby.

On the morning of All Hallows' Day, Dorsey presented himself at the kitchen table at six-thirty, dressed in khaki and wearing his tall brown leather boots, still speckled with tiny brown flecks of his own blood. Bright, dawdling over a bowl of oatmeal, leapt gape-mouthed from her chair. "Papa!" she cried, half-afraid he would collapse at her feet, then seeing the way he held himself very erect, very carefully under control. It must have taken a great effort to prepare himself, she thought.

"What on earth you think you doin', Mr. Dorsey?" Hosanna scolded, setting a pitcher of milk on the counter by the sink with a clatter. "Exertion done gone to yo' head."

"I'm going to work," he said simply.

"No, you ain't!"

"Yes, I am."

"Yes, he is," Elise said from the doorway, and they all turned to look at her. She had a strange look on her face, Bright thought, something wistful there. She tried a smile, but it didn't quite work. "Perhaps for just a little while," she said.

"I'm a lumberman." Dorsey nodded. "I've got to get my business back in order. Might as well start today."

"Can I go?" Bright said, pulling at his sleeve.

"Course not!" Hosanna broke in. "You needs to be in school. First report card say you needs heaps of work at figurin'."

"We'll have her there by ten o'clock," Dorsey said evenly, looking Hosanna straight in the eye. "I think just this once won't hurt."

Hosanna, miffed, turned back to the sink, mumbling darkly. But within a half hour she was helping all of them settle into the car. Mose

< 289 >

had put the top back so Dorsey could see everything, and Hosanna bustled about, tucking a lap robe around his legs, instructing Mose on how to drive. "This here is a big day," she said. "You steer clear of potholes, you hear. Don't rattle Mr. Dorsey's bones." As they pulled out of the yard, Bright turned from her place in the front seat and looked back at Hosanna, standing next to the curb in flour-sack dress and bright white apron and slopped-over shoes, waving them off like a brood of mischievous children. Bright gave her a wave and then she looked at her father, sitting very straight in the back seat, hat clamped firmly to his head, coat buttoned over the leather corset that held his wasted arm. The bright morning made the lines and angles of his gaunt face seem very sharp, the skin very pale. He had aged a great deal, she thought. But he was here, there was a determined set to his jaw, and he was going back to his lumberyard. He gave Bright a big smile and then he took Elise's hand and gave it a pat.

Word had preceded them. The men were waiting in a crowd by the tiny office and they began waving and shouting as the car turned in at the gate by the river. There should be a band, Bright thought, trombones and a big oompah bass playing Sousa. Mose took a wide turn around the lumberyard, past the triangular stacks of fresh-cut, drying lumber, the planer mill, the sawdust pile, the big steam engine. And as the car drew up in front of the office building, one of the men let loose with a long, wailing blast of the steam whistle—the first time it had ever sounded at any time but noon and day's end. Dorsey drank it all in like a man slaking his thirst after a long agonizing trek across a desert, a big grin wreathing his face.

When the echo of the whistle died away, he raised his hand for a moment until the crowd quieted and the men moved in close around the car. Dorsey looked slowly around the gathering, lingering on each face, and then he took a long, deep breath. "I feel like the president of the United States," he said. Then his voice broke and the tears came and ran down his cheeks. He wept unashamedly and the men averted their eyes, giving him a moment to compose himself. Bright thought suddenly, *This has all made him very fragile.* Elise took a handkerchief from her purse and handed it to him, and he blew his nose loudly and then cleared his throat. He looked again around the circle of men. "Well, I am raised from the dead," he said, and a ripple of "Amen's" went through the crowd. "I am here by the grace of God and the love of my dear family and all of you." He looked around the lumberyard again, his gaze lingering here and there. "It looks pretty good to me. It has not only survived, it has prospered. I have all of you to thank for that, for carrying on in my absence." He stopped, thought for a mo-

< 290 >

ment. "I'm going home to rest in just a moment, but I will be back for a little longer tomorrow, and more the day after that. Before I go, I'm going to make you two promises." His face was grave now, and they were all very quiet, waiting for him. "No man but I will ever run this lumberyard as long as I live. There will be no more foremen from outside. And ten percent of the profits of this business will go into a bank account for your future. If you stay with me, if you continue to give me the same kind of loyalty you have given during these past few weeks, then when you decide it is time to retire, the account will pay you a modest wage for the rest of your life. So every time you fell a tree, every time you tote a board into a boxcar, you're putting money in your own bank account. This is *our* business." His voice was strong and clear and there were echoes of the old Dorsey Bascombe. He would be back in the woods before long, the tall leather boots striding over the fallen logs, the old smile creasing his face. Perhaps, Bright thought, he might even become a giant again.

"God bless you, Mr. Dorsey," Mose murmured from the front seat next to Bright, and the crowd pressed in on him then, murmuring their thanks and pressing his good hand, patting him on the shoulder. Bright sat and watched and she thought for a moment that her heart would burst. It was a dazzling day, the air cool and sharp with the sweet smell of wood, the duskiness of the black men, the tang of autumn. Mose started the car again and the engine throbbed beneath them, a deep rhythm. Music welled up in her, high and light, filled with wonderment and magic, life and hope renewed.

And then she turned in the seat and looked back at her mother. Elise's mouth was open slightly and there was a look of perplexity on her face. And hurt. Her hands were in her lap, clasped tightly, the fingers kneading each other. She stared at them, unseeing. Then she looked up at Bright, forlorn and lost and frightened, a small girl again. She turned her head away with a jerk and Bright realized suddenly, *He didn't say anything about her, about all she's done. He didn't mention her name.* Oh, Mama! she wanted to cry out. But she could not, not here in front of the men. Did they see? Or did they see only Dorsey Bascombe? And what did Dorsey see? If he turned to Elise just now he would see that she was drifting away from them before their eyes, drifting into a gray silence that would soon entomb the house, their lives. But Dorsey did not turn to her. He seemed to grow in size and she to shrink beside him. He was enveloped by the touch of his men, his life reaching out to touch him and welcome him back. Bright felt a rush of cold dread, spoiling everything. It should have been so fine, so perfect.

"Time to go now," Dorsey said, and his voice sounded hollow and

< 291 >

far away. "I've tuckered myself out." The men drew back as Mose eased the car into gear and pulled away, making another swing about the lumberyard as the whistle let loose with another long, powerful blast. It was not until they were out the gate that Dorsey finally turned to Elise. "Well, that was just bully!" he said. "By God, it's good to be back!" Elise did not answer and he did not seem to see what Bright had seen. *How could he miss it?* "Mose," he said, turning again to the front, "that pine in the number-ten stack. Where did it come from?"

"We took it out the place up near Harmony Springs, Mr. Dorsey, that three hundred acres you bought last summer," Mose answered from the front seat. "Some them trees so big you couldn't walk around 'em 'fore dinnertime."

Dorsey laughed. "We'll go take a look tomorrow. It'll do me good to get out in the country."

They chattered on about the lumberyard, he and Mose, while they left the road by the river and puttered through town on the way to drop Bright at the schoolhouse. Bright turned and sat deep in the seat, losing herself in the rumble of the car's engine. She could not bear to look into the back seat again. From there, she heard the profound emptiness of disappointed silence, the sound of ashes.

<   >

They took Elise to the train station in Columbus in early December. She would ride all day, down through the South toward New Orleans, pulling into the station at midevening. Her father, the cotton broker, would be waiting for her with a carriage and a servant to handle the big steamer trunk that contained Elise's clothes. Traditionally, it was the one time each year when all three of them went—Dorsey taking time from his business, a week with Elise's parents in the big house off St. Charles, then back in time for Christmas at home.

This time, Elise would go alone.

"I'm afraid I'm not going to make it to New Orleans," Dorsey had said at Sunday dinner two weeks before. "There's just too much catching up to do."

Elise looked down at her plate, poked at her food, then nodded at him. "I understand."

Dorsey shifted about in his chair, wiped his mouth with his napkin. "And perhaps Bright should stay here with me." He said it so casually that she wondered for a moment exactly what he had said. It hung there in the air over the table and Bright realized how terribly quiet it was. Not a sound from Hosanna in the kitchen.

Then Elise said simply, "As you wish."

< 292 >

And that was all she heard, though she wondered what her father and mother said to each other in the privacy of their room, in the unavoidable intimate moments when there was nothing left to do but confront each other.

They rode to Columbus in silence on an overcast, blustery morning with wind gusts nibbling at the isinglass flaps over the car's windows. Hosanna had kept her own counsel when Dorsey insisted on driving himself and he was preoccupied with the car, fussing one-handedly with the gearshift and steering wheel, back and forth, brow knit in concentration. Bright sat in front with him, her face and ears tingling with cold, the rest of her warm under the rough wool of a lap robe, alternately watching Dorsey and the countryside. The fields were plucked bare except for meandering rows of corn stubble, the river a slate-gray ribbon through the barren trees until the road curved away from it. The wind and the car made music, an odd dancing tune played by panpipe and kettledrum. In the green-on-gray pine forests on either side of the rushing car, she imagined strange and mystical animals that heard it too, pricked up their pointed ears and looked about them with small almond eyes, searching for the panpiper—half man, half beast, thumping a drumbeat on his round, full tummy while the music-smoke from his pipe made a wreath about his head. Bright let the notes carry her—now sweet, now harshly discordant. *I know,* they sang. *I know.*

Elise looked very pretty, standing on the platform at the train station. The cold air brought out the color in her cheeks and the wind nibbled at the soft strands of hair that peeked from under her crushed velvet hat. She and Bright stood together next to the car where Elise would ride while Dorsey saw to the handling of the steamer trunk. The train wheezed softly, the big engine emitting tiny puffs of steam that hovered for an instant above the gravel of the roadbed before the wind snatched them away.

"I suppose you'll have a grand time in New Orleans," Bright said.

Elise looked down at her, buried her hands deep in the wool muff she carried. "Yes, I think so."

"I imagine Grandma Poncie will have the house all decorated," Bright said. "She likes to put up the Christmas things before the Thanksgiving turkey is scarcely gone. I think she hopes it will turn cold, but it never does."

"Well, Grandma grew up in Missouri. It's usually cold in Missouri by this time of year."

"She probably misses it," Bright said.

Elise knelt suddenly beside Bright, dropping the muff on the platform between them, and took Bright's hands in her own. "I want you

< 293 >

to go straight home and get out all the Christmas things and put them up. You and Hosanna. Make Papa go to the woods and cut a tree right away." She squeezed Bright's hands almost painfully. There was an urgency, almost a desperation in her voice. "And play the piano a lot. All your favorite things."

"Yes, Mama," Bright answered.

Elise searched her face, looking for something. "You're a most uncommon young lady, Bright. I've scarcely known what to do with you. Sometimes I think you're very much older than I am." Elise dropped her hands then and enveloped Bright in a fierce hug. Bright clung to Elise, burying her face in her mother's coat, breathing deeply the smell of wool and perfume, winter and summer. Then Elise kissed her on the forehead and held her at arm's length. "I love you," she said.

"I love you too, Mama."

"Practice the piano, now."

"Yes, Mama."

"And take care of Papa."

"Yes. I will."

Elise stood and Dorsey joined them then on the platform, towering above them. He was dressed in his Sunday best today, a tweed suit with a vest, the coat buttoned over the leather sling that encased his left arm. He took off his felt hat, leaned down to kiss Elise on the cheek. "Have a safe trip," he said.

"I will."

"I wish . . ."

"No, I think not."

Dorsey knelt, picked up the muff she had dropped, handed it to her. Their hands met, lingered for a moment. "You'll need this," he said. "These railroad cars can get awfully drafty. Don't want you to catch cold and reach New Orleans with a runny nose."

Elise looked at him for a long moment. "All I wanted was to be needed," she said.

"You were. Are."

"No. Not truly."

Bright looked up at them, saw the defeat, the resignation in both their faces. Their hands parted. Elise knelt, gave Bright another quick peck on the cheek, and then turned to the open door of the train car. Dorsey reached to help her, but she stepped nimbly up and his hand hung there in the empty air for a moment. The conductor leaned from the car in front of them and called out, "Board!" as Elise disappeared into the car. Bright watched for her to appear at the window, but as the train rattled and lurched and began to move, she realized that Elise

< 294 >

had taken a seat on the far side, away from them, even though there seemed to be plenty of empty places on this side.

The train moved away, groaning irritably like a dragon awakened from a nap. Bright craned her neck, trying to see into the car, walking alongside until she reached the end of the platform and it left her standing there, gathering force for the long journey south. As the distance between them widened, she thought for an instant that she saw her mother's face at the window above the rear platform, but it was too far now to be sure. She watched for a long time until she felt her father's hand on her shoulder. She looked up to see that he too was staring at the empty space where the train had been, down where the tracks curved into the woods. The wind sang at her ears, carrying away the sound of the receding train, and finally, the last wisps of its gray smoke on the horizon.

She turned to Dorsey then. "She won't be back for Christmas," she said. And she could hear the accusing thing in her voice, mean and spiteful. And then she felt a pang of remorse. Whom was she accusing? She reached and took his hand.

He squeezed his eyes shut for a moment. "No. I think not."

"Mama told me to put up the tree and play all your favorite songs on the piano."

"Yes," he said softly. Then he looked down at her for a long moment before he said, "Bright, don't ever leave me."

Bright gave his hand a squeeze. "Of course not, Papa." And she thought, *What a strange thing to say.*

< 295 >

18

*T*he Atlanta Conservatory of Music was an aging, nondescript three-story red brick building, constructed in the early years of Atlanta's rebirth after the devastation of Sherman. As Bright Bascombe stepped from her taxi on a late August morning in 1929, she looked up at the building with sinking heart and thought, *It's dreadful.* But then she heard the lilting music of a clarinet from an open window upstairs. The clarinetist was running scales—up and down, up and down—and it reminded her of a fawn hopping nimbly across a meadow, water tripping over stones in a shallow brook. There was an exuberance and a technical skill to it that made her breath catch in her throat. *Music. That's what I've come for.* And then she thought, *I dare not fail here. There is too much at stake.*

Bright had not intended to eavesdrop, but she came upon the conversation between Hosanna and Dorsey quite by accident, two days after she had received the invitation from the Atlanta Conservatory to audition for a prized scholarship. She stopped outside the door to the kitchen and listened to their voices, quite clear on the other side. She knew she should go away, was afraid of what she might hear. But she was unable to move.

"It's none of your damned business!" Dorsey said angrily beyond the door.

His voice, once so clear and strong, quavered now. He was an old man, old before his time, wasted physically, his business in decline because he seemed to have lost the will to make it prosper. Still, it could be, when he was sufficiently aroused, a voice that brooked no argument. Except from Hosanna. "Course it's my bidness," she flashed now. "I raised that young'un, much as anybody did. Difference is, I know when to turn loose."

< 296 >

Bright heard a strangled snarl and her hand went to her mouth in fear. *Don't!*

"Git mad if you want to, Mr. Dorsey. I'm jest an old nigger woman. You can slap me down if you want. Go ahead!"

There was a moment of terrible silence, then a thump and scrape as Dorsey sat down in a kitchen chair. "I'm sorry," he said after a moment. "I'd never raise a hand to you, Hosanna."

Hosanna was unrelenting. "Did I speak the truth?"

"I don't know."

"You know I did! You know deep down what's right for that girl. She got to live her own life, Mr. Dorsey. Bad as you need her, she need to be her ownself even badder."

"But this music business . . ."

"It's *her* bidness," Hosanna said. "I don't know how good she is. She play mighty good to me, but ain't me or you got sense enough to know the difference. Thing is, she got to strike out and you got to loose your hold. Least a little. You keep this up, you gone mark that young'un for life. If you ain't already."

Bright wanted to rush through the door and throw her arms around Dorsey, tell him it was all right, she didn't really want to go to the Atlanta Conservatory, she didn't want to leave him. But she stood in the dim hallway outside the kitchen and did battle with her mortal soul because she *did* want to go. Not to leave him, but to seek herself. She jammed her fist against her mouth to keep from crying out. It was his fault! He had encouraged her to think her own thoughts and speak her own mind. And now she must do exactly that, even if it led her away from him for a time, even if it caused a terrible rending of her mortal soul. So she went quietly away from the kitchen door, and into the world.

And thus, the Atlanta Conservatory of Music. She had won the scholarship and there was no earthly reason not to take it. The faculty had said, in awarding it to her, that she had talent. She might, with prodigious hard work, make a pianist.

There were seventy students, about evenly divided between male and female. The men boarded in the community; the young ladies occupied cramped cubicles on the third floor of the red brick Conservatory building. The second floor was devoted to practice rooms and closetlike offices for the ten members of the faculty. The first floor contained a dining room, a recital hall, and a spacious foyer where students could entertain visitors. It had formerly been the home of a medical college, and when the windows were closed for very long at a time, you could still get faint whiffs of its past life.

< 297 >

There had been a frightening beginning back in May at the audition. All the way to Atlanta on the train by herself to find the head of the faculty, Oscar Hogarth, waiting for her in the recital hall, slumped in a seat in the front row with his legs stretched out in front of him, head resting on his chest. Bright thought at first he was asleep. Or perhaps dead. He was a small ancient man with a large head crowned by an unruly mop of steel-gray hair. He wore a goatee, and a monocle tucked in one eye. He looked very European, or what Bright thought might pass for European. She walked to the front of the hall, stopped in front of him, waited for a moment. Finally, she cleared her throat. "Professor Hogarth?"

"Bascombe," he said without opening his eyes.

"Yes sir," Bright said. "Bright Bascombe."

He pointed a bony finger toward the stage, where a Steinway grand piano stood huge and black and gleaming like a piece of the night sky. "Play," he said.

Bright shrugged, mounted the stage, sat at the piano, got up and adjusted the seat, sat again. She looked down at Hogarth. He hadn't moved a muscle. She raised her hands, went ripping into her first piece.

"Stop!" Oscar Hogarth roared. Bright froze, badly frightened, surprised by the volume he had suddenly summoned from that tiny, shriveled body. "Aren't you going to announce yourself, Miss Bascombe?" he said dryly. "What are you going to play?"

Bright stammered. "I'm, ah, I'm going to play . . ." *Good God, what am I going to play? What was I playing just then? Right. The Rachmaninoff.* "I'm going to play Rachmaninoff's Prelude in G Major."

"Is that all?"

"No sir."

"Well," he boomed, "what else, then?"

"I'm going to play Schumann's *Traümerei* and Chopin's Mazurka in F Minor."

"Hmmmm," he hummed. "The F Minor."

"Yes sir."

"I've heard it done right only once. By Rubinstein. And he's Polish."

Bright stared at him. Great God! The man was a monster! She started shivering. It was cold in the recital hall and she was unnerved by Oscar Hogarth and she felt miserable. She wanted to get up and walk out. Damn him!

Then he asked, "Are you nervous, Miss Bascombe?"

"Of course I'm nervous, Professor Hogarth."

< 298 >

And he surprised her totally by giving her a nice little smile, his eyes still closed and his head propped on his chest. "Entirely to be expected. Just play. You have three nice selections, so give them your best." And he gave a little wave of his hand, signaling her to start.

She got her trembling hands under control, took a deep breath, and launched again into the Rachmaninoff. She started badly, tripped over a note or two, but soon began to get the feel of the piano and to lose herself in the music. By the time she began the Schumann she was entirely in control, and she fairly congratulated herself on the zest of the Chopin. As the last notes died away, she lifted her hands from the keyboard and put them in her lap, then looked at Hogarth again. His eyes were open now and the left one, peering up at her through the monocle, made him look like some terrible fish. They sat looking at each other for a long moment before he finally said, "Hmmm. Yes. Well, that was very nice, Miss Bascombe." His voice was flat and non-committal.

"Thank you, sir," she said, and stood up. "Is that all?"

"Yes. Quite. We'll be in touch, Miss Bascombe." And he closed his eyes again, dismissing her.

In the foyer, Bright stood awhile, feeling quite numb. Then she saw the young couple standing off to the side—a girl about her age, a boy slightly older. More than a boy. Midtwenties, perhaps, rather thin, wearing a tweed suit and holding a snap-brim hat in his hands. He was looking at her and when he caught her eye he walked over, followed by the young woman.

"That was beautiful," he said.

"What?"

"I was listening from the foyer here. The last piece. It was so beautiful it made me cry."

She stared at him, wondering what kind of young fool he was. A fairly handsome young fool, with quick blue eyes and high cheekbones.

"Fitzhugh Birdsong," he said, offering his hand. "Bright Bascombe," she replied. She took his hand and he gave hers a quick squeeze. "My sister, Catherine," he said, introducing the young woman. "She's auditioning too."

Catherine Birdsong looked a bit frail, as if she might be affected by spells. But she had lovely slim hands that held a small stack of sheet music against her chest. Bright smiled and shook Catherine's hand. "Professor Hogarth is a bit of a bear," she said. "Don't let him scare you."

"Oh, he won't," Catherine said, putting her arm through her brother's. "I've got Fitzhugh here to protect me."

< 299 >

"Where are you from?" Bright asked.

"Savannah," Fitzhugh Birdsong answered. "But I'm in law school at Emory here in Atlanta. So I met Catherine's train this morning."

He was a rather odd young man, Bright decided. He had a way of leaning a bit toward you as he talked, just enough to make you feel that he was speaking to you and only you—that you were the only person in the world worth talking to at that particular moment. At this particular moment, he was leaning slightly toward Bright and she was aware of being riveted by his gaze, immobilized by those bright blue eyes. In a rank stranger, it was somewhat unsettling.

She tore her eyes away from him. "Well, good luck," she said to Catherine.

"Perhaps you'll both get accepted," Fitzhugh said. "That would be awfully nice." He fished in a pocket of his coat for a watch, snapped it open. "Almost time," he said. "Miss Bascombe, I hope to have the pleasure again." He gave her a tiny bow and then he opened the door of the recital hall and followed Catherine through with a last quick look back at Bright.

Alone in the foyer, Bright flushed. *My goodness,* she thought to herself. *How odd. But not at all unpleasant.*

<   >

"I hope you're quite happy with yourself," Catherine Birdsong said to her on the day they arrived for classes in August, assigned as roommates.

"I beg your pardon," Bright said, barely remembering their encounter months earlier.

"He broke his engagement," Catherine said.

"Who?"

"My brother. He has embarrassed the family and made an utter fool of himself."

"Why, for goodness' sakes?"

"He doesn't say. But you're all he talks about."

"Merciful heavens," Bright said, incredulous. She had given the young man—Fitzmorris, was that his name?—scarcely a thought since the afternoon he had introduced himself. She had certainly given him no encouragement.

"Do you know anything about the Savannah Birdsongs?" Catherine asked.

"Not a morsel," Bright said. Nor did she care.

"Well, we've got a great deal of money and even more social standing."

< 300 >

Bright bristled. This thin, pale young woman appeared to be a snob of the worst order. Bright dreaded the thought of sharing lodgings with her. Perhaps . . .

"We're also incredibly stuffy and, on the whole, boring," Catherine went on, her eyes twinkling. "And Fitzhugh's former fiancée is a ninny and plays the piano like it was a kettledrum."

Bright was quite taken aback. "I hardly know what to say," she said. "And I haven't the foggiest notion what to say to your brother."

"Well, you'd better think of something," Catherine said. "He's coming to see you on Sunday afternoon."

She spent the week in dread of it. But as it turned out, Fitzhugh Birdsong was altogether proper and pleasant and charming. He sent around a note during the early part of the week, asking permission to call on Sunday, and arrived in the early afternoon, after dinner was finished. She half expected him to present himself moon-eyed with an armful of flowers, pressing himself upon her. But he came empty-handed, pleasantly casual, as if he were simply an old friend who had stopped by to chat for a moment. He seemed to sense her wariness, and though he was attentive, he was careful not to appear in the least bit familiar.

"It's been a good first week?" he asked as they sat on a divan under the watchful eye of one of the female faculty members, who perched behind a desk at one end of the room.

"Mostly," Bright answered. She had decided that she would not help him by appearing interested. In fact, she was not. She was here to study music, not young men. And if she wanted to think at all about young men, there was Harley Gibbons, who had already written to her from the University to tell about pledging Sigma Nu and beginning his classes.

"How are you getting on with Catherine?" he asked.

"Just fine, thank you."

"She's a bit of a pickle sometimes," he said. "Don't let her bully you."

"Mr. Birdsong, I've never been bullied in my life."

He smiled. "I can believe that."

"Your sister, in fact, has been very pleasant company and has had the good sense to ship most of her wardrobe back home."

"The quarters are cramped?"

"Practically nonexistent."

"A Spartan environment here," he said. "The young artists, forsaking creature comfort to pursue truth and beauty."

< 301 >

"No," she said, "just music."

"Ah," he said, "surely in a place like this there's no such thing as 'just music.'"

Then she realized with a jolt that he was leaning toward her just a bit, drawing her to him without so much as a gesture. His eyes never left her face. Those bright blue eyes and that way of listening very carefully to everything you said, making you feel that it was the only thing in the world worth hearing just now. *Good God. He makes you want to get up and go with him.* Bright shook her head, trying to rid herself of the notion.

"Mr. Birdsong, sit back," she said.

"What?"

"Over there." She pointed to the other end of the divan.

He moved away from her a few inches with a slightly amused look on his face. "Am I bothering you?"

"No. Yes. You have a way of looking at people."

"Oh?" He seemed genuinely surprised. "I don't mean to offend."

"It's not offensive," she said. "It's just . . . disconcerting."

He smiled, a very nice smile that showed his even white teeth. "Then I shall sit way over here and try very hard not to disconcert."

They talked for a while longer and then Bright rose to go. "I have to go practice now, Mr. Birdsong."

"On Sunday afternoon?"

"Yes, if I dare face Professor Hogarth on Monday morning."

He studied her for an instant and then he said, "I'd like to call again. Next Sunday?"

She hung fire for a moment. "Mr. Birdsong, are you an impetuous young man?"

He leaned toward her just a bit and filled the rest of the space between them with his smile. "About most things, no. I'm usually very careful."

"It's a good habit," she said, and turned and left him there in the foyer, feeling his eyes as she mounted the stairs without a backward glance. Enough of him, she thought. He was interesting, perhaps even a little fascinating. She thought of him once or twice as she sat in the cramped practice room through the afternoon, but she pushed the thought away. She had not come to the Atlanta Conservatory of Music at the great expense of her father's disapproval to spend her time and energy on a young man, no matter how fascinating. She vowed not to let him bother her. Not a bit.

But he did. He bothered her considerably, and in the nicest way. And as Atlanta slipped into autumn, as Bright began the metamorphosis

< 302 >

into musician under Oscar Hogarth's grueling tutelage, she found herself falling in love with Fitzhugh Birdsong. Catherine took note and kept her own counsel, but the blossoming relationship between Bright and her brother became an unspoken aspect of Catherine and Bright's own friendship.

Catherine was a bit of a pickle, as Fitzhugh had said. She could be peevish and petulant at times; and at others, gloomy and silent. She frequently was unwell—white-faced and short of breath. But Bright learned that Catherine's physical frailty masked a wry, fierce independence and a great capacity for laughing at herself and her important family. "It's hell being a Savannah Birdsong," she liked to say. "They walk about like they've got cucumbers stuffed up their fannies." She was mildly profane and she could do a devastating imitation of Oscar Hogarth, playing the alternate roles of terrified student and tyrannical teacher, leaving Bright and the other fellow-suffering students weak with laughter. She was candid about her own health, which was precarious at best. "I have a bad heart," she said. "The doctors said I would live no longer than my sixteenth birthday. If you find me stiff as a board in my bed some morning, call them first thing and tell them they were wrong."

What she did not do was interfere in the least with the courtship. And it fairly quickly became that: a courtship. Bright found herself alternately perplexed and fascinated by Fitzhugh. He was a very earnest young man. But he was also much aware of his earnestness and went to great lengths to keep it from putting people off. Still, it popped through in bursts of enthusiasm despite his best efforts. He was handsome enough, she thought—not to the point of preciousness, but quite nice-looking, with good strong features and those snapping blue eyes. He had a quick, analytical mind and he was passionate about a few things in life—the law, for one; and, it became increasingly clear, Bright Bascombe. He visited her on Sunday afternoons and Wednesday evenings, those starchily restricted times when suitors were tolerated on the premises.

"I hope you'll come to visit Catherine sometime in Savannah," he said one mid-October Sunday afternoon as they sat on a divan in the foyer. It was still warm, as Atlanta can be for spells in October, and a ceiling fan whooshed listlessly overhead, stirring the close air in the room. Still, there was just a hint of autumn, a quickness, a sense of things turning. "You should meet our family."

Bright smiled, thinking of what Catherine had said of them. "Are they terribly fascinating?"

"Fascinating, perhaps. But not terribly. They came down from upstate South Carolina just after the Revolution and settled for a while

< 303 >

in Charleston. But they didn't consider Charleston good enough for them, if you can imagine that. So they moved on to Savannah."

She didn't want to seem forward, but she was intrigued. "What is their business?"

"Money," he said simply. "Originally, land speculation and shipping. Now, just money. Papa manages money."

"How does one manage money?"

"Oh"—he waved his hand—"you push it around from pile to pile and somehow it grows. Stocks and bonds, that sort of thing. I think Papa considers land and ships rather grubby by comparison."

"I don't mean to pry," she said.

"Not at all."

"And do you plan to go back to Savannah when you've finished law school?"

"Good Lord, no. I'll try to clerk for a judge here in Atlanta, then join a good firm somewhere. A few years from now, I'll go to Congress."

She marveled. "Just like that? Does one get elected to these things, or anointed?"

"Elected, of course," he smiled, slightly abashed at the way he had let his earnestness get out of hand.

Bright tried to think of him being in Congress. He was an attractive man and he dressed well and had good manners, and she supposed his earnestness would be an asset. But she was not at all sure what people did in Congress. In fact, she had hardly considered Congress at all. "What do you plan to do in Congress?" she asked.

"Do? Why, serve. Make a mark." He seemed surprised at the question.

"Does a Savannah Birdsong really need to make a mark?" she teased.

"By all means," he said vigorously. "I intend to be my own man." He paused, thinking about it. "It's not easy being a Savannah Birdsong."

"It's quite easy being a Bascombe," she said. "All you have to remember is that Bascombes are always right. At least that's what my father says."

"You speak a lot of your father."

"Yes. He's the best man I know. In his own words, he will do to hunt with."

Fitzhugh considered that, then smiled. "I like the sound of that. A man who will do to hunt with. And are Bascombes always right?"

"Of course."

He sat silent for a moment and then he said very carefully, "I should hope you would be right about me."

< 304 >

"And I should hope you would not press me to be right or wrong," she answered.

"No," he said emphatically. "I have all the time in the world, Miss Bascombe."

< >

As it turned out, neither of them had all the time in the world. Time very suddenly became an irrelevancy. The world turned upside down. In late October, the stock market crashed. At first, Bright paid scant attention to the bold black headlines across the front page of the *Constitution*. Bad news, but it didn't concern her. But one evening several days later, Catherine didn't appear at supper, and Bright went looking for her. She found Catherine in their room, ashen-faced.

"What on earth is the matter?" she asked. "Are you ill?"

"I've got to leave." Her voice was leaden.

"Why?"

"My father's been wiped out. He had all the family money in stocks."

Bright sat down next to her on Catherine's bed. "Everything?"

"Everything. All we have left is the house. And our pride, I suppose. God knows, we've always had plenty of that. Even a stock market collapse couldn't wipe out the Birdsong pride."

"What will you do?"

"We'll stay in the house because it's been in the family for nearly a hundred years. What little money there is will go to help Fitzhugh finish law school. He's too close to the end now to quit. But there's no money for little sister to fritter away her time playing the piano."

"My father will help," Bright said instantly.

"No!"

"But Catherine—"

"Did you hear me?" she cried. "We've still got our pride!"

"Don't let it ruin you," Bright snapped back.

Catherine's face softened. She looked incredibly tired, very frail. "It may kill me, but it won't ruin me."

Catherine's father arrived by motorcar the next day to fetch her. By the time he arrived, Fitzhugh had Catherine's trunk and suitcases at the front door. He and the girls stood at the top of the steps, Fitzhugh silent and grim-faced, Catherine tight-lipped, none of them trying to make conversation. There didn't seem to be much worth saying.

"There they are," Fitzhugh said, and Bright looked to see a gleaming Packard pull up to the curb, driven by a Negro in chauffeur's uniform and narrow-brimmed cap, a white man sitting in the back, staring

< 305 >

straight ahead. He seemed not to see them there on the steps. The car stopped and the Negro got out and walked around to the back door.

"Morning, Hobart," Fitzhugh called as he descended the steps.

The Negro nodded, but he didn't say anything. He looked sullen and put-upon, and Bright wondered for an instant if he too had lost heavily in the stock market. He opened the car door and Fitzhugh's father stepped out.

"Father," Fitzhugh said simply.

Fletcher Birdsong had the look of a shipwreck survivor, slack-jawed in disbelief. She could see Fitzhugh in him—the same trim carriage, the bright blue eyes. Only his eyes were bleak now, uncomprehending, and he stood blinking on the sidewalk in the gray morning. It struck Bright how personal a thing this was, this business on Wall Street, how deeply it cut into people's lives and changed the way they regarded themselves, perhaps forever. Fletcher Birdsong might be a proud man, but this morning his tailored pin-striped suit looked a size too big for him.

Catherine gave him a quick hug. "Father, this is my friend Bright Bascombe."

"Yes, yes," he said absently and shook the hand she offered. "Pleased to meet you."

They stood in awkward silence for a moment and then Catherine said, "Well, I'm ready."

He stared at her, then he seemed to come to himself. He turned with a jerk to the Negro. "Go fetch Miss Catherine's things, Hobart," he snapped, "and be quick about it."

But Hobart didn't move. Bright could see him tense, the muscles of his face twitching. Then he said, "Fetch 'em yo'self."

It took an instant to sink in; then a crimson flush spread across Fletcher Birdsong's face. "You sonofa—"

"Father!" Fitzhugh grabbed his father's arm.

Hobart stepped back a couple of paces, out of harm's way, eyes flashing with defiance. "I ain't been paid and it don't look like no prospect."

"You're fired!" Birdsong exploded.

"No," Hobart said, "I quits. I get back to Savannah best I can." He took off the chauffeur's cap and tossed it on the sidewalk at Fletcher Birdsong's feet. "You kin have this, Mr. Birdsong. You gone need it 'fore long. See how you like bein' on the other end." Then he turned abruptly and walked away, leaving them there on the sidewalk, staring at his back.

< 306 >

Bright turned then to see the look of utter humiliation on Fitz-hugh's face. It was a terrible thing, seeing him so vulnerable, so na-kedly ashamed, and she wanted to cry out and throw her arms around him. But it would not do, of course. So instead she wished to flee from their misery, to go home to her father, where things were safe and untroubled, where she could sort out the chaos that had suddenly turned things upside down.

Fletcher Birdsong drew himself up. "Well, to hell with him." Then he thought for a moment and said, "But I can't drive."

Fitzhugh released his father's arm. "Here, get in the car, Father. I'll drive you to Savannah. I can come back on the train tonight." He helped Fletcher into the back seat and closed the door gently behind him. Then he opened the trunk and put Catherine's things inside while she and Bright stood on the sidewalk, miserable in their silence. It was done quickly and Fitzhugh opened the back door on the other side.

Catherine gave Bright a fierce hug, then drew back a bit. "Take care of yourself."

"And you." Bright felt tears quicken and fought them back. "You'll write?"

"No. I think not." She turned to go, but then she stopped herself. "It's probably not a good match," she said. "You're both too sure of yourselves."

Then she was gone. As the Packard pulled away from the curb, none of them looked back at her standing there on the sidewalk.

< >

And then, quickly on the heels of Catherine Birdsong's departure, there was the letter:

> Dear Miss Bright,
>   I'm writing this letter for my mama, who is mighty worried about Mister Dorsey. We think things has gone bad for him. He is spending a lot of time out at the camp house these days and Mama believes he has took to drinking more than he ought to. And he is drinking alone, which Mama says is the worst way.
>   Mama says it is time you come home directly and see what you can do.
>   Flavo Richardson

She found him at the camp house, sitting at a small table in the middle of the darkened room, a near-empty bottle in front of him. He stared uncomprehendingly as she pushed open the door, flooding the room with the slanting light of late afternoon. The room reeked of whiskey and his own stench, the smell of death and defeat, and her hand went involuntarily to her mouth as she tried to stifle a rush of nausea. She was aware of a terrible clutter, clothes tossed about, furniture overturned—the abiding place of a soul in agony.

She realized that he didn't recognize her at first, profiled as she was in the open doorway with the afternoon light at her back. "Papa," she said, and he flinched at the sound and turned his face from her. She crossed to him and knelt beside the chair. "Papa, I love you."

He began to weep softly and she held him, cradling his head in her arms as she would an infant. She hurt deeply for him, the most terrible hurt she had ever known, far worse than the dull empty ache when her mother had boarded the train for New Orleans. Elise had been a tiny, frightened animal, running from her life in order to survive it. But her father was the strong one, the proud one. To see him like this wrenched the core of her being. She wanted to flee from the awful sight and smell of him, from the shame of his impoverished strength and pride. But she couldn't flee. After Dorsey, there was simply no place to go. So now she must stay and be the strong one. She struggled against herself, gained control.

He calmed himself after a while, but he wouldn't look at her. "I'm ashamed for you to see me like this."

"I know."

"I want you to go away."

"No, Papa. I'm going to stay with you. Can you tell me what's wrong?"

"I'm wretched," he whispered. "That's what's wrong."

"Why, Papa?"

"I've suffered some great losses."

"The crash?"

He nodded. Then after a moment he said, "And this." He reached into the pocket of his flannel shirt and pulled out a piece of yellow paper. It was folded into a square, the creases worn from much handling. She opened it, squinted at the bold black words of the telegram in the fading light.

ELISE DIED TODAY.

JOHN FOURNIER.

Then she saw the date. October 3.

"Papa," she said softly, "it's been more than a month. Why didn't you tell anybody?"

He shook his head. "I couldn't. I'm ashamed."

< 308 >

"Why, Papa?"

He looked up at her then, showed her the ravages of his face. He was old and withered, held prisoner inside the hated leather corset that bound his wasted arm. "I killed her, Bright,"

She wanted to cry out, *No! No!* But then she thought, *What if he is right? What then?* Bright had neither the capacity nor the will to judge either of them. The only thing that mattered right now was that one was gone and the other remained. So she said, "Don't kill yourself, Papa."

"I'm afraid."

"Yes. I know."

"It has all turned out badly, Bright. I've lost everything."

"No, not everything." She rose, put her hand under his elbow. "Come, Papa. We're going home. Flavo's outside with the car, and we're going to take you home. And that's where we'll stay."

He didn't protest. Instead, he looked up at her with the pitifully grateful eyes of a man being thrown a lifeline. Perhaps the last one that existed.

< >

She quite forgot Fitzhugh Birdsong for a time. She dispatched Flavo to Atlanta to get her things from the Conservatory and she got about the business of caring for her father. They put him to bed, she and Hosanna, began tending to him as they would an invalid. And she began sifting through Dorsey's affairs, learning the extent of his financial troubles. He had indeed lost money in the stock market debacle, but the worst of it was that the lumber business was in disarray, more the victim of his neglect than anything. And that alone was proof enough of his decline. It had been his great pride, his great achievement. Now he seemed to have lost interest.

What to do? She sat down with Pegram Gibbons and they talked through the options. Bright could try to persuade Dorsey to sell the business, but in its present state, and with the nation's affairs in even more dire straits, there seemed little hope of getting much for it. And Bright could not run things by herself. The alternatives, Pegram suggested, were to close it down entirely or find someone to manage it. Closing it, Bright decided, was no option at all. How would they live? Dorsey had some landholdings, but who wanted to buy land, now that people could barely afford essentials? No, the timber business was all they had.

Bright left the bank in a daze and stood on the sidewalk for a moment in the thin January sunshine, staring at the pavement, her

< 309 >

mind aswirl. Then she looked up and saw Monkey Deloach. He was pushing a dray cart full of potato sacks along the sidewalk in front of Putnam's Mercantile, wearing a canvas apron, a pencil tucked behind his ear.

"Monkey!" she cried.

He stopped, peered over the top of his glasses at her. At nineteen, Monkey was already beginning to look like a wizened old man, features pinched, brow eternally furrowed. "Bright!" he called out with a grin.

She walked swiftly to him, gave him a hug. "My goodness, I'm glad to see you!"

"Oh?" He gave her a bemused smile.

"What are you doing?" she asked.

Monkey looked down at his dray cart. "Hauling potatoes."

"I mean"—she waved her hand—"in general."

"Learning the mercantile business."

There was a calm earnestness about Monkey Deloach, she thought. He seemed to know exactly who he was, and how he might contend with that. Good, solid Monkey. She looked him up and down, took a deep breath. "Monkey," she said, "have you ever thought about the lumber business?"

Monkey gave her back an equally honest appraisal. Then he said, "Not until just now."

"It's not an easy business," she said.

Monkey looked down at his dray cart, smiled. "Neither are potatoes."

"I need help."

"Yes. I know you do."

"Would you be interested . . ."

He was already reaching behind him to untie the strings of his apron. "If you'll give me a moment," he said, "I'll give notice."

Bright went straight home and told Dorsey what she had done. He was sitting on the front porch in a rocking chair, wrapped in a thick shawl that Hosanna had no doubt forced upon him. He was beginning to get a little color back in his cheeks, but his eyes were sunken and his bony knees poked at the fabric of his trousers. She sat down next to him. "You've just hired Monkey Deloach," she said.

He stared at her for a moment. "For what?"

"To help you. I want you to teach him the lumber business, Papa. He's as solid a young man as you'll find anywhere. Monkey will, as you like to say, do to hunt with."

He looked away from her for a long while, stared out at the street beyond the stark branches of the oak tree in the front yard. His lips

< 310 >

moved ever so slightly, but no sound came out. Finally, he turned back. "It's my business," he said.

There was nothing to do but be plainspoken. "It is not much of a business at all right now."

She saw just a hint of something then in the tired gray eyes. A tiny glint of interest. "Take him to Mose and Jester," Dorsey said. "Tell them to work him in the woods until his rear end drags the ground and his tongue hangs out. It's the only way to learn the timber business. If he's still around when they get through with him, I'll come see." He poked the air between them with a finger. "Tell them just exactly that. Just the way I said it."

"Yes, Papa." And she did.

Bright and Fitzhugh exchanged letters through the winter. When would she return to the Conservatory? She put him off. Her father was quite ill, he needed her. She could not think beyond that. Fitzhugh had finished law school, had begun his clerkship. His letters were full of the future, a guarded optimism in the face of such terrible times. And she could hear the clear echoes of the unspoken in them: the future meant Bright Bascombe. She replied politely and noncommittally, put the letters aside and Fitzhugh Birdsong out of her mind.

And then Fitzhugh showed up on her front porch on an April afternoon. In fact, he had progressed from the porch to the kitchen by the time she arrived from errands. He was seated at the kitchen table with a glass of iced tea in front of him, listening to a steady stream of chatter from Hosanna, when Bright stopped in the doorway and stared at the both of them. Hosanna was halfway to the stove with a pan of biscuits. She turned, saw Bright, waved the biscuit pan in Fitzhugh's direction. "You didn't tell me you had a beau in Atlanta," she said without missing a beat. "He look a little frail, but I might could fatten him up a bit."

Fitzhugh rose, gave Bright a slight bow. "Bright," he said simply.

She opened her mouth, closed it again.

Hosanna opened the oven door, shoved the biscuit pan in with a clatter, turned back to them with her hands on her hips. Then she fixed Fitzhugh with a hard stare. "She the one you can't do without, Mr. Fitzhugh?"

Fitzhugh blushed deeply. Then he drew himself up, looked into Bright's eyes. "Yes, Miz Hosanna, she is that."

"I thought so," Hosanna said. "You look like you 'bout to bust a gusset. Well, God help you. She a handful." Then she flapped her arms at both of them. "Y'all get out of my kitchen and go work it out."

* * *

< 311 >

He sat next to her on the parlor sofa but he was careful not to come too close, careful not to lean too much. Even at a distance, though, he had the effect of fixing her absolutely in his attention, drawing a curtain about them.

"Are you going to give it all up?" he asked. "Your music, the Conservatory?"

Bright was peeved to find him here, especially unannounced. She did not want to be pressed.

"Yes," she answered. "For now."

"They're very disappointed. I talked with Professor Hogarth. He thinks you have a fine talent."

Bright sat very still on her end of the sofa, hands clasped in her lap. "At the moment, that doesn't seem to be very relevant."

"You love your father very much."

"I'm all he has left."

Fitzhugh looked around. "Is he here?"

"He's at the lumberyard. He's started going back for a few hours each day."

"Then he's better."

"Somewhat. Still very fragile, I'm afraid." Bright tried to keep her voice firm. She knew full well what she had to do, and she was determined to do it. She would be civil and then send him away. If she was indeed the one he could not do without, he would wait.

But then Fitzhugh said, "Bright, I want to marry you."

It was suddenly very quiet. Not a sound from the kitchen or the street outside. Only the beating of Bright's heart, which became much faster and louder, thumping in her ears. She felt weak. She shook her head. "No," she managed to get out. "Not now."

"Of course now." His voice was urgent, insistent. "Now, of all times. Because the world is upside down, Bright. Yours and mine."

"That's not reason enough to marry," she said.

"Yes! It's a very good reason. But it's not the most important one. I love you, Bright. I'm wretched without you!" He moved close to her now, reached for her hand. She started at his touch.

"Fitzhugh, please!" she cried. And then she looked up to see Dorsey Bascombe standing in the doorway. They both froze.

He was wearing his brown leather boots and puttees and a khaki shirt, and there was the faint smell of the woods about him, even at a distance. With the afternoon light just so, he looked ten years younger—tall and lean like a sturdy sapling, bent just a bit in the wind, perhaps. There was only the leather corset to give him away.

"What is this?" he asked quietly.

< 312 >

Fitzhugh let go of her hand and rose immediately. "My name is Fitzhugh Birdsong, Mr. Bascombe." He took a breath. "I've come to ask for your daughter's hand in marriage."

Dorsey looked down at where Bright sat on the sofa. She wanted to run from both of them, to seek a quiet hiding place. "I didn't know my daughter had a suitor of such serious nature," Dorsey said.

"Papa . . ."

But then he turned abruptly and was gone, his boots making a heavy, measured tread as he mounted the stairs.

She didn't look at Fitzhugh. "Go," she said.

"I will," he said softly. "But not far."

She turned to him then. "What do you mean?"

"I have come to live here," he said simply.

"Here?"

"In this town. If you're not coming back to Atlanta, I'm staying here. I intend to be a lawyer here and marry you and raise a family. In this very town, Bright Bascombe." He thrust his jaw out. "I mean it."

She stood in misery, torn between her father's hard displeasure, still lingering like acrid smoke in the air, and Fitzhugh's great presence next to her. She felt quite overwhelmed by it all, by the sea change in all their lives, the grimness, the urge to cling to the few things that were solid and dependable. Fitzhugh Birdsong seemed quite solid and dependable, and there was a set to his jaw now, a determination that hadn't been there before. What had remained of the boy was gone, perhaps left behind on the sidewalk in front of the Conservatory when he had driven away in humiliation at the wheel of his father's Packard. He would make his mark, she was quite sure of that. He would be devoted to her and to whatever he decided was his life's work because he was earnest and honorable. He might even be passionate. He seemed to have the capacity for that. But there was Dorsey. She could not defy him, not now. Forced to choose, she must choose him because his need was greatest.

She sat down finally on the sofa. "Leave me," she said. "I can't think now. Just go. Please."

He hesitated for a moment. Then he said, "All right. I'll be at the hotel. I'm prepared to wait for you as long as it takes, Bright. There simply isn't any other way." He bent and kissed her forehead. And then he left her alone there in her agony.

There were two days of stony quiet in the house. And then something happened. Bright was never sure exactly what. Dorsey came to her late on the second night, knocked on her door. She had already turned out

< 313 >

the light, but she sat up in bed and flicked it on again and he opened the door gently. "Talk?" he asked, and she nodded, afraid of her voice. He sat on the side of her bed. He seemed frightfully old and worn now, his hair entirely gray, thinning quickly, a great pink bald spot at the crown. Bright reached up, touched his cheek. "Papa . . ."

He pressed his fingers gently over her lips. "I've been to see your young man tonight," he said. His voice was calm, clear, the strongest she had heard it in some time. "He apparently means what he says. He's taken up residence at the hotel and he intends to open a law practice. He seems quite stubborn about it, in fact." Dorsey sat quietly for a moment, studying her. "Do you love him, Bright?"

"Yes. I think so, Papa. But . . ."

"You can't be burdened forever by my failures."

"Papa," she cried, "you're not a failure!"

"I'm a disappointment," he said. "I've disappointed myself most of all. And you'll have your own disappointments, Bright. No one's immune from that. But the root of the matter is, we both have to get on with things. Especially you. If you love him, marry him. Take his name and have his children. Just don't forget who *you* are."

Bright felt relief flooding her, a great lifting of the burden. She would not have to choose after all! Dorsey Bascombe was wise and good. He gave himself no mercy, but there was a kind of courage in that. And Fitzhugh Birdsong was a fine and honorable young man who loved her deeply. His eyes were warm and deep, a place you might abide in peace. And she did need such a place where she was loved unreservedly by someone who was strong and constant and would be so for a great long while.

She began to cry now, leaning her head against his chest, feeling the hardness of the leather corset against her cheek. Dorsey put his good arm around her shoulders, held her close.

"Just remember what I told you a long time ago," Dorsey said. "Live where you are. Make a place for yourself and put yourself into it. This is your place, Bright."

She nodded. "Yes, Papa."

Only Hosanna seemed oddly troubled by the turn of affairs. "I 'spected him to pitch a fit," she said darkly.

"Why, for goodness' sake?" Bright asked.

"'Cause you goin' off."

"I'm not going anywhere," Bright said firmly. "That's the whole idea. I came back when he needed me. And I'll be right here whenever he needs me again."

< 314 >

"Does young Mr. Fitzhugh understand that?"

"Of course. What on earth is wrong with you?"

Hosanna pressed her lips together, shook her head. Finally she said, "I tole you long time ago to pick the one you can't do without. I just hope you ain't got *two* you can't do without. 'Cause then you'll have to choose betwixt 'em."

"Nonsense," Bright cried. "That's just the point. That's what Papa has done. Made it so I *don't* have to choose. Don't you see?"

"I see," Hosanna said quietly. "But I'm not sure jes' *what* I see."

< 315 >

19

*B*right and Fitzhugh were married at Christmas. And while people remarked on what a handsome young couple they made, they took equal notice of the bracing effect the nuptials seemed to have on Dorsey Bascombe.

He took renewed interest in the lumberyard and began to rejuvenate its operation with the help of Monkey Deloach. He told one and all that Mose and Jester had nearly killed young Deloach with hard work, but that he might, in time, make a lumberman. Dorsey set into motion two building projects—the house at the end of Claxton Street that the newlyweds would occupy and a two-room frame office for Fitzhugh's law practice halfway between the house and the bridge. And when he escorted Bright down the aisle of the Methodist Church on a Sunday afternoon, the congregation took note that he looked more like the old Dorsey Bascombe than they could remember in some time.

Dorsey also surprised the community by announcing that he would not be a candidate for mayor when the spring of 1932 came around. He had in truth not been much of a mayor during the time of his latest illness, but now he seemed pretty much recovered. All he would say was "It's time for somebody else." So Pegram Gibbons ran unopposed and Dorsey stepped back from the town's affairs. Some thought it was fitting. For one thing, there was the Depression. All across the desperate country, people were ready to try something new, anything to help them claw their way out of the grip of disaster. New leadership, they said. Like this fellow Roosevelt.

There was another thing too, and Fitzhugh remarked on it one evening at dinner just after Dorsey had quietly passed the word that he would not run again. "Not everyone's upset," he said.

"What do you mean?" Bright asked, glancing up at him.

"Well, people are careful how they talk around a new fellow in

< 316 >

town, especially the mayor's son-in-law. But if you listen carefully, you hear things."

"Like what?" she demanded.

"Like maybe some folks believe Dorsey Bascombe has straw-bossed the town long enough."

Bright could feel her hackles rising. "What do you mean, straw-bossed?"

"Well," he said carefully, "you can abide one man getting his way about everything for just so long. He might be right and another fellow might be wrong. But the other fellow has a right to speak his piece and have his ideas considered."

"If my father hadn't done all he's done for this town, it would be a one-horse crossroads," Bright said hotly, dropping her fork with a clatter onto her plate.

"Whoa, now." Fitzhugh raised his hands in surrender. "I didn't mean to start a ruckus."

"Then don't!" she shot back.

"I'm just telling you what I hear."

"Maybe you listen to the wrong people."

It was their first real argument and it left a chill on the winter evening. They spent the rest of it in a gloomy silence, and later in bed, Bright turned away from him, pulling the covers tight around her neck. They lay there awhile in their separateness and finally he put his arm around her and nuzzled her neck. "How can I make love to you if you stay mad?"

"You can't," she said.

"Then stop being mad."

"Apologize."

"All right," he said without hesitation. "I'm sorry. What am I sorry about?"

"My father."

"Ah, yes," he sighed. "I'm beginning to learn that when I put my foot in certain places, it ends up in my mouth."

"Yes, it does."

"I don't intend to compete with him, Bright. I couldn't if I tried. I intend to make my own mark. And I am truly and abjectly sorry if I have offended you." He began to nibble at her ear then, something she had come to like a great deal, and she felt herself stirring, turning to him in the darkness, opening. He was, as she had suspected before they married, a passionate man. She was beginning to learn of her own capacity for passion. There were, she thought, all kinds of music.

* * *

< 317 >

An uncommon young man, that's what they said about Fitzhugh Birdsong. By the end of 1932 he was quite established in his law practice. At first, before the marriage, he had taken a room in a widow's home and rented a tiny cubbyhole of an office upstairs over Pegram Gibbons's bank. But he was not inclined to sit behind his desk and wait for business to come in the door. He was out and about—making the rounds of the business district, meeting merchants in their stores, stopping people on the sidewalks to introduce himself. He seemed never to forget a name or face. He noted the connections among the interlocking families of the community and sniffed out the sources of power and influence. And he had the most peculiar quality of making you feel, even in a crowd, that you were the only person worth talking to, that you had his absolute, undivided attention. It was a bit disconcerting at first, but people decided eventually that Fitzhugh Birdsong was genuine. He was new and he was from Savannah and that in itself could make folks suspicious of a fellow. But he didn't push himself. He seemed like a young man who had his eye on something but could bide his time about getting to it.

So by the time he and Bright married, he had already made his presence felt in the community. And with the marriage, he moved his law practice to the small frame building fronting on Claxton that Dorsey Bascombe had built for him. It carried a sort of endorsement. Fitzhugh was careful not to exploit it, but if it meant a measure of acceptability, so be it. His practice began to grow, as much as a small-town lawyer's business could in hard times. There was precious little money in folks' pockets for legal doings. It was easier, they said, to shoot a fellow than to sue him. And if they sent you to prison, at least the food and lodging were free. But business trickled in as people came to learn that Fitzhugh Birdsong was a tireless, meticulous, and entirely discreet young lawyer. Then in the fall of 1932, Fitzhugh won a difficult civil case against a prominent lawyer from Columbus. The word spread quickly. The next morning, the elderly Miss Eugenia Putnam showed up at Fitzhugh's office with a large envelope. "My affairs," she said, laying the envelope on Fitzhugh's desk. "I trust them to you until you make a ninny of yourself in court."

The one thing Fitzhugh would not do was foreclosures. When Pegram Gibbons offered work from the bank, Fitzhugh turned it down. "I'm going to run for Congress one day," he told Bright, "and I don't want to be remembered as the lawyer who took people's land away from them."

It was Bright who actually became the first to hold office, appointive though it was. Pegram Gibbons dropped by the house one afternoon and asked her to take a vacancy on the Library Board. Bright was

< 318 >

surprised. The Library Board was notorious for its decrepit and lethargic membership. "My father sent you," she said.

"No, your father suggested that you might be willing."

"Well, he was right. I am."

At the first meeting, Bright urged the board to double its annual appropriation for book purchases. No money, her aging fellow members said when they roused themselves to stare at her. "Then I'll raise it," she said. Bright made the rounds of the community's merchants and prominent citizens, wheedling and cajoling, until she came back with enough pledges to quadruple the meager book budget.

Fitzhugh and Bright were both careful to let people know that Fitzhugh, not Dorsey, supported them. Neither would have considered accepting help from Dorsey, had there been any offered beyond the house and office. Bright began to take in piano students, teaching them on the Story and Clark upright that Dorsey had moved from his own home for her. She became the pianist for the Methodist Church and was in demand for musical programs before social and civic groups throughout the area. People admired her talent and wondered, sometimes to her face, why she had not pursued the musical career she had gone to Atlanta to study for. In her own mind, the Conservatory became a brief and almost dreamlike interlude in her life, something unavoidably unfulfilled. She might ask herself whether she would have indeed made a concert pianist, whether she would have had the talent and drive it took, the willingness to sacrifice. But there was no use in belaboring that. She had left because it was the only thing to do at the time. She had made that choice and there was nothing to do but move on beyond it. So when people asked, she said simply, "This is where I belong." After a while, they stopped asking. And Bright all but stopped remembering.

Bright remained a devoted daughter. She visited Dorsey at least once a day, usually in the late afternoon. She would often be waiting when he arrived from the lumberyard and they would sit for a while on the front porch, if the weather were suitable, and talk. Fitzhugh and Bright came for Sunday dinner. It was a ritual.

There was a wariness to Dorsey and Fitzhugh's relationship that neither man could ever quite overcome, a studied cordiality. Bright would have wished them to be friends, but she realized that in truth they were rivals. It must be thus with any man and his son-in-law, she assumed, especially a man in Dorsey Bascombe's circumstances and given all that had happened before Fitzhugh Birdsong had come along. As men, they were much alike—intelligent, ambitious, sure of themselves. But their interests were poles apart. Fitzhugh was fascinated by the world at large, intrigued by the vast changes taking place in the

< 319 >

world's politics and economics, especially those being driven pell-mell by Franklin D. Roosevelt. Dorsey thought the only world worth being fascinated by was the one he could drive through in a day. His vision narrowed, his outlook became more provincial. Roosevelt, he said, would be a better president if he had left the aristocracy of the Hudson River elite and spent some time at honest work such as lumbering. Like his cousin Teddy. Now there, Dorsey Bascombe said, was a real president. A real Roosevelt. Fitzhugh did not argue with his father-in-law. He kept his own counsel, steered clear of even the hint of conflict. He was deferential without being subservient. Fitzhugh Birdsong had other fish to fry.

<   >

In the autumn of 1934, Bright discovered that she was pregnant. She knew it well before there were any physical manifestations. She woke one morning to an almost imperceptible change in the rhythm of her body, and she said to herself, "There is a baby."

It was the most private thing she ever did. Fitzhugh might have planted the seed, but the growing life inside was hers alone to nurture into fullness. And once she had told Fitzhugh, she retreated into herself while he clucked and fussed about her, trying to *do* something, anything. From the first, he was captivated by her changing body— touching, listening, poking gently, asking a thousand questions.

"He can't help it," Hosanna said. "Biggest thing a man ever do is begat. Every time a woman get with child, you see the man struttin' around like a peahen, 'cause he done begat. Hell, ain't nothin' to begattin'. It's after the begattin' that you gets down to bidness. And that drive the man near about crazy 'cause he can't run the bidness."

So Bright told Fitzhugh, "It's all right. Don't try so hard. We're doing fine."

She was patient, but she was aware of being aloof with him, distant. She had gone someplace he could not go, and there was a magnificent aloneness to it. She and the baby shared a dark, warm cocoon, both undergoing metamorphosis, quite apart from the light and air of the ordinary world. Her body sang to her, a pure, primal music. She rarely touched the piano. What she could coax from it seemed discordant by comparison.

The only thing that troubled Bright during her pregnancy was her father. Dorsey seemed taken aback by the business, at a loss for what to say or do, almost embarrassed. For the first time there was an awkwardness between them, long silences as they sat and rocked together on the front porch of his house in the late afternoons. He rarely

< 320 >

remarked about her condition and avoided looking at her swelling belly.

Again, Hosanna: "He's grieving," she said. "A man don't truly give up his daughter 'til she gets with child. Then he has to admit that his daughter does the things women does with men. From that time on, she's more a woman, and another man's woman, than she is his daughter. And for yo' daddy, that's 'specially hard."

"Why?" Bright asked.

"'Cause he messed up with his own woman," she said simply. "And he put all his stock in you. It's high time he gave you up, but it ain't easy. So he grieves."

He came to her almost shyly when she gave birth, bringing a lovely hand-carved walnut crib for the baby. Emotion played in open conflict in his face: joy, sadness. She studied him as he sat down in the chair by her bed, truly seeing him for the first time in months as she emerged from her own long self-absorbed solitude. And she thought he looked very fragile again, his health and perhaps his will beginning to slip. She felt a pang of guilt at having been so preoccupied, at having neglected him. And she longed now to make him see and feel the miracle of a grandson, to share it with her. Perhaps, she thought, an atonement.

"A boy," she said, nestling the baby in the crook of her arm. "A Bascombe boy. Even if his name is Birdsong."

"Yes," he said softly. "He looks a good deal like Fitzhugh, but that doesn't mean anything. There's no such thing as a half-Bascombe. Is he ornery?"

She smiled. "No, he seems to be a sweet baby. He comes from the gentle side of the family, I'd say. We've named him Dorsey Fitzhugh Birdsong."

"Well, I'm honored. But you call him Fitzhugh, you hear?"

"Yes, Papa. I suppose there's only room for one Dorsey around here."

"That's right."

She understood then a little of what he must have experienced these last few months—indeed, all her life. A giving up, as she had just done with the baby. It was a reluctant thing, letting him go from the safe warm place where she had kept him. She longed to hold him inside just a while longer, to listen to the primal music, to sing to him and savor his closeness and keep him from all harm. But he struggled to be free of her and she released him finally into the light and air. It was, as Hosanna had said, a kind of grieving.

She was very tired and she closed her eyes for a moment, heard a

< 321 >

blur of voices—Hosanna gently lifting the baby from her side, Fitzhugh and Dorsey talking quietly. When she awoke, it was dark outside and Dorsey was gone. It was Fitzhugh who sat in the chair next to her bed, holding her hand. "We did well," he said. "He's a fine boy." She saw then that there were tears in his eyes. *He is a fine and gentle man*, she thought. *He will be a good father, and he has been a good husband. He does love me without reservation, and what more could I ask. And I do truly love him. I do.* But she felt oddly riven now. The exquisite aloneness she had enjoyed these past few months, the sense of abiding in the still place deep inside herself, was gone. Now there were three men in her life. All laying claim to her in their own ways. And there was a fine sadness to that.

< >

It surprised people, and then again it didn't, when Fitzhugh decided to run for Congress in 1936. People could picture him as a congressman someday. He had the looks and bearing. But now? It was rushing things a bit. His youth was one thing, but more important, the seat was held by a man in his midfifties who had had no opposition whatsoever the past two elections, so safely was he ensconced in office. He was backed by conservative business interests that could count on him not to go too far down the New Deal path with Roosevelt. He had been part of that staunch core of Southern Democrats who had helped block some of Roosevelt's wilder schemes.

At one time, Dorsey Bascombe had been a leading spokesman for business interests in his part of the state. He might be progressive, but he was no fool when it came to government meddling in the affairs of free enterprise. So when his son-in-law announced plans to seek the seat in Congress, the men who had known him the longest sent Pegram Gibbons to see Dorsey. And Dorsey in turn went to see Bright.

"Fitzhugh will make a fool of himself," Dorsey told her as they sat on her front porch one warmish late-winter afternoon. "Oscar Gainous is a good congressman, a levelheaded man, and he has a hammerlock on that seat. If Fitzhugh will bide his time, pay his dues in the party, his turn will come. But if he goes tearing off into the underbrush like this, he'll alienate the very people he needs later."

"Then why don't you tell Fitzhugh that," Bright said.

"You tell him."

"No, Papa." He looked at her in surprise. "I'm not going to get involved in Fitzhugh's politics. And I'm not going to get crossways between you and him."

"If he gets into politics, you will be involved whether you like it or not," he said gruffly.

< 322 >

In fact, she thought, she *was* involved because she and Fitzhugh had been through all the arguments pro and con already. She knew as well as her father what the political rules and givens were, and Fitzhugh could see quite well what the odds were. And beyond that, they were in no position financially for Fitzhugh to mount a campaign. It would mean long hours away from a law practice that was still struggling, long hours away from his wife and small son. But in the end, despite anything Bright or Dorsey said, his sheer determination wore her down.

"I mean to go to Congress," he said.

They were in Little Fitz's bedroom, Fitzhugh standing in the doorway while she put the baby down for his afternoon nap. They had argued all through dinner and Bright was worn out with it, prickly with irritation. "Then go!" she snapped. "Leave us here and go!" And then she added, "If you can get there."

"I'll get there." There was steel in his voice. She had learned in just over five years of marriage that he could be single-mindedly obstinate when he wanted something badly. In fact, she thought, it went back further than that. He had wanted *her*, hadn't he?

"Papa says Oscar Gainous will beat you like a drum," she said, then regretted it.

There was a moment of pained silence before Fitzhugh said, "Oscar Gainous is no longer in the mainstream of politics hereabouts. Neither is your father."

She tucked Little Fitz's blanket carefully about him in the crib and then turned to Fitzhugh. "I'll forget you said that."

"Suit yourself," he said.

"If you persist in this, Fitzhugh, it's your business. Just yours. I won't get involved."

"Fine," he said. "I won't count on you."

She heard the front door close behind him as he left the house, left behind an empty silence that filled the long afternoon as painfully as if it had been a blaring noise. *Why does he need this?* she kept asking herself. *Aren't we enough?* For the first time in their marriage, she felt a sense of abandonment, an ancient grief she thought she had put aside.

So Fitzhugh ran for Congress, more on sheer instinct than anything else. He demonstrated for the first time his ability to sniff the wind and smell change and adapt himself to it. Throughout his career it would mark him mostly as a cautious man, because change comes to political process only occasionally. But there were a few times when he made bold strokes, sweeping aside convention and leaving the so-called experts and political soothsayers dumbfounded. This first time was perhaps the most remarkable because he had no experience to rely on, just his nose and his intuition.

< 323 >

The more notable folk across the district were polite to him. He was a nice young man, rather fascinating in the odd way he acted face-to-face. And if he behaved himself in this campaign they would forgive him his folly and perhaps take another look at him when he had grown up. But Fitzhugh didn't concern himself much with the more notable folk.

His allies were a few young businessmen across the district, beginning in his own town with Monkey Deloach and Harley Gibbons. Monkey was by now taking an increasingly active role in the day-to-day operation of Dorsey's lumber business. Harley, home from college, had joined his father at the bank, and together they had saved it from ruin by pledging everything they owned personally to its full faith and credit. This too was an act of faith for people like Harley and Monkey—running at crosscurrents with the established business interests that Dorsey and Pegram represented. They took some heat because of it, but there was something compelling about Fitzhugh Birdsong. It might be a foolhardy and radical enterprise, as Dorsey and Pegram argued, but they argued back that young men were due some foolhardiness. And the times demanded radicality. So they went about their business—forming a small, tight network of men like themselves throughout the district, raising a little money, riding the back roads in their automobiles and stopping to tack up campaign posters on fence posts. And talking. Always talking. Stirring up trouble, the establishment said. But the establishment didn't take them seriously.

Lesser folk began to before long, because the message Fitzhugh Birdsong preached made sense. It was simple: Roosevelt needed help. Sure, some of what he tried didn't work. But he was trying. People were hungry, cold, ill, homeless, hurting. Business was indeed the engine that pulled the train, but when the engine faltered, the folks back in the boxcars needed help—public jobs, security for their old age. Roosevelt was trying to help the people in the boxcars at the same time he tried to get the engine going again. Send Fitzhugh Birdsong to Congress, and he would make sure the folks in this district got a fair hearing in Washington, and that Franklin D. Roosevelt got a fair hearing in Congress. So the people across the district began to take a long hard look at this trim, neatly dressed young fellow who came calling at their homes and stores across the district. He started campaigning early in the spring, while Congress was still in session, and by the time Oscar Gainous came home to announce himself in mid-May at a grand rally on the courthouse lawn in Columbus, Fitzhugh had already covered the back roads of the district once and was beginning a second round.

Gainous made two fatal mistakes: he underestimated the depth of his constituents' misery; and he underestimated the energy of his

< 324 >

young opponent. It seemed that Fitzhugh was everywhere. He had nothing to assist him but an old automobile he had borrowed from Monkey Deloach, a good pair of shoes, his handful of allies, and what turned out to be considerable powers of persuasion. This young fellow, they said around the district, was the best campaigner they had seen in a long time. He shook your hand, looked you in the eye, captured you with his message. He made you feel that your vote was the only one that counted at that particular moment.

Oscar Gainous was rather cavalier about the whole thing until the last week before the primary in early June, when certain members of the district's Democratic Committee began to whisper in his ear that this young Birdsong fellow might have to be reckoned with after all. He had people riled. Gainous bestirred himself to make a few luncheon speeches to some of the more prominent civic groups in the district. But by then it was too late.

Bright was detached from all this, watching it as one would look out the window at passersby on the sidewalk. She knew only that Fitzhugh was gone from early morning until late at night, dragging himself in to collapse exhausted in bed beside her. It would have been more of a strained and prickly thing between them, but he simply was not there most of the time. She asked him little and he volunteered almost nothing, not until the very end, when he could smell blood and his own blood was high and he was flushed with the sense of what was happening to him. His excitement overcame his reticence.

"I think I may win," he said to her two days before the vote.

He was near collapse, eyes bloodshot, right hand swollen from handshaking, face gaunt from the weight he had lost. But there was a fierce gleam in his eye, a zeal that almost matched the ardor with which he had pursued her. And she softened, seeing how very badly he wanted this, remembering that this very quality was what had attracted her to him in the first place. She touched his cheek gently. "I hope you do win," she said. "I truly do. And if you do win, what will you do with it?"

"Serve," he said simply. "I can't think very far ahead. In fact," he laughed, "I can't think what I'm supposed to do a half hour from now."

It took three days to count and recount the votes. At first tally, Fitzhugh astonishingly led by slightly more than five hundred. But Oscar Gainous kept demanding recounts and the district Democratic Committee kept obliging him. Each time its members sifted through the ballots, they found a few more for Gainous. And, mysteriously, there were three boxes from the far reaches of the district that somehow had not made their way to the courthouse in Columbus to be tallied.

< 325 >

"They're stealing the damn thing!" Monkey Deloach howled. "Fitzhugh, you've got to do something!" So Fitzhugh went to court. He found a maverick judge in Columbus who heard Fitzhugh and his allies out, then ordered the sheriff to confiscate the ballot boxes and bring them to his courtroom. There, in front of his bench with the judge glaring down at them, the members of the Democratic Committee counted again, including the three wayward boxes that had now magically appeared. It was seven o'clock at night when they finished. The district chairman got up slowly and walked to the bench, handed the judge a piece of paper with the final tally on it. "The sonofabitch won," the chairman said.

Fitzhugh stood up from his seat in the front row of the spectator section of the courtroom. "Which sonofabitch, Your Honor?"

The judge looked down at the paper in his hand. "Birdsong by thirty-seven votes," he said.

"Well, I'll be a sonofabitch for thirty-seven votes," Fitzhugh said. And even the district chairman laughed.

< >

She heard the telephone ringing in the front hall through the pounding in her ears, ignored it for a long time. She had him now deep in the secret recesses of her body where they both touched gold and honey, set off explosions of light, whimpered and then cried with pleasure, the sweat-slickness of their bodies mingling in the hot June midnight.

But the telephone would not quit. It intruded, beckoning her back from the brink, until finally she said in exasperation, "Go answer the damned thing! And hurry." He withdrew with a shudder of pleasure, rose and wrapped a robe around his nakedness and padded down the hall to the telephone.

He was gone for several minutes. When he returned, instead of removing his robe and sliding into bed beside her, he sat on the edge, pensive.

"Who on earth?" she asked.

"Franklin Delano Roosevelt."

His voice was so low she could hardly hear him. "Of course," she laughed. "Who else this time of night?" Then he turned to her and she saw in the dim light from the window the look of wonder on his face. "It really was, wasn't it."

"Yes. It really was."

She waited for a moment. "Well, what did he say?"

"He said 'Congratulations.'"

< 326 >

"Is that all?"

Fitzhugh shook his head, returning to her. "No. He talked for several minutes. I don't know who told him about me, but he said he'd been following my campaign, knew what I was saying about him. He knew the exact words, in fact, all that business about the folks back in the boxcars."

"You're sure it was him."

"Goodness, yes. I'd recognize the voice anywhere. And the laugh. He has a great big laugh. You can feel the power of it, even all the way down here over the telephone line. He kept saying, 'I love it! I love it!'"

"Well, what did you say?" she asked.

"I was as tongue-tied as a schoolboy. But he didn't give me much of a chance, anyway. He said as soon as he disposes of Landon in November, we've got work to do. *We*. He said *we*."

Bright felt suddenly very alone, very much at the edge of things. And ashamed that she felt that way just now when he was savoring this very great triumph. She took his hand, held it tightly in hers. "I'm very proud of you, Fitzhugh. To have the president of the United States calling our home. That's rather nice, don't you think?"

"Yes," he smiled. Then, his voice urgent: "You'll come with me. You and Fitz."

"Come with you?"

"Of course. To Washington. There'll be so much to do, to see. What a great education for him, growing up there."

She drew away from him, felt a sudden rise of panic. "That's out of the question, Fitzhugh. We don't belong in Washington. And there's Papa . . ."

"Papa."

"Yes," she cried. "He's old and he's sick and he needs me."

"And what about me?"

She shook her head in frustration. "No! You're not going to do this."

"Do what?"

"Make me choose. I won't be forced to choose!"

He got up then, walked over to the window and stood there for a long time looking out at the yard while she huddled in the bed, feeling wretched, trapped. "Well," he said after a while, turning back to her, "Congress isn't in session but a few months out of the year. We'll make do for now. No sense in disrupting things, I suppose."

"No. No sense," she answered.

"I don't want to make you choose, Bright."

< 327 >

"Then don't," she said bitterly.

"Perhaps later . . ."

But she didn't answer that.

< >

Fitzhugh went to Washington to take his seat in January of 1937. And Dorsey Bascombe began slowly to lose his mind.

Bright was jarred awake by the telephone in the middle of the night, several days after Fitzhugh had boarded the train. "Bright," Dorsey said, "I can't find your mother's things." His voice was very calm, very matter-of-fact.

She fought through the grogginess of sleep. "What things, Papa?"

"All her things," he said. "You know. I've looked all over the house for them, but I can't find them. Can you come help me?"

She was wide awake now, alarmed. "Papa, it's the middle of the night."

He seemed not to hear her. "The cameo brooch. The one I bought her in San Francisco. It's missing, and I'm afraid somebody has broken in and stolen it."

"Papa, nobody's broken in . . ."

"But if he comes back, I'm ready for him. I've got my gun here, and I'll blow his goddamned head off."

He never cursed, certainly not around her. "Papa, you put the gun away. I'll be right there."

But by the time she arrived, carrying a sleep-logged Little Fitz in her arms, Dorsey seemed to be perfectly all right. He was sitting in the parlor in his pajamas and robe. There was no sign of a gun. The front door was unlocked and she let herself in, looked quickly around the parlor, saw him there in the dim light from a lamp on the telephone table. "Papa?"

He looked up, gave her a thin smile. "Hello there."

"Are you all right, Papa?"

"Of course I'm all right. I couldn't sleep, so I got up and had a glass of milk and thought I'd just sit here for a while."

"You . . ." She hung fire, not knowing how much to say. She crossed the room, sat down next to him on the sofa. "You called me."

He looked surprised. "Called?"

"On the telephone. Just now."

He looked over at the telephone. "No, it's just your imagination."

He seemed very composed, his voice even. *Am I crazy? No. There is something desperately wrong here.*

"I think I'll go back to bed now. And you go home and get some

< 328 >

rest, for heaven's sake." Then he got up abruptly and left her there, staring at his back and feeling the cold fist of dread squeezing her insides until she could hardly breathe.

He came and went as the weeks passed, often quite lucid and in control of his faculties—if anything, even sharper of mind than he had been previously. He made elaborate lists, plans, took great notice of the smallest details. But other times he was either in the grip of fantasy or wrapped in a cocoon of silence in which he barely acknowledged his surroundings or the people who spoke to him. He was never violent, but his behavior was unpredictable. He might be at the lumberyard conducting business with perfect clarity one moment, then suddenly get up from his desk and wander off on some fanciful errand only he knew about. He disappeared altogether one April afternoon and turned up in Columbus the next day, asking for directions from a policeman. Bright, wild with fear, drove with Monkey Deloach to fetch him and found him sitting calmly on a bench in the police station. He seemed to have not the foggiest idea what the fuss was all about.

Dr. Finus Tillman was little help. "It may be temporary, or not."

"Is he going mad?"

"I suppose in the clinical sense, you could say so. In a more practical way, he just goes off by himself, off to places both physical and mental where we can't follow. It's a way of coping, I think."

"Coping with what?"

"With whatever is bothering him," Tillman said simply.

His wanderings drove both Bright and Hosanna to distraction. But then in the early summer they ceased, and Dorsey seemed to come to himself. He simply said to Bright one day, "I'm tired. I'm ready to sit for a spell."

"What do you mean, Papa?"

"You handle things."

"The lumberyard?"

"That. All the rest."

She kissed him softly on the forehead, smoothed the thin gray strands of his hair. His skin looked very transparent, like paper. He was a ghost inhabiting the wasted remains of his body. "Yes, Papa. You rest now. You've done enough."

She went to Monkey, told him to take charge of the lumberyard operation. She did not think Dorsey would be back for a good while. Monkey was obliging, as ever. Yes, he would take over. He would keep Dorsey Bascombe's business on its feet. It would be there when Dorsey was ready to return. Bright knew in her heart he never would. He was

< 329 >

quietly drifting away from them now, disappearing into the temple of his disappointment.

< >

In 1938, Fitzhugh ran for a second term, but it was a hideous business. Oscar Gainous ran again, swearing revenge, giving no quarter, thundering condemnations. Fitzhugh Birdsong, he fumed, was no true Southerner, but rather a captive of the Mad Hatter in the White House, part of a sinister cabal that was leading the country down the road to socialism or worse. That was what he said in public. In private, he and his supporters carried on a brutal whispering campaign. The worst of it was directed against Dorsey Bascombe. He was, they said, a drunk and a lunatic who kept company with a black woman. Gainous was well financed. His advertisements filled the newspapers in the district. His slanderous smear sheets were everywhere. The windows of Fitzhugh's car were smashed. The Ku Klux Klan burned a cross on their front yard, though nobody could quite figure out why. Midway into the campaign, it became clear that Gainous's tactics were working. The steady drumbeat of his criticisms and accusations, public and private, had Fitzhugh in deep trouble.

Bright was stung and furious. "How can you let this go on?" she railed to Fitzhugh. "Do you know what he's saying about Papa?"

"Yes. I know every word of it. He says things about you and me too."

"Well, stop him," she demanded.

"I'll stop him by beating him." But there was no conviction in his voice. He looked whipped already.

"And what if you do," she said bitterly. "What will you do about the hurt and the humiliation?"

His eyes were bleak with the frustration of it. But all he could say was "Bright, I'm sorry. For your father, for all of us."

Surprisingly, it was Dorsey who energized him. She found him on the back steps of his house one morning two weeks before the election, staring out across the yard. It was warm, but he wore an old brown sweater with a moth hole on one sleeve, a faded pair of pants, and a straw hat. He hadn't shaved for several days and his cheeks were flecked with the white stubble of his beard. She sat down beside him, grieving at the sight of him, the pain of what was being done to him. He didn't acknowledge her at first. "Good morning," she said, trying to keep her voice under control.

"It's right nice out here," he said after a moment. "I always liked the backyard. It's big and open, and if you sit here long enough, you

< 330 >

can fill it with your thoughts. That's why I never wanted to plant much of anything back here."

He seemed talkative this morning. Many days, he barely gave her a mumble. He seemed so deep inside himself most of the time. "I never knew you for a backyard sitter," she said.

There was a long silence and she wondered if he had heard her. Finally he said, "I used to come out here at night years ago. Just sit for a while and take stock of things. It seemed I could reason things out if it was just me and the darkness and the backyard. There's plenty of room out here for your thoughts to wander about without bumping into anything." He looked at her then, studied her for a moment. "You look a little peaked this morning."

"Oh?"

"Election bothering you?"

"No," she lied. Then, "Yes. It is. I'm mad as hell. At Oscar Gainous. And at Fitzhugh. I don't know what to do."

"Remember who you are," he said without hesitation. "You're a Bascombe. And a man doesn't go around spitting on Bascombes and get away with it. The best way to get even is for Fitzhugh to win this election."

She gave him a close look, saw the set of his jaw and the way the hair stood up on the back of his neck. "You're fighting mad, aren't you," she said with a trace of wonder.

"No, I'm not mad about anything anymore. But Fitzhugh had better be. It's the only way he'll win. You tell him that."

Bright went home and told Fitzhugh what he had said. And it seemed to give him a sudden surge of strength and conviction. In the waning days of the campaign he attacked Gainous head-on, lashing out at the personal smears, charging that Gainous and the moneyed interests he represented were only trying to get back to the public trough by climbing over the backs of little people who still had nothing. He was ferocious in his assault, and people responded. By the time the vote was taken, he had turned the election upside down. He won comfortably, the results confirmed by a recount of the state elections board. And it was the instant consensus that, having survived so mighty a challenge, Fitzhugh Birdsong was in Congress for as long as he wanted to stay. But Fitzhugh never forgot what a brutal thing it had been. It would haunt him for the rest of his political career.

< 331 >

20

*I*n the spring of 1939, the river flooded. Back in the time of Dorsey's mayorship, he had warned that the river would eventually rise up and spread itself across the broad flatland at its banks, into the streets and homes and businesses. He could look at the lay of the land and tell how the river had helped to shape it. "Nature," he said, "is inevitable. This whole valley belongs to the river. We're temporary squatters here." Indeed, there had been a few minor floods over the years—a foot or two of water in the pasture bottomland, the yellow water lapping at the udders of cows that had been stranded and, petrified by fear, refused to move until it subsided. But people generally took the minor flooding as proof that Dorsey, who was right about many things, was wrong about this one. And by 1939, few people paid much mind at all to Dorsey Bascombe. He was part of the town's history, not its present. Few people even saw him anymore.

The late winter of 1939 was unusually wet—dreary, unending days of cold, miserable rain; never great torrents of it, but a steady downpour that kept people cooped up inside, staring morosely out of their streaked windows, and soaked the soil to a spongy saturation. There had been a drought the previous summer, so the rain was welcome at first. But by the beginning of March, folks had had enough of a good thing. Fields were so waterlogged it would take a month for them to dry out before the farmers could plant their spring crops. And townspeople half joked about being devoured by mildew as they slept.

On March 11, the weather broke suddenly. The rain stopped, the skies cleared, and it turned unseasonably warm. Dazed people threw open their windows, left their houses, wandered the streets of the town, stepping around puddles glistening in the sunshine. In the afternoon, the temperature warmed to eighty-five and steam began to rise from the sidewalks. The school superintendent declared a one-day hol-

< 332 >

iday on March 12 to calm the frayed nerves of his faculty. Crowds gathered on the riverbank to gape at the angry orange water, carrying tree limbs and other debris as it surged along. A log floated by with a rooster clinging to it. The river was swollen and dangerous, but it was still where it was supposed to be, even after more rain than anyone could remember.

On March 13, the bottom fell out. It started late in the afternoon with thick gray clouds boiling in from the southwest. From near Columbus, there was a report of a tornado—a barn destroyed, a cow pierced through the side by a flying board. At dusk, a sprinkle of rain drove people back inside. By eight o'clock it was raining heavily. By nine, there were sheets of water so thick people could not see past their front porches. They went to bed grumbling. They woke the next morning to find it was still raining and the river was in their yards.

Bright woke to the raucous yammering of a flock of crows in a tree outside her window, the barking of a dog, and a strange swishing sound under the house below her bed. She rose, put on her robe and slippers, went to the front door, opened it and looked out, saw the sea of reddish-brown stretching out from the front steps under the pecan trees on the front lawn, down Claxton toward the river as far as she could see. A block away, a boy splashed furiously along in the middle of what had been the street, the water already up to his waist. He was the only sign of humanity.

"Oh, my God," she said softly. She thought instantly of Dorsey, then of her child sleeping in the back bedroom. She looked in on Little Fitz, curled in a knot under his blanket. Then she went back to the front hall, clicked the light switch. Nothing. The power was out. The hydroelectric plant at the small dam upstream was probably completely underwater by now, she imagined. She took the telephone receiver off its hook, gave the hand crank several furious turns. Nothing. Either the operator at Central had abandoned her switchboard or the lines were waterlogged and useless. Probably both. She went back to the front porch and stood there staring at the water, saw how it was creeping up the front steps. She began to hear shouts now as the neighbors woke—Buster Putnam's elderly grandparents beyond the high hedge to her left, Clayton Pulyard the barber over to the right.

"Bright! Bright Birdsong!" Clayton called to her from his front porch. She couldn't see him for the crepe myrtle bush between them.

"Yes, Clayton. We're all right. How about you?"

"What the hell are we going to do?" he cried.

Bright looked at the water again. It was midway up the steps now, lapping against the concrete. If you studied it for a moment, you could

< 333 >

see how the great mass of water moved off toward the right. It struck her. They were now in the middle of the river. It covered the entire town. She looked across the street at the small grocery store on the corner of Claxton. The water had pushed open the front door, like a throng of eager shoppers, and was floating items out through the opening—a parade of vegetables, boxes of flour and salt, joining the growing tide of household items swirling about in the streets, as if they were setting up house on their own. The buildings along Claxton seemed to bob in the tide, and she wondered if they would float away, if the river would sweep the town clean and leave the land as bare as a baby's bottom.

"I'm worried about my father," she called back to Clayton.

"Hell, he's got an upstairs," Clayton said. "He'll be fine. What about us?"

Bright felt a rush of sheer, mindless panic. That, and boiling anger. Fitzhugh Birdsong, off in Washington saving the country from itself. And who would save her from the flood? She was a twenty-eight-year-old woman, at home with a child not quite four years old. And about to have a house full of water. Damn Fitzhugh. Damn Franklin D. Roosevelt.

Then she calmed herself. There was simply nothing else to do. She would deal with Fitzhugh and the president later. Right now, she had all she could take care of right here.

"Something will come along, Clayton," she cried out. "You and Myrna just hold on over there." Then she called to the Putnams in the other direction. "Mr. Putnam. Are you folks all right?"

"Gardenia is worried about her fur," Mr. Putnam called back in a tremulous voice. "She's had it since we went to the World's Fair. It wouldn't do to get it wet."

Bright considered that for a moment. "Tell her to hang it from a light fixture, Mr. Putnam. Surely the water won't get up as high as the light fixtures."

"Yes!" he called back. "That's the ticket! I'll tell her to do that."

"Just hold on for a little while, Mr. Putnam," Bright said. "Someone will come along presently to get us, I'm sure of it."

It helped her to say it. They wouldn't drown. If necessary, they could climb up on the roof. She wasn't exactly sure how she would do that with a small child, but she would think of something. But she imagined that help would arrive before she had to do that. So she went back inside and packed a small valise and woke Little Fitz. "Honey, I've got a surprise for you," she said. She picked him up, tucking a blanket around his pajamas, and carried him to the front door. He slumped

< 334 >

against her, still groggy with sleep, then finally rubbed his eyes with his fists and looked out. "Where did all the water come from?" he asked, wide-eyed now.

"That's the river. It's flooded."

"Will we float off to China?"

"Maybe so. If you see any Chinamen come by, you'll know we already did. Right now, I think we best get ready to take a trip."

"Where to?"

"Wherever we can get to from here. As long as it's dry."

"Are we going to walk?" he asked, staring at the water.

"No, it's too deep for that now. I imagine we'll go in a boat. Or the bathtub."

He giggled at that, looking over his shoulder at the water as she carried him back to the bedroom and dressed him. Then she sat him and her valise on the dining room table and went back to check the water. It was at the top step now, only inches from the porch. Another few minutes and it would be into the house. She took off her shoes, went to the dining room and put them on the table next to Fitz, dragged up a chair and sat on the edge of the table with her bare feet on the chair seat. This would do for now.

"Mama," said Fitz, "it's not nice to sit on the table."

"I know, honey. Just this once, all right? Let's imagine it's a boat."

"I've got to wee-wee," he said.

She looked toward the front hall a few feet away, saw the first trickle of water nudging its way in the open front door. Then she felt the house shudder, heard the groan of protesting beams. *My God!* she thought, *the house is going to float off its foundation.* The water would start seeping up through the floor any moment, and then it would lift the house off the brick piers. She sensed the immense ominous power of the water, like a huge growling beast under the house, rising up to smash them . . .

"Mama, I've got to *wee-wee!*"

"Then *do* it!" she bellowed, frightening him. He began to cry.

Bright reached for Fitz, hugged him to her. "It's all right, honey," she said. "Mama didn't mean to scare you. We're going to be all right. Here." She released him. "Just stand up at the edge of the table and wee-wee on the floor."

Fitz stared at her, wide-eyed. "It'll mess up the floor."

She stared back, then started laughing. "Oh, I don't imagine that's going to matter," she said. "Just this once, it won't matter even a little bit. Do you need some help?"

"No, Mama," he said solemnly. "I can do it by myself."

< 335 >

He stood up and turned his back to her, and in a moment she heard the dribble of water hitting the floor. And then a loud bump out on the front porch. She jumped, thinking something big had hit the house.

"Miz Bright!" the voice called.

"Flavo?"

"Yes'm. I've got a rowboat out here. Y'all come on out so I can take you someplace."

Flavo! God bless Flavo Richardson! "We're coming!" she cried. She helped Fitz button his trousers, handed him her shoes, then took him in one hand and the valise in the other and headed for the door. By the time she reached the front porch she was sloshing in cold, red water.

Flavo had the rowboat right up on the porch where the wicker furniture had been. She saw a piece of it now, floating out near one of the pecan trees in the front yard. Flavo was sitting in the rear of the boat with the oars shipped, holding on to one of the porch pillars to steady the boat. "I'da been here sooner, but I had to get Miz Estelle Dockery out of a tree," he said.

"Flavo, you're a sight for sore eyes," Bright said.

Flavo leaned forward to take Bright's valise and then helped them over the gunwale onto the small wooden seat.

"My father . . ."

"He's fine. I just come from there. He's upstairs, looking out his window and directing traffic."

"Directing traffic?"

"Yelling instructions out the window. Like he was still the mayor or something. He seemed pretty excited."

"Can you take me over there?"

Flavo looked out at the sea of water swirling about the trees in the front yard. "That's where we're going. Mama said for me not to come back without you."

Fitz stared at Flavo, eyes wide, mouth open. "Are we gonna drown, Flavo?" he asked.

"No sir," Flavo said. "Not if you hold on tight. You take care of your mama while I row the boat, you hear?"

"Yes sir," Fitz said, gripping Bright's hand tightly.

Flavo took one of the oars in both hands and used it to shove them away from the porch. When they were clear, he placed it back in the oarlock and began rowing toward the street, the ropy muscles of his arms straining with every stroke.

She thought suddenly of Hosanna and Mose. "Flavo, where are your folks?"

< 336 >

"Mama's at the house with Mr. Dorsey, and Daddy's gone to get the trucks," he said.

"What trucks?"

"From the lumberyard. He and Jester went to see could they get the trucks out 'fore the water got to 'em."

Bright looked back, saw the water well up in the house now, probably a foot deep or so. It was rising very rapidly. There must have been an enormous amount of rainfall, even more upstream than here. The river had reclaimed the land, just as Dorsey Bascombe had said it would. She wondered if it would have made any difference if people had believed him. Probably not. They had built their town on the banks of the river and made a life here—a middling good life—and they would rebuild it when the river had given the land back. People could be incredibly stoical, she thought. Or stupid. Or both.

They were out onto what had been Hill Street now, and as she watched the house receding behind them, her mind wandered through its rooms, taking inventory of all the things the floodwaters would soil and plunder—furniture, bedding, clothing, photographs, her piano. It would be ruined, she thought. The piano Dorsey Bascombe had bought for his young wife some thirty years before, had insisted that Bright take to her new home. You could refinish furniture, you could wash clothing. But a piano would never be the same. Cold, muddy water would destroy the delicate balance of rare woods and strings and felt and ivory. Another piece of her life gone. Things seemed to be forever slipping away from her. Things and people. *I will not cry,* she thought. *I just damned well will not cry.*

She had never realized there were so many rowboats in town. Every third house or so must have had a boat stored away in a backyard shed, and they were all out now, a veritable armada of small wooden craft, gliding about in the floodwaters and occasionally bumping into each other, the town trying to save itself. As Flavo rowed their own boat the three blocks to Dorsey's house, they passed perhaps a dozen others, many of them loaded to the gunwales with entire families, others with a lone man at the oars, looking for somebody to rescue, turning suddenly toward a house where people yelled for help from the windows or roof or stood knee-deep in water on their front porches.

One boat precariously held a large Victrola cabinet and two men who were arguing at the top of their lungs about where to take it. Their dilemma was solved when the current carried them under a maple tree and a limb caught the cabinet and sent everything into the water. When the men came up, the water was at their armpits. They climbed into the tree, soaked to the skin but still fuming at each other.

Another boat held the police chief, a large florid man named

< 337 >

Burkhalter, who seemed fairly angry at what the river was doing to his town. Another man rowed and Burkhalter sat at the bow with a shotgun cradled in his arms, calling out to everybody who passed, "You see any looters, let me know. I'll blow their damn heads off." Looters? Here? This wasn't Chicago or Munich, for goodness' sake. *My God,* Bright thought, *it's made them all a little crazy!* There was an air of frantic unreality to it: the town submerged—trees without trunks, only branches; houses half their normal height, the whole business appearing to sink into the water; people dazed and irrational. They clearly needed somebody to take charge. They needed Dorsey Bascombe the way he used to be. Where the devil was Pegram Gibbons? Probably saving his own hide, she thought, or at the back door of his bank with a rowboat, loading money. Pegram was not a bold man, not the way Dorsey had been. It was, she supposed, the difference between a man who spent money and one who lent it.

Flavo could sense the panic. He rowed hard, his eyes wide and his breath coming in labored gasps. He steered well clear of the other boats, stopping against a tree or the edge of a building to let them pass. It took perhaps twenty minutes to reach Dorsey's house, and as they glided through the gate, she saw her father stick his head out the window of the second-floor bedroom where she had spent her childhood. He had a huge pistol in his hand, and before she could open her mouth, he lowered the barrel of the pistol and fired, aiming somewhere just ahead of their boat. The sound was enormous. "Papa!" she screamed, grabbing Fitz and pulling him against her, trying to shield him with her body. Another shot, then another, the roaring echo ricocheting across the hard flat surface of the water and off the house across the street. There was a violent thrashing behind her as Flavo tried to stop the progress of the boat and put it into reverse. Swirls of angry red water from his flailing oars eddied around them. Fitz bellowed with fright. Dorsey fired again, and then she looked in horror as two halves of a blasted water moccasin went flying from a lower branch of the big oak tree in the front yard and flopped into the water.

"Papa, don't shoot us!" Fitz cried.

"Mr. Dorsey, put the gun away!" Flavo yelled from behind them.

Dorsey stared at them, blinking, bewildered. Bright could see the wild, fevered look in his eyes. "Bright!" he cried out. "Look what they've done to my town!"

"It's all right, Papa!" she called up to him. "The river will go away. It'll be all right. We're here now." She turned to Flavo. "How are we going to get up there? Can you row into the house?"

Flavo surveyed the situation. "No'm, I don't think so. The boat

< 338 >

won't fit in the front door, even if it was open, which it ain't. I reckon y'all gone have to climb up on the porch roof and get in the winder."

The water was halfway up the front porch now. The weight of it had smashed in the windowpanes and the river was all in the downstairs. She could see smaller pieces of furniture floating about inside. Flavo maneuvered the boat to the edge of the porch and grabbed one of the porch pillars, hugging it tightly to steady the boat. The roof was just a few feet over their heads. Bright rose gingerly with Fitz in her arms. "Honey, I'm going to lift you up onto the roof and I want you to crawl up to Grandpa's window and climb inside."

Fitz gaped at her, clung to her neck fiercely. "No!" he whimpered. "I'm 'fraid, Mama!"

"Fitz, stop it this instant! Hitch up your britches, boy, and do what I tell you! Exactly what I tell you!"

He clamped his mouth shut, but his eyes were wide with terror and silent tears streamed down his face. She couldn't let it take hold of them. *I have to get him up. I have to get up myself. I have to get to Papa!* She hoisted him very slowly, trying not to rock the boat and spill them all into the water. She got the upper half of his body over the edge, but he froze there with his legs dangling off. "I want my daddy!" he wailed.

She smacked him on the fanny, perhaps harder than she needed to, but it got him moving again and he wriggled up the rest of the way. "Don't stand up now," she commanded. "The roof's slick. Crawl on your stomach. Like an alligator." He disappeared and she heard him slithering across the roof and then scrambling in the window, finally cutting loose with a scream of fright as he reached the safety of his grandfather's arms.

Bright sat down for a moment to catch her breath and compose herself.

"If you wait a little bit, maybe the water'll go on up some more and that'll make it easier for you," Flavo said.

"No!" she said fiercely.

She took off her shoes, tossed one of them in a curving arc up on the roof above, trying to aim in the general direction of Dorsey's open window. She heard it hit, then rattle across the shingles as it tumbled back down and toppled off the edge into the water, ten feet or so from the front edge of the boat. The shoe floated for a moment; then a tiny wave hit it and it took on water and went down at the heel.

She stared at the spot where it had gone under, beginning to feel a little hysterical.

"You want me to go get it?" Flavo said softly.

Bright turned and stared at him, and then they both started

< 339 >

laughing. Bright felt instantly better. God bless Flavo Richardson. Perhaps the truest and sanest man in the entire town right this moment. She tossed the other shoe after the first, and it hit the water with a splash and disappeared. "Hosanna always told me never to go barefoot before the first of May, but what the devil!"

"Here, I got an idea," Flavo said. He eased up amidships, still holding on tightly to the porch post. "You step up real slow-like on my shoulders, and that'll give you a little boost." He knelt in the bottom of the boat, facing her, and she did as he said, planting her feet on his broad shoulders, digging her toes into the hard muscles of his upper back, using the post to steady herself. She reached for the roof and then began to pull herself over the edge as Flavo straightened up below. She threw one leg over the edge of the roof, then the other, and she was up and she could see Dorsey and Fitz in the open window. Dorsey didn't have the gun now. Fitz had stopped crying and he was watching her, fascinated. "Like an alligator, Mama," he called out. She eased slowly toward them on her belly, reached the open window, where Dorsey reached out with his good arm and helped her crawl through. She threw her arms around his neck. "Are you all right?"

"The town," he said, his voice quavering. "And my lumberyard."

"I know, Papa. We'll fix everything. Don't you worry about it."

"I've got to get to the lumberyard!" he insisted. "I've got to save my logs! It's all that's left!"

He grabbed her arm, his grip so firm that it hurt. "Papa!" She squeezed his hand with her own, trying to stay calm, trying to soothe him. "It's all right, Papa. The water will go down soon, and we'll get to the lumberyard. You'll see. It's all right."

"It's gone," he said, his voice a paper-thin whisper. "All gone down the river."

"Will it float off to China?" Fitz asked, staring up at his grandfather.

"Shhh," Bright hushed him. "Papa doesn't feel well, honey." She tried to edge him toward the doorway. "You need to lie down for a while, Papa. Get some sleep. We'll take care of everything now."

He gave in to her then with a great sigh, peered up at her with his pale, watery eyes. There was a tiny glimmer for just a moment, a flicker of light in the bleakness. He released his iron grip on her arm and she could feel the blood coursing back through her veins with a flash of heat. "It's all yours," he said. "All of it."

She led him gently to his own bedroom and he sat quietly on the edge of the bed while she took off his shoes. Then she lifted his thin legs onto the bed and pulled the covers over him. He lay there, staring

< 340 >

at the ceiling for a moment. "It's all yours," he said again. "You can have it."

"Sleep, Papa. You'll feel better."

She pulled down the shades, darkening the room, kissed him on the forehead, then left him there in the stillness, closing the door softly behind her.

She froze in the doorway to her own room. Fitz was sitting in a chair, holding the great weight of the pistol with both hands, pointing it out the window.

"Fitz!"

He jerked around toward her, startled, and the gun went off with a roar that shattered the room, and a vase on top of the dresser beside Bright exploded as the bullet hit. She felt shards of it sting her face. Then Fitz dropped the gun and it clattered to the floor. He bellowed with fright and she rushed to him, kicking the pistol furiously aside with her foot, and enveloped him in her arms. She crushed him to her, felt the blood wet on her face. Everything inside her seemed to break loose at once. She screamed, giving way to the rage and hurt, the terror. *Oh God! Fitzhugh, come home and save us!*

< >

The river crested at fifteen feet above flood stage at midafternoon of the first day, and at that depth it had invaded every structure in town. On the smaller houses only the roofs were showing, and the only automobile to be seen was one that had floated on the rising tide and been wedged sideways in an alleyway behind Putnam's Mercantile downtown. Not that anybody was downtown to see it, once the rowboats finished their scurrying about. They ferried many of the townspeople to higher ground east of the river, where a steady stream of cars began arriving from nearby communities to pick up the chilled, soaked refugees and take them to temporary shelter. Every two-story house in town was packed, the windows filled with dazed people staring out at the swirling red water. Late in the afternoon, they heard a drone overhead and looked up to see an Army Air Corps biplane circling the town. The man in the front seat was leaning over the side with a large camera, taking pictures. Some of the flood victims shook their fists at the plane. To hell with pictures, they said. When darkness came, they closed their windows and bedded down wherever there was room, exhausted and hungry.

They awoke the next morning to find that the river had receded during the night, leaving small ponds of standing water in low places. The town looked as if it had been ravaged by war—trees pushed over

< 341 >

by the relentless force of the water, automobiles and wagons overturned, several houses tilted crazily off their foundations. There was an
incredible tangle of debris everywhere—furniture, pieces of clothing,
mattresses, tree limbs—all of it coated with a dull red slime of mud.

Bright and Hosanna looked out the front window of the Bascombe home and watched a dog feasting on a ham that had floated out
of somebody's kitchen.

"Ain't gone take much for me to go fight that dog over that ham
bone," Hosanna said. "I don't believe I ever been so hungry."

It was a bright, blustery day. The wind rippled the surface of the
standing water and picked at the raw faces of the handful of people
who wandered out of their ruined houses and stood ankle-deep in mud,
gaping at the destruction, blinking with disbelief in the sunlight. The
morning crackled with intermittent gunfire: People shooting at snakes.
One thing they had rescued from the rising water was their guns.

"The lumberyard," Bright said.

"Ain't nothin' to do for the lumberyard," Hosanna scoffed. "They
lots of trees where those come from."

"But the machinery. It'll ruin."

"Humph. I 'magine it done ruint already."

"Maybe we can save at least some of it," she insisted. "It's the only
thing I can do for Papa."

She dispatched Flavo and Mose, told them to scavenge for grease
and oil and do what they could to lubricate the big saws in the planer
mill and the steam engine before rust set in. With the trucks saved, she
thought, Dorsey could be back in operation fairly soon.

Help started arriving by midmorning. At first it was a motley collection of cars and trucks from neighboring communities, loaded with
blankets, food, and clothing. People who didn't have very much in the
first place had stripped their beds and cupboards and sent the supplies
to the towns along the river that had been ravaged by the floodwaters.
The vehicles couldn't get into the town proper, but word spread
quickly, and people began to slog through the muck to a hill on the
edge of town where a temporary relief headquarters had been set up in
a farmer's barn.

The upstairs of the Bascombe house was packed to the rafters with
refugees, thirty people or so, young and old. They were tired and sore
from sleeping on the hard pine floors through the chilled night, hungry
and thirsty. Nobody seemed to know much what to do now. In another
time, Dorsey would have been issuing orders, organizing the chaos. But
he lay now in his bed with the covers clutched up around his chin,
staring at the ceiling. He seemed not to hear when Bright spoke to

< 342 >

him. So she took charge, organized a delegation to go for help—several of the able-bodied men, among them Clayton Pulyard and Buster Putnam's younger brother Donnell. They returned two hours later, covered with mud but laden with supplies including a jerry can of drinking water and several cardboard boxes of foodstuffs. A scouting party she sent out came back with an iron washpot, an ax, and some dry boards they had found in the rafters of a woodshed. Bright had them pile up pieces of brick debris in the front yard to make a cook stand, and she and Hosanna built a fire under the washpot and began to make a huge stew. It bubbled and simmered for hours, cooking vegetables and bits of meat into a thick, rich concoction. The aroma drifted down the street, taking the edge off the stench of river mud, and others brought what they could find to the mixture. At midafternoon, Bright and Hosanna served it up to a crowd of more than fifty people—red-eyed, dazed, grimy, exhausted folk who ate ravenously using whatever utensils they could find, or their fingers. Bright carried a bowl of it up to her father and sat by his bed, spoon-feeding him. He ate, but his mind seemed to be far away. She didn't try to talk to him. *Let him be. Let him seek refuge where he can.*

Police Chief Burkhalter came by in the afternoon on a horse, picking his way carefully down the littered street, stopping where he found people to tell them the National Guard was on the way. A convoy of trucks from the state capital would be there by dark and would take everyone to Columbus, where emergency shelter had been set up in church basements and the high school gymnasium. Burkhalter got off his horse at the Bascombe house long enough to have a bowl of stew.

"Miz Bright," he said when he was finished, "you run a good soup kitchen."

"We're making do."

Burkhalter wiped his mouth on the sleeve of his coat, looked around at the ruination. "I'll be glad to get everybody out of here. Can't get a thing done with folks wandering around getting in the way." He looked like he had been without a drink of whiskey for a good while and needed one badly.

"We're not leaving," she said.

He looked at her, surprised. "But Miz Bright . . ."

"We'll be all right for another night, Chief. Papa and Fitz and I will stay here until Fitzhugh comes home. Hosanna and her family will stay with us."

"But . . ."

"And that's that." She was determined to stay, determined to

< 343 >

make Fitzhugh come and fetch her. She wanted him to see all this, to be shocked by it.

Burkhalter shrugged, thanked her for the stew, got on his horse and left. Just about everybody else left over the next hour or so as word came that the convoy had arrived at the relief headquarters. They straggled out in knots, carrying the few pitiful possessions they had saved, their feet making awful sucking sounds as they labored through the mud.

Bright stood on the porch and watched them go, and when the street was dark and empty she went back inside. Flavo and Mose arrived soon after, lighting their way with a coal oil lantern. They looked as if they had spent the day wallowing in a grease pit. Monkey Deloach, they reported, had been there when they arrived, and the three of them had spent the day dismantling the lumberyard machinery and coating it with grease and oil. *God bless Monkey.* Flavo and Mose helped themselves to the contents of the stewpot and then they all went back inside, leaving the remains to whatever animals were roaming about in the dark.

She woke in the bed she had slept in as a child, felt the movement of her own child next to her as he stretched his small body, still deep in sleep. She blinked in the sunlight splattering the wall next to her, turned over and saw Fitzhugh standing in the doorway.

He crossed the room, treading softly so as not to wake Little Fitz, and sat on the bed next to her. There were tears in his eyes. He truly did love them, she thought, and the hurt and anger left her. Then he took her in his arms and they clung silently to each other for a long time. "It's all right now," he whispered. "I'm home."

"Don't leave me," she said softly. "Don't ever leave me again."

Outside now, she could hear men's voices, one of them shouting orders, the roar of a truck's big engine. Men come to take them to safety.

<   >

When they returned two months later, the town seemed a shell of its former self. It had been picked clean by the water—smaller structures smashed and washed away, much of what people owned carried far downriver. The debris had been cleaned up and hauled off, houses righted and repaired. But there were only buildings and streets here now, none of the things large and small that marked a place as inhabited: ferns hanging in baskets on porches, bicycles leaning against picket fences, street lamps casting a soft glow against the summer evening. It would be a long time before it had the comfortable, scruffy

< 344 >

look of a lived-in place. And there would be reminders of the disaster for years, particularly the dull red stain that went to a certain height on trees and buildings. No use in trying to wash it away. It was deep in the pores of wood and brick. Only time would fade it.

Fitzhugh had moved them during the interim to a large, rambling boardinghouse in Columbus—Bright and Little Fitz in one room, Dorsey in another next door—while he stayed to help organize the restoration. He came to them on the weekends, but in between there were long, silent hours. Dorsey spent most of them in a rocking chair on the wide front porch of the house as the weather warmed into April and May, his eyes unfocused, his jaw slack. He asked no questions about his town or his lumberyard. He seemed to be wasting away, sad and defeated.

Franklin Delano Roosevelt had taken a personal interest in the enterprise. He federalized the National Guard and sent in an additional contingent of regular Army troops with heavy machinery and a company of young CCC men. They all set up camp in a pasture on the edge of town, rows of big green Army tents and a field kitchen and young officers puttering about in jeeps with clipboards. Good training, FDR said. They might be pitching their tents in Europe before long, he told Fitzhugh privately. FDR depended upon Fitzhugh for regular progress reports. He had come to depend upon him for many things. The young congressman was already one of his mainstays in the House at a time when Republicans and Democrats alike yapped at his heels like puppies, bleeding his domestic initiatives and thwarting his cautious attempts to prepare the nation for war. Fitzhugh had stuck with him. This, this rescue effort, was payback. And there was to be more, he promised. Roosevelt told the WPA to draw up plans for a levee around the town, with a canal to drain off the river's excess and floodgates at the bridges. There would be a new, metal bridge across the river at the foot of Claxton Street to replace the old wooden one the flood had washed away. Fitzhugh Birdsong's town would not flood again, not if FDR had anything to say about it.

Fitzhugh Birdsong's town. That's what they began to call it now, in the way they had called it Dorsey Bascombe's town for so many years. He could hold their seat in Congress for as long as he drew breath, they said. Damn the man who dared run against him.

Fitzhugh steered the car, a new Buick, into the driveway and helped them out, and they stood there for a moment, looking at the house.

"Did you build us a new house, Papa?" Little Fitz asked, eyeing it suspiciously.

"No," he laughed, "it just looks that way."

< 345 >

Indeed, it was a different house from the one Bright had departed from in Flavo's rowboat two months before. It had a fresh coat of white paint and dark green shutters. But the most striking change was the attic addition with windows peeking out of the roofline. They would never again have to flee in a rowboat, she thought. There was a nice new set of wicker on the front porch, white with bright green cushions, two rocking chairs and a settee and two tables. It looked very comfortable, the kind of porch where you could spend a warm soft evening and feel safe and at peace. Inside, there were a few familiar pieces of furniture, all cleaned up and refinished. But there was much that was new, including the gleaming white Kelvinator refrigerator in the kitchen with its motor in a round housing on top. It hummed ever so faintly, and when Bright opened the door, she felt a wave of cool air wash over her. No more ice deliveries. And in the parlor, a new tall black Story and Clark upright piano to replace the one the flood had ruined. She sat down for a moment and ran her fingers lightly over the keys. It had a nice touch, a nice sound. Hopeful. A beginning. Then they clomped up the new set of stairs built off the back porch to the attic and stood in the middle of the big room shaped like a cross, with a double set of windows on each of the four sides and four small closets tucked under the roofline at the inside corners. A big empty room, waiting to be filled with things.

Fitz ran quickly to the window that looked out over the backyard. "Papa," he called. "I can see all over!"

"It's a pretty good view, huh?"

"Can you see the whole world from up here?" Fitz asked.

"Well, not all. But a good bit of it, I guess."

"I feel like we're starting over," Bright said, taking Fitzhugh's hand.

"In a way, we are," he said ruefully. "We're in hock up to our eyeballs."

"All this . . ."

"Borrowed, of course. The car, the furniture, the piano, the attic." He smiled, ticking off their debts. "I'm not sure I even own my underwear outright. But we're no different than anybody else in town. People have to rebuild, get on with their lives. Pegram and Harley Gibbons are lending, folks are borrowing. It's an act of faith."

"Then you'd better get busy," she said. "And maybe I'd best think about finding some more piano students."

"That would help. I've got the law office cleaned up. Even managed to save a few books that were on the top shelves. And I have some more on order. Maybe I can sweet-talk a few little old ladies out of their life savings before we go back in session in September."

< 346 >

"I thought perhaps you'd stay home," she said quietly.

He gave her a surprised look. "These people elected me. I can't just walk away from it."

She dropped his hand. "You could. If you wanted to. You could stay home and tend to your own business."

"It *is* my business. Mine and theirs. Especially now, after what's happened here." His voice pleaded for understanding. "It's what I've chosen to do, Bright. It's good work, with a purpose. I can make things happen for people, not just here but all over the country. And the president needs me."

She turned away, walked over to the front window of the attic, looked out through the bright green of the pecan trees on the lawn. From this high, you could see above the trees all the way to the foot of the street where the river had torn away the old bridge. It dropped off precipitously there, and the Army troops had put up barricades to keep people from driving off into the river. The river. For most of its life it had seemed a placid thing, meandering nowhere in particular. Now the river took on a whole new meaning—ominous, threatening. It could take away your very life in a heartbeat. It could wrench your soul from your body.

"Bright," Fitzhugh pleaded. "Let's don't argue." He came to her, put his arm around her. "We're home now. All back together. I've tried to make it nice for you."

She turned to him, looked directly into his eyes. "I need *you*, Fitzhugh. That's what would make it nice for me."

"Then come with me," he said urgently. "Come to Washington. Just for the session. There's so much to do, so much to show Fitz. They'd love you there."

"I can't leave Papa."

"Then bring him too. A change will do him good."

"Oh, Fitzhugh," she said with an impatient shake of her head, "don't! I'm not going to Washington, Papa's not going to Washington! You're the only one who's going to Washington!"

"Mama." They looked down to see Little Fitz standing next to them, one hand on his father's pants leg, the other tugging on his mother's dress. "Are you fussing?"

Bright knelt to him, enclosed him in her arms. "Just a little, honey."

"Well," he said gravely, "I don't want you to fuss."

She pulled his small head to her breast, stroking his hair. Then she looked up; their eyes met. "Stay with us."

"I can't," he whispered, his voice anguished.

He cared, deeply and honestly, she thought. He was a good and

< 347 >

honest man, a passionate man. And that was why she needed him so badly just now, when the other good and honest man in her life seemed to be slipping away by the day. She wanted to wail, be angry, be selfish, be terribly hurt. Instead, she said, "All right, Fitzhugh. Go to Washington. But next spring, when the session is over . . ."

She saw the great pain in his face, the agony of choosing, of being forced to choose. He closed his eyes, nodded. "Next spring . . ." But he didn't finish the sentence. Instead, he turned away and went downstairs to unload the car.

<   >

Perhaps it was the horribly hot summer that took what was left of Dorsey Bascombe's mind. Days on end of it, waking to a quiet predawn still fetid from the day before, the air so thick and heavy with humidity that every breath was labored, the bedsheets damp with perspiration. And then, the moment the great unyielding sun began to splinter the tops of the trees beyond the river, it began again—a new day feeding like a dragon on the heat-blast of the one before; people moving like torpid slugs, seeking shade.

There was rain, a late-afternoon shower every few days when the heat and humidity turned the sky into a boiling mass of cumulonimbus and suddenly erupted with sheets of water and violent lightning and thunder. But it was little relief. Storms passed and steam rose thick from the pavement and the roofs of houses, the land giving back the moisture to start the whole process anew, and the temperature instantly shot up again. It was, young Ortho Noblett wrote in the newspaper, like pouring a bucket of water on Hades.

The refugees from the flood straggled back into town through June as homes and stores were repaired, and there was a good deal of brave talk about starting over, building something even better, the indomitability of the spirit. But then the heat took hold. By mid-July, it was a wilted, defeated place—ground down by ten years of Depression, a devastating flood, and now the most terrible heat wave to hit the area in fifty years or so.

The first meeting of the reconvened town council degenerated into raucous argument over a proposed resolution to commend Police Chief Burkhalter for his service during the flood crisis. Mayor Pegram Gibbons and Councilman Clayton Pulyard had to be physically restrained after Clayton called Burkhalter a "worthless drunk who did nothing but shoot snakes and get in the way." Burkhalter tossed his badge on the council table and stormed out of the chambers just as Pegram, normally the mildest of souls, but also the man who had hired

< 348 >

Burkhalter the year before, started climbing across the table toward Clayton. It had the makings of farce, but people didn't see much humor in it.

People in fact didn't see much humor in anything. The accumulated misery made them fractious. They said it was what sent Dorsey Bascombe over the edge.

It happened suddenly. Hosanna sent Flavo running to Bright's house on an early July afternoon. Telephone service had not yet been restored. Flavo banged urgently on the back door. "Miz Bright. Come quick!"

She was in the parlor, reading a magazine while Fitz took his nap in the front bedroom.

"Flavo, for goodness' sakes," she scolded as she headed for the door; then she saw his eyes wide with fear.

"Mama says you got to come right now! Mr. Dorsey locked himself in his room and he's yelling his head off!"

She left Flavo there to listen out for Little Fitz and ran the three blocks to Dorsey's house in the fierce heat, feeling the perspiration coursing down her back and face and the air pulling at her lungs. She found Hosanna in the hallway outside Dorsey's room. "Mr. Dorsey," she was pleading to the closed door, "you come on out now. I'll get you some dinner, that make you feel better. We got fresh tomatoes today, Mr. Dorsey." Her eyes were bleak with fright. Behind the door, she could hear Dorsey shouting incoherently.

Bright rattled the doorknob. "Papa. It's me, Papa. Open the door."

The shouts turned to sobbing. He made no move toward the door. He seemed far away, on the other side of the room somewhere. She ran down the stairs to the parlor, found the passkey in a drawer in the tall walnut secretary, returned to the hallway. She steadied her trembling hands and inserted the key in the latch, turned it with a click, opened the door slowly.

A blast of heat struck her in the face. The window was closed, the shade drawn, the room dim and fevered. She didn't see him at first, and then she spied the top of his head and his lower body, hunkered in a far corner between the wall and a chifforobe. His breath came in great labored gasps, as if his lungs were on fire. The terrible sound of it rasped against the heat.

She crossed the room quickly and knelt in front of him. "Papa," she said, "what's the matter?"

He would not show her his face at first, but then she put her hand gently on his forehead and he looked up at her and she could see the

< 349 >

madness in his eyes, the froth of spittle on his lips, the flaring of his nostrils. And then suddenly he grabbed her by the shoulders, pulled her roughly to him, pressed his mouth against hers. The stench of his breath, his body, was terrible. She recoiled in horror, pulled away from him, stumbled back against the bed while he cowered there in the corner. "Elise, don't leave me!" he cried.

Bright pressed her fist to her mouth, shaken to the core, repelled and sickened with shame. She ran from him, from the sight and smell of him, past Hosanna, who had seen it all and who stood bug-eyed in the doorway. She reached quickly and caught Bright with one hand and closed the doorway with the other as Bright collapsed against her, sobbing wildly. "Oh, Hosanna! He's mad! Oh, God!"

Hosanna let her cry for a long time, pouring out her grief and anguish until she was numb and empty. "Come away now," Hosanna said gently. "I'll fetch the doctor."

When Finus Tillman had come and given Dorsey a strong sedative, Bright sat in the kitchen and summoned the strength to ask Hosanna what had happened.

"I don't know," she said. "I just know Mr. Dorsey sent for Mose this morning, told him he wanted to go to the lumberyard. Mose come in one of the trucks and took him over there 'bout eleven, I reckon. When he come back, he look real strange and he just come up here to his room and closed the door. 'Bout an hour later I heard him hollerin'."

She went to him again in the late afternoon after Finus had left, sat for a long time by his bed, fanning him with a small cardboard church fan while he slept fitfully, mumbling and turning about, unable to find peace even under the spell of the sedative. His body seemed as dry as a desert, the skin parched and paper-thin, body and soul wasted.

Finus came again in the evening. Bright waited downstairs while he examined Dorsey, and when he came down, Bright asked, "What's wrong with him?"

Finus hesitated, shook his head. "I don't know, Bright. About this today, I just don't know. It may well be the shock of seeing the lumberyard for the first time since the flood. It may be an accumulation of things." He looked down at the black bag in his hand. "What's in there can't heal the mind. Maybe nothing can."

"Is my father insane?"

"Your father, my old and dear friend, is very fragile," he said gently.

"He's only sixty-four!" she cried.

"That has very little to do with it." He could sense her despair. He took her hand. "Stay with him, Bright. Do all you can humanly do, and take solace in that."

< 350 >

Tears sprang to her eyes. "Is he dying?"

"We're all dying," he said, his voice heavy with the twilight weariness of the many years he had carried the worn black bag in and out of dim rooms, of a doctor's inevitable ultimate failure. "We're all dying," he repeated. "It's the only way out."

<   >

On the fifth morning after Dorsey's fit of madness, Bright woke very early in the bedroom next to his and felt a great stillness. Outside, the first dim gray of daylight was giving faint outline to the leaves on the tree in the front yard. Silence. It was too early for Hosanna, but there was something else—a void from which life itself seemed to have been sucked. She lay in her bed for a while, listening, but the house itself seemed deadened. Finally she rose, pulled on a robe, and opened the door to her father's room. The bed was empty. Not only that, but neatly made, with the chintz spread tucked underneath the pillows. It looked as if no one had ever slept there, as if this were a room preserved in memory.

Bright's hand went to her mouth. "Oh, no!" she cried softly.

The lumberyard was a barren place. The flood had swept it clean, smashing the great stacks of lumber and carrying them away. Monkey had scouted downriver to see what he could salvage and had come back empty-handed. The operation would have to start over. The big shed housing the planer mill was just now being rebuilt, but it would be some time yet before Bascombe Lumber would be back in business. Here in the long-shadowed moments of early morning it was empty and lifeless, a wasteland. Years of accumulated sawdust that had made the ground spongy and sweet-smelling underfoot had been washed away. In its place the river had left a coating of red that was parched and cracked by the heat. How it must have grieved him when he saw it, the wreckage of his dreams and honor.

Bright found him in the tiny office, set back on its foundation since the flood had gone. The door was ajar, and just inside in the dim light she saw first the hated leather corset, cast aside on the floor. She closed her eyes tightly, sick with dread, afraid to see. She wanted desperately to turn and go, close the door quietly behind her. But she forced herself to stand her ground. She began to cry now, to give way to the great encompassing ache that settled over her like a shroud. Then she opened her eyes, and through the shiny film of her tears she saw the brown leather boots. She moved behind the desk and knelt beside him. "Oh, Papa!" she cried. "Oh, dear Papa!" His unseeing eyes stared at her, pierced straight through to her heart. The huge black

< 351 >

pistol lay on the floor next to his outstretched hand. And beneath it, the note, barely legible in his fevered scrawl:

Bright,

It's all gone. Everything. I can't bear the sight of it, or of myself. I love you, but I am so ashamed. It's up to you now. Don't run from it, as I have done. I have failed. You must not.

The bullet had gone through his heart. It was the place where he hurt the most.

< 352 >

21

*F*itzhugh meant to enlist, and as soon as possible. It would be a young man's war, as all wars are, but there would be a place for men who were no longer young, and they too were signing up. They wouldn't let him at the front at his age, but there were important things he could do. Perhaps a commission in Army Intelligence. That was something akin to politics.

But FDR got wind of it and called Fitzhugh to the White House on a gray late December afternoon in 1941. He sat Fitzhugh down in front of a crackling fire in his office and said, "Fitz, I don't want you tooling off to the Pescadores now. I need you here. We've got to have soldiers on the Hill too, because that's where some of the most important battles will be fought. Just because there's a war on doesn't mean the hyenas will roll over and play dead." Roosevelt cocked his eye and took a drag on his cigarette, peering at Fitzhugh over the top of his glasses, and that was that.

So Fitzhugh resigned himself to staying home and tried to hide his disappointment. But it was there. His war, the one for his generation, and he was missing it. The president could talk convincingly about manning the battlements in Congress, but it wasn't the same as going in harm's way. So a dinner at the White House with Winston Churchill was important, at least in making Fitzhugh Birdsong feel that a little bit of the war was being waged where he could get to it.

Bright went with him back to Washington after New Year's. There seemed little else to do, he was so insistent, so excited about the dinner, almost pleading. They left Little Fitz in Hosanna's care and drove to Columbus to catch the train, then rode all day and through the night, making love as the train rocked gently under their urgent bodies, waking to a Virginia countryside brilliant with frost, so clean and dazzling it could make your heart ache.

She sat watching it from their table in the dining car as the train approached Washington, feeling for the first time in two and a half

< 353 >

years that things might be made right again. Not the same, but made right and whole. She felt herself awakening from a long sleep in which nothing had mattered but dreams and the memory of dreams. She thought suddenly of her mother, of the long deep silences in which she had wrapped herself and the household during Bright's childhood. She understood something about that now, how an injured or fearful soul sought refuge in the quiet dark, trying to heal itself. Bright had existed since her father's death as two people: one who functioned, one who hid behind a curtain. She played the piano; she heard no music.

She blinked now in the sunlight, felt the warm glowing place deep in her body that Fitzhugh had stirred in the night.

He took her hand. "I'm so glad you came. I was afraid you wouldn't."

She looked at him, searched his face, studied the lines and angles as if seeing them for the first time. There were tiny crow's-feet around his eyes, slivers of gray in his hair, a softness about his lips. He had always been an attractive man. Now there was the grace of maturity, an ease that came of accomplishment. Fitzhugh Birdsong was one of the most influential young members of the Congress, a confidant of the master politician in the White House. Moreover, he had staked out his ground—foreign policy—just at the moment when it had seized the nation's consciousness. He was gaining influence on the House Foreign Affairs Committee, a builder of consensus, a gently persuasive man who could, nonetheless, drive a ruthless bargain when he had to. Most of the time, he didn't have to. Fitzhugh Birdsong combined charm and just the merest hint of vulnerability. It made you want to agree with him if you possibly could.

She could scarcely remember the moment in 1940 when he had told her he intended to run for reelection. He couldn't leave now, he said. Neither could FDR. They were both men who saw the world, and America's place in the world, in a new light. And the world they saw was spinning out of control. It was no time for such men to shrink back. He paraphrased Emerson: "Events are in the saddle, and ride mankind." She had heard him numbly. It didn't matter. Nothing seemed to matter very much in 1940. She felt alone. Whether Fitzhugh was there with her or off in Washington, she still felt alone.

Now, on this bright Virginia morning with the frost in the broad grassy fields fracturing the new sun into a million pinpoints of light, had it come to matter, at least a little? Was there an end to the aloneness? She couldn't answer that yet. She was here with him, that was all.

She smiled. "I'm a country girl come to town. Will I be terribly frightened?"

< 354 >

"No," he said gravely. "I won't allow that. They'll love you. You'll see."

They stepped from the train in the middle of the morning into the middle of the war. Union Station was a madhouse, a surging throng—young men in a rainbow of uniforms, young women clutching suitcases with one hand and holding their hats on their heads with the other, men with fedoras carrying briefcases, everyone in a terrible hurry but nobody particularly put out by the whole thing. While Fitzhugh fetched the bags, Bright clung to a broad marble column and saw the great ethnic diversity of America pass before her, the faces of Europe and Asia, the babble of strange accents and foreign tongues. It struck her: how provincial her upbringing, how sheltered her life, how narrow her perspective. These were strange, even exotic people, many of them with ideas and ideals that would undoubtedly be alien to her. But all God's creatures. Great heavens, what a stew he had cooked! It was a bit breathtaking.

She marveled at Fitzhugh, making his way back to her, so self-assured, moving so easily in the noise and crush. "Where did all these foreigners come from?" she asked when he reached her.

He laughed. "Brooklyn and Des Moines, probably. Quite a hodgepodge, isn't it. We're going to war with our ancestors."

They crammed into a taxicab with a Navy captain, an Air Corps lieutenant, and a young woman who had just arrived from Richmond to take a job in the Office of Production Management. The cabbie let them off first at the Hay-Adams and Bright sat on a sofa in the dark-paneled lobby, watching the scurrying about of people who looked incredibly important and busy, while Fitzhugh checked them in. He shared a small apartment behind the Capitol with three other congressmen, but there was no privacy for them there.

They lunched in the Hay-Adams dining room, lobster bisque and mountain trout, interrupted by a stream of passersby who stopped to say hello to Fitzhugh—a senator, an undersecretary of something, various bureaucrats and congressional aides, and, most notably, Tommy Corcoran. Bright recognized the name instantly—a key member of the Roosevelt brain trust, one of the great behind-the-scenes powers at the White House. Fitzhugh greeted him warmly and he sat with them for a brief moment, talking about the great upheaval of Washington, the difficulty of getting a suit of clothes pressed.

When he had gone, Bright said, "I thought he looked a little sad."

"He's on the outside looking in now. Practicing law in New York and wishing he were back with his hands on the levers. He tried to wangle an appointment as solicitor general, but he couldn't muster up the support."

< 355 >

"I thought he was one of the most important men in Washington."

Fitzhugh shook his head. "Not anymore. Tommy's no longer useful. He and folks like Ben Cohen and Rex Tugwell, the ones who helped put the New Deal together, have been left behind. The important thing now is the war, and they couldn't reconcile themselves to that. They're still talking about social programs, and Roosevelt and Churchill are over there in the White House right this minute talking about bombers and heavy cruisers."

"Good heavens." It was a bit unsettling, the thought of the two most powerful men in the world deep in strategy a few hundred yards away from where they sat eating a leisurely lunch.

"What Tommy and the rest of the New Dealers can't see," he went on, "is that they've already won. They've changed the basic way the country operates. Government is a major player now, where ten years ago it was pretty much a benign observer. Government is as important as business in determining how people live, how they work, how they raise their families. The war can't do anything but reinforce that."

"You said he's no longer useful. Does the president toss aside people who are no longer useful?"

"Of course," Fitzhugh said without hesitation. "The president is first and foremost a politician, probably the best that ever was, and the most pragmatic. If he likes your ideas and the way you back them up, he'll let you approach him. But not get too close. And you can stay only so long as you serve his purposes. Forget that, and he can break your heart. He doesn't do it overtly. He has no stomach for direct confrontation. But suddenly one day you find yourself on the outside. That's what happened to Tommy."

"But that hasn't happened to you."

"Not yet."

"Do you always agree with him?"

"No. But on the important things, usually. I respect his vision. He saw the war coming a long time ago."

She marveled at him. He was so clearly at home here. Washington seemed to fit him like a glove. "I'm very proud of you," she said suddenly.

He looked up from his plate, surprised. "You are?"

"Of course." She sat back in her chair, folded her napkin and placed it next to her plate. "Now finish your lunch and take me to bed."

He blushed deeply, and then gave her a rather incredible smile.

*　*　*

< 356 >

He undressed her slowly and lovingly in the dim, high-ceilinged room, worshiping each part of her body with his hands and mouth as he bared it until she shivered with delight. Then they made love through the long, slow afternoon, discovering each other again. She felt like a butterfly loosed from its cocoon—lighter than air, free to go where the breeze and her passions took her, unfettered and unashamed.

He slept in her arms and she lay awake, floating, hearing music again in the deep recesses of her mind for the first time in many months. She drifted back in half-dreams to her childhood, to the smell and feel of tall brown boots rubbed to a deep luster with neat's-foot oil; to the tinkle of laughter as a mother and daughter played at tea in a sunstruck upstairs bedroom with an array of dolls for company; to the exquisite sight of bodies rising and falling against each other in front of the camp house fireplace, all golden in the flickering light. It was, even after what had happened, the most beautiful thing she had ever seen. And now, locked in the long echoing hall of time, the saddest. Fitzhugh stirred against her, nuzzled her breast. This, here and now, was what mattered, and she spoke of it silently to Fitzhugh. *I've been adrift, shut away. But perhaps I can find my way back. I make no promises, but perhaps I can even come away with you. There will be time enough to speak of it . . .* She looked down at him, flesh against her flesh, eyes closed and face soft, and joined him in sleep.

But time rushed, with the urgency of war. The next day, January 6, Bright sat in the packed House gallery as President Roosevelt delivered his State of the Union address and called America to arms. His fine, measured voice stirred them: "The militarists of Berlin and Tokyo started this war. But the massed, angered forces of common humanity will finish it." He called for a staggering arsenal of destruction—sixty thousand planes a year, seventy-five thousand tanks by 1943. His audience gasped and cheered. Bright could not imagine sixty thousand airplanes, but the force of it struck her—the incredible latent power of the nation, the grim stakes of the conflict. Boys from small towns like hers would fly those airplanes and man those tanks. Many would die in them. She thought of Buster Putnam, a captain now in the Marine Corps. He had enlisted just after high school, when the Depression held the country in its grip and the chances of a young man finding a decent job were slight. He had undoubtedly made a good Marine. They had sent him to Annapolis and so he was a college graduate, an officer, and a gentleman. He was twenty-eight now, two years younger than she. He would lead men into battle. Little Buster Putnam. Imagine that. She realized, sitting here and listening to

< 357 >

President Roosevelt, that it would probably be a long war and that even the winners would pay dearly. She thought of the boys who sat at her piano, laboring over Chopin and Schumann. The war wouldn't have to last very long at all to take the oldest of them. Boys at war. It saddened her.

She and Fitzhugh stood together in the wide hallway outside the chamber after FDR had finished his speech and gone, and Bright met the great and near-great who knew Fitzhugh Birdsong by first name: Hugo Black, the Supreme Court justice from Alabama; bespectacled congressman Sol Bloom of New York, chairman of the Foreign Affairs Committee that Fitzhugh sat on; and a short, dapper senator from Missouri with snappy eyes named Truman.

"Take a good look," Fitzhugh said to her. "You're seeing the last of an era."

She studied the crowd. They were mostly older men, Dorsey Bascombe's generation. They looked, somehow, a bit bewildered tonight. "Dinosaurs?"

"Exactly." Fitzhugh smiled. "They don't know what's hit them. This place"—he indicated the portrait-covered walls with a wave of his hand—"has been a fossilized gentleman's club. The Depression barely caused a ripple in the way things get done—or mostly not done—around here. But the war . . ." He shook his head. "It's turned everything upside down. Congress can't run the war. We're too old and fat and slow. We can't move fast enough, we don't know enough. We have no choice but to leave that to the president and his generals and admirals. They'll get exactly what they want, because nobody up here dares do any differently. There'll be a good bit of grousing around the hallways, but when Roosevelt says sixty thousand planes, we'll open the treasure chest and say, 'How much?' "

"But the war won't last forever," she said.

"Long enough to change everything. The old hands will stick around until it's over, but then the boys will come home and kick them out. It'll never be the same, Bright. Nothing will be the same."

"And what about you?"

He looked away for a moment, his gaze roaming the hallway as the last of the crowd emptied from the chamber, the diplomatic corps in their frocked coats, members of the president's cabinet. Bright recognized General Marshall, erect and distinguished in his uniform. Fitzhugh turned back to her, chose his words carefully. "I can be a power here, Bright."

"Is that important to you?"

"Not as an end, no. Power corrupts, but it also gets things done.

< 358 >

What the war means, more than anything else, is that America is part of the world. We don't have any choice but to care about what happens in China or Russia or anywhere else. It's heady business, but risky, too. It means Congress has to keep a check on what presidents do. We'll have to make sure they don't go galloping off getting us up to our eyeballs in trouble." There was a high boyish color in his cheeks. Standing here, in the midst of power you could feel, the power now of life and death, she understood what brought him to Washington, what enthralled him like a mistress. Could she expect less of him? Could she ask less? Perhaps not. The decision, she understood now, was hers.

<   >

She intended to be as quiet as a mouse at the White House, to be unobtrusive and observant and take away every tiny detail she could store in her heart and mind. One might visit the White House again, if one were the wife of an up-and-coming young congressman. But one would never again be here on such a night when the air fairly crackled.

Fitzhugh had told her that the White House was a comfortable, rumpled place under the Roosevelts, busy with the casual comings and goings of family, friends, political cronies, some of whom stayed for weeks or even months. No one seemed to be entirely certain at any one time just who occupied the place.

But tonight it seemed to be a dazzling palace, even with the grounds dimly lit and blackout curtains on the windows and soldiers with rifles and bayonets in clusters at the entrances and spaced along the fence. There was a small knot of people on the sidewalk out front, as there always seemed to be these days, even on a bitterly cold night like this one. Ordinary people, bundled in overcoats, silent, gazing at the broad sweep of the building as if they might catch a glimpse of their future.

Fitzhugh showed their invitation and his congressional identification card to a Secret Service man at the front gate, and they walked up the curving driveway, Bright clinging to him for warmth. The door opened to a sparkling world with young officers just inside in dress blues and greens to escort them to the state dining room, where a Marine Corps orchestra played a Strauss waltz in one corner and a protocol officer announced them formally to the receiving line. And there they were. *What the devil*, she thought, *not a one of them has a shred more common sense than Hosanna Richardson.* She smiled to herself, thinking of Hosanna sitting in on an Allied strategy session, plotting invasions and bombing strategies. Hosanna would make quick work of the Axis.

< 359 >

Franklin Roosevelt beamed up from his wheelchair as he took her hand, "Ah, Mrs. Birdsong. Fitzhugh has finally let us see what he's been so jealously keeping to himself. Fitz, my boy, my estimate of you has increased a thousandfold."

She felt the warm glow of his famous charm, almost a palpable thing. He was still quite handsome, she thought, despite the weariness around his eyes, the mottled complexion. She could imagine him in the years before polio had crippled him. How the ladies must have cut their eyes at him. "Mr. President," she said, "it took an invitation from you to bring me to Washington."

Roosevelt threw back his head. "I love it," he chortled. "I love it." He handed her to Winston Churchill, at his right. "Winston, this is Fitz Birdsong's lady. She's a Southern belle, so be careful."

He took her hand and bowed slightly, and she found herself looking at the top of his balding head, marveling at his slight stature, the way he seemed to exude energy. His small eyes danced as he looked up at her. "Bright Birdsong," she murmured.

"Ah," he said, the voice rich and lovely, the music of old ale and pheasant, "could a bird song be any other than bright? And what is this about being careful of Southern belles?"

"Well," she said, "I suppose we Southern belles are the reason Southern warriors fight so fiercely."

"Ah," he said with a smile. "Then you are our greatest asset in the fight against Mr. Hitler."

And then she was past him, taking Eleanor Roosevelt's hand, looking into gray, clever eyes. If you saw the eyes first, you didn't notice the plain, almost shy face. "I'm so glad you've come," Mrs. Roosevelt said. "I hope we'll get a chance to chat."

"Thank you," Bright said, and then they were being escorted to their table by another young officer.

It was not an especially large crowd, and for the most part decidedly male and military—the brain trusts of the American and British war machines. They had been meeting almost around-the-clock since Churchill had arrived in mid-December. At their own table were an American Army Air Corps general named Arnold, a British field marshal named Dill, and Harry Hopkins. "My goodness, Mr. Hopkins, I would have thought you were ten feet tall, after all I've read in the newspapers," Bright said. That drew a great laugh from the others. She blushed. "I shall try to make that the last silly thing I say tonight."

"Nonsense," Hopkins said as he held her chair. "It's refreshing, Mrs. Birdsong, after all our grim business."

"Oh," she said innocently, "what business is that?"

< 360 >

"Why, making war," he said gravely, taking the chair next to her. He was a tall man with a broad, intense forehead that wrinkled when he spoke. He pointed out some of the notables in the room—Ickes and Hull and Stimson from the cabinet; the American and British military men, among them, Beaverbrook and Marshall and King; Connally and Vandenberg from the Senate. "And your husband," he said with a smile. "He and the Speaker are the only members of the House who are here."

She glanced at Fitzhugh, across the table from her, deep in conversation with General Arnold. "And why is that?"

"Because the president thinks a very great deal of him," Hopkins said simply. "Fitz had the good sense to see all this coming a long time ago. If we hadn't had not only his vote but his very vocal support on the military draft and lend-lease bills . . . well, it might have been an entirely different story. He took a great deal of heat over that."

"Congressman, how was the president's speech received on the Hill last night?" Field Marshal Dill asked Fitzhugh.

"We're like lambs," Fitzhugh said with a smile. "Don't be surprised if you see Borah and the rest of the isolationist crowd driving rivets on bombers before long."

That drew a laugh from the rest of the table as the first course was served, and as they began their soup, Bright thought with a rush of pleasure how very much this must mean to Fitzhugh. Politics, her father had told her years before when he had been the mayor, was a matter of rewards. People elect you, you reward them with good faith and good service. And for the politician, there were rewards in return. Like tonight.

They were well into the main course when a young Army officer bent over Bright's shoulder. "Mrs. Birdsong," he said quietly, "might Mrs. Roosevelt have a word with you?" Bright looked around at him in astonishment, then at Fitzhugh, then at the empty chair next to the president at the head table. Eleanor Roosevelt had said she wanted to chat, but Bright had assumed it was just a pleasantry. Even if it wasn't, why now, in the middle of dinner?

"If you'll just come with me, please, ma'am," the young officer said.

She gave Fitzhugh a puzzled shrug, then followed the lieutenant down the hall to an anteroom where Mrs. Roosevelt was in deep conversation with another woman, who was saying, ". . . simply snockered, Mrs. Roosevelt. He threw up on the rug."

Eleanor Roosevelt gave an exasperated shake of her head, then turned to see Bright in the doorway and flashed a smile. "Ah, Mrs.

< 361 >

Birdsong. I'm sorry to take you away from your dinner. Won't you have a seat?"

They both sat in rather stiff armchairs while the other woman withdrew, and Bright tried to compose herself. *Whatever's going on here*, she thought, *don't look and act like a ninny. Remember who you are.*

"I have a very great favor to ask of you," Mrs. Roosevelt said. Her voice trilled like quick fingers on the upper octaves of a piano.

"Me?"

"Yes. You see, we were to be entertained tonight by a concert pianist. You'd recognize his name immediately if I mentioned it, but the poor man has taken ill and we've got him upstairs stretched out on a bed. I'm afraid he's, ah, quite indisposed."

"I'm sorry."

"Could you?" Mrs. Roosevelt asked.

There was a long silence while Bright's heart thumped in her ears. "Could I what?"

"Why, play, of course."

"Play what?"

"The piano." Eleanor Roosevelt's laugh tinkled. "Your reputation precedes you, Mrs. Birdsong."

"My husband . . ."

"Likes to brag on you. It's one of his most charming qualities."

Bright folded her hands in her lap, her mind racing. "All those important people . . ."

"Just people, that's all. Some people who've been working very hard, trying to do their best in a difficult time, and who need a bit of entertainment tonight. You needn't play for very long. Perhaps fifteen or twenty minutes would be lovely." Her voice was pleasant but insistent.

"A contribution to the war effort," Bright said.

"Of course."

Bright nodded. "Well, why not."

"Indeed! Do you need music? We have something of a library of it. A leftover from Mrs. Harding, I think. Or was it Mrs. Wilson?"

Bright thought for a moment. "No," she decided. "What I do best, I know from memory. Do you have any suggestions?"

"Goodness, me?" Mrs. Roosevelt shot her eyes toward the ceiling. "I can barely carry a tune, Mrs. Birdsong. You're quite the expert here. Just anything you think appropriate."

The young officer escorted her back to her table, held her chair, disappeared. She could feel their eyes on her, but she sat quietly for a

< 362 >

bit, then picked up her fork and resumed her meal. Fitzhugh's eyebrows were at full mast. She chewed demurely, swallowed, smiled at him.

After dinner, President Roosevelt spoke for a moment from his wheelchair, proposed a toast to Winston Churchill and the British Empire, and then Churchill got to his feet and responded. Bright barely heard what they said. The music in her head took over, calmed her. She heard each piece clearly, her fingers tingling in her lap as she went through them mentally, note by note, stopping only to raise her glass or applaud when those around her did. When Mrs. Roosevelt got up, Bright was ready.

"We have a very special treat tonight," Mrs. Roosevelt said. Her voice was controlled and measured, and Bright got the impression of a woman who had tried very hard to master public speaking. It was a voice that ran the risk of grating, with little grace notes in it that could get out of control if you let them and run amok among the upper octaves. But Mrs. Roosevelt had turned it into a lovely thing. "Our British guests will appreciate the fact that we Americans honor our Old World heritage in things artistic and cultural, but insist on putting our own stamp upon them. We are, after all, an independent lot." That drew a laugh from the room. "So we value our artists. And tonight, we have an accomplished artist in our midst who has consented to bring us an entertaining interlude in the grave affairs in which you gentlemen are so engrossed these days. Without further ado, Mrs. Bright Birdsong."

Bright looked at Fitzhugh and gave him a little wink as his face broke into an astonished smile. She walked to the grand piano next to the head table to polite applause, adjusted the bench and sat. She lifted her hands to play, then thought better of it and turned to the audience. "I want to dedicate my opening number to the people of Poland. It's a Polish folk dance, a mazurka, by the greatest musician that nation has ever produced, Frederic Chopin."

She heard a murmur of assent from the room as she launched into the F minor mazurka, the one that had won her admission to the Conservatory thirteen years before. She summoned images of wide, green fields and exuberant youths with their heels flying, the Poland that Chopin had painted so exquisitely. Midway through the piece, it suddenly struck her. *I'm playing a concert in the White House! Good grief! Old Oscar Hogarth, dead now, would say that this was what I prepared for. To perform. To summon forth a little truth and beauty.* She felt a little catch in her throat, thinking of all she had given up back then, and why. But then she turned away from it and concentrated on her playing. She finished the mazurka with a flourish and received an

< 363 >

appreciative burst of applause, then gave the audience a little bow from the waist, glancing as she did at the head table. Roosevelt had his cigarette holder clenched in his teeth, a wreath of smoke drifting up around his head. He applauded, but he seemed pensive. Churchill nodded, gave a little wiggle of the cigar he held in his right hand.

Bright played on, mixing her selections—a Mozart sonata, an allegro movement from a Beethoven concerto, a Stephen Foster medley, and then the Schumann *Träumerei*. She played it slowly and lovingly, summoning the heart to listen to its secrets, caressing each note and finally freeing it to take flight in the golden, dazzling light of the room. "Bully!" someone shouted from the rear, and the room erupted into applause. Bright started to rise from the piano, but then she thought, *No, that's not the way to leave them. The* Träumerei *is a bit sad and wistful. These men have enough sadness to contend with.*

She let the applause die away, and then she said, "And finally, a salute to brave men, and victory!" She raised her hands and went crashing into "It's a Long Way to Tipperary," and the entire assemblage rose with a shout, everybody except Franklin D. Roosevelt, who beamed from his wheelchair. They began to clap in time to the music, a great rhythmic undercurrent to her piano. She played it through again, and the Britishers and some of the Americans who knew the words sang along. And when she came to the end of the piece, she glided smoothly into "The Stars and Stripes Forever." The room was in an uproar now. From the corner of her eye, Bright could see that Churchill had his cigar clamped firmly in his mouth and was pounding his hands together, eyes flashing with delight. The piece had a mind of its own now, and Bright let it carry her, riding the crest of Sousa's masterpiece, even adding the piccolo part with her right hand in the upper reaches of the treble notes and then finishing with a crescendo as the room burst forth with a shout and prolonged applause. And then Churchill was at her side, bending to take her hand and kiss it. "By heavens, that was rousing!" he growled, wringing the words with his teeth like a bulldog. "You shall play again, Mrs. Birdsong. In Berlin, after we have slain the wretched German dragon!"

Bright was quite beyond words. So she simply smiled up at him, and then Fitzhugh was there, bending to kiss her cheek and helping her up from the piano bench. The audience was still on its feet, surrounding her with waves of applause.

She thought suddenly of Dorsey Bascombe. She could hear ever so faintly the echoes of his golden trombone, feel the soft warmth of a summer night when he played on the front porch of the camp house. *Oh, Papa, I wish you could see me now!* Perhaps he did.

< 364 >

Bright was exhausted, drained, a bit weak in the knees. "I want to go home now," she said to Fitzhugh with a smile. "I'm not used to being famous."

<   >

She was packing for her afternoon train when the call came. Fitzhugh was at the Capitol for a meeting of the Foreign Affairs Committee, but he would be back for an early lunch before he took her to Union Station.

"Mrs. Birdsong?"

Bright recognized the voice instantly. "Mrs. Roosevelt. Good morning."

"I had hoped I would catch you. Is it possible you could join me for tea?"

"Goodness." Bright looked at her watch. "Well, I suppose . . ."

"It's nine now. Shall we say ten? I'll tell them downstairs to expect you."

She walked the short block to the White House, feeling a little giddy with the unexpectedness of it. Mrs. Roosevelt, from all Bright had read and heard from Fitzhugh, was a human whirlwind, a doggedly determined woman, a personage quite apart from the inescapable fact of her husband. She wrote, she spoke, she did things. Sometimes, Fitzhugh said, she exasperated people. But in all things, she was steadfast in what she saw as her duty. Fitzhugh admired her a great deal. Now, on this January morning when the world was turning upside down, when Eleanor Roosevelt's notion of her duty must be magnified a thousandfold, why on earth would she want to sip tea with Bright Birdsong?

Bright paused at the edge of Lafayette Park to let a convoy of Army trucks rumble past, their canvas flaps tied securely at the rear, concealing whatever cargo might be inside. Men? Secret weapons? Toilet paper? It was a brisk, overcast day and people hurried by on the sidewalks, bundled against the cold. In front of the White House, the soldiers looked miserably red-nosed at their guard stations. A young lieutenant and a Secret Service man at the gate were talking about the promise of snow in the forecast. Bright thought it would be good to be heading south before that happened. Both men examined her driver's license and checked her name on a clipboard, and then she walked up the curving driveway to the front portico where they had entered the night before.

Mrs. Roosevelt's secretary, Malvina Thompson, was waiting for her in the foyer, and she took her up in the elevator and down a long hallway through the Roosevelts' living quarters. It was almost like a

< 365 >

hotel corridor, a cluttered and bustling place with all manner of people wandering about, doors slamming, the rattle of carts as the household staff made their morning rounds. As they passed one doorway, she could hear the laughter of children.

"Gracious," Bright said, "is it always like this?"

"Oh, this is calm," Malvina Thompson laughed. "We had to clear out some of the guests when we heard Mr. Churchill was coming."

"He's staying here?" Bright marveled.

"Of course."

"What's he like?" Bright found herself asking.

Mrs. Thompson lowered her voice confidentially. "Actually, he's quite a character. He stays in bed until late morning, smoking cigars and reading the dispatches and the papers. Then he keeps the president up much too late at night."

At the end of the corridor, they arrived at a second-floor sitting room with tall windows and low, comfortable sofas and chairs around the walls, a small table in the middle with two chairs and a tea service. It was a warm and inviting room, safe from the stark-limbed cold outside. Eleanor Roosevelt was seated at the table, writing on a tablet, and she looked up as Bright and Mrs. Thompson appeared in the doorway, flashing a smile. "Oh, I'm so glad you could come," she said, rising to offer Bright her hand. "I know you have a train to catch, but I did so want to have a moment with you before you go." She looked out the window toward the South Lawn. "It's very bracing out this morning."

"You've been out?" Bright asked.

"Yes. I went for a ride early this morning in Rock Creek Park. The Army keeps my horse at Fort Myers, and they bring it over for me. It's a frightfully lot of trouble, I'm afraid, but I do so enjoy it. It helps me get my day organized to start with a little exercise."

They sat at the table. "This is a lovely room," Bright said.

Mrs. Roosevelt smiled. "It's where the family gathers. Mrs. Hoover had it looking like a tropical rain forest, with bamboo furniture and palm trees and birds. I rather like it like this."

"It feels like home."

"I'm glad you think so. Now. Some tea?"

"Yes. Thank you."

She reached for the silver teapot and poured for both of them. "Last night was magnificent, and I'm very deeply in your debt."

Bright blushed. "I'm afraid I got quite carried away with myself."

"I'm so glad you did!"

Bright felt suddenly quite at ease. There was an appealing earnestness in Eleanor Roosevelt, almost childlike. A wanting to be liked? Bright found herself fascinated.

< 366 >

"I did so want things to go well last night," Mrs. Roosevelt said. "I suppose that is the last grand dinner we'll have here for a while."

"Oh?"

"Well, wartime is hardly the time for much entertaining, I think. Actually, I've never had much stomach for it." She handed Bright her cup and offered sugar and milk. "I first came to Washington as the young wife of the assistant naval secretary, and in those days it was the custom of every officer's lady to call at the secretary's home. They were all terribly nice, of course, but I began to think, 'What's the use of it?' There were so many other things to do that made more sense." She took a sip of her tea, placed the cup back in the saucer with a clatter. "At any rate, if last night was to be our last gala for a while, I'm glad it turned out so well."

"It was a very distinguished gathering," Bright said. "I sat next to Mr. Hopkins. He was very nice."

"Ah, Mr. Hopkins," Mrs. Roosevelt said. "What would we do without Mr. Hopkins! He lives here, you know."

"Here?"

"Right down the hall there," Mrs. Roosevelt nodded.

Bright detected a bit of an edge. A rivalry? "Is he a bother?" Bright blurted before she could catch herself.

Mrs. Roosevelt gave her a tiny smile, and when she spoke her words were very carefully chosen. "Every president, I suppose, must have a Mr. Hopkins to get things done for him. And now, with the war upon us, Mr. Hopkins has become fairly indispensable. I don't suppose we could win the war without Mr. Hopkins."

There is something very odd here, Bright thought. *This is a very complex woman, and not an entirely happy one. But quite remarkably in control of herself, despite everything.*

"Well," Mrs. Roosevelt said, shaking her head vigorously as if to rid herself of Mr. Hopkins, "have you had a good visit to Washington? I'm told it's your first."

"Yes. It's sort of overwhelming, especially now. All these people, all from somewhere else. At Union Station, when we got here, I just stood and gawked. Everyone looked so foreign."

Mrs. Roosevelt was pensive. "It's a big country," she said, "and sometimes we seem like we have no kinship to each other except geography. But I hope the past few years have taught us how interdependent we are. No region of the nation has been immune from misery. Perhaps the result will be that we all realize that we're responsible for each other."

"I imagine the war will help," Bright said.

"In what way?" She cocked her head, attentive. Bright could see

< 367 >

the bright snap of her eyes, a quick mind at work, waiting for some new morsel.

"All those young men. They come from all over, but they'll be going off to war together. I imagine that when a boy from Georgia shares a foxhole with a boy from Montana, they'll learn a lot about each other."

"Yes!" Mrs. Roosevelt burst out, taking hold of the idea. "Just Americans! My goodness, I must write that down." And she pulled the writing tablet toward her, picked up her pen, and scribbled a few words.

"My father used to say," Bright said, "that you can't stay mad at a fellow when you have to look him in the eye every day."

Mrs. Roosevelt jerked her head up. "Say that again," she commanded, and Bright repeated it while she wrote it down. "Splendid! I'm giving a speech tomorrow to the USO volunteers, and I shall quote your father. With your permission, of course."

"Of course," Bright laughed.

"He must be a very wise man."

"Was," Bright said, and looked away quickly out the window. She felt herself suddenly very close to tears. She fought them back, wanting desperately not to embarrass herself, not here in this grand house in the presence of this remarkable woman she hardly knew. But Dorsey Bascombe seemed to be very close now, perhaps just outside in the cold morning, listening. There was a sudden pain, the ancient agony of giving up. Why now?

"Our fathers are a very great influence on us," Mrs. Roosevelt said gently. "My father died when I was very young, but he shapes my life, even today. We honor our fathers by keeping alive the good things they did and were."

Bright looked back at her. "Mrs. Roosevelt, you're a very kind person."

"Ah, nothing of the sort." She blushed self-consciously. And then she said, "Mrs. Birdsong, I want you to come back to Washington."

"Well, perhaps someday . . ."

"No, right away." She paused for a moment, musing over something, then rushed on. "What this town, this country needs more than anything else right now is some uncommon young women. Like yourself." Bright started to protest, but Mrs. Roosevelt raised her hand. "The men alone won't win the war. The whole country has to do it, and more important, the whole country has to believe that it has a stake in the winning of it. I'm very involved now with Mayor La-Guardia in the Office of Civilian Defense. It has enormous possibilities, Mrs. Birdsong, for mobilizing the home front—women, children,

< 368 >

the elderly, all those who can't bear arms. We must do things together. And not just rolling bandages and collecting scrap metal. We must play and sing and dance together."

"Dance?" Bright thought Mrs. Roosevelt sounded just a tad cock-eyed, but she was so utterly earnest you wanted very much to agree with her.

"Yes! Of course!" She leaned forward in her chair, the words coming in a torrent now. "Mayris Chaney, the dancer, has joined us in the physical fitness division. Mayris and I believe that when people dance together, they're more likely to work together. It's like your father said, Mrs. Birdsong. Looking another person in the eye. And there's the exercise. Don't you feel better when you exercise?"

"I feel better when I've had a good night's sleep," Bright said.

"Well, that too, naturally. But exercise gets the blood racing. This country has got to get the blood racing! And it's about time!" She punched the air with a triumphant fist and Bright smiled. She was infectious. "And you, Mrs. Birdsong. You can bring us music. We need someone like yourself who is an accomplished musician, and not afraid to get up before a crowd and be an advocate for music. America must sing and play!" She ended abruptly, sank back in the chair, folded her hands on the table, and looked at Bright expectantly.

Bright sat staring for a moment, then realized that her mouth was open. She closed it. She felt giddy. Things were happening too fast.

"Well, what do you say? We can pay you, of course. Say, perhaps four thousand a year? And your expenses when you travel."

"Travel?"

"Goodness, yes. I foresee programs all over the country, all run by volunteers, but set up initially by the staff of our Washington office. You and Mayris will be a positive inspiration to the local people."

Bright looked at her hands, knotted tightly in her lap, the fingers that so deftly played the music she heard in the secret places of her mind and heart. To be given such a gift . . . But then there was all the other. It came upon her in a great rush and suddenly she felt home-sick. She wanted to be gone from here, from this great vibrant house and this bustling city, to wake up in her own bed with the early light filtering through the branches of the pecan tree outside her window, to smell Hosanna's cooking, to sit on the porch of the camp house and hear the murmur of the river behind her and the soughing of the trees at the edge of the clearing, to marvel at a heron taking flight. She wanted Washington and the war and Eleanor Roosevelt, dear woman that she was, to be far away. She just wanted to be Bright Bascombe again. She wanted her father back.

Bright gathered her wits, brought herself forcibly back to this

< 369 >

warm cluttered room. Mrs. Roosevelt waited. She took a deep breath. "I have a small son," she said quietly, "and a home and a hometown. I have a life there and work to do that I find very compelling. And comfortable, I admit. So even though you do me an incomparable honor, Mrs. Roosevelt, I can't. I have to go home." She could barely hear her own voice, it was so very small.

Mrs. Roosevelt's face fell. "I'm sorry," she said. "I had hoped . . . how silly of me . . ." Her voice trailed off, and she looked away.

She is angry with me, Bright thought. No, not angry. Disappointed. But there is something else here. A woman who has been disappointed often before, but who goes on despite that. A woman who has conquered a thousand disappointments and hurts and made her own way. She is the strong one in this house.

Mrs. Roosevelt seemed lost in her thoughts for a moment; then she composed herself and shook her head and looked back at Bright. "Home. It must be very special to you."

"Yes."

"I never really had a home of my own," Eleanor Roosevelt said. "I grew up with relatives after my parents died, and then after I married, my mother-in-law always seemed to . . . well, direct things. And now"—she looked about her, gave a wistful wave of her hand—"I am still living in someone else's house. I'm living in *everybody's* house."

"I should think that would be very hard," Bright said. "But I should think you are very much up to it." She hesitated. "I'm sorry, Mrs. Roosevelt, truly I am. But I have to be honest with you."

"Yes." She nodded. "I appreciate that. The country needs strong young women, wherever they are." She rose, dismissing Bright. She had important things to do, other projects and persuasions. Bright stood, and Mrs. Roosevelt offered her hand. "I just ask one thing."

"Yes?"

"Make a difference, Mrs. Birdsong. Wherever you are, do something that matters."

"Yes," Bright said softly. "I can see that. I will."

<   >

She was waiting for Fitzhugh in the lobby of the Hay-Adams, her bags all packed and waiting upstairs. He bustled in from the cold, red-cheeked and smiling. He had a thin square package under his arm, plain brown wrapping tied with string. He crossed to her, pulling off his gloves and rubbing his hands together. "By George, that'll get the blood up. I had to run half a block to chase down a taxi with one seat

< 370 >

vacant. I have a feeling this is about to become a town of walkers." He bent and kissed her cheek, then put the package down on the settee, took off his overcoat and folded it across his lap as he sat next to her.

"Well . . . ," she said.

"Well, what?"

"What's in the package?"

"Oh," he said airily, "a little something I picked up on the way back from the Hill." He drummed his fingers together and looked about the room. "A little something for the most famous pianist in Washington." He smiled. "You've got the whole darn town talking this morning. I could have booked you into the best club in Washington in an instant."

He handed her the package, watched as she opened it. "Oh, Fitzhugh!" Gershwin. A two-record album, sixteen-inch discs with *Rhapsody in Blue* and *An American in Paris*. A very modernistic drawing on the front of a piano with notes rising from it like bubbles from champagne. Paul Whiteman and his orchestra. A brilliant blend of jazz and classical. She had heard it performed on the radio.

"The lady at the department store told me it was quite the thing," Fitzhugh said.

"Oh, it is!" she cried, clutching the album to her. "But we don't have a Victrola to play it on. It got ruined in the Flood, remember?"

"You do now," he said slyly. "I believe it's being delivered at home just as we speak."

"I could kiss you right here," she said.

"Fine," he said. "Go right ahead."

So she placed the album on the settee beside her and flung her arms around his neck and kissed him long and deeply. A young naval officer passing them gave a low whistle and said, "Atta way to go, lady."

She released him, blushing, and they sat looking at each other for a moment, laughing.

Finally he asked, "Have you had a good morning?"

It brought her back to earth. She hesitated, wondering if he knew. Of course he knew. "Interesting," she said.

"Did you . . ." He hung fire, looking at her quizzically.

"Go to the White House? Yes."

He smiled. "She's quite marvelous, isn't she."

"Quite a presence," Bright said. "I don't think I've ever met anyone quite like her."

Fitzhugh chuckled. "I think she pesters the horns off the president sometimes, but she generally gets what she wants."

She could tell it in his face. He knew exactly what Mrs. Roosevelt

< 371 >

had planned to propose to her. But he didn't know what the answer had been.

She took a moment. And then she said softly, "I said 'No thank you.'"

His smile froze and she could see the color drain from behind it, leaving a mask. The hotel lobby was filling with people now at lunchtime, a surging babble that smelled of cologne and tobacco smoke and the cold midday outside. Bright felt lost, alien. And, again, homesick.

"Why?" Fitzhugh asked.

She thought of all the perfectly good excuses. Wartime Washington was no place for a young child. Why, you couldn't find decent housing. And it might well be a dangerous place. If an enemy attacked, certainly here. Plus the weather. Snow on the way. What if Little Fitz got sick? All these strangers.

But what she said was "It's not home."

"Bright, for God's sake." He looked around the lobby, at the growing crowd. "We can't talk here," he said. "Let's go to our room."

She recoiled at that, at the thought of being closed up in the small room with him, with his disappointment and disapproval, with the thing that stood most between them now. "No," she said. "Let's go for a walk."

They sat on a concrete bench in a corner of Lafayette Park, away from the foot traffic, and they had the place much to themselves. A biting wind sent the noontime crowd scudding along the sidewalks, quick about the business of seeking shelter. Only the squirrels and pigeons eyed them curiously. Lafayette, green with age on his horse across the way, seemed forever en route to distant battles, unheeding of a man and woman who huddled together with the rawness of the midday stinging their eyes and plucking at their hair. Fitzhugh watched Lafayette for a moment, seeming to seek direction. And then he turned to her finally and there was a nakedness, a vulnerability, in his face that made her long to touch him. But she kept her gloved hands burrowed deep in the folds of her coat. "I had hoped you would stay," he said. "I had hoped that very much."

"I can't," she said simply. "I'm sorry, but I can't. It's just not something I'm capable of."

"Yes, you are," he insisted. "You're very much up to it. Haven't you seen that these past few days? And last night . . ."

"It's not a matter of that. It's simply that this is not my place."

"For God's sake," he exploded. "It's the *nation*, Bright. This is . . ." He waved his hand, searching for the word.

< 372 >

"Indispensable?" she finished for him.

"Yes," he said emphatically. "Especially now."

"To the nation, perhaps. To you. But my God, Fitzhugh. Washington in wartime? It's no place for a family."

He shook his head, but then he took a long time to speak, and when he did he weighed his words very carefully. It had the tenor of something he had been saying in his mind for quite a while. He said, "Your father's dead, Bright."

"Of course he's dead," she shot back. "I don't need you to remind me of that."

"Then bury Dorsey Bascombe and be done with it."

She felt the sudden rush of a great rage then—at Fitzhugh, at circumstance. And yes, at Dorsey. All of it locked away for a long time behind the numbness that had become the door to her heart. "How dare you!" she lashed at him, full of the fury of it. "You have no right to speak of him! You couldn't . . ."

And then she caught herself. The enormity of what she was about to say and all that it meant seized her like huge hands plucking her powerfully from the park bench as if to fling her into the bare wicked limbs of the trees. Her voice froze in her throat. *No!*

But it was too late. He stared at her for a moment, saw the anger and then the fear. He blinked once, slowly, with the fine agony of it. And then he said softly, his words almost lost in a gust of wind. "No. I couldn't. I have seen that for a long time. But then, I don't need to."

She looked away quickly, unable to face him. But she could feel his gaze on her. After a moment she summoned her voice. It seemed a strange, unconnected thing. "My father once told me to be whatever I wanted to be and not worry about what other people thought. That was a very great thing for a man to say to a daughter. Men are supposed to think that way, but not women. And then, he said that when you live in a place, you put your heart into it. And I've done that."

That was all true, she thought. And it might explain her. But it was not sufficient for now. Perhaps nothing was. She turned finally, touched his sleeve, and as she did so she understood with perfect clarity that everything hung in the balance. Everything about them.

"I just want . . ." His voice trailed off, but she knew. And that was when she began to cry, when it all flooded out, and she was powerless to stop it, even here in this most public place in this profound city on this wretchedly cold day with the world turning itself inside out. She felt small and inadequate, threatened by great forces over which she had no control, by the unfairness of being forced to choose, and once having chosen, being forced to face the consequences of

< 373 >

choice. She sobbed, and he put his arm around her and pulled her against him and didn't try to stop the tears. She cried for a very long time and when she finally began to regain control she looked up and saw Fitzhugh's own deep weary sadness. He reached into his coat pocket for a handkerchief and handed it to her and she dabbed at her eyes.

"We're a great deal alike," he said. "We both want the same kinds of things. Only they happen to be in different places. Now what are we going to do about that?"

"Perhaps we can live with it," she said.

He thought about that for a moment and then he nodded. "Perhaps we can. If that's the only way." Then he looked down into her eyes and said the most gallant thing he ever said in his life. "I will not give you up."

"I love you," she said. And she did, truly.

But he said, "I suppose I could say that if you loved me you would come away with me. But it's not that simple, is it?"

"No, it's not."

"Then love really doesn't have a great deal to do with it."

They sat for a while longer, letting the midday slip past into a gray afternoon when the overcast seemed to get thicker and somehow softer, as if the snow might come any moment—big wet flakes that would cover the streets and park benches and deaden the sounds of the great hurrying about. Perhaps over there in the White House, Winston Churchill might push Franklin Delano Roosevelt's wheelchair to a broad window and they would look out on the South Lawn stretching white toward the monuments and believe for a moment that gentleness and beauty might one day return to the earth. The earth, even at war, could mask its wretchedness under a snowfall. A heart, Bright Birdsong thought, could not.

<   >

She barely remembered the afternoon, the taxi ride to the station, the terrible crush of the crowd, Fitzhugh kissing her before he handed her up to the conductor. She seemed to be in a well, sounds bouncing hollowly off the walls around her, a round hole of light far above, beyond her reach. The train started to move almost as soon as she sat down and she looked out the window, searching for him in the throng as they pulled away. He stood silently, hands thrust deep in the pockets of his overcoat, trying to spot her as the train picked up speed. Then their eyes met for an instant and she could see the pain there. He nodded, and then he was gone and she was leaving Washington behind.

< 374 >

They went south into snowfall and the Virginia countryside faded into winter darkness with white flakes flashing by in the light from her window. She sat clutching the Gershwin albums in her arms, declining the conductor's invitation to go to the dining car. She was not hungry. She thought she would go to bed early, taking refuge in sleep as the train clicked and rumbled southward toward home. She began, after a while, to come to herself. And as she did she began to think of all the people and things waiting for her. There were Little Fitz and Hosanna, and all her music students. And the school board—at odds now over expanding the library at the high school. Can't do it with a war on, some said. Can't let a war stand in the way, Bright Birdsong countered. And there was the lumber business, or what remained of it. She intended to turn it over to Monkey Deloach when she got home. It would be his, to salvage if he could. Monkey was made of the stuff it took to do such things. It would be her way of repaying a debt long due. There was that, and so much else to be taken care of. So much to do.

So Bright went to bed early and let the night and the rolling music of the train settle around her. She woke in the morning to a strong, clear light at the edges of the window shade. She climbed down from the bunk and pulled up the shade and saw that the train was hurtling through dense woodland, the track a narrow ribbon through the towering green and brown blur. The smell of it, clean and fresh, was strong even through the closed window of the car and she inhaled it hungrily. It was powerful, like opium, and she felt it lifting her. She heard music, imagined the majestic sweep of orchestra, strings and brass. And the sweet golden notes of a trombone. *The sound of God's breathing, he said.*

< 375 >

22

*B*right told herself in the years after the war that even if she had agreed to what Fitzhugh wanted there in Washington in January of 1942, she could not have made good on her promise. She was barely home when she discovered that she was pregnant. Piteously, convulsively pregnant.

Nothing about it was easy or pleasant. She was first a slave to her roiling stomach. It refused anything, snarled at her even when abjectly empty, left her weak and gaunt. When that had passed she was virtually emaciated. Dr. Finus Tillman, grown old and mottled-skinned now, said that he had never known a woman to *lose* weight in her first weeks of pregnancy. Bright hated being sick for any reason. She particularly hated being sick at the whim of this barest of lives growing like a nettle in her womb.

Hosanna took it all calmly. "Different baby," she said. "This one get through announcin' hisself, he'll settle down." Hosanna always spoke of babies as *he*. She was partial to boy children, she said. She was especially partial to Little Fritz. Bright had had a relatively easy pregnancy with him, and now he was quiet, bright-eyed, eager to please. He was in awe of Hosanna, who filled him with the same nuggets of myth and wisdom she had showered upon Bright in her own youth. Little Fitz seemed to prove that Hosanna's partiality to boy children was correct, ordained.

The baby did indeed settle down for a while, but Bright did not. Her ankles swelled horribly, she felt bloated and distended through the sickeningly hot months of the summer. Her pregnancy was a wound that would not heal, and just when she thought that she might be gaining a measure of control, she would suffer some other indignity. At seven months, her belly turned into a cement mixer. The baby thrashed about like a caged animal, poking and knocking Bright's insides, particularly her bladder. Fitzhugh, finally home from Congress

< 376 >

after the end of a session that had dragged on far past its usual length, stood back just beyond her torment with a perpetual look of bafflement on his face.

"Arrrgggghhh," she bellowed in the middle of one night, "be still for one instant, for God's sake!"

Fitzhugh sat bolt upright in bed beside her. His mere presence infuriated Bright.

"Is there anything I can do to help?" he asked innocently.

"Help?" she cried. "Help?"

"A damp washcloth?" he tried.

"Get out!" She turned away from him, pummeled the pillow with her fists. "Just get out!"

He did, taking his own pillow with him to Little Fitz's room, where they slept fitfully, waking each other the rest of the night with their tossing. The next morning, everyone in the house was cross. Except for Hosanna, "Y'all look like the fellow up in the tree with the bobcat," she said at breakfast as they all glowered at each other through reddened eyes. "He say, 'Somebody shoot up here amongst us, 'cause one of us has got to have some relief.'"

"I've had enough of your folk wisdom," Bright snapped.

"No," Hosanna said. "You've had enough young'un."

The baby came, as babies must, but Bright discovered that the ordeal had not ended, simply taken a new direction. She woke in the middle of the night after her delivery to Roseann's hideous screams down the hall in the room where Hosanna had set up camp. After a moment, the door opened and Hosanna stood there with the bellowing infant in her arms. "This one different all right," she said. "She got a burr under her saddle." Hosanna brought Roseann to the bed, where she attacked Bright's breast with the same fury in which she had leapt and tumbled in the womb—pummeling and sucking until Bright thought she would be turned inside out. "I'm sore," she cried. But Hosanna insisted. "Baby got to eat. She don't get some satisfaction, we all gone be loony 'fore morning." She drained Bright dry—first one breast and then the other. Still she cried.

"Is she still hungry?" Bright asked, astonished.

"No," Hosanna said, "I think she just ornery."

Bright looked up to see Fitzhugh in the doorway, robe-clad, shuffling in his slippers, rubbing the sleep from his eyes. "Let me," he said. And while Hosanna stepped back and watched, he took Roseann from Bright and nestled her against his chest and walked out. They heard the baby's fitful cries echoing in the hall and down the stairway. And then silence. Blessed silence.

< 377 >

It was to set the pattern for their days, until Fitzhugh died in 1971. Through Roseann's infancy and childhood, Fitzhugh was the one who could calm her rages, still the terrible restless energy. In the months when he was away, Roseann tormented Bright and herself and anyone else within reach—plucking at her hair, disrupting meals, breaking things. When he was at home, she was more reasonable, more pliable. She demanded and got his attention. In fact, she demanded and got everyone's attention, but usually with upsets and tantrums. With Fitzhugh, it was freely given. There was just never enough of it. She cried inconsolably when he left. Still, he left.

Roseann was not quite three when the war ended, and Bright held out a brief hope that he might now reconsider his future. But when he announced that he would run for reelection in 1946, she was not surprised. Fitzhugh Birdsong was clearly a man for postwar Washington. With Roosevelt dead and the great conflagration over, Congress was beginning to reassert itself in policy, domestic and foreign. And Fitzhugh had emerged from the war as one of Congress's most effective and influential members in the shaping of the nation's role in the world.

For a time, he kept Washington and home separate, as much as any congressman could. He did not bring that part of his work home with him. He might be a student of the world in Washington, a man whose pronouncements affected Indochina and Greece and Eastern Europe. But when he was home he was the congressman who catered to the needs of his constituents—farm subsidies, Social Security, government loans. He was husband and father. He maintained an active and fairly lucrative law practice in the postwar years and took in a younger attorney to help with the business and manage affairs when he was away.

But increasingly, the world held his attention. It was a global age, he said, fraught with perils large and small. America might have emerged from the war as the bulwark of democracy and the underpinning of the world's economy, but that also meant that its stakes were extraordinarily high. And the wolves were at every door. So Washington drew Fitzhugh Birdsong away. In the prewar years, Congress had met for at most five months out of the year. It was a leisurely business. But now the sessions stretched on for months longer. And when recesses came, the world called—trips to Berlin and Istanbul, Buenos Aires and Manila. Journalists called them junkets. Fitzhugh took them as serious business. And he did not take his wife.

It had come to a head with them fairly early—in 1948. Fitzhugh and three other members of the Foreign Affairs Committee would take

< 378 >

a two-week trip to the Far East: Toyko, Manila, Hong Kong, Sydney, Auckland. He called from Washington. "I want you to go," he said. "All the wives are going."

The miles of telephone line between them sizzled with static. "I thought you would come home," she said. "Isn't it enough to spend all this time in Washington without tooting off around the world?"

"I'm not tooting off, as you put it. This is my job. It's important."

"So is what I'm doing," she snapped. "I'm raising two children. And they could stand a dose of their father."

"Hosanna can take care of them for two weeks," he insisted.

"Hosanna is getting old. God knows, she's too old to handle Rose-ann."

More silence. Finally, she could hear him take a deep breath on the other end. "You know what I think?"

"What do you think, Fitzhugh?"

"I think you're still afraid of your mother. At least, what happened to her."

"What?"

"She probably never should have left New Orleans. And you're afraid you'll make the same mistake."

He had become more combative, she thought. He was embold-ened by his success, by his *place.* And by the fact that they had both made their choices, of sound mind, without coercion. If she would not do what he wanted, he felt no great need to tread softly. And given that, there was always the very great danger that their tacit agreement to accommodate could come undone. Because, as she frankly ad-mitted, she was sharp-tongued enough to begin the unraveling. And now he was sure enough of himself to do his part.

So there was increasingly a brink there, and it fell to one or the other to decide whether to step back from it. "I don't need to be psy-choanalyzed," she said quietly.

And then he followed her lead. "No. I'm sorry. I understand how you feel. I'll miss you."

"Then hurry home."

"Yes." And he hung up.

And so they accommodated. They were both very busy—Fitz-hugh with the world at large, Bright with her own world. She became chairman of the school board, a member of the administrative board at the Methodist Church as well as chief musician, and immersed herself in a hundred projects and causes, large and small. She remembered Eleanor Roosevelt's admonition: make a difference. And increasingly, with Fitzhugh away much of the time, she raised the children. When

< 379 >

Hosanna died in 1952, withered by arthritis and finally felled by a massive heart attack, Bright thought to herself, "Well, I am the last of the Bascombes." She thought more and more of *her* town, *her* people. She tried not to bully people about what she wanted. But she admitted to being provincial and proprietary. How else did one get things done unless one cared and acted?

It became clear that Fitzhugh would be little help in raising the children. He was simply not there most of the time, and when he was it was with a growing sense of estrangement. It was not that he didn't care for them, and care deeply. But he was not a part of their world. So when he came home from Washington, it was like a man stepping into a dim room from bright sunshine, fumbling about and bumping into the furniture until his eyes became adjusted to the different quality of light. He could not know the thousand small things and happenings that made up their lives. And try as he might, there was a gulf of understanding. Fitzhugh might sit for hours in a front porch rocker reading to Roseann from a book he had brought home, and she might rest against his chest, calm for the first time in weeks. But the moments were all too short and the partings all too keenly felt.

And then there was Little Fitz. He seemed often in a state of perpetual puzzlement as he entered his teen years, as if he could not quite put his finger on things. He was a handsome boy, eager to please, with a great warm smile. And when he turned its glow upon you, he made you feel that he was the keeper of some good secret that blessed everything upon which his gaze fell. He seemed outgoing, loquacious. But Bright knew that it masked an uncertainty. It was as if he had some things he wanted to tell, and had some questions he wanted to ask, but was not quite sure how to go about it. When Fitzhugh was home, they had long conversations, but there was a certain formality about them. Fitzhugh asked about what Little Fitz was doing, how he felt about things. Fitz answered. They talked about Fitzhugh's work, about the world at large. But Little Fitz went away from them with a look on his face that said, "We didn't quite get to the meat of things." And he was, forever, Little Fitz. Fitzhugh Birdsong's son. And Bright's. In search of that essential thing that said, "I am me. Just me."

But it took her a long time to fathom the depth of his feeling. It came in 1956, with Fitz in his senior year in college. After his earlier brush with academic disaster and Bright's precipitate intervention, he had become a fair student, a political science major with designs on law school. The University was celebrating its one hundredth birthday, and it planned a special convocation. The distinguished congressman Fitzhugh Birdsong, recently installed as chairman of the House For-

< 380 >

eign Affairs Committee, would speak. And his son would introduce him.

They planned a family weekend of it in early November. Fitzhugh came home by train at midweek and they drove to the University on Saturday, up through the heart of the state with late fall blazing the countryside. Roseann, at fourteen, was beginning to emerge from the gawky wretchedness of her adolescence and she seemed determined just now to be very much the young lady. She and Bright maintained a tenuous truce through the trip.

Fitz was waiting for them on the steps of the Phi Gam house when they arrived at midafternoon, wearing a dark blazer with his fraternity crest on the pocket. And as he walked across the lawn to meet them, Bright's heart caught in her throat. *He looks like Dorsey Bascombe. And he is a man, no longer just mine.* He was taller than Fitzhugh, and he called his father "Dad" now. Roseann seemed almost in awe of him. He was quite handsome, very poised. He had that great winning smile and just enough reserve to give it some authority. He was the vice president of the student body this year, and he had mentioned casually to Bright the previous summer that he might one day be interested in politics. At dinner that night, he and his father talked animatedly of events in the Middle East, the Israeli invasion of Egypt a few days before, the strategic importance of the Suez Canal.

"That's the best talk we've had in a long time," Fitzhugh said when they were alone later. "He's quite an impressive young man, actually."

Bright was sitting in her slip at the dressing table in their room, face caked with cold cream. Fitzhugh, already in his pajamas, was propped on the bed, scanning a State Department briefing paper he had brought along with him. He was forever toting along papers, scholarly journals, newspapers, and books, and he read voraciously. It was another irritant. "I'm glad you had time to notice," she said now. And then she regretted the tone of it. She didn't want to spoil anything this weekend. It held the promise of some semblance of normality. The four of them together for the first time in a good while, their lives all moving along separate paths, the distances between them widening. A drift—some of it natural, some the product of their peculiar circumstance. She thought often of the families of celebrities, how easily they seemed to become estranged. She had managed to protect Fitz and Roseann from most of that, but there was still a price.

Fitzhugh turned down the edge of the page he was reading and put the briefing paper on the bed beside him. They looked at each other for a long moment in the mirror. "I've missed a lot," he said. "I know that."

< 381 >

"Yes, you have. There's been quite a change. Fitz has grown up. I think I just realized it myself today."

"He seems quite at ease with himself. He speaks well. He'll make a good lawyer."

"He made a nice boy," Bright said, and heard a trace of the bitterness creeping in. *Don't spoil it, Bright.*

"And I missed that."

"Yes, you did." *I am unable to help myself.* "That conversation tonight, that was all about your life, Fitzhugh. Israel and Egypt and the Suez Canal. He's meeting you on your own ground. But did you ever talk to Fitz about snakes and snails and puppy dog tails?"

"Some," Fitzhugh said quietly. "Not enough."

"I'm sorry you didn't." She picked up a tissue and turned to him as she began to wipe off the cold cream. "And if you had it to do over?"

"I don't, though," he said emphatically. "There doesn't seem to be much use in looking back."

"Oh, I don't know," she said. "There's nothing wrong with a little honest regret, Fitzhugh."

"We both made choices."

"Yes. But it doesn't keep me from regretting that things haven't been different."

"Then," he said with some urgency, "change things. You could come to Washington. Even now. Especially now. It's nothing like during the war. It's truly a gracious place at times, not at all bad for a family."

She shook her head. "It's entirely too late for that. Roseann—"

"I know." He stopped her. "There's always something."

"Well," she snapped, "you come home and try to deal with her on a full-time basis! She is a maddening child!"

"The trouble is, you take everything Roseann does or says personally."

"Dammit, Fitzhugh," she exploded, "don't give me any of your long-range strategic analysis!"

They glared at each other for a moment and then he picked up his briefing paper again. "Let's not fight," he said.

"No," she said wearily. "Let's not."

The hotel manager himself interrupted their breakfast in the dining room the next morning. "Congressman Birdsong, there's a telephone call for you. The White House," he said, impressed. "You can take it in my office."

Fitzhugh pursed his lips, then looked at the rest of them apologetically. "Excuse me," he said. "I'll be just a moment." He dabbed at his

< 382 >

mouth with his napkin, then folded it neatly and slid it under the edge of his plate and got up and followed the manager.

He was gone for a long time. Bright and Fitz and Roseann finished their breakfast and then Bright had another cup of coffee and finally she paid the bill, and they went to sit in the hotel lobby and wait for him. Roseann fidgeted in a chair, pulling and tugging at her hair, and Bright fought the urge to bark at her. She talked with Fitz instead. He volunteered in an offhand way that he had been seeing a good deal of a young lady. An Alpha Chi. They would meet her this afternoon after the convocation. And would it do for him to bring her home with him for Thanksgiving? Bright's eyebrows shot up. Of course, she smiled. Bright had long ago resolved not to put her son through the agony of female rivalries.

She looked up finally, saw Fitzhugh walking toward them across the lobby. He looked very intense and a little unsure of himself. Unlike Fitzhugh. He sat down on a sofa next to Bright and they all looked at him expectantly. "Britain and France have invaded Egypt," he said. "At Port Said and Port Faud. They apparently mean to take back the canal. Ike's having a fit. Everybody's having a fit. I think Eden has put his foot in it this time."

Bright didn't want to ask the question, but she knew it was inevitable. "And you? What about you, Fitzhugh?"

His eyes went bleak with the conflict. *You would rather take a whipping than tell us, wouldn't you.* "I've got to go back to Washington. Ike's sending a plane."

Little Fitz stared at him, dumbfounded. "Now?"

Fitzhugh nodded. "I'm sorry, son. I've called the president of the University. He was very understanding."

Roseann hunkered deep in her chair, her hands a whirlwind about her head, grabbing fistfuls of hair. "Stop it, Roseann!" Bright snapped at her.

They sat in wretched silence for a few moments, and then Bright said, trying to hold things together, "Can't they do without you for just a few hours?"

"The president's asked the cabinet and congressional leadership to be at the White House at three o'clock." He shook his head. "Ike needs all the help he can get on this one."

"Daddy, is there gonna be a war?" Roseann asked. She looked small and frightened, a child again.

"I hope not," he said. He seemed grateful for the question, for a chance to explain himself, but he did it all wrong, Bright thought. A child needed reassuring, but Fitzhugh was suddenly the congressman, the foreign affairs expert. "The Soviets are threatening to intervene.

< 383 >

The UN is hopping mad. Yes, there could be a war. If we don't handle things just right."

But it was Little Fitz who surprised them all. He stood up suddenly and Bright saw the sudden flash of anger and knew instinctively that it had been there for a long time. It stunned her. "And if we do get in a war, Dad," Fitz said, "where will you be? At your post like a good soldier. And we'll be here."

Fitzhugh blanched. He looked down at his hands. "Son, really. I hate this. I'm sorry."

"Do we always have to take a back seat to the rest of the world?"

"No." He shook his head. "It's just that this . . ." But when Fitzhugh looked up, it was to see the ramrod-straight back of his son striding across the hotel lobby away from them, and there was a quick, naked grief in Fitzhugh's eyes. Bright did not speak. There seemed to be absolutely nothing to say.

They did not see Little Fitz again. Fitzhugh caught a cab to the airport and Bright and Roseann drove home, refusing the University president's invitation to stay for the afternoon activities. He did not press. They would have been in the way, Bright thought, another reminder of the mess that had been made of things. The congressman had to respond to the call to duty, of course, but it left a pall over things. No, he did not press.

Fitzhugh called late that night, waking Bright. "I just wanted you to know, I think everything's going to be all right." He waited for her answer, got only silence. "Britain and France are having second thoughts. They're looking for a graceful way out." More silence. "Bright?"

"Don't come home, Fitzhugh," she said.

It took him a moment. "You don't mean that."

"Nobody at the White House said anything like that to you, did they? Everybody at the White House said, 'Yes, Congressman.' And, 'What do you think, Congressman?' Didn't they."

"Bright, for God's sake . . ."

She hung up on him.

But by the time he arrived home, she had already withered in her resolve. She didn't let him know that, not at first. She exacted a measure of blood from him. And she made him confess. "If you leave me, I'm finished," he said. He sat on the sofa with his shoulders slumped, abject in his sorrow.

"You mean your political career," she said. "People in the South don't vote for congressmen who can't hold on to their women."

"No, it's not just that."

< 384 >

"Not *just* that. But some that."

"Yes, but . . ."

"I'm just indispensable to you, aren't I."

"Think of the children if nothing else."

"Oh, I have. Believe me, I have. For years."

But finally he had enough of wallowing in apology and he rose up angrily. "You chose," he said bitterly. "We both chose. We both agreed we'd try to live with it. I chose my life's work, and it happened to be in Washington and there is a great price to pay for that. But you raised the price, Bright. You! Because you've been unable to tear yourself away from this town and your father and all that means to you. So we knew damn well what we were doing. We're big boys and girls. And we've just tried to do the best we could!"

And that, she thought, was the truth. They raged at each other, slinging bitter words and stripping away layer after layer of flesh until they got down to where they both bled. But at the bottom of it was the truth, and Fitzhugh had spoken it. So when they were spent with their outpouring, the truth was still there. And both of them had in the end to either face it or turn their backs on it. The terrible thing was, they were both honest people, not much given to self-delusion.

So in the end, they accommodated—or rather, continued the accommodation they had settled upon a good while ago. There was mutual need, things shared, what remained of love. And that was no small thing in itself, the business of love. Amazing how bits and pieces of it could survive much abuse. Perhaps, Bright thought, enough to think of someday mending the broken parts and filling in the empty spaces.

It was, in truth, not so terribly long until Fitzhugh began to talk of coming home. The fifties became the sixties, and being a Southern congressman became a wrenching thing if you had much integrity about you. And then came Vietnam and Fitzhugh agonized over the deepening void it became, swallowing presidents and congressmen and young boys in its maw. He harbored a great distrust of it from the beginning, but again his Southernness bedeviled him. It was the hunt, the match, fourth and goal on the one-yard line. Manhood. Fitzhugh Birdsong was too gentle for all that, and Bright realized that it would only be a matter of time until Fitzhugh could no longer reconcile himself to the duality of the job. Then he would come home to her and they would knit the tattered threads of their lives into new cloth.

There would always be a certain amount of regret. But they would make things as right as possible. And there would be no more choices.

< 385 >

BOOK 5

23

The river. It began as a small creek in the uplands, falling over itself as it tumbled like a playful child, end over end, and joined forces with other streams. Then it slid gray-green past the capital through the rich heartland of the state, beckoning towns and farms and forests to its banks as it went. Bright had to stretch her imagination to think of it as the long ribbon of water it was. In her lifetime, it had been just the river that flowed past her town, the one she had seen from Ollie Doubleday's biplane on that bright March day in 1919, making a sweeping curve past her father's sawmill. And later, an invader. But always there. A constant.

Downstream, the river was something of a disappointment. Nowhere along its course was it very deep, but it turned brown and torpid as it entered the sand and scrub pine of the coastal plain and began to meander, as if it had grown weary with the journey and lost its way. It had also been a disappointment for Dorsey Bascombe in his day. He had envisioned it as a commercial boon to the state, made navigable with a series of locks and dams along its length. But in this instance he failed to make others see his vision. He had organized committees, lobbied the legislature, to no avail. Just not worth the trouble and expense, people said. It had been something of a source of irritation between Dorsey and his son-in-law in Fitzhugh's early days in Congress too. Fitzhugh was more interested in rivers as geopolitical boundaries of Europe and the Orient, not as pathways of domestic commerce. Dorsey and Fitzhugh avoided open disagreement, but Dorsey was apt to say on occasion, "I can't see Heathen China from my front porch."

So the river had remained much as God had made it. Man figured little in its destiny. And on this early morning, Bright Birdsong was glad that, in this one instance, Dorsey Bascombe had not gotten his way.

There was the river. And there was new sun. She stood on the

< 389 >

front porch of the camp house, feeling the first warmth of the new sun peeking just over the tops of the trees at the edge of the clearing and bathing the porch with soft golden light. She was clad only in her slip, her feet bare. She raised her arms slowly, held them outstretched toward the sun like some pagan at worship, felt the warmth flooding her, reaching down into the soft secret places. She thought of Hosanna with a smile. *New sun got power to heal and clean.*

The clearing began to awake from its cool grayness. Birds chattered in the trees, arguing over breakfast. Two squirrels chased madly around the trunk of a gnarled oak and then one of them zipped into the green bosom of the upper branches and sat chattering, unseen. Behind the house, the river slid like a broad green snake with just the faintest of sighs, an undercurrent to the morning. A quiet splash at its edge. The heron, feeding. Bright's stomach rumbled.

"What are you doing?" Jimbo asked from the doorway at her back.

She didn't turn around. "Energizing."

"Why are you standing out here in your gilhoolies?"

Bright lowered her arms. "My what?"

"Gilhoolies. That's what Rupert calls underwear."

She turned to him now. "And what's that you're wearing, buster?"

His hair was askew, eyes puffy from sleep. He wore only white jockey shorts. He looked down at himself, grinned self-consciously. "Gilhoolies."

"Want to go for a swim?"

He shrugged. "I reckon." *Three days with his dotty old grandmother, and nothing seems to surprise him anymore. It is progress.*

They splashed about at the edge of the water, Bright holding her slip up just above her knees, wading about in the sandy shallows and scattering minnows with her feet. Jimbo stood ankle-deep for a moment, looking out at midstream, hesitant.

"Well," Bright said, "are you going to swim or just wish you did?"

"I'll get my underwear wet," he muttered, kicking at the water with a big toe. "It's the only pair I've got with me."

"Then take 'em off," she said.

He turned, stared at her. She gave him a wave of her hand. "Good heavens, haven't you ever been skinny-dipping before?"

"No."

"Well, give it a try." He shivered a bit, looked down at his underpants. She smiled. "Nothing's going to bite you. I used to bring your mother and your uncle Fitz out here when they were little and let them swim bare-butt."

"You did?"

< 390 >

"Yes. Them and their dog."

"Dogs don't swim bare-butt."

"Have you ever seen a dog in gilhoolies?"

He thought about that for a moment. "I reckon not." He cocked his head, still uncertain. "Are you going to take off your clothes?"

"No. I'm too old to skinny-dip. Only old dogs and children get to skinny-dip. But don't let that stop you."

He turned and looked out at the water. She could see him wrestling with himself, giving in finally. "Well, don't look." She turned her back to him, gazing off downriver where it made another wide bend and disappeared into the forest that grew close to its banks. She spied the heron perched on a low branch overhanging the water, looking back at her. She started to wave, then thought how silly that would be. A sixty-eight-year-old woman waving at a bird. Maybe when she was seventy. But not yet. She heard Jimbo behind her at the edge, then splashing out toward the middle. She turned back in time to see his scrawny bare bottom disappear as he reached midstream and settled into the water, making small waves with a sweep of his thin arms.

"How is it?" she called.

"It feels good. A little cool." His eyes were wide, surprised at what he had done, still a bit uncertain that it was the right thing. But he stayed there, moved about in the water. It flowed gently here, just enough to caress the skin.

"Don't get out too far. I don't want to have to fetch you." She thought suddenly of Flavo Richardson's grandson, the small brown lifeless body lifted from the dark water underneath the bridge. She felt a small rush of panic, started to call out to Jimbo again to be careful. But she thought better of it. Instead, she turned her back on Jimbo and walked out of the water and stood on the narrow sandbar. *The river is not dangerous here. It is a good place.*

Bright smoothed out a place in the sand and sat, feeling the coolness beneath her slip, the warmth of the sun on the back of her head as it rose now well above the treetops, glinting off the ripples that Jimbo made in the water as he moved about, testing the bottom with his feet.

She thought then of her father, and strangely enough she thought of his resting place. It came seldom to mind, and she rarely visited it. It was in the old part of the cemetery where there were trees, weathering gravestones among gnarled brown trunks, shaded by thick branches. The old families were there. In the newer sections, there were no trees and no true tombstones, only small granite markers set flush with the ground so that mowers could pass over them. Perpetual care. In the old part where Dorsey lay, "perpetual care" meant the

< 391 >

families, several times a year with rakes and hoes, tending and honoring their dead. She went enough to keep it up, but it was here—in this still place by the river—that Dorsey Bascombe haunted. She had always been able to hear him in this place. But not this time.

I've been waiting all night, Papa. Waiting for you to speak to me, to tell me what to do. All I heard was the night and echoes from your trombone. Is that what you do now? Sit around and trade music with God? Does his breathing really sound like a low E-flat? Is he tone-deaf? Does he, or you, care a whit about our miserable human fidgetings? Or do you both just say, "Work it out. We've got better things to do"?

No, Dorsey Bascombe hadn't spoken. So here she sat on the sandbar in her gilhoolies. Still waiting.

"Ow!" Jimbo yelled from midstream.

"What's the matter?"

"I stubbed my toe."

"Is it bleeding?"

He reached down to feel his foot, lost his balance, toppled and disappeared under the surface, came up spewing and grinning. "No, I don't think it's bleeding."

"Good. Nothing for the sharks to smell."

The water came halfway up his torso where he was now and he stood, splashing his hands back and forth, sending water volleys across the surface that sparkled in the new sun. "Aw, there ain't no sharks in here."

"No," she said, "I reckon there ain't."

He shrugged, then arched forward into the water and disappeared again, leaving the surface roiled. He frolicked in and out as she watched, losing himself in play.

She thought about Dorsey again, about the thing he had said so often in her youth. "Something will always come along." And she had always believed it. It was a Bascombe credo. But later, when he was gone, she realized that he had not truly believed it himself, at least not there at the last. Dorsey had discovered that there might be a time when you stood with your back to the wall, the wolves snapping at your throat, waiting for something to come along, and nothing did. "Okay, God, DO IT!" you said, and got only silence in return—or, if God is a bit perverse, a faint snicker.

Maybe that's what Dorsey was trying to tell her now with his own silence. Sometimes, nothing comes along. Then you're left with nothing but your own wits and ingenuity and stubbornness. So what do you do? Dorsey had had his own final answer. Dorsey Bascombe had simply gone away. Was it a cowardly thing to do? Or the most sensible under

< 392 >

the circumstances? She didn't know that, either. She didn't judge. *We all simply make choices. I know all about that.*

Then she thought suddenly of Fitzhugh. He had wanted to be cremated. The logical thing, he said. None of this business of filling you up with embalming fluid and putting you on display with a boutonniere in your buttonhole for everybody to gawk over. Nothing there anymore, just a shell. Better to have just the memory. Fitzhugh prided himself on his logic. But when the time came . . . "Ah," he must have thought, "another disappointment. But what could I expect? She never did a damn thing I wanted."

And perhaps that was the root and sum of what bothered her now and had for a good number of years. Disappointment, a long string of it going back as far as she could remember. People she loved, disappointing her. Elise and Dorsey, to begin with. And she in turn, disappointing others. Was it an inheritance, a family curse born of some unnatural orneriness of the Bascombes? The thing of it was, Bright had tried to stave off disappointment by accommodating, accepting half of this and half of that in order to make less than a whole but more than nothing at all. But accommodation, she was beginning to realize, was no substitute for having lived a life, dangers and all. She realized that by doing so, she might have done greater harm to those for whose very sake she accommodated. Fitz and Roseann, and now this slip of a boy who heard and felt the echoes of a past of which he hadn't the foggiest notion.

So now, at this very late time, a basic question: Was there such a thing as atonement? And should she attempt it? Or should she simply let sleeping old dogs lie?

She sat pondering it all, the questions swirling in her brain, as Jimbo cavorted in the water, losing his self-consciousness. The shining water made his thin, pale body sleek. He thrashed about, battling some imaginary foe—a crocodile, perhaps. There was something about the sheer abandonment of it that struck a deep, resonant chord in Bright's heart. Nothing of choices here. Simply play, in the way only a child can understand. A thin strand of naked boy in the current, as natural as God could make a thing. Too soon, it would end for him. It made her heart ache to see it.

He stopped suddenly, stood panting in the water for a moment, catching his breath, then turned to her, squinted as if he had forgotten she was there, had forgotten that anything existed but himself and this small piece of the river-universe.

He shook his head and diamonds sprayed from his hair. "I'm hungry."

*   *   *

< 393 >

She heard the car then. It had a familiar sound to it, something she couldn't quite put her finger on, as it lurched along the rutted narrow path from the road to the camp house, the sound of its engine echoing off the trees. Then she realized that it wasn't a car at all, but a truck. Buster Putnam's truck. It rumbled into the clearing and stopped. The engine died and she heard the door slam. "Bright!"

"Back here," she called.

Buster eased his way down the sandy bank, planting his feet carefully so as not to lose his balance. He was wearing an old pair of ankle-high boots, the kind her father had referred to as brogans. Dorsey Bascombe wouldn't be caught dead with a pair of brogans on. They weren't a gentleman's kind of boot. Buster was wearing the same brown pants and faded flannel shirt that had been his uniform all week. When he sat down next to her on the sand with a grunt, she expected to smell its rankness. Instead, it had a clean, fresh aroma. "You old dog, you've been washing those clothes," she said.

"Hmmmm," he acknowledged.

"Is it all an act, Buster?"

"Of course not," he said. "I simply feel comfortable in these clothes, but I spent enough of my life in the dirt to loathe uncleanliness. At least, when I'm sober."

"And you're sober this morning," she said.

"As the proverbial judge." He waved to Jimbo out in the river. "Looks like an amphibious assault," he called.

"A what?"

"Attacking by water. Who's winning?"

"Nobody," Jimbo said solemnly. "I'm just playing."

"Ah," Buster said with a nod. "Much better than attacking."

Jimbo answered by disappearing under the surface again, kicking up explosions of water with his feet.

"I thought I might find you out here," Buster said to Bright.

"How did you know about this place?"

"Oh," he said, "everybody knows about your old camp house. After you went off to the Conservatory, kids used to come out here and neck. We all figured it was abandoned."

"It was, in a way."

Buster looked back over his shoulder at the house, just the roofline visible from here through the trees at the sandbar's edge. "Looks in pretty good shape now."

"I had it fixed up when the children were small. We used to come out here a lot, spend the night, swim in the river."

"Like Jimbo."

"Yes, like Jimbo. I'd like to bring him out here a lot."

< 394 >

Jimbo called to them now from the river. "I'm ready to come out now."

"Well, come ahead, then," Bright answered.

"Turn your heads," he said.

Buster stifled a snort, and they turned their heads and looked off downriver. The heron was gone now from its perch above the sluggish water. Off fishing where there wasn't so much commotion, no doubt. These clumsy, wingless creatures, invading its sanctuary, just at the best time of the day. A bother.

Bright heard Jimbo splash toward them then, out of the water, the soft crunch of his bare feet across the sand. "You'll find a towel in the bottom drawer of the dresser," she said. "Check for spiders." Then he was past them, climbing the bank, and they turned to see his backside disappear, and the white of the underpants he held in his hand.

"There's food in the front seat of the truck," Buster called after him. "Some ham and biscuits. Help yourself."

"All right."

"He could be a fairly normal boy," Buster said to Bright.

"How would you know about boys, normal or otherwise?" Bright tossed back. "You never had any children."

"Oh, yes. I had thousands of them. All mine. A little bigger than Jimbo, but my kids, just the same."

Someday, she thought, she might ask Buster about all that, about being a Marine Corps general and about not becoming the commandant, the way people had expected. The thing in Korea. But she didn't want to know about that right now. She didn't want to know much about anybody else's expectations or failures.

"Have you been out here all night?" Buster asked.

"Yes."

"Doing what?"

"Listening."

"Did you hear anything?"

"Not what I had hoped."

"And what was that?" he asked.

"Some answers."

"Ahhhh, yes. We do tend to go back to our old haunts in search of answers, don't we."

She studied him for a moment. He looked very much in control of himself this morning, more so than she had seen in a good long while. More Marine-like, perhaps. "Is that why you're bumping about in that ruin of a house?"

"No." He shook his head. "I'm just looking for a little peace and quiet. I've had all the answers I can say grace over."

< 395 >

"I thought I had," she confessed. "But here I am at sixty-eight with all the answers turned upside down and becoming questions again."

Buster looked around at the river, the sandbar, up the slope at the tin roof of the camp house. "And nothing here."

"Not even so much as a ghost." She smiled.

"Then you might as well go back home," Buster said. "At least there, you've got a house full of food. And I mean a house full."

"Why?"

"Folks started toting it in late yesterday, when word got out you and Jimbo were missing."

"We're not missing. And if we were, who in God's name would eat it?"

"That's not the point, apparently. I guess I've been too long in the Marines. I forgot that when people don't know what to do in an uncertain situation, they bring food. When Marines don't know what to do, they start shooting. Come to think of it, food isn't a bad alternative. Anyhow, Xuripha Deloach arrived with potato salad about two o'clock. That was right after the Rescue Squad took Roseann to the hospital."

She stared at him, trying to find evidence in his face that it was some bit of foolishness. In truth, Buster had never been much for foolishness, at least not in their youth, when she had known him best. He was the small boy in overalls, standing just at the edge of the crowd, gravely earnest. And despite all his attempts to go to seed now, there was still an earnestness that he couldn't quite escape. There was something rather appealing about it, in fact. A bit of the little boy remained, always would. At this age, you had shed all the baggage you were going to shed.

"All right," she said, "tell me what's going on."

"The old Booker T. Washington High School burned down last night," he said.

"Yes, I know that. When we topped the River Bridge, I could see the flames. So I just turned around and came out here."

"Well, there's a good-sized contingent of highway patrol in town right now. They've sealed off the Quarter. And there's a good-sized search on for you and Jimbo between here and the state capital."

"Good Lord! Why on earth? There's nothing wrong with us."

"A batty old woman and a kid and fifty thousand dollars in a beat-up piece of Plymouth?"

"I beg your pardon . . . ," she started hotly.

"Yes?" He looked amused. Had she made herself ridiculous? Of course she had.

< 396 >

"Nothing. What's this about Roseann?"

"I believe they said she had an asthma attack. Got overexcited about something." He raised his eyebrows at her. "Any idea what?"

"Perhaps," she said, rising from the sand beside Buster. *All I wanted to do three days ago was be quiet. Now I am at the center of an incredible commotion only partly of my own making. What in the devil is going on here?* She realized then that she was still clad only in her slip. She felt a flush of embarrassment. "Gilhoolies," she said lamely.

"Don't believe I know 'em," Buster said. "They from around here?"

< >

Rupert was sitting in one of the wicker chairs on the front porch when she turned into the driveway, and he came out of it like a shot when he spotted the car. It was the fastest Bright had ever seen Rupert move. By the time she rolled to a stop behind the big tan Winnebago, he was at the bottom of the steps, the color high in his face, smoke billowing from his pipe like a tobacco factory gone haywire. "Where in the hell have you been?" he cried. He was wearing a pair of madras Bermuda shorts and a knit shirt, long black socks and the jogging shoes with the big red stars on the sides. He looked exhausted, as if he had been up all night. He probably had, Bright thought. Roseann could keep a man up all night. But then, Roseann wasn't the only problem here, was she?

"Hi, Rupert," Jimbo called out. "We've got fifty thousand dollars in a briefcase."

Bright left the engine running while she and Jimbo got out of the car.

"Are you all right?" Rupert asked him, his eyes searching for signs of damage.

"Of course I'm all right," Jimbo said. "I've been with Mama Bright."

"You have scared the bejesus out of us," Rupert said. "Both of you." He was exhausted, almost at the point of tears. She could see that. *How marvelous for both of them,* she thought, *to have a man who truly cares.*

"I'm sorry for all the confusion," Bright said, trying to sound at least a little contrite. That was the least she could do, she thought. "Roseann . . ."

Rupert took a deep breath. "She's in the hospital."

"Yes. Buster told me."

"Mama's in the hospital?" Jimbo cried, alarmed, staring up at Rupert.

Rupert put his hand on Jimbo's shoulder, reassuring. "She's all right. Just had an asthma seizure. The doctor gave her a shot, and she's sleeping now."

"I'm sorry," Bright said again.

Rupert ran his fingers wearily through his thinning hair. "You had no right to do that, Bright. Taking Jimbo off and keeping him all night. We've been worried to death."

"We were okay, Rupert," Jimbo said, trying to console. "We took our check to the bank and spent the night at the camp house and I went skinny-dipping this morning."

Rupert opened his mouth, shut it again, looked the both of them over head to toe. "Bright," he said finally, "what's gotten into you?"

"I'm not sure I know," she said truthfully. "I haven't had time to stop and figure it out. Maybe tomorrow." She opened the door of the car, got back in, looked out the window at Jimbo and Rupert. "I'm going to the hospital to see Roseann," she said. "But I've got a couple of other stops to make on the way. I just wanted to get Jimbo home first, let you know he was all right."

"Can I come, Mama Bright?" Jimbo asked.

"No!" Rupert barked.

"I think you probably need a break from your dotty old grand-mother," Bright said gently. "Rupert, get him something to eat and a book to read."

"I had a good time, Mama Bright," Jimbo said. "It was fun."

"We'll do it again sometime. Next time we win fifty thousand dollars."

"Okay," he said solemnly. Then he cocked his head to one side and gave her a funny look. "I love you, Mama Bright."

"I love you too, Jimbo. You're my kind of man." She looked up at Rupert and gave him a wink and she could see him soften. How could you be mad at an old lady and a kid? Such a pair. She realized that she would miss Jimbo a great deal when Roseann and Rupert took him away. And they would, very soon.

Bright put the old Plymouth into gear and backed out of the drive-way, then stopped at the curb and leaned out the window. "Feed Gladys!" she called to Jimbo. "She's probably starving. I hope she hasn't eaten Josephus!" Jimbo grinned back at her, a grin as big as the new sun popping over the treetops. She lurched into Birdsong Boule-vard and pulled away with a roar and a cloud of exhaust.

< >

She had quite forgotten about the parade until she saw the huge ban-ner strung above the main street downtown just in front of City Hall: WELCOME HOME, LITTLE FITZ. Big red letters across a white background, neatly printed. A professional job, just like you would

< 398 >

have for a returning hero, Bright thought. WELCOME HOME, AU-
DIE MURPHY. Crepe paper streamers hung limply in the heat from
the utility poles. There hadn't been any streamers or banners when
Congressman Fitzhugh Birdsong came home from Washington. Only
punch and cookies at City Hall, the way Fitzhugh had asked them to
do it. No fuss, just a simple affair so he could thank the folks. But Little
Fitz loved a good show—a parade, a band, dancing girls, lots of applause. His picture on the front page of the paper.

The Live Eye 5 van was parked in front of the police station, and
Bright pulled up to the curb next to it. Through the big plate glass
window, she could see a sizable contingent of law enforcement folk
inside—Homer Sipsey, the police chief; the county sheriff; a major
from the highway patrol; and several minor officers of various stripe.
Over in a corner, talking on the telephone, was Holly Hardee, the TV
reporter, and, lounging in a chair with his camera cradled in his lap,
the cameraman who had been with her yesterday at the Dixie Vittles
Supermarket. And there was Big Deal O'Neill, his forehead glistening
with sweat and his gold neck chain hanging out of his open-front shirt.
Big Deal and the law enforcement people were huddled in conference
around a table in the middle of the room, scrutinizing a map laid out
before them, drinking coffee from Styrofoam cups and eating dough-
nuts from a big platter.

They didn't see Bright until she pushed open the door and stepped
inside. "Good morning," she said politely.

The group around the conference table fairly exploded. "Good
Lord, Miz Bright!" Homer cried. "Are you all right?"

"She's here!" Holly Hardee barked in the phone. "Get right back
to you!" She slammed the receiver down and the cameraman leapt to
his feet and hefted the camera onto his shoulder.

Big Deal O'Neill almost upset the table getting to her. "We've
been worried sick about you."

Holly Hardee bore down on her with the cameraman in tow, microphone thrust in front like a jousting pole. She shouldered her way
past the others. "Mrs. Birdsong, can you tell us what happened to
you?"

"Nothing happened to me," Bright said.

"Were you abducted?"

"Of course not."

"Where have you been all night?"

Bright started to say "Drinking and carousing," but then she
thought, *No, this is no time to be flippant.* So instead she said, "Camping out."

< 399 >

"Does this have anything to do with your son's political troubles here at the end of the campaign?"

All right, enough now. Bright turned to Homer Sipsey. "Homer, can you escort this young lady out of here? I believe she's interfering with a police investigation, isn't she?"

"Yes," Homer said with an emphatic nod. "She's doing just that." And he grabbed Holly Hardee by the arm and started hustling her toward the door.

"Get your hands offa me!" Holly Hardee cried. But Homer muscled her out the door, the cameraman backing along behind them, still trying to take pictures. Homer turned the dead bolt on the front door and Holly Hardee glared through the plate glass at them. "Just lemme use the phone!" she cried, tapping loudly on the glass. "Dammit, I'm just tryin' to do my job!"

Homer turned back to Bright. "Miz Bright, are you okay?"

"Of course I'm all right."

"Well, where in the thunder have you been all night?" the sheriff asked.

"Minding my business," she said. "I went to the bank and then took my sweet time getting home. That's the be-all and end-all of it. I can't imagine what all the fuss is about."

"We've had an all-points bulletin out for you, Miz Birdsong," the highway patrol major rumbled. He had thick black wavy hair and one temple of his dark glasses was stuck through the top buttonhole of his shirt. Bright thought he looked like a man who probably liked to drive fast with his siren on.

"Well, you can tell all points that I'm safe and sound," Bright said.

The major scratched his head for a moment, then picked up his cap from the table and jammed it on his head. "Yeah, I reckon I better." He headed for the door. "I'll check in with the command post and let the guv'nah know you're okay."

"Miz Bright, you gave us quite a scare," Homer said. "When you didn't show up yesterday afternoon, we started checking around and found that you'd been up to the capital and cashed your check. And then disappeared."

"Homer, I'm sorry. I didn't mean to cause any fuss."

"Well, coming with all the other . . ."

"What other?"

"Trouble up at the Quarter. The old schoolhouse burned last night, and things have been pretty tense. The major's folks have got everything under control, though."

"Under control," she repeated.

< 400 >

"Yes ma'am. Little Fitz ain't had to declare martial law yet, but that's an option if there's any more trouble."

Bright turned to Big Deal O'Neill. "Francis, where's my son?"

"He'll be here any time now," Big Deal said. He looked wretched. Probably up all night, chain-smoking and drinking coffee. Men his age collapsed from heart attacks. "I tell you," he went on, "if you hadn't showed up just now, we'da just called off Fitz Birdsong Day and the parade and luncheon and all."

"Perhaps you should anyway. With all the trouble at the Quarter."

"No ma'am!" Big Deal said emphatically. "We ain't gonna let Flavo and his folks interfere with Fitz's big day. No ma'am!"

Flavo and his folks. Bright turned to the door. "Well, I'll be going now. Just wanted to let you know I'm all right. Thank you all for your concern." She left them all there gawking, all except for Homer, who followed her out to the sidewalk. Holly Hardee and the Live Eye 5 van were gone.

"Miz Bright, I hope you've about finished now."

"What do you mean, Homer?"

"Causing an uproar."

She gave him what she hoped was a blank look. It didn't work. Homer sighed. "Miz Bright, you been awful quiet down there in your house for a good while now. And all of a sudden you've got the whole town upset. The swimming pool . . ."

"The swimming pool business is an abomination," Bright snapped.

He held up his hands, a peace sign. "I don't make the rules, Miz Bright. I just pick up folks' mess." He looked awfully tired this morning, she thought. Even more so than he had at the bridge when Flavo's grandson drowned. That seemed like an eternity ago. "Anyhow," Homer went on. "The swimming pool, and the money, and the trouble up in the Quarter, and then going off and disappearing like that."

"I didn't burn down Booker T. Washington," she said evenly.

"No'm. I don't reckon you did." But the unsaid hung there between them. *Troublemaker. Agitator.*

She stared at him for a moment, hands on hips. "Well, what do you want me to do?"

"Go home and be quiet. Like you been being." He opened the door of her car and held it for her. She hesitated for a moment, then slid behind the steering wheel. No sense upsetting Homer Sipsey any more than she had already. Homer had a long day ahead of him. Fitz Birdsong Day. He would be powerfully glad to be done with the Birdsongs. Homer should go home at nightfall and fix himself a good drink.

< 401 >

"I'm sorry for all the trouble, Homer," she said as he closed the door behind her. She tried again to sound contrite, but she was not at all sure it was convincing.

Homer shook his head, dismissing his great burdens. Then he said, "Miz Bright, you still got all that money with you?"

"Yes," she said.

"Don't you want me to follow you around to the bank so you can put it where it's safe?"

"No, thank you. Not the bank. Definitely not the bank."

"Well, you don't want to just tote it around with you."

"Yes," she said, "that's exactly what I want to do."

Homer shrugged. "Suit yourself. It's your money. Just be careful."

"I will, Homer." She cranked the car and he stepped up onto the sidewalk and watched her pull away. She could imagine what he must be thinking. *An old woman made crazy by fifty thousand dollars.* Well, that wasn't the half of it. In fact, that wasn't it at all. Fifty thousand dollars, and it didn't make a hill of beans. It had caused an upheaval of sorts. But it was all this other. And you couldn't blame that on fifty thousand dollars.

"Good Lord," she said softly to herself, and realized that it was the second time she had invoked the Lord this morning. The Lord must be weary with all this invoking. *Go away,* He must be thinking. *Pull your own wagon. I'm busy. Listening to trombone music.*

< 402 >

24

There were two highway patrol cars parked across the road leading into the Quarter, nose to nose like big gray animals sniffing each other. She could see them a block away, from the point where the first patrolman stopped her with an outstretched hand.

"Can't go in there, ma'am," he said.

She looked up at him. He looked barely out of high school. He was wearing a broad-brimmed hat and sunglasses and his uniform was neatly pressed with razor-sharp creases down his trouser legs. But there were big wet blotches under his armpits, and a trickle of perspiration coursed down the side of his face. It was nine o'clock in the morning and already scorching, the heat blasting up from the asphalt. In another hour, it would bake through the soles of your shoes.

"Of course I can go in there," Bright said. "I have friends there and I am going to visit them."

"No ma'am," he said firmly. "The area's sealed off. We've had trouble in there."

Sealed off. As if you could seal off the Quarter or bottle it up or define its boundaries. There were no doubt a thousand worn paths leading in and out of the Quarter through the woods and along the river. If Flavo Richardson had a mind, he could evacuate the entire place in thirty minutes and the state highway patrol would be none the wiser. But beyond that, the Quarter wasn't really a place. It was a state of mind—unfathomable to white folks, even those who had been coming here for years. And especially now that there had been trouble. That was probably what worried Homer Sipsey and Harley Gibbons and the state highway patrol more than anything. Not knowing what was next. Black folks were one thing. Unpredictable black folks were something else altogether. One thing Flavo and his people had not

< 403 >

been until now was unpredictable. But now they must be bothering the hell out of Homer and Harley and the rest with their unpredictability.

Bright didn't want to get the young highway patrolman in trouble. He looked nice enough. Probably a Beta Club member in high school, maybe a baseball player. So she said, "Turn around."

"What?"

"Turn around," she repeated. And when he did, she simply drove off.

"Hey!" he yelled. In her rearview mirror, she could see him reach to his belt. *My God, he's going to shoot me!* She tensed, bent forward toward the steering wheel. But then she saw him talking on a small hand-held radio, and up ahead there was a flurry of activity among the half dozen or so patrolmen clustered about the roadblock. Those men had shotguns and they were waving their arms and shouting. Along either side of the roadway, she could see a scattering of people, standing in their yards or on their porches. The white folks who lived at the edge of the Quarter, milling about and waiting for something to happen. Now it had, and they were pointing at her car, edging up toward the roadside as she passed them and bore down on the roadblock. The patrolmen were running toward her now, guns held across their chests at the ready. And one of them crouched in the road and brought the barrel of his gun up, aiming it squarely at the front of the car. It looked enormous. *She stared at it, transfixed suddenly by the memory of another shotgun barrel, the flash of flame, blood everywhere . . .*

"Hold your fire!" someone yelled. Bright jammed on the brakes, bringing the old Plymouth to a shuddering stop perhaps twenty yards from the crouching patrolman.

Bright sat there for a moment, feeling a wave of nausea sweep over her, fighting the urge to open the door and retch onto the pavement. *This is too much. I am not capable of this.* She wished suddenly for a strong presence to prop her up, perhaps take her home, where it was quiet. She thought fleetingly of Buster Putnam. But no, that would not do. This was none of Buster's business.

It was the major, the one she had met at the police station. He was standing at the open window of Bright's car now, peering in at her. He peered for a good while and when she looked up at him she saw that his jaw was working slowly, like a cow chewing a cud. Bright had always thought that cows were thoughtful animals. Finally the major said, "Mrs. Birdsong, I want you to go home. The authorities are in charge here, and we have everything under control." He was trying to keep his voice low, but she could tell that he was a man who did not put up with much tommyrot.

< 404 >

She really should do that, she thought. She should let the major take care of things. But then she thought that the major didn't live here, that he would do whatever it was that he had come to do and then get in his highway patrol car and drive back to the capital. Probably very fast with the siren on. And that would leave the home folks here to deal with things. And that made Bright angry. She let it build in her for a moment, shoving her fear and nausea aside.

"Move your roadblock," she said.

"No ma'am. I can't do that."

Then she opened the door of the car and the major backed away a couple of steps to let her out. She reached in and got her purse and tucked it under her arm, closed the door and said, "All right. If you won't let me drive into the Quarter, I'll walk. But I'm going to see Flavo."

"No, you're not," the major said flatly.

"You might shoot an old lady," Bright said, "but I don't think you'll shoot the governor's mother. Will you?"

The major pursed his lips and then he took off his wide-brimmed hat and ran his fingers through his hair. And then he put his hat back on. And then he took off his sunglasses and blinked at her in the bright morning and put them back on. And finally he said, "No."

So Bright was on foot, feeling the sun on her scalp, wishing she had thought to bring a hat. A hot breeze riffled the drooping leaves on the trees at the edge of the roadway, but it was the only thing stirring. The street was deserted, the porches of the houses empty, the windows gaping blankly as she walked toward Flavo's grocery store. Every single time she had been here before, going back to her girlhood, she had had a sense of the street watching her, eyes that saw more than they let on. But now, there was none of that. Simply emptiness. And she began to wonder if Flavo had indeed evacuated, if they had all lit out for the promised land. She wished for someone to come to a front door and at least look at her, acknowledge her presence. *If no one looks at you, are you truly there? Perhaps not.*

She had gone scarcely a block when she rounded the bend in the road and saw the ruin of Booker T. Washington High School. The fire had somehow spared much of one side wall, but the rest of it was a blackened hulk, charred timbers poking crazily from the rubble, thin wisps of smoke still rising here and there. Bright stopped for a moment to look at it, to pay her respects. Lumber from Dorsey's sprawling yard by the river had built this school fifty years before, in a time before most towns their size had even considered a high school for Negroes.

< 405 >

Dorsey had seen it as a measure of the town's progressivism. *Now look at it. Another piece of the past—mine, his, theirs—gone.*

She was struck again by the emptiness, the quiet. There was no sound here except the singing of some crickets in the tall grass at the edge of the burned-out building, the raucous call of a crow in a tree down the way. Across the street, the yard in front of Flavo Richardson's store and house was bare—no cars, no people. Bright felt the hair on the back of her neck tingle. There was something ominously wrong here. Will a shot ring out? Will a rock come sailing from behind a bush to bounce off her skull? *Run!* somebody cried out, and she looked around wildly, searching for cover, jerking her head this way and that, gripping her purse with both hands. Then she realized that the voice was in her own head, terrified of the unknown. *Stop it! Of course there's something wrong here. Flavo's grandson is dead and the school-house has burned down and the highway patrol is up the road with shot-guns. But not a soul has raised a finger or a voice against you. The worst of it is, they're ignoring you.*

She took a deep breath and crossed the street, took refuge for a moment in the shade of the big oak tree in front of the store. The ground was bare and hard-packed and oil-spattered from the comings and goings of four generations of vehicles and people. Flavo had built the store in the late thirties, when times were still desperate, when white folks had little and black folks had nothing at all. People had marveled at his ability to keep it going in those first years until the war and economic revival came along. It had never been closed on a week-day, not even when Flavo's wife or his mother, Hosanna, died. He had returned from the funeral and opened for business. But now a black wreath hung on the shuttered door, holding commerce at bay.

Bright heard a siren now back toward town, heading in her gen-eral direction. Homer Sipsey, she guessed, called to the battlefront by the highway patrol major. *Come do something about this squirrelly old woman!* Poor Homer. The siren grew louder and then groaned to a halt about the spot where the patrol cars were blocking the road. *The old bat's down there! Just tucked her purse under her arm and started walk-ing! Like she owned the place!*

Well, they would come after her before long, Bright imagined. Engines roaring, sirens blaring, shotguns bristling. A SWAT team, perhaps, in an armored car. Coming to rescue the governor's mother. So she walked across the yard to Flavo's house and up the steps and knocked at the front door. After a moment, Flavo opened it and blinked out at her.

"Good morning," Bright said.

"Good morning yourself."

< 406 >

Bright looked around at the empty morning. "Where is everybody?"

Flavo took stock of the street. "Probably at the church." Bright thought he looked calm, well rested. Like a man who had set things in motion and then sat back to watch what happened. He stood there now with the screen between them, giving Bright Birdsong a good sizing up.

"Ah, yes," she said. "The funeral is at ten."

"That's right."

"I imagine everybody will be there."

"Not much else to do, I suppose," Flavo said, deadpan. "Travel is somewhat restricted this morning."

"Hmmmm. I noticed. Well, are you going to invite me in?"

"No," he said, "I believe I'll invite myself out." He opened the screen and stepped onto the porch. "Too nice a morning to be settin' inside in the gloom." He indicated two aging cane-bottomed rocking chairs at one end of the porch. "Why don't we just sit down over here and take the mornin' for a few minutes before I have to get off to the service."

"That would be fine," Bright said, and they sat down and rocked for a few moments with the smoking hulk of Booker T. Washington High School staring at them from across the street. "You've had a fire, I see," Bright said eventually.

"Yes, we certainly have."

Bright decided to get right to the point. "Did you burn down the schoolhouse, Flavo?"

He turned to her with a jerk, eyes wide with wounded surprise. "Of course not. What makes you think anybody *burned* it down? That"—he pointed to the ruin—"is an ancient building, made entirely of wood. Heart pine in the floors. Burns like a lightwood knot when it gets caught. Probably a million ways it could have caught fire. Who knows? Who will ever know?"

Bright unsnapped her purse, took out a handkerchief, and dabbed at the perspiration on her forehead, wished again she had fetched a hat from the house. "Well, I get the distinct impression that folks in town think you torched it. You or somebody"—she waved at the Quarter—"up here."

"Hmmmm," Flavo hummed. "I can see how they might think that. Especially after some young ruffian threw a rock at the fire truck when it came up here last night."

"A rock."

"A single rock. I was standing here on the porch and I distinctly heard it bounce off the fire truck. That was right before the explosion."

< 407 >

"What explosion?"

"Oh, I think some of the brothers had been storing a little light-nin' in a closet over at Booker T. It gave off a pretty good bang when it went up."

"Good Lord. What happened then?"

Flavo crossed one knee slowly over the other and massaged the top kneecap for a moment. Then he smiled a tiny smile and said, "The brave volunteers of the fire department cut and ran. They turned around and went lickety-split back to town and let old Booker T. burn. Never put a drop of water on it."

Bright studied him for a moment. When Flavo Richardson wanted you to know exactly what he was thinking, exactly what he was up to, he would tell you in exact terms. Right now was not one of those times. He wore a black mask, and all you could see was the eyes. And they revealed little. But they saw everything *you* did. And were.

"How long has the roadblock been up?"

"I have no idea," Flavo said with an impatient wave of his hand. "That's not something I'm concerned about just now."

"Maybe later," she said.

"Oh, yes," he said. "Definitely later. I'll want some answers, I 'spect."

"I believe Harley Gibbons and the highway patrol think you are about to rampage through town burning and looting."

Flavo snorted. "We may be." He stood up and walked to the edge of the porch, looked across the road at the school building. Then he turned back to her. "I told you to take care of things."

"*Told* me?"

"Told you, asked you. Whatever. I explained things so you could understand them, I think."

"Well, I tried," she said. Then she felt a rush of anger, remember-ing the town council meeting, the blank stares, the pigheaded recita-tion of rules and procedures. "I tried!" she said again, hotly. "I did your dirty work, just like I've done it before, Flavo Richardson!"

"My dirty work?"

Bright shrugged. "A bad choice of words. But you always come to me, Flavo. Always in the past, you come lay the burden on my door-step."

"This time, you failed," he said flatly.

She was on her feet then, brandishing her purse. "Yes. And what did you go and do? Burn down the schoolhouse and bring the highway patrol out in force!"

"I tell you again, *I did not burn down the schoolhouse!*" he thun-dered, and they stood there for a moment, glowering at each other.

< 408 >

Just the two of them alone in the hot vacant morning, squared off like aging gladiators. The mask was down now and Flavo Richardson had fire in his eyes. Daggers flew. And then just as suddenly they broke it off and both sat back down and looked at Booker T. for a while.

"All right," Bright said after a moment. "What are you going to do now?"

"I'm going to go bury my grandbaby," Flavo said softly, sadly.

"Then what?"

"Still depends on you, Bright."

"Me? Why me?"

"We been through all this before."

"I can't answer for my daddy any longer!" Bright snapped. "I've toted him around on my shoulders long enough! I've come to the realization over the past couple of days that I made some bad mistakes trying to do that. So I'm finished with that business. No more guilt over Papa, Flavo. So just don't try that tactic with me anymore."

Flavo turned and looked at her for a long time. "All right, then don't," he said. "Do it because you *matter.*"

"Did, perhaps."

"Still do. Good people always do, Bright. When things need doing, good people *have* to matter. You've done some good in this town in your time, Bright. Regardless of why. Your daddy did some good in his day, and some bad." He sat rocking for a moment, pondering. Then: "I never told you this, but he gave me the money to start my store. It was not long before he died, and I don't think he really had it to give." Flavo shook his head. "But that's all really beside the point. He's been dead and gone for a long time, Bright. Any old debts involving Dorsey Bascombe have long been settled. Yours and mine. But you and me, we're still here."

Bright sighed, feeling the dead weight of an ancient burden. "Flavo, you have been using me for a long, long time. Manipulating me to get what you wanted. And putting me in tight places because of it."

She expected him to take hot issue with that, but instead he rubbed his chin for a moment and looked out across the yard. Finally he said, "I'm sad to hear you put that kind of definition on it."

"I always thought of you as my friend," she went on. "But I don't know that friends do that to each other."

"Well," he said slowly, "I like to think of it this way: I came to you as a friend in need and you recognized the need and helped. And did a lot of good in the process. A friend does that, and if she says 'Damn the consequences' in doing that, it's a great measure of the friendship."

Bright nodded. "And you're doing that again."

"No," he said firmly, "it's different this time. I'm quite prepared to

< 409 >

meet my own need, if you're not willing or able. And damn the consequences. You will still be my friend, but not my friend in need."

"And that makes the friendship different."

"Yes. That it does."

They sat and rocked for a while longer, and then Flavo got up from his chair, took his watch out of his pocket, flipped open the cover and looked at it. "Time to go," he said.

"Do you want me to go with you?"

"No. This is a private grief, Bright."

She stood alongside him. "What's going to happen after the funeral, Flavo?"

"I suspect there will have to be an accounting of some sort. Folks are mad as hell."

"Are you going to disrupt the parade?"

"No. Not that. I won't let that happen."

Bright nodded. "I'm glad. I wouldn't have Fitz come home this morning and be humiliated. I would not take kindly to anyone who did that or allowed that."

"Neither would I."

Flavo got his hat from the rack just inside the door and they walked together down the steps and stood for a moment in the yard. Bright could hear singing now up the way, about the place where the small white frame church would be. The church Dorsey Bascombe had built. The one where she had sat with Hosanna and heard God in the powerful dusky voices. Where now a small casket would sit in front of the altar, covered with greenery. She turned to Flavo. "I'm sorry," she said gently, taking his hand. "I grieve with you."

"I know." And she saw the deep, abiding pain in his eyes, the great loss.

"I hope you don't want retribution," she said.

"No. I just want a wrong made right."

She sighed, released his hand. "We hand down our history like family Bibles, don't we."

"Yes."

And then they parted, he toward the church and she toward the roadblock where the highway patrol waited with their shotguns. She understood, as she walked, that it was a deadly serious business here, that it could become very nasty. And that just would not do.

But what to do? What could *she* do, even if she were inclined to act? She hadn't the foggiest idea at the moment. Perhaps, just this one more time, something would turn up.

Meantime, there was this other thing.

<   >

< 410 >

The Winnebago was in the parking lot at the hospital, baking in the midmorning sun, dancing in its own heat shimmers. Bright parked the Plymouth beside it, sat for a moment and gathered her wits before she went in. *Now. Perhaps the hardest part of all.*

Jimbo was sitting on the side of Roseann's bed and Rupert was perched on the edge of a chair when Bright edged the door open and peered in. "Anybody home?"

"Hi, Mama Bright!" Jimbo cried, hopping off the bed. "Didja know the highway patrol's captured all the black people?"

"No, they haven't," Bright said, pushing the door farther open. "I've just been there. They've got a roadblock and a bunch of young men with shotguns. But there's no trouble." His next visit, she thought, she would take him to the Quarter. Let him spend a day at Flavo Richardson's grocery store, maybe go to Wednesday night prayer meeting at the little white frame church. A child should know more than what he's told by adults.

The room was dim, a haven against the bright day outside. The venetian blinds were drawn and only slivers of light peeked around the edges. Bright stepped into the room and closed the door behind her. The head of the hospital bed had been raised and Roseann was sitting up, pillows fluffed at her back. She stared at Bright for a moment and then said, "What are you doing here?" Her voice was thick.

Rupert cleared his throat and then stood up and jammed his pipe in his mouth. The first line of defense. "Ahhhh, hummmm," he said around the stem of the pipe. "Jimbo, let's you and me give the ladies a few minutes by themselves."

Jimbo's eyes darted from Bright to Roseann. Uncertainty there, perhaps a little fear. *Something is wrong, something mysterious and grown-up. Was it his fault?* Bright wanted to kneel and reassure him. But this was not the time.

"We'll be outside," Rupert said, and he put his arm on Jimbo's shoulder and led him out, leaving behind the sweet aroma of his pipe. There was something solid and reassuring about it, something for Roseann to cling to. Bright was glad.

Bright stood at the foot of Roseann's bed for a moment; then she sat down in the chair and folded her hands across her purse. Roseann was disheveled and bleary-eyed. She seemed for a moment to have a hard time focusing on Bright and she turned her head away, looked at a spot high up on the wall across from her bed. Then her jaw tightened and she said, "That was a terrible thing to do."

"It was the wrong way to do it," Bright said, "but Jimbo and I had a wonderful time. He's a right remarkable young man."

"I would kill anyone who touched a hair on his head," Roseann

< 411 >

said, her voice flat and hard. "You put me through hell, Mama. I'll never forgive you for that."

Bright sat for a moment thinking how, oddly, that tied together so much of what had happened already this morning—the fierce protectiveness of parents. Flavo with his grandson, Roseann with Jimbo, Bright with Fitz. And how that same thread ran through much of her own life, her great dilemma. *We shelter our children from harm,* as Dorsey had done with Bright, and Bright in turn had done with Fitz and Roseann. And now full circle. It was the most natural thing on earth. And damn the consequences. If that was a sin, surely it was a sin of the heart. But there were consequences just the same. And sometimes you find that despite all good intention, you have failed in some basic ways.

She got up after a moment and opened the venetian blinds, flooding the room with the bright morning. Outside, the parking lot was nearly empty except for the Winnebago and the Plymouth. Nobody wanted to go to the hospital in June if they could help it. You would choose a quiet riverbank in June, or a cool place on the front porch, but not a hospital.

Bright sat back down in the chair and studied the dust motes dancing in the air between them. "I came to say I'm sorry," she said. "For the fight, for frightening you. For anything else you think I ought to be sorry about."

Roseann stared at the spot high on the wall and Bright could see a flush of color in her cheeks. But she didn't speak.

"Will you talk to me about it?"

A shake of the head.

"Well, I'll sit here until you do. We have some things to settle."

Roseann turned on her then, eyes flashing. "*Settle?* That has a nice neat sound to it, doesn't it! I don't want to settle anything with you!"

"That won't do, Roseann," Bright said calmly. "I'm not going to let you off the hook. Or me."

Roseann gave an angry shake of her head, grabbed a handful of the sheet and crushed it fiercely against her breasts. "Damn you!" she cried. "You slap me in the face and then run off with my child, and now it's *me* who's feeling wretched!" She began to sob, rocking back and forth in the bed. "You always make me feel like a bad little girl!"

Oh, you were! The question is, Did I love you in spite of it? "I've thought a lot about that the past few days," Bright said.

"I've been thinking about it all my life," Roseann wailed. Then her hands went to her hair and Bright flinched, seeing how hatefully

< 412 >

she tugged and pulled, fingers entwined in the brown strands, clawing at herself.

"Roseann, please," she said softly. "Please don't."

"Don't what?"

"Don't . . ." *Ah, but what? Punish yourself? Punish me? What is it here? What has it always been? Why can't we . . . TALK! Instead of clawing at each other. And ourselves.* "Put your hands in your lap," Bright said finally, imploring.

Roseann stared at her, then at her hands. And then she wiped her eyes with them and folded them slowly into the sheet and squeezed her eyes shut. They sat there for a long time in the silence of the room. It, and they, seemed to be carved into neat lines by the shafts of light from the window blinds. A prison cell of sorts, or a confessional box. Just the two of them now. Bright could not remember when it had been just the two of them with no escape and no place to hide. In truth, either or both could cut and run, flee down the tiled corridor of the hospital and out into the blazing day. But they would not. It was time . . .

"I don't think I ever told you much about my own mother," Bright said after a while. There was no answer from Roseann, no evidence of the slightest interest. "She left when I was nine years old. She got on the train and went to New Orleans and I never heard from her again. I hated her for that. I felt alone and abandoned, and I blamed it all on my mother."

Roseann opened her eyes now, looked at Bright.

"But I'm not quite so sure anymore," Bright went on. "I'm afraid it's a good deal more complicated than that. I can't explain it yet, to myself or anyone else. But I'm beginning to see how it must have been for her. And how others bear blame. I think she felt very much alone, too. And that was a terrible thing."

"I know," Roseann said quietly.

"You do?"

"Yes." Her eyes were bleak with an ancient despair. "I know what it's like to be alone. That's the way I always felt with you."

It stung her. And it took her a moment to recover. "Why did you feel alone, Roseann?"

"Because you . . ." Roseann's voice broke again and she struggled for a moment to get it under control. Then she shook her head fiercely. "You were always so right about everything! So perfect! So busy! And Papa was never there to make it better!"

Ah, yes. I can see now how it must have been, how intimidating I must have been. Like Dorsey Bascombe. I am indeed my father's daugh-

< 413 >

ter in ways neither of us ever intended. And we were ever at odds—
Roseann so filled with spite, so combative, so belligerent; and me, determined to make the course I chose the right one.

"I never intended for you to feel alone," Bright said. "In fact, that
was the whole idea behind staying here, not going to Washington. I
wanted you and Fitz to grow up here among the people you knew, the
people who cared about you."

"But we weren't a family," Roseann said bitterly.

"Not in the best sense of the word," Bright said. "But we stayed
together. Even through some times when we might not have. Your
father and I made choices, compromises. We both did the best we
knew how to do at the time. And now I'm left to live with the consequences."

"Yes," Roseann said, "and so am I."

And that too was true. Again, things come full circle. So much
of the past skewing the present, defining the future. Beautiful, frightened Elise in a soft summer dress, smiling dreamily at the ladies of the
Study Club and then quietly just going away. It had been ever thus. A
going away. A train disappearing into the distance, a crumpled telegram. Then beyond that, Dorsey, in whom Bright invested everything
once Elise had gone. He too had abandoned her in his own way. And
Fitzhugh? Was that a kind of abandonment? Yes, on both their parts.
A failure to hold on in the truest sense.

But there was something else too. Roseann had uttered a great
wisdom just now without realizing it. The burden of it was not Bright's
alone. There were three of them left, keepers of the legacy, bad and
good. She and Roseann and Fitz. They were the survivors, however
scarred, and there might be something worth reaching for there. If it
were not too late, if they could each find a little grace.

So Bright climbed up from the well of memory and looked up into
her daughter's eyes. "I know you missed your father terribly," she said.
"We both share the blame for that."

Roseann looked away, out the window at the morning. "I always
dreamed that you would die first and Papa would come to live with me.
Or I'd come back home and live with him and take care of him when
he got old. But," she whispered, "it didn't work out that way."

Ah, does anything truly ever work out? Or does it just happen, and
if it happens the way we wish, we say it worked out. If not . . . "And
I always thought that one day your father would come home and we
would put our lives back together. And that didn't work out either. I
grieve for that."

Roseann looked back at Bright now and there was the old stub-

< 414 >

bornness there. And most painful of all, dismissal. "I hope you do," she said. "And now I just want to get out of here and take my family and go home." She fixed Bright with her hard eyes, unflinching. "I want you to leave me alone, Mama. Me and Jimbo and Rupert. Just leave us alone."

"No," Bright said, "I won't do that."

"I'm not coming down here anymore," Roseann flashed.

Bright stood, smoothing the front of her dress, tucking her purse under her arm. "All right. I've discovered that my old car will make it to the capital. I'm sure it will get to your place."

"Don't bother," Roseann said.

Bright started to retort, but then she thought, *There has been enough said for the moment. I cannot explain it all, or make it all right, because I only understand it dimly myself. What we need now is time. Perhaps there is something beyond time. Or perhaps not.*

Monkey Deloach was standing in the hallway outside Roseann's room. Bright closed the door and stood there staring at him for a moment.

"How is . . . hmmmmmmm . . . Roseann?" Monkey asked.

"She'll be all right," Bright said. "Just a little too much excitement. We've all had a little too much excitement."

"Xuripha used to think Donald . . . hmmmmmm . . . should have married her," Monkey said. "But I . . . hmmmmmm . . . thought she was too . . . hmmmmmm . . . much for him." He smiled.

"Well," Bright nodded, "Xuripha's not right about everything."

"But . . . hmmmmmm . . . most things."

She looked Monkey over head to toe, thinking again of the small boy who had come to her aid on a wintry playground so many years before, the one she had kissed on the cheek. Good, true, loyal Monkey. There was an abiding sadness about him now.

"Monkey," she said suddenly, "go back to the lumberyard."

He studied her for a moment. "But I turned all that over to Donald."

"Fine. Let Donald run it. But go back. Do something. Chop down trees. Drive a truck. Get in the way."

"But Xuripha—"

"As I said, Xuripha is not right about everything," Bright interrupted. "You are too young to go to seed."

Monkey looked down at the linoleum of the hallway. "You . . . hmmmmmm . . . think that's what I'm doing?"

"Yes. And so am I. Or have been, that is."

< 415 >

Monkey looked up at her again. "You can't . . . hmmmmmm . . . teach an old dog new tricks," he said.

"No, but old dogs know some old tricks the young'uns have never thought of."

Monkey ruminated on that. Then a small, sly smile crept across his face. He drew himself up, threw back his shoulders. "Maybe you're right," he said, as clearly as you please.

Bright leaned over and kissed Monkey on the cheek. Sixty years, it had been. And this time he didn't look astonished.

Rupert and Jimbo were in the lobby, and Little Fitz was with them, looking very distinguished this morning in a blue suit and a bold red tie. They all stared at her curiously and she realized she must look a fright. "Mama . . . ," Fitz said. And then he came to her and put his arms around her. "Are you all right?"

"I've been better," she said. In truth, she wanted to go somewhere quiet and dark just now, to escape into sleep or just the absence of thought. To drift, in the comfortable place she had inhabited for the past eight years, an eternal summertime where torpor settled like mist. There was great temptation to do that now, enveloped as she was in her son's arms, aching with the sting of her daughter's bitterness.

But then she thought, *There is a great deal to do, even if I don't have the faintest notion of what it is.* So she gave Fitz a pat on the back and he released her. "What time is it?" she asked.

He looked at his watch. "Almost eleven. Almost time for the parade."

"What parade?"

He gave her a rueful smile. "Fitz Birdsong Day, Mama. The parade, and then the luncheon at the high school. Welcome home, conquering hero, all that rot."

She fixed him with a hard look. "There's not a bit of rot about it, Fitz Birdsong. These are your people."

"Despite everything?"

"Let's hope so."

He nodded. "You're going to ride in the parade with me."

"Me? Lord, no."

"Please, Mama."

Through the double glass doors of the hospital entrance, she could see his entourage drawn up out front—the big Lincoln limousine, flanked by two highway patrol cars. There was a goodly little knot of men standing around the cars, some in uniform and the rest in suits. She saw Big Deal O'Neill and Doyle Butterworth, Fitz's campaign

< 416 >

manager. And the highway patrol major she had defied at the roadblock. Big Deal gave them a wave and pointed to his watch.

She saw then how much it meant to Fitz. He had played the fool
for all the world to see and he was shot through with remorse. He
needed his mother by his side to say to the world, "Look, he may be
way out on a limb with his fanny flapping in the breeze, but he's my
boy. Take note of that."

So, other things would wait. Bright reached up and patted his
cheek. "All right. On one condition."

"What's that?"

"Take down that silly roadblock at the Quarter."

"Mama, they've had trouble up there . . . ," he started.

"Nonsense. The old schoolhouse burned down and somebody
threw a rock. That's no cause to put the place under siege. It's an insult
to Flavo and everybody who lives there."

"But the parade . . ."

"Flavo promised me there would be no trouble."

Fitz shrugged. "All right. I'll pull the state people out. But it's up
to Harley and Chief Sipsey about the local boys."

"No, I want you to take care of that too. Go talk to them. Don't
you have a radio gizmo or something in your car?"

"All right," he said wearily. "There's never been any use arguing
with you, Mama."

"I'll be right out."

He left her there, went through the double doors into the hot
morning to take care of his business.

She turned to Rupert and Jimbo. "I think Roseann is ready to go
home now."

Rupert chewed on the stem of his pipe for a moment and Jimbo
looked up at her, still waiting for someone to explain things to him. So
she took him by the hand and led him to a nearby sofa, and they sat
while Rupert stood back, giving them the moment.

"Jimbo," Bright said, "you and Rupert and your mother are going
home now, and it may be a while before I see you again."

"Why?"

She thought of making some light thing of it, but then she decided, *No, that's not fair. Why should you be anything but honest with a
child? I was not entirely honest with my own. So only the truth here.* And
she said, "Your mother is very angry with me."

"Because we ran away?"

Bright smiled. "Is that what we did? Maybe so. Yes, that has something to do with it. The main thing is, your mother and I haven't

< 417 >

gotten along very well for a long time." He looked at her intently, all curiosity. "That happens sometimes, and we're trying to sort it all out. But it has absolutely nothing to do with you. Your mother loves you very much, and she is a very good mother, and I want you to always mind her and take care of her."

"Why don't you get along?" he asked.

"I'm not sure I understand it completely. But I'm trying. Do you ever get mad at a friend?"

"Sure," he said.

"Well, it's a little like that. Except that grown-ups aren't so good at patching things up."

"Are you and Mama gonna patch things up?"

"I hope so. Will you help us?"

"Sure," he said earnestly.

"And there is one other thing. Half the money is yours. Do you know what that comes to?"

"Twenty-five thousand dollars," he said matter-of-factly.

"Will you accept that as a token of my esteem and a remembrance of a good adventure?"

A smile tugged at the corners of his mouth. "I reckon."

"Excellent. I'm going to find me a good lawyer and have it put in a trust account in your name. When it comes time to go to college, it'll be there for you." She patted him on the knee and started to rise, but Jimbo flung his arms around her neck and squeezed her very hard. She came a bit undone then, and didn't mind very much at all.

< 418 >

25

It wasn't really much of a parade as parades went. A color guard from the Army National Guard leading the way—two men with flags flanked by two more with rifles, all of them in khaki and wearing chrome helmets that shone like beacons in the sunlight; then Chief Homer Sipsey in his police car; the high school band (those who weren't on summer jobs or at the beach with their parents); a highway patrol cruiser; several automobiles carrying assorted local dignitaries—Mayor Harley Gibbons, the chairman of the county commission, the head of the soil and water conservation board; a marching assortment of Boy and Girl Scouts, Cubs, and Brownies; the county sheriff in his own sedan with a blue bubble on top; a truck towing a flatbed trailer with the attendees of the First Baptist Church Vacation Bible School dressed in biblical attire; another city police car; then the open-top convertible carrying Fitz and Bright, driven by Big Deal O'Neill. And finally, to flesh out the procession, a city street sweeper with a big sign on the side of the cab that read A CLEAN SWEEP FOR LITTLE FITZ. Big Deal had tried to get Holly Hardee and the Live Eye 5 van to join the parade, but Holly Hardee had been in no mood for parading, Big Deal said.

It wouldn't be much of a parade route, either. From the Methodist Church parking lot, down Fitzhugh Birdsong Boulevard past Bright's house, then left along Bascombe, the main business street, for several blocks, and finally left again across Claxton and a straight shot to the high school. It was the same route the Christmas parade followed each year, and Big Deal O'Neill, who had organized the affair, allowed that there was no use in getting folks confused by changing things around. Big Deal allowed that several times while he scurried about the Methodist Church parking lot (the staging area, he called it) trying to get things moving, shouting instructions, arguing with one of the Baptist mothers who fussed at him from the flatbed trailer while the children

< 419 >

fidgeted irritably in the heat. When Fitz and Bright swept up in the limousine with the highway patrol cars wailing front and rear, they were already fifteen minutes late. Big Deal was bathed in sweat, his thinning hair matted to his head, his baby blue button-down dress shirt splotched with sweat, tie loose at the collar. Bright sympathized. Francis O'Neill was Little Fitz Birdsong's oldest friend, boyhood companion, adult confidant, buddy. He wanted things to go just right, especially with all that had transpired in the past few days. Big Deal wanted to show the rest of the state that, warts and all, Fitz Birdsong's hometown thought he was the finest thing since sliced bread.

Heat phantoms rose from the black asphalt of the parking lot, and Bright could feel the sun baking right through the hat they had stopped by her house to fetch. The orchid corsage Big Deal's wife had pinned to her dress just before they climbed into the convertible was already beginning to show signs of heatstroke. Her brain was in ferment, a swirling caldron of all the things she had set in motion in the space of a few hours.

"Mama, are you gonna be all right?" Fitz asked. "You want me to get you an umbrella?"

"No. I look foolish enough without an umbrella."

"You don't look foolish. You look like the governor's mother. That's a very nice dress. I don't believe I've seen it before."

"Yes," she said, "you've seen it before. I wore it to your inauguration. I don't believe anybody noticed my dress. They were all gawking at Flavo Richardson."

"Speaking of which, the roadblocks are down."

"Good. He buried his grandson this morning."

"I know. I should have been there."

"No," she said, "he didn't want us. He called it a private grief. I respect that."

"I hope there's not any trouble. There's never been any around here, not with the blacks."

"You know all about the business with the swimming pool?"

"Yes." He nodded. "Harley told me." He started to say something else, but there was a commotion up ahead of them now and the parade began to lurch into motion, the units easing out of the parking lot one by one, the color guard and Homer Sipsey's car up front, his siren competing with the bleating of the high school band. Just behind them, the street sweeper roared to life, its diesel spouting puffs of smoke. Big Deal sprinted back to the convertible and slid in behind the wheel, gasping for breath. Bright took a tight grip on the hot leather of the seat.

< 420 >

She felt like a ninny, perched on the back of the convertible next to Fitz, directly behind Big Deal, with her feet resting on the rear seat next to her purse. It was a rather snazzy-looking Ford convertible, white with red leather upholstery. But Bright was not much for display. She leaned over, tapped Big Deal on the shoulder. "Francis, don't you hot-rod this car, you hear?"

"Yes ma'am," he grinned back at her. "No danger of that." He pointed over his left shoulder. "The parade can't go no faster than the street sweeper, and it's kinda slow. So we'll just take 'er real easy, okay?" He looked back at her. "After the parade's over, I can work out a good deal for you on this car, Miz Bright. Low mileage, one owner. Little bit down, easy payments. You ought to get a new car."

"Francis," she said, "I've got a perfectly good automobile. Low mileage, one owner. Nothing down, no payments."

The city police car just ahead of them began to move then and Big Deal shifted into gear. Bright held on to Fitz's arm as the convertible pulled away with a bit of a lurch, and she glanced back at the street sweeper. It was a big green machine with a small enclosed cab up top for the driver. The big round brush in front was held high off the pavement by two thick metal arms. It looked like a huge insect with a great bushy mustache. Big Deal looked back and waved it forward, and it growled into motion with a clashing of gears. It was very loud and very slow. It would take a long time to get to the high school. The street sweeper was not a good idea, she thought. It bordered on the ridiculous. But she didn't say anything to Big Deal.

Birdsong Boulevard was empty except for the units of the parade, with barricades at every intersection to keep other traffic at bay. There weren't any people along the street here either, just a few up on their porches out of the sun, mostly old folks. Bright could see her own house ahead, and Buster Putnam's sagging monstrosity next door. She didn't expect much of a crowd until they got to where Birdsong intersected with Bascombe. At the Christmas parade every year, the crowd mostly gathered along Bascombe.

"Francis . . . ," she said loudly.

Big Deal sat like a statue in the front seat. He couldn't hear her, she realized, with the street sweeper groaning and grinding behind them. It drowned out everything except the occasional whumping of the bass drum in the band up ahead. That was just fine, she thought. They could have a private conversation, right here in the middle of the parade. She turned to Fitz, leaned close to his ear. "We've got to talk about the money."

"Yes." He nodded. "We do."

< 421 >

"I've got it all in cash," she said.

Fitz pursed his lips. "Yes, I know. Remember, you called me from the bank. You've cut a pretty wide swath since yesterday."

"A what?" She craned her ear toward him, trying to catch the word.

"A wide SWATH." He held his hands wide. "Two banks, the highway patrol, and the National Guard."

"Two banks?"

"Harley Gibbons told me about that, too."

"Oh."

Fitz smiled. "Seems everybody wants your money."

"Yes. Before I won it, I didn't need it. Now that I've got it, I need about three times as much. One thing I'm not going to do is give it to the government."

Big Deal turned to them from the front seat. "Y'all say something?" he yelled.

"No!" Fitz yelled back. "Mama and I were talking to each other."

"Oh." Big Deal looked back at the street sweeper. "Kinda loud!"

"Yeah!" Fitz stuck his fingers in his ears. Big Deal grinned and went back to his driving.

"You've got to pay taxes on the money, regardless of what you do with it," Fitz said.

She tossed her head. "What are they going to do with an old lady, send me to jail?"

"Yes, Mama. They will do exactly that."

Bright looked ahead, over the top of the city police car in front of them, and she could see that the parade was beginning to spread out. The units up front were making good time, but the street sweeper was slowing things down here at the tail end. The driver of the truck towing the Vacation Bible School flatbed kept leaning out his window, looking back. There was a considerable gap developing between the flatbed and the sheriff's car just ahead of it. And time was taking its toll on the flatbed's occupants. Two of the kids on the rear were struggling over a shepherd's crook and one of the teachers was trying to separate them. Bright thought if they could get a full-scale riot going, it might keep the crowd along Bascombe entertained until Fitz's convertible got there.

They were at the intersection where Claxton joined from the left now, with the Dixie Vittles Supermarket on the corner, and there was a small knot of people standing in front of the store under the awning—Doris Hawkins and Hank Foscoe the manager, wearing their little white hats and red jackets, and several other people she assumed were customers.

< 422 >

"Hey, who's that up yonder on the back seat of that fancy car with Miz Bright Birdsong?" Doris yelled with a horselaugh. "Miz Bright, you spent all that money yet?"

"Howdy, Miz Doris, Hank," Fitz called back.

Bright smiled and waved. She wasn't about to start yelling back at people in the crowd. And it was really none of Doris Hawkins's business what she had done, or planned to do, with the money.

Bright looked to her right, over at her own house. The Winnebago gone, and she thought with a pang of Rupert and Roseann and Jimbo, driving back home now. Then she thought about the briefcase. She really must get it back to Mr. Purcell at the bank in the capital. Perhaps, she thought, Fitz could carry it back with him in his limousine after the luncheon, drop it off at the bank. She tapped Fitz on the arm, pointed. "I've got the money in my car there."

His eyes widened. "The cash?"

"Under the front seat."

"My God, Mama!"

"As safe a place as any," she said. "Who would think to look under the front seat of a car for fifty thousand dollars?"

Fitz laughed, then shook his head. "I don't know why I'm surprised."

"Me either."

"You've never been one to do the usual thing."

Bright shrugged.

"Do you remember the time you stood in front of Putnam's Mercantile with the sign that said THIS BUSINESS UNFAIR TO WOMEN?"

"Of course I remember it," she said.

It had been when Fitz was a teenager. O. P. Putnam had girlie magazines under the counter, which he sold on the sly to men and older boys. Bright found one under Fitz's mattress, made him tell her where he got it, then marched downtown and demanded that O. P. sell her one. He refused; she returned with the sign. O. P. could either sell to everybody or nobody, she said, planting herself on the sidewalk just in front of the door. When people passed by and asked what the sign meant, she said, "Go ask Mr. Putnam." It took perhaps thirty minutes, because O. P. was a stubborn man. But he came out finally with his hands up. And he went out of the girlie magazine business, at least as far as teenaged boys were concerned. Bright remembered it even now with a bit of satisfaction. She had cut a wide swath then too. But that had been a good while ago.

Fitz gave the house another long look. "The house needs a coat of paint, Mama. And a new roof."

< 423 >

She pointed to the house next door. "Well, it's not as bad as Buster's. The roofing man fell clean through his roof around in the back." She searched his face. "Do you think I'm going to seed, Fitz?"

He scrunched up his mouth, considering it. "No, Mama, I don't. A few days ago, I might have. But now . . ." He shrugged.

Now. Yes, she thought, things had changed. And the fifty thousand dollars was the least of it. Bright leaned close to Fitz's ear. "I've thought about you a great deal the past few days."

He stared at her for a moment. "Oh? In what way?"

"Mistakes," she said bluntly. "Mine."

Fitz's mouth formed a big O of surprise. "Yours? What kind?"

"I thought it had mostly to do with going to Washington. Or rather, not going. But I'm beginning to believe that was only part of it." She paused a moment and then said, "You've always been very angry with your father, haven't you."

She saw the flash of pain in his eyes then and he turned away from her. *I shouldn't have brought it up. Not here, not now.* Then he looked back and said, "Yes."

"And with me."

He considered it. She could see the struggle there. Fitz was ever the good son, chary of giving offense. But he nodded slowly. "Maybe so."

"It's been a hard thing for you, hasn't it."

"Yes." No argument there. She remembered Fitzhugh's funeral. It had been Little Fitz who had been inconsolable. And after that, they had not had a great deal to say to each other. There was a good deal they should have spoken about. But he got on with his life, and she retreated into hers. A drifting away. History repeating itself.

"Why did you go into politics, Fitz?" she asked him now.

He pondered it for a moment. "I'm good at it," he said. "And I got that from Papa. But I think in a way I was trying to find something I lost somewhere. Does that make sense?"

"Yes."

"That's why I can't figure out why I've made such a complete ass of myself. When I intended just the opposite."

"Don't be too hard . . ."

He nodded.

She studied him. "We should have had this conversation a long time ago."

"Probably."

"I'm trying to figure out some things myself."

He nodded. They would talk. There was a good deal to say. Some of it would be difficult, but that made it all the more worth saying.

< 424 >

Big Deal turned around in the front seat, grinned back at them. "You folks all right back there?" he yelled.

She and Fitz stared at him; then Fitz grinned and gave him a thumbs-up. "Just fine, pardner. Just hold 'er in the road."

"Crowd's a little thin right now," Big Deal shouted. "Most folks are probably around on Bascombe." He looked very hopeful. He did so want things to go well. Bright leaned over toward him. "It'll be just fine, Francis. You'll see."

"Yes ma'am." He gave her a big smile.

Then the band up ahead struck up a march. "The Stars and Stripes Forever." Bright gave Fitz's arm a squeeze, remembering with a smile the night in the glittering ballroom at the White House. That had been very fine, something to treasure. Nothing, not all the mistakes before and after, could take that away.

They could see the corner of Birdsong and Bascombe now, and yes, there was a good-sized knot of people on the left near corner, another on the far side in front of the Gulf station, some of them sitting on the hoods of cars. The color guard and Homer Sipsey's patrol car and the high school band and the highway patrol car had already made the turn, and the dark blue Cadillac carrying Mayor Harley Gibbons was easing into the intersection. The tinted windows of Harley's car were rolled up, and she could barely see the driver on the near side. Harley rode in air-conditioned comfort. Bright thought that only a mayor who had been in office as long as Harley, and probably one who was a banker too, could get away with riding in a parade in a Cadillac. She heard Hosanna's voice: *Big-Ikey*. As Harley's car cleared the intersection and headed up Bascombe, several kids edged off the curb into the street, peering back down the parade route toward them. A police officer herded them back.

There was a sprinkling of people along the sidewalk on either side of the street here too. Fitz straightened, coming to life, waving and flashing his big sunshine smile. She watched his eyes, saw how he did it. They darted quickly from one onlooker to the next, fixing for just a split second on each individual face so that every single person could say later, "The governor looked right at me." He nodded and waved, reaching out to them with his eyes and his hands and his smile, pulling them toward him. They seemed to lean forward. Remarkable.

He turned suddenly, caught her watching him. "What's the matter?"

"Your father," she said.

"What?"

"You looked exactly like him just now. He had a way of making you feel you were the only person in the world worth talking to."

< 425 >

Fitz lowered his hand then, looked directly at her, ignoring the people alongside the street. For just a moment, it seemed it was just the two of them there, surrounded by the grinding noise of the street sweeper and the whumping of the band up ahead. "I blew it," he said.

"You don't have to tell me anything," she said.

"Yes, I do. You're my mama. I could always tell you anything."

She felt tears spring to her eyes. "And you're my boy." She wanted to put her arm around him, draw him very close to her. But that would not do just here, just now.

His face went very soft then, the way she remembered it when he was a small boy, when he would curl up next to her on the wicker love seat on the front porch on a summer night, just the two of them there with Roseann finally asleep inside after her nightly tantrum, filling the evening with their talk of things great and small, mostly small. Books read, ideas pondered, the thousand small incidents that made a day and accumulated into a life. It was in those quiet shared moments that Bright Birdsong believed most fervently that she had done the right thing by staying here, by giving him that time and this place to grow to maturity. And looking back on it, was that so wrong? There were those things, and others, that were fine and true about all their lives, going back to the beginning. If they were all lucky, there would be time enough to dwell on that too.

"Yes." He smiled now. "I'm your boy."

Big Deal turned around to them again just at that moment, breaking into their little world. "What'd I tell you!" he yelped. "Just look at 'em."

They were at the intersection—Birdsong and Bascombe. The meeting of this town's two most famous names, she thought. If there was one piece of this town that belonged to her, to her and everything connected to her, this was it. As they began to turn the corner, she could see the people thick along both sides of the street here at the intersection, and on down Bascombe, more people lining the sidewalks, four and five deep, it appeared, with a huge crowd down around City Hall, midway the street. Big Deal gave two loud honks on the horn, and people in the crowd called back, yelling and waving. Up ahead, the band launched into another chorus of "The Stars and Stripes Forever." Then the street sweeper lumbered around the corner behind them and its roar echoed off the sides of the buildings, crashing around them like continuous rolling thunder. It was deafening.

"Good heavens!" she called out to Fitz. "I didn't know there were this many people in the whole town!"

"There aren't," he shouted back with a grin. "Big Deal ran buses from all over the county."

< 426 >

It was a big, noisy, friendly crowd. These were Little Fitz Bird-song's home folks, and regardless of the pickle he had gotten himself into, they were still with him. They held hand-lettered signs: GIVE 'EM HELL, LITTLE FITZ and FOUR MORE YEARS!; and big blue and white printed campaign posters that said simply BIRDSONG. It was a sea of noise and color, and Bright felt her skin tingle. Fitz grabbed her right hand with his left and held it up high and the crowd screamed with delight. Bright smiled back at the spectators, waving to an occasional person she knew.

They passed the first intersection on Bascombe, recognizable only by the gap in the buildings. The crowd was unbroken along the street, held in check by a wooden barricade guarded by a sheriff's deputy who gave a little salute as the car passed.

Then she spotted Buster Putnam, standing right in the front of the crowd on the corner outside Putnam's Mercantile. Buster, wearing the flannel shirt and faded pants, but clean-shaven now, his hair slicked down. And right next to him, Gladys. *Gladys?*

"Is that Gladys?" Fitz yelled into her ear.

"The dog hasn't ventured past the backyard in ten years," she said incredulously. Good Lord! The aging beast could die of heatstroke out here on the street like this. And all these people. Gladys wasn't used to people. But there she sat on her haunches next to Buster, head cocked quizzically, looking rather satisfied with herself. And then she thought, *Perhaps no stranger for Gladys to be sitting there on the curb than it is for me to be sitting up here in this convertible.*

Fitz gave Buster a wave and Buster blew back a kiss to Bright. She blushed with embarrassment.

Fitz leaned close to her again. "Has General Putnam come court-ing?"

She looked at him sharply. "Buster Putnam's too young for me." Fitz threw his head back and laughed.

They were nearing City Hall now, and the band had stopped there and re-formed on the opposite side of the street. In front of City Hall itself, just under the big banner that said WELCOME HOME, LITTLE FITZ, Big Deal and his committee had set up a platform with a microphone so Fitz could get out of the car and make a speech. There was a row of chairs at the rear of the platform where the dignitaries could sit, and Bright could see Harley Gibbons and the other bigwigs up there already. Then she spotted Holly Hardee and her Live Eye 5 cameraman at the front edge of the platform, edging now toward the car as it approached.

She studied Fitz for a moment. What could he say to the crowd? No doubt a stem-winding, rip-roaring political speech full of fighting

< 427 >

words. She had heard him give that kind a few times before, and in that he was more the master than his father had been. Congressman Fitzhugh Birdsong's speeches had been full of gentle wit and calm wisdom, the kind you expected from a man who held the nation's security and destiny in his hands, or at least wanted you to think he did. He could give a speech like that to the simplest of people and make them believe that they too had a hand in the nation's security and destiny, that he had shared with them a vision handed straight from the fellows who signed the Constitution. Governors, on the other hand, weren't security-and-destiny people. You expected them to do the mundane things like patch the roads and hire the teachers and put crooks in prison and pay old folks' pensions and send in the National Guard when there was a disaster. And you were lucky if they didn't steal you blind in the process. Fitz was a governor-type politician, and his speeches evoked the earthy business of everydayness—going to school and church, raising a family, holding a job. Governor Fitz Birdsong could make people feel like he was one of them, but one who had made it, at least for a moment. Bright remembered Hosanna talking about how people regarded God. *Folks want God to be just like them, but cuter.* It was a little bit like that with a successful politician. Fitz Birdsong and his father wore the mantle as if it had been made for them. Perhaps it had.

The car stopped at the edge of the platform and Doyle Butterworth stepped from the crowd to open the door on the passenger side, reaching up with a broad smile for Bright's hand. A flash of light blinded her momentarily, and then she saw Ortho Noblett from the newspaper holding up his Speed Graphic camera, getting a photo of them perched there on the back of the car. Behind them, the street sweeper ground to a halt and the driver cut the engine back to a dull, throaty roar. She entertained the brief hope that it would proceed on without them, but there really wasn't room for it to get through. The crowd from across the way was edging out into the street now, moving in a mass toward the platform, cheering and applauding as they came. The high school band was playing "I'm Looking Over a Four Leaf Clover," and the strong beat of the music pulsed through the crowd. It was, if anything, even noisier here than on the parade route, and Bright felt smothered by the waves of sound, the people pressing in close to the car. *Good Lord, don't let me faint and embarrass us all.* She reached down and fetched her purse from the seat and then Fitz and Doyle Butterworth helped her out of the convertible and through the crowd up to the little stage. Fitz followed, the Live Eye 5 camera almost in his face, with Holly Hardee yammering questions that Bright

< 428 >

couldn't hear for the noise. He was ignoring her, smiling, reaching out to shake hands as he went, clapping people on the back.

Bright sat in a folding chair between Harley Gibbons and the chairman of the soil and water conservation board, her purse in her lap, and felt the perspiration gushing in a river down her back. She was sorely tempted to ask if she couldn't just duck inside City Hall and cool off for a moment. But that wouldn't do. Then she looked to her right, past the line of dignitaries, and saw the big blue and white boxy Rescue Squad truck parked next to the reviewing stand. If she fell out here in the heat, they would just have to rescue her, the way they had done Buster's roofer.

She leaned over to Harley. "It's quite a crowd," she said. "Fitz is very proud."

Harley gave her a long look. Some patching up to do there, she thought. Harley had been too good a friend for too long to let it rest the way it was. But on the other hand, there was still this matter of business to be taken care of. They would see about that.

Harley shook his head, a grudging admiration. "The boy's got the touch," he said. "He may just pull this thing out."

They didn't even try to introduce Fitz. He simply stepped to the microphone and flashed his great beaming smile and the crowd went wild. To hell with the rest of the state and the big-city newspapers and the other fellow running for governor. This was the hometown boy. Little Fitz.

He tried several times to begin his speech, and they kept cheering and he kept smiling, standing there with both hands gripping the tall microphone stand. Finally the noise subsided a bit and he said, the words booming out of the loudspeakers mounted on the utility poles to his left and right, "It's good to be home!" And the cheering broke loose again, flooding over him in waves.

Bright felt a great rush of pride, the awesome noise of the crowd lifting her up. Home! Their town! The Birdsongs and the Bascombes before them. The place where they had sunk their roots and to which they had given their hearts, through thick and thin, right and wrong. She wished Dorsey Bascombe could be here now to see it. And Fitz-hugh, who had finally wanted nothing better than to come back here—to her and to the honorable practice of law in the small white frame building down on Claxton Street. Fitzhugh would have put a great deal of himself into this town, into its everydayness. He would have been devoted to it, as he was devoted to anything he considered honorable. And that meant something too.

The crowd calmed finally, and Fitz stood there for a moment,

< 429 >

looking out over the sea of faces. When he spoke, his voice was measured, the rich baritone rolling out over the packed street. "It's too hot for long speeches, but I don't want to let this wonderful day go by without saying some things that need to be said." His voice quieted them and they stood, expectant, in the glaring sun. "First, I want to thank two people who made this possible. The best friend I've got in the world, my boyhood buddy Francis O'Neill. Big Deal!" He turned, held out his hand, beckoning Big Deal forward, and he stepped out of the crowd of people at the rear of the platform, a huge smile splitting his blushing face. He stood next to Fitz, their arms around each other's shoulders, while the crowd gave Big Deal an appreciative cheer. Then he waved and stepped back again. Bright opened her purse, looking for a handkerchief to dab at the perspiration on her brow. "And," Fitz said when they had quieted, "the greatest single influence on my life, then and now. My mama." It startled her and she jerked her head up, her mouth open, as he crossed the platform with two quick steps, bent down and kissed her on the cheek, his lips lingering there softly for a long moment. "I love you, Mama," he said in her ear.

"Fitz . . ."

She reached up to him, but he was already turning back to the microphone now while the crowd applauded Bright Birdsong. She sat there with what she imagined was an incredibly stupid smile on her face and dabbed at her eyes instead of her brow.

Fitz took off his suit jacket and handed it down to Doyle Butterworth at the edge of the platform. Bright could see only his broad back now, the wide streak of dark blue following his spine under the light blue of his shirt. But there must be something in his face that quieted the crowd again. The man who was running the street sweeper cut the ignition and the engine died with a cough, and it was almost quiet there in the open space between City Hall and the storefronts along the way. The big banner over the street flapped softly in a midday breeze and the crowd moved restlessly, waiting for him. Finally, he spoke again:

"I want to thank all of you, the people of my hometown and my home county, simply for being my people. It is a good place to be a boy and become a man." He spoke slowly, playing out the words, one hand on the microphone stand, the other jammed in a pants pocket. "I got a good education here. I went to a good church, read books from a good library, had good friends and a good river to go skinny-dipping in." He drew an appreciative laugh from the crowd, and Bright remembered him as a boy at the back door on late summer afternoons, clothes dry but hair still damp, the flush of rambunctious, unfettered fun still in his face and eyes.

< 430 >

"But most of all," he went on, "I had a lot of people who simply cared about me, cared about all the young'uns who grew up here. And still do, I imagine. The kind of folks, whether they were kin to you or not, who picked you up and dusted you off when you made a mistake, and who bragged on you when you did something right. You, all of you, let me know you expected me to do the right thing." He paused, his gaze sweeping the crowd. "And you let me know you loved me even when I didn't." Fitz ducked his head for a moment, then looked them in the eye again. "Thank you for saying that again today, simply by being here. I love you all. I'm proud to be one of you. And I'm mighty glad to be back."

Bright realized that he was finished. They simply stood there looking at each other for a long moment, Little Fitz Birdsong and the sweltering mass of people at his feet. Bright sat, stunned by what he had said and what he had not and felt a great ache for him swelling inside her; that, and pride. They seemed not to know what to do, and then a smattering of applause started and built and rolled through the crowd—not a raucous political cheer, but a great warm reaching out that enfolded him and seemed to lift him up.

Then they heard the whistle. *Whooooooooo-whoooot-whoooo.* High noon, the joyous wail of steam from the lumberyard across town by the riverbank, summoning folk from labor to an hour of cool rest and sustenance. *God bless Monkey Deloach,* she thought. When he had bought Dorsey's timber business, he had decreed that the whistle would continue to blow every workday—noon and evening—in honor of the man who built it and taught Monkey all he knew about tall trees and honest work. *Whooooooooo-whoooot-whooooooo.*

"Time for dinner!" Fitz Birdsong cried. "Come on, Mama, let's finish this parade and get to the fried chicken." The crowd roared, and on the sidewalk across the street, the band swung quickly into "There'll Be a Hot Time in the Old Town Tonight." Bright rose from her chair as Fitz reached out for her, and they climbed down and started toward the convertible waiting at the edge of the platform. Big Deal was there with the passenger-side door open and Doyle Butterworth was holding Fitz's coat. But the crowd came to them in a rush, reaching out to touch, their hands eager but gentle, calling out, "Little Fitz! Little Fitz!" and some of them even calling Bright's name, people she didn't recognize, a few whose faces seemed vaguely familiar. They couldn't move an inch, so they stood there side by side, sweating like field hands, Fitz reaching to shake every hand he could grab. Bright clutched her purse tightly and Fitz held one arm firmly around her for protection. The noise and the heat were awesome, and Bright felt light-headed.

< 431 >

But then Homer Sipsey and some of his boys reached them and began to clear a path so they could get to the car. Big Deal and Doyle Butterworth helped her up and Fitz spread his suit jacket on the top of the scorching leather of the back seat. She could feel the heat even through the fabric when she sat, still holding her purse. Behind them, the street sweeper roared to life again, its thunder crashing over them, drowning out even the hooting, hollering crowd. Fitz leaned over the back of the car, grinning broadly, still shaking hands. Big Deal climbed in, sliding across the passenger seat behind the wheel, and Homer began waving his arms in front of the car, moving the crowd back so they could resume the parade. The other units, including the Vacation Bible School flatbed, had mercifully gone on ahead when Fitz's car had stopped. But the tail end of the procession still had two blocks to go before it would make a left turn off Bascombe and head for the high school. The high school band was making a valiant effort to regroup in the middle of the street. Finally the band director, a young fellow dressed all in white, from his shirt to his buck shoes, and sweating profusely, yelled "Charge!" and the high schoolers galloped off the sidewalk and into the fray, their gleaming instruments bobbing in the crowd. They more or less formed up, with people darting between their ranks, and began to play a ragged version of "Camptown Races." Just ahead of them, Harley Gibbons climbed into the passenger side of Homer Sipsey's police car and Homer jumped behind the wheel and turned on the siren and all the lights, and the entire business began to inch forward. Big Deal gave the convertible a shot of gas and it lurched into motion, and Bright grabbed Fitz's arm and held on to her hat.

"Whoooo, dogies!" Fitz cried. "You all right, Mama?"

"I don't know," she said.

They were under way now, the crowd parting on the street in front of them, moving up onto the sidewalks to give them room, still yelling and applauding. The noise swelled—Homer's siren, the band, the street sweeper behind them.

And then suddenly they popped free of the crowd and picked up speed, moving toward the corner two blocks away where they would turn to head for the high school.

"Good Lord!" Bright said. "I thought we were goners."

"That was quite a reception," Fitz said.

"That was quite a speech," she countered.

He looked straight ahead, finding something terribly interesting up there at the back of the band. Then he turned and said, "It's over."

"What is?"

"The election." He drew his hand across his neck. "I'm a dead duck."

< 432 >

She stared at him; then she reached over with the handkerchief still clutched in her hand and wiped the sweat from his forehead.

"I don't want the money," he said. "It would be throwing good after bad."

She opened her mouth, snapped it shut again.

"Lavonia's left me," he said. "I didn't intend to tell you that, but she has. Another mess there."

Well, what to say about that? Bright had never been the kind of mother who thought no girl was good enough for her boy. Lavonia had her shortcomings, but she was pleasant enough and she had taken good care of Fitz. And, no doubt, put up with a lot. "I'm sorry," Bright said.

"I'm coming home."

"Here?"

"Yeah. I'm going to practice law and try to get my self-respect back."

She started to say something, but then out of the corner of her eye she saw a commotion up ahead and she turned her head to see Homer's police car pulling over to curbside, Homer jumping out and waving the band around him. They kept marching, playing "Camptown Races."

Fitz leaned over to Big Deal. "What's the matter?"

"I don't know," Big Deal called back. "I'll pull in here behind Homer and find out."

Harley Gibbons was out of the police car now, and Bright thought he looked awfully perturbed. Homer was leaning in the window on the driver's side, talking on his radio. Big Deal eased the convertible in behind them and Harley started striding back toward the car, arms flapping. "Damn Flavo!" he cried out.

Flavo. She had quite forgotten him, what with Roseann and Fitz and the parade and the speech. Too much for a sixty-eight-year-old woman to keep track of at once. But Flavo Richardson would not go away. Never had, never would. Harley was right. Damn Flavo!

"Harley, what on earth?" she called out to him.

Harley reached them, puffing, eyes wide, face flushed. "They're marching, Bright! Flavo and all his folks. The whole damn bunch of 'em. Heading this way out of the Quarter." He glared at Fitz. "I told you we ought not to take down the roadblocks!"

They both looked at Bright. *All right, this is all my doing, is it? Well, I suppose it is. I have put my foot right in the middle of it. Now what?* She thought first to be angry with Flavo. He had double-crossed her. Or had he? No, what he had said was that they would not disrupt the parade. But the parade was over, or would be by the time . . .

< 433 >

"The swimming pool," she said.

"Oh, my God," Harley said, as if she had said "The nuclear power plant."

Bright leaned down to Big Deal. "Francis, go to the swimming pool. Now!"

"Mama . . . ," Fitz started to say, and Big Deal turned in the seat to look back at him, eyebrows at full mast.

"Fitz, go to the luncheon. This is my business," she said firmly.

But Fitz just shrugged. "What the hell. Let's go to the swimming pool."

Big Deal threw the convertible into gear and Fitz grabbed her and they slid down into the back seat as Big Deal swung out into the street, leaving Harley standing there. "Bright!" he called after her. "Dammit, Bright!" She dared not look back.

<   >

"All right, Mama. What's up?" Fitz asked as they sped toward the swimming pool. Behind them, she could hear the siren on Homer's patrol car whine to life as it took off after them.

She turned and stared at Fitz. The wind was loud in her ears and she had to raise her voice to hear herself. "I think Flavo's decided to take the bull by the horns."

"What does that mean?"

"I don't know for sure. But I'd guess he's willing to kick up a good-sized commotion and get a good number of folks arrested."

Fitz sat back in the seat and pondered that. Things at war there. The politician's nose for trouble. And a slightly bemused expression too. "And what are you going to do?"

"I don't know." And that was the gospel truth, she thought. She would have to make it up as she went along. Something would turn up. *You hear that, Papa?* Her hat blew off then, went sailing up above the convertible and drifted behind them, hit the road and tumbled into the gutter. She looked back, waved her hand at it in disgust. The wind felt good on her sweat-matted hair. "It may be messy," she said, more to herself than Fitz.

Homer's patrol car had almost caught up with them when they pulled up to the swimming pool, and it was creating a great racket, siren howling and tires screeching, as Homer made the turn and rocketed down the slope into the parking lot. Bright looked back and saw two more vehicles in hot pursuit—the Live Eye 5 van and an old Ford sedan she recognized as Ortho Noblett's. She had never seen Ortho in this much of a hurry. Perhaps Ortho had never been to this much of a news story.

< 434 >

There was a good-sized crowd at the pool, more than Bright would have expected with such big doings in town. A line of children was gathering inside the chain-link fence, dripping water on the grass and staring at the police car. Beyond them, the ice-blue water shimmered in the midday and bright orange and white umbrellas sprouted protectively over the line of chaise longues on the concrete apron around the pool. The chaise longues were full of teenagers and mothers.

Big Deal opened the door and scrambled out, pulling his seat forward so Bright could exit. Bright picked up her purse and tucked it underneath her arm and wished for a fleeting moment that she still had her hat. A woman should be armed with both purse and hat at a time like this.

Harley and Homer piled out of the patrol car and bore down on the convertible. Homer had one hand on the butt of his pistol and Bright blanched. *My Lord, I hope we don't have any shooting here. Surely not.* "Bright," Harley huffed, "what the hell's going on here?"

Bright and Fitz climbed out of the back seat of the convertible and Fitz stood with a protective hand at Bright's elbow.

"I don't know, Harley," Bright said. "I don't know what Flavo has in mind. But I think this could all have been avoided with a little reasonableness."

"Hah!" Harley cried. "I'll tell you about reasonableness! While you were off tooting around the country last night, Flavo's folks burned down Booker T. and threw rocks at the fire truck. We've got lawlessness on our hands here! Marchers, for God's sake! We've never had marchers, Bright. Not until now. Not until you stirred things up!"

"Now wait just a damned minute . . . ," Fitz started hotly.

"And you, *Governor*,"—he whirled on Fitz—"have taken down the barricades and left my town wide open!"

"*Your* town!" Bright yelped. "Who ever told you it was *your* town, Harley? That's what this whole business is about. Whose town is it? Yours or mine, or everybody's?"

Harley opened his mouth to bark back, but it was just at that moment they heard the singing. It drifted to them on the hot noontime like a puff of breeze floating across an open field, sending shivers through the grass. It stopped them all in their tracks, even Holly Hardee, who was on the run from the Live Eye 5 van, her cameraman scrambling to keep up with her. They all stopped and they looked up toward the bridge and they listened. And then Bright began to make out the tune. It was an ancient spiritual, an echo from her childhood when she had sat in the pew of the little white frame church at Hosanna's side and heard the sound of God in the powerful ring of a hundred voices. But there were more than that now, all of them in a great

< 435 >

swelling chorus that was pure sound and then after a moment a mass of people moving out across the bridge. *My God. It must be every single person in the Quarter.*

"Well, Harley," Bright said quietly, so as not to disturb the music, "I think we're about to get down to business here."

Harley turned to her, mouth open. "What in the hell's going on? What are they doing?"

"Going swimming, I imagine."

They heard more sirens then, and in a moment two police cars flashed by the marchers on the bridge and roared down the incline into the swimming pool parking lot. They were packed with policemen. Every officer in town, apparently, all armed to the teeth. Several of them had shotguns. The two cars screeched to a halt and the men piled out. "Riot gear!" Homer Sipsey bellowed. "Get on your riot gear!"

"Good Lord, Harley. Stop this!" Bright cried. But Harley just stared at her, hands on hips, while the police officers popped open the trunks of the cars and began hauling out helmets and gas masks. Holly Hardee and her cameraman crowded up to them, getting pictures of the officers donning their battle dress.

"Sonofabitch!" Big Deal said softly. He looked truly frightened. "Fitz, we gotta get you out of here. This ain't gonna look good on TV. Fitz . . ."

But Fitz ignored him. Instead, he stepped between Bright and Harley, grabbed Harley by the arm. "Harley, you're going to have a disaster on your hands if you don't do something!"

Harley pointed angrily at the singing black mass up on the bridge, nearing the halfway point now. "If there's a disaster, it's *their* fault! Go talk to Flavo Richardson!" he said, shaking off Fitz's grip. Then he turned to Homer. "Chief Sipsey, I want to make damn sure that not a single person without a season ticket gets in the swimming pool. That's an order!"

"Yes sir," Homer said, giving Bright a long hard look. He was angry too, bone-weary and up to his eyeballs with trouble. *Go home and be quiet,* he had told Bright. Well, so much for being quiet.

"Harley," Fitz said, "are you sure you want to be hard-nosed about this?"

Harley turned on him, and Bright could see a good deal of pent-up resentment there—the business of the bank, possibly some other burrs under Harley's political saddle that she had no idea of. "Governor," he said carefully, "now that your folks have turned tail, I see this as strictly a local problem. So maybe you ought to be getting on to the luncheon. All your folks are waiting for you there."

< 436 >

"Damn right," Big Deal said. "Come on, Fitz, Miz Bright. Let's go. Right NOW!"

But nobody budged. They all stood their ground and glared at each other, and Bright could feel it all piling in on them very quickly, getting out of hand. The great mass of Flavo's folks making the turn now from the bridge, the surge of their voices making the air dance and the hair stand up on the nape of Bright's neck. The police officers grimly strapping on their bulletproof vests and clamping visored helmets on their heads. And the rest of them just standing there, watching. Like knots on a log.

Bright took a deep breath. *Dear Lord in heaven, give me a sign.* Nothing. *All right, then. If something's going to turn up, it'll have to be Bright Birdsong. God help us.* Bright turned abruptly on her heel and headed toward the gate to the swimming pool.

"Bright . . . ," Harley called after her, his voice rising a bit as if somebody had tightened his underwear a notch. She could hear the scuffle of feet across the grass behind her, people following.

"Mama—" Fitz tried to hold her up, but she didn't look back. She went through the gate, ignoring Roger Sipsey gaping at her from his ticket booth, and never stopped. Across the concrete apron, past the curious stares of the women and teenagers under the umbrellas, and then right on down the steps into the water, holding her purse up to keep it from getting wet. "Ohhh!" she cried as the cold hit her, and she heard a woman behind her say, "Good Godawmighty!" Then an excited babble of voices, everybody yelling at once. And Homer's police whistle tweeting shrilly. Bright kept moving and her dress began to billow up around her, and she suddenly had to choose between modesty and keeping her purse dry. She opted for modesty, mashing the dress down around her in the water. She waded on, out to where it was just above her waist, the water so icy that it took her breath and made her eyes pop. She was stunned by it, and she remembered now that it came from an underground spring. All the city did was shoot a little chlorine into it before they pumped it into the pool. The water was a shock, and so was the sudden realization of what she had done. She stood there for a moment, wondering what Dorsey Bascombe would have thought about all this business, about his daughter the piano student up to her keister in ice water and ruckus. But no use in dwelling on that. She turned around gingerly, trying to keep her balance, thinking what a fortunate thing it was that she had decided to wear one-inch heels today.

Up on the concrete apron surrounding the pool, it was pandemonium. Adults gawking, teenagers laughing and pointing, little kids screaming with surprised delight. And the men all standing there,

< 437 >

stunned and gape-mouthed. A good-sized army of flies could have camped out in their open craws, she thought. Holly Hardee and her cameraman were going a little crazy, hopping around the edge of the pool, getting pictures of everything. And Ortho was snapping away with his Speed Graphic. *Well,* she thought, *I have ripped it now. It's a matter of public record.* And she wished that Jimbo were here to see it all. See it, the dickens. To *do* it. There would have been the most delicious look of wonderment on his face, she imagined, the kind that only a ten-year-old boy could have after he had done something totally unexpected and outrageous. But Jimbo was not here. She felt very much alone out there in the middle of the swimming pool. And she felt a rush of despair. Why was she here? With all that needed seeing about, why on earth was she *here?* But, then, she knew the answer to that as surely as she knew the question. *Because I am who I am, bag and baggage. I can't escape it. To deny that makes all the past a waste, a repudiation of all that's good and true. And that would leave only the mistakes.*

Harley finally found his voice. "Bright, get out of there!"

"No, Harley. I will not."

"This is ridiculous!" he cried.

"No, it's not, it's civil disobedience." She waved her dripping purse defiantly. "I am in the swimming pool without a season ticket, Harley. Now you can either change the rules and let me swim, or you can arrest me."

Then a small boy on a bright red inner tube paddled up from the rear and nudged against Bright. "You wanna play dibble-dabble?" he asked.

"In a moment," she said, but as she turned to him, her foot caught on the rough concrete bottom of the pool and she lost her balance and toppled over. The cold water rushed over her and she lost her grip on her purse. She fought against the water, opened her eyes and saw the surface above her, shimmering in the noon sun as she sank toward the bottom. Then she heard a dull pounding as other bodies hit the water. Fitz was the first to reach her. He reached down and grabbed Bright under her armpits and hauled her quickly to the surface, and they stood there gawking at each other, water dripping from their hair and clothing. Fitz's nice blue suit was a soggy ruin. The water was full of people, all splashing in her direction.

"My purse," she managed. "I dropped my purse." He looked down, spied her purse on the bottom of the pool, ducked under and retrieved it. He came up sputtering, then handed it to her.

"The water's cold," he said. "I didn't remember. It's been a long time."

< 438 >

"Yes," Bright said, "it has."

"Get a shot! Close-ups!" Holly Hardee was screaming to her cameraman and then to Fitz. "Governor! Governor!"

Bright looked back beyond the crowd now and she could see the marchers bearing down on the swimming pool and, between them and the gate, the knot of policemen milling about. Riot gear. What on earth did anyone in this town need riot gear for? This wasn't Chicago, for God's sake. She could see Flavo at the head of the crowd, straining to get a look at what was happening beyond the swimming pool fence. The marchers had stopped singing, but the measured tramp of their feet was stirring up a dust storm in the parking lot and their voices buzzed angrily like a swarm of aroused insects.

"Well, Harley?" she demanded.

Harley stared at her, eyes bulging. She thought it would probably take Harley a good while to get over this. "Dammit!" he cried. "You Bascombes have been trying to run this town as long as I can remember!"

She shouldn't have said it, but she did. "And most of the time we're right, Harley. That's the way it is with Bascombes."

That did it. "Arrest her!" he bellowed, pointing a long arm and finger.

Homer Sipsey looked at Harley for a moment. "Now!" Harley shouted, and Homer shrugged and stepped down into the water, wincing at the cold.

"The hell you say," Fitz cried, moving toward Homer.

But Bright grabbed his arm. "No, Fitz. It's all right." Fitz stopped, stared at her. "Please. Just let me handle this." His eyebrows went up. *No, of course I don't know what I'm doing. I'm making it up as I go.* She released her grip. "Stay there, Homer," she said. "I'm coming." She waded slowly over to Homer, hands outstretched, holding her purse in one. "Aren't you going to put handcuffs on me?"

Homer blanched. "What for?"

"Because I broke the law." She looked up at Harley. Beyond the chain-link fence, Flavo's crowd of marchers was milling about, shouting now at the squad of policemen. It was beginning to sound ugly. "Harley, we've got a mess here."

"We?" he snapped. "We didn't do this, Bright, *you* did."

"Maybe so, but now we're all in it together. You and me and Flavo and everybody else. Now if you'll just have Chief Sipsey put the handcuffs on me and take me out to where Flavo is, maybe we can defuse the situation. I think the handcuffs might help."

"Do it," Harley said between clenched teeth. And Homer took

< 439 >

the pair of shiny handcuffs off his wide leather belt and snapped them around Bright's wrists.

"What about me?" Fitz said at her back. "I don't have a season ticket, Harley."

"No, we're not gonna arrest you!" Harley bawled.

"Why not?"

Harley waved his arms in frustration. "Hell, I don't know. Diplomatic immunity. You're the governor of the state, for God's sake. Fitz, just get out of the water and go to the luncheon."

"Harley's right, Fitz," Bright said. "Go take care of your business."

Bright climbed out of the water then, with Homer's firm hand at her elbow to steady her, and stood dripping on the concrete apron next to the pool. "Now if you'll just take me out to Flavo, I'll see what I can do," she said quietly.

The crowd parted to let them through and they marched through the gate toward Homer's patrol car, Homer and Harley flanking her, Fitz close behind. Flavo spotted her then and she saw his eyes go wide. There was a good deal of pushing and shoving at the front of the crowd where Flavo stood. Suddenly, one of the policemen stumbled and went down, and the officer next to him let out a bellow and swung the butt of his shotgun, narrowly missing Flavo's head. The rest of the policemen rushed forward and an angry roar went up from the crowd. Bright's heart caught in her throat. It was dangerously close to bloodshed here, to unhealable rift. Homer tightened his grip on Bright's arm and tried to steer her away from the melee, but she dug in her heels and cried out, "Stop! Stop it right now! Flavo!" She broke free from Homer and plunged into the middle of the fracas, holding her purse in her manacled hands in front of her for protection. "Mama!" she heard Fitz cry out behind her. The noise and jostling bodies boiled around her, and she was shoved roughly from one side and then the other and she lost her purse. "Flavo! Stop! Don't!" she shouted, and she thought, *It's too late!*

Then all at once she was on her rump in the middle of the melee and everybody was staring at her. She looked up at the circle of faces, black and white, sweat-streaked and flushed with anger and surprise. Fitz burst through the crowd behind her, shouldering people aside. "Get outta the way!" he commanded, and they parted and let him through and he stopped, looked down at Bright, then around at the crowd. He flashed with anger. "What the hell do you mean! Get back! All of you! Get back away from my mama!"

They backed away from his fury, all but Flavo. And the two of them squared off over Bright. "Flavo, what the hell's going on here? You trying to cause a riot?"

< 440 >

"No, Guv'nah," Flavo said evenly. "Just come to see what the swimming pool looks like. See all these nice white folks at the swimming pool."

"Would you gentlemen like to help me up?" Bright asked, looking up at them. They glared at each other for another instant, then down at her. She offered her outstretched arms and they reached down, pulled her gently to her feet. She stood for a moment, wobbling a bit and trying to catch her breath and compose herself.

Bright looked into Flavo's eyes. There was the dust of old battles there, smoke and fire and ashes. A woman like Bright Birdsong could never truly *know*. But she had been present at enough of it to *feel*, at least a little. They were both too old for this, she thought. But that didn't really make any difference. Sometimes only the old ones could remember back far enough to make sense of things.

She could feel all their eyes on her now, the crowd waiting. "Flavo," she said quietly, "I have committed an act of civil disobedience. I have been swimming in the municipal pool without a season pass. Chief Sipsey has arrested me, as was his duty."

Flavo looked at her for a long moment, then drew himself up and dusted off the sleeves of his coat. "Yes," he said dryly. "I see. And what made you do a thing like that, Bright?"

"Making a point, I suppose."

"So, what now?"

She thought about it, still playing it by ear. Then she looked around at Homer and Harley. "Chief Sipsey will take me to jail, and I will refuse to post bond until the town council changes the rule on season passes at the swimming pool."

And Flavo said, "My, my."

"So if you want to do something helpful, you might organize a vigil at the jail." She looked at the sea of angry black faces behind Flavo. They might do his bidding, or they might not. "A very determined vigil," she said. "But no ruckus."

Flavo stood there for a long time looking at her and she could tell exactly what he was thinking. *Now who is manipulating whom, Bright Birdsong?* And she answered him with just a trace of a smile, letting it play at the corners of her mouth.

It was still very touchy here, the air thick with hostility and tension and a painful breath holding. Then Flavo blinked. Once, very slowly. "Yes," he said. "That will have to do, I suppose." And there was a great sigh, a thing with a life of its own, from black and white. They all stood there looking at each other, faces still hard, but everybody knowing at the same instant that things would be all right, at least here in the short run.

< 441 >

Holly Hardee and her cameraman broke through the crowd at Fitz's elbow and she thrust the microphone into his face. "Governor—"

"Hush up!" he commanded. "Just hush up a minute. We've got a situation here, can't you see? Now don't make it any worse than it is." Holly Hardee backed away a pace or two, eyes wide.

Flavo looked Fitz up and down. "Guv'nah," he said, "you cut a fine figure there."

Fitz looked down at himself, the sodden blue suit now covered with a fine mat of dust. Flavo pulled a handkerchief from his back pocket, handed it to Fitz, who unfolded it carefully and wiped the grime off his face. Then he handed the handkerchief back. "I'm obliged," he said.

"I believe you got some politickin' to do," Flavo said, wrinkling his nose. "While we local folks take care of our bidness here."

"Perhaps."

"Go kick up a fuss, Guv'nah. Like yo' mama here."

Fitz turned to Bright, stared at her for a moment. "Are you all right?"

"Perfectly. Go on, now."

Fitz shook his head. There was a trace of a smile there. "You always did just what you wanted to do," he said. "Come hell or high water."

"Yes," she said. "I suppose I did. Even when it hurt."

He shrugged. "We'll have to talk about that, too."

"Yes, we will." Then she turned to Homer Sipsey. "I'm ready to go, Homer. My father used to say the farther a monkey goes up a flagpole, the more of its rear end you can see. And I'm just about as far up the flagpole as I want to go."

< 442 >

26

*T*he most magic of moments are those just before dawn—moments when things can be as you wish them, unencumbered by light and shadow. You know the vague outline of a familiar place, but you can shape it to the whim of your imagination, people it only with those you wish to have near. Call them ghosts if you wish, or memory. Is there any difference? You can summon them whole and fresh, unravaged by time and the wasting of flesh. You can say to them all the things you always wished you had said, would have said in a more perfect time. That is magic.

It helps if you are older, because then there is more to draw upon. The great burden of old age is that there is so much history to deal with; the great blessing is the gift of forgetfulness, so that you can fashion your own particular history as a carver would work at a piece of wood, smoothing out the rough edges. That is part of the magic.

Thus it is that Bright Birdsong sits this early morning on the sandbar beside her river, conjuring thoughts of magic while she waits for the sky to pale above the treetops. It is quiet except for the soft sound the water makes as it slides against itself and the occasional stirring of a small animal or a bird, anticipating day.

She is alone now. Her ghosts have come and gone: Dorsey Bascombe, tall and lean in his big brown boots that smell of worn leather and neat's-foot oil and pine tar, his arms strong and his voice confident; Elise, her pale skin luminescent, reflecting firelight, her smile shy and her voice musical; Hosanna, her eyes sparkling with some morsel of wisdom so close to the earth that it smells like a freshly turned field in springtime; and Fitzhugh, the color high in his cheeks from the brisk midday of a Washington winter, his face attentive as if she were the only person in the world worth talking to at that particular moment. Bright Birdsong has not made peace with them, because peace depends

< 443 >

on things being certain and settled, and here in these moments before dawn, nothing is certain. It is simply here for the instant—a thing of fancy, not reality. Instead, she has imagined them for a brief time as she wished them, as she wished herself with them. In doing so, she has taken some comfort from them, from the parts of their mutual history that she chooses to remember just now. And that too is part of the magic.

But now the magic time is fading into morning, objects taking their own unalterable shape, ghosts receding, imagination giving way to reality. And reality is something else altogether.

Bright sighs, stretches her stiff limbs, wriggles about a bit in the soft sand underneath. She looks up at the sky. There were stars when she came an hour ago, clearheaded from a night of deep and dreamless sleep in the soft camp house bed. But the bright pinpoints have given way now to a general lightness. It will start as a clear day, a blue sky wiped clean. Perhaps a shower in the afternoon, the first big round droplets speckling the greenish-brown surface of the river and then a sudden downpour emptying the hot mugginess of a June day.

June. Most of a summer yet to come. And what of this summer? A week ago, she expected a still, quiet summer, a time and place where the mind drifts like the river along a familiar and comfortable route, seeking places where it can go unimpeded—Gladys asleep under the house; traffic moving slowly on Claxton Avenue, pausing near the River Bridge as the light winks red-green-yellow-red; quiet notes floating from the old Story and Clark upright piano in the parlor; and somewhere beyond them, the faint echo of a golden trombone. *Träumerei.* And the sound of God breathing.

But all is changed. There is something quick and lively and unsettled in the air, like the moment just before the summer storm rushes in to rattle the bones of old dogs and children alike, shaking loose ancient dust and cobwebs. A small boy in the spare bedroom, an alligator under the house, fifty thousand dollars in a briefcase. That alone is enough to unsettle, not to mention all the other. A public unraveling, messy with human commerce. Good Lord!

So Bright sits here on her riverbank pondering how all these extraneous things have come tumbling in on her life, altering the course of her summer. But she is an honest woman above all else, in the way her father taught her to be. Too honest, perhaps, for her own good. So she arrives eventually at a truth: that alligators and little boys and stacks of money have little to do with all this unsettling. They are only the instruments by which she has been forced to come out of hiding. And *confront.* Oh, God, this business of confronting! What she has confronted won't go away like all the ghosts who came stealing across

< 444 >

the sandbar in the predawn hour. There is this business of conse-
quence—of the Dorsey who left his mark so indelibly on her, then
surrendered to the battle with his demons; the Elise who fled in perplexed defeat; the Hosanna who, despite her great native wisdom, was
no match for dark abidings. And most recently, Fitzhugh. In death, he
had worn a perplexity the undertaker had not been able to smooth
away. *Ah, Fitzhugh. It may have all been a very grave error. And now,
unrectifiable.* Finally, there were those who remained—Roseann and
Fitz, chiefly. They must be dealt with, and no matter the outcome,
there would always be a deep ache there, a certain sense of failure.

But dealing with all that, that was the thing. And that was the
difference a week had made. Confronting, and then dealing. Dust
shaken loose, objects tumbling from locked attic closets. Sixty-eight
years old, and she couldn't be quiet and still. Not anymore, she
couldn't. There was first a small boy, the possibilities he represented.
She had barely scratched the surface there. There was the money, or
what was left of it, demanding to be dealt with. She had thought about
it now and then as she sat in the cramped jail cell waiting for the town
council to give way, as it finally had, wanting no more of the tackiness
she had created. But she had reached no conclusions. It remained a
bother. And of course there was Flavo Richardson. Let her close her
eyes in peace and he would surely show up on her front porch, arthritic
and irascible, demanding something else. Friend enough to drive an
old woman to distraction, now that she had loosed the old furies again.
It made her weary to think about it. All of it.

And finally, Buster Putnam. He wouldn't go away, either.

Sitting with him on her back steps late yesterday afternoon, she
had succumbed to a brief moment of confession, had opened her devil's
box of regrets and uncertainties and hauntings.

Errors of the heart, Buster Putnam had said. But that hadn't been
enough. Errors they were, nonetheless.

"Well, then," he said, "maybe not even errors, Bright. I'm not so
sure of right and wrong, outside a few narrow boundaries. Maybe the
only sane measure for most of it is how it turns out. And we don't find
that out until it's woefully too late."

"You know so much?" she asked.

"Some."

"Korea?" Then regretted it.

There was a little flicker of pain there in his face. It gave him
character, she thought. And when she looked more closely she could
see the fine lines that pain had etched over his warrior's lifetime. They
were different from wrinkles, more subtle yet more profound.

"Yes," he said after a moment.

< 445 >

"What of it?"

"None of your business," he said, but there was no malice in it. He looked at his hands for a moment, flicked a wood shaving off the cuff of his flannel shirt. He smelled of sawdust and varnish.

"Of course not," she said. "But just answer me this. Would you do it any differently, Buster?"

He shook his head firmly. "Hell, no. Goddammit to hell, no, I wouldn't. Would you?"

"Perhaps. But I can't."

"No. So what's the use?"

She let the evening soften things a bit and then she said, "You always did like to be a little foul-mouth, as I remember. When you were five years old, living next door, I remember you standing at my back steps and saying . . . well, I won't say what you were saying."

Buster smiled. "Back there when I was five, I used to think you were a little prissy."

"What do you mean?"

"Oh, a little too full of yourself."

"Maybe I was," she said. "My father always told me I was the smartest and best-looking girl in town."

He nodded. "I suppose he was right."

"And how about now? Am I still prissy?"

He thought about it a moment. "You've mellowed some, I reckon. You still need to loosen up a little, though. You ought to go out carousing with me some night, get sloppy drunk and sing along with Waylon Jennings on the jukebox at the Dew Drop Inn."

She thought to be prissy about that, but then she started thinking about being sloppy drunk at the Dew Drop and she smiled in spite of herself. "Well, who knows," she said.

And she thought to herself, *I don't need any scandal here. Not with all the other. Well, not much, anyhow.*

She is suddenly aware of the morning. The first dazzling burst of sun on the thick branches of a maple across the way, flooding the sandbar with soft gold, the shards of light chasing the last vestiges of the magic hour like a mirror shattering. A new sun, full of life and energy. *Hosanna,* she thought. *She may have been the wisest, sanest one of us all.*

Bright Birdsong stands and turns, feeling the new sun warm and full on her face. Then she lifts her nightgown over her head and drops it in the sand at her feet and lifts her arms to welcome the sun, feeling it flood the deep, secret places of her body. Perhaps, she thinks, there is a bit of magic here too.

< 446 >

Too soon, it is over. Then sun pops full and robust into the sky above the camp house and soft gold becomes a clean white heat and Bright feels tiny beads of perspiration on her upper lip. She turns back, looks longingly at the river, then laughs. *Sinner, baptize thyself.* She wades in, feeling its coolness salve her thighs, her belly, her breasts. At midstream she stops, then thinks how utterly foolish she must look just now, a wrinkled old woman skinny-dipping in the river. She looks downriver then, sees the heron on a low overhanging branch, sees him take sudden flight, straight toward her this time, the ungainly body launching from the branch and becoming a graceful thing, all wing and long neck. He passes perhaps ten feet overhead and Bright turns in the water, watching until the heron rounds the bend and disappears.

Bright thinks suddenly of her father, goes back to the very beginning. "I will take care of everything," he had said. He had been wrong in that, wrong to try. But he had said something else too. He had said, "Something will always come along."

She understood now what he meant.

< 447 >